C000228786

Where the Rivers Meet

Also by John Wain

Poetry
A Word Carved on a Sill
Weep Before God
Wildtrack
Letters to Five Artists
Feng
Open Country

Fiction
Hurry on Down
Living in the Present
The Contenders
A Travelling Woman
Nuncle and Other Stories
Strike the Father Dead
The Young Visitors
Death of the Hind Legs and Other Stories
The Smaller Sky
A Winter in the Hills
The Life Guard
The Pardoner's Tale
Young Shoulders

Autobiography
Sprightly Running
Dear Shadows: Portraits from Memory

Criticism
Preliminary Essays
Essays on Literature and Ideas
The Living World of Shakespeare
A House for the Truth
Professing Poetry

Biography
Samuel Johnson

John Wain has also edited
Johnson as Critic
Johnson on Johnson
Interpretations
Contemporary Reviews of Romantic Poetry
Selected Poems of Thomas Hardy
Personal Choice: A Poetry Anthology
Anthology of Contemporary Poetry
An Edmund Wilson Celebration
Everyman's Book of English Verse
The Oxford Library of English Poetry

Where the Rivers Meet

John Wain

Hutchinson
London · Melbourne · Auckland · Johannesburg

© John Wain 1988

All rights reserved

First published in Great Britain by Hutchinson, an imprint of
Century Hutchinson Ltd, Brookmount House, 62-65 Chandos Place,
London WC2N 4NW

Century Hutchinson Australia Pty Ltd
PO Box 496, 16-22 Church Street, Hawthorn, Victoria 3122, Australia

Century Hutchinson New Zealand Limited
PO Box 40-086, Glenfield, Auckland 10, New Zealand

Century Hutchinson South Africa (Pty) Ltd
PO Box 337, Berglvei, 2012 South Africa

Photoset in North Wales by
Derek Doyle & Associates, Mold, Clwyd.
Printed and bound in Great Britain by
Butler and Tanner Ltd, Frome and London

British Library Cataloguing in Publication Data

Wain, John, *1925–*
Where the rivers meet.
I. Title.
823′.914[F]

ISBN 0-09-173617-X

Dedication

To William, to Ianto and most of all to Toby, who helped at a bad time; and to Raymond Hodgkins, for his unfailingly genial readiness to 'summon up remembrance of things past'; and to the college where I was young.

… who will deny that Oxford, by her ineffable charm, keeps ever calling us nearer to the true goal of all of us, to the ideal, to perfection, – to beauty, in a word, which is only truth seen from another side?

– Matthew Arnold, *Essays in Criticism*

– Does you worship mean to geld and spay all the youth of the city?
– No, Pompey.
– Truly, sir, in my humble opinion, they will to 't then.

Measure for Measure

Note

This novel is complete in itself, though the fact that its narrative ends at 1933 does give me the option of continuing it in further volumes, and I expect to bring the story of Peter Leonard, his friends and enemies, loves and hates, down to our own days. But there is another, and more important, motive for beginning well back in time. The setting is Oxford, both City and University; and Oxford was a different place before the 1920s, when this story opens. My central character is an historian; it is still fashionable to deny that history is or can be made by individuals. But when in 1919 Mr William Morris, later Lord Nuffield, started up his motor factory at Cowley, a village just across the fields from Oxford, one decision by one man altered the destiny of an important city and a famous university.

I wanted to begin at the beginning of that change. It made Oxford into a very complex place; too complex I fear for most of the people who have written novels about it, who prefer to scissor out a neat selection, which they then present satirically or sentimentally according to taste. But Oxford life is not made up of neat sections. My purpose is to deal imaginatively with the full range of that life.

J.W.
June 1988

Chapter 1

It was a spring day, afternoon just merging into evening and I was walking along the towpath, breathing hard. As I walked I looked at the river. It was very full. There had been a lot of rain at the end of the winter, and the level had not gone down yet although it was April now, the trees were in bud and the new season was coming in fast. The water pushed ahead so purposefully that it looked more like a solid than a liquid, a wide moving band of smooth glass. Only here and there, where it swished round some obstacle, was it streaked and cross-hatched. There were some mallards trying to live out their normal lives on top of this steadily flowing mass, but the current was too strong for their webbed feet to push against. They would be hurried downstream fifty yards or so, then take to the air, wings whirring, and splash down more or less where they had started. If they were not facing dead upstream when they hit the water, they would be spun round and round. It didn't seem to worry them much.

The reason I was breathing hard was because I was in a hurry to get home by six. I had gone down the towpath to see if the fritillaries had started to come out in the fields round about Iffley Lock.

There was in fact no sign of the fritillaries yet, and I decided not to tell Brian I had been down to look. He would call me a fool for going down so early, when anyone could tell there would be no fritillaries out. Brian was sixteen, two years older than I. We were brothers and lived with our parents at a pub called the Bargeman's Arms, which they kept. Brian never made allowances for the fact that I could not do things as well as he, with his two years' head start. He just put it down to stupidity.

There was always an unpleasant scene if we were not both there for tea at six o'clock sharp. It was 'high tea', of course, a substantial meal based on meat or fish though it shaded off, as it were, into things like bread and butter and jam, cakes and scones. The household routine was that we two boys ate with our mother and then our father came in for his. The pub opened at six, Dad took the first half-hour behind the bar and at six-thirty Mother took over. If Brian or I showed up even five minutes late, the machine-like precision of this timing was jarred and everybody got irritable. When Dad had eaten, he went into the bar and then the two of them were there till ten, when the pub closed.

On this particular evening I knew I was cutting it fine if I was going to get back by six, but I still hoped to make it. As I came along the stretch on the opposite side from Christ Church Meadow I listened anxiously for the clocks to begin striking. There was always one that was a bit earlier than the others and once that broke the silence the chiming would go on until it died out with the last one or two that were noticeably later than the rest. The whole business of striking the hour would take four or five minutes, so that a boy running at his best pace had still some hope of covering a quarter of a mile or so and still claiming that it 'hasn't gone six yet, honest Mum.'

The bells were still silent when I got to Folly Bridge and came up from the towpath briefly to cross the Abingdon Road, diving back down again to run on towards Oseney Town, where the Bargeman's Arms stood on its pleasant corner site within a few feet of the calmly flowing river. This last stretch, with the gasworks on one's left hand and various railway bridges and sidings on the right, was the drabbest part of the route. Not that I cared about such things, then or for years afterwards. It was simply an irritating slab of distance which separated me from home, the next meal and a row or non-row according to my punctuality.

Summoning all the fleetness of foot natural to my age, I pounded over the last few hundred yards of towpath, pursued now by the beginning of that horological debate from the classic towers and spires of the region known vaguely as 'the Colleges'. What actually went on in 'the Colleges' I had never troubled to enquire, and neither had most people in my circle, though some of them were college servants and necessarily had their own perspectives on that world.

As I reached Oseney Lock, the breath flaring in my lungs as I put on a last sprint, I heard from behind me a strange yet familiar noise, midway between a flutter and a rasp. I knew what this was. Brian was overtaking me on his bicycle. Ignoring the notice that said 'No Cycling at the Lock', he was lunging at the pedals and urging his well-worn bike, mostly put together from scrap parts, in the same direction as I was running but far faster. As I got clear of the lock footbridge he was barely a yard behind me, and as I entered the last ten yards of towpath he accelerated past, all the while making that strange noise.

The noise came from two strips of stiff cardboard he had wedged into the brakes, so that they hit the spokes of the back wheel as it revolved.

This procedure was unsatisfactory in a number of ways. By creating a certain amount of drag, it must have slowed him down. By drumming on the thin wire spokes it must have tended to loosen them. And the sound-effect, in any case, lasted only a few minutes, after which the strips of cardboard became fatigued and began to shred away. But Brian would just fit new strips and go on from there. What mattered was that he was riding along astride something that, as it moved, made a *noise*. The noise was not very impressive, the whole process was time-wasting, but for Brian it was a necessity. It was the symbol of his deep longing for a motor-cycle.

We were just in time. The cottage pie landed on the table just as we took our seats. We ate in abstracted silence, just about returning answers to our mother's mechanical questions about how we had 'got on'. She was always hoping in a vague, kindly way that we would 'get on' all right, but she was not ambitious for us; she merely wished our unremarkable welfare and happiness. I was slogging away at school, and Brian, who had hated school and insisted on leaving on the very day when the law allowed him to, was in his third or fourth blind-alley job. When we had eaten, Mother told me to go and tell Dad to come in five minutes. By that time his food would be on the table and she, with her kitchen apron off and her hair tidied, would be ready to take over behind the bar.

I went into the bar. The circle of regulars, five or six in number, were sitting about as usual. Old Trundle was speaking. I don't suppose his name really was Trundle, it was probably Trumbull or something like that, but it fell on my ear as Trundle, which suited him because he was a slow-moving old man of enormous girth. When he moved, you had the impression that he was, so to speak, trundling his belly in front of him. His constant companion was a long, thin man called Peake, who had a lined, brown, watchful face and never took his eyes off yours when he was speaking to you. Peake was there now, listening.

As I went in old Trundle was saying, 'And to finish off with.' He took a swig from his beer tankard and looked round at his audience. 'Do you know what they done to finish off with?'

'Well, go on,' said my father in his capacity as chairman.

'They puts a bullet through each one of his eyes,' old Trundle said. 'They shoots his eyes out. And 'im lying dead in the road.'

'With flies round him, I shouldn't wonder,' added Peake. 'Flies starting to gather.'

'What they done that for?' asked another man, the youngest of the circle. He was listening so intently to the narrative that his loosely-rolled cigarette had gone out. 'His eyes? What they done that for?'

'Haven't you never heard,' said my father slightly condescendingly, from his magisterial position behind the dark wooden bar, 'how they say when you dies, the last person you see is printed on your eyeballs?'

'No,' said the youngish man. 'I can't say as I have 'eard that.' He picked up his beer mug and buried his face in it, as if feeling slightly put down.

'I don't know as I believe it meself,' said Peake judicially.

'Well, them two fellers believed it,' said old Trundle.

'P'raps they was just taking no chances, like,' said another man. 'They might have heard it and not known whether it was true, and thought they'd be on the safe side, like.'

'Ay,' said my father, 'we might all do some pretty rum things, at a time like that.'

'At a time like what?' someone asked.

'Just arter shootin' a man, of course.'

'I don't suppose it ever could happen, to the likes of you and me,' Peake said. 'We're not the type to go round shootin' people.'

'We're not the type to be on the run in a stolen motor, if it comes to that,' my father said, 'and have the police out looking for us all over the county.'

'Was it in the paper?' asked the youngish man.

'The robbery was,' said old Trundle. 'That was in last night. But the murder worn't in tonight's.'

'I got it here,' said my father, displaying the *Oxford Mail*. 'But I haven't had time to look at it yet.'

'It come too late for 'em, the murder,' said Peake, nodding.

'Even too late for the Stop Press,' said Trundle.

'How is it you knows about it then?' the younger man asked Trundle. 'Was you there watching 'em?'

'Nigh enough,' said old Trundle with quiet satisfaction. 'You might nigh enough say I worr there.' He looked round again, savouring the moment. 'It happened just outside Buckland Village. The policeman's body was found about ten minutes after they drove off –'

'How do they know?' Peake put in. 'How do they make out it was ten minutes?'

''Cause people in the village see the car goin' through and they agrees about the time. Car traffic isn't so common out there as people don't look up when they hears the noise of one.'

This point cleared up, he continued his story.

'When they finds the body they pulls it to the side of the road. The next one that come along was Bert West with his steam-engine. They asks him to go to the police station and give the news so they can start telephoning round. Bert goes to the police station and comes straight on to Oxford, takes him about half an hour, and I meets him coming over Folly Bridge and he stops dead in the middle of the bridge and leans down and tells me what's happened.'

He settled back and drank, pleased with the solemn effect of his words. At that moment my mother appeared in the narrow doorway behind where my father stood.

'What's keeping you, Jack? I sent Peter through to tell you to come.' At this they all turned and looked accusingly at me. I was standing over by the door.

'Peter said nothing to me,' said my father severely.

I felt my face growing hot and knew I must be blushing at all the attention. I hated blushing, but there was no way of controlling it. 'I didn't want to interrupt,' I said.

'Giving a message isn't interrupting,' my father said. He turned and went through into the kitchen. I knew he was clearing himself with my mother, putting the blame on me for his slowness in coming to the table. Of course he would never have left the bar until old Trundle's story was complete.

My mother now took up her stance behind the bar and I went out into the street. It was, if possible, an even finer evening than when I had gone in. The slanting sun shone with a crystal brightness, making the dull houses and ordinary gardens seem suddenly worth looking at. I turned my head, taking everything in. The colours of the pub sign stood out in jubilant clarity. Even the official lettering over the doorway seemed freshly picked out: JOHN EDWARD LEONARD. LICENSED TO SELL BEER AND WINE. FOR CONSUMPTION ON OR OFF THE PREMISES. The bit about wine was just fancy talk. There may have been a bottle or two of sweet sherry, of which a few glasses would go at Christmas time, but mainly the Bargeman's was a beer house. As I lounged on the pavement outside the door, Brian came out. We stood for a moment on the pavement together: two ordinary middle-sized lads with the usual snub features of youth. Brian was more broad-shouldered than I was; Dad's strong build had missed me, for I was slender like Mother, but quite healthy. Brian now spoke to me, a rare occurrence.

'You're doing the sandwiches tomorrow.'

'Why the hell? I did them this morning, it's your turn.'

'Mum says,' he returned indifferently, already moving past me along the pavement.

'But it's your bloody *turn*.'

He stopped and faced me for a moment. 'You got plenty of time before you go to the swot pot. You did them this morning, do them tomorrow morning.'

'Why not you? Just *tell* me that. Why not –'

'I'm going for a new job,' he said over his shoulder. 'Got to be at Cowley at eight.'

'How you getting there?' I called. He was already receding.

'Bike,' he said over his shoulder.

'Better take that bloody silly cardboard out of your wheel, then,' I called vindictively. 'They'll think you're daft.'

He ignored me, of course, and I went back into the house to have it confirmed that I had to do the sandwiches the next morning. This was a job that Brian and I both hated. We had to do it by turns. The Bargeman's offered, in addition to beer, two items only of solid food: cheese sandwiches and pickled onions. In an average week-day lunchtime, half a dozen sandwiches would be asked for. Brian or I had to get these ready before we went out in the morning. Then a damp cloth was put over them and they were, as a card behind the bar announced, 'Freshly Cut' for the rest of the day. Without such small acts of assistance, my mother could not have tended the pub single-handed all through the day; and single-handed she had to be, for my father had a part-time job at the brewery that kept him out till mid-afternoon. So I had to take Brian's sandwich stint the next morning. A long wrangle ensued as I tried to make sure that he would do two successive stints to make up. I forget how it came out. But that would be another reason for me to remember that evening. It was the last day of Brian's working life that was not given to (in one form or another) Morris Motors.

*

The reason I had been scouting for fritillaries was because they were a source of pocket-money for me and Brian. There was a florist's shop in George Street where you could get sixpence for a bunch of thirty. Sixpence in those days was the price of two visits to the cinema (if you were a juvenile) or a week's supply of cheap sweets at a ha'penny an ounce. Brian used to organize a posse of six or eight boys and we used to work each field relentlessly, everyone marking out an imaginary strip about three yards wide and picking every single fritillary in it. Lovely little flowers they were, white or very pale pink, with that elegant head that earns them the name of snake's-head fritillaries.

Focusing more clearly on that April evening, I realize it must have been in 1926, which meant, since my birthday is in July, that I was coming up to fourteen and Brian was sixteen. I know it was 1926 because in that summer three things happened. Brian went to Morris Motors; I decided, largely through inertia and a general preference for the devil I knew over the devil I didn't know, to stay on at school; and we had our Last Fritillary Expedition. Although Morris Motors took Brian on that morning when I had to make the sandwiches, his pay as an apprentice was so low that the fritillary business, for all its associations with his childhood, was too useful a source of income for him to let it go just like that. One Saturday afternoon in May, due notice having been given, he rallied the motley crew who were his picking team. Brian eyed them dubiously as they assembled in the pub yard. Several of them were girls; this was an innovation that had crept in only towards the end of the previous season, and against Brian's will, but the fact was that girls tended to be good pickers: they had sharp eyes and nimble little hands, and were more industrious than boys. Boys allowed themselves to be distracted: they took offence at chance remarks and squared up for a fight, or if a brightly-coloured butterfly zig-zagged by they would run after it and try to throw their jackets over it. Girls worked on much more steadily; on the other hand they had certain built-in disadvantages. However young they were, they tended to have even younger brothers and sisters whom they had to look after, which of course meant bringing them along. This made the walk along the towpath very slow, and it had to be a walk and not a bike ride because naturally the little kids didn't have bikes. Brian fairly exuded dissatisfaction as he looked over this mob, but they were what he had to work with and he adopted a fatalistic attitude similar to that of the Duke of Wellington on the eve of Waterloo. There were some bright spots: one of the girls, Dorothy by name, was a superlative worker, with a picking rate far higher than anyone else's; my presence, too, was an advantage in its way, because I had experience and was amenable to discipline; and solidity came from Brian and another boy of his own age, named Ivan. This Ivan was a fellow apprentice at Morris Motors. He looked a good-natured fellow, and indeed the fact that Brian was willing to tell him about the fritillary-picking business and invite him to join us showed that he knew Ivan would not laugh at him for playing such a kids' game. Ivan had a long-boned, humorous face with a pleasant smile and there seemed to me, in an indefinable way, something unusual about him, something I could not place.

In the end about a dozen of us, not counting the small children too young to be anything but a nuisance, set out. We went down the street to the river towpath, along to Folly Bridge, across the road, and along the towpath again, past the point where the Cherwell flows into the Thames and makes it suddenly into a much bigger river, and not far downstream of that we were opposite the fields we had come to plunder. We eyed them longingly; if we had had any kind of boat we could have ferried ourselves across and started work, but we had to trudge on to Iffley Lock and go over the bridge there, and then come back about a quarter of a mile. (Donnington Bridge, of course, was still thirty years into the future.)

At last, however, with all the delays and hold-ups and tantrums, we approached the wide meadow we meant to strip of its fritillaries. In another week or so they would be past their best, and in any case the meadows would probably be mown. It was today or never. But Brian's face set hard as the field came in sight, and he pointed over to the far end.

'We're not the first,' he said shortly. And indeed there was a row of figures, bent double and picking away. About six of them. About our own average age and size.

We stopped and Ivan asked Brian, 'Does it matter?'

'Does what matter?'

'Them being there. There's enough to go round, en't there?'

'No,' said Brian firmly. 'This is the best field and we planned on picking this 'un and we're going to pick it. They'll have to find somewhere else.'

'Seems a bit rough on them,' Ivan said dubiously. I liked him for being fair-minded, but I could see Brian wasn't having any. The Thames-side fritillaries were his personal property. He was not a ruthless boy, at any rate not more so than most boys, but he did not like having his plans interfered with.

'I'll go and talk to 'em,' said Ivan. 'If we offer to leave them a *part* of the field, say about a third of it – down to that big tree there, p'raps....'

'What's the matter with you?' Brian said bad-temperedly. 'They're in the field we come to do. We've lugged ourselves all this way with these bloody kids and all the rest of the carry-on, this en't the time to start getting soft on some gang of locals that – '

Ivan had already started to walk down the length of the big field. One by one the other pickers saw him, stopped work and straightened up. Their leader, from the way he held himself and the way the others glanced across as if to take their cue from him, was a thick-set boy with a mop of very black hair.

‘What’re you picking?’ Ivan called when the intervening space was short enough for him to be heard.

‘Fri’illaries,’ was the reply. The letter ‘t’, except at the beginning of a word, does not exist in the dialect of Oxfordshire.

‘Well, let’s share the field, eh? You have it to yourselves down to that big tree, and we’ll – ’

Ivan stopped abruptly as he was forced to duck. The black-haired boy, immediately on discerning his drift, had bent down, picked up a stone, and hurled it fast and accurately at Ivan’s head. What was more, he took the stone not from the ground – there are usually very few stones lying about in meadows – but from a basket that stood ready.

‘They’ve got ammunition, by God!’ Brian exclaimed.

The rival party had in fact brought that basket of stones, carefully selected to be suitable in size and weight as missiles, to enable them to launch a volley at short notice at any advancing party. They did so now. One caught me painfully on the shoulder. Some of the younger children sent up a wail of fright. The defenders gathered stones for another shower, and stood watching to see if we would retreat.

‘Spread out,’ Brian ordered. ‘Come at ’em from different sides.’ He was enjoying this. Generalship was more fun than picking fritillaries.

‘You lot sod off,’ the black-haired boy shouted. ‘We was here first. Sod off out of it.’

‘Get the little kids back,’ I said to Dorothy. ‘Keep ’em out of the way.’

Hasty arrangements were made for the protection of non-combatants; but the battle, when joined, was something of an anti-climax. We outnumbered the other party, and moreover their side had little stomach for a fight. Only the black-haired leader and his immediate lieutenant, a bouncy fat boy who seemed to have plenty of spirit, put up any strong resistance, and they withdrew soon after Brian had managed to capture the basket of ammunition. Shouting insults, they receded into the distance.

With the terrain to ourselves we worked away steadily, and at the end of a couple of hours the keenest-eyed botanist could not have found a single fritillary in that wide field. Sitting in a ring, we counted the flowers out into bunches of thirty and slid elastic bands round the delicate stems. One, two, three, we counted them methodically, and found we had forty bunches – a whole pound’s worth. The money would have to be divided by eight, the number of effective pickers, but that still gave us thirty pence each, in other words half a crown. (In my case, that meant five weeks’ pocket-money.) Still working methodically, we put some large dock-leaves into the stout brown-paper carrier we had brought for the harvest, and on this moist green floor we gently laid the forty precious bunches. The job was done, the swag was in its brown-paper carrier, and we were off towards Iffley Lock. Then it happened.

Our path was shadowed on its left-hand side by a tall, thick hedge. The area was, and still is, a patchwork of waste ground and allotments, and at one point the hedge was interrupted by a stile over which we had to climb one at a time. Brian went first, then Ivan, then I. The girls and younger children came after, as in an Oriental society. And undoubtedly it was this that saved the fritillaries. Dorothy was carrying them, and she was due to get over the stile next. But before she had done more than put a foot over it, the three of us in the van were suddenly assaulted by a party that had been waiting in the green shelter of the hedge. I knew nothing of the attack till I was sent spinning into a bed of nettles by a vicious shoulder-charge that caught me on the wrong foot. I staggered, trying to avoid going full-length; my sleeves were rolled up and the fiery stings instantly made themselves felt all over my arms and hands. Turning, I saw that our attackers were the boys we had driven away, plus reinforcements. Fair enough that they should answer force with force! Not that there was any question of an equal contest; the force they had now put into the field was overwhelming. The black-haired boy was there, and so was the bouncy fat boy, but the latter had now been joined by three members of his family, which was evidently one of those families in which the resemblance is so close as to be almost comical. They all had exactly the same appearance, and the way you told them apart was simply by size. There was one about a third as big again as the original fat boy, another about half as big again, and a third about twice as big. This last was doubtless the eldest brother or perhaps the father, if they had a young-looking father. The sight of them all together might, as I say, have struck me as amusing if they had not been so ferociously intent on doing us the maximum of damage. Obviously they were going to give us a good hiding and take our fritillaries into the bargain.

With a sudden, silent rush, they had Brian down on his back beside the stile. Ivan at once stood over him to prevent his getting kicked in the ribs, and began exchanging punches with the biggest of the fat characters. Glancing rapidly over the stile, I saw that the girls and children were in ragged flight, Dorothy still clutching the paper carrier with its precious quid's worth. The sight gave me a flash of inspiration. The boy with the mop of black hair had his back momentarily turned to me; darting forward, I gave him as hard a push from behind as I could manage, sending him heavily forward into one of his companions, and in the same instant I vaulted over the stile and ran after the girls. When I caught up with Dorothy I snatched the brown-paper bag from her, turned, and held it up mockingly in the sight of our attackers. The black-haired boy was staring angrily after me, as if hesitating whether to give chase. 'I've got the flowers!' I shouted. 'Come and get 'em!' And I went off like the wind.

My motive was simply to draw off some of the invaders and give a better chance to Brian and Ivan. In so far as, in those breathless moments, I had a plan, it was simply to run until they were on the point of catching me up, and then throw the carrier into the hedge so that they would stop to pick it up and I would escape. I was running along a gravel path that flanked a patch of allotments and led more or less straight in the direction of the Iffley Road. At a turn of the path I risked a backward glance and saw that the black-haired boy and one of the fat ones were some thirty yards behind me. Not enough margin to allow of any slackening of speed. I put my head down and ran like a greyhound, and to my surprise was still ahead when the gravel path widened and became straighter, and I realized that I knew where I was: this was Jackdaw Lane, running between the big Victorian church on the Iffley Road and the University athletics ground. In a few moments I should be on the main road, with people walking along and traffic going by, and though my pursuers would obviously be able to grab the fritillaries from me, it would not be possible for them to do much more. A few quick punches and a kick or two, before melting unobtrusively away, yes; a full-scale beating-up, there in full view of the passers-by, no. My plan had worked. Then, as I covered the last few yards to the pavement, I saw through a red mist of exertion that it had worked better than I would have dared hope. A few yards to one side was a bus stop; a bus was approaching it; slowing down; stopping. I was saved. I ran, I jumped on, I went down far into the interior of the bus, under the watchful eye of the conductor, and sank gasping into a seat.

What I needed now, of course, was for the bus to move off. In theory there was nothing to stop the two boys from boarding it and travelling to whatever stop I chose to get off at, then beginning the process again when we were all out in the street. Seconds ticked by; the bus stood as if sunk in concrete; the two hounds came right up to the entrance and peered inside. I was finished, I thought; I had so nearly made it, and now my luck had turned bad and everything was spoilt. But they stopped, hesitated, conferred, and finally drew back and watched helplessly as the bus, as slowly as a bus in a nightmare, pulled away from the stop.

I sank back, feeling suddenly faint with relief. I had not realised until that moment how afraid I had been. I slumped back in my seat, shuddering uncontrollably from sheer nervous reaction from the fear and tension.

Then the conductor was by my side, saying, 'I said where *to*, lad.' Evidently he had said it once and I hadn't heard him.

The last few minutes had been so crowded that I had had no time to hoist in the fact that, although I carried booty worth a princely pound, in terms of actual currency I was penniless. Not one piece of legal tender lurked anywhere in my clothing. There was nothing for it but a spot of play-acting. I dived a hand into one trouser pocket and wiggled it about. Then, simulating the dawn of a mood of bafflement and unease, I did the same on the other side. Finally I got out of my seat and stood in the aisle and repeated the performance more furiously. People began to look at me. I did not need to simulate blushing. I felt the dark crimson creeping up to the roots of my hair.

'Sorry,' I mumbled to the conductor. 'Thought I had a penny. Could have sworn. Must have dropped it somewhere.'

He reached up and with one decisive jerk pulled the cord which rang the bell to stop. The 'ting!' had to my ear a contemptuous note. The bus wearily halted at a stop where no one was waiting. We were just opposite the Cricketer's Arms, an establishment in which I have since spent many convivial evenings.

'Off,' said the conductor with a curt motion of his head towards the exit. 'And next time you gets on a bus, have a look in your pockets first. We haven't got all day to waste on sloppy kids.'

As I went down the aisle I heard him say to a lady passenger, 'Did it on purpose, I shouldn't wonder.'

'They're too saucy these days,' she replied.

After the bus had gone I hurried over Magdalen Bridge and took the bag of fritillaries to George Street. The florist bought them, though he grumbled and said he could have sold them much more easily if he had had them earlier. He said it was getting on for closing time, and the next day he was shut, and how could he expect to sell them before they wilted?

I said nothing. I knew he had a stall outside the Radcliffe Infirmary on Sundays and did a roaring trade. He would easily get rid of them the next morning. His grumble was probably a routine, to see if he could force down the price. I just stood there and waited for the pound note, and when I got it I went straight home.

Brian was already there. I was relieved to see him, not much the worse for the fight, though he was holding a cold compress to one of his eyes, and when he took the compress away I saw that the eye was already turning purple. Our mother, crossing and re-crossing the room as she went about her tasks, informed him each time she passed his chair that it was a disgrace and he ought to know better and she was ashamed to look at him.

'I got the money,' I said to him, and put it on the table.

What I wanted him to do, of course, was to praise me for my quick-wittedness in saving our cargo from certain confiscation. But it hardly surprised me when he did not.

'If you'd stayed and helped us to put up more of a fight,' he said, 'we could've kept them.'

This was so absurd that I didn't bother to argue with it. I just said, pacifically, 'Perhaps, but it'd have taken time. We'd never have got to the shop before it closed. It's better this way, honest.'

'It's a disgrace,' Mother said from the scullery doorway. 'Fighting at your age, and coming home with a black eye. I don't know what you'll be up to next.'

Brian folded the pound note and put it in his shirt pocket. I had complete confidence that he would share it out fairly among everyone who had picked the fritillaries. But I suddenly felt very tired, and rather low-spirited. For the first time since I had been pushed into the nettles, I became aware of the angry cluster of stings all over my hands and arms.

*

A week or two after that, quite early on in that summer term, a major shift in my life occurred, in the quiet casual way in which these things sometimes happen; it altered my relationship with the authorities at school, pointed in a new direction, and determined the channel along which my energies, such as they were, would henceforth flow. It was all because several of my schoolfellows and I were caught smoking behind the bicycle sheds. It so happens that I have never cared for smoking, and didn't then, but one can't afford to be left out of these mild acts of rebellion in the long welter of tedium that makes up a school career. We were caught; the master who caught us threatened that if any of us stepped over the line again he would report us to the headmaster, which meant a caning.

I had a rooted objection to the idea of being caned by the headmaster, a bald-headed vulture of a man of the physical type now usually selected by casting directors to play the part of a concentration-camp *kommandant* or mad scientist, and this spurred me on to take an unusual amount of trouble in my entry for the Essay Competition. It seemed the simplest way, given that I could string sentences together fairly easily, to get myself out of this bad patch.

We were all entered for this competition automatically; it was simply one of those routines by which schools try to ensure that there will be a long enough list of things to give out at Speech Day when parents are present. We were given a subject and a date by which it had to be handed in and that was that. Most of the boys produced some sort of scrawl, three or four sides of school paper, enough to avoid punishment. But I decided to have a real go.

The subject was 'An English River', and I decided to write about the Thames, which I saw every day of my life and yet knew almost nothing about. Once started, I made the discovery that I was actually enjoying the job. I forgot the original motive, to avoid the indignity of a caning from that bald-headed caricature of a sadist, and began to do the job for its own sake; in other words, my intellectual life began at that point. I got maps and traced the river's course from where it rises in Gloucestershire right down to where it washes muddily into the sea. I went to the Public Library and took out books that told me something about the fish that lived in the river and the water-birds that preyed on them; and about the days when the Thames had been an artery for trade and vessels had plied ceaselessly up and down, and of the fights that continually broke out between the boat people who wanted a clear channel for navigation, and the fishing people who wanted to build dams as an easy way of catching hundreds of fish, in the days when river fish were an important part of everyone's diet. I mentioned places like Reading Abbey and Windsor Castle and the Tower of London.

It took me two or three weeks to write the essay, and they were weeks that changed my life. In that short span, history laid her spell on me. It is a strange thing, this passion to understand the past; though perhaps 'understand' is not quite the right word, for the more we immerse ourselves in the past the stronger grows the half-secret conviction that we shall never understand it, only become involved with it in the same compulsive way that a musician is involved with music or a painter with pictures.

What those weeks revealed in me was that the bias of my mind was towards the historical. Since my assignment was to write about a river, from any point of view at all, I might easily have concentrated on the fact that rivers are made up of water. Water, when you come to think of it, is a worthy subject for an essay on its own. Not only is it a component in every living being, but in itself it is one of the great abiding mysteries. The amount of it on the earth is in equilibrium; it neither diminishes nor increases. It is perfectly possible to manufacture water in a laboratory by mixing two parts of hydrogen with one of oxygen, but no busy scientist is going to trouble to do so when there is so much water available simply by turning on the tap. And so the quantity remains fixed. Every drop of water that exists has existed since the world began, endlessly recycled, drawn up by the heat of the sun into clouds, sent wandering across the sky, releasing itself in rain, falling into seas and rivers, or on to the earth that filters it into seas and rivers or sends it up again as vapour, on and on without end. An awesome thought! But, although I was aware of the timeless mystery of water, I had to see that mystery as endlessly impinging on the moving, changing, shifting, evanescent human scene, which is never the same today as yesterday though it is founded on elements that do not change.

This is the fascination of history, that it blends the timeless mysteries with the day-to-day concreteness of here-and-now. Its materials are unchanging. The patterns it makes with those materials are endlessly varying. The deep-down stuff of the human being – the need to survive, the fear of failure, the urge to triumph over one's rivals, the need to give and receive love, the dread of loneliness and of being forgotten – are as changeless as water. But the shapes that human beings fashion from these materials are never quite the same in one place as another, one time as another. When I looked at the river that flowed past the doorstep of my parents' house I knew that a mile to the north, at Wolvercote, there was a mill. Its slender chimney greeted me on the northward skyline whenever I walked out as far as Port Meadow. I found out now that there had been a mill in that spot for a thousand years. For about the last hundred it had been exclusively a paper mill, but before that, century after century, it had driven machinery for any and every purpose – grinding corn, turning lathes and spindles, anything. And why had there been a mill for so long in that spot? Because some Anglo-Saxon, or group of Anglo-Saxons, had taken note of the fact that as the Thames rounds the bend at the foot of Wytham Hill it increases slightly in speed, evidently because the slope of the ground is intensified at that point. The timeless physical fact – water flows downhill – produces a succession of specified historical effects in local life – the flow of trade, the pattern of settlement, the kind of work people did. The fundamental truth, too deep and settled to be called historical, meets the swirl and flow that is history, because history is never *merely* a swirl and flow but always reflects the everlasting bones that underlie it. To study it is to study the changing and the unchanging. It is the one study that includes *everything.*

Green as I was, an adolescent boy with no reading, no travel, no breadth of experience or information, I became a scholar in those weeks before I knew what scholarship was, because the passion for scholarly immersion entered my soul. I had only the vaguest notion of what historical study consisted in, but I knew that whatever it was it called me and that more than anything else I wanted to answer that call. From that time I date my omnivorous reading; my passion for consulting maps, charts, lists, anything that will yield some information about how things used to be; my willingness to listen to people with long memories. I became ready to get out of bed early in the morning to grapple with some speculative problem while my mind was fresh from sleep, or to stay up late at night in order to finish reading a long book while I had the momentum to absorb page after page without stopping. I had no sense of merit in doing these things; I was merely obeying my nature.

All this revealed itself in me for the first time when I got down to work in an effort to turn in a respectable entry for the Essay Prize. When I had finished, my contribution was so long that I handed it in with a certain amount of fear and trembling; the average schoolmaster (and our lot were mostly very average) was quite capable of seeing it as some kind of insult, a sign that I was trying to make the whole enterprise look ridiculous by turning in this mammoth overplus of information. As it turned out, I had misjudged them; they liked it, and I won the prize.

This removed me from the penumbra of having been caught smoking, but I realized at once that I had filled one hole by digging another. When Brian heard that I had won something called an Essay Prize, his worst intuitions about my character would be confirmed. I had managed to keep from him the sight of the stack of books I gathered from the library, and to do my reading and writing behind a firmly closed door. No one in the family had so much as heard of the Essay Prize, but once I had been declared the winner, some busybody dropped the word in at home within twelve hours. The matter was, naturally, discussed the next time we all met at table, and I can remember the contempt with which Brian's eyes rested for a moment on my face.

'What d'you get for it?' he asked in his off-hand way.

'Get for it?'

'Yes, get for it, don't y' understand, what's the *prize*? You've won it, haven't you? What d'you *get*?'

With everyone's eyes on me I felt my face growing hot. In a low voice, doubtless only just audible, I said, 'I think they give you a book.'

Brian said nothing to this. He simply shifted his attention to his plate and left me to get on with my strange, effeminate half-life. Brian considered book-reading one of those skills that girls had, like flower-arranging or embroidery. That a brother of his had read through a lot of books and written an essay about what he found there – it was easy to see how the mere thought irritated him.

Still, the two of us continued to share a few activities, until he finally shook me off, and one of these was going for bike-rides. You didn't, in those days and that setting, get a new bike until you had earned it as the glittering prize for some tremendous achievement. You had old bikes, usually with cannibalized parts. It takes a long time for a bicycle to wear out, but some of the ones we had as kids must have been close to completing even that lengthy process. They were far, far older than we were, and some of them had fixed wheels, and back-steps for mounting because the saddle was so high, and other relics of Edwardian days. Usually one of the tyres , thinned by long wear, developed a puncture before you had gone a mile. We got to the stage where we could mend a puncture by the roadside in about seven minutes. Otherwise we could never have gone on a bike-ride.

Suddenly I see an image, one of memory's glossy photographs. The two of us are coming down the hill from Shotover. It is very steep and, since it has not yet been macadamized, has a shifting surface of gravel and dust. Brian is ahead – he was always ahead as a matter of course, being older and stronger and more of a hastener than I was. But coming down this hill he would have gone ahead anyway, because the brakes on my bike were good – my father had adjusted them for me the previous evening – and those on Brian's were very, very faulty. The blocks had worn down almost to nothing, and his wheels were so buckled that during part of each revolution they made no contact with the brakes anyway. By pulling at them with full force, he could slow himself down a trifle, to the accompaniment of a rhythmic groaning sound, but to stop altogether he had to put his left foot down on the ground and bring the bike round broadside, like a speedway rider.

None of this deterred him from shooting off down the hill so fast that he soon began to dwindle in the distance. I followed at a cautious pace. We didn't, in fact, meet again till I got home, about fifteen minutes later, Brian having already been there for a while. What I shall never forget is the sight of Brian, his jacket flying open in the wind, negotiating the sharp left-hand bend that took him out of my vision. He was going at what I should have thought an impossible pace, and to get round the corner at all he had to bank over so hard that his left elbow, jutting out, actually rubbed on the ground. I looked at his jacket, when I got home, and saw the patch of dust at that point on the sleeve.

I suppose if anything had been coming the other way it might have been the end of Brian then and there. But probably there was no risk of that. He had an exceptional nerve, but he was not foolhardy. Cars in those days made a loud noise as they slowly climbed steep hills, and, because very few roads had yet been paved, also went along in a cloud of white dust. If there had been a car coming, Brian would have read the signs, thought quickly, and managed somehow to skitter round it.

I couldn't do things like that. But I admired Brian for being able to do them. He had a reckless dash that was entirely missing from my character. He had animal courage and animal high spirits, and he never bothered about whether people liked him or not, just blasted on through life. All this was very different from me, and when you add to that the fact that he took after our father and I after our mother, with soft pale hair and a more slender build, it was natural for him to think me no better than a girl.

Chapter 2

One night, after I had been sent up to bed, I came down to fetch something, and through the half-open door of the main living-room, where we both ate and sat about, I saw Brian and Dad sitting with their heads together, earnestly discussing something that evidently had to do with facts and figures. 'I'm not convinced yet as it's something I need,' I heard my father say, and Brian reply, 'It's the coming thing, Dad – you might as well be the first in your neighbourhood.' I paused and eavesdropped.

'You talk like an advertisement,' Dad said. He pronounced it 'adverteyesment.'

'P'raps I do. What the adverteyesments say is true, anyway. In a few years, it'll be only the failures who –' Then Brian saw me listening and said, 'Hop it, young 'un. This is man's talk.'

I got what I had come down for and went back upstairs. I didn't much resent his speaking to me in that way. I was too used to it. But I wondered, as I drifted off to sleep, what could they be talking about. What was being advertised? It'll be only the failures who what?

I didn't have to wait long to find out. A couple of afternoons later, when I got back from school, my parents were hanging about and my father seemed nervous, keyed-up. My mother was cutting sandwiches at the kitchen table.

'Are we going somewhere, Dad?' I said.

'We could be,' he said. (It was June, and beautiful weather.)

'The sandwiches, I mean,' I said.

'We might be going on a little outing,' he said, half embarrassed, half excited, in a way I had never seen in him before; and my mother added, 'I'm just cutting these in case we don't get back till right on six and there's no time to get a meal.'

It was nearly five by then,so I knew we couldn't be going on much of an outing, but what was the excitement? Then there was a tinny drumming sound from the street and Dad said, 'That'll be him.'

'They're all ready,' said my mother, wrapping the sandwiches in a damp cloth ready to be put in a basket; doing her part, as usual.

My father hurried out into the street, with me at his heels, and there it was. A bull-nosed Morris Cowley, its coachwork painted the kind of drab green you generally see on garden sheds, and its brass radiator gleaming a rich yellow in the sunlight. Perched aloft – cars were very high-built in those days – were Brian, in the driving seat, and beside him a thin man in a bowler hat. I had never seen the man before. He had a grave, deliberate expression, as if he expected to be consulted only about matters of the greatest importance and complexity and otherwise not troubled.

Brian stopped the engine by some process that seemed akin to strangulation. It choked, and died.

'Here it is, Dad,' he called out. 'One brand-new Morris Cowley tourer, complete with all equipment, ex-works, road-taxed, insured, and it's yours.'

My father approached cautiously and looked up at the bowler-hatted man.

'Mr Prothero, from the works,' Brian explained. 'Assembly line foreman. He lives over this way so it was convenient for him to have a lift, and he gave me a few wrinkles about handling the car in traffic.'

There was, of course, no driving test in those days. You just bought a car in a showroom and drove it away, even if you had never seen one before.

'I should hope he did,' Dad said. 'I should think you need a few wrinkles, what with it being the first time you've driven on the road. How d'you do, Mr Prothero.'

Mr Prothero opened the door on his side, clambered out on to the running-board, and stepped thence to the ground.

'How d'you do, Mr Leonard. I think you'll find the car satisfactory. And the young man here drives quite safely. He's got a lot of confidence and that's what you need.'

'Not too much, I hope,' said my father.

'Come on, Dad, get in,' said Brian. 'Let's have a spin before you have to work. Where's Mum?'

He did not invite me, but I was determined to go anyway. The car was an open four-seater, and I was as excited as anyone at the prospect of riding in it.

My mother now appeared on the pavement, with the basket of sandwiches, and said uncertainly, 'Is Brian driving?' She looked at Mr

Prothero as if hoping he would introduce himself as a professional chauffeur hired for the occasion.

Mr Prothero, after greeting her with perfunctory politeness, turned back to my father and said, 'You've got a good buy here, Mr Leonard. You won't regret it. This model has been very successful. And the servicing facilities are ample. Oh, yes, ample.'

His Adam's apple moved up and down in his stringy neck as he talked. Standing there talking about the car, resting a hand on one of the front mudguards, he seemed to be drawing authority from it. It was only when he got away from the car and existed within his own aura, so to speak, that he became an ordinary little man trying to look dignified. But the bowler hat did help him a little.

'Course I'm driving, who else?' said Brian to his mother. 'I've done lots of driving. I have to, it's part of my job.'

'Just within the works, of course,' Mr Prothero confirmed. 'But he's got plenty of confidence.'

'Will you be all right getting home, Mr Prothero?' Dad asked considerately. 'Or shall Brian take you home and come back for us?'

'No, no,' said Mr Prothero benignly. 'It's just a few minutes' walk for me now. And before I go I want to see you all set off. Your first family trip.'

We got aboard. Cars in those days were rather like boats, and I remember leaning back in my corner as if I expected to trail one hand in the water.

Brian was the last to get in; he paused to swing the starting-handle. The car shuddered into life, the gear-lever shaking, the flimsy mudguards trembling, a deep throb coming up through the leather of the seats (yes, leather, in those days).

We moved off, made our way through side streets to the Abingdon Road, and then swung right towards open country. My mother, clutching her basket, leaned forward and called nervously over the noise of the engine, 'Where are we going?' She could feel the wave of male excitement coming from the front of the car, and her feminine realism and sense of nest-building responsibility were coming into play. She could see the two of them getting so high on pride of ownership and the thrill of motion, driving on and on, leaving the pub doors shut, discontented patrons gathering on the pavement, complaints to the brewery, Jack losing his licence, the family destitute... Women of my mother's class and generation took the attitude that men were big children, that the fabric of life was held together by women, the ones with the grown-up sense, the foresight, the savvy. I have still not decided, even after all the years that have gone by, whether this view was right or wrong; what I do know is that they held it, firmly, unquestioningly.

Brian shouted back over his shoulder, addressing partly her and partly Dad, 'We're going up Boar's Hill – I'm going to show you how she can climb!'

He stamped on the accelerator. We had left the paved street of the city behind now and clouds of white dust were billowing from the tyres. The car lurched and swung to the foot of Boar's Hill and began the climb. Brian changed down to second, then to first. The engine went on to a high sobbing note. But we climbed evenly, and even at the steepest point we were doing twelve or fifteen miles an hour.

'See her climb! And with four up!' Brian exulted.

'Goes well!' Dad agreed. He was pretending not to be excited; no one was fooled.

When we got to the top, steam was coming from the radiator cap, but Brian said that was normal. We chugged into Wootton village and stopped to eat our sandwiches. The car hissed and sighed quietly to itself. I think we were all very happy. I know I was. We were a motoring family!

'It'll make nothing of getting to the seaside, this will,' Dad said to Mother. 'Just chuck everything in and off we go. No waiting for trains.'

'If it doesn't go wrong on the way,' she said.

'Oh, we'll have Brian along. He'll have a box of tools and if anything gives trouble he'll have it right in no time.'

Brian grinned, round a mouthful of ham sandwich. No wonder he was enjoying the motor age. It was making a king of him, or at least a dauphin. My own way of life seemed as usual drab, ineffectual, utterly overshadowed. But on that magic evening, by the village green at Wootton, with the woods waving on the skyline and the long white road stretching ahead and behind, I didn't care. I was sharing in it; for a brief time I, too, was part of the motor age.

*

As an employee at Cowley, Brian had been able to buy the bull-nose car at a discount. Second-hand cars were of course very plentiful by the later 1920s, and many people who expected to have a car as a matter of course never looked further than the second-hand market. Brian, with one powerful shove, had placed his father in the new car bracket, and the fact only served to buttress his position as the effective son of the family, the achiever. He was living *now* whereas I, by staying on at school, was plodding along year after year in pursuit of some distant and largely unguessable reward. He owned a succession of motor-bikes so bewilderingly rapid that one never knew at any given time whether the machine in the yard was a settled possession, or on loan to be tried out, or in the process of being tinkered up to be sold the following week. Tools, the blue exhaust of engines, spare parts, mechanical noises, absorbed him at home as they absorbed him at work; except for those mysterious absences which were, I was quietly convinced, something to do with the complex, mysterious, beckoning and forbidden region known as Girls.

As my body grew larger, and began to grow hair in the appropriate places, I spent a lot of time thinking about Girls, and making tentative sorties, but I never got anywhere. I had no wage-packet, I had no motor conveyance, I didn't know about anything interesting. I don't think I resented it because I accepted myself as a totally uninteresting person. Such gifts as I had did not seem likely to open the way to a colourful, eventful life. They just seemed a recipe for work, work and still more boring work.

This attitude was so solidly fixed, both in me and in everyone in the family, that it hardly caused a ripple when one day, when I was about fifteen, the school headmaster gave me a letter to take home to my parents. With the usual never-sleeping sense of guilt that the educational system is, or was then, designed to implant in the young, I immediately assumed that I had been guilty of some crime so monstrous that my father was being brought into the matter; warned, perhaps, of my impending expulsion from school, or urged to discipline me in some way. I had no consciousness of having done anything in particular, but that made no difference because I was aware of so many anarchic wishes and impulses in my own inner being that I thought it only natural that older and wiser people, who doubtless could read my thoughts, should see them and take account of them. If I sat day-dreaming in, say, a maths lesson, and not just day-dreaming about something innocent but quite specifically day-dreaming about the attractive girl who worked in our local newsagent's shop and how much I would enjoy pulling down her little white knickers, I might (I felt) just as well have handed in a signed confession at the end of the lesson.

So I took the letter home and, under the pretext of making a cup of tea for my mother and myself, got the kettle boiling and steamed the envelope open. To my relief – not unmixed with a certain sense of anti-climax and boredom – all it concerned was my scholastic prowess and my possible trajectory in the educational world. The headmaster assured my father that I was potential University material, the stuff of which scholarship-winners were made, and if my father would consider the matter seriously and give me encouragement at home (i.e. not take me away and put me into a wage-earning job) the school, for its part, would do its best to further and to bring out, etc, etc. Probably the head wrote this kind of letter to the parents of anyone who looked even faintly promising, to try to get a strong Sixth Form and a respectable number of ex-pupils at the University, to look good in his own professional record. All in the day's work. I re-gummed the envelope, making a bit of a soggy mess of it which fortunately passed unnoticed, and handed it to Dad when he came through for his tea at six-thirty.

He read it slowly and with attention, his jaws moving as he consumed liver and bacon but his eyes moving carefully along each line of the letter. Then he said to me, 'You're clever at your studies, seemingly, Peter.'

'I get along all right,' I said.

He looked up at me and I can see him so clearly now, with a friendly and rather puzzled smile on his broad, honest face.

'I don't know where you get it from. I was never much of a hand at it. Must be your mother. She was bright at school.'

'She's bright now, come to that,' I said.

'Oh, she's bright,' he said. 'My Katie's a clever woman. But she doesn't have to be bright in that way, not these days. That stops when you leave school. Or College I suppose. That's education brightness. I never had it myself. I was more the way Brian is.'

Brian, Brian, always Brian.

'Your teacher's written,' he went on, tapping the letter. 'But of course you know that. You brought it home. What I can't make out is, what does he want me to do?'

'Nothing,' I said quickly. I forgot, in my eagerness to pass the whole thing over without fuss, that I was not supposed to know what was in the letter.

'What he seems to be saying,' my father went on, staring hard at the letter as if hoping to read between the lines, 'is that if you stay at school you've got a good future. You can try for college and that. Well, we know already. You're *at* school, aren't you? If you was going to leave school you'd ha' done it six months ago. So what's he after?'

'Nothing, Dad, I'm sure,' I said. 'He just wants to warn you that if I really do go in for all these... scholarships and stuff, it'll mean stopping at school a long time.'

'How long?'

'Three years, more or less,' I said.

He thought for a moment and then said, 'Well, I don't see why not. Suits you, does it?'

'Well, it's boring most of the time, but I – '

'We don't need another wage-earner in the family,' he said, talking to himself more than to me. 'Not say really *need*. We got enough. Of course, if times gets any *worse*...' he shrugged. 'But Brian's in a steady job and the pub won't fall down. You can stay on at school and take all these exams and papers and that, if it's what you want to do. Your mother and I won't stand in your light.' He looked down at the letter. 'He says here he'd be glad to see me any time, to discuss your future. Not much use discussing it with me. It's all things I don't know about.'

'There's no need,' I said. 'I expect he put that bit in just to be polite. There's no need for you to spend time going and sitting around talking to him.'

'Well,' he said, 'I got enough to do, that's for certain.'

Those few minutes' talk were the only discussion my father and I ever had about my career. And it was logical enough, for what, as he very reasonably said, could he be expected to know about these things?

*

If the headmaster's letter, and my father's tranquil acceptance of it, marked some kind of tiny little Rubicon, the passage from being a very ordinary nonentity to being someone who, however much a nonentity, had plans and ambitions, I can recollect no actual difference made by the crossing. Except, perhaps, that the whole forbidden topic of Girls became even more fraught with danger and disapproval. This was brought home to me, if it needed any bringing home, by the episode of the Kiss on the Way Home from Tennis.

One of my cronies at school was called Tupper Boardman. The name 'Boardman' was well known in the town, since his father ran a business hiring out punts and canoes on the river, beside Folly Bridge. But no one knew where 'Tupper' came from; it was lost in the mists of his boyhood. He was a big, round-faced lad, with no brains to speak of but a pleasant, easy-going disposition and a knack of getting on well with people. He and I shared one thing in particular: our sexual fantasies. We both had the same devouring interest in Girls, and came from the same kind of family backgrounds where our parents thought they were giving us a good upbringing if they placed obstacle after immovable obstacle in the way of our ever satisfying our natural curiosity. So, of course, it all spilled out of our mouths in dirty talk. We used to speculate, and weave fantasies, for hours together, lounging about on interminable Sunday afternoons.

One day in early summer, when we were about sixteen, Tupper declared that we must put the whole thing on a more practical basis and really decide on some Way of Getting to Know Girls. I thought for a while and said listlessly, 'What about tennis?' I was hardly serious, more than half fantasizing, because I had no tennis racquet and didn't know anyone who would teach me to play, or where one went to play, or anything about it. But Tupper leapt on the idea and his energy shoved me along. He said there were some municipal courts not far off where we could play without joining a club or anything, and he would show me the rudiments. We went along to the courts and somehow I managed to get hold of a clumsy, out-of-date, heavy tenth-hand racquet and, evening by summer evening, got up to the state of proficiency at which it wasn't utterly absurd to contemplate playing doubles. All the time, naturally, we kept our eyes open to spot any other regular frequenters of the place who might do to make a start on: that is, persons of the female sex, able to hold a tennis racquet and willing to be approached by that particular avenue. And of course both Tupper and I took it for granted that if we succeeded in Getting to Know a Girl to any satisfactory depth, the tennis business could be quietly forgotten.

And behold, after about three weeks we did actually get to know a pair of girls, about our own age, who always came together and played together. Tupper, who had more nerve than I had (it would have been difficult to have less), suggested to them that it would bring our game on if we played doubles regularly, and they agreed so readily that I concluded that their motive for taking up tennis was the same as ours, or more accurately its appropriate converse.

The girls were called Jean and Susan. Neither of them could have been called attractive, except in one over-arching respect: they were female. Jean was tall and lanky with spots, which I found off-putting, but Susan, though undeniably plain, had qualities that anyone determined to be attracted to her could build up into selling points. She was little and skinny, so in my imaginary dialogues about her, lying in bed and talking it over with my *alter ego*, I was able to use words like *petite* and *svelte*. I don't know whether Tupper got anything going with Jean – he *said* he did, and gave me a lot of succulent details, but I didn't have to believe him; it was just a game between us – but for a couple of weeks a small, half-hearted spark flickered between myself and Susan. I did my best, but my heart wasn't really in the business and neither was hers, it was like trying to build a fire with a few wisps of damp straw, and after about a fortnight she went away with her family on their annual seaside holiday and when they came back we just didn't bother to pick up again. I could see, so plainly, that there wasn't going to be any real help coming from that quarter. I didn't resent it or feel rebuffed, it was just one of those situations that aren't ever going to amount to anything.

Still, that's how it came about that one warm, dusky summer evening, at about half-past nine, I was standing at what I hoped was an unfrequented point of a quiet street near my home, with my arms round a girl, and I was kissing her. I had never kissed a girl before, so even kissing Susan was quite a big bang. It was, I found out, not quite the simple matter that people made it seem on the cinema screen. The first time, I went at it too frontally and bumped her nose with mine. She giggled, and for one dread moment I thought it was all going to collapse into a Jolly Good Joke, but I tilted my face over a bit on the second run-in, missed her nose and homed in quite satisfactorily on her mouth. She seemed to have no objection, and as for me, what the next ten minutes or so revealed clearly was that this kissing lark was definitely to my liking and that when circumstances permitted I intended to take it up as a better use of leisure time than lawn tennis. It was my first kissing session and I daresay it was also Susan's , so I remember it with interest and a kind of affection and I hope she does too, if she's still on this earth, but it obviously wasn't going to lead to anything very exciting. I was just thinking of closing the proceedings with a vote of thanks and walking on to Susan's bus stop when a figure that seemed vaguely familiar pattered rapidly by. This figure turned its head as it drew level with me, shot me a swift, recognizing look and was gone. After a moment's searching in my mind I recalled the name and identity. It was a little sharp-nosed woman like an old weasel, called Mrs Walker, who was an acquaintance of my mother's; I had seen them talking together outside our local shop.

No alarm bells rang in my head. I had stopped to give Susan a few friendly kisses and Mrs Walker-Weasel had come by and seen us, so what?

So what was that my mother came into the kitchen a couple of afternoons later and, finding me for some reason in there by myself, moved straight in to the attack. She must have been holding the matter all ready in her mind, waiting for the right moment to hit me with it, because without any preamble she said, 'Peter, I think you ought to know that you were seen on Wednesday night.'

Seen? I thought. *Seen*? What happened to me on Monday and Tuesday nights, was I invisible then? But of course I knew what she meant. Seen getting up to something. Immediately I flushed crimson with alarm; I couldn't see myself but I could feel the heat of it and I knew I was crimson.

'Seen doing what?' I parried feebly.

'Don't pretend, Peter,' she said in her quiet, serious voice, the one she used when it was something important. 'Seen with that girl.'

'Yes, I was with a girl. I was seeing her to her bus stop. She had to get to Kidlington or somewhere. We'd been playing tennis.'

'Well,' she said, resting one hand on the table and looking straight into my eyes, 'you weren't playing tennis when Mrs Walker saw you.'

'No. I didn't say we were playing tennis at that *exact moment*. I said we *had* been. At that exact moment we were – '

'Peter, I'm not going to argue with you. You know what you were doing and you know why I'm speaking to you about it.'

'I don't,' I said recklessly.

'I don't know whether it was wrong in itself,' my mother said, still in this very composed voice, 'but you've got to look at it this way. You're at the beginning of a long road. You won't be in a position to take a girl into your life for a good many years yet.'

So what was I supposed to do? Take up raffia work?

'It'd be different if Brian took up with someone,' she went on. (Oh, yes, Brian, Brian.) 'He's in a position to start making plans if he wants to and in any case he's older than you. But if you start at your age, *already*, getting to know girls, it's going to make a lot of difficulties.'

'I won't make difficulties.'

'You may not think you're going to. But difficulties come along, once you get interested in a girl and she gets interested in you.'

Come along?

'It'd be more fair all round,' she concluded,' if you'd let all that side of life wait till you're ready to deal with it. More fair to everybody.'

I knew exactly what she meant. It was as near as she could come to telling me that in order for me to have an education my parents were going to have to Make Sacrifices. Even if I got some help from the education authorities, I would still not be bringing a wage into the house, and the best way for me to show gratitude was to keep my head down to my studies and, presumably, stun my developing sexuality into submission by drinking a bucketful of bromide every four hours.

In addition, of course, to the whole thorny topic of Sacrifices, there was the general sexual puritanism of that epoch. In a tiny remote area inhabited by 'advanced' and 'progressive' people, attitudes had changed since Queen Victoria died, but it hadn't happened in our neck of the social woods, the respectable upper-working and lower-middle classes. No, siree. Youthful sexual relationships, even those that stayed very much on the surface, were viewed very warily. At the first hint of a relationship between boy and girl, even of the lightest kind, parents, teachers and grown-ups in general lifted their nostrils and sniffed danger in the wind. When a young man had been in a job for some years and started earning a decent wage, he could start 'going steady' with a girl and in that case it would be all right to bring her home – in fact, before they had been going steady for more than a few weeks it would be *de rigueur* to bring her home, for the ritual looking-over. This, as it were, purified her. No allowance was made – in the official code, that is – for the need to get to know a number of girls, short-term, in order to find out which kind suited you, and was suited by you, best. Monogamy was lifelong, and as far as possible it came into force at birth. The ideal thing was to grow up next door to a nice girl, have her as a childhood sweetheart, and in due course sign her up for matrimony and children: and if circumstances prevented you from hitting this target exactly, you were at least supposed to stay as close to it as possible.

A more perfect recipe for encouraging furtive debauchery could hardly be imagined. If even innocent relationships with girls had to be swept under the carpet, how could one ever discuss those that were... I was going to write 'not innocent', but stopped myself in time. Because of course there was no such thing as an innocent relationship with a girl. The mere fact that the boy had been endowed by nature with a penis and the girl with a vagina, made it highly dangerous even for them to stand within three yards of each other. Innocence had ended when our first parents were turned out of the Garden of Eden; the Bible said so.

Chapter 3

So my life became largely a matter of work, work, work and more work. Since history was my main subject, and as I got into the University by doing well in it, I suppose our Sixth-Form history master at school must be regarded as having played an important part in my life, but I don't remember feeling much gratitude to him. It was a straight working arrangement, with no sentiment on either side. He was shoe-horning historical information into me until I was sufficiently crammed to pass muster, and he was doing it because to have scholarship-winners among his pupils was his mark of professional success. His name was Grayson. He was a countryman by origin, and spoke in an only slightly modified version of the slow bucolic burr of Charlbury or Rissington – as those places were in those days, I mean, before they became commuter villages.

I can see Grayson now. He had very pale blue eyes set in an expressionless meat-face, and the general impression he gave was of a walking corpse. I suppose he had begun life at the bottom of some large hungry rural family, the son of a farm labourer or at best a struggling tenant on a few acres, and he had pulled his way up to the position of being not only a schoolmaster but a Sixth-Form master, a history specialist, preparing boys to enter the universities. He had done it by the same kind of immovable, patient doggedness that he would have shown in following the plough fourteen hours a day. He had no opinions about anything. He regarded opinions as a waste of time, just as he regarded the idea of taking pleasure in history as a misdirection of energy, or would have regarded it that way if he had ever thought about it. His task, as he saw it, was simple. Our heads were empty; historical facts lay waiting in neatly arranged heaps known as 'periods'; all he had to do was take the empty young head in one large capable hand, gather up the appropriate sheaf of knowledge in the other, and force the one into the other. He was not unkind; he was not kind. He was a machine. One of the marks of his early poverty was that he distrusted books. The book, the real book with lettering on the spine and all those printed pages and perhaps a frontispiece, he regarded as a luxury. What you did with a book was to gut it and take out a dozen or so pages of 'essential facts', as he always called them. (It hadn't occurred to him that a fact might be essential in one perspective, inessential in another, and *vice versa*.) These facts you stored methodically. He showed us his method.

Grayson's technology for storing essential facts, after which the book itself could be thrown aside like a squeezed orange, was to take sheets of regulation school paper and fold them so that the lines ran vertically instead of horizontally. He then took a ruler and made a thick marginal line, about an inch in from the left-hand side of each half-page. Then he was ready to 'read' the book, which was a matter of picking off 'essential facts' in exactly the way the old Cockney hop-pickers used to strip the Kentish hops from the bines, and write them on his vertically-lined pages. The space on the left of the margin could be left for various asterisks or comments, or a supplementary date or two. When this process was complete, and the book itself ready for the discard, he took two paper-fasteners of the old-fashioned sort, with brass heads, and drove them through to hold the pages together. Those facts, that book, were henceforth his property. He had domesticated, tamed, disciplined them, brought them into his system. He applied this not only to historical books, but to every book he read. I remember once, during a history period when we were getting on with some piece of work while he sat at his desk and supervised us, noticing that he was reading a book about Japan, subjecting it to the folded-paper and brasshead-fastener routine. For some reason it has stuck in my mind – the thought of the strange, complex, mad, sinister, beautiful, teeming mass of contradictions that is Japan, being first of all crushed into a book – that is bad enough – but then dehydrated and hung up to dry in one of Grayson's home-made information-folders.

He insisted that we all, the boys in his 'set', made these notebooks too, and for two whole years I tried to go along with it. Up to a point, of course, such methods do work, at that stage in one's intellectual life when the sheer absorption of new information counts for so much. But I am glad to say that Grayson never succeeded in communicating to me his own narrow utilitarian contempt for the book, the book unprocessed, unsystematized, the book still in possession of its own identity. To me, a book is something to be lived with, to be taken down in odd moments, to be read in different settings and in different moods; to yield up, at a third or fourth reading, some hitherto unnoticed fact, lying about somewhere in tiny print, that suddenly makes one see the whole subject in a new perspective.

I already had that attitude when I was sixteen, but of course I had it in an inchoate, unconfident form. I thought that serious, grown-up, motivated people regarded knowledge as Grayson regarded it. I thought study, historical or otherwise, was the two round eyes of the paper-fasteners, staring at me reproachfully, their colour the dull gold of perseverance.

That was one of the two pillars of my life when I was sixteen and seventeen – Work, the endless dour succession of tasks under the eyes of Grayson and his paper-fasteners. The other was Girls, that undiscovered country about which I day-dreamed and speculated. Perhaps the second was so richly extravagant, just because the first was so grimly down to a standard of 'reality' that wasn't realistic at all. Grayson was trying to cram into me a notion of historical truth that was too dead, too cut and dried, to bear any relation to the capricious nature of human experience as it actually is. So perhaps I compensated in my sexual fantasies, which were not hindered by any empirical knowledge.

When I was eighteen, however, my interest in Girls received an injection of new intensity (if that were possible) and of realism, both at the same time – a heady mixture. This experience came at the very outset of my life as a University student. It came so early, in fact, that it was before the start of my first autumn term: a beginning before the beginning.

It happened during the interim between getting a place at Episcopus College and actually going to the University. I didn't consciously choose Episcopus. It was just that I went along in November of the year in which I was seventeen and took the scholarship paper for a group of Oxford colleges, and it was Episcopus that offered me a small bursary. In those days, going to the University on somebody else's money was rather like collecting trading stamps. You got a bit of money from your local authority, a bit from the State (if you were very lucky or very bright) and a bit from the college that took you. When I put the bursary together with my other bits and pieces I had just enough to get by, with care.

Episcopus was a middle-of-the-road college with no particularly brilliant intellectual tradition but with graceful buildings, a beautiful garden, and lots of money in the bank. I didn't, of course, know how it was regarded within the University, nor concern myself with such matters at all. For me, a college was just a college. I knew that going to one would involve changes in my life so unimaginably huge that it was better not even to think about them in advance, just let them happen and try to react as they came at me. It was all too much to comprehend. I was going to be an Oxford undergraduate, one of those mysterious beings who lived on the other side of the magic barrier. The barrier was magic because, like all magic, it existed purely in the mind. Both sides kept to their allotted territory, not because there was any physical reason for it, but because the magic said so. They walked in Christ Church Meadow, our kind stuck to the towpath or the lanes round Ferry Hinksey. They drank beer in pubs like the Bear and the Lamb and Flag, our kind drank the same beer in pubs like the Bargeman's. They punted or rowed on the river, we fished in it. Except for a few recesses of the colleges, virtually everywhere in Oxford was open to the public, so that theoretically there was no reason why either side should not infiltrate the other's territory, but no one ever did.

And here I was, just about to cease being the younger son of the landlord of a side-street pub and become an undergraduate, with a gown, going to lectures, eating my meals in the College Hall, and having a servant, called a 'scout', to clean my rooms. ('Rooms', not 'room': the standard allowance was two, one that doubled as a study and sitting-room and one that was a tiny cell-like bedroom.) How was it all going to seem, to one who was, permanently and inescapably, the younger son of the landlord of a side-street pub? The question was too remote for speculation; I would just wait and see.

Before being formally taken on I had to go through the formality of the 'interview'. In those days timing was not as strict as it is now, when the University has become one more factory and production schedules have to be kept up. Nowadays, any student coming up in October is interviewed in the previous December and that's that. But my youth fell in a less mechanized era, and I was summoned along to Episcopus to be listlessly eyed by a committee of dons one fine day towards the end of March. I hardly remember the interview, which was pretty much a formality. I was asked a few questions about my 'interests', to which I would have replied, had I been candid, that I hadn't any, my life being taken up entirely by working and fantasizing about girls; but I had made up a few in advance, just in case.

The Senior Tutor was presiding over the interviews – they had ten or a dozen to get through – and after mine was over he asked me if I would mind waiting about for a little and coming to see him in his rooms at midday. I had never before been asked whether I would 'mind' doing this or that; either it was something I had to do, in which case I was just told to get on with it, or the matter was not brought up at all.

Thinking of this, I strolled in the garden, trying to feel that it belonged to me, or that I belonged there, or something. But of course it didn't work. There were a few undergraduates walking or standing around in the sunshine; their voices, as I moved in and out of earshot, sounded dreadfully posh, the sort of standard governing-class bark that I knew I could never imitate. How was I ever going to talk to people like this? Then I passed a bunch where a man was talking to two others, holding their attention with something he was explaining, and I noticed to my relief that this man had a broad northern accent; I didn't know whether it was Yorkshire or Lancashire or what, never having been north of about Banbury, but I recognized it as an accent I had previously heard only from music-hall comedians.

I cheered up at this – it was, surely, evidence that you could meet all types at College, not just upper-class barkers – and cheered up still more at the reflection that by getting in at Episcopus I had already cleared a hurdle I had been secretly dreading. For the last six months I had been haunted by the nightmare that the only college to offer me a place might have been Pembroke.

Had I anything against Pembroke College, did I know anything to its discredit? Certainly not. But my father had an elder brother who was a college servant. And, though I had vaguely registered the fact that Uncle Ernest worked for a college and was a 'scout', it was not until some six months previously that I had learnt, from casual conversation, that it was Pembroke he worked for. Nervous as I was already, unsure of my standing among all these self-assured Public Schoolites, my blood ran cold at the thought of my uncle, a man with the same surname as myself, quite possibly with some facial resemblance invisible to me but visible to everyone else, serving food and making beds, his relationship to me an immediate bar to my desperate efforts to blend in and avoid being noticed. I speak, remember, of the year 1930. Thirty years later, when undergraduates began trying to ape the working class and anyone who actually *was* proletarian was at a distinct social advantage, it would have been another story; but by then it would have been someone else's story.

So I meditated on my lucky escape as I walked about on that velvet lawn and under those stately trees. With any luck, I reflected, I ought to get by without being actually persecuted; and if I could stick it for three years I could put 'B.A. Oxon.' after my name, and that would be a meal ticket for the rest of my life. That was my eighteen-year-old view of the world.

It was twelve. Through the clear spring air came the chimes of one clock, then another, then two or three more. The first one had just about finished all twelve strokes as the last one began. I knocked on the dark wooden door and heard a voice say reflectively, as if talking to itself, 'Come in.'

The Senior Tutor was called Gadsby. He was a long, bony man with sad eyes and a gentle voice. He wore a bow tie. Everything he said and did was gently dignified. You could never imagine him guffawing with laughter or raising his voice in anger. He was polite to me. He rose, briefly, when I entered the room, asked me to sit down, and sat down himself. He apologized for asking me to wait. Nobody had ever treated me like this before. It was a heady sensation: I was a gentleman already, a scholar and a gentleman. I imagined, and on the evidence I had I don't see how I could have imagined anything else, that all Oxford dons treated students in this way, that it was their standard manner. That belief was not true, though it was less untrue in 1930 than it would be today.

Gadsby said that he had a suggestion which, if I accepted it, would take up a couple of weeks of my summer vacation. He asked me if I had any particular plans for the summer, as if he half expected me to say that I was going to Interlaken or reading in the Vatican library. He knew, of course, that I wasn't, but to act as if I *might* be was part of his politeness, part of the Oxford politeness of those days.

When I mumbled that I had no special plans, he told me that the College was involved in something called the Oxford and Poplar Boys' Club. This existed to bring boys from the poorest quarters of London, the real hard core of dockland, out into the country at week-ends and in particular to give them a summer holiday in Oxford. They stayed in a North Oxford boarding-school which was empty for the holidays, and in order to get some sort of social mixture, illuminating for both sides, they tried to get at least one Oxford undergraduate to be there with them.

Gadsby didn't explain why it was that they were scraping the bottom of the barrel by getting me to masquerade as an Oxford undergraduate. Obviously the College must have tried and failed to get anyone else. It was a time when the European currencies were in a very low relation to the pound, and you could go to France or Italy with £15 in your pocket and live comfortably for two months. With this kind of thing beckoning them across the Channel, it was evident that none of the undergraduates at Episcopus felt particularly seized by the thought of staying on in Oxford, sleeping in the dormitory of a prep. school, and helping dockland lads kick a football about and swim in the river. There had, clearly, been no takers. Gadsby did his best with this situation.

'The function of the Oxford, ah, participant,' he said in his beautifully modulated but so sad voice, 'is to represent, in all sorts of little ways and without necessarily thinking about it, the Oxford... attitude to things.'

It was a good job I didn't have to think about it, I told myself silently, because I wouldn't have known what to think about.

'And of course you have the advantage,' he pursued, leaning back in his chair and looking at me thoughtfully, 'of having grown up in Oxford. That is... an undoubted advantage.'

'I can show them round,' I said.

'Show them round, yes,' he said, 'and communicate to them what it feels like to have become, ah, very familiar with... Oxford surroundings. And, as I say, without consciously thinking about the matter at all. It will be... instinctive with you.'

Looking back, I see what he was doing was to reassure me that I would have something to offer these London lads, however absurd it seemed to be sending me in to bat for 'Oxford'. It was part of his politeness, and it must also have soothed any misgivings he had about getting off the hook in that way. The plain fact was that the Oxford and Poplar Boys' Club were being short-changed. They had asked the College to provide an undergraduate and the College hadn't been able to find one. So Gadsby had picked me out, at the interview, as a half-way decent substitute.

We talked a bit more, settling dates and details, and then he stood up, rearing in front of me in his bony length.

'Thank you, Leonard, for taking this job on,' he said. 'It won't go... unappreciated.'

'I'm glad to, sir,' I said.

'It should prove... not without its, ah, illuminations.'

'I expect,' I said.

He held out his hand.

'We shall see you in October. Congratulations again, and I hope you'll be happy here.'

The handshake business was so unexpected that for a moment I just let him stand there with his hand out in front of him, then I grabbed it (much too hard), mumbled something and went away. As the door of his panelled room closed behind me I realized that I still had a long distance to go before I could think of myself as a scholar and a gentleman.

All the same, I had, it seemed, to try to be enough of an s. and g. to represent that point of view among a crowd of boys from the East End, and not just the East End but Dockland. As I put a few things into a bag one August afternoon, preparatory to cycling over and joining them, I wondered for the first time, now that the experience was actually here, what it was going to be like. Words like 'East End' and 'Dockland' had a great deal of power in those days, when England was very much divided into compartments and people lived territorial lives. I had a mental picture that sprang into life when someone said 'East End', and it was on the whole a Victorian picture, and the horrifying side of Victorian life at that, compounded of flaming gas-jets, puddles of gin-scented urine in the gutters, dark alleys where ruffians waited to leap out and murder you for the sake of your small change; of huddled, weeping women in shawls and pallid children with tear-stained faces outside pubs that had no closing-time. In my vision of the East End, every street was dirty, every window-pane was broken, no one was well dressed or well fed, and the constables walked in twos. It was a vision of ordinary working-class life, as I had seen it in Oxford, stripped of everything that made it cosy and comfortable, and with its harsh and difficult side made incomparably harsher and saturated with criminality.

Where exactly this mental picture came from, I reflected as I strapped the hold-all on to my bike and pumped up the tyres, was not clear to me. But there it was, and I was about to spend a whole fortnight in the company of a pack of young wolves from this jungle. According to a note I had had from the organizers in London, the club rented premises in Oxford for two weeks and most of the boys came for one week, with an almost complete change of personnel at the first week-end. Well, at least if any of them took a particular spite against me I would, in all probability, only have to stick them for the seven days.

The two weeks began on a Saturday afternoon; the boys came down after lunch and the first meal they had was high tea, served at six o'clock as it was in my own home. The place they rented was the Gryphon School, a place where the dons sent their children so that they could start being little dons at the age of eight or nine, without ever going out of the leafy sanctum of North Oxford. The Cherwell was in front of us, the University Parks on one side, and (in those days) open country on the other. It was high summer in Oxford, with all the typical things: the hint of smoky mist early in the mornings, already whispering the message of the autumn that will begin in a month or so, the long seedy grasses, the cow-parsley very high along the lanes and footpaths, the river flowing as if the water were moving in its sleep. In those days, before the tourist trade was as highly organized as it is now, and before the Summer School industry had begun, Oxford was a very sleepy place in August. The University people were all away – I'm sure many dons went through a fifty-year career and never set eyes on Oxford in August – and there was nobody in the streets except the visitors. Even they didn't descend in huge, disciplined coach-loads; they came by train in ones and twos, got off at Oxford station and wandered the streets with guide-books, looking slightly lost.

I had been told to get there about five o'clock, but when I did so the place was as silent as a beautiful painting of summer hung on the wall of a quiet room. The buildings, the playing fields, the gardens, the tool shed and the bicycle racks, stood in absolute tranquillity. It was one of those perfect late-summer afternoons when England suddenly seems the most attractive country in the world and Oxford the most attractive place in England.

I leaned my bike against a wall of the main school-house and went in at the front door. It opened on a wide hallway with rooms going off it on both sides. One was a dining-room with long tables already laid for a meal. Still no one about and no sound of feet or voices. Quite clearly they had not arrived yet, this was the calm before the storm, and a perfect calm it was. Looking out through the big windows, I could see that the sun, as it gradually levelled its rays, was picking out every leaf, twig and blade of grass in an individual clarity as if it were something unique and precious. Then I heard gentle footsteps behind me and turned to see a middle-aged woman in a large white apron, who smiled at me.

'You're not with the party, are you?' she asked, and in those few words she told me she was Irish. I had not, in my short life, met with many Irish people, and it was a pleasure to hear her melodious way of pronouncing English, 'No? You'll be Mr Leonard, I suppose – Peter Leonard, isn't it?' She held out a soft, strong hand. 'I'm Mrs Finnegan. I do the cooking here, I'm the school cook on a regular basis but I come in a couple of weeks in the summer to cook for the Poplar boys. It helps to make ends meet, you know? My husband's a college servant and in the summer he's laid off for thirteen weeks, so we have that problem every year, but besides, if we didn't have it, I'd still come and cook for the London boys because it's a pleasure to put some good meals in front of them. It's my belief the most of them don't get the best food in the world in their own homes, not the food growing boys should get, not by a long way.'

That was how Mrs Finnegan talked: not volubly but in a steady stream, and always in this soft Irish voice with its instinctively beautiful modulations. I could have listened to her for ever.

'Of course you can't go too far with it,' she went on. She didn't of course say 'with it'; the consonant of 'with' was that soft sound the Irish make that is sometimes represented in print by a 'd', though actually it is half-way, not so hard as a 'd' but not so totally breathed as a 'th'. 'You have to give them what they're used to or they'll torn their noses up at it, even when they're hungry.' She laughed. 'I gave them steak and kidney pudding once, I made six great big puddings and beautiful they were though I do say it myself, and do you know there were five or six of them pushed their plates away? I wouldn't have thought that was a rich people's dish, but I suppose anything with steak in it, even shin of beef cut up into odd bits, must be too expensive for some of the poorest people there. I think they live on things like pig's trotters. And of course jellied eels.'

'Jellied eels?' I asked wonderingly. It was a dish that only flourished in the tidal stretches of the Thames and was virtually unknown to the populace upstream of Teddington.

'Yes, bless you, jellied eels they will have at least once during their week here or it's not a real holiday for them. Of course it's a rest for me that evening because they eat them cold, just with thick doorsteps of bread and butter and mugs of strong tea, but then it's mugs of strong tea with everything, even roast beef.' She looked at me with amused concern. 'If you find any of the meals a bit strange, and you don't fancy them, do your best and sit there with the others and make it look as if you're eating, and when the meal's cleared away you come and see me in the kitchen and I'll do you an omelette or find you some nice cold ham or something, we can't have you going hungry.'

'That's very kind of you, Mrs Finnegan,' I said.

'Ah, it's not anything at all to do for a young fellow that's giving up part of his holiday to come and help boys that aren't so fortunate as himself.'

I hadn't quite seen it in that light, but I realized that that was how she must see me and I had no objections to her approving of me. I liked her, already, a great deal. Her eyes, above broad cheekbones, were very honest and very kind. For her sake I became, instantaneously, a friend and admirer of the whole Irish nation.

'You'll be a College man, of course?' she asked me.

'Yes,' I said. 'Episcopus.'

'Sure and that is a beautiful place. I had an old uncle that worked in the garden there. My uncle Sean. He was the one that gave my parents the advice to come and find work in Oxford. So he's responsible for us being here as a family. He spent his life working in that garden and by the time he finished he knew more about plants and flowers and everything than any man alive. So that's how I came to be born in Jericho all those many years ago. I'm an Oxford woman born and bred, though I dare say I don't seem much like one. We were always an Irish family once the door was closed behind us.' She laughed, inviting me to share her amusement at the oddness of life.

A short, stocky man of about forty now entered. He was wearing shorts, an open-necked khaki shirt, and gym shoes. His features were coarse but not unpleasant, and his head, already, was bald and shiny across its central dome. He looked at me appraisingly, then turned to my companion.

'All ready for the invasion, Mrs Finnegan?'

'We're well provided for, sir,' she smiled. 'I've just been talking to Mr Leonard. He's just after arriving.'

'Good,' he said crisply. 'Hello there. I'm Bill Robinson, everybody just calls me Robbo, and I run this show. During this fortnight I give the instructions and a certain proportion of them get obeyed a certain amount of the time. I give a lead in most matters and some people follow my lead some of the time. It's the best we can hope for. You done any youth work before?'

'N...no,' I said.

'Ah, well, I wouldn't have expected it. You're only just over the stage of being youth club material yourself. Well, it's all to the good. Help you to see things from the same perspective as the lads. They told me at Episcopus you were a good mixer.'

They did, did they? Who the hell had told him that?

'You'll be sleeping in one of the dorms,' Robbo went on in his no-nonsense way. 'There are three. They're on the first landing. You might as well take your stuff up and stake out a claim to a bed before the hosts of Midian get here.'

I thanked him for the advice and took my grip upstairs. The dormitories lay tranced in the beautiful sunlight. They were small and domestic, with ten or twelve beds in each. I pictured the young sons of the upper middle classes curled up there in cosy, protected sleep. Now the beds were going to be occupied by not only the working class, but the working class of the East End, by denizens temporarily released from the bizarre circle of hell which in my mind's eye was 'Dockland'.

Alone, in that silent sunlit room, I chose the bed next to the window. I wanted to be near the outside world, not only for fresh air in case the room became foetid, but for a deeper, more obscurely felt reason: what lay outside the window was my accustomed world where I knew I was at home. What lay inside was going to Dockland. I felt fairly sure I could cope, but I didn't know how pleasant or unpleasant it was going to be, and I wanted reassurance. Then I thought of Mrs Finnegan and felt slightly ashamed. She was reassurance in herself. If she could feel benevolence towards these uncouth and doubtless unwashed lads, so could I.

As I stood there thinking these thoughts, my eyes were fixed absent-mindedly on the street outside, which was as quiet and empty as a well-arranged stage set just before the curtain goes up and the first entrances are made. Into this set there now came something that announced that from that moment everything was to be changed. A forty-seater coach with 'Somebody-or-other's Motors, Bermondsey' painted on the side drew up outside the school gates, and immediately the wheels had stopped revolving the door had been wrenched open and a tide of humanity began rapidly spilling out, all boys and all shouting. In a moment they were out and milling round the driver as he opened the luggage compartment in the belly of the coach and began tossing out bags, bundles and here and there a small suitcase or two. Even from where I stood the luggage looked pitifully skimpy; the suitcases, I surmised, were cardboard, and most of the bundles looked too small to hold what a person, even a boy from a poor street, would need for a week. But there was no doubting their high spirits. Released from some hours of having to sit (relatively) still in the coach, they were reacting into frenetic movement, elbowing, grabbing for belongings, scuffling, jumping on one another's backs, or just making short rushes aimlessly up and down, a few yards here and a few there, as if testing that their legs could still run. Then, as I watched, one boy, who seemed no taller than the rest but about twice as broad, went back into the coach for a moment and came out with an old, worn, greasy-looking football, which he launched into the air with a tremendous kick. It soared up past the window where I stood watching, and disappeared out of my field of vision, and in that second Robbo came out of the house and called out, 'Wotcher, lads!'

This was so far from his natural idiom that I recognized it as a ritual greeting, doubtless a yearly tradition. They gave him an answering 'Wotcher, Robbo' but before there was time for anything else the ball fell back down among them and a furious barging, kicking and running started. Robbo, stepping back adroitly to avoid the flying arms and legs, shouted above the noise, 'Twenty minutes to let off steam. Then come in to get organized!' The broadly-built youth kicked the ball clear over into the centre of the playground and the boys whipped off after it, leaving Robbo and the coach driver standing looking at each other in the suddenly quiet gravel yard, and me looking down at them from the dormitory window.

'Any trouble on the way down?' I heard Robbo ask.

'Not to say *trouble*,' the driver said. 'They didn't damage the bus nor nothing like that. There was the usual, like, imperdence.'

'I can imagine,' Robbo said.

'Some of the things they was calling out. They had the windows wound down and they was shouting out remarks to everything else on the road. Fair chronic, some of it was.' The driver suddenly laughed.

'Oh, well,' Robbo said. 'As long as it's just letting off steam through the mouth. Well, you know where the kitchen is, don't you? Mrs Finnegan's got some tea for you.'

The driver departed. I waited about, wondering whether I ought to show myself a good sport by going out and kicking the football about with them or whether it would be better to wait till I was introduced. That little problem lasted for the twenty-minute period of letting off steam, and when they came in Robbo told them to get upstairs and find themselves beds and then come down for their meal. At this meal he made a short statement about me, simply presenting me as 'an Oxford chap who was going to spend the holiday with them and help them to have a good time, not that he thought they'd need much helping.' He made me stand up and be recognized; the boys looked over at me half-interestedly and went on eating, but the ones sitting near me chatted a little and were friendly enough.

That was how it was, pretty much, for the next fortnight. The lads were absorbed in the job of getting as much fun as possible out of their holiday; they accepted my presence as they accepted Robbo's – all just part of the way the thing was set up – and that was it. They all came from the same few streets and had known each other all their lives, so they brought with them their long-standing friendships and rivalries and enmities, they knew the jokes and catch-phrases, and half the time I felt rather left out, but it didn't worry me because my attitude was that I was doing my fair share just by being there and breathing in and out. I wasn't all that keen to be brought into everything, so long as they didn't think me standoffish. And they didn't seem to, in fact for the most part they didn't seem to think about me one way or another, which was fair enough.

I was a little afraid, to begin with, that they would twig me for an impostor, a chap wished on to them as a real live Oxford student who had never in fact spent a day of his life in a college. But after the first day or so, I was ready to smile at my simplicity in having had this worry. The whole issue simply wasn't real to them, wasn't part of their world. They never asked me a single question about what it was like to be at college, so I was spared the trouble of inventing any lies about it. (I wasn't going to tell them that I was nothing but a local yokel, the son of a side-street pub landlord.) It all passed off pretty easily, and I began to feel that I could start well with Gadsby by reporting to him that I had managed the assignment with credit. (In the event, he never asked me.) I gained confidence, too, from the fact that, whereas the boys had all seemed to me much the same on that first evening, I soon began to sort them out into individual characters whose names and faces I knew and whose behaviour I could to some extent predict.

The only two I remember at all clearly across the years are Alf and Chucker. Alf was a thin, narrow-faced boy, lively and restless, who communicated entirely by making jokes. He was the archetypal Cockney humorist. He had, in particular, a vein of sexual humour which was an eye-opener to me. He referred familiarly to things I had only dimly surmised might happen. Apart from that he has almost entirely vanished from my mind, but Chucker is still there very clearly. He was the one I had noticed first, the thick-set chap who had kicked the football up into the air.

Why he was called Chucker, I don't know. It may have been some kind of reference to his physical strength – one could imagine him not merely lifting bags of cement, for instance, but chucking them about – or it may have been something more arcane. Perhaps it should be spelt 'Chukka', but none of them ever had occasion to spell it and most certainly would not have cared. It fell on my ear as 'Chucker', and that was how I thought of him.

Chucker was the king of these lads. Most of them were three or four years younger than I was, but he was the same age or a bit older. He was a man, where the rest of them were boys. He was already in work as a docker, and the scheme was really meant for boys who were either still at school (i.e. under fourteen) or in their first year or so of looking for work, usually as errand-boys or the like. Chucker was probably bending the rules by coming on the holiday at all, but if so Robbo turned a blind eye to it. He was such a natural leader that the boys felt more secure in venturing out of their environment when he was with them. Whether he was a 'good influence' I would find it hard to say, but at any rate he never bullied any of the boys. With his basic good nature and his unquestioned authority, he would not have stooped to it.

This authority of Chucker's came primarily from his colossal physical strength. With poor food, and overcrowding, and living in airless streets, many of the boys were poor enough physical specimens, but Chucker could have posed in the publicity for a body-building school. Short and immensely broad, he had shoulders like a house, enormous hands, and muscles so developed by constantly lifting heavy weights that they had become almost a deformity. Not that his mates would have considered them a deformity; these lads inhabited a world where muscle was well worth having, and the more of it the better.

Chucker had a calm assurance. People deferred to him, and what he wanted came to him, without his having to push or to prove anything. This, it soon became clear to me, extended to the little matter of sex. In the dormitory, after lights out, Chucker would sometimes favour us with brief accounts of some of his sexual encounters. I didn't think then and don't think now that he made any of them up; he would have no need to impress us, his natural inferiors, and in any case I doubt whether he had the imagination to invent anything. Alf was different. His stories, however scabrous, were always farcical, always aimed at laughter, and they always culminated in some *riposte* he had made to the girl. 'So I give her a two-bob piece. 'Ere, she says, this won't cover it. So I says, Well, try a bloody frying-pan, that will.'

I didn't believe Alf's stories, they were just stories, but when Chucker mentioned anything that had happened to him, one saw for a moment into his world and it was completely authentic. His name for any young female was 'tart'. All girls and young women were tarts to him, whether they were in business as prostitutes or not. 'So this tart come up to me,' his stories usually began. And one soon realized that the favours of tarts were to him part of the ordinary amenities of life, like having a pint of beer at the pub or some jellied eels from a kerbside stall.

Night after hot August night I lay in the dark and listened. An important part of my education was beginning, though, in common with most education, it was difficult to know what use it could ever be put to. You had to accept the education first, to take it on trust, and later on, when you had become educated, your opportunities might arrive. One thing I now understood clearly: sexual experiences with girls, which were to me a closed, far-off area to be speculated about, were for Chucker and his kind merely casual. It was what tarts were for, part of the laid-down order of things, and you just got on with it.

To this day, the notion of sexual desire is associated in my mind with the physical feel of Oxford in August, when the warm blanket of Thames Valley summer has been lying on everything till the maggots have had time to breed in everyone's mind. All plant life has reached its full growth and is just about to topple over and start to slide down into the compost of autumn, while as for human beings, most of them – the young ones, anyway – move about as if they were in a sexual trance, mesmerized by the immense parade of fertility going on all around them, their consciousness dwindled to a single focus; the girls in particular, it used to seem to me, walked the pavements in a swaying pelvic pavane, staring straight ahead as if their heads had been emptied of brains and somehow pumped full of semen.

I had, of course, spent every August of my life in Oxford, saving the odd spell of a week or so at the seaside, or at Scout camp or something. But this, my eighteenth, was in an important respect my first. It was the summer when I became urgently aware of sexual desire. I had been no stranger to it during the last three or four years, but it had been a matter of vague, almost unlocalized day-dreaming, hours and hours of reverie in which in imagination I trod the magic groves of the enchanted territory called Girls. Now, suddenly, in August 1930, sexual need became a hard, focused, specific longing.

The actual event that cracked the barrier is quite easy to describe. I had been out somewhere for the evening with about half a dozen of the lads, and we were coming back through Jericho. In those days this was a purely working-class area, its close-set terraces inhabited by employees of the University Press, college servants, railway workers. The different quarters of Oxford were much more differentiated then, and people kept to their own quarter or similar ones. I think the Poplar boys picked up the vibrations from this; certainly they liked Jericho more than they liked the spacious, arboreal area where the Gryphon was situated, and as we walked homeward through Jericho they instinctively slackened their pace and looked about them as if ready to strike up acquaintanceships, get into talk, make new friends. Or were they, in the case of the older ones, simply on the look-out for tarts?

We walked in a long, straggling procession, two and three together. It was just beginning to grow dark, a deep velvet dusk; when we got to North Oxford, the street-lamps would be shining lyrically on the thick green foliage of the trees beside them; here, they merely threw circles of light on the narrow pavements. As we turned the corner at the intersection of Hart Street and Jericho Street, two girls were standing, one defiantly in the centre of one of these circles of lamplight, the other more timidly, half in shadow.

I was walking with the first two or three boys, and as it happened Alf and Chucker were bringing up the rear. As I went past the two girls I took in every detail of the one standing in the lamplight. She was looking into our faces as we went past, coolly and levelly, daring us not to notice that she was there. Her companion, taller and more shadowy, had the ampler body, but she was almost invisible in the presence of such brazen assurance. The smaller, slenderer girl – she looked scarcely full-grown – had a fringe of dark brown hair which shone chestnut under the street-lamp, and brown eyes to match, eyes that searched, probed, challenged. Her skimpy body was dressed in a simple green jersey and dark-red skirt, with a light raincoat thrown like a cloak over her narrow shoulders. My heart gave a great lurch of excitement as her eyes brushed across my face and, for an instant, held my gaze. I had never seen that cool, challenging effrontery in a feminine face before. I have seen it since.

My feet kept on walking, and I believe I even continued the sentence I was in the middle of uttering to the boy at my side. I felt a wild desire to halt and simply plant myself on the pavement in front of the brown-haired girl, to see if she would say anything to me, make any kind of initiatory move. But in the presence of the Poplar boys it was out of the question, and in my heart of hearts I knew that even if I had been alone I would not have had the courage to stop. The challenge she presented was too big and too unexpected. I would simply have walked on with my heart hammering faster, as I did now.

As we reached the point where Jericho Street runs into Walton Street, however, I had to stop and make sure everyone knew that we were turning left. It was my responsibility to see that no one got lost and wandered the streets, and we were supposed to be in by ten-fifteen. I looked back. And I saw that Alf and Chucker had halted beneath the lamp-post and were in conversation, or something that served for conversation, with the two girls.

'Chucker. Alf!' I called. Nervousness made my voice high-pitched. 'We're turning left here.'

I saw Chucker nod his head, but neither he nor Alf made any move to follow the rest of us. I did not know what to do.

'Don't get lost!' I called desperately.

Chucker called something in reply that I didn't catch. It must have been a quip of some kind because I heard the girl laugh, a single clear chuckle that floated to me very distinctly along the empty street.

I turned and walked on with the others. They didn't seem as affected by the sight of the slim girl as I was: the younger ones because they were younger, no doubt, and the ones nearer my own age because in their big-city environment they had seen so much more than I had. Someone passed a remark and there was a laugh or two – more or less on the lines of 'Wonder what Alf and Chucker's saying to them two tarts.' 'Give yer three guesses' – and then we just went on with the evening. I did myself, outwardly. But I kept sneaking a look back to see if Alf and Chucker were in sight behind us, and they never were.

Biscuits and malted milk drinks were laid on in the school's dining-hall at ten-fifteen. Robbo kept it going for exactly a quarter of an hour and then, at ten-thirty, the dishes were wheeled away and there was positively no more. It was his only disciplinary way of making sure that people came in reasonably on time. After the biscuits and milk, you went to bed. We – the main body of our party, that is – got in just as the big jugs of milk were being brought in. Everybody crowded round to get served, and I took advantage of having nobody's eyes on me to slip out into the school-yard and across to the side gate. There was an enormous chestnut tree right beside it, and its bulk hid me as I crossed the yard, and stood just inside the fence, very close to the gate. Something prompted me to do that. I had an instinctive feeling that situations were developing that would be beyond my power to handle, yet in the curious position I was in, with one foot in the official organization and the other among the boys themselves, I might feel obliged to try to handle them. I might, of course, have stayed comfortably inside the school hall, having my bedtime snack and chatting to all and sundry. But I was drawn by a hankering curiosity to station myself outside, in that warm and now fully dark night. There was a jungle scent in it that spoke to something very deep in my being.

I only just gained the tree in time because a figure swung in at the gate at that exact second. It was Alf, walking rapidly and obviously thinking of nothing but getting in before the supplies ran out. He passed within a yard of me, but he was looking neither to right nor left. I stood still for a moment, letting my eyes get used to the night. It was not so black that your eyes could not distinguish objects, and faces, perfectly well.

I stood still, listening and watching. It was scarcely more than a minute before two figures came along the lane and halted by the gate. Evidently to gain a little privacy, they moved to one side of the gate and stood directly by the tree. There was nothing but the gnarled, massive trunk between them and me. Since one was a small, lightly structured figure and the other only a little taller but immensely broad, I did not need to puzzle over their identity. They halted by the tree and there was a silence in which they had obviously other things to do with their mouths than talk. I froze. Already it was too late to cough or make some other harmless noise to advertise my presence in a non-annoying way. Chucker would be angry with me for spying on him, and at the thought of Chucker's anger my legs felt weak. I have heard of people's knees knocking together with fear, and I can certainly testify that an intense trembling in the legs is one of the symptoms of fear because I felt it then.

In between kisses they began speaking in low voices. I could also hear a sound which must have been her moving her hand, or both hands, over the upper part of his body.

'You've got great muscles.' I heard her voice.

'Yerr.'

'I like feeling them.'

'Yerr. I got a great something else too. You can feel that any time.'

'I know,' she said.

She brought out the two words in a calm, matter-of-fact way – no giggle, no coyness, just a straight accceptance of a straight offer. This coolness, when I looked back on it later, excited me immensely. But at the moment all I could feel was panic. Good God! Was she going to take it out, there beside the school gates, at a time of night when there were still a lot of people about? I pictured her hand making its way towards the no doubt Alpine bulge at his fork, but I pictured it not with excitement but with pure dread. Someone would be bound to come by and see them – there would be an outcry, a rumpus – my presence would undoubtedly be discovered- what on God's earth was I to *do*?

Rapid footsteps came from behind me: someone had emerged from the school-house. I turned to look, uttering a quick wordless prayer that the swivelling motion of my body would be without sound. It was Robbo, shorts flapping against his muscular thighs. He made straight for the gate beside the chestnut tree. I am certain he saw me standing there, but he said nothing, only walked on and opened the gate. Now, I thought, he will see Chucker and the girl, he will turn to me and ask why I didn't stop what must be going on, and later on tonight Chucker will kill me. I suddenly saw his huge, knotty fists, felt them already pounding into my face and body. He would break me across his knee like a rotten stick. He would teach me what happened to people who spied on Chucker when he was busy with a tart.

Immediately on top of the wave of despairing terror came the instantaneous, the unbelievable, the almost unrealizable deliverance. Robbo, having opened the gate, walked quickly through it, swung round to his right – thus presenting his back view to the couple – and disappeared down the lane.

Many a time, in the years that have come since, I have speculated on where Robbo could have been off to, walking so determinedly and so obviously with an all-engrossing purpose. Sometimes it has seemed to me possible that he had a mistress who lived in one of the nearby houses, already at that time beginning to be carved into flats. I don't want to seem to have a one-track mind, but when a youngish man walks with that kind of determination through a summer night, there is usually a strong motive and it is usually that one.

He wasn't off duty yet; if he had a girl-friend he may have just been going round to make sure she was in and set up a meeting later on. The snack-time had another ten minutes to run, and then he would have to be back to shoo us upstairs. Perhaps that was why he was hurrying, with so much to fit in. But these speculations are an historian's indulgence.

For whatever reason, Robbo hurried past and saw nothing. And the next instant the school-house door burst open and two or three boys ran out, chasing each other and laughing. This was my opportunity and I seized it. Half-a-dozen flying steps took me close enough to them, as they weaved across the yard, for it to seem that I had been with them when they came out of the door. Unless Chucker had been staring directly across in my direction, I was safe. And the chances were that he was still staring after Robbo.

After a few minutes of aimless horseplay and running to and fro, we were all indoors, Chucker included, and soon Robbo came back and herded us all upstairs as usual. We got into bed, ten minutes later the lights were put out as per discipline, and the standard dormitory talk – football, smut, tribal jokes – ran its course. One by one the beds fell silent as sleep took over. I think I lay awake longer than most. My bed was next to Chucker's, as it happened. I had the end bed, by the window, and he was next. I watched the mound made by his thick strong body lying motionless. So it has all passed over, I thought. For him, just a little fun on the wing. Something to remember his Oxford holiday by, for a week or two, before being swallowed up in more exciting impressions. Then I began thinking about the slim brown-haired girl with her devouring eyes. I had only spent about three seconds looking at her, but it was enough to change my view of life. Hitherto I had accepted the convention that the female role is passive, the male active. But the way she had stood in the middle of that circle of lamplight, looking with that brazen challenge into the faces of the boys as they went past, revealed to me that some girls, at least – for she couldn't be the only one in the world – were predatory. At that thought all my adolescent sexuality, which I had managed for a few weeks to keep fairly quiescent, began bubbling up like Vesuvian lava. I sank into a web of uneasy dreams, and down through them into deeper sleep.

After I don't know how long, something woke me. It was not the time of full moon, but there was enough light of one kind and another coming in through the window for me to see, four feet away from me, Chucker's bulk. I did not – at first – realize what he was doing, but he wasn't asleep; that much I took in immediately. I froze, as I had done beside the tree, and lay there exactly as I had before except that my eyes were wide open. If Chucker had looked towards me he might have seen them faintly gleaming in the dim light from the window. But he didn't look. He had other things to attend to, for now I saw that there were two silhouetted shapes, his and another. The other was slight and weasel-like.

I lay absolutely still while the performance went on, accelerated, eased off, ceased, then in a little while started again. I was not terrified as I had been beside the tree, but I was determined to be very, very careful. Nothing, absolutely nothing, was going to draw me into this business which was so much more extreme, more shocking, more reckless than anything I had ever imagined. How the two of them had managed it I could only conjecture. She must have hung about in the school grounds until everything went quiet and then he must have managed somehow to get her into the dormitory. Through the window, no doubt, though it was a good twelve feet from the ground and I could not recall anything that would help her to get a footing. I had vaguely heard of people 'shinning up drainpipes', but as I lay there and searched my memory I couldn't even remember whether there was a substantial drainpipe anywhere near that window. Still, whatever they had done, it had worked, and she was here, the two of them were within four feet of where I lay and they were... I tried to say it in my mind, to say that they were fucking, but I could not shape the word even silently. It was too raw, too powerful, too anarchic for me. If I uttered it, even conceptually, the ceiling would fall in because of the pressure of the sky above it. They, being strong and lawless, could get away *doing* it, but I knew that I could not get away with even *thinking* it. These two, slithering and pumping in this bed beside me, were the buccaneers, the ones outside the law, the ones who saw something they wanted and went straight towards it, not caring a damn about Robbo or being sent home or making a scandal. I did care about these things. They had nothing to lose. I had a whole world to lose.

And then of course the next thought came to me: was the world that I was afraid of losing as good as the world they were enjoying now, this minute, right beside me? Good God, I was going mad with the sound of their single-minded pleasure. Was anyone else awake? Were they all sitting on their beds, watching? I did not raise myself and look. All I could do was lie absolutely motionless. In the end Chucker and the girl lay motionless too. I became convinced that they were sleeping. And, in spite of the tumult of thoughts in my head, I, too, slept.

I woke to the sound of voices and a general stir of activity. There was an alarm clock in the dormitory which woke us at half-past seven, and it must have gone off without my hearing it. Most people were out of bed by the time I became fully conscious, and were pulling on shirts and trousers and fooling around. We were supposed to go along the corridor to the shower-room, but most of the boys didn't bother. I lay still, coming round, remembering where I was and what I was doing. I had turned over in my sleep and was lying now with my back towards Chucker's bed. I remembered that I was with the Oxford and Poplar Boys' Club, in the Gryphon School, a second or two before I remembered the events of the night before. When I did remember about Chucker and the girl, I went rigid and then, very slowly and cautiously, rolled over with my eyes open.

Chucker was sitting on his bed. He had his trousers on and was doing up the buttons of his shirt. His bulky body as usual dwarfed his surroundings, and it was only because I knew what to look for that I saw the thin shape lying under the bedclothes behind him. To the casual eye it looked simply like an unmade bed, or as if he had carelessly left a pair of pyjamas under the counterpane. Except that Chucker did not wear pyjamas. He slept in an old shirt, or on hot nights nothing at all. Last night it had been nothing at all.

As I came face to face with him I saw to my fright and confusion that he was looking straight into my eyes, as if trying to read in them whether I knew anything or not. I immediately rolled over on to my back, jack-knifed upright and sprang out of bed on the side furthest away from him. My towel was hanging on a hook above the head of my bed, and I grabbed it and hurried off to the shower-room. Usually I followed the example of most of the boys and didn't bother with a shower, but this morning I wanted to get into another room, to steer clear of the whole situation, to play for time until Chucker had got the girl out. Till I was sure she was gone I wanted to see nothing, hear nothing, know nothing.

I had a long shower and as I was towelling myself I heard the breakfast-bell ring down below and the usual stampede on the staircase. I had the shower-room to myself, the sun was shining in at the windows and making great golden oblongs on the floor, and suddenly it all felt very peaceful.

I was dry now. I picked up my pyjamas, which I had thrown on a chair, and with them and my towel bundled under my arm I made for the door. At that exact second, it opened and in came Chucker and the thin brown-haired girl. He was behind her, his broad body screening hers from the sight of anyone looking along the landing from the direction of the dormitory and the stair-head. Not that there was anyone. He was fully dressed. She was naked.

They came straight past me with the kind of cursory glance you give to a dog or a cat. Chucker swished aside the curtain of one of the showers and explained his plan of campaign.

'You gets in here, see, and you turns the water on. If you hear anybody come in, turn it up high and splash about. They won't bother you.'

'When will you be back?'

'Quarter of an hour. Less'n that. Ten minutes. Then I'll bring the towel and your clothes.'

'Quarter of an *hour*? I've got to stay under this thing for – '

'Look, if you stays in the sleeping room somebody'll come in and find you. Try and get down the stairs now and they'll all see you, Robbo and all the lot. Just give 'em a few minutes to have breakfast and then they goes off to their different jobs and that. Then I'll get you out easy. No fuss, no arguments. Why mess it up now when we're doing fine? You've been here all night and nobody's seen you.'

'He's seen me,' she said, nodding towards me.

'Oh, Pete's seen you,' Chucker said casually. 'But he won't make no trouble.'

His tone conveyed no threat, only a simple statement of fact.

'I haven't seen you,' I said. 'I'm not here. I don't exist.'

'Well then,' Chucker said to the girl.

All this time I had been standing stock-still. I was staring at the girl. It so happened that I had never seen a stark naked girl before. I had never even seen a photograph of one. In 1930, such things were heavily censored. We were innocent, and ignorant, to a degree that no one in the world is now. I stood there, unable to move, hypnotized by the sight of the girl's pubic hair. It clustered thickly round the lips of her vagina and then, as it journeyed upwards across the *mons Veneris*, narrowed to a relatively thin streak and then spread out, with a kind of fan-vaulting effect, to the straight line of its boundary.

That moment corrupted me. I became, and remained for years, avidly curious about girls' pubic hair and its individual variations. Something told me even then that no two are exactly alike.

I stood there mesmerized, oblivious for a moment of my situation, of the advisability of getting lost. The girl stepped into the shower cubicle.

'How does it work?' she said bad-temperedly. 'Christ, I never thought you'd put me through all this.'

'Have a shower,' said Chucker indifferently. 'It'll give you summink to do.' He reached past her and turned on the tap. It was the kind that makes the water hotter as you turn it to the right. He gave it a good turn, but of course the first douche of water that came out was cold, and the girl yelped.

'It's bloody freezing!'

'Keep yer voice down.' He twisted the tap again. The water came out hot. She gave a cry of, 'Stop the fucking thing. It's boiling me!'

The spectacle had me riveted. Chucker was leaning forward, water cascading down his back. His shirt clung to his powerful body. His huge shoulders blocked my view of the girl's lower half, which at that moment of excitement seemed to me a tragedy. I wanted to see her sexual hair with water coursing down through it. But since I could only see her upper body, I concentrated on her small, pert breasts. The dash of cold water had made her nipples stand out like pink thimbles. I stood there staring: I could not have moved if the floor had been a sheet of flame.

Finally Chucker got the water right for her and straightened up. He stripped off his soaking shirt, wrung it out, and swished the shower curtain to so that the girl was hidden. Then he turned and saw me.

'Hop it, mate,' he said; but quite pleasantly.

I hopped it. My clothes were back in the dormitory, so I covered my nakedness with the damp, clinging towel. I was still bemused at what I had seen, and when I got to the dormitory I was confused and frightened to see that I had a tremendous erection. Confused, because after all this was hardly the moment for sex to rear its head; frightened, because I felt I must at all costs conceal this tell-tale sight from Chucker, who would probably see it as a kind of insubordination. I dressed hastily, buttoning my still stubborn *membrum virile* into a severe concealment, and hurried down to breakfast. Chucker was just sitting down when I got there. He was next to last, and I was last.

After breakfast I was detailed for some job or other which kept me busy for about half an hour. At the end of that time, I stepped out into the school-yard. There were lots of people standing about. Suddenly the brown-haired girl appeared, walking casually round the corner of the building, having evidently come out through a side door. With no attempt at concealment, walking like someone who had a perfect right to be there, she went across to the gate beside the chestnut tree, out into the lane, and off. Obviously boldness was the best cover. By this time – about nine o'clock – she might have had a dozen legitimate reasons for being on the school premises. Chucker, who had presumably guided her to the side door, was nowhere to be seen.

The last I saw of her was the swing of her dark red skirt below the thin raincoat she wore, as she had last night, thrown loosely over her shoulders. I stood gazing after her. Was she hungry? I wondered. Would she go straight and have breakfast?

Chapter 4

By that time, the Oxford and Poplar holiday was nearly at the end of its first week. Most of the boys, Alf and Chucker included, went home on the Saturday; a new wave flooded in; I, now a veteran with a week's service behind me, took it all in my stride. Mrs Finnegan, kindly soul, kept me going through the difficult times when I had to pretend to pick at revolting food like jellied eels; she fed me behind the scenes and talked to me in her beautiful Irish voice. Subconsciously, I was learning a lesson that was to stay with me all my life: that the complex and unwieldy structure of Oxford academic and scholastic life is sustained by a resilient infrastructure of people who cater and cook and clean and scrub and sew and mend equipment and dig flower-beds over, and without the second, the first would crumble immediately.

Nothing in that second week approached in guilty excitement the episode of the brown-haired girl with the fan-vault tracery of pubic hair – not surprisingly, since there was no one like Chucker to act as the magnet for such feline exciting prowlers of the night – and the week passed quietly; soon enough the afternoon came when I strapped my bag on to the bike again and cycled back across town, a changed character from when I had made the outward journey fourteen days earlier: more alert, more watchful, more discontented, and more specifically aware of what I was discontented *about*. August was nearly over, but I still had September to get through with nothing to do, nowhere to go, and no release for my rampant energies.

I came through it, of course. One always does come through those things, since the merciful Creator decreed that it is the nature of time to tick by. Most of that last month at home, then, is just a warm, hazy blur in my memory. But one long, golden Sunday afternoon will stay with me for ever. It began, just after our family dinner (we didn't call the mid-day meal 'lunch' in those days), as a happy mood of shared relaxation, with jokes and friendliness, and it finished some four hours later with an experience so shatteringly awful that it still comes back to me in nightmares.

We had dinner – roast beef, roast potatoes, greens, apple pie, the whole works – and then, after the inevitable washing-up, I sauntered out into the sunshine to find the yard full of Brian's friends. They had every conceivable kind of motor vehicle except one: the one kind being, of course, the sedate family car. There were heavy motor-bikes, light motor-bikes, a stripped-down Austin Seven, and two or three stark sidecar outfits. More were arriving all the time, parking in the street outside. I knew what was happening because Brian had been talking about it at table; not to me, of course, but in my hearing. There was a grass-track race meeting out in the country, somewhere near Cropredy, and the lads and girls were all going out for an afternoon's fun. Yes, girls too. They were there in all shapes and sizes, all the way from typical motor-cyclists' molls who wore leathers and helmets to pretty, feminine ones in pretty, feminine clothes. I wandered about among them enjoying the stir and bustle and good humour, expecting that in a few minutes some signal would be given and they would all roar off as collectively as a flight of starlings, leaving the street quiet, the yard empty, and the long Sunday afternoon thoughtful and lonely like most of my afternoons. These few minutes, when they were all there and all joking and laughing, was my afternoon's cup of enjoyment, and I drained it right down to the bottom, moving here and there, looking at the strange machines, hearing the jokes and banter, getting a good view of the girls.

Brian seemed to be the chief organizer, which I suppose was why they had assembled at the Bargeman's Arms, and when he was ready he waved his arms above his head and they all began to move off in convoy, their engines crackling and thundering. I stood and watched them go. I wasn't feeling any self-pity at not being invited. I hadn't expected it or hoped for it. Outings like this, particularly outings to watch racing, were – as the kids of the 1960s were to say three decades later – 'not my scene'. But it did rather point up the solitariness of my life as compared with the gregariousness of Brian's.

I was standing in the Sunday-afternoon quiet and just turning to go back into the house, when a rapidly approaching noise became audible in the street at right-angles to me, the one I couldn't see. It was like nothing so much as a prolonged and rather irregular roll on the kettledrums. I turned, knowing that it must come from a vehicle of the same general tendency as the ones that had just gone off in a cloud of noise and *bonhomie.* The vehicle swung round into the street I was standing in, and halted beside me. It was Ivan and his Morgan.

Most of Brian's mates were an undifferentiated mass to me – they looked and sounded rather similar, and I didn't see them frequently enough to sort out one from another, especially as they rarely said anything to me or noticed my existence. But I remember Ivan very clearly for three reasons. One was that, from the day of the Last Fritillary Expedition, Ivan had always been friendly to me and often spoke to me – even, on occasion, addressing me by name. The second reason was that his name was a somewhat unusual one in that place and at that time. Most of the lads had names like Jack and Bob and Phil, but Ivan was Ivan. The third reason, on its own, would have made him indelible in my memory. Ivan was the one with the Morgan.

The Morgan three-wheeler of the 'twenties and 'thirties was the nearest approach to a fast sports car that could be bought and run on a low income. It was made, basically, of the same ingredients as a motor-cycle and sidecar, except that the engine was stuck out in front, with two wheels on either side of it and the third, driven by a chain, at the rear. Driver and passenger sat side by side in a cramped cockpit very like that of a light aeroplane of the period; in fact James Thurber, trying to find words to describe a Morgan owned by a handyman who worked for him in France, said that it resembled the cockpit of a wrecked plane. It was stubby, purposeful, noisy and fast. The engine, out there in the open, got plenty of air to cool it; the exhaust pipes ran gleaming down the sides of the cockpit; the little windscreen was just big enough to keep the rain off your face. All the lads wanted a Morgan. Morgans raced at Brooklands. They raced on grass tracks. They raced along country roads, scattering chickens and dogs. What the rich young man could have from his Bugatti or his Bentley, the poor young man could have from his Morgan, especially if he was handy with a spanner and could buy and maintain a second-hand one.

Ivan's Morgan was doubtless third- or fourth-hand. But it looked wonderfully dashing to me as it stood there in the afternoon sunshine, throbbing and vibrating. Ivan had stopped it and turned the engine right down, but a Morgan always trembled violently if the engine was running at all, like a washing machine.

'Have they gone, Peter?' he asked me.

'Just gone,' I said. 'About a minute ago.'

'Oh, well, I'll catch them up then,' he said. 'I'd have been here half an hour ago, but,' he gave a kind of shrug, 'I had a bit of trouble with Hazel.'

I had no idea what he meant by this quasi-explanation. Perhaps Hazel was his girl-friend and he had been expecting to take her to the meeting, but some kind of tiff had arisen and she had ended by refusing to join him. (I knew Hazel couldn't be the pet name he gave his car because people who drove Morgans didn't give them pet names.) Whatever lay behind it, the upshot was that he was going by himself, and he was a bit late.

Ivan was driving to this place near Cropredy, some twenty miles away, by himself in a Morgan made for two. I looked down at the empty seat beside him and for the first and only time I can remember I experienced the magical attraction of the sports car. Motor cars have not meant much to me in my life. They have been, so to speak, a counter-tradition to the tradition within which I have lived and worked. But in that moment, with Ivan's dark green Morgan pulsating away at about my knee-level, and that empty leather seat beside him, I experienced a spasm of pure longing. I felt that I wanted to get down into that cockpit with him, and rip off down our street and away to Cropredy, more than I wanted anything in the world. More than to go to College. More than to get to know a Girl. More than –

Ivan was a kindly lad and I suppose he must have caught the look in my eyes, because he said simply and affably, 'Like to come along?'

There were no words to express the gratitude I felt to him, so I didn't bother to search for any. Without a word I got myself into the passenger's seat. There were no doors, so you just lifted yourself up and lowered yourself in somehow and snuggled down behind the little windscreen. Ivan let in the clutch, trod on the accelerator, and the back of the leather seat pushed me hard in the back as we accelerated away down the street.

I don't know how long it took us to get to Cropredy – something like half-an-hour, I expect. What I do know is that that half-hour was the most purely happy I have ever spent. 'Pleasure' is, as moral philosophers know, a difficult concept. Some of the pleasure that comes our way is very akin to pain in its devouring intensity, and it is often shot through with emotions that are not pleasurable or happy in themselves. But this was pure, innocent, Eden-like pleasure: what I would have described, in those days, as 'fun'. Everything about it was fun: the swaying and bouncing of the little projectile, which, coupled with one's closeness to the ground, gave an impression of tremendous speed as soon as we got above about forty-five miles an hour; the rush of the wind past one's face; the clatter and snarl of the engine. The countryside in September is not as fragrant as it is in June, when all the foliage is full of sap and the wild flowers are full of scent, but what smells there were came straight into the cockpit and were an added dimension in the experience: dust, the occasional weedy smell of a river, a whiff of resin from where some conifers had been cut down, and, for one savoury moment, the hot tar on a road that was being repaired, melting gently in the sun. Ivan, enjoying my enjoyment, slammed up and down through the gears, braked and accelerated dramatically, overtook everything we came up behind, and we swung and lurched and zoomed. There was, by modern standards, hardly any traffic on the roads. One of the things that make the memory of that Morgan ride seem so Arcadian is that it would be totally impossible today, when to go out on the road at all is dangerous enough, but to go out in a vehicle as frail, and as fast-moving, as Ivan's Morgan would be asking to get killed in the first quarter of an hour.

As we drew near the farm on which the race meeting was being held, we had to slow down because the road was lined with people walking or bicycling towards it: neighbouring villagers, attracted by the prospect of a bit of fun. There were motor-cycles coming in from all points of the compass, and a few cars, and even one other Morgan – not as smart as Ivan's, though, and not in British racing green, which types like Ivan regarded as obligatory. He rolled our three wheels to a stop in the field that was set aside for parking, and we went to pay our entrance money – it was something incredibly low, like a shilling – and join the spectators who were strung out along the roped-off course. I saw Brian and the others, clustered at the top of a small hillock, and at the same moment Ivan saw them and waved. I knew I should soon be losing him, so I made my little speech of thanks.

'Fine, Peter, fine,' he said with that easy affability. 'Nice having you along. Look out for me at the end. There may be spare capacity going back too.'

That 'may be' struck some anxiety into me (how was I going to get back to Oxford if the man who'd brought me didn't take me back?), but I was still in the afterglow of that wonderful half-hour's fun, and the anxiety passed quickly through my nervous system and out the other side. Let what happens happen, I thought. I'm here and I came here by Morgan. At that moment I could have faced the thought of walking the twenty miles back if I had to.

For the next two-and-a-half hours I simply watched the racing. I found myself a good spot by the fence and enjoyed every minute of it. This, on the face of it, is strange. Any kind of motor racing, whether it involves two wheels or four, whether it is Grand Prix, stock car, road, track, whatever, is something that you are either born with a taste for or not. I was not and Brian was. But for that one afternoon I seem to have strayed, or perhaps been magically transported by the ride in the Morgan, over to the other side of the dividing-line. I relished it all – the helmeted figures crouching over their handlebars, the speed, the noise, the fierce competition, the smell of high-octane petrol. Even the sight of a perfectly good arable field getting chewed up to mud as these contraptions thundered around a roped-off course did not bother me; the farmer would be getting a good fee, and in any case he was probably going to plough this ground any time now: the skidding, spinning racers would have done half the job for him.

There was a beer tent, but I hadn't any money to go to it, and with the strong bladder of youth I didn't need to relieve myself, so I just stood where I was, in my good vantage point, and watched everything. I remember thinking that that programme of races, put on by the South Oxon and Bucks Motor Cycle Club or some such outfit, must be the best shilling's worth on offer in England that day. Then, at last, it was over, people began to thin out and move off, engines chugged as the parking field began to empty, and I moved off towards where Ivan and I had left the Morgan.

I was just in time to see him moving off, joining the queue of traffic that was going through a gate on to the road. In the seat beside him, the one I had so joyfully occupied, was a girl wearing a brightly coloured head-scarf. Was she Hazel? Or had he, during that golden afternoon, made acquaintance with the girl who was to be Hazel's successor? Either way, I was there, in a field outside Cropredy, with only my own two legs as locomotion. Buses existed, of course – far more of them then than now, in country areas – but I could not muster the fare.

Then I saw Brian, kick-starting his motor-bike over in a corner of the parking field. He seemed to be by himself; the original, noisy, happy group had evidently, by some general understanding, succumbed to centrifugal forces as the meeting ended. I hesitated, not knowing whether I wanted him to see me or not. But he did see me, and with a swirl of muddy tyres he came up alongside me.

'On your own?' he asked curtly.

'Yes,' I said. 'I came here with Ivan –'

'I saw,' he said. 'I'm getting back home, so get on.'

I looked at the pillion seat. Did I want to ride back on it? On the other hand, what else could I do?

'Get *on*,' he said. 'I haven't got all night. I'm going out after tea.'

I pulled down the rear foot-rests, which were folded upwards, into the riding position and got astride the bike. It felt terribly exposed. Brian started us moving forward before I was ready, and I nearly toppled off the back. I grabbed him round the waist. He stopped and turned round fiercely.

'Now look, don't do that,' he said. 'The place for your hands is on your knees. Don't hang on to me or else both of us'll bloody fall off. Just sit easy and balance with the bike.'

I put my hands on my knees. We went forward again, slowly at first. There were so many cars, so many motor-cycles and push-bikes, such a narrow and crowded space that at first we went at a walking pace and I felt I was getting used to it. The bike was a big A.J.S., twin cylinder, with an exhaust pipe running down each side under our feet. The speedometer, I saw apprehensively over Brian's shoulder, went up to 120 m.p.h. I tried to tell myself that didn't mean anything. You could mark any figures on the dial of a speedometer, just to look impressive. There was no need to conclude that the bike would actually go as fast as that.

Then we were through the gate and with a roar we swung off down the road. Once again I nearly flew off the back and it was only by a colossal effort of will that I kept myself from grabbing Brian round the waist. A wave of giddiness swept over me and I wondered if I were going to black out. We accelerated, going up through the gears, as traffic thinned and the road opened out ahead of us. The foot gear-lever for motor-cycles had not yet come in, and Brian changed gear by moving a lever from notch to notch with his left hand, which of course meant letting go of the handlebars on that side every time he changed up or down. The hedges on either side became a green blur. I fought hard not to think, not to feel, just to keep my hands on my knees and sit there and go with the bike, tilting when it tilted, swaying when it swayed, like some diabolical sexual act with a demented centaur.

What had happened up to now was frightening enough, but far worse began when we reached the main road from Banbury to Oxford. Brian twisted the grip of the throttle and we really leapt forward. The wind tore at my clothes and tried to pull me off on to the road that whirled under us. The engine dinned in my ears like a perpetual yell of mockery, as if a crowd of fiends was witnessing my torment. If the motor-cycle had existed in the thirteenth century, Dante would surely have depicted one of the circles of the Inferno as a race-track round and round which drivers like Brian, for ever and ever, conveyed passengers like me; because what I went through on that ride was truly, without a flicker of exaggeration, an agony worthy of any hell that can be devised. Abandon hope all ye who enter here. I abandoned it about half a mile along the Banbury Road. I ceased, that is. to be afraid I was going to be killed: I knew for a fact that I was. The only question was, when? How long would it be before I fainted from pure terror, and collapsed into the road, my broken body bouncing over and over, my face set in a hideous rictus of pain and fear as the flesh was torn from cheekbone and jawline. I knew there was no hope; I despaired. I knew, now, that all the years of solitary effort, of reading books and making notes, had been wasted, that I would never get to Episcopus, never take even the first steps in my real education. It had all been a hollow fraud, a promise that Fate never even intended to keep.

The supreme peak of my terror was when Brian accelerated to what must have been maximum speed, even for that fiendish A.J.S., to overtake a long procession of cars that were running nose to tail. Long, I mean, for those days – seven or eight, I suppose. They were held down to a slow speed by a lorry, so after overtaking all of them he had to overtake the lorry, and there was another one coming in the opposite direction. I knew, as a scientific fact, that we could never hope to survive, that this was death. As we screamed past the lorry on our left, and at the same instant managed somehow to swerve out of the path of the one coming on our right, I took my hands off my knees and convulsively clutched Brian round the waist. He kept going at full speed for a moment or two, just enough to get a clear space between us and the lumbering caravan to our rear, and then skidded savagely to a halt.

'Look,' he said, twisting round to glare at me, 'for the last time, keep your hands on your knees and ride easy. Don't grab me round the middle like a bloody monkey on a stick.'

'I can't help it,' I said faintly.

'You can walk home, then,' he said.

The words fell on my ear like a benediction. I was just opening my mouth to say 'Yes, please,' when Brian twisted the accelerator-grip again and we shot off like a bat out of hell. The lorry we had overtaken was nearly on us again, and as we swung out into the road I had a sickening vision of myself somersaulting backwards under its huge wheels and being pasted on to the road like a hedgehog.

There was no getting off now. I went back to facing death. Brian did not stop until we swung into the yard of the Bargeman's Arms. Then he throttled back to the 'off' position and the engine spluttered out. The silence that came in at my ears was more beautiful than the most exquisite music I have heard in a concert hall, more beautiful than the song of a nightingale, more beautiful than the passionate breathing of a woman I loved who was giving herself to me. It was the silence of reprieve. Soldiers who survive intensive bombardment must have heard it. Survivors of thousand-bomber air raids must have heard it. I heard it.

I sat there, breathing in and out. 'Well, get *off*,' said Brian. It was difficult for him to dismount until I did.

I tried to move, but at first my body felt paralysed. Would I have to spend the rest of my life in a wheelchair? Concentrating hard, I moved one leg, then the other. I was off. I was standing on the concrete paving of the pub yard. I was alive, I was going to live, I was going to get to Episcopus and be educated.

'If you're going to stand there looking as if you've seen a bloody ghost,' Brian said, 'I'm going somewhere where I don't have to look at you.'

He went into the house. I knew our meal would be served when he went in but I didn't feel hungry. I walked along the road to the river towpath and stood there relaxing, watching the water flow past. I had never known before what it was to be thankful, as deeply thankful as it was possible to feel, simply for being alive. I felt my muscles relaxing. But my forehead was still cold and sweaty. Suddenly, I went down on my knees in the grass of the river's verge. With great convulsive, shuddering spasms, I vomited once, twice, three times, into the water. I had had nothing to eat for so long that there was nothing solid to come up, it was just bile and digestive juices, but it came anyway.

That night, having successfully resisted my mother's demands that I should eat something, I lay in bed and tried to make sense of the experiences of those few hours. I felt that I had been punished; I had crossed over into Brian's country by riding out to Cropredy in Ivan's Morgan. By enjoying the racing, by beginning to see what Brian and his cronies saw in all this business of engines and petrol and tyres, I had lingered beyond the permissible few minutes in that country. Coming home – traversing exactly the same ground as on that delightful ride with Ivan – I had gone through the floor of hell, I had been terrified and despairing and wretched.

Only one question remained, but there was no one to answer it for me. Was Brian deliberately teaching me a lesson, setting out to frighten me, involving me, even, in real danger of being killed? Doing it as a warning to keep out of his patch? Or was it just his ordinary way of riding his motor-cycle? Would he have driven just like that if the pillion passenger had been a girl, or one of his tried and trusted mates?

I went to sleep that night not knowing the answer. And now I know that I shall go to my grave not knowing the answer. The one person I could have asked would never, never have told me. It was all part of the deep, tightly-folded mystery of the brother-relationship.

*

September passed into October, a few last days trickled by like grains of sand from an hour-glass, and then it had come, the time for me to leave my old life. Brian and my parents, in those last few days, hardly mentioned the impending change. It was too big for them to be able to handle directly. There had been, back in the early summer, a mild stir of excitement when I got my scholarship and it was finally clear that I was going to the University; and since then my mother had been shopping with me a few times, to get the things that were on the official list, linen and crockery and what-not. Beyond that, the family had had no way of dealing with this big, strange intrusion except by underplaying it. References to it at meal-times and so forth actually became rarer as the date approached.

On my last evening as Peter Leonard, son of the licensee of the Bargeman's Arms, I had high tea with Brian and Mother as usual. Nobody remarked on the fact that the next evening I should be having dinner in the hall at Episcopus College, with my gown on, and scouts waiting at table as Uncle Ernest waited at Pembroke. The thought was very present to me, and I was sure to Mother; whether Brian registered it at all I had simply no means of knowing. We ate pretty much in silence, and then Mother put out Dad's meal and went through into the bar to take his place. Brian silently disappeared. I sat on in my chair. Dad came in, sat down, and began to eat. He acknowledged my presence with one or two casual remarks, but it was not until he had finished eating and pushed his plate away that he said, in the same casual tone, 'What time have you got to be there tomorrow?'

'About five would be right, I think,' I said. 'I just need to settle in to my room, unpack my stuff and all that, and then go in to dinner.'

He nodded. 'I'll run you along there in the car.'

'Oh,' I protested unconvincingly, 'there's no need to trouble... I can...'

'No trouble,' he said. 'I'm not needed here till six.'

That was that, and the next day,towards the end of afternoon with the descending sun beaming long rays down our little street, he helped me to carry my luggage from my room and stow it in the car. My mother came out through the bar and stood on the pavement, watching us. The clear sunlight brought her sharply into focus, as if under a photographer's arc-lights. She seemed to be wishing to speak but unable to think of anything to say. I looked at her, a slight, fair-haired figure, still not old, though of course she seemed old to me; I suppose she was barely forty, but it was so long since anything had changed in her life, except gradually, that she had sunk deep roots into the clay of time and become middle-aged in her thinking. On my side, like most boys, I had thought of my mother simply as part of the furniture. She was the person who kept the house going and cooked meals, who uttered predictable admonitions and predictable rebukes; even, at certain clearly defined times, predictable endearments. I thought to myself, standing there looking at her in the brilliant autumn air, 'For the first time I am seeing her as a person.' But I wasn't. I was putting her into another box, typecasting her again. It so happened that I had recently seen for the first time Ford Madox Brown's painting 'The Last of England', and it struck me that her face, particularly the eyes, recalled the woman staring with sorrowful intensity over the aft rail of the ship. Probably what she was really feeling was much more complex, but I simplified partly because I was young and shallow but mainly because at that moment, with the unknown yawning in front of me, I was simply not able to take on anything new. If I had really seen my mother, Katie Leonard, as a real person, taken her in for what she was and what she was capable of becoming, it would have been too much: the new knowledge would have submerged me with its weight. So, while with my conscious mind I was feeling a surge of fondness for her and regret at parting from her, what I did in practice was to push her away.

'Shall I come with you?' she suggested. 'Just for the ride?'

I knew she didn't need the ride, that it was a plea she was uttering, to keep us all together in the old relationship for another few minutes. But I felt as a swimmer must feel on a high diving-board, with muscles tensed and nerve braced for the leap out and down: no diversions now – a clean move forward or it won't happen ever!

'I shouldn't bother, Mum,' I said off-handedly, as if we were going on a half-hour shopping trip. 'Hardly worth it. I'll see you very soon anyway.'

And I stepped forward and gave her a kiss on the cheek. Her body, as it touched mine, felt rigid, held-in.

My father, ignoring our moment of farewell, swung the starting-handle a few times, till the engine fired, then walked round and settled into the driving seat. 'Well, let's get off,' he said.

'Cheerio, Mum,' I said. There was no sign of Brian.

I remember it so well, that seven-minute car journey from one life to another. The sky was very blue and tranquil, with a few golden clouds in it, and Oxford was looking unreally beautiful, like a colour film. We went along to the Abingdon Road, turned left and chugged over Folly Bridge and up St Aldate's. The car was a bullnose Morris, like the first one Brian had got at employees' discount for his father. It was not the original bullnose, of course – that came out before the First World War

– but one of the later ones; the last, I think, to have the familiar smooth-snout radiator. It was an open tourer with a hood, and we had the hood folded back in the fine afternoon and my father wore his leather motoring coat as if he had been driving down from Windermere or somewhere. With our heads out in the air, we could feel the fine autumn afternoon and see the magnificence all round us. At Carfax we had to ease back and almost stop – there was a fair amount of traffic even in those days – but presently we were up to twenty miles an hour again and we pulled up in fine style outside Episcopus.

I had two big cases. I took one and my father took the other. There was also a soft carpet-bag which I carried in my other hand. We went into the lodge, put them down, then straightened up and looked at each other. It was goodbye, we both knew. Goodbye to my childhood, and therefore, in most ways, goodbye to him.

'Well, thanks a lot, Dad,' I said.

'Like me to give you a hand taking them to your room?' he asked.

'Oh, no, don't trouble. I'm sure it won't be...'

I babbled for a few moments, just as I had babbled to my mother when she suggested coming with us for the ride. What I meant in both cases was the same: Don't crowd me, just go away, let me handle this.

My father understood. He nodded and said, 'Well, drop round any time. I expect you'll be pretty busy at first.'

'Oh, I'll drop round,' I said. 'And when I get settled in my room, wherever it is, you must bring Mum round for a cup of tea. Just as often as she likes to come.'

'We shan't bother you,' he said. 'Well, good luck, son.'

He turned and went out through the lodge gate. I stood there for a moment and heard him start the engine, then its note rising as he gathered speed, moving away. He was going back to another evening's routine work, serving beer to the locals; all cosy and foreseeable and familiar. But what was I going to?

Well, whatever happened, the first person I had to face was the porter in the lodge. He looked up my name on a list and told me where my room was. It was confusing, or at any rate I was confused, and I did not follow his directions very well. I came out only half convinced I knew where Twelve, Eight was. But I thought it would be better to carry my bags over there at once. On the other hand, not having three hands, I could not take the whole lot. I ought to have accepted my father's offer of help. I went back into the porter's den and asked him to keep an eye on one of the cases while I took the other one, plus the carpet bag, across. He told me, unconcernedly, to leave it and it would be all right.

He did not say that he would, or wouldn't, keep an eye on it. I set off with the other two items. I got lost. After going through archways and down passageways and sweating up and down steep wooden staircases I found that I had forgotten whether I lived in Twelve, Eight, or Eight, Twelve. And was it the custom to put the staircase, or the number of one's room, first? I had to take a fresh grip on the whole thing. I put my suitcase down at the foot of a staircase and trudged back to the lodge to start all over again. My other suitcase was still there. I got the porter to repeat where my room was. His eye, as it rested briefly on me, seemed sardonic, or had it been sardonic all along? As I came out, still sweating, still flustered, another student was just entering through the lodge gate. He had come in a taxi – from the station, I supposed – and the taxi-driver was walking heavily after him with two enormous suitcases. The young man himself carried nothing. I halted for an instant, not meaning to stare rudely, but stopped in my tracks by a sudden curiosity. I had never taken a taxi in my life, and if I had been in this student's place I would not have known how much to tip the driver or in what kind of tone I was expected to address him.

'How much?' the undergraduate asked. Though that phrase contains only two words, it happens that each of the words contains a vowel of the kind that instantly indicates a provincial or dialect speaker. I now heard it pronounced as the governing class pronounce it.

'Half a crown, sir,' said the driver.

The undergraduate fished in his pocket and produced a florin and two sixpences. It seems odd that I should have noticed the exact coins, and that I should still remember them. But I can see them, lying there in the driver's palm. Three shillings. So that was what you tipped a taxi-driver: sixpence on half a crown. I wondered, as I walked away, whether sixpence was the usual flat-rate tip, whether he would have given the man sixpence if the fare had been, say, a pound; or whether, since there were eight half-crowns in a pound, the tip in that case would have been four shillings. (I learnt later that it would have stayed at sixpence or risen at the most to a shilling.) The thing that remained fixed in my mind was that I was from this hour onward to mix with young men of my own age but in other respects nothing like me; with men who were accustomed to having people work for them and serve them, who knew how to give these people instructions and pay them and, for that matter, give them the correct tip.

As for me, I had all this still to learn and it would be just as much of an effort to assimilate all those things as to assimilate what they put in front of me in the way of formal study. What a beginner I was, what a greenhorn: worse than a greenhorn, an intruder, someone who had inveigled himself into a club and didn't know its rules and procedures.

Thinking these thoughts, I resumed trying to find my room, and when I did find it I couldn't find the suitcase I had left at the foot of another staircase somewhere. By this time all the staircases looked pretty well identical to me, and I began to wonder if someone had taken my suitcase by mistake, or if it had been stolen. My mind filled up with nightmare fantasies about starting my University career with a scandal, of being put into a position of appearing to accuse a fellow-student of being a thief, of the resentment of the accused man and his friends. I saw myself an outcast, a pariah, alternately ignored or made the butt of cruel practical jokes, till after a major nervous breakdown I was driven back to the Bargeman's Arms, broken on the threshold of life, an object of my parents' pity and Brian's scorn. I lived through the whole saga in the ten minutes it took me to lope round the bewildering maze of the College until I found my suitcase.

Having got my belongings together at last, I shut the door of my room behind me, glad to have that haven, glad even before I had given myself time to look round the place I was to inhabit and form any impression of it. Almost like an animal that feels itself pursued, I wanted above everything to get inside and be safe. I set down my two bags, went back down the staircase to get the third one, panted up the stairs with it (my rooms were right at the top) and only then, when all my possessions were present and correct and the door shut behind me, did I straighten up, look round, and take in the place.

It was smallish; longer than it was broad, by a good deal; on the floor a carpet, not new but not very worn; on the walls, plain yellow wallpaper not new but not very faded. The light came from two windows set fairly high up in the wall, so that to look out of them you had to mount up on to a kind of platform. In each one was a window-seat, thinly but adequately cushioned. In between the windows was the fireplace. On the opposite side to the fireplace was the door leading into a spartan little bedroom with washstand, chair, and iron bedstead of the kind you see in a barracks.

That was all, it was not magnificent, but it was mine and I had an undisputed right to it: the only thing in the world, as far as I could see, that I *did* have an undisputed right to. The grate was empty, with no sign of coal or kindling, and I decided not to try to heat the place; presumably that was something my scout would do, in his own good time, and my young blood kept me warm as I moved about the room, unpacking, putting things into drawers, hanging up the only picture I had brought (a framed print of the ruins of Tintern Abbey), and generally putting my faint, tentative thumb-print on the place. At about ten to six my scout knocked on the door. He was a leathery old man with rheumy, suspicious eyes, in whose watery light I was just another lazy, disorganized lump of undergraduate humanity, ready to be a nuisance to him for the next couple of years. I asked him about a fire and he said he would light one before I got up in the morning. He didn't specify when he expected me to get up, nor say what I was supposed to do if I wanted to sit in the room that evening, with the chill autumn night coming down outside the windows. I hadn't enough spirit to protest. He told me his name was Arthur; not knowing that scouts were always called by their Christian names, I was uncertain whether he was Arthur Something or Something Arthur, so I avoided calling him anything except You. But it was a milestone: I had met my scout, and from now on I knew whom to ask if I wanted anything – wanted it enough, that is, to pluck up the courage to ask for it.

After Arthur had closed the door and thumped off down the stairs, I sat for a while thinking about my Uncle Ernest. He had been a benign and somewhat remote figure all through my childhood. I had always known he was a college scout, but never until this moment had I pictured him at work, toiling up and down staircases, carrying trays and pails and coal-buckets, lighting fires and cleaning rooms, one of that unsung army of caryatids on whose shoulders seven hundred years of scholarship have rested. As a matter of fact the chief thing I had associated my Uncle Ernest with had been an aeroplane crash among a fringe of trees on the bank of the Thames just north of Port Meadow. Two RFC officers, Betterton and Hotchkiss, were piloting their comical little aeroplane down to land on the broad grassy space when a wire running along the side of the fusilage had pulled away because its quick-release catch had come open. The wire slashed across the fabric of one wing and ripped it off, making the wing into a wooden skeleton. Though the plane was no more than fifty or sixty feet from the ground, just about to touch down, it canted over immediately. One of the fliers – Uncle Ernest knew which one – fell out of his seat and was killed by hitting the ground. The other died when the plane hit the trees. The incident caused an enormous stir of interest. People came out from Oxford, to the number of thousands, to stand and gaze silently at the wreckage and then, for weeks and months, at the broken trees where the wreckage had been. When a polished granite plaque had been put up to Betterton and Hotchkiss on Wolvercote toll-bridge they had again come out in their thousands. An aeroplane in those days aroused the same kind of interest as a flying saucer from outer space would in our time. And aviators were a new race, a breed of Wellsian super-heroes who were going to take us into the super-wonderful twentieth century. At the time Betterton and Hotchkiss hit the ground that dream had about twelve months to live. No wonder Uncle Ernest remembered it. He was there, gazing at the wreckage. He was there again, straining to catch the words of the big-wig who had unveiled the memorial on the bridge. And on that occasion he had sternly compelled his younger brother, Jack, my father, to accompany him. Not to have turned out on such an occasion would have seemed to him not only a failure of patriotism but also an act of disrespect towards the goddess History. My mother, a busy young housewife, had refused to take the time to go and stand about on the fringe of a vast crowd, but she had been glad of a chance to get rid of Brian (aged three) and me (aged one) for a while, so we had been along, though I don't remember the occasion. It is merged with many scores of Sunday morning walks Uncle Ernest used to take the pair of us on, till Brian at about eight rebelled and said he had more interesting things to do. I was more docile but in any case, even at that age, more interested in the old man's reminiscences and the bits of local information he would impart as we walked along, my chubby legs in the early years just about able to keep up with his tireless bony shanks. For of course it was as an old man that I thought of him, though in my infancy I don't suppose he was more than forty-five and, even in the years I remembered best, barely into his fifties. He was grey-haired and moved stiffly and, child-like, I thought of old people as a race apart, not belonging with the rest of humanity, the Struldbrugs of Swift's imagination, though of course there were good Struldbrugs and bad Struldbrugs.

But wherever we started out to walk to, it was always at Port Meadow we finished up, and then it was to the little bridge and the plaque, and Betterton and Hotchkiss, Betterton and Hotchkiss, till I knew their brave, ill-fated names as well as my own. And here I was thinking about them again, sitting in my room at Episcopus, waiting for my new life to begin, and a few streets away Uncle Ernest was no doubt taking his stiffening hocks up and down some staircase just like this one, looking after some set of whippersnappers just like me.

Well, getting to know Arthur by sight and name was surmounting a hurdle, and at dinner that night I surmounted another. I talked to a fellow-student. The lift this gave me was all the more pronounced because a few minutes earlier I had been sliding rapidly down into a depressing sense of isolation.

At Episcopus, dinner was served at seven-fifteen sharp. You could get away with being three or four minutes late, but as time went on you successively missed courses and in the end you missed your dinner. The scouts were always in a hurry to get the meal over and clear up and go off duty, and they usually managed to get the undergraduates through by the time the dons, on their dais at the far end of the hall, were half-way through their stately and elaborate meal. (No point in hurrying *them*. Those were still the days when High Table dressed for dinner, dinner-jacket every week-night and full evening dress on Sundays, and to try to hurry them would have been like trying to drive a flock of penguins past a trough of fresh mackerel.) And if the scouts did not allow the undergraduates to linger over their food, they were equally firm about letting them in before it was served. While they were laying the tables, they had the hall door solidly closed, and opened it on the dot of seven-fifteen. The result was that undergraduates tended to drift in just before the door was opened, and stand about for a few minutes in a long, ill-lit passage running down the side of the hall.

The archetypal timid newcomer, eager only to be lost in the crowd, I drifted in with the others and stood in the passage, wearing my gown. Because I had won a scholarship I had a gown that was long and voluminous and dignified, especially by comparison with the short square of black cloth, sleeveless and just covering one's back, the irreducible minimum of a gown, that the Commoners wore, the students who were paying their own way. On that first evening I made a problem and a hesitation even of that. Did wearing a Scholar's gown mark one out as an upward toiler from a humble home? Surely the men who came from a moneyed background, from homes where the expenses of a university education were of no account, formed the *élite* here as they would have done anywhere? In the dim light I looked timidly from face to face, wondering if I could discern any difference between the faces of those wearing different gowns. But I couldn't. Standing just beside me was a knot of obviously Public School men, talking in loud, assured voices, all obviously well known to each other, and several of them wore Scholars' gowns. I was so green, so new to everything, that I had not yet heard of the existence of 'closed' scholarships, endowed for this or that particular school. Some of the major public schools, at that time, had so many closed scholarships to individual colleges at Oxford or Cambridge that a Sixth-Former would have had to be practically subnormal to miss getting one.

I knew nothing of this. All I knew was that when I looked round and tried to see whether the men in the Scholars' gowns looked more 'my type', I could not see that they did. Any kind of gown might be surmounted by any kind of face, with any kind of voice coming out of it. There was no clue anywhere. The one obvious thing was that the Public-Schoolites, besides being more numerous, were totally in control when it came to setting the tone of the place. In those few minutes of waiting for my first College meal, knowing nobody, confident about nothing, I had the feeling of being among a pack of large, strong dogs. Their physical vitality and restlessness, the rough texture of their tweed jackets, and above all the loud bark, bark, bark of their voices, all seemed totally dog-like. Some of them gave the impression of being leaders, others ordinary pack members, but the one thing certain was that these beings, among whom I was to spend the next three years, were dogs who would hunt together, pull down their prey together, and act together to starve out weak or diseased creatures that tried to share the life of the pack.

The door was opened, we filed in and I just let myself be drawn along by the movement of the pack. At some colleges, I was later to discover, Scholars sat together at dinner and third-year men sat together and this and that and the other, but at Episcopus we all just sat anywhere, fitting in wherever there was a vacant space on one of the long benches. I found myself sitting next to half a dozen big barking dogs who had obviously been known to each other for years; probably they had all been at school together. My food was put in front of me and as I silently ate it I listened to their voices. At first it seemed to me impossible to tell which of them were actually arrogant and which were merely made to sound arrogant by the curt, rather loud way in which they had all been trained to speak, exactly alike. But even after five minutes I began to detect differences. Some of them seemed modest, humorous, self-parodying; in others, the sahib accent seemed exactly to match an inner need to assert authority, to look down on people and order them about. One man in particular, tall and fleshy and with glasses and close-cut curly hair, seemed to exude loftiness and disdain. The others often addressed remarks to him, to which he answered shortly and dismissively with phrases like, 'Sounds like a damn' bad idea to me,' or 'Chap like that would be bound to make a mess of it.' He was, I decided, the type who had been absolutely in his element as a prefect, with a labour force of much smaller boys, helpless and cringing fags, whom he was not only permitted but actually required to set to menial work and cane for any one of a host of petty and largely unavoidable offences. I determined to steer clear of him.

All this took shape in my mind so quickly that the meal had been going on for hardly more than five minutes when the man on my right, the side not occupied by the barking dogs, asked me to pass the water-jug or something of the sort. We fell into conversation; he too was a freshman, he too knew no one there, and we immediately formed a relationship born of loneliness and gratitude. He was broad-shouldered and fresh-faced, with round glasses, and his name was Wilmot. I liked him for his friendliness, his ordinariness, the fact that he spoke with a pleasant West-Country burr and even had (it was the first time I had heard it) the intrusive 'l' of the Bristolian.

Towards the end of the meal Wilmot asked me if I would care for a cup of coffee in his rooms. 'I've got the fire going,' he said. 'It's the only thing I've had time to do since I got here.' How sensible, I thought, my mind going back to the dead cold hearth of my own study. I accepted gladly, and for what remained of the meal just sat there eating, not saying much, enjoying the let-down of tension. Another fence cleared, and a big one.

One more thing I recall from that first College dinner, so nervously begun and so reassuringly concluded. My gaze wandered down the table past the group of barkers on my left-hand side, and a few places down I saw a face that for some reason stuck in my mind. It was a face of extraordinary intentness, pale in colour and surmounted by thick, very dark hair. The eyes, which were set back in deep sockets as if to protect themselves from the world, were moving from face to face of the knot of hearty, careless laughers and talkers next to him, the Public School barkers. It was clear that he was listening intently to their conversation, but with no ambition to join in: storing up information about what kind of things they talked about, and in what manner. Most of the faces I saw round me were youthful, and wore the expressions that young faces generally wear – amused, animated, vacuous, brooding, melancholy, the whole range. But of this man's face I can only say that, for all his eighteen years, I never saw a face that less suggested the artlessness, the impulsiveness, the unpreparedness of youth. It was, already, the face of one accustomed to calculating life's chances and keeping a shrewd eye on the competition.

The meal over, we went to Wilmot's room and sat by the fire and drank watery coffee and talked about our Sixth Forms and where we had been for our holidays and what we thought of this and that. Good, decent, innocent Wilmot, I shall always remember him with fondness. It often happens in a crowd of people thrown together for the first time that a person who, at the beginning, occupies the foreground of one's attention moves to the background when things settle down. I saw Wilmot a few times in my first term, sat by his fireside and had him sit by mine, but inevitably we formed our own more particular friendships and for the last couple of years that we were fellow undergraduates I rarely talked much with him, though we always had a cheerful word for each other. I do know that after graduating he got a job as a country schoolmaster, an excellent destiny for a kindly, approachable and not very clever man. Peace be to Wilmot, and to the gentle, unassuming Wilmots of all the world.

Chapter 5

My scout woke me the next morning by clumping into the tiny bedroom and saying loudly, in his rasping old voice, 'A quarter to eight, sir.'

I had been very deeply asleep – a subconscious defence, perhaps, against these new and still fearsome surroundings. His voice reached down like some abrasive steel cable and dragged me up through layer after swirling layer of the dim, translucent ocean of dreams. As I neared the surface and became aware that there was someone else in the room, someone who had addressed me, I passed through a stage of believing that this person was my Uncle Ernest.

'What will you want for breakfast, sir?' the old man rasped out.

'I'll get it, Uncle,' I said. 'I have to get up anyway. I can do Brian's as well while I'm...'

My voice trailed off as daylight flooded through my eyes into my brain.

The man, ignoring my murmurings, had turned and was going. What was his name? Oh yes, Arthur. His taut, bowed shoulders said, 'I can't hang about for ever till this young whippersnapper chooses to make up his mind.' In the doorway he turned and faced me long enough to say, 'Most gennlemen has bacon and eggs.'

'All right,' I said. 'Bacon and eggs, please.'

'And coffee, they mostly has,' he said, as he turned away.

I would have preferred tea, which is what we always had at home – coffee was for special occasions – but he was already banging away down the twisting staircase and I lacked the nerve to call him back and ask if I could have tea. *Lacked* it? I fell a million miles short of getting anywhere near it.

A little later I heard him come up again and start moving about in the larger room, making the fire. In those days there was a coal bunker on every landing, between every pair of rooms, and your scout lit your study fire before you got up and then laid out your breakfast in front of it. We still had, then, an England of masters and servants, and you had no choice but to be one or the other. I pulled the bedclothes up round my chin and lay there looking up at the ceiling, thinking about this, wondering whether it was necessary to take any special steps to turn oneself into a master or whether it would just happen naturally with time. I couldn't believe it would just rub off on me from all those barking Public School men. They seemed so different from myself that I couldn't imagine anything just rubbing off from them to me.

Oh well, I decided, just let it happen. I got up and put on a dressing-gown. This action, trivial as it was, constituted another novelty. At home, back at the good old Bargeman's, I never put on my dressing-gown unless I happened to be ill and needed for some reason to be out of bed for a while. Being a healthy lad, this meant that I had worn my dressing-gown half a dozen times in a year, and recently it had become too small for me and I could hardly get it on. My mother had bought me a new one, thick and sensible, as part of my going-away equipment. How had she known I would need it? I certainly did need it, because to get to the bath-house one had to go out and walk a hundred yards or so, in all weathers. Had my mother just guessed that? Or had she perhaps, on the quiet, consulted Uncle Ernest? She had also, whether intentionally or not, read my mind, for I had decided that in my new life I would have a bath every morning, before starting the day. I had read somewhere that gentlemen did that. 'The matutinal tub', I remember reading, was a mark of the governing class and it seemed a fairly easy one to acquire, much easier than changing one's accent or bearing. I stood there getting ready to sally forth, assembling my sponge-bag, towel, even my razor though at that time I only needed to shave every third day and I had shaved the day before. Then I heard the door shoved open and more clumping and scraping in my study. It was Arthur with the breakfast. I heard him put the dishes down, and in the same instant I noticed for the first time that when he woke me he had brought into my bedroom a large metal jug full of hot water. He had folded my face-towel and put it over the jug to keep the heat in. I had a wash-stand with a basin and ewer, and an earthenware slop-bucket with a lid on it such as men in prison are issued with.

I took the dressing-gown off again, put it on the bed, and had a quick wash in the basin. To go all that way to get a bath, as my breakfast went cold, seemed suddenly too much trouble. It was my first compromise, and I made it before breakfast on my first day.

For any newcomer in any situation, the first few days are mostly spent in finding out what one has to do. Anxiously approaching the notice-board in the lodge after breakfast, I saw some half-dozen notices meticulously set up, well spaced out and with a drawing-pin at each corner. My name was on one of them. Somebody called R.S.C. Bax wanted to see 'those gentlemen intending to read for the Honours School of Mediaeval and Modern History'. There followed a list of about eight names, including mine. So it was official: I was a gentleman. R.S.C. Bax said so.

I already knew that Bax was the History tutor at Episcopus, though I had never met him. No doubt I had seen him, because he must have been one of the dons who had interviewed me for admission, but I had not been introduced to these people individually. I went along to his rooms at the stated time and found myself waiting with the others. So these were my fellow historians. Already the blurred, amorphous mass of the College population was separating itself out into identifiable strands; a pattern was beginning to appear.

We were all freshmen. We looked at each other with, for the most part, guarded friendliness. We all wore the same sort of clothes – tweed jackets, pullovers, thick grey flannel bags, and ties. No one in those days went to see his tutor without wearing a tie; and of course we all had our gowns on. Someone knocked gently on the door, but there was no answer from inside Bax's study. We just stood there, taking each other in.

Two faces stand out in my memory. One is that of a tall, loose-limbed youth, with a genial, humorous expression. Though obviously Public School, he struck one immediately as being easy-going and with a sense of humour. The other was the face I had noticed at dinner, the pallid, observant one with the thatch of dark hair. Here, too, he was looking round him with an air of concentrating mightily, noticing every detail and storing it away. I had a sudden curiosity to hear him speak, to know what kind of voice and accent came out. I said something to him, I have forgotten what. But it did not elicit a reply. He simply looked at me, with those deep-set, watchful eyes, and nodded: acknowledging my existence but giving nothing away.

I noticed, just as another piece in the jigsaw, that the tall man wore the elaborate gown of a Scholar, and the pallid watchful man the unceremonious bum-freezer of a non-Scholar. But Wilmot had explained a few things to me on the previous evening – he was somewhat better briefed than I was, which wouldn't have been difficult – and I knew by now about closed scholarships, and also that Exhibitioners, men who had won certain cash awards that could be almost as valuable as a scholarship – wore short gowns like Commoners. I knew, in short, that in this place nothing, absolutely nothing at all, was what it seemed to be on the surface.

Then Bax came up the staircase behind us, apologized lightly for keeping us waiting, and led the way into his room. Obviously his not being there had been totally intentional, to give us time to assemble so that he would not have to keep breaking off to admit some new arrival. Everything Bax did was totally intentional; he was an entirely organized man. Of somewhat more than average height, wiry and active, with dark hair beginning to turn iron-grey, he seemed to my boyish eyes to be middle-aged, but I suppose he was about thirty-five. He got us all sitting down and then went into a very clear and economical explanation of our scheme of work. He did not speak quickly, nor did he seem to be holding back his speed to suit our comprehension; he just had the one pace at which he always spoke, and you had the distinct impression that he would be displeased at being asked to repeat anything or put it in other words. What he told us was, in its way, as impersonal as a printed hand-out. He had thought out his subject matter clearly before beginning to speak, he had found the logical words for it, and those words would have to do: there were no more where they came from. His eyes, behind round and fairly thick lenses, struck me as cold.

We all, it seemed, were hoping to read for an Honours degree in Modern History. (In those days the Pass degree still existed and a minority chose to take it.) Before being admitted to read for an Honours degree you had to spend two terms getting through something called Honour Moderations, in which you did a bit of Latin, a bit of Political Theory, a bit of this and that. So Bax was not going to be dealing with us very much before next May, but he had been put in charge to keep a general eye on us while we went to other tutors for our this and that.

He checked off our names against a list when we first went in, and from this I gathered that the watchful man was called Carshalton and the big good-natured Public-School man Knowlton. As I sat quietly hoisting everything in, my fellow-students began to take on names, faces, personalities even. There was one man, Lamont by name, who impressed me deeply, though I had not noticed him in those first few moments on the staircase. He was very good-looking, with a large and (if the term isn't too absurd to apply to an eighteen-year-old) noble head. His brow, across which a lock of hair perpetually strayed, was lofty and his eyes had a steadiness and depth that spoke of concentrated thought. He alone, among that roomful of adolescents, gave the impression of being totally grown-up. (Carshalton was not so much grown-up as psychologically stunted; he had not outgrown his boyhood, merely by-passed it.) Lamont was the only one who – not with any kind of impudent familiarity but with perfect courtesy, as if they were two learned gentlemen encountering one another in the course of their studies – spoke to Bax as to an equal.

Bax himself was going to take us for the Political Theory paper, and he obviously regarded it as a very simple matter, something we could do on our heads.

'There's no need for tutorials and essays,' he said. 'We'll just meet once a week as a class and go over the ground very straightforwardly. We start with Aristotle but I don't propose to do it in chronological order. We're going to radiate out from the Enlightenment. We shall be meeting on Tuesday morning, and as that doesn't give you much time just get an acquaintance with Montesquieu's *L'Esprit des Lois*. You won't have time to read it all, but just get a grip on the main themes.'

One of the students asked if there was a reliable translation. Bax's cold eyes rested on him for a moment, as if to remember his face.

'I wouldn't know,' he said. 'If your French needs brushing up you'd better brush it up. You won't get anywhere in the Modern History School if you can only read English.'

There was a short silence and then Bax spoke again. 'I think that just about sets everything up for the present, gentlemen, so I won't keep you.'

'I won't keep you,' I was soon to learn, is Oxford don's language for 'Go away.' As we went down the stairs the youth who had asked about a translation of Montesquieu began to build up his grievance. I have forgotten his name, but he was sandy-haired and narrow-faced, with a high, squealing voice, one of nature's grumblers.

'Christ, we'll never get through all that. We couldn't even if we had nothing else to do. Have you seen that Montesquieu thing? It's a bloody great row of volumes. It must be at least –'

'I don't think there's anything to bother about,' said big Knowlton calmly. 'He said himself we wouldn't have time to read it all. Best thing is just to look him up in the encyclopaedia and get a line on what this *Esprit* stunt is all about. Total time, ten minutes. Then get the full version and have a skim through and pick out a few quotes. Total time, another ten minutes.'

Behind his words I guessed at years of placidly getting by, moving up his school year by year with as little friction as possible, doing the minimum of work that would keep him out of trouble; and behind that in turn I surmised a background of complete economic security, a *milieu* where there was no need to push and shove and certainly not much need to excel, where a place would be found for you if you were a decent chap and got along all right with the people about you. If I had had to find one word for Knowlton I think I would have chosen 'unassailable'.

We had got down the staircase by now and were standing in the quad. It was almost ten o'clock.

'I'm going to brew a pot of coffee,' Lamont said. 'Anybody care to join me?'

'Is it the tail-end of breakfast,' someone asked, 'or an early elevenses?'

'Categorize it anyhow you like,' said Lamont, smiling. 'I feel like coffee and I feel like talking to people.'

Most of the others had things they wanted to get on with, and declined his offer, but I wasn't going to miss this. I still couldn't quite believe Lamont. I thought if I got a chance to talk to him at more leisure, I might begin to get some clues to the secret of his perfect assurance. Slightly to my surprise, the watchful man, Carshalton, also accepted, and the three of us went along to Lamont's rooms. His scout had just finished making the bed and roughly tidying the sitting-room; he was going out as we entered. Lamont greeted him with casual cheerfulness and gave him some instruction about things he wanted fetched over from the buttery. He addressed him as Joe. I now knew that my scout's name, Arthur, must be a Christian name and that one was expected to call him by it.

While Lamont busied himself with the coffee-pot, I looked along his bookshelves. The books I had on my shelves, except for a couple of thrillers, were all to do with modern history; mostly they were just the recommended text-books. Anyone entering my room could have told immediately that I was reading for a history degree. But Lamont's shelves gave no clue; he might have been reading anything. There was a Sophocles play in Greek. I had heard of Sophocles though I had never read that play and knew no Greek, but the rest of his books seemed to be by people who were not even names to me. Spengler's *Decline of the West*. W.H.Auden, *Poems*. Van Wyck Brooks's *The Ordeal of Mark Twain*. A translation of the Tibetan Book of the Dead. T.S. Eliot, *Prufrock and Other Observations*: what kind of book was that?

Lamont had now entered into conversation with Carshalton and I was therefore enabled at last to hear Carshalton's speaking voice. It was unlike any other I had ever heard. He spoke exactly like a robot. If we had been in the 1980s instead of the 'thirties, I would have said that he talked like a computer. The syllables all came out with about equal emphasis and the vowels were phonetically pure and entirely without character. His speech was as flavourless as a glass of tap-water.

Lamont, warming to some theme, had a beautiful blend of dreaminess and concentration; he always looked as if he were seeing a vision inside his head, and not just seeing it but examining it very scrupulously before it vanished. I have completely forgotten what he was talking about; perhaps I didn't register it even then.

Carshalton led the talk round to practical matters to do with our work; which parts of the syllabus were going to be heaviest, he wondered.

'I've made up my mind not to care too much,' Lamont said. 'Just as long as I avoid getting sent down. I want three years in Oxford because I've heard it's a place where poets are tolerated.'

'Is that what you are?' I said. 'A poet?'

He smiled, but his eyes were very serious. 'That's what I'd like to be. At all events I can't stop my thoughts going in that particular direction.'

Carshalton said, in his computer voice, 'I would have expected you to be reading English. That's what most literary types do, isn't it?'

'Oh, that wouldn't be much use,' said Lamont. 'Reading a lot of other people's poems isn't going to train one, especially as one will inevitably do a lot of that unofficially. No, a poet needs information. I want to amass some hard facts.'

Facts, I thought. What kind of facts are there in the Tibetan Book of the Dead? But perhaps Prufrock was a fact, though he didn't sound like one.

'I shall be quite happy,' Lamont continued, 'just to get the Poet's Third. I believe it's regarded here as an institution.'

At that moment he looked out of the window and caught sight of a tall undergraduate in a black corduroy jacket and scarlet trousers of the same material, walking across the quad. Rapidly crossing the room to the window, he opened it and called, 'Gerard, come and have some coffee.'

The young man stopped, recognized him and approached. As he came through the doorway I took stock of him: another type to learn about, not quite like anyone I had met so far. Very tall; fair-haired; a long, humorous face with eyebrows that formed perfectly symmetrical arches over his strikingly blue eyes and gave him a perpetual air of being slightly surprised; an appearance that combined untidiness with elegance in a way I had never quite seen before.

Come to that, why had I not seen this actual man before? Was he at Episcopus, or not?

'Hello, Gerard,' Lamont said. 'I've just made a pot of coffee. Have some. These are –' he waved a genial hand towards Carshalton and myself, 'chaps.'

'Leonard,' I said. 'Peter Leonard.' Carshalton merely stared at the newcomer and said nothing.

'Hello,' Gerard said easily. Was it a surname or a Christian name?

Once again I had the same problem as with Arthur. Was life ever to be anything but problems, problems, problems? I would watch and wait. Like Carshalton. No, not like Carshalton.

I noticed, as they chatted, that Gerard addressed Lamont as 'Gavin'. So they were on Christian-name terms. So 'Gerard' was not his surname. Later I discovered it was Urquhart.

Lamont handed out mugs of coffee and plunged into conversation with Gerard, who had led off with the words, 'I don't think I'm going to be able to stand three years of this.'

'It may not be as bad as you think,' Lamont said. 'One's only in fact here for half the year. And at least it's convenient. Everything happens in a small compass.'

'Happens?' The surprised expression on Gerard's face intensified. 'Would you mind telling me *what* exactly happens?'

'Well – ' Lamont shrugged tolerantly. 'People read books and talk about their ideas. And get to know each other.'

'Oh, yes, *people*. I know people are important, but they're not the only important thing. I mean, where can you go in Oxford to look at paintings? Where are the galleries?'

'There's the Ashmolean.'

'I've been there this morning and I can tell you it isn't going to last me three years. There's some Pissarro and a few Samuel Palmers – you can't keep going on that.'

'Nonsense, they've got lots of other things. There's the Print Room. Of course you have to get permission to look at things, but it's quite easy. And anyway the Ashmolean isn't all. There are some nice things in Christ Church picture gallery.'

'All right, but what else? There's no concert hall. I'm not going to sit and listen to family-night-out all-Tchaikovsky programmes in that awful Victorian town hall. That's the only – '

'I believe there's quite a lot of chamber music. You'll just have to give it a try, Gerard.'

'Oh, I'll give it a try. I've started exploring already.'

'Is that why you weren't in to dinner last night?' (So Gerard was at Episcopus.)

'Yes, I was round at Magdalen. I know two or three people there. We had a bottle of something and then went out to see if there were any decent films on.'

'Were there?'

'Nothing we hadn't seen before in town. And of course there's no proper theatre. I can't see how anyone survives.'

'You really are going to suffer, aren't you, Gerard?' said Lamont, enjoying the joke of his friend's over-acting. 'Well, Oxford isn't London, there's no denying that. But perhaps you'll be able to put a bit of life into it.'

'Well,' Gerard said, 'when I get settled in I shall see if anything's possible. Is there a film club, d'you know?'

'Sure to be. And there are any number of dramatic societies that do productions.'

Gerard brightened. 'Yes, one could try working through some of those. I'd like to put some of the German stuff on. I was in Germany in the summer.'

'Oh, that's why I didn't see you.'

'Yes. It's really worth a visit. I went to a few plays and films, but my German isn't good enough to follow everything. I wish to God I'd got myself taken on to read German instead of French. The French aren't doing anything interesting. They're so self-congratulatory about their marvellous bloody tradition that all they do is repeat it. The Germans know they haven't got much tradition, and anyway their society's been all smashed up and put together anyhow, so they're looking for new outlets and they're full of energy. Brecht – '

I became aware of a movement beside me. Carshalton put down his empty coffee mug, stood up, thanked Lamont, nodded to Gerard, and took himself off. It was as if he had suddenly made up his mind that this was no place for him, that he was wasting his time here. So, like a good robot, he buzzed out his correctly programmed politeness-words and clicked away.

Lamont and Gerard, deep in conversation about these mysterious matters that so obviously made up the essential business of their lives, appeared hardly to notice that Carshalton had gone or that I had stayed. Gerard was telling, with little puffs of laughter, a cautionary tale about a man of his acquaintance who was actually reading German, as Gerard wished to do, but had elicited by enquiry the fact that his tutor had not even heard of Franz Kafka.

While they were both marvelling at this, I happened to be looking out of the window into the sunlit quadrangle when my gaze was caught and held by the tall, slender figure of a girl walking across it. She had on a long, orange skirt – other things too, of course, but it is only the orange skirt I remember – which came down to her ankles, and walked in a graceful way that seemed almost floating. She was bare-headed, and the sun glowed on glossy wings of bronze-coloured hair that were swept back from her forehead on either side. I forgot Gerard, I forgot Lamont,

I stared. Then Gerard's voice exclaimed, 'Hey, there's Annabel!'

'So there is,' Lamont agreed.

'That means it must be eleven. I asked her to come round then but I hadn't realized it was so late. Good thing she didn't get to my lair and find no one at home – that always makes her furious. Annabel!' he called through the still open window. 'We're in here!'

The girl approached, and now that I saw her in full face I saw that her countenance was heart-shaped, with a wide brow perfectly set off by those great wings of bronze. She wore an expression of cool amusement. Her clothes were loose-fitting, so that one did not see her shape in much detail, but it was obvious from the way she walked and held herself that her body was graceful and lissom, the kind that gets called 'willowy'. She seemed to me a vision of perfect beauty.

She came into the room, smiling, looking from face to face. Gerard took her hands in his for an instant, and said, 'You know Gavin, don't you?'

'Do I?' she asked: not nastily, not haughtily, just trying to remember, perfectly at ease among equals.

'I'm not surprised you don't remember,' Lamont said. 'We met for about two minutes at the Redfern and you were looking very hard at the pictures.'

'Oh, yes, of course I remember,' she said. 'Yes, I was looking hard at the pictures. Gerard always makes me do that when we go to a gallery. He *grills* me afterwards on what I remember.'

'In other words, I try to have an intelligent conversation,' Gerard said. 'But I admit it's uphill work.'

'I'm afraid we've come to the end of the coffee,' said Lamont, looking into the pot, 'but I can easily make some more.'

'No, please don't bother,' she said. 'As a matter of fact I had all I could drink before I came away from L.M.H. Everybody's *madly* getting to know everybody and the only way they seem to know how is to brew *oceans* of coffee and dish it out to one another.'

'Poor you,' said Gerard.

'Well, seriously,' she said, 'I don't know that I'll be able to stick three years of it.'

'Just what I was saying.' he agreed.

'Well, I'm landed with it,' said Lamont placidly. 'There's enough in Oxford to keep me occupied for three years. How do you feel about it, Leonard?'

I almost jumped as he addressed me. I had become so accustomed to my role as listener and onlooker that I thought of myself as no more perceptible than a fly on the wall.

'Oh, I – yes, it suits me all right,' I said, knowing how lame it sounded but utterly unable to think of anything more intelligent.

Annabel was looking at me in that cool but perfectly friendly way. 'I expect it'll turn out that I've met you, too,' she said. 'Do forgive me if I have. My memory's *shocking*.'

'No, you haven't,' I assured her. (Did I look the type that would hang around exclusive London art galleries?)

'Sorry,' Lamont interposed. 'Leonard, of this College.'

'Leonard what?' she said.

'Peter Leonard,' I said. 'Leonard's my surname.'

She nodded and said, 'I'm Annabel.'

'Annabel Graveney,' Lamont completed the name.

'Clever of you to remember my surname, and only meeting me once,' she said. 'Gerard forgets it half the time.'

'Well, it's an unmemorable name,' said Gerard, unruffled, 'and you'd be better without it.'

'As far as you're concerned I *am* without it.'

'So you don't think,' Lamont asked, 'that L.M.H. is going to be much fun?'

'*Fun*? It'll be the reverse of fun, whatever that is. Nuff. Yes, it'll quite definitely be nuff. Everybody's so *dowdy* and they all seem to come either from Cheltenham or from Northern grammar schools.'

'Snob,' Gerard said casually.

'Well, if it's being a snob to find those people boring...' she shrugged. 'I've got to stick it, all the same, for a term or two. I couldn't face the *ructions* at home if I just turned straight round and walked out.'

'Get pregnant, then they'll whip you out fast enough,' Gerard suggested.

'You needn't be *coarse*.'

'There's nothing coarse about pregnancy, surely,' Lamont put in.

'There is if you're at L.M.H.'

Gerard now uncoiled his long, scarlet-clad limbs from the armchair. 'Time we were off, best beloved,' he said to Annabel.

'Why, what have we got to do?'

'You've forgotten. That memory of yours again.'

'Oh, yes, buy some records.'

'No, not just *buy* some records as baldly as that. We're going to make the rounds of the music shops, go through their stocks, insist on hearing lots and lots of records, then see what money we've got available, put our heads together, choose carefully and select a batch to tide us over the next few weeks. Then we're going to come back to my room and sit by the fire and play them on my gramophone.'

'Well,' she said, acquiescing, 'your gramophone's better than mine.'

'Yes, and my room's nicer than yours too.'

'How d'you know that? You haven't even *seen* my room.'

'No, but it's inevitable. Part of the order of things. The women's colleges are horrible and the rooms in them are horrible.'

'I know,' she said. 'It's all beastly unfair. It's enough to turn one into a Mrs Parkhurst.'

I felt an impulse to tell her that the name she was after was 'Pankhurst', but it was an impulse I had no difficulty in stifling. If I never met Annabel again, I didn't want her to remember me as the uncouth pedant whose only contribution had been to put her right over one letter in a name.

The sun was shining brightly now, the early mist had dried off and it was a fine, diamond-clear mid-morning with all the autumn colours standing out with an intensity that as usual made everything seem unreal. Gerard and Annabel were off on their search for music they could use to build an insulating wall round their sensibilities, Lamont was obviously ready to sink into his nest of poetic thoughts, from which he would arise like some fabulous bird with a sheet of verses in his bill, and I thought it was time I went about my humbler occupations. Did people like these three ever do any *work*, I wondered, or were they just born knowing everything already? I thanked Lamont for the coffee, and, outside in the sunlit quadrangle, murmured some kind of valediction to Gerard and Annabel, who smiled at me and went off arm in arm. The last impression I had of them, as they disappeared through a perfectly proportioned arch, was the sweeping rapidity of their walk, and the way she kept in step with him and inclined her body slightly towards his in a way that said, gently and undemonstratively but very clearly, 'I love this man.'

I pulled myself out of my trance, went off and started moling away, chasing the necessary books in the library, looking up references, and generally getting ready to field a few questions on Montesquieu's *L'Esprit des Lois* so that I should not make a fool of myself under Bax's sardonic, appraising eye. The day passed quickly. Almost the only events in it were that I took my meals in Hall and drank a pint of beer standing at the bar of the buttery. As I went in to dinner for the second time, I reflected that the place no longer seemed so frightening. I was beginning to pick out familiar faces and even attach names to them. I happened once again to sit near the tall, spectacled, curly-haired man whose manner was so cold and arrogant, the one I had already set down as the type who had never got over being a prefect at school; though I was not, thank God, near enough to speak to or be spoken to by him. I heard someone address him as 'Dick'.

In the evening Wilmot asked me round again, and I found two or three others there. They were all in very much my situation – timid grammar-school freshmen, glad and relieved at finding congenial companionship – and we clubbed together for a large jug of draught beer that loosened our tongues very satisfactorily. I realized, looking round the circle as we chatted away, that I would be perfectly content to hang around with men like this during the whole of my three years. There were in those days a lot of people who saw the ancient Universities as primarily turnstiles to the ruling class. For a person not already in that class to get to Oxford, or Cambridge, seemed to them first and foremost an act of social climbing. Not to me. I had (I now realized) never considered the matter. What brought me here was the opportunity to study history. I didn't care who my friends were, as long as they *were* friends.

*

Incredible though it must seem nowadays, the Bargeman's Arms, as it was in 1930, had no telephone. The lower orders of society, in those days, did not run to telephones unless their trade required one, and the trade arrangements at the Bargeman's Arms were of the very simplest. My father very rarely needed to vary the weekly delivery of mild and bitter beer (in barrels), light and brown ale (in crated bottles), and if he did need to he could always file his request at the brewery where, after all, he spent some hours every day.

The matter is germane to my own story because had my parents possessed a telephone I would have gone into the coin-operated call-box in the lodge at Episcopus and spoken to them quite often in those first few weeks. As it was, I wrote them a letter on my third or fourth day, assuring them that I was 'getting on all right' and would be down to see them 'any time now'. As my new life claimed me more and more thoroughly, any time now became easier and easier to push into the future. The Bargeman's was so close, it was no more than ten minutes on the bike, one of these days I would find I had a couple of hours with nothing much to do, and of course if it was *important*, if they *needed* me for anything they could always... Finally, with a shock, I realized that almost a month had gone by since my father had driven me across town in the old bullnose and deposited me at the lodge to start my new life.

A *month*... at least, by the next weekend it would be a month. This was serious. To drop in for half an hour would no longer do. I must make a real visit of it; that meant a mealtime, and, by an inescapably tightening chain of logic, a 'Sunday dinner', as of course we called the large, stupefying meal to which we all sat down after closing the pub at two o'clock.

So I got a note into the post inviting myself home for dinner the next Sunday, with a few lame words of excuse for my neglect ('You just wouldn't believe how busy,' 'so many things crowd in,' 'looking forward to hearing all news'), and put the matter out of my mind for the intervening two or three days.

Sunday dawned crisp and bright, and as I ate the breakfast that Arthur had brought up and sat beside my damply smouldering fire (in forty years as a scout he had never become *good* at laying fires), it occurred to me that my digestive pattern had altered in the last four weeks. Owing to the demands of the bar, it was always about half-past two before we sat down to Sunday dinner at home; it was eight-thirty now and I had almost finished breakfast. Could I, with the appetite of youth, wait six hours for my next meal? Would it not be better to have lunch in Hall at one, and then go home at 2.30 and, since I couldn't eat two lunches, just sit with the family while they ate? No, no, impossible. It would look stand-offish, as if my new mysterious life had already begun to push me away from them.

I decided to go and look in at home in the middle of the morning, before the pub opened at noon. My mother would be in the kitchen, preparing vegetables and what-not, and as I chatted to her she would certainly offer me a cup of tea, and with it I could have a few biscuits or a bun or something, enabling my young metabolism to hold out till half-past two.

So it came about that I entered my home premises by the back door at eleven that morning, instead of my announced time, and found not only Mother in the kitchen but Brian, sitting among the fragments of a late breakfast. He looked up at me unconcernedly and said, 'Let you out, have they?'

'Yes, they've opened the cage,' I said, deciding to play it all on a nice easy note. 'Yes, thanks, Mum, I'd love a cup. Do I see some of your home-made scones over there? Thanks, I'd love one.'

Brian looked at me with distaste as I began eating and said, 'Don't they feed you?'

'Never mind me,' I said. 'I'm having dinner with you all here and this is just to keep me going. Where's Dad?'

'In the cellar.'

'Well, I'll eat and you talk,' I said. 'Tell me your news.'

'How much news d'you think there is,' he said defensively, 'when it's only three or four weeks since I saw you? You're the one that's got the –'

'I bet you have got some news. I bet there's always something happening in your life.'

I was pushing him a little, because I was determined to build a bridge to him if I could.

'Oh, well,' he said, relaxing a bit. 'There is some news, as it happens. You know I'm with M.G. now. Well, we're going to have a factory of our own.'

'Excellent,' I said, washing down my scone with a draught of hot tea.

'You bet it's excellent. It's a triumph for Cecil Kimber. It's taken him years, quietly pushing on, putting the arguments in front of the Old Man, having them pushed to one side and quietly putting them back on the desk again.'

'Whose desk?' I asked. 'Could you begin at the beginning? No, I'm interested, I really want to know.'

'Whose desk?' Brian demanded contemptuously. 'Who the hell's desk d'you think I'm talking about? Who runs the show up at our place?'

'Morris, I suppose,' I said.

'Correct,' he said witheringly. 'Full marks to our bright boy. Morris Motors Limited is run by Mr Morris, right?'

'Yes,' I said. 'The one you call the Old Man.'

'That's what everybody calls him. And he's been the big stumbling-block in Cecil Kimber's way all these years. How he ever managed to talk the Old Man into it, I'll never know. Nobody'll ever know.'

He seemed ready to lapse into wondering silence, but I determined to keep after him. 'Oh, come on, Brian,' I said. 'Help a poor ignorant sod who doesn't know who Cecil Kimber even *is*, let alone what he's done that's so marvellous.'

For once Brian really seemed to hear me. My words evidently stunned him. He put down his tea-cup and stared at me.

'You mean you've never... Well, stone the flaming crows. You've lived in Oxford all your life and you don't know who Cecil Kimber is?'

At this, my mother laughed: a sound rarely heard, for though she had plenty of humour the responsibilities of her life tended to induce in her a mood of grave deliberation that seldom quite lifted. She often smiled, but rarely laughed.

'Brian, Brian,' she said, 'you are funny with your one-track mind.'

'Thanks very much,' he said.

'No, but honestly,' she said and laughed again. 'You'd do better to turn it round and ask, How many people that have lived in Oxford all their life *do* know who Cecil Kimber is?'

'Well, you do, for one.'

'Only because you talk about him so much. D'you want some tea?'

'I'm not the only person in Oxford that talks about Cecil Kimber,' Brian said doggedly. 'And before long there won't be anybody in Oxford that hasn't heard of him. And bloody few in England, if it comes to that.'

'Now then, Brian,' she said. 'If you can't talk about Mr Kimber without swearing I'd rather you –'

'All right, all right, I'm sorry.'

'There's never been bad language at our table and there's never going to be.'

'All *right*, Mother.'

'Well, tell me, with or without swearing,' I said, 'who Cecil Kimber is before I go raving mad.'

'If you haven't heard of him you're raving mad already. Or at least daft.'

'No, I'm not. I've just been busy with other things. Now cut out the insults and tell me who this joker is or I shall begin to believe you've dreamt him.'

My showing a bit of spirit may have been the right thing to do, because Brian began to explain the matter to me in what were, for him, patient and courteous tones.

'Number One. D'you know what M.G. is?'

'Yes. It's a sign you see up outside garages. I expect it means Mouldy Grease or something.'

'It means Morris Garages. The Old Man set them up as an after-sales organization. They're there to service Morris cars and sell spares and that.'

'Right,' I said. 'So what has Cecil Kimber –'

'Cecil Kimber is one of the directors of Morris Motors and his job is to run Morris Garages. He's always been very efficient at his job and he's made them a lot of money. So they have to listen to him. But there's one subject the Old Man has never liked listening to him about.'

'Don't tell me,' I said. 'Grass-track racing.'

'You're just trying to take the micky, but funnily enough you're nearly right. Racing of any sort. The Old Man doesn't like fast cars and he isn't interested in the sporting side of motoring. His idea of a car is a little tin box that trundles along from A to B without breaking down and without costing a lot of money.'

'Well, there's a certain amount of sense in –'

'There may be sense but there's no *fun*. No excitement. And no development, if it comes to that. It's racing that tests a car.'

Not knowing what to say to this, I said nothing, and at this point my father, who had indeed been occupied in the cellar, came in and sat down with us. Routine greetings, and routine questions and answers, followed. Soon afterwards, I took my leave, promising to return towards 2.30. I was rather behind with an assignment for Bax's class, and I could use a couple of hours' quiet reading.

Just after two I was back, and helped to clear up the bar and set the table, as I had done every Sunday for years; these little observances, this slipping back into the habits of home, suddenly stood out as deeply reassuring, sources of real strength. Of course I would have to leave them sooner or later, but not yet, not yet.

So my father carved the joint, and my mother handed out Yorkshire pudding and vegetables, and I ate two large helpings and drank a bottle of light ale on the house (a sign that my father considered this a special occasion), and sat about afterwards and chatted in a low voice to my mother while my father dozed in his armchair, and the peace and ordinariness of it all, with the quiet Sunday-afternoon streets outside and the quiet river flowing by, seemed to me blessings for which I was profoundly grateful.

Brian had gone off somewhere, so I took the opportunity to ask Mother about this M.G. business, and whether it all amounted to anything important.

'Well,' she said, glancing over at my father to make sure that he had fallen asleep, 'it's important to Brian because it's what he's interested in. He loves working on those racing cars. As for Mr Kimber, well, for Brian there's nobody on earth like him. But I think,' she lowered her voice carefully,' I think Dad's a bit worried.'

'Yes? What about?'

'Well, the way he sees it, the racing side of the motor business isn't the bread and butter side. It's a luxury, and if times get bad and the company starts feeling the draught they'll close it before they close anything else.'

'Not if they do well, surely,' I said.

'Well, I don't know anything about it, of course, but your Dad's a bit worried. He does want Brian to get into something solid. Unemployment's a terrible thing.'

She went to the kitchen to make the pot of strong tea that would bring us all round from our post-prandial heaviness, and I sat there, pondering her words. Like her, I knew nothing of Brian's world, and only one specific truth emerged to me from what she said. But it was an important truth, that Brian and I really were kin, that we were united by the same blood and deep similarities: for was not his leap into the unknown every bit as great as mine?

Chapter 6

November was here. The clocks had gone back an hour, the long, dark, drizzling evenings had come, and the world out of doors no longer seemed very attractive. For the next few months one's comforts would consist of things like bright fires, hot buttered toast, cosy little suppers, and a general sense of getting one's head down and letting the world go by.

One afternoon at about three-thirty I was crossing the quad on my way to my room. I was going to re-light the fire, which had gone out since breakfast-time, have some tea and toast, and settle down for a good spell of reading.

I was so absorbed, and happily absorbed, in this programme that I almost bumped into Gerard and Annabel, who were just passing through the archway between the first quadrangle and the second, where his rooms were. The last time I had set eyes on the two of them together they had been moving away from me through this elegant arch, and now they were moving towards me through it. How the mind hangs on to these visual details. It must be something to do with the structure of memory.

They were walking arm in arm, as usual, and Annabel was on the side nearest me. I didn't quite touch her, but she passed so close to me that I felt the disturbance of air made by the swirl of the cloak she had across her shoulders, and her face, framed in that great bronze loop of hair, was for an instant very close to mine. She gave me a smile of recognition – no words, just the smile – and they passed on.

These two beautiful, intelligent creatures, so obviously living intensely in the magic of one another, made me feel what I was: awkward, shy, solitary. For some reason I needed to turn my head and stare after them. I didn't want to, I was sure it was a slightly ridiculous and slightly discreditable thing to do, but a power stronger than any will of mine rooted my feet to the paving-stones, there in that archway, and at the same time pivoted my head. I watched, as Gerard and Annabel stepped lightly across the empty quad towards the corner staircase, where Gerard lived. His rooms were on the ground floor. Still trying to pull my eyes off them, still unable to, I watched him open the door, usher her in and pause for a moment in the doorway. What was he doing? Ah, yes, I saw now. He was sporting his oak.

It's possible that the expression 'sport one's oak' may not be understood in the present generation. In my youth, and for at least a century before, every set of rooms in an Oxford college had two doors: an ordinary one through which you went in and out in an ordinary way, and a thick outer door of oak. The oak had no handle on the outside. Once it was shut, the occupant of the room could not be disturbed; at least, people could bang on the oak and shout, but they couldn't open it.

The legal fiction, of course, was that since Oxford was a place of study, a man needed to protect himself against interruptions when he meant to settle down to a spell of hard reading. And no doubt, like all legal fictions, it was sometimes true. Some men did read hard, and sometimes they sported their oak for exactly the official reason. But even the College authorities can hardly have been simple-minded enough to imagine that there was one reason, and one reason only, for needing the privacy and security of that oak door.

Gerard's reason was obvious enough.

Discipline at the University was much stricter than it is today, and in particular every obstacle was put in the way of dealing with the opposite sex, even in the most ordinary and blameless companionship; if you had a female visitor she must not arrive before two in the afternoon and by seven she had to be out – but *out*. Still, there was no regulation that stopped her from coming in at two o'clock and staying five hours, and in five hours behind a sported oak there is time for a lot to happen.

I went on across the darkening quadrangle and up the narrow, twisting wooden stairs to my room. As I entered it I realized that I had an oak, too. I had hardly noticed it before. The possibility of my ever needing to use it was too remote to make it an object of interest to me. My friends were drawn from a circle of pretty serious-minded types who worked when it was usual to work and didn't come round for a casual chat when you were settling down to Montesquieu. And as for Gerard and Annabel and *their* reason for sporting the oak – well, that was a territory I didn't see myself visiting except in dreams, dreams of the waking and the sleeping variety.

The first day-dream took over then and there. I got the fire going, ate my toast – in a rather off-hand, preoccupied way, not really noticing it –

and then I settled down in the armchair by the fire to read Gilbert Murray's *Five Stages of Greek Religion*, which Bax had mentioned as a good popular introduction to the Ancient Greek way of seeing things. But I got no further than reading the same sentence over and over again. Images of Gerard and Annabel kept forming between me and the page. I saw them building a blazing fire. I saw them piling cushions on the floor in front of it. I saw this, I saw that. There is no need to particularize; everybody's sexual fantasies are much the same, and about equally boring to anybody else. Every so often I laid down the book and looked round my room. With its flickering firelight, with my possessions scattered about, with my print of Tintern Abbey on the wall, it had been coming of late to seem quite welcoming and home-like; but now, suddenly, it seemed incredibly bare and lonely.

It was almost the end of term, seven weeks behind me and one to go. Holly and tinsel and paper-chains had appeared in the shops, and there was a spirit of mild festivity in the air, a general relaxing of effort and tension. I remembered, with something approaching surprise, that in an ordinary normal life there was something called 'having fun'. Ever since I had entered Episcopus, my attention had been so entirely engrossed in just getting by, just avoiding notice and keeping up with the work, that I had quite genuinely forgotten there was such a thing as ordinary frivolous fun, kicking up harmlessly and enjoying oneself.

I must have been thinking these thoughts, one evening that week, as I walked from Hall after dinner, with the vague intention of going up to my room and reading, as I did most evenings. Knowlton was standing in the quad with four or five companions, Public School barkers to a man, but not, I realized as I went by and saw their faces, including any of the really objectionable types like the creature they called Dick. They were grinning and cracking jokes, waiting apparently to be joined by some lagging member of their party before going out. They were in holiday mood: they were going to have some of this same 'fun' I had just been thinking about. I went past them; I had a great wish, suddenly, that I were going out somewhere.

I don't know whether Knowlton caught the vibrations; probably it was just his natural geniality coming automatically into play; but he peered through the darkness, recognized me, and called out, 'I say, it's Leonard. He comes to classes with me. A good bloke. Perhaps he likes beer.'

'Scoop him up,' said one of the barkers. 'We need numbers. Numbers are cheerful. Scoop him up.'

'He's not just numbers, he's a good man,' Knowlton said. 'How about it, old sport?' he addressed me. 'Care to sally forth into the big wide-open night?'

I said Yes first. Second I said I would go up to my room for my overcoat and join them straight away. Only third did I ask what they were going out *for*.

'Oh, just a cosy little pub-crawl,' said Knowlton. 'Better leave your gown upstairs, natch.'

'Natch,' I said and bounded up the narrow stairs. Down went my gown on a chair, off its peg came my overcoat, and in forty seconds I was with them. The other man had arrived now and we moved off in a body.

Knowlton's caution about the gown was a very pertinent one. In those days, and in fact right up to the Second World War, you were supposed to wear your gown if you went out in the street in the evening. If found without it by the University Proctors, you were fined. It was a medieval throwback. And one, obviously, that we were not going to be bothered with when setting out on a pub-crawl.

So there I was, cheerfully breaking University statutes for the first time and thinking the better of myself for it, sitting in one pub and then another and then another, in company with Knowlton and his barking friends. I was very happy that evening. These men were an easy-going lot compared with a natural excluder and bully like Dick Who'sit, whose surname, I now learnt since the conversation touched briefly on personalities, was Kent. Their opinion of him, I learnt to my surprise, was not much different from mine; they were less appalled by his arrogance, having been steeped for so many years in the atmosphere that nurtured it; but they could see, as clearly as I could, that a man does not develop into a Kent, even in a Public School, unless he was originally born with the temperament of a *Gauleiter*. I began to expand and glow. In the third pub we went to I bought a round of drinks. I had a pound note in my wallet, the thrifty residue of the spending money I had budgeted for the term, which meant that I was wealthy; a pound, in 1930, would buy thirty pints of beer, far more than the lot of us were likely to get through in an evening. I was rich, I was able to stand a round and be a good bloke, and what was more I could carry a few pints of beer better than some of the party, who were beginning to slur their words and repeat themselves. Growing up in a pub seemed to have given me a certain immunity, not that my father encouraged either me or Brian to drink more than a very occasional glass until we were well turned eighteen; I suppose I must have just breathed in the stuff. Certainly I had, and always have had, a good tolerance of it.

That evening we had drunk about half-way through the round I had provided with such an inner swelling of quiet pride, when the landlord, a burly patriarch with a shock of white hair, happened to look out of the window into the street, stiffened to attention, and immediately whirled round and called out, 'Everybody upstairs!' As he uttered this, loudly enough to be heard over the conversation in every corner of the pub, he pointed to the staircase which could be seen through an open door at the far end of the room. For a moment I was too surprised to move, but some of the other men must have met this situation before and they took prompt action. The big shambling Knowlton, I was interested to see, was one of the first on his feet, and put a large hand on the shoulder of the man next to him, who was beginning to be slightly drunk.

'Come on, Teddy,' he said in a voice that obviously expected to be obeyed. 'Progs.'

'Progs? Oh, my God... Wha'...'

Knowlton jerked him to a standing position and within ten seconds we were all on the staircase, moving up. Two undergraduates from some other college, men we did not know, were suddenly with us. At the top of the stairs was a landing. We stood there, feeling rather sheepish, not talking. A door opened, and a stout, apple-cheeked woman, doubtless the landlord's wife, came out and surveyed us with a tolerant grin. She looked like Mrs. Noah in a picture-book. To her, we must have looked like a gang of truant schoolboys hiding from the master.

'Usual thing, I s'pose?' she asked, looking along the line of us.

'Usual thing, mother,' said Knowlton, recovering his easy good humour.

'Ah, you're lucky Fred saw 'em coming,' she said, shaking her head and still looking amused. 'Sometimes they Proctors just pops in the side door before you can say "knife" and it's Name and College? Name and College? all round the room. Ah well, they got their reasons I suppose. And you got away with it this time. They never stays long.'

She went back into her sanctum and sure enough, after a couple of minutes, the landlord called up the stairs that the coast was clear and we all filed downstairs, feeling no longer foolish but suddenly rather heroic, as if we had been involved in a skirmish with a powerful enemy and come off best. Knowlton was joking with the two men from another college: the common emergency had brought us all together. Five minutes after the original alarm we were all back at the same places in which we had been sitting, in front of the same half-empty glasses. None of the other customers took the slightest notice of us. To them, we were a different species of animal, and what we did held no interest for them.

Flushed with success, and feeling pretty confident that the Proctors, after a perfunctory walk through the town, would soon go back to their comfortable quarters, we visited a couple more pubs before closing time – ten o'clock – and wound up at College singing in a spirited but ragged chorus 'Pale Hands I Loved Beside the Shalimar'. There were the usual suggestions that we should have a nightcap in someone's rooms, but it turned out that no one had any stock of beer in, the buttery of course was closed, and as sobriety descended we became sleepy and drifted away to our beds. How innocent it all was, how Arcadian. Yet to me it was an initiation into manhood; or rather, perhaps, gentlemanhood.

*

That was on, I think, the Wednesday of that last week of term. On the Friday evening, everyone was expected to be at dinner in Hall, and when the meal was over the Dean got up from his seat at High Table and said to us, 'Well, gentlemen, I hope you've had a good term. Now go away and have a good vacation, and remember, I don't want to see you till next term. You will be welcome back any time from lunchtime on Friday, January the 16th. But not a minute before. Thank you and have a good Christmas with your people.'

That was how it was. Undergraduates were encouraged to regard Oxford as their province for three stretches of eight weeks, and for the rest of the year they were politely but firmly invited to stay away. Not that their space was needed for anything else. The colleges simply went into suspended animation. Of the several hundred undergraduates in that Hall, I did not expect to run into any in the street, or come through from the living quarters into the bar of the Bargeman's Arms and find them sitting there.

After the Dean had spoken his little piece, people began to drift away, but quite a lot ordered a fresh tankard and lingered at the table a little. It seemed to be an evening when people expected to get a fair skinful of beer, and I noticed the conversation becoming rather boisterous, with bursts of loud laughter, at some points around the Hall. Opposite me, Lamont and Urquhart were sitting together. Lamont was trying to persuade Urquhart to come with him to a concert at the Town Hall. Urquhart seemed hardly able to believe his ears at the suggestion.

'What, and sit through the Emperor Concerto for the ten millionth time?'

'Well, I don't choose the programme, Gerard,' said Lamont, smiling tolerantly, 'but how long is it since you sat and listened to the Emperor Concerto? I mean really from beginning to end?'

'Oh, probably on some Sunday evening when I was at prep school and it was either that or vaulting practice in the gym or something.'

'Precisely, and it's been associated with vaulting practice in your mind ever since.'

'With avoiding vaulting practice, you mean. And now I've at last managed to get to a stage of life where I can avoid both of them.'

'There's some César Franck, too.'

'Nineteenth-century Romanticism in deliquescence. Once all that warm treacle starts washing round me I'll just sink down and drown in it.'

'Well,' said Lamont, beginning to rise from his place at the long bench, 'you'd be much better off coming with me to hear some music than hanging about in College listening to a lot of drunken louts whooping around.'

Why was Lamont so sure there would be drunks about tonight? Evidently he knew something I didn't, but what? Had the word gone round that there was to be a specially rowdy party somewhere in College, or was it simply a custom on the last night of term?

As I sat considering the matter, Kent and some of his friends came past on their way out. They all seemed so large, so fierce, and – Kent in particular – so overbearing.

I felt a hand on my shoulder and I must have been feeling tense because it made me start quite violently. But it was only Wilmot, friendly, uncompetitive, reassuring Wilmot.

'Doing anything this evening?' he asked. 'I'm going to get in a big jug of beer and there are two or three other chaps coming. Might as well have a bit of an end-of-term celebration.'

'Excellent,' I said. 'I'll get a jug, too.'

He nodded and said, 'Come over whenever you like.'

So I went and spent the last evening of term where I had spent the first – beside Wilmot's fire. His friends, three or four in number, were much the same as I had met there on previous evenings: either the same individuals, or so exactly the same type as to be more or less interchangeable. Only two names, apart from Wilmot's, have stayed with me. One was McFarlane, a medical student from somewhere like Dundee. He was exceptionally young in University terms, being not yet eighteen; and he looked at least two years younger than he was, with a fresh schoolboy face and his hair brushed straight forward, without a parting, which was the way you brushed little boys' hair in those days, till they got to be eleven or twelve. He had a clear, not very strong Scots voice. He had not started shaving, and the line of soft dark down on his upper lip proclaimed that this decision would have to be taken soon, but it was impossible to imagine McFarlane going into a shop and buying a shaving-brush and a razor and blades and all the rest of it. One felt that he wouldn't have known which part of the shop to go to. I suppose, looking back, that his thrifty parents, recognizing that the training of a medical man takes a long time, had packed him off to University as soon as he had got through the necessary examinations. He would be about twenty-four when he ultimately qualified, and they probably thought that was long enough to have him consuming resources and earning no money. McFarlane always seemed perfectly confident. He never gave the impression of feeling insecure at finding himself in an environment that must have been as strange to him as to any of us. It was almost as if, being still a child, he was simply not troubled by questions of status or prestige. He had his own concerns, as a child will play with its toys in a corner of the room while its parents are agonizing over some career decision or facing bankruptcy.

The other man whose name I remember was called Armitage. He was the son of a Yorkshire miner, a real product of the Scholarship manner. He was tall and raw-boned, with a long, gentle, rather equine face. Armitage had a fortunate temperament. Though he was unmistakably Northern working-class and never pretended to be anything else, he, like McFarlane, seemed to have no difficulty in fitting in to Oxford. He had a rather wide-eyed look, as if he always found everything slightly amazing. His attitude seemed to be that Oxford was a tremendous show, full of glitter and achievement and strangeness, and that he, Fred Armitage, had earned by his own efforts a ring-side seat at that show. He watched it all without any sign of wanting to join in and emulate it.

The talk drifted on, interestingly enough. Some of it was about our work and how we coped with it; to all of us, this was an important sector of our lives, and comparing experiences we found that none of us had had much idea, before we got here, of the standard that would be expected of us and whether we would be able to live with it. We had seen ourselves pitchforked into a world where everyone else was better educated than ourselves, where they had all had marvellous teaching at famous schools, backed up by private tuition if they needed it, and had picked up foreign languages on all those holidays abroad that they took for granted. After eight weeks' contact with the reality of that daydream, we found that very few of the men from that background had read any more than we had and that some of them were astonishingly simple-minded.

'Where they score,' said Wilmot reflectively, 'is that they just damn' well don't care whether they're simple-minded or not. They've been taught that they're the governing class, so what they do is right and it isn't for the peasants to question it.'

'I think a few cracks are beginning to appear in that structure,' another student put in. 'The Public School man hasn't got the world in a jug the way he had before the War.'

Armitage, who seemed to have been lost in his thoughts for a while, now revealed that those thoughts were about Lamont. He had sat near Lamont in Hall a few times and been amazed at the snatches of his conversation that he had heard. 'The number of books he knows about, he must have done nothing sin' he was born except sit in a library and read.' Some of his awe of Lamont had also attached itself to me, because he had noticed that I knew Lamont and had occasionally been to his rooms. I did not disillusion him by pointing out that this was merely the casualness of Lamont's genial hospitality. I was no more Lamont's intellectual equal than I was Bax's. He asked me now if I had read any of Lamont's poetry, and rather unwisely I revealed that I had. He published quite a lot in the undergraduate magazines of the time, and as it happened I had been reading one only the day before.

'What's it like?' Armitage asked. 'What kind of stuff is it?'

When reading idly through Lamont's verse I had not expected ever to have to tell anyone what it was 'like', and I now discovered that this is not the easiest of tasks.

'It's – well, it's – I'm not very good at saying what poetry's *like*,' I said. 'I mean, it's all just poetry, isn't it?'

Someone, with vague memories of 'English' at school, asked if it was 'romantic'. This again threw me. I knew that if it was not Romantic it had to be Classical, because apparently you had to run on to the field wearing the colours of one team or the other; so much had stayed with me from my school textbooks. What was Lamont?

'It's pretty classical,' I said. 'I mean, it's got a lot of classical names in it. Ancient Greek gods and stuff. There was one poem, I remember, it was about Circe.'

'She's not a god, she's a character in Homer,' someone put in.

'I can never tell,' said Wilmot, 'which of the people in Homer are gods and which are just characters. They all seem to behave in the same way. I suppose it's because they're all Greeks.'

'Anybody happen to know what school Lamont's from?' I asked, steering the conversation back to what interested me.

'Why does it matter?' someone asked.

'Well, it's just curiosity. But I think it does matter, in a way. You sometimes meet men like him. There aren't many of them but they're a recognizable type. They've got the self-confidence of these Public School men but they're not Philistine. As far as I can see there's only one other man in College here who's anything like that same type, and that's Urquhart, the fellow that wears those red trousers. They seem to have a natural relationship with the arts. You can't imagine any of these Public School hearties having that. If they ever had any interest in those things, it was crushed out of them long ago. So what I want to know is, Where have men like that spent the last five years before they came to College?'

No one knew the answer. As time went on I was to learn that Lamont had been at one of the more liberal of the minor Public Schools, a place where to take an interest in the arts did not necessarily land you in a morass of odium and persecution. As for Gerard, a Londoner through and through, he had rather absent-mindedly gone to school at Highgate, and his home background had been one of those households in which poets and painters and actors are as familiar as gas-inspectors and odd-job men. All very different from the Bargeman's Arms, West Oxford.

We talked on, in the comfortable firelight, and no doubt most of us were thinking that it was a fine, snug life, after all, that this College existence had turned out to be. But as the hands of the clock on Wilmot's shelf moved from ten towards ten-thirty, a distant, and at times not very distant, noise began to reach our ears. It was a noise of young male voices, at first predominantly in a ragged attempt at song, then increasingly into a roaring like that of a football crowd, and finally – intruding decisively and forcing us to drop our conversation and attend to it – burst after burst of cheering. Under the cheering were some other vocal sounds which the cheering almost totally drowned: shouts, I thought, of protest.

'What gang of louts is that?' someone asked, rather uneasily.

'Whoever they are, they're in the other quad,' said Wilmot.

Yes, I thought, the one I live in.

There was a sound that sounded like a crash of breaking timbers, and another wild outburst of cheering. We began speculating.

'Good God – they're going it, whoever they are,' said McFarlane, in his precise little voice.

'Not much doubt who they are. I could give you half a dozen names I'd guarantee are on that particular scene.'

'Who?'

'Oh, well, obviously,' and a string of names among which I recognized Kent's.

'What on earth,' I asked, keeping my voice very calm, 'can they be *doing*?'

'You must remember,' said Wilmot, 'that the tradition of the Rag is far from extinct in this venerable seat of learning.'

For a few minutes we discussed, amateur scholars, the precise signification of the word 'rag.' We concluded that it had originally meant something more or less planned and purposive, a hoax or practical joke, and had deteriorated into meaning any outburst of unruly behaviour, even the mobbing of one undergraduate by a gang of others.

'It sounds,' said one, 'as if they were breaking up someone's rooms.'

'Stupid, mindless cretins,' said Wilmot. In the firelight I could see Armitage shaking his head sadly, as if lamenting this blot on the beautiful Oxford he had come so far to share in.

We tried to ignore the noise. It would have been impossible to see what was happening from the windows of Wilmot's room. All this action, whatever it was, was happening in the other quad, through the archway. The only way to find out was to go and see, and this no one felt inclined to do.

But our cosy beer-jug and fireside-talk evening was ruined. The air seemed suddenly loaded with menace; the dark, crisp winter night seemed full of wild animals emerging from their lairs, snuffling for the scent of prey. Fitfully, the noise spread to Wilmot's quadrangle, and we heard thumping feet, raised voices, a high, off-key solo voice trying to sing a popular song. At one point, feet thundered briefly on Wilmot's staircase, further down.

'I've a good mind to sport the oak,' said Wilmot.

No one commented on this suggestion. Looking back, I suppose we were all unwilling to show fear by urging him to carry it out; equally, we did not want to oppose it. So no one spoke and no one stirred.

About eleven a man who lived on the next staircase said in an attempt at casualness, 'Well, I've got a long journey tomorrow. I think I'll get some sleep. Good-night, chaps all.'

He opened the door and was gone. I envied him. I couldn't get back to the sanctuary of my rooms without going through the area of all that hideous mob-noise.

But the other men, glad of the excuse provided by that first departure, were saying good-night and leaving in ones and twos. I lingered for a few moments with Wilmot. Even more than on that lonely first evening, his fireside seemed a beautiful place to linger in.

'D'you want to stay here?' he suddenly asked me. 'You might be better off on my sofa than trying to force your way through that howling pack.'

I think I opened my mouth to say 'Yes, please,' but to my own surprise

I heard my voice say, 'No, thanks, I'll be all right.'

'As you like,' he said. 'I shall turn in anyway.'

We wished each other good-night. As I went down the stairs I wondered, with real curiosity, what on earth had possessed me to refuse Wilmot's offer of sanctuary. Some sort of pride, perhaps, but pride in what? My vanity had never been invested in physical prowess, in the ability to punch my way through a gang of rowdies; and as for fear, I had been no stranger to it since I clung giddily to Brian's motor-bike.

Pondering this, I halted at the foot of Wilmot's staircase. His rooms were on Staircase 6, in the Victorian quad – a building solid, substantial, useful and not at all interesting to look at, rather like Wilmot himself. It was cut off from the other two quadrangles by the Hall and chapel. A passageway led to the main quad, where I lived, and to get to the one that lay nearest the garden, where Urquhart and Lamont lived, and Bax too for that matter, you turned left and went through another passageway, this one gracefully arched. The noise was coming from the main quad, the one I lived in; I could hear it coming in waves over the Hall-and-chapel roof. It was the sort of noise you would instinctively walk away from; but to get to the sanctuary of my room I had to walk towards it. I did so, as calmly as possible. The sound became muffled for a moment as I went through the dark, quiet passageway between Hall and chapel, then burst on my ears with renewed loudness as I came out into the open. And not only the sound, but the sight that greeted me was enough to freeze my blood. Over in the far corner, where the J.C.R. staircase was, I saw the leap of flames and the whirling of sparks. These drunken dervishes were making a bonfire. What of? Someone's possessions? For an instant I wondered if they, whoever 'they' might be, had run completely mad and were throwing on to the flames shelf after shelf of books looted from the library. The thought passed over my mind as rapidly as an actor running across the stage, but what it revealed during that brief time was my own attitude of profound mistrust: I really did not put *anything* past these overfed, over-privileged louts.

Hugging the wall, as reluctant as a cat to trust myself to the open space of the quadrangle, I went along to the porter's lodge. The head porter was on duty that night. His name was Frank Penney. He had a large, flat, expressionless face pitted with large open pores, a face that confronted the world and gave nothing away.

I opened the door of his sanctum, timidly. As a member of the College, I had a perfect right to go into the lodge, but I still went in timidly. There was nothing welcoming about Frank's manner. Or repelling, to be fair. It was simply a non-manner, an absence of reaction.

'Seems to be a hell of a row going on, Frank,' I ventured.

'Nothing new,' he said. 'Specially not for the last night of term.'

His matter-of-fact acceptance cheered me slightly.

'There seems to be a fire burning over there,' I pursued.

'Shouldn't wonder.'

'But look here, Frank, if they're burning somebody's furniture or something, surely that's against the law?'

Frank Penney turned his big, flat, expressionless face towards me and looked at me through his large round glasses.

'If you think that,' he said, 'I'll open the gate for you and you go out into the town and fetch a policeman.'

'Well, but...'

'Or I got a telephone here. You're welcome to use it.'

'Well, thanks, but I hardly think it's my place to –'

'When they gets a few drinks inside 'em,' Frank said, jerking his head in the appropriate direction, 'there's always some of 'em gets an itch. They wants to break something, or burn something, or tear something up by the roots. I've known two or three of 'em pile up the furniture from their own rooms and make a bonfire in the quad with it.'

'But it isn't *theirs*,' I objected. 'It's College furniture.'

'Some of it is and some of it en't. A lot of 'em bring chairs and tables and the Lord knows what with 'em. One brought a four-poster bed once. It wouldn't go up the staircase, so he put in for a room on the ground floor. Got one, too. Viscount Something,' and he gave a name that has faded from my memory, 'he was. Owned half of Durrbyshire, they used to say. And if they was to set fire to furniture that was from College, well, College charged 'em for it and they paid up. 'Tworn't no trouble to them. Money to burn, they had.'

I glanced at him to see if these last words were intended as a joke, but his face was as expressionless as always.

'Who was it who burnt the grand piano?' I asked. It was a story I had heard, but never believed.

'Oh, aye, him. It was after a Boat Club supper. They had a bonfire going and this chap appears and says to 'em, If you'd like the piano from my room, he says, to make a nice hot fire, you can have it, he says. I never liked that piano, he says. And they carries it out and burns it. I can still smell it. The varnish was a'bubblin' off it. And the keys didn't melt, of course. One of the scouts picked 'em out of the ashes in the morning. Got a price for 'em.'

So the fantastic story was *true*. It was within the experience of this living piece of history here.

'But,' I said, appalled, 'what about the dons who live in College? They must have seen what was going on. I mean, burning a grand –'

'The dons knows when to keep their heads down,' said Frank. 'They knows there's nothing to be done with 'em while the fit's on 'em. Next morning'll be a different story. When they're hung over and tired out and can't hardly remember what they was doing. *That's* when they brings 'em to book.' He stared at me briefly, as if for emphasis. 'I s'pose you're going up to your room now.'

'You bet I am. I'm not going to hang about with that lot of –'

'Well,' he said, 'when you goes, keep an eye out and you'll see Hungerford lurking about somewhere, or hanging out of a window p'raps.' (Hungerford was the Junior Dean.) 'He won't come out. He knows he's safe where he is. But he'll be noticing. He'll be remembering names. And in the morning, at nine o'clock sharp, the ones that are doing it'll be called up and made to explain theirselves. And of course,' he concluded, picking up his newspaper in readiness to continue reading, 'they won't have no explanation and it'll be like Bow Street – next please, pay up and move along.'

He went back to the *Oxford Mail* in a gesture of dismissal as decisive as a don's 'I mustn't keep you.' I went out of the lodge with the intention of hurrying straight up to my room. The bonfire with the whooping crowd round it was, mercifully, over on the far side and in the opposite corner from my staircase; it was bad enough to have such things going on in the quad I lived in, but, given that, I was as far from it as one could hope to be. And yet something gripped my feet and held me there for a moment, staring, instead of hurrying on and diving into the safe darkness of my staircase. I had known, as one knows a fact intellectually, that hooliganism and destructiveness existed at Oxford and sometimes got out of hand. But now that I was seeing these abstractions as they actually took shape in real experience, the effect was so phantasmagoric, so totally at variance with what I had accepted as the guiding spirit of the place, that I was hypnotized by sheer amazement. I just stood there, staring across at the glare of the bonfire. Figures, outlined against it, flitted to and fro. I heard a crash, then some more whooping. It was like some sort of antechamber of hell, with the devils busy at their work.

I don't think I shall ever forget that scene. I saw others like it during the next three years, but this was the first and it went in deepest.

The bonfire, rather choked and smoky now, was burning in the middle of the quad. One glance showed that it was fuelled by furniture; the legs and backs of chairs and the top of a desk were clearly identifiable. My blood chilled at the thought of those yobs dragging out *my* desk and throwing it on a fire; all those notebooks and files.... Had they emptied this man's desk of its papers beforehand? It was hard to believe that they would have so much consideration. This was persecution. Someone was being punished: either for doing something that was felt to be out of line, or just for existing. The quad was lined with figures, some gesticulating and shouting, some standing still and watching; over in the far corner a struggle was going on, one man being pinned in a helpless position by three or four others. As I stared across, the man who was being set on turned his head in my direction and I recognized him. His name was Walters or Waters or something like that; I never knew him well; he was rather a morose, solitary, somewhat badger-like creature who kept himself very much to himself. As I stood there, staring in horrified disbelief, two things happened. One was that Kent came hurrying past me, calling out, 'Get him ready – we'll do it here.' *Do* what? I thought with a sinking feeling of utter horror. In his hand Kent carried one of those boxes that people use for shoe-cleaning kit. He went over to the struggling knot in the corner. The second thing that happened was that, as the bonfire began visibly fading – there was a mattress lying on top which was stifling it somewhat – a figure moved forward into the circle of the firelight and began stirring it energetically with a long metal poker which I recognized as one of those normally kept beside the fireplace in Hall. It was Carshalton. He stirred the blaze into more life and stood back looking at it. His eyes, in their dark caverns, seemed to me to be envying the flames their light and warmth. But perhaps all he was envying was their power to destroy.

I had seen enough. No one was paying any attention to me; I walked to the foot of my staircase as little hindered as if this were eleven o'clock in the morning and no one about. But if my body was unmolested, my mind was full of fear and disgust. As I went up the stairs I thought of Hungerford. Had he really been lurking somewhere? I had not seen him.

*

I was woken in the morning by Arthur rapping on the impregnable surface of my oak and calling out in a querulous tone, 'I shall 'ave to get this door open, sir.' Waking from a sleep shot through with nightmares, I welcomed the homelinessof his voice. He talked like my Uncle Ernest.

I got out of bed and opened the inner door, and then the oak. He looked at me crossly. 'Everything upside down this mornin',' he said. 'Upside down, it is.'

I could believe it. Even I had been pretty confused. I had no memory, for instance, of shutting the oak behind me as I came in.

'What exactly went on, Arthur?' I asked, hungry for information.

'All I knows,' he said dismissively, coming past me into the room and setting down my jug of hot water, 'is there's a lot of blasted young fools about.' I can hear it now, the way he came out with that Oxfordshire 'blaarsted'.

He stumped off out. I washed and dressed, and when he brought my breakfast I ate it quickly by the smoking, half-lit fire. Then I went out into the quad. Curiosity, overcoming my disgust and timidity, took me over to where the bonfire had been.An under-gardener was busy with broom and barrow, clearing up the unsightly remains. As I was looking at this sight, Lamont passed by. I wondered where he had been while all this was going on. He had his usual air of being so deeply involved in his private world that the mundane made very little impression; but he paused long enough to look at the scene. His face stiffened; then, noticing me standing there, he moved towards me and said, 'This is the kind of thing that makes one think it would be a good idea to bring back the stocks. The people who did this ought to sit in the middle of the quad till nightfall in wooden gaiters so that everyone could come and have a good look at them and see them for what they are.'

'What will actually happen to them, d'you know?' I asked.

'Oh, they'll be hauled up before the dons and fined, and they'll have to pay for the stuff they burnt, and if Hungerford can identify a ringleader he'll probably be gated for about the first fortnight of next term. None of it will worry them much. They'd rather have the reputation of hooligans even if it has to be bought at a price.'

He passed on, probably beginning already to think about something more interesting, and I went up to my room to pack. Some of the undergraduates who had to make a long journey and catch an early train were already in the lodge with their trunks and suitcases, pestering the porter about taxis and sweetening the pester with his termly *baksheesh*. For myself, I knew all I had to do was to leave my luggage in the lodge and cycle down to the Bargeman's. My father would doubtless drive me round at about tea-time to collect the heavy bags.

It was all simple, there was no pressure on me, and I ought to have been feeling cheerful at having surmounted the various obstacles and got through my first term. Instead, I felt heavy and apprehensive. The events of last night had opened a door through which I had caught a glimpse of a very nasty landscape. I thought of the victim, Walters or Waters. No doubt the College would replace his furniture, charging it up to Kent and company. What upset me was the thought of such a violation, the shredding of a man's privacy and dignity. They must have caught him by surprise or he would have sported his oak. I pictured him sitting quietly reading, or listening to music, and those whooping brutes suddenly appearing, throwing open the door and rushing into the room.

This was 1930. In another three or four years, things like this, only on a huge scale and much more extreme, were being done to people in Germany who happened to be Jews. By those standards, what had happened to Walters/Waters was trivial, and so was the bullying of tear-stained little boys in boarding schools. But trivial or not, they were ugly, and what made them uglier was that they were inflicted by the upper classes, those destined to be in control of society.

As I stood outside the lodge I saw Carshalton coming across the quad. I felt a surge of dislike and that gave me the energy to confront him, far more brusquely than I would have done normally. I barred his way as he was about to enter the lodge.

'What happened to Walters last night?' I demanded.

'I don't know,' he replied, not looking at me and trying to walk past as if I weren't there.

'Yes, you do,' I said. I took hold of his arm. 'And you can spare a minute to tell me. You were there all right. I saw you working on the bonfire.'

'Let go,' he said in that neutral machine-voice.

'I'll let go when you tell me what I'm asking. What did they do to Walters? I heard Kent saying *Get him ready, we'll do it out here.* Do what? What had he got in that box he was carrying?'

'If you must know,' Carshalton said, 'they debagged him and put some shoe polish on his bum.'

'How revolting,' I said, letting my hand fall away from his arm.

'He wasn't hurt,' Carshalton said. 'It would just take him some time to get it off, that's all.'

'And wrecking his rooms,' I said. 'And burning all his stuff.'

Carshalton shrugged. 'He's been asking for something like that all term. He's too damned stand-offish.'

This was so obviously a phrase taken over from Kent that I ignored it and walked away. I had Carshalton tagged by now. He was the type who would be careful to go along with whatever was the ruling power-group in any *milieu* in which he found himself. Not that he was fined on this occasion, or hauled up before the dons. He had been, as usual, discreet: making up the bonfire when it seemed to be flagging, but not bursting into anyone's rooms and dragging out the furniture, or committing any assault. He would always support the ruling group to the extent that he stood well with them, but not to the extent of getting into the trajectory of any possible backlash. He was clever, that one.

Chapter 7

One of the things I certainly wasn't ready for, when I came back to the Bargeman's after that first term, was how strange it was going to seem at first. Things I had been used to, and taken for granted all my life, suddenly seemed very odd, and after only a couple of months away. (Was that *really* all it had been?) Having high tea at six o'clock, for instance, with Mother and Brian. Not only had my metabolism adjusted to eating an hour and a quarter later – no great problem since I could soon adjust back – but the atmosphere round the table was so different. In College, I usually found a seat near somebody I could chat to; if I sat near a man who ignored me, that was because he was immersed in his own thoughts, which I knew nothing of, and had a perfect right to ignore me. But Brian had a special, elder-brotherly way of ignoring me, the one he had developed and polished through the years ever since I could remember. He simply came in and sat down to his food as if I were not there. If Mother made a remark or asked him anything, he answered amiably enough; but if I spoke to him he looked at me in a startled way, as if the furniture had suddenly begun talking.

Settling back, for the four weeks of the vacation, into life at the Bargeman's, I soon discovered that Brian's attitude hadn't changed: he still largely ignored me. My doings did not interest him, and he did not care enough about my reaction to tell me anything about his. Fair enough, I thought. If I could bear it for eighteen years I could go on bearing it. One evening, however, he came home with a piece of news so exciting, so engrossing, so all-important that he was willing – unstoppably eager, indeed – to talk about it to anyone who was in the room, even me. After months, and probably years, of string-pulling and negotiating, M.G. were going to Abingdon.

Clearly it was Dad he really wanted to talk to, but that would have to wait till closing time, so he poured out a not very coherent half-account of the matter to the uninitiated ears of Mother and myself.

'It'll give us much more scope for research and development,' he said, pouring a blob of tomato sauce on to the plate next to his grilled chops.

'The Old Man,' Brian went on, holding me with his fiercely proselytizing eye, 'hates the thought of spending money on a fast car. If you mention racing to him he doesn't sleep for a week. It's money down the drain as far as he's concerned. He'd only want to build a racing car if you came to him with proof that England had fifty million racing drivers. He goes for big numbers. He doesn't understand about research and development.Cecil Kimber does.'

Even at that tender age, even in those early days, I knew that when Brian used words like that, *research, development* and the rest, he was uttering runes rather than arguing. His notion was that prosaic, hard-headed men in board-rooms would think kindly of racing if you could get them to see it in terms of *research and development* and thus, ultimately, of *market prestige* and *money*. Deep down, or rather about one millimetre down, he, Brian, didn't care a fig for research and markets and money. What gripped him fast was the excitement and glamour of motor-racing. He loved the howl of highly-tuned engines, the sharp smell of high-octane fuel, the begoggled heroes at the wheel, the swish of the chequered flag at the end. He loved the thrills and spills and slides and phenomenal avoidances at high speed; he loved the champagne celebrations and big silver cups that greeted the winner. He was a man in love, I thought as I looked across the table at him, hopelessly and for ever in love.

Mother now brought out our father's meal, which we generally took as a signal to finish what was on our plates and leave the table to give him a bit of peace. This time, though, Brian stayed where he was and so did I. The occasion was too important to yield to the petty restrictions of household routine.

There was a momentary pause during which neither of our parents was present, and even this seemed to Brian, in his state of excitement, worth filling with words, if only to me.

'Short-sighted, that's what it is. He's after the big numbers and the big money; all right, fair enough, but so's Henry Ford.'

I waited.

'Henry Ford makes cars for the masses. Nothing fancy. The Old Man must've taken a leaf or two out of old Ford's book – pity he didn't take this one.'

'Which one?'

'Racing. Building a car he believed in enough to put it out there where the racing fans could see it. They're the ones that *know* cars, after all.'

'And Henry Ford did that? Went racing?'

'One of the first things Ford ever did was to build a special and hire Barney Oldfield to drive it. Barney Oldfield was the top racing driver in America, and Ford entered this special in a big race in Long Island, I think it was, with Barney Oldfield driving.'

'How did he get on?' I asked innocently.

'Get on? He *won*, damn it!'

'Oh. Well, I wasn't to know.'

'Look, chump,' said Brian, leaning across the table and looking straight into my face. 'He didn't only win. He finished ten minutes before the bloke that came second. *Ten minutes.* A gap like that's pretty near unheard-of in racing!'

He glared at me as if I were trying to take away from Mr Oldfield some of the glory of his achievement.

'Oh,' I said lamely. 'Pretty good, eh?'

'*Good*? It launched Henry Ford. Got the name out where people could see it.'

My father entered as he spoke, sat down at the table, and said, 'What launched Henry Ford?'

'Winning a big race with Barney Oldfield up,' Brian said.

'Oh,' said Dad. He began to eat, meditatively, then said, 'I thought it was the Model T launched him.'

'That and winning the race. The two together.'

'Oh,' said Dad. 'Well, you ought to know. You're in the motor business.'

'In the best bit of it, too,' Brian grinned. 'From today. It's been all hole and corner up to now.'

'Hole and corner?'

'M.G. have been making racing cars,' Brian said, 'in any odd bits of space in any of the Morris Garages. Using their equipment and their storage space when it didn't happen to be needed for the family-car trade. And as for money –' he spread his hands in a gesture of hopelessness – 'you could pretty near say they didn't *have* any money. Scraped it up out of the Morris Garages budget.'

'Must have been quite a headache,' Dad agreed, 'when it came to balancing the books.'

'Only a man like Cecil Kimber could have done it. He had the patience and he knew what he wanted. He was tough enough to get in there and wear the Old Man down.'

'Then again,' said our father, scraping his plate, 'I daresay Billy Morris has got his own way of looking at these things.'

I had noticed before, listening at odd times to their conversation, that each of them had his own habitual way of referring to the proprietor of Morris Motors. Brian called him the Old Man. Our father called him Billy Morris. Behind each sobriquet, of course, lay an attitude. Brian saw him rather like the miserly grandfather of some hungry peasant family, cautious, penny-pinching and stick-in-the-mud, refusing to release funds to enable the younger members to show initiative and energy. My father saw him as a conventional Oxford tradesman, immensely rich but in no other way different from the average grocer or timber-merchant: thrifty, unadventurous, content with these two qualities and distrusting their opposites.

The discussion now broke up because our father was needed at his station behind the bar. Brian disappeared somewhere, no doubt to spread the word among his cronies that he was to be one of the first wave of M.G. workers in their proud new little factory at Abingdon. I sat mooning over the kitchen fire. After about half an hour I got up and washed the dishes from our evening meal, not because I had been told to but because I wanted to avoid any possible stigma of idleness. Then I sat down by the fire again, reviewing my life and trying somehow to compare it with Brian's.

I couldn't, of course, find any point of contact between the two. Brian's world, whatever it was, clearly had nothing at all in common with the world of Bax and Gadsby and of my fellow-students, of people like Knowlton and Lamont, right down to the more ordinary ones like Wilmot and Armitage. Even a swine like Kent could at least be disliked within a framework I had grown to understand, whereas in Brian's world I had no compass-bearings at all. What was Cecil Kimber, so idolized by Brian, actually *like*? In the totally improbable event of my ever meeting him, would I like him? And if so, what qualities would I like him for?

As I brooded over this, there came to me a memory, one of those fresh, vivid memories that are like dreams: and not just any dreams, but the kind that are coloured, and stylized, and held in a frame, so that the people we dream about, both ourselves and others, move as formally and deliberately as the actors in a Noh play. It was a memory of the previous September: not a long time ago, in calendar terms, but very distant in terms of my life because it was before the Great Divide, was indeed in that dream-like interlude when, knowing that I was to be a student of history, I wandered about Oxford in a continuous reverie of the past, hearing voices from open doorways where no doorways were, and the rattle of spurs and the drumming of hoofs on silent turf, and the peal of bells from towers that now rang to a different sound or had collapsed. I had walked the streets in a continuous hallucination, seeing with the eyes of the body the Oxford of 1930 – box-like motor-cars, clumsy suits and heavy hats on the men, long tubular dresses on the women – but because I had read myself silly and dreamed myself crazy I was also seeing with the eyes of the mind the Oxford of the Middle Ages, the Civil War, the eighteenth century. One hot, bright morning I had gone into Episcopus to walk for a while in the garden, and on coming out I went across St Giles and entered Alfred Street. This is the street that is now called Pusey Street, and the narrow lane going off to its left, now called Pusey Lane, was Alfred Lane. This lane was bordered by what used to be coach-houses and, since the coming of the motor-car, had been turned into garages. It must once have been heavy with the scent of leather, and oats, and the urine of horses, and from the cool shadowy interiors there would have come the sound of jingling and champing and the occasional stamp of an iron-shod hoof. Now, cars lived there, and the alley was silent because the cars were either out serving their owners or resting motionless on their concrete floors.

Only from one of these coach-houses-turned-garage was any sound issuing. As I drew near I saw it was not one garage but two, side by side. The intervening wall had not been demolished, so that anyone working there had to keep coming out into the lane and back into the building through the other door. I was still ten yards away when Brian, head down, hurrying, concentrating hard, came out of one door and went in at the other. He was carrying a metal tray on which lay a mass of what looked like cog-wheels of various sizes: the inside of a gear-box, perhaps. He did not see me. I halted for a moment, from sheer surprise. He had never told me where he worked and I had always taken for granted that it was Cowley. But now, as I stood in the cobbled lane, I saw that the octagonal M.G. sign was displayed over both doors.

M.G.? What was that? I thought Brian worked for Morris Motors. Well, he did, so this must be a branch or subdivision of them. Should I ask him? Reveal myself? I shuddered at the thought. He would think I was spying, poking my nose into his life. I walked past at a normal pace, throwing no more than a casual-seeming glance into the shadowy interiors of the two workshops. In one, I saw a stubby little car with the engine exposed. In the other, what looked like a heap of sheer junk. I had to assume that they knew what they were doing, whoever 'they' were, and that Brian had thrown in his lot with them. And now they, and he, were off to Abingdon.

At about half-past ten the family assembled again at the table, for our customary bedtime snack. (It was a folk-belief in those days that you didn't sleep well if you went to bed with an empty stomach.) It was clear that Dad had been thinking, and perhaps worrying, about Brian's crusading devotion to M.G. and what M.G. stood for, because we had hardly all settled into our chairs when he moved into the attack. Brian had in fact begun the conversation by praising the racing version of the Austin Seven.

'Herbert Austin's our best friend,' he was saying. 'If he didn't have those racing seven-fifties, M.G.'d never have got a factory out of the Old Man. In fact I'd take a bet M.G.'d have been scrapped by now.'

'You're sure anybody'd miss them?' Dad said, deliberately provocative and dead-pan.

'They might not know they were missing them, but they would be. No racing – no progress. That's where the development is.'

'Come off it,' Dad said roughly. He seemed to have decided that it was time to challenge Brian's assumptions. 'Racing can only develop other racing cars.'

'Why does Herbert Austin race his Sevens, then?' Brian demanded. 'Because he knows that's how to breed 'em tough. If a seven-fifty like that can finish in the T.T., and win its class, it's got to be good. That's why the Austin Seven's a success.'

''Course it isn't. The typical bloke who goes to a showroom and buys an Austin Seven, he's never heard of the T.T. and he wouldn't know what it means for a car to win its class. He just wants a cheap car to –'

'Do you think,' Brian exploded, 'that any firm can put a cheap car on the road and have it reliable and good, with every component tested, without a racing department?'

'Yes, I do. And I'll tell you somebody else as thinks so too. Billy Morris.'

'That's true, but if you think I'm going to –'

'Billy Morris has made a lot of money selling ordinary motor-cars to the ordinary bloke. He don't want your Cecil Kimber throwing his money down the drain, making a lot of freak racers.'

'Freak? *Freak*? You don't know the first thing about –'

'It's like horses,' Dad said. I can see him now, putting down his empty cup with a rattle into its saucer, and lighting a cigarette. 'These millionaires that run racing stables, trying to breed a horse that'll win the Grand National. All right, if they win they get the purse, but all the rest of them in the field have spent their money for nothing. And the horses are freaks. They're no good for anything else. You can't open a riding school with a racehorse, or pull a milk-cart with him.'

'Ask anybody who runs a stud farm,' Brian countered, 'where the best blood comes from. Your riding stables'd soon close down if they didn't have some good blood in the horses.'

It was unwise of Brian to let himself be drawn off his own ground and on to Dad's, because Dad knew something about horses and Brian didn't – made, indeed, a point of not knowing anything about any form of transport that rivalled his beloved internal combustion engine. He was scathing about railways, for instance, consigning them with one wave of the hand to the scrap-heap of history. A locomotive to him was 'a steam-kettle'.

There was now an excursion from the main argument while our father flattened Brian by factual references to such matters as the breeds of horses favoured by the Metropolitan Police. Brian waited for him to get finished and then said, 'Yes, there's all these different breeds, but one thing's true of all of 'em. They've got to be kept up, improved, else they'll go down. Cars the same.'

'Testing, yes,' said the old man. 'Development, yes, I can see that. But not freaks.'

'How many times do I have to tell you that –'

'You put one of your fancy racers,' said Dad, speaking slowly and loudly, 'side by side with an ordinary family man's car. You're looking at two completely different things. The ordinary bloke thinks the way Billy Morris thinks. He just wants a comfortable –'

'Different? Is the transmission different? Is the carburettor different? Are the tyres different?'

'Yes, the tyres are different, for a start. These racers you build, the tyres look like the kind you get on an aeroplane. Nothing like the ordinary –'

'They've got air in 'em, haven't they?' Brian demanded. 'And the steering and the brakes and the plugs are all the same as you got in your own car out there, only they're tested, tested!' He was almost shouting now. These matters were his life, and he could not see them undermined and take it calmly. It was obvious that the placid approval with which his father brought out the name 'Billy Morris', as if Billy Morris were some reasonable, level-headed geezer you might meet at the local bowls club, got to him most of all. To Brian, after only two years in the rapidly growing organization, the 'Old Man' was the enemy, whose short-sighted, play-it-safe attitudes were threatening to take all the poetry and adventure out of life.

He now dived his hand into his inside jacket pocket and brought out an envelope. This he carefully opened and took out a photograph, which he held out to our father.

'Is that a freak?' he demanded. 'D'you call that a freak? Isn't it a better design than Morris Motors ever turned out?'

Dad studied the photograph without putting out his hand to take it. 'I can see it's all right,' he conceded, 'if you like that sort of thing.'

'That sort of thing!' Brian spat out the words. 'It's got class, it's got style, it's a real car!'

'What is it, anyway?'

'It's the first M.G.,' Brian said lovingly. He took the photograph back and gazed at it. 'Built in nineteen twenty-three. A one-off. Hotchkiss o.h.v. engine on a Morris Oxford chassis. Cecil Kimber used to drive it himself. Got more than eighty miles an hour out of it. In 'twenty-three! I was thirteen!'

I stood up and moved round so that I could see over his shoulder. The photograph showed a very stark single-seater racing car with tiny cycle-type mudguards and a general air of being stripped down for business. One detail has stuck in my mind: the fuselage was so narrow that the hand-brake was mounted outside in the open air.

Our father now seemed to think that this infatuation had gone far enough. He spoke seriously, holding Brian's eyes with his own.

'If you want to know what I think,' he said, 'I think you made a mistake getting so deep in with Kimber and that wildcat outfit up there.'

'A mistake? A *mistake*? A man like that, who's respected by the whole –'

'Morris Motors has a future. The motor car's here to stay, more and more ordinary blokes are going to want one, they'll be busy at Cowley no matter whether trade's good or bad. There's hard times coming. You hear some funny things, all these stocks and shares and that. I don't pretend to understand it, but the chap from the brewery was in here, talking figures. A lot of men as are in work now won't be in work in a few years' time. And you' – he jabbed his forefinger towards Brian – 'you choose this time to get out of the safe part of Morris, the part that'll go on through thick and thin, and join Kimber's gang.'

'Kimber's gang. That's a nice way to put it. Go anywhere in the world and you'll find –'

'I don't know about anywhere in the world,' Dad said, 'because I'm a stay-at-home sort of chap. The bit of France I saw in nineteen-seventeen was enough of foreign parts for me, enough and plenty to spare.' (A little older than most of the conscripts, he had arrived in France rather late, servicing field telephones or something of the sort, but still managed to be hit by a sniper's bullet which almost severed his arm.) 'I'm an Oxford man born and bred and I know another when I see one, and I know how Billy Morris thinks. I know how his mind works.

Billy Morris is the man you're working for. He runs that factory, and he'll be running it till the day he dies, and that'll be long after your Cecil Kimber has come and gone.'

As he said the last three words he spaced them out and brought the flat of his hand down on the table three times; not violently, but with emphasis. It stuck in my mind, that *come – and – gone*; it came back to me years later; it comes back to me now.

'Come and gone?' Brian was fighting back. 'Cecil Kimber's there as long as he wants to be. M.G. couldn't exist without him.'

'That's just it,' the old man said. He picked up his cup again. 'The way I see it, that's just it. Billy Morris doesn't like Cecil Kimber and he doesn't like M.G. And that means, when you come right down to it, that he doesn't like Brian Leonard, or wouldn't if he knew who Brian Leonard was, which he don't.'

Brian may have been going to reply, but at this point Mother made one of her shows of firmness that always brought the family to heel. She pointed out that our bedtime snack was intended to be soothing and help us to sleep. She asked what was the point of her going to the trouble of putting it on if while we were consuming it we were going to argue and get ourselves into a state?

We had no answer to this, so we finished our biscuits and cocoa; rather an unhealthy bedtime snack, I should have thought, but very usual in our social class at that time; and went to bed with no further discussion.

I don't remember much else about that first vacation at home. I did an occasional spell of duty behind the bar, which was a new experience for me; until I was eighteen the law would not have permitted it. But now, able to rest on my oars to some extent, and of age to make myself useful, I was installed behind the bar during slack times of the day. It is, I suppose, another pointer to the great difference between Oxford then and Oxford now that I would have been distinctly uneasy if any of my acquaintances from Episcopus had happened into the pub and seen me serving pints of beer to the populace. It was the kind of thing that was, decidedly, 'not done'. But I neither worried nor needed to worry. The chances of my being discovered by any of my University acquaintances in the public bar of the Bargeman's Arms in the middle of the Christmas vacation were just about nil. Virtually the whole University, certainly at undergraduate level, had gone away, and the occasional one who might find himself in Oxford for the odd day or half-day would not have penetrated down here.

So I served beer, at first under my father's watchful eye till I got to know the craft and could pull a pint with just the right amount of head on it, and got used to rapid addition and subtraction of change, and knew what the various drinks were called, the difference between a Light Special and a Light and Bitter and Mixed and this and that, and not to be thrown by the traditional jokey names such as an Old and Bitter being called a Mother-in-law; and my father showed me the art of pouring out bottled beer in such a way that it never foams over the top of the glass. (The trick is to 'pour it over your finger', i.e. the hand that holds the glass should have a forefinger curved round the glass just below the top. That creates a band of slight warmth, which – for some scientific reason I don't know – inhibits the foam from piling up into a tall head and overflowing.) And I think I acquitted myself reasonably well and was a help to my hard-working parents at a busy time.

One evening, I took over the six to six-thirty spot because my father was out somewhere. He wouldn't normally have ceded it to me because it was the bit of the working day he enjoyed most, with old Trundle, Peake and the rest of them; not much to do and his daily dose of gossip. I could see the *cénacle* regarded me as a poor substitute for him, so I just drew the beer and kept my mouth shut. They were talking about a man called Bert Nutt. At least, they were not so much talking about him as going off into fits of laughter every time his name was uttered. The laughter was of that sidelong, rib-digging nature which, in those days, always accompanied any mention of sexual intercourse between human beings, or any topic cognate to, conditional upon, or ancillary to such intercourse.

Peake, with his long, thin, brown face, had managed to wrench his mind off the subject of Bert Nutt for long enough to remark that he had seen a couple of gallon drums of paint going cheap at So-and-So's warehouse that morning and had bought them. He intended to spring-clean and redecorate his house; not until Easter, but there was no harm in laying in the materials now, especially if he could get a bargain.

'If you 'as any left when you done the 'ouse,' said Trundle, beginning to puff with mirth, 'you better let old Bert Nutt have it.'

After the obligatory snigger, someone asked why.

'Well, stands to reason,' said Trundle triumphantly, pleased to find that his thinking was one jump ahead of theirs. 'He'll be on paintin' work every summer of his life from now on. He'll need a few good – ' The end of the sentence was drowned in gales of laughter.

To me, keeping quiet behind the bar, it had the interest of a puzzle. Why would Bert Nutt be on painting duty every summer? What had he done that was so funny?

'You could go round and do a deal with his missis, if you got all this paint,' said the younger man who was usually there. His name, I gathered, was Ted. 'Knock on the back door and say you got two gallons of paint to keep Bert out o' mischief.'

'It en't paint she'll be looking to buy,' said Peake. 'What she'll be in the market for'll be a nice big bucket of tar and a hundredweight o'feathers.'

Everybody laughed again. I sat down behind the bar – everybody had his pint and obviously nobody was going to want a refill – and began patiently to piece it out. This was no bad training for an historian, who so often has to reconstruct an episode, or an epoch, from a few fragments of authentic evidence in very much the same way that palaeontologists had to build the first dinosaur replicas from a claw, a tooth or two, and a fossil footprint.

In the end I got it pieced together. Bert Nutt was a college scout. One afternoon, during his spell of free time between two-thirty and seven, his house had been invaded by a red-haired young woman. Nutt had answered the door. When he saw who the caller was he did not invite her to come in, so she stood on the doorstep calling him a string of names in a shrill, powerful voice that soon had all the neighbouring housewives out on their doorsteps and all the neighbouring children three deep round the red-haired girl in a staring semi-circle. The names she called Nutt included 'Betrayer' and 'Seducer'. Fortunately Mrs Nutt happened to be out shopping, and Nutt bundled the visitor into the house and got the door safely closed behind her while he tried, unsuccessfully, to quieten her and, with even less hope of success, to get her to go away. It was not long before Mrs Nutt returned, accompanied on the last quarter-mile of her journey home by a succession of friends and acquaintances drawn from her own sex and generation, all offering her information and advice.

The scene when Mrs Nutt actually reached home and let herself in had been witnessed by no one but the three participants, but the Muse of fiction had willingly taken over from the Muse of history, and the conversation was described many times over in rich detail – the detail, of course, being replaceable as between one version and the next.

One solid fact emerged. The red-haired young woman was a chambermaid at an hotel on the South Coast somewhere. Bert Nutt, working at the hotel for thirteen weeks the previous summer, had been thrown into her company a good deal and, being a persuasive fellow, had trifled with her emotions. He was, according to Peake, 'known for it'. Old Trundle characterized Nutt as 'a feller that would pretty near walk round the streets with his whatsername hangin' out'. Ted corrected this to 'juttin' out, you means', and another loud laugh went round.

As for me, as I stood passively behind the bar, my thoughts on the matter were social in character; even what people would nowadays call 'sociological.' The reason why Bert Nutt was at an hotel on the South Coast for thirteen sultry weeks in the summer, rather than at home with Mrs Nutt, was that it was the custom of the Oxford colleges to lay off their scouts during the summer vacation. It was an accepted fact that the scout lost his job at the beginning of July and was given it back in October. During the vacation there was no work for him to do (this, of course, was before the colleges went into the Conference business) and so he was not employed and not paid. It was quite usual to fill the gap by working at a seaside hotel. The only exception to this was that there were a few jobs going, for scouts who volunteered, doing maintenance work on the staircases, which mostly meant painting the woodwork.

All this, as an Oxford lad whose uncle was a college scout, I knew already. The blanks I had to fill in (the identity of Nutt, the probable cause of the young woman's visit) were not beyond the powers of a nascent historian. Nor was it beyond my compassion to reflect that it was probably unfair to make a youngish man leave his wife for over three months, under the crudest kind of economic coercion, and expect him to behave himself; especially a man that would pretty near walk round the streets with his whatsername hanging out.

Trundle and his mates made a joke of Bert Nutt's misadventure because it was sexual in character, and sex was for making jokes about. But, at a deeper level which did not get into their talk, they knew that the situation of men like Nutt, and women like Mrs Nutt, was serious enough, because it was their own situation. They were working men and therefore subject to the harsh economic discipline of those times.

*

Christmas Day, in that year of 1930, fell some time in the middle of the week, and on the preceding Sunday morning my father received a message at the pub saying that Uncle Ernest would be glad to see him at Pembroke College. The message, which was delivered by a breathless small boy who then waited about for his penny and went off rejoicing when he got it, did not seem to surprise my father much, nor did he need telling that it would be necessary to take the car. Uncle Ernest, as a scout, had access to some good pickings in those days when the upper classes wasted food as naturally as they breathed air; and he usually found us something at Christmas time. So, at about eleven in the morning, an hour before he had to open the doors of the pub, my father trundled out the old bull-nose Morris and I went with him for the ride.

Dad parked the car in Littlegate Street and went into Pembroke by the service entrance, not the lodge-gate. He knew his way to the kitchens. Uncle Ernest was waiting for us. He was a spry little man with brisk movements and no spare flesh, even now when he was close to retiring age. He had little black button eyes and his hair, which lay in a neat half-circle round the base of his head with a shining bald isthmus in the middle, was the purest silver. As a child I used to feel an impulse to reach out and touch Uncle Ernest's hair, but of course I never did anything so familiar; I just listened while he told me over again about Betterton and Hotchiss, or explained some point of local topography, such as where the Castle mill Stream was, or the difference between King's Cut and Duke's Cut. He was kindly and often good to me, giving me a penny or a stick of toffee when he visited us, but his dignity was immense. I felt it again now. He had on a linen jacket, one of those unlined jackets too light to impede the movement of arm and shoulder but just enough to keep out the chill air. It was black, which suited his discreet, sober manner. He stood there now with the great kitchen forming a superb theatrical backdrop, twinkling at us with his bright little black eyes (Where did he get them? My father's eyes were brown), and looking the very image of the responsible, dignified, trusted college servant. Men like him, I reflected, had made possible the smooth running of these colleges for hundreds of years, as they had made possible the smooth running of the great country houses. It occurred to me to hope that they were appreciated at their true value. He came forward a few steps, welcoming.

'All ready for you, Jack,' he said; and to me, 'How are you, then, Peter?'

'Fine, Uncle Ernest,' I said.

'They looking after you all right at Episcopus?' he asked benignly, though his expression suggested that he was ready to disbelieve my answer, whatever it turned out to be.

I said 'Fine' again and faded into the background while my elders did business.

Uncle Ernest was my father's eldest brother, the oldest in fact of a large family. A college scout was very far from being well off, in money terms, but he was in a position to dispense certain kinds of largesse, and I think Ernest saw it as all part of looking after Jack and his child bride:

that was obviously how he thought of this hard-working, responsible couple. He treated my father as a promising young lad who might one day grow up and earn a decent income. You could see the satisfaction it gave him to weigh in with some of the goods of this world.

He led us now to a large oaken cupboard at the back of the kitchen. Colleges did not have refrigerators then, but the great stone walls made everything fairly cool as long as you kept it away from the ovens and stoves. He opened the cupboard with a flourish and stood back. Inside were three large carving-dishes with clean white cloths over whatever was on them. My father and I lifted them out on to a table and took the cloths off. One was a turkey, only about one-third eaten; the next a beautiful York ham, ditto; the third, about half of an outsize game pie. The cupboards also contained two bottles of hock which had been broached but not emptied. Uncle Ernest had re-corked them. One was nearly empty, but the other was nearly full.

'That'll keep us going for a bit,' my father said. 'Very good of you, Ernie.'

'That's not all,' the dignified old man replied. Moving majestically, almost sacerdotally, like some god-like personification of Liberality, he walked over to another cupboard and produced a huge slab of Cheshire cheese, three or four pounds of it, evidently cut from one of the authentic large round ones the farmers sold in the market.

'What about you and Bessie?' my father asked. 'You're not going short, are you?'

'Bessie and I are All Right,' Ernest replied. 'We don't need a lot to eat at our age, and we've got some very nice stuff in for Christmas. You knows me, Jack. I gets round everybody all fair and square. Everybody that has a claim on me gets their fair look-in, and this morning it's your turn, you and Kate and the lads. How's that other one, by the way?'

'All right,' my father said. 'Come and see for yourself one evening. Drop by the Bargeman's and it'll be my pleasure to draw you the best pint on the house.'

'All right, Jack, all right. I'll get down and see you one side of Christmas or the other. Now, I can find you a basket for all that stuff, as long as you brings it back.'

'Where did it all come from, Uncle Ernest?' I asked as my father loaded the basket.

He grinned. 'Some of 'em had a party last night, and this is the stuff that didn't get finished. Leastways, it's *some* of the stuff. There was two of us on and the other chap had his half.'

'They left all this?'

'They left more'n twice all this. Bless you, it's nothing to what I've seen.'

'The undergrads here must be rich,' I commented.

' 'Tworn't undergrads, 'twere dons.'

That explained it, I thought. Dons were well known to be gluttonous and to have eyes bigger than their bellies, so that they ordered enormous quantities of food and wasted half of it. Well known to whom? To folklore, of course.

*

Amid all this preoccupation with eating and drinking and fetching and carrying, the few vacation weeks passed smoothly enough. My fears of friction with Brian were not seriously confirmed. Life was regular, rather empty, and, in a mildly boring way, quite pleasant. Until one afternoon about a week after Christmas. Then the big jolt came.

I had some shopping to do and had gone to Cornmarket Street. It was already the end of the short winter afternoon light, and the shop windows were theatrically lit by contrast with the dusky pavement. My mind absorbed by the trivia of my arrangements for the new term, I was walking thoughtfully past a large shoe-shop whose display was divided into two windows, men's shoes on one side of the entrance, women's on the other. I wasn't thinking about shoes. My eyes merely happened to be drifting over one window-display after another, like a trawl net that picked up things automatically and unselectively. But in one half of the window, the feminine half, they suddenly registered a slender figure, also feminine. This figure, clad in a neat blue and white overall, was bending over a display stand of elegant evening shoes. The last time I had seen this figure, it had been clad in a dark red skirt and a green jersey, but the blue and white outfit, obviously some sort of staff uniform at the shop, didn't hold me up for an instant. Total recognition was immediate. It was the girl from Jericho, the girl with the fringe of dark brown hair, the girl with the narrow, sinuous body I had seen naked. The girl whose sounds of pleasure I had listened to as I lay rigidly awake in the next bed to Chucker's. The girl. The girl. It was *the girl*.

She was balancing those smart, flimsy, high-heeled shoes on little platforms on the stand, a fussy job. They were displayed in pairs; and there was evidently just room for a pair on each of the little platforms. She had to concentrate hard to get them balanced so that they wouldn't fall off, and also at an angle to one another that would be attractive to the onlooker from outside the window. She was standing sideways on to me, and at the moment when I first caught sight of her she was turning her head to talk, or listen, to someone in the interior of the shop. But just as I came level with her she turned towards her task again, and her face was exactly in profile and just about on a level with mine. Only the glass was between us, the glass and about eighteen inches of space.

For the next few minutes of my life it was my feet that seemed to have taken over the decision-making role. They walked straight on, without my consciously deciding to walk. Then, about ten yards past the shop, they halted, without my consciously deciding to halt. After a brief pause they turned me round and carried me back, again without volition on my part. And to my mounting panic, they carried me straight into the shop.

Now, I thought, I *have* done it. This is it, total chaos, the finish, the nose-dive.

For men's shoes you had to turn one way and for women's the other way. I could see assistants lurking about, the girls in blue and white overalls, the men in dark suits. I, or rather my feet on my behalf, got inside the door and then simply went and stood as close as possible to the window where the girl was. I was afraid to stand with my back to her looking into the shop in case an assistant came up to me. I was afraid to stand and gaze full at her. So I stood in profile, as if I were studying the wall at one side of the window, the one that was behind her as she worked.

Nobody took any notice of me for a moment or two, but I knew it couldn't last. Sooner or later someone was going to come and try to sell me some shoes. Or perhaps they would just call the police. As sometimes happens in an hallucinatory state, I was standing both inside and outside the situation, both enacting these absurdities and looking at myself enacting them. With one half of my mind, or one lobe of my brain or something, I knew clear-sightedly why I was there. It was not really my feet that had brought me into the shop, it was my prick. I wanted to do what Chucker had done, and to do it again and again and again. There was, my observing half noted dispassionately, nothing I would not do, no humiliation or disaster I would not lay myself open to, if it would give me even an outside chance of some day, somehow, getting to that objective. All other thoughts, motives, considerations, were simply blown away by the violence of that hot wind, a sirocco from the baking desert of sexual need I had been carrying around inside me.

I stood there, with this self-knowledge sand-blasting my mind, and as I did so the girl stepped out of the window and, finding herself face to face with me, said, 'The gents' department is down that side.'

That was how shop assistants talked in those days. 'The gents' department', things like that.

As she spoke to me her hazel eyes brushed over my face very much as they had done when I walked past her on that sweltering night in Jericho. But the expression was different. Then, standing on the pavement while a procession of male creatures went by, she had been like a wild vixen scenting the appropriate smell of musk or whatever it is that sets them off on the mating trail. She had had that challenging watchfulness in her eyes then, even for me, just because I was male and present. Now, in her shop uniform, bored and probably tired, she had no expression at all. I was just another faceless customer, one without even the sense to see where to go to buy himself some shoes.

I opened my mouth to speak, but before I could think of anything to say she had walked on into the sanctuary of the ladies' department. I had lost my chance. Chance to do what? I had no idea, except that I had this compulsion to reach out towards her, to make some sort of grab for her, any sort of grab.

I walked out of the shop and went straight home. I needed to think out a plan of campaign and I had to do it in solitude. I sat there most of the evening, once I could get free of the six o'clock meal, but at the end of it all I could think of was to go into the shop and buy a pair of shoes. I had no need of shoes; I had two pairs and both were in good repair; I should have to conceal them from my parents, who would naturally want to know why I had lashed out the money – money that I should in any case have to take out of my Post Office savings account, which was distinctly anaemic.

But of course I did it, I went back to the shop the next morning and bought that unnecessary pair of shoes, taking a long time over choosing, craning round all the time to see if I could get a glimpse of her. Several glimpses I did get, but she flitted about the shop without ever coming near enough for me to catch her eye or get any chance to speak to her, not that I would have known what to say. So that was Stage One: I was a pair of shoes to the good, which I didn't need, and everything else to the bad.

I went home and hid the shoes carefully, and that afternoon at the hour when the shops closed I was lurking on the other side of Cornmarket Street, determined to follow her and establish where she lived. She was so long in coming out that I began to feel she must have left by a back entrance or something, but finally she did come out, wearing a raincoat and with a yellow scarf tied round her head. She was with another girl. The two of them went up Cornmarket Street and along St Giles till they reached Little Clarendon Street, where the other girl went straight on but mine turned to the left and went down the street. I allowed myself to get close, about twenty yards behind, not because I had the nerve to accost her but because it was dark by now and I didn't dare lose sight of her. I followed her across Walton Street, down Walton Crescent and into that maze of little streets behind the University Press. Finally she went into a house in Canal Street. I took careful note of the number. It was just possible that she was paying a call on someone else, but the chances were very strongly that this was where she lived. I now had the two fixed points, her place of work and her home, and all I had to do was patrol the space in between until I ran into her, and then...

I still couldn't think what I was going to do 'then', but I had no choice but to hang about anyway. The craving in my blood was so strong that electric fences and guard dogs would not have kept me away. Which of the gods played this practical joke on us? Or is it, so far from being a joke, the only serious thing in the universe?

Two or three evenings of skulking about went by without incident. Just about the only thing I achieved was that I wore the new shoes all the time, conscientiously getting them wet and muddy so that when they were discovered at home, as inevitably they would be, they wouldn't stand out as new shoes and might pass unnoticed. To such picayune subterfuges was my strong young mind brought down, that mind which ought to have been soaring among the mountain peaks of historical knowledge. But so it was. All that counted was my biological craving for this slip of a girl. Once I saw her in the distance, briefly illuminated by a shop window she was passing, and a couple of times I failed to get a sighting at all. Then it came. I was loafing at a street corner, near one of those little pubs they have in that area, the Globe or the Bookbinder's Arms or something, when I saw her coming along. I felt sick with tension, but I knew it had to be now, so as she came level with me I lurched forward and almost bumped into her, so that she had to stop.

'Oh, sorry,' I said, as if I had done it just out of clumsiness. Then I looked straight into her face. That fringe of dark brown hair and that narrow, intent little countenance seemed to go right through me like a knife. 'Oh, hello,' I said, trying to put a bit of surprise into my voice. I expect the whole performance was abysmally awful.

'What d'you mean, hello?' she said. Her voice was high-pitched and yet soft, like a clarinet. I was scarcely sane; I hardly knew what I was doing.

'Why, we met last summer, don't you remember?' I mouthed.

'Last summer? No, we didn't.' She was moving sideways, trying to get past me on the pavement.

'Yes, we did,' I said. 'At the Gryphon School.' I could hardly go on and say, 'I was the one who was standing in the shower-room when you came in stark naked and I got a good look at your pubic hair. I could describe its formation to you in detail, standing right here on the pavement.' So I just said, 'I was with the lads. The London lads, at the Gryphon School.'

She had stopped moving sideways now, but she didn't seem to want to be bothered with me, for all that.

'You mean that place where they were all staying? Over by the Banbury Road somewhere?'

She spoke with the local accent, as I did. After all we were just two Oxford kids. I plucked up a bit more courage.

'You... paid a visit there,' I said. 'One evening.' I wasn't going to add 'with Chucker.' I didn't want to have his shadow coming between us.

She then looked at me levelly and said, 'You were in the next bed to that big chap.'

'So you have met me before,' I said. 'So you do remember.'

'I wouldn't exactly call it meeting,' she said. 'But in any case, what about it?'

'I want to buy you a drink,' I said.

'Buy me a drink? What d'you want to do that for?'

'Because I want to talk to you,' I said.

'Talk to me? What about?'

'Your pubic hair,' I nearly said. I was beginning to get the desperate feeling that it was all getting nowhere, when she suddenly said, 'Well, you might as well buy me a drink as just stand out here in the cold.'

Cold? My body was burning. But I knew, objectively, it *was* a cold evening.

We went into the pub, which had only been open a few minutes. They were different in those days, before they started to make the bars look like suburban living-rooms to attract the women in. That happened in the 1950s. In 1930 they were very simple and bare, with wooden tables and lino on the floor. And she couldn't order some kind of fancy drink, a Snowball or a Pina Colada, like a modern shopgirl. They were just beer-houses then. There was only one other customer in there, reading the newspaper by the fire. He took no notice of us.

She had a cider, a half-pint bottle of sweet cider. I had a pint of beer. It was unpleasant beer, rather flat and sticky, but I didn't mind. We sat at the bar on stools and she unbuttoned her raincoat and took off her head-scarf. Under the coat she was wearing the dark red skirt I had first seen her in, but with a heavier pullover because this was winter. She must have left her blue and white overalls back at the shop. She looked at me over the rim of her glass and said, 'What d'you want to talk about?'

'You asked me that outside,' I said.

'Well, it's natural, isn't it? You said you wanted to talk to me. What's so great about talking, anyway?'

Privately I agreed with her. Chucker certainly hadn't talked much. On the other hand I wasn't such a fool as to think I could simply walk up to her and take what I wanted, as he had done. I hadn't the obvious attractions.

'There's nothing great about talking, just in itself,' I said. 'It depends who you talk to. It depends if it's somebody you'd like to get to know.'

'What d'you want to get to know *me* for?' she returned indifferently. 'If that's what you mean. Why don't you talk straight out? Are you a college boy or something?'

'Yes and no,' I said. 'I am and I'm not.'

'Look,' she said, 'if you've got something to talk about, get on and talk about it. I've been working all day and I want to get home to my tea. I can't sit listening to a load of rubbish, you are a college boy and you're not, and blah blah blah, as if I cared what you are.'

'Don't take on,' I said, 'I'm not trying to be annoying. It's just that my father keeps a pub in Oseney and I grew up there, and now I go to Episcopus College.'

That 'go to' was a piece of subtlety on my part. Kids at school said 'I go to Such-and-such a school.' Nobody at the University would ever have said 'I go to Balliol' or 'I go to Magdalen'. By deliberately slipping back into school idiom, I was domesticating the issue for her, taking care to minimize any social gulf she might feel had to be bridged.

Like most subtleties, this was unnoticed, useless and a complete waste of time. She just put her glass down on the bar and said, 'Well, I shall have to be going.'

'Oh, don't go yet,' I said. 'Or at least not till you've told me when I can see you again.'

She got down from her stool. 'What d'you want to see me again for? You're just trying to get off with me, that's all.'

As she used that down-to-earth, commonplace expression I felt a surge of something like relief. It was like being back in the old simpler days, before I was at the University, when lads at school turned up on Monday morning with tales of having gone to dance-halls in the town on Saturday night and 'got off with' this or that girl, complete with lurid accounts of sequels which were doubtless almost entirely wishful thinking. That was her world, and I did not care if it were my world too. It was basic, and that was a good enough word for the way I felt about her.

'All right,' I said. I had about four inches of beer left in my pint glass, and I downed it in one big swallow and put the glass down. 'All right. I'm trying to get off with you. Is there something wrong with that? You're the kind of girl chaps do try to get off with, so you must be used to it.'

'Used to it, yes.' She gave me a cool, level look from under that brown fringe. 'But that's not to say I can't please myself what I do.'

'Who said it did?' I said. 'I mean, who said you can't?' I was beginning to get confused with these double negatives. Grammatically, I had forgotten where I was. 'Look, all I want to say is, do what you want to do. Only I want a turn if I can get one.'

'A turn?'

'A place in the queue,' I said. 'I can wait, but I want you to know I'm waiting.'

'Waiting?' she said. 'What for?'

'Anything I can get,' I said.

She stood stock-still for a moment and then said, 'Nerve. I call that nerve.'

'All right,' I said. 'It's nerve. But I've got nothing to lose. Where would we be without nerve?' I felt like a puppet, in the grip of some much stronger force. It hardly mattered what I said or did. I could not feel embarrassed or guilty: the responsibility so clearly belonged elsewhere. 'All I want,' I said, 'is to get to know you. In a way, you might say I know you already.' I was light-headed by this time. 'You might say we started at the deep end.'

'The deep end?' She came back to the bar and leaned her elbow on it, staring into my face. 'What d'you mean, the deep end? Are you some kind of loony or something?'

'Look,' I said. 'I saw you without a stitch of clothes on, before I knew your name. If it comes to that, I *still* don't know your name.'

'It's Vinnie,' she said.

This simple reaction threw me. Compared with what I had just reminded (or informed) her of, it seemed a trivial detail that I did, or didn't, know her name. And what kind of name was Vinnie, anyway? What was it short for? Virginia or something? She didn't *look* like the kind of girl whose parents would christen her Virginia. It wasn't a Canal Street name. But what the hell, if it was what she called herself?

A cold dementia had possessed me. I no longer cared what she, or any living creature, thought of me. I had shrunk to a dried-up skin and a chalky skeleton mustering between them enough strength to support a pair of ram's balls and an enormous distended phallus. Logic, memory, reason, conscience, were not even words, they were meaningless explosions of breath. I faced Vinnie and looked straight into her eyes. The customer by the fireside went on reading the *Oxford Mail.* The landlord was fiddling with something under the bar.

'You were in the shower-room at that school,' I said. 'At eight o'clock in the morning. You were with Chucker. When you came in I was standing there.'

'All right,' she said. 'You were standing there.'

'You had no clothes on,' I said.

'I hadn't taken them off for you.'

'I know that. You didn't have to remind me of it. I know it. I know other things too. But look – it means I do at least know something about you.'

'Yes,' she said. 'You know what I look like with no clothes on.'

The man reading the *Oxford Mail* turned his head and stared at her briefly.

'I know more than that,' I said. And we stood there, in that quiet, empty bar, staring at each other.

Finally she said, 'I'm going.'

'Pictures one night this week?' I said. 'There's some quite good things on.'

'The pictures' was what my generation of English kids called the cinema. It wasn't 'the movies', still less the cinema. It was the pictures. I suppose mentally we were still living in the old bioscope era. But it was a dark, anonymous private place where relationships of a furtive kind could grow – and in those days all sexual relationships were furtive.

Suddenly she said, 'I wouldn't mind the pictures one night. Meet me here on Thursday, six-thirty,' and with a quick, lithe movement she was through the door and gone, swallowed up in the dark street and then, doubtless, in her nearby home.

I stayed and had another pint of beer. It cleaned me out of spending money, but I needed it.

*

So there I was, lumbered with a pair of shoes I didn't want, with no money, and a date to take Vinnie to the pictures later that week. I spent the interval getting ready. I had my hair cut to give me a smart appearance, and the man took too much off and made my head look like a gooseberry. I borrowed some money from Brian to finance the evening out; he wasn't even interested enough to ask what I needed it for. When the day came, and the hour approached, I put on the shirt and jacket I had decided on, and at the last minute switched to another shirt and my other jacket, and nearly made myself late. But in the end there we were, at the pictures, with Vinnie sitting beside me as if she were my girl-friend or something.

I even remember what the film was: *Tugboat Annie*, with Marie Dressler and Wallace Beery. A tale of simple, rugged heroism in New York harbour. Then there was a Mickey Mouse, which amused Vinnie a lot. I felt the shaking of her silent laughter. The reason I could feel it was because I had my arm along the back of her seat, trying to pluck up the courage to put it round her shoulders. But I was too inhibited.

Afterwards I took her for some kind of snack somewhere and the next memory shows us sitting in a pub. Vinnie had some more of that sweet cider. At this point I began to think of the evening as definitely ruined, because two other girls, friends of hers, came over and talked to her. They were with two blokes who were playing darts at the other end of the bar. Vinnie rattled away to these girls and none of them bothered to bring me into the conversation. I expected that when the game of darts ended the two other chaps would join us and then I should be irretrievably the odd one out. Vinnie seemed entirely oblivious of my presence. My God, was it to be nothing but failure, failure, failure?

Then, with one of those sudden reversals of fortune that make life perpetually surprising, the two chaps suddenly came up and said they wanted to go to some other pub where the dart-board was better or something, and gathered the girls up and took them off. I was terrified for a moment that Vinnie would simply up and go with them, but she just smiled and let them go. The pub was getting more crowded now, towards closing-time, and to prevent anyone from pushing in between us I got down from my bar stool and stood beside her where she sat on hers. I filled her glass up again with that cider stuff. Suddenly I had her attention. A moment ago I would have said she didn't know I was on the earth, and now she was looking into my eyes, and as I stood there without speaking she shifted slightly so that one of her thighs was pressing lightly against me. In a most inconvenient place, I may say. As I stood there without speaking, gripped by her magnetism, she began moving the thigh up and down in a slow, deliberate rhythm.

'What's it like being at college?' she asked me. 'D'you have wards, no, that's not the word...' She wrinkled her brow under the dark fringe, searching for the unfamiliar word, 'dormitories, that's it – d'you have dormitories?'

'No,' I said. 'Everybody has his own bedroom. Two rooms, one to sit about in, make a fire, have toast and stuff and drinks and stuff. And a bedroom.'

'You have all that to yourself?'

'Yes.'

'Coo,' she said reflectively. 'I'm trying to picture it. There's five of us at our house. Never get a bit of space to yourself. Can't live your own life.'

'It's the same for me, too,' I said, 'in the holidays.' I said 'holidays' rather than 'vacation' for the same reason that I had said 'I go to Episcopus'. 'But when term starts and I move back into College, there's nobody to bother me.'

'No interruptions, eh?' she murmured. She was still keeping up the thigh-brushing movement.

'None at all. None of any kind.'

'I can't picture it,' she said. 'I think if I had a place where I could invite people and live my own life, I'd never do any studying.'

'I do a bit of studying,' I said, 'but I'm always ready to lay it aside if... something better crops up.'

She slid down from her stool and said, 'Let's walk.'

Outside, it was cold. The moon was shining on a hard frost that would be lying thickly by morning. Already the roofs were beginning to sparkle. We moved into a shop doorway and I began to kiss her. She went along with it all right, but after a few minutes the cold must have begun to get through to her, because she drew her overcoat round her more tightly and shivered.

'It's cold,' she said. 'Too cold for this kind of thing out of doors. And we've got nowhere to go indoors.'

'We shall have soon,' I said. 'Term starts in,' I calculated rapidly, 'eight days.'

'Can you wait eight days?'

I felt I would go crazy if I waited eight *seconds*, but there seemed nothing for it, and I said, 'I suppose I can wait that long if I have to.'

She opened my overcoat and put her hand where I had seen her put it with Chucker. 'I'm glad you're impatient,' she said.

*

Oxford terms, then as now, began and ended on a Sunday. You were expected to get back to College by Thursday night so that on Friday you could see your tutor, get books from the library, settle in and make arrangements generally. Saturday was for socializing and generally fooling about. On the Sunday itself there was nothing much doing; no lectures or tutorials, obviously, just a quiet day for digging in before the work routines began. So the obvious day to show Vinnie my College rooms and initiate her into their delightful possibilities was the Sunday. I issued the invitation as I walked her home, slowly and lingeringly, from that Jericho shop-doorway.

'Sunday afternoon,' I said. 'As early as you like. Straight after lunch. I could come and pick you up.'

'Don't you dare,' she said. 'I have to be at home for Sunday dinner else my parents never stop going on at me. We don't have it till two, it isn't cleared away till three and then I have to stay and help with the washing up. And I don't want my mother looking out of the window and seeing you hanging about.'

'Why not?' I said. 'She must know you have boy-friends.'

'She does *not*. She'd have *fits*. She'd have two fits and die in the first.'

'Come on, Vinnie. You mean your mother really doesn't know that you're not exactly a stranger to boys?'

'My mother thinks,' Vinnie said, 'that I think the stork brings babies. She wants me to be clean in thought, word and deed. She wants me to see a prick for the first time in my life on the night I get married, and then only out of the corner of my eye when my husband gets into bed.'

'But why is she like that?'

'They're all the same,' Vinnie said. I knew she meant grown-ups, people who had been through that mysterious change that would for ever afterwards prevent them from taking any pleasure in anything. 'When I was little, about five, she was taking me along the street and we saw two dogs having their fun on the pavement. A dog and a bitch, I mean. She got hold of my hand and dragged me across the street to the other side. And I looked back over my shoulder to see what they were doing and she walloped me for it. I didn't know what it was all about and I asked her why it was wrong to look at them and she walloped me again.'

'Look, what about Sunday?' I said. We were getting near her house.

'Well, I don't know,' she said. 'I was going out with Doreen.'

'Yes, but surely...' I was at a loss for words. 'I mean, that can't be half as much fun as –'

'Course it's fun. I like Doreen. We have a good time. We go to her house and try clothes on and play records.'

'No matter how much fun you have with another *girl*,' I said, determined to spell it out, 'it can't possibly be the same *kind* of fun you can have with a chap.'

'Yes it can, it's called being a Lezz.'

I was taken aback. What had we got into now? Was she up to something with this Doreen?

'I didn't... know you were that kind,' I said.

'I'm not that kind. I'm just saying. It is possible to have that kind of fun, as you call it, with anyone.'

'Well,' I said desperately, 'if it's possible with anyone, why not with me?'

She laughed softly and said, 'All right. I'll go out with Doreen tomorrow night.'

'So what time Sunday afternoon?'

'Oh, when I'm ready.'

'You'll have to be out by seven,' I warned.

'Oh, I'll come before then. Just stay in and wait for me.'

'You won't know where to find my rooms,' I said.

'You can draw me a map. See you,' and she was gone.

*

So I drew a careful map and took it round and handed it to her, quickly and stealthily, at the shoe-shop the next morning. We managed it so that no one saw us. She put it in the pocket of her overall without appearing to see me. I came out of the shop with my *membrum virile* struggling for freedom like a full-grown ferret. Trousers didn't have metal zips in those days, they had buttons, and there was a nasty moment when I thought it was going to fire them off like bullets in the middle of Cornmarket Street, breaking windows and causing injury to passers-by.

Thursday came, Dad drove me along to College in the Morris – it was getting to be a ritual – and there I was, installed in the now familiar surroundings, able to put a name to just about every face I saw. The euphoria I had felt after that 'Everybody upstairs!' pub-crawl was still, of course, tarnished by my memory of the horrible scenes on that last night of term, but even they had not actually altered the nature of the universe; Walters or Waters was still there, his rooms doubtless fitted up with new furniture over the vacation, and he seemed to be his previous self, badger-like and solitary, neither more nor less so than before that barbaric mob assault.

But of course one sees these things through subjective eyes, and I was feeling happy and confident because I was on a crest. Vinnie had come into my life, and my lonely, cold, monastic, womanless existence was done with. From now on there was some point in having a nice cosy little sitting-room and bedroom, with an oak, and a bright fire in the grate, and all the requirements for the odd snack carefully assembled in the cupboard. Thursday night seemed very long, and as for Friday, it almost convinced me that some sort of disaster had befallen the planetary system and that time was actually standing still.

When Saturday dawned I was already regretting that I had not nailed Vinnie down for this afternoon rather than the next one. It seemed that the enormous empty time would never go by. But then something did happen. I was pottering about in my study just after lunch when there was a loud, peremptory double knock on the door. I called to whoever it was to come in, and it turned out to be Kent. He was carrying a clip-board with a list of names on it, and behind him, less assertively, hovered another man of the same type, minus the arrogance.

'Good, you're in,' said Kent, advancing to the centre of the room and dividing his attention between me and the clip-board. 'I'm arranging the rota for tubbing.We ought to have done it at the end of last term but the equipment wasn't ready.'

'Most colleges don't start tubbing till after the Christmas vac,' the other man said over Kent's shoulder. 'It's quite easy to fit it in.'

'Ideally,' said Kent coldly, putting him down, 'tubbing ought to be over by the time people go down at Christmas, so that the ones who are picked can start training.' He turned back to me. 'Tomorrow morning at nine-thirty. Or you could have this afternoon at three. That's not quite so good. I can't be there myself.'

'I shan't be needing either, thanks,' I said.

'I didn't ask you what you needed,' Kent said. His eyes behind his glasses were cold with an impersonal authority. 'Those are the times available for you to be tubbed. Choose one and let me get on, I've got a lot of people to see.'

'Look, Kent,' I said, 'if you've got a lot of people to see you'd better go and see them. I don't intend to take up rowing and so there's no point in my turning up to be tubbed.'

'Tubbing', by the way, was the first stage in an oarsman's career. You sat in a punt-like structure that was firmly moored to the bank, and handled an oar that had no blade, only the outline of a blade in metal. It taught you the weight and feel of an oar and then you were ready to get into a boat and handle the real thing. It was the custom then, and persisted right into the nineteen-forties, for all freshmen to be tubbed as a matter of course. The ones who showed no idea of how to handle an oar never got any further.

A few weeks earlier I would have consented meekly to be tubbed, taken my place with the other sheep and gone through the business. It would have cost me nothing but a slice out of an afternoon and I would have done it for the sake of peace, taking care not to make a good showing that would have involved me in a boat trial. But now, I was a changed man. The prospect of sexual initiation with Vinnie had given me confidence and pride; so important are these things in our growing-up years. I had also come to dislike Kent so much that it would have pained me to fall in with any wish of his, even on such a neutral matter as this. Being a peaceable, slightly cowardly creature and wanting a quiet life, I knew I ought to go along with convention and not draw attention to myself. Even as I talked back to Kent I knew it was a mistake. But I couldn't force myself to kow-tow to him, in just the same way that some people couldn't force themselves to pick up a centipede.

'Now look here, Leonard,' said Kent. As he uttered my name he took a swift look at the list on his clip-board, conveying the impression that under normal circumstances I was a being so far beneath his notice that he wouldn't have known my name. He knew it perfectly well, having, among other things, just read it on the door lintel, but that glance at his list said, 'Now look here, Whatever-your-name-is.' That little jab inserted, he went on, 'You're being obstructive and you're wasting my time.'

'No, I'm not. You're perfectly free to go on to the next name on your list, which is probably that of someone who's burning to be tubbed and then given a trial and finally to get to row in the College Eight. I just don't happen to want any of those things. If I did turn up I'd be wasting your time. As well as my own,' I added for good measure.

Kent shot me a look of outrage. From his point of view, freshmen weren't supposed to have a commodity called 'time' that they wished to avoid wasting. He wanted to be back at school, with a crowd of fags who likewise didn't have any such thing as their own time, who could be beaten for 'side' if they showed the slightest reluctance to drop what they were doing and rush to carry out his bidding. I had done what was, for him, the worst thing in the book. I had reminded him that an Oxford college was not the same as a boarding-school.

'Come on, Dick,' the other man now said, peaceably enough. 'The man isn't interested in rowing.'

'I don't give a damn what he's interested in,' Kent said slowly and very distinctly. 'This College tubs freshmen. All freshmen without exception. It always has and it always will.'

'Not me,' I said. 'And now, if you'll excuse me,' and I turned my back on him and went over to my bookshelf as if to take down a volume.

For a moment I wondered whether I had gone too far. In the tense silence I was ready for the sound of Kent's footstep coming after me to give me a good hiding there and then. Perhaps if the other man, the secretary of the Boat Club or whatever he was, had not been there, that might have happened. But it didn't and they left. I stood there, in the suddenly empty and peaceful room, listening to the hammering of my pulse.

As I heard their footsteps clattering down the stairs, my spirits plummeted and for about five minutes I tasted the stale, bitter flavour of insecurity, self-doubt and, yes, I admit it, fear. Kent was a brainless oaf, but on the other hand he was a power in my immediate environment: he was a storm-trooper with the bully-boys at his heels. He must have enjoyed this status ever since he was about fifteen, and pretty soon he would have to give it up and settle down to grown-up life. I could tell he wasn't relishing the prospect, and that during his remaining time in College he would put himself at the head of any hooliganism that was going forward.

I knew my cover was blown, as people say today. By temperament I was an opponent of Kent and his ilk, an outsider, an enemy. Up to now I had kept out of trouble simply by not being visible; but now, at the beginning of only my second term, I had emerged as exactly the type Kent was out looking for. And all in a burst of impatient defiance lasting about two minutes.

I knew I had laid up trouble for myself. But I didn't, in the next twenty-four hours, think about it much. The simple reason was that I couldn't. My mind, both in its foreground and its background, was occupied by only one thought: Vinnie was coming to see me, Vinnie was coming, Vinnie was coming, Vinnie.

Chapter 8

When Sunday lunch-time came I could hardly eat anything, but I made myself swallow down some of the cold meat and salad because I thought I was going to need fuel. Armitage, who sat opposite me, made a few efforts to engage me in conversation, but it was hopeless. Finally, as we were getting up to leave, he asked if I would like to go and have tea with him about four o'clock. I thanked him but said I expected to be very busy that afternoon.

'I've got a big essay I'm half-way through,' I lied, in order to keep my tracks well covered. Not even people sympathetic to me were going to know what I was up to. You never knew who might talk.

'It must be a gradely big one,' he smiled. 'You've been deep in your thoughts all through lunch. Made a New Year resolution to work hard, I'll be bound.'

'Not that exactly,' I said. 'It's just something I'm very interested in.'

'Wouldn't mean anything to me, I don't suppose,' he said, 'even if you told me about it.' He was reading Chemistry.

'I'll talk about it when it's finished,' I said and hurried away to my rooms.

That was a mistake. Vinnie might well not turn up for at least a couple of hours. On the other hand I didn't dare go out in case she happened to arrive earlier, and, finding me not there, took herself off. The thought of that brought me out in a cold sweat.

So I made up the fire and sat by it. The weather was quite warm, in fact it was one of those muggy days you sometimes get in an English midwinter. Just to have something to do, I made an enormous fire, with the only result that the room became too hot to sit in, so I opened the windows. Then the horrible idea struck me that someone might drop in and be difficult to get rid of. I didn't want to sport the oak till Vinnie was safely inside – the sight of that blank, handle-less wall of hard wood might have sent her away – so I arranged some books and papers on the desk to look as if I were working. That would give me an excuse for cutting short the visit of anyone else who turned up.

I think after that I must have gone into an actual trance of nervous tension, a kind of catalepsy, because I actually don't remember anything from that moment of stage-managing my desk until, possibly an hour and a half later, I heard light, rapid footsteps on the stairs and a knock on the door.

I suppose I was in a state of hyper-excitement that made me ready for any kind of sudden, hallucinatory mental impression. Whatever the reason, when I first whipped the door open I was, for a few seconds, back in that sultry August evening at the corner of Hart and Jericho Streets, with Vinnie standing in the ring of light on the pavement, looking with such cool sexual effrontery into the faces of the boys going by. As she came forward into the room, with a brief 'hello', and took off her overcoat, I saw that underneath it she had on exactly the same clothes as on the night when she had it with Chucker, the green jersey and dark red skirt. Perhaps that was the outfit she always wore for sexual adventures, or perhaps it was just coincidence. The green of the jersey went with her hazel eyes, and the red of the skirt set off her dark brown hair.

I had the oak sported and the inner door closed in a twinkling. When I turned and came back into the room, Vinnie had thrown her overcoat on to the armchair and was kneeling by the fire, warming her hands, while she swivelled her head to take in the details of my room.

'Funny old place,' she said. 'They don't give you a sofa, it's more like an overgrown armchair.'

My room contained the usual outfit of two lumpy armchairs and, instead of a sofa, a *chaise longue*. Evidently she had never seen a *chaise longue* before, but then neither had I before I came to College. It occurred to me, in that moment, to wonder whether this was not a deliberate policy, a *chaise longue* being slightly more difficult to misbehave on than a sofa; but then, I reflected immmediately, any couple who had got to that stage were less likely to be put off than to regard it as an interesting challenge.

'It's warm, at any rate,' Vinnie said, in the tone of one making the best of a bad job. She spread her fingers before the blaze of the fire.

I stood there gripped with a sudden paralyzing shyness. If she had risen and come towards me, offering herself to be embraced and kissed, I could have moved. But she just knelt in front of the fire, appraising my living-space, as if she were my sister. I was immobile, my feet frozen to the carpet, the great boiling mass of sexual longing inside me congealed to a menhir of cold stone.

Then, as abruptly and decisively as she always moved, Vinnie got up, turned, and moved across to the bedroom. She disappeared inside it and I heard the springs creak as she sat down on the bed. Should I follow? Immediately, before the question had fully formed itself, she reappeared with a discontented expression.

'No good in there,' she said. 'It's too bloody cold. The heat from the fire just doesn't reach beyond this room.'

'Well, no, it doesn't,' I had to admit. They were the first words I had spoken, and they came out with a damp, dispirited sound.

'It's too cold in there,' she said as if thinking aloud, 'and too uncomfortable in here with no sofa. If there were just some cushions we could put on the floor.'

Bemused as I was, I realized at that moment what she was doing: planning the action, taking over the whole strategic field like a general.

'There's only one thing to do,' she said. 'Come and help me,' and with this terse command she disappeared into the bedroom again.

I followed. She had moved the bed out and edged into the narrow space between it and the wall. 'Get hold of the mattress,' she said. 'Come on, lift.' As I lifted it she stripped off the two blankets and let them slide to the floor. We moved the mattress into the sitting-room and laid it down in front of the fire. Vinnie went back and fetched the eiderdown. 'We may not need this,' she said, putting it down beside the mattress, 'but just in case it's draughty.'

I was in a daze. Her matter-of-factness, completely unmixed with any show of passion, reduced my blood to chilled yoghurt. The coolness, the off-handedness, of her manner seemed so completely at variance with any kind of physical desire. She looked, moved and spoke as if she were setting up a loom to give me a lesson in hand-weaving or something. This threw me, and it combined with my natural sexual shyness, the shyness that goes along with the last few minutes of one's virginity, to make me stand there looking fixedly ahead of me like a wax dummy in a shop window. But of course she was used to shop windows.

And still she took no notice of me. Exactly as if she were alone, she lay down on the mattress and shifted around on it as if to test its springiness. Apparently satisfied, she got up and walked over to me. I was like a rabbit in front of a snake. If she had stuck a knife into me I wouldn't have had the nerve to back away. Or to move forward, for that matter. Still working coolly and impersonally, she unbuttoned my fly.

'Come on,' she said in her hand-weaving teacher's voice, 'Let's see what you've got for me.'

She took it out, but even that didn't work, I was so nonplussed. My prick simply lay in her hand, as heavy and unresponsive as a black pudding. Not at all disconcerted by this, she simply let go of it and used both hands to unhook her skirt, slid it off and threw it to the chair on top of her overcoat. In another moment she had stepped out of her knickers and was back on the mattress, stretching out luxuriously as the warmth of the fire played on her thighs. As she did so I saw again the fan-tracery of pubic hair that had so unsettled me, unsettled me to the core and for ever, that morning in the shower-room of the Gryphon School. That did it. In a trice my garments had followed hers on to the chair and I was beside her on the mattress.

No need to go into any more details. Let it be enough to say that once we got going, we kept going. God, the potency one has at that time of life! And the cruelty of a system that forces, or at any rate in those days forced, freshly-grown youths to dam that potency up, to batten it down, deny it any outlet till it festered and came out at last as a leprous rash that covered the soul rather than the body! Well, I, Peter Leonard, had beaten that system, if only for this one afternoon. The oak was firmly shut, the fire was burning well, and Vinnie was here, enjoying it all in her coolly inventive way.

I was just coming for the fourth time (in three hours!) when an alien sound penetrated my consciousness, a sound that seemed to come from some far-off planet. It was the tolling of the bell that announced dinner in Hall; it started at five past seven and went on for five minutes, which meant, among other things, that Vinnie ought to have been out five minutes ago. I say it penetrated my consciousness, but it would be more accurate to say that it lay on top of my consciousness, which was busy elsewhere, rather as a dead fish might lie across a clump of reeds.

When the spasm ended and we fell back into our separate existences, the bell had stopped. But I knew I had heard it. The fire was sinking and there was no coal; Vinnie had to be out and the quad would be full of people going across to Hall. The party was over.

'I have to get you out, I'm afraid,' I said to Vinnie. I felt undignified and juvenile; after all the big show of independence, having my own place where we could be together, my own fortified private space, to have to bring up the petty realities of College discipline. 'You see, they have this rule –'

'Oh, don't worry,' she said, off-hand as ever. 'I don't mind going.' She seemed almost to be conveying that there was nothing much to hang around here for anyway.

We got dressed quickly, like two strangers side by side on a crowded beach. Vinnie put on her overcoat. I opened the inner door, then the oak, and stood there irresolute.

'Perhaps we ought to wait a few minutes,' I said. 'Let them all get into Hall.'

'Ashamed to be seen with me, are you?' she said levelly.

'It's not a matter of being ashamed – it's just that they're so sticky about...'

Vinnie brushed past me and started down the stairs. I knew I had to go with her. I had just enough presence of mind to dive back into my room and grab an outdoor coat. I wasn't going into Hall and I wasn't coming back here. That meant I was going out, into the town. A cold rain was falling.

Vinnie walked straight down the two flights of stairs, holding her back very straight as she always did, and with her overcoat loosely round her shoulders so that it swung as she walked, like a cloak. That was how she had worn her light mackintosh on that hot summer evening. She was a natural cloak-wearer.

She had picked the exact time to give us maximum exposure. There was a steady stream of figures, among whom I recognized both undergraduates and dons, moving towards the lighted archway that led to the Hall. For an instant I toyed with the utterly unworthy thought of hanging back and letting Vinnie walk across to the lodge by herself. But with all my cowardice I hadn't sunk as low as that. Besides which, I needed Vinnie in my life and was afraid if she walked across the quad and disappeared into the night unaccompanied I would never establish contact with her again. I felt curiously light-headed as I caught up and took my place beside her. The top layer of my mind was full of tension and anxiety, but at a deeper level I was at peace, fulfilled, reckless of what might become of me.

Vinnie walked straight ahead. At one point she almost bumped into a knot of men who were moving across, talking, laughing, settling their gowns on their shoulders. One of them, I noticed, was Knowlton. And on the fringe of the group was Kent. Of course he would have to be there. Of course he would have to take a good look at Vinnie as she walked past, full in the glow of light from a window.

We went out into the street and Vinnie turned towards her home. I walked beside her, silent. I had no idea what to say to her; all my energies had spent themselves in that three-hour encounter, and in any case I could tell absolutely nothing about what she was feeling or thinking, so I had no guideline as to what kind of remark she might have found welcome. As a last resort I might have suggested taking her somewhere for a drink or a meal, but apart from a shilling or two I had no money, so that was out.

As we went along St John Street I took her hand and drew her arm through mine. She didn't pull it away, just let it lie there, as it were absent-mindedly. She seemed to have gone completely inside herself.

Approaching her house I became desperate to say something before we parted. I grabbed her arm and brought her to a halt on a dark stretch of pavement, midway between two street-lamps. 'Vinnie,' I said.

'Yes?' she responded calmly.

'That was – it was just the most – you were wonderful.' I gabbled. 'I mean it was the best thing that ever happened to me.'

'It was pretty nice for me too,' she said and smiled. It was a contained little smile, but I had to be content with it. She stopped me coming any nearer to where she lived. Apparently it was all right for her to hide me away from her family, but not all right for me to try to hide her away from the College. I called after her something about fixing up a 'next time', but she didn't choose to answer. It would have to be back to the shoe-shop again.

Standing there in the street, hideously alone now, I became aware that I was very hungry. In view of my youthful appetite, and the rate at which my body had been consuming its own cells, that was only to be expected. What was not to be expected was dinner. I had of course missed Hall, and would in any case have to nerve myself before I could go among that crowd again.

I walked slowly along, rain slanting against me, hunger gnawing my belly. It seemed that society was dead set against allowing me to satisfy more than one of my bodily needs at a time. Nowadays, of course, there would have been snack-bars open of one kind and another, and quite a lot of pubs would have offered food, if only the left-overs from the roaring trade they did at lunchtime. But this was 1930, and a Sunday in 1930 to boot. It was, at that time and for about another twenty years, a completely unquestioned article of faith among the English that if you were outside your own home, unfed, on a Sunday evening you must be up to no good. And who would want to cater for people who are up to no good?

My couple of shillings would buy some beer, at any rate. I went into a pub. Once I was inside I noticed that it was the one I had gone into with Vinnie on that first evening, when I had found the boldness to tell her what I wanted of her. At least, I thought, I've carried that part of the operation through all right, no matter what other problems have been raised in the process. I ordered a pint of beer and as I sat drinking it I suddenly began to think of Gavin and Annabel. Obviously this kind of anti-climax never happened to them. They were stylish, independent, on top of things, and above all they were unquestioningly devoted to one another. If Gavin had been hungry, Annabel would have produced delicious home-baked biscuits or a game pie from Harrods or something. Nor would they skulk in fear of College discipline; they would have their organization perfected to a point where such things simply did not exist for them.

Well, I thought, some people are born into the freedom that a couple like that enjoy. Others just have to climb up to it, step by step. Nor was it, I went on to think, just a matter of being born low down or high up in the social scale. It was difficult to imagine Brian, for instance, being put in the position of having to do without food because he had been making love to a girl. He would have planned ahead, guarded against it somehow.

At that moment I felt an almost irresistible urge to walk rapidly through the streets to the Bargeman's Arms, which after all was scarcely fifteen minutes' walk away, and sit by the fire in the back parlour and ask my mother for some bread and cheese. But I didn't. I wanted to cope on my own. However awkward life was turning out to be, I needed the feeling that I could manage it without help from anyone. You learnt more that way.

The two pints of beer on an empty stomach, coupled with the languidness I was feeling anyway, began to make me feel tipsy. I thought with longing of my bed, then remembered that I hadn't got a bed, just a mattress in front of a dead hearth. Never mind, that would do. I walked back to College, went up to my room, and gathered up the remaining sheets and blankets into an untidy bundle. This bundle I chucked down on the mattress, rolled myself up in it, and dived into sleep.

It was Arthur who woke me, banging in at his usual time of 7.45 with the intention, I suppose, of taking out my empty coal-scuttle, filling it, and coming back to start the fire. But as soon as he got through the door he stopped dead and uttered an exclamation. I know what that exclamation was because, doubtless owing to my having a totally empty stomach, I had already begun to float up towards consciousness and was only just still asleep when he pushed the door open.

'Gaw struth!' he said. His tone conveyed disbelief and anger simultaneously.

I kept quite still, just opened my eyes. He came over and stood looking down at me.

'What's been goin' on 'ere, sir?' he rasped.

My mind raced, and came up with what seemed to me the only way out. 'I think I must be ill, Arthur,' I said. 'Perhaps I'm getting... flu or something.' It sounded wretchedly thin. 'I just couldn't get warm in the night. I was... shivering and everything. In the end I had to get up and make a big fire and lie in front of it. I did manage to get some sleep then.'

About half-way through this fabrication Arthur seemed to lose interest, as if it were simply not worth his while to pay attention to such piffle. He straightened up and started looking round the room.

'Goin' to take a bit o' puttin' straight, this is,' he remarked into the dank air.

'I'll help,' I said quickly.

'Thought you was ill,' he said.

'I think I've turned the corner,' I said. 'I'll see how I feel when I get –'

'All this'll have to be shifted,' he said, nudging at the mattress with the toe of his boot, 'if I'm going to get at the fire.'

I would have leapt up then and there and helped him to put the mattress back, but I remembered that, being too dead-beat to hunt round for my pyjamas, I had simply crashed into bed in my shirt and undervest, and I felt he would despise me if I revealed myself like that. So I just lay there, helplessly.

'I'll go and do the other gennlemen's fires,' he said. 'The ones I can get at.'

'They may all be ill,' I said spitefully. 'It may be an epidemic.'

He was half-way to the door now, and he turned and gave me a look that made me wish I hadn't tried to be clever.

'It's my belief,' he said slowly and murderously, 'as there's no sick gennlemen on this staircase.'

The door closed and he was gone. No mention of a fire, nor of breakfast. I felt cold and half-starved, a great need for physical comfort swept over me. I decided to go across to the bath-house and have a good long soak in hot water. I found my pyjamas, put them on – that at least made me look like a normal bedraggled early-riser – threw my overcoat on over them, and with towel and sponge-bag walked over there and got into a deep bath whose warmth penetrated my body and mind. Lying there, idly staring up at the steamy wooden ceiling, I got back my sensuous appetite for life and began to think, for the first time since it had happened, of the time I had had with Vinnie. I re-lived it detail by detail, wonderingly, scarcely able to believe it had happened to me and not someone else, someone I had been reading or dreaming about. The water began to cool; I ran some off and replenished it. I didn't care how long I stayed in the bath. I thought some more about the things Vinnie and I had done. Those three hours had changed everything. I was different: though exactly in what ways, and exactly how it would appear in my behaviour, I could not tell.

At last I had to get out of the water. My skin was becoming ridged, I had washed out so much of the oil that lay under it. I stood up, towelled and got back into my pyjamas and overcoat. I wished now that I had brought my clothes. I had intended to shave, using one of the hand-basins, but I was shivering too much. I started back across the quad.

Arthur was in the room when I got up there. He had his back to me, sweeping the carpet, and did not turn round. The mattress was gone from in front of the fire, but the bedclothes were still heaped over the armchair. Yesterday's dead ashes still lay in the grate.

'I could do with some breakfast, Arthur,' I said to his back.

'It's off by now,' he said. 'By the time I'd started to clear this place up, the kitchen'd closed.'

I felt pretty sure he was lying, but there was nothing I could do about it. If he wouldn't go down and get my breakfast, I couldn't go for it myself. Demarcation lines, in the society of those days, were like electric fences.

I picked up my clothes and went into the bedroom to put them on. But before I could do so he had turned round and was facing me.

'I'm afraid the Dean'll 'ave to hear about all this, sir,' he said, fixing me with his eyes.

'All what?' I faltered.

'You 'ad a lady visitor yestday. And this morning your bedding was disarranged and laid all over the floor. It's not my job to go in for guess-work. It'll be up to the Dean to decide whether you've broke College discipline when I puts the facks to him.'

A lady visitor? How had that got about?

'So, Arthur,' I said, 'you simply don't believe my statement that I felt ill during the night and had to get warm by the fire?'

He turned away again and resumed prodding at the carpet with his brush. 'It's not my job to believe or disbelieve. It's for the Dean when 'e has the facks.'

'But, Arthur,' I said, standing there with my clothes over my arm, feeling empty and feeble and utterly at a disadvantage compared with this entrenched old reptile, 'assuming I did have a visit from a young lady yesterday, that's not a breach of discipline. She just came to tea and went out again before Hall.'

'Come to tea, did she?' Arthur stopped sweeping, put one hand in his waistcoat pocket, took it out and stretched it out to me. There were two objects lying in his palm. For an instant I stared at them not knowing what they were. Then I realized. They were hairpins. I had not even realized that Vinnie used hairpins. I just thought her hair lay in its neat shape by nature.

'Don't use these, do you, sir?' Arthur asked sarcastically. 'Leastways, I never –'

'No,' I said. 'I don't use hairpins.' And I walked into the bedroom to get dressed. But for a minute or so I was too shaken to start putting my clothes on. I just shut the door and leaned against it with my heart hammering. So the case against me was unbreakable. Vinnie had shed her hairpins on to the mattress. Fetch the firing-squad, rig up the guillotine.

There seemed to be nothing to do but get dressed and go out. There were of course things like lectures going on, and later that week I was due for a tutorial with Bax at which I would have to show up an essay; since not a word of the essay was written, I had planned to spend today steadily working. Somewhere in the back of my mind was the vision I had had of myself today, how I would be at peace with the world after the fulfilment of Sunday afternoon, how I would sit contentedly in the library, consulting this book and that, weighing evidence and argument, constructing a first-rate essay, and all the time feeling happy and secure, friendly and affable with the people I sat among at meals. Now that today had actually come, all I was feeling was a numb anxiety. The fulfilment had happened all right, I was here, the library was open; but it had all been spoilt by a rumpled mattress in the wrong room and two hairpins.

I had no idea what would happen to me when Arthur reported me to the Dean, but I wouldn't have laid a bet that my tutorial with Bax would now take place at all. I had only the vaguest idea of College discipline, of what punishments were customary for what offences, but I knew enough to be sure that offences against chastity were at the very top of the list. As I stood there in my narrow little bedroom, knotting my tie, hearing grumpy old Arthur clattering about in my sitting-room, I faced the prospect of being sent down, my University career at an end before my second term was well started.

Hunger gnawed at my belly, which had now been empty for some twenty hours. At least, I thought, I'll eat. There were cafés in the town which made a speciality of serving sumptuous breakfasts to undergraduates who had been unable to wake up early enough to face the College hand-out. I planned to go to one of them – Lyons in

Cornmarket, I thought, would do very well – and at least line my stomach. That would give me the confidence to face what was coming to me.

In my desk drawer was my Post Office Savings Book with two pounds in it, exactly two pounds: my spending money for the whole eight-week term. Given the value of money as it was in those days, that was not too bad. I didn't have to buy clothes, I had no fares to pay, and I could sign for things like bread and butter and marmalade in the College buttery; my scholarship would cover those at the end of term, plus the occasional jug of beer when I had friends in. The two pounds – five bob a week – was really just walking-around money, enough to cover the odd visit to a cinema or a pub. Well, now it was going to cover a solid breakfast. I went into my sitting-room, skirted the slowly-moving figure of Arthur, and took the Post Office book out of the drawer.

The small positive step lifted my spirits, and as I thumped down the wooden stairs, I clutched the slim cardboard-covered book tightly in my mackintosh pocket. There was a Post Office in Broad Street in those days, and as I walked I forced myself to think in a calm, matter-of-fact way about the fact that very soon – by next weekend, say – I would be an ex-member of Oxford University, on the labour market and looking for a job as a clerk or a shop assistant. The thought struck me that I might get a job in the shop where Vinnie worked, able to steal glances at her down the length of the shop and chat to her several times a day during our breaks from work. For a moment I almost felt glad about what had happened, glad that the burden of a studious life had been lifted from my unformed shoulders and with it that other burden of social adjustment, the endless imperative to stop seeing the world from the viewpoint of the Bargeman's Arms, West Oxford, and move towards seeing it as the University saw it. Let it fall away, I thought, let it fall away like a heavy stone.

But this feeling vanished in its turn. As I turned the corner by the front of Balliol and got ready to cross the road, I glanced along the length of Broad Street and took it all in: the wide graceful thoroughfare, at the far end of it the elegant prow of the Sheldonian Theatre and the sturdy pillars of the Clarendon Building, the row of weatherbeaten heads on their pedestals, with the Indian Institute closing off the scene at the far end, and in between people walking along in twos and threes, many of them obvious at a glance as undergraduates, pausing now and then to look into the windows of the big bookshops whose array of thousands of volumes always gave me a shiver of nervous excitement as I walked past them. I paused no longer than was necessary to let a couple of cars go by before crossing the road, but that time was enough for me to be drawn back into the magnetic field and to know that the prospect that faced me, of ceasing to be a student and going back to the ordinary workaday life of Oxford as a prosaic midland city, was unbearable in its sadness.

I went into the Post Office, filled out the withdrawal form and picked up my two pounds. The bored girl behind the grille pointed out that this closed the account; was this intentional? I was too far gone to care, but I hadn't meant to give up my savings book altogether, so I changed one of the notes and put five shillings back in the account to keep it open, emerging into the winter sunlight with a pound note, a ten-shilling note, and two half-crowns. Now for the filling of my clamorous stomach! And about time too. I thought of crisp bacon, slippery fried eggs, toast and butter, hot coffee. That was what I had come out for, wasn't it?

Well, yes. But, as I started to walk, another cluster of thoughts came pushing in: of rich armfuls of leather-bound books from the college library, of neat stacks of unused paper, of the circle of light cast by the lamp on my desk; of meditative, idea-gathering walks in Christ Church Meadow or across the Parks; of the sheer joy of harvesting, however piecemeal and however slowly, knowledge from here and there, bringing large, misty issues into something like clarity and discussability. Was this all to be snatched from me, just when the happiness of it was at last within my reach? – That happiness that I had known intuitively must exist, ever since I went in for the Essay Prize: was it to be taken away so soon?

My situation, at that moment, showed itself to me in stark outline. I had pursued Vinnie, and moved heaven and earth to entice her to my room, because my whole nature passionately rejected the monastic tradition, which in Oxford was accepted without question. But I dreaded being cut off from the University because, equally, my whole nature desired the life of the mind, and I knew of no other setting in which I could find it. Being a good student involved two things: taking a burning interest in one's work, and accepting the monastic, anti-sexual discipline. The first I could provide; the second, never. All I could do was to improvise various makeshift ways of getting my emotional needs satisfied, and work hard at not being found out.

The other alternative – that of pursuing the intellectual life in some setting where the monastic discipline did not prevail – did not enter my head. I knew too little of the world to be aware that such places existed. My world was Oxford; and within Oxford, the choice was between Episcopus College and the Bargeman's Arms.

The decision as to which of these two worlds I was to inhabit did not rest with me. It rested with a curmudgeonly, watery-eyed old man in shirt-sleeves and an apron. At that thought I stopped, fingered the two notes in my pocket, and turned back in the direction of College. Breakfast would have to go. Hunger would have to be endured.

I walked quickly back to Episcopus and set about finding Arthur. He was not on my staircase, but he had charge of two others, and as I got to the top of the adjacent one I met him coming out of someone's rooms, carrying a slop-pail and looking, as usual, fiercely depressed.

'Arthur, just a word,' I said.

'I got a lot to do,' he said, making as if to push past me.

'I shan't keep you a second,' I said. My heart was pounding: I *had* to get this one right. 'I've been thinking,' I went on. 'I was a bit spent up at the end of last term, and I wasn't left with enough to give you a decent Christmas box.' In fact I had given him ten shillings, which was quite normal for all but the well-heeled undergraduates. 'I'd like to make it up,' I said rapidly, suddenly ashamed of the whole charade, and I whipped out the two notes, the pound one and the ten-shilling one, and held them out to him. 'Do take them,' I said. 'I don't like... feeling mean.' And for good measure I laid the two half-crowns on top of the heap.

To be fair to him, Arthur didn't torture me by making it a matter of suspense. He took the notes, folded them carefully, and put them into one of his waistcoat pockets. The half-crowns disappeared into the other. I can see him now. He had an old-fashioned stem-winding watch in one pocket and he put the notes on the other side.

'Much obliged,' he said. His expression remained exactly the same.

Of course neither of us brought up the matter of his reporting me to the Dean. I was reasonably sure he couldn't have done it yet, because I had only been out a few minutes, during which he had had time to whisk round all the rooms on my staircase and get up here.

Sometimes, now, I look back on that episode and wonder whether Arthur would really have reported me. It is impossible to be certain, but my belief is that he would. Not out of pure love for the college system and its discipline, but out of pique. My adventure had caused him extra work, and he had nothing to lose by getting me sent down: the room would have been occupied by someone else, someone who in his eyes would have been indistinguishable from me.

As I turned away and went down the stairs, I could not, of course, know that my bribe had worked. For the rest of that day I was nervous when going in and out through the lodge, in case the porter called to me and said I had to see the Dean: to climb those stairs, knock on the door and confront pale, podgy Hungerford who had total power over my life. But the tension was a little lighter by the evening, and by mid-morning the next day, when the summons still had not come, it vanished altogether. In theory, I know, bribery is a corrupt way of solving one's problems, but it was the only way open to me, and I thought then and think now that I was right to take it.

To go back to that morning. Once the money was handed over and I had come out into the empty quad, I was faced with the problem of how to fill in the hours. I needed two things: food, and a cessation of my anxiety about the Dean. The first would be provided at one o'clock and not a moment before, which meant that I had two and a half hours of hunger ahead of me. The second would come, if it came at all, in successive stages. Either of my two pressing needs was enough on its own to come between me and any book I tried to concentrate on.

I stood there, shivering. The morning was chilly in any case, but my totally empty stomach had resulted in a lowering of my body temperature. I felt as miserable as a lost dog. Naturally, in such a situation, I thought of home. A short brisk walk would bring me to the Bargeman's Arms; Dad would be at the brewery, but Mother would be around, either in the house or in one of the little neighbourhood shops, and I could count on her for steaming hot tea and a scone or a piece of toast. The thought gripped me with intense longing, but my feet made no move in that direction. For whatever complex of reasons, I just couldn't face home, the atmosphere of the family circle and the background of what had been my daily life, with all this hanging over me. My mother would ask, more or less mechanically, how I was 'getting on', and at the moment I wasn't getting on and I couldn't explain any of it to her.

So I went for a walk instead. I knew it would make my hunger worse, but at least if I walked rapidly enough it kept me from thinking. I went across the Parks and over the Rainbow Bridge and out to Marston, which in those days was a small, pretty rural village. When I got there it was still only half-past ten, so I went on and climbed up the hill to Elsfield, from which I had one of those famous views of Oxford, the Oxford of the storybooks, with its cluster of towers and spires pointing up into a clear sky from that riverside hollow: sacred ground if ever there was sacred ground, though despoiled and insulted in my lifetime. Away to the east I could see the smudge of smoke that was Cowley; not black, belching smoke of the kind you got with the old Northern industrial towns that burnt coal, more like a dark, oily haze from all those engines.

Coming back, I felt faint and had to lean up against a wall and rest, and when I got to the Parks I sat down on a bench and gathered strength before walking the last bit. Like most people in the industrial countries, I have lived a very pampered life as far as food was concerned, and this was the only time I have known real hunger and the weakness that comes from it. I ought to be able to say that the experience did me good, made me better equipped to live sympathetically in a world where millions have died of hunger as I munched an endless succession of good meals, but to be honest I just remember it as an unpleasant experience, part of the punishment for flying in the face of the College system by obeying my natural need to get into bed with a girl.

I hung back from being actually the first one in to Hall when they started handing out the lunch. I think I was second or third. College meals were very good in those days, though lunch, by tradition, was not as elaborate as dinner, and I had to content myself with a couple of pork chops, peas, roast potatoes and apple sauce, followed by a chocolate pudding. I remember every mouthful. It was only towards the end of the second course that I got my head up enough to notice the people around me. The first person I knowingly saw, as it happened, was Kent. He was sitting some places down the table, talking to a knot of his fellow-barkers, and it seemed to me that his gaze rested on me for a moment, coldly, and then he turned and said something to the others. Something about me? How could I tell?

Chapter 9

All this time I had not thought of Vinnie. The very idea of her existence had not so much as floated into my consciousness since I left the bath-house. But now, with the immediate crisis shading off into a twilight of wait-and-see, and my bodily life coming back into its own with the comfort of a satisfied stomach, the thought of her returned swiftly and imperiously. I went straight out of College and over to Cornmarket Street. It was only about half-past one and I thought she might still be having her lunch break, but she was there, standing about among the racks of shoes. I went in and moved towards her. She was wearing her neat shop outfit of the blue overall picked out with white at the collar and cuffs. The effect of her slender, upright figure – she always had very good carriage – and smooth, lustrous brown hair set my desire for her thrashing within me as if it had not been whole-heartedly surfeited less than twenty-four hours earlier.

She didn't see me immediately, but as I drew near she looked straight at me and a forbidding expression appeared on her pale, intent little face.

'Go away,' she hissed, glancing rapidly from side to side to try to see if I had already been spotted as an intruder from that forbidden country, her personal life.

'I just wanted to –'

'Not in the shop! You mustn't come into the shop!'

I hung on another second to see if she would suggest that I met her outside when the shop closed, but she didn't, so I did.

'I'll wait outside when they close.'

She gave a little shrug that said 'Please yourself,' turned away, and started to look busy by rearranging some evening shoes that didn't need rearranging. The first she picked up was a narrow gold one that shone very brightly in the electric light. I knew I would never forget the sight of her long, pale fingers holding this shiny golden shoe. It has remained with me all my life as the ultimate erotic symbol.

I went out and spent the afternoon scratching about for a few facts that might build up into the essay I had to write for Bax. Not that I got far. My mind obstinately refused to stay on the topic, whatever it was. It simply slid off, like an object placed again and again on a sloping block of ice. I knew I would have to make some progress with it later that evening, even if it meant working far into the night, but at least by then I would, all being well, have got out from under the cloud of anxiety about being summoned to see the Dean. If he didn't ask for me soon, it would mean Arthur had tacitly accepted the bribe and I was reprieved.

At five-thirty I was able to stop pretending and go over to Cornmarket Street. The shops in those days, instead of being mostly chain-stores off-loading cheap trash made in Taiwan, were solidly established businesses selling goods that were worth buying. The window displays were discreet, and the Clarendon Hotel, on the right going towards Carfax, kept up the standard of dignity with its elegant doors and windows, as if it knew it was the last of Oxford's great coaching inns. I felt faintly guilty, skulking about there at the behest of my appetites. I lurked in the doorway of a shop opposite the one where Vinnie worked, and kept the door unwinkingly in view.

She came out; I fell in about ten yards behind her, and when we were some distance from the shop I drew level.

'Hello,' I said. 'I'm here.'

'Yes,' she said, giving me one neutral glance and then going back to looking straight ahead.

I thought perhaps she wasn't stopping to talk because the pavement was too crowded with all the people spilling out of the shops. But when we turned into Beaumont Street she just kept walking steadily onward.

'When am I going to see you again?' I asked.

She gave that shrug again.

'There's – there's nothing the matter, is there?'

'No,' she said unconcernedly.

I felt I ought to make some concrete suggestion, but since my spending money was all gone there was nowhere I could offer to take her, and all I could think of was to get her up to my room again, if circumstances permitted.

'Like to come to tea again next weekend?' I hazarded.

'No, thanks,' she said.

This threw me completely. What was she telling me? Had I somehow failed her? Or was it my room she didn't like? Or what?

'I'm a bit skint just now,' I said, trying to keep my tone light. 'I'd like to suggest the pictures or something, but finances...' I could hear my voice trailing off.

Suddenly she said, 'If you want to do something you can take me dancing.'

'Dancing?' I echoed as if I had never heard the word before.

'Yes, at Holyoake Hall. Mondays, Thursdays and Saturdays. They have a band.'

This was the last thing on earth I wanted to do. Only the fact that the suggestion came from Vinnie could have made me consider it for a single second. Going to a dance would (i) cost money which I hadn't got, (ii) put the pair of us in public for a whole evening instead of in private, (iii) doubtless involve me in making a fool of myself, because my notion of ballroom dancing was extremely vague. I would be at a disadvantage all the way round. The evening was quite likely to be (iv) such a catastrophe that Vinnie would never want to see me again, in which case I would have spent money (and where was I going to get it?) and invested colossal effort and endured humiliation, all for nothing. For worse than nothing, for a shattering kick in the guts, viz., losing such hold as I had on Vinnie.

That hold was pretty fragile in any case. Ought I to get out now, while I could at least chalk up one blissful success? (Or was it a success? Was there perhaps a note from the Dean, pale, silent, withdrawn Hungerford, waiting for me in the lodge even now?)

Vinnie must have decided to go along St John Street, because when we came opposite it she stopped and waited to cross the road. This put her in the first position in which I had ever seen her – standing near a street-lamp, with that pale light falling on her slender shape and accentuating the dramatic effect of that dark brown fringe, surmounting her face like a helmet. As I looked at her I knew there was no point in trying to break away. I would do anything, *anything*, to keep my hat in the ring.

'What night d'you want to go?' I asked.

'Any night you like.'

'I don't dance very well.'

'You needn't come if you don't want to,' she said reasonably.

'Oh, I do want to,' I said hastily. 'Look, it's Monday now. You say they have it on Thursdays. Let's go then.'

The traffic had paused and she began to walk across to St John Street. 'All right,' she said.

'Thursday, then.' I was already beginning to work out what I could sell to get hold of some money. I had that spare pair of shoes at home, the ones I had bought so as to have an excuse for going into the shop. I could go and collect those and sell them. But where did one go to sell shoes? Who would buy them?

'What time does it start?' I asked Vinnie. Does she go often, I thought, and will it be full of people she knows, coming up and claiming her attention, dancing with her, perhaps taking her home? What fantastic spiral of disaster was I getting myself into?

'It starts at half-past seven,' she said, 'but we don't have to get there at the beginning. We can meet about eight, if you've got to eat your dinner or something.'

Her words made me feel uncomfortable, carrying with them the reminder that we had completely different patterns of life, that there was a gulf fixed between us. But I was already so uncomfortable for other reasons that I hardly noticed the increase. And I was grateful for her permission to have dinner in College, at least. I already had no idea how I was going to finance the expedition without paying for food on top of the price of admission to the dance-hall.

'All right,' I said, putting a false ring of confidence into my voice. 'Thursday, then. Where is this place?'

'Top of Headington Hill,' she said. 'Don't you know that?'

'I must have passed it often enough,' I said, 'but I never noticed it. I haven't been much of a dancing man.'

'Well, you can be one on Thursday,' she said. 'We'll get the bus in Cornmarket. Be there at ten to eight.' And after that neither of us spoke till we got within a hundred yards of her home, when she stopped and told me not to come any further.

I put my arms round her, clumsily; but I would have been less clumsy if she had shown any eagerness, if she had swayed towards me or moulded her shape to mine the slightest bit. I went for her mouth but she turned her head sideways and gave me one cheek, then the other.

'There's nothing wrong, is there, Vinnie?' I murmured.

'Have I said there's anything wrong?'

'No, but... well, you know...'

She pulled away from me. 'I've been standing on my feet all day and I want to go home and have my tea.'

That was reasonable enough. I watched her walk away and then I went back to College.

*

Later that week, perhaps the following day, I happened to find myself, at lunch in Hall, sitting near Gerard and Lamont. (I always thought of them by those names, though by now I was clear that 'Gerard' was Gerard Urquhart's Christian name and 'Lamont' was Gavin Lamont's surname.) I had gone in a few minutes late and there was not much space left on the benches. But there was an empty place laid beside Lamont, and he gave me a friendly smile as I approached, while Gerard gave me a cheerful nod from the other side of the table. This encouraged me to sit down. Though I had of course a perfect right to sit anywhere I chose, I still needed this slight encouragement because I felt, as I had when I first met them, somewhat in awe of these two.

Seated there, I could hardly help overhearing their conversation. It emerged that Lamont was trying to help Gerard not to feel so discontented with his life at Oxford.

'It's so *unproductive,*' Gerard was saying, scowling at the baked potato on his plate. 'Month after month goes by and I think about the things that are going on in Paris and Berlin and Vienna, even in London... And here, no one's initiating *anything*. No one's launching out. If they put on a production of what they call an *avant-garde* play or opera or something, it always turns out to be some well-worn thing seven or eight years old, already stale.'

'If it's good art it won't be stale in seven years, or in seventy,' Lamont said calmly. 'Personally I'm rather glad to have a few years of quiet, to get some reading in, and polish my techniques a bit, before I have to step out into the full glare of day.'

'I want that glare. I feel it's the only thing that'll bring me on. It'll make me open up, whereas here I'm clenched tight. I feel myself getting as boring and provincial as everyone else.'

I listened in my usual open-mouthed way. It had never occurred to me to wonder whether I was boring and provincial. I just got on with the tasks that were put in front of me. What was it to be provincial? Was Brian provincial? Was Cecil Kimber boring? I supposed Gerard would think they were.

'I know why it is, of course,' Lamont was saying. 'Why this place suits me and doesn't suit you. It's because, though we're both artists, we're different kinds. When I'm contemplating a poem, I have to be by myself. I don't want stimulating company or any company. All right, when I've finished the poem, I might want to show it to people, get their reactions to it. I might even want to go to places where I meet other poets, gangs of them. But essentially I don't work with other people, and you do.'

'I ought to, you mean,' Gerard said moodily. 'If there were any who were the slightest bit interested in what I'm interested in.'

'Well, what about this Theatre Club or whatever it is, that you belong to?'

'Sixth-Formers,' said Gerard. 'I just have to clue them in on everything. Their idea of experimental theatre is Granville-Barker.'

'You mean to tell me that of all the people there are at the University, several thousand of them, you haven't found kindred spirits to the tune of, say, half-a-dozen?'

Gerard considered for a moment before answering. 'It's not exactly that they don't exist. I expect they do exist, if one could find them. In fact I *have* found them, in certain cases. It's just that they find it impossible to function creatively because they're so *diluted*.'

Diluted? I thought. What with?

'For every one person with any ideas,' Gerard went on, as if answering my unspoken question, 'and any notion of what a contemporary sensibility would be like, there are hundreds of such devastating *ordinariness*.' His eyes, as he spoke, moved briefly along the table, ranged as it was with thoughtless, feeding faces. 'All the hearties, and the worker ants who never do anything but read and make notes for their next essay, and the fops who think about nothing but their appearance and are always running up to Town to see their tailor and get measured for something, and the churchy ones with crucifixes up on their walls who burn candles and go to retreats, and the ones who aren't even any of those things, just Public School prefects who still haven't got over being deprived of their fags...' He finished with an explosion of breath, conveying despair.

'Well,' Lamont said mildly, 'that's all true enough, but what would you do if you went down?'

'Get into the theatre as an Assistant Stage Manager. And if there wasn't an A.S.M. job going for the moment, sell programmes, work in the box office, sweep the carpets.'

'Why not shift scenery? That'd get you closer to the action.'

'Difficult to get in. They've got a Union and they're fairly solid.' Gerard seemed lost in his thoughts for a moment, then spoke again, emphatically. 'I'd go down tomorrow. Or at least, at the end of this term. I'm hitting my head against a brick wall here. I *ought* to go down. And d'you know why I don't?'

'Annabel,' said Lamont, smiling, 'at a guess.'

'Exactly. She won't leave till she's had her full three years, if you please, because she says it would *upset her parents*. A totally boring, conventional-to-the-backbone couple who *ought* to be upset. But that's her trouble, Annabel – she's so damned *nice*.'

Putting cheese on a piece of bread, I thought of Annabel and how damned nice she was. The great bronze wings sweeping back from her forehead, perfectly setting off her heart-shaped face... Had she always, I wondered, worn her hair like that? After all, twelve or eighteen months ago she must have been a schoolgirl. What did she look like then? Leggy and gawky, in school uniform and a boater? Was her hair bobbed, or in pigtails? Annabel Graveney, 5c. First reserve in the house netball team. Or did people like that have private tutors, or go to exotic schools in Switzerland? How, in any case, had she gone from that stage to the stage she was at now, totally poised, totally beautiful? Gradually? Or in one giant stride? Had Gerard helped?

Lamont was saying something, but his voice receded into a remote background as I had a sudden vision of Gerard and Annabel making love. It was just their faces I saw. The glowing bronze of her hair spread out on the pillow. His piercingly blue eyes, under the perfectly symmetrical arches of his eyebrows, boring into hers as if searching in them for the depths of her being while he invaded her down below.

The vision must have lasted no more than a second or two, but when I came back to my actual surroundings Lamont was saying, 'Well, I must be off.'

'Me too,' said Gerard.

They departed, leaving me thoughtfully picking up the last crumbs from my plate of bread and cheese. Dick Kent walked out, throwing me a brief hostile stare as he went past. How, I thought, was there room in the same universe, let alone in the same college, for someone like him and someone like Gerard?

*

As the evening approached when I was to take Vinnie to Holyoake Hall, a chill depression settled on me. It was all so grey, so anxious and, above all, so humiliating. I took absolutely no pleasure in contemplating the prospect; what I wanted to do with Vinnie was to fuck her, not dance with her, and of course I had agreed to take her dancing merely for the sake of keeping our relationship going on the off-chance that my preferred choice might become available again some time. I had never been to Holyoake Hall, but I knew that its reputation was very much as a night-time haunt of Town, which in those days meant that it was automatically barred, banned and bolted against Gown. Just the sort of place, in short, that the Proctors would go for if they happened to be making their rounds that evening. They would see it as their duty to protect from their own worst impulses any undergraduates who had gone there with the intention of meeting girls from the town. Girls like Vinnie.

So I was running a heavy risk, and in addition, of course, I had no money because all my cash had gone on the bribe to Arthur. But money I must have, or I would let Vinnie down and inevitably lose her. Burning with shame, I walked down to the pub one night – ah, those childhood-familiar streets – and asked my father for two pounds. I told him I needed to buy some extra books that had become necessary for the course I was reading. He made a fuss, of course – said that he had understood my various scholarships and grants were enough to pay for books, and also asked what impossible amount of books I needed to buy, that cost as much as *two pounds*? (In those days the price of a brand-new, good-quality hardback book was usually about five shillings or seven and sixpence.) I told him they were specialized academic books. He asked if everyone had to buy these books, and I told him everyone did, if he was serious about the work we were doing. I said one or two of the chaps were not going to bother, but I was taking a serious interest and I thought this was a chance to get my nose out in front. That worked, as I knew it would. He took two pound notes out of the till and gave them to me, making sure as he did so that I understood it was a loan.

I had the money, I had the resolve, I had the arrangement to meet Vinnie at the bus stop, and now only a few hours stood between me and the desperate adventure, in which I was once again going to put my whole career in jeopardy for the sake of an outside chance of dousing the furnace I was carrying about inside my body. As I went into Hall for that last meal – for so, amid my forebodings, I found myself thinking of it – I felt a numbing sense of having already made some irretrievable mistake, of having ruined everything for myself once and for all. The food was put in front of me; I could hardly eat any of it; Fred Armitage, opposite me, tried one or two conversational openings and then sank into silence.

I toyed with the meal until it was time to go up to my rooms and get my overcoat and go along to the bus stop in Cornmarket Street. As I walked along the street I actually had to fight down an impulse to turn and run, blindly, heedlessly, into the night, anywhere so that I put distance between myself and the *débâcle* I felt sure was coming. But my feet just kept moving me along, and when I drew near the bus stop and saw that beguiling, weasel-slender figure standing beside it, a wave of reckless excitement went through me. At least in *that* area of my life I knew exactly what my feelings were and exactly what I wanted. I would go for it, and let the chips fall where they might.

Vinnie greeted me tranquilly but cheerfully, and in a few minutes the bus appeared. I was glad to get into its large, lighted interior, comfortably ordinary and reassuring. I felt safe now. Vinnie and I were just two young people riding in a bus, safe from surveillance at any rate until we alighted. (If this sounds paranoid, remember that technically I was breaking a University regulation by going out into the streets after dinner without my gown on, and that that regulation, preposterous as it was, had not quite become a dead letter.)

The bus ground its way up Headington Hill, the driver shifting down through the gears to tackle the short stretch where the gradient was steep. Bus engines in those days were petrol, not diesel, and in the lower gears they made a peculiar sound that you never hear nowadays, a high-pitched whine that seemed about to break into a fit of sobbing. It ought to have been a sorrowful noise, but actually what it conveyed was not sorrow, just honest effort. I shifted slightly on the seat beside Vinnie, bringing myself discreetly closer to her. Why had I suddenly become so wary of her, so circumspect that I hesitated before the slightest bodily contact, when only a few days ago we had been wrestling around on the floor of my room like a pair of polecats? What had changed? Something in Vinnie, of course, was the answer. After opening herself out to me so completely, she had closed again, withdrawn into her own inner citadel. I caught a whiff of perfume from her neck or ears or wherever she had dabbed it; only a cheap scent, I suppose, but it stabbed right through my being and seemed to sharpen all my senses. Well, I thought, when I dance with her I'll get my arm round her and draw her close to me. You're allowed to do that, in dancing, in fact it's compulsory. That may warm her up. The thought flashed across my mind that perhaps she had suggested we go dancing as a way of getting back into some sort of body-relationship with me, dispersing the chill that had fallen on her.

Holyoake Hall was not exactly in competition with the Savoy Ballroom. It was a pretty down-to-earth place that said to the customers, 'You're here to dance – well, get on with it and dance.' It cost half a crown to get in, *each*, and there was a Cloaks where you had to leave your coat, if you didn't want somebody stealing it, and that set you back another sixpence, *each*. I could see that the two pounds I had chiselled out of my father were by no means a wild over-estimate, allowing for possible emergencies. On the other hand there was no need for expensive rounds at the bar, because the City Fathers in their wisdom had ordained that there was to be no bar. It was bad enough having the young men and women putting their arms round each other without allowing them to become excited with alcohol. You could buy soft drinks, but they were very cheap in those days, and so nasty that I couldn't imagine Vinnie wanting to consume more than two or three in the evening.

The band was playing when we went in, and the first ten minutes of the evening raised my spirits a good deal; which was just as well, since as it turned out they were the only bit I enjoyed. Everything became steadily worse from about minute eleven onward, so let me linger for a moment on the enchantment of being close to Vinnie and feeling our limbs moving to the same rhythm. She simply turned to me, wordlessly but with a faint smile, and put her hands in the position usual for the female partner in the dancing of those days; I got one arm firmly round her narrow waist and grasped her right hand in my left, and we were off. I'm sure my inexperience caused me to dance very badly – I had only the most rudimentary notion of the correct steps – but on the other hand I have always had a good natural sense of rhythm, and the pumping beat of the twelve-piece band flowed very naturally down from my ears to my feet. Vinnie was close to me, moving with me, and I was really getting her perfume now. She must have sprayed it on her hair or something. It went to my blood like a forbidden elixir. All the time I was trucking her around, moving her backwards and sideways, inhaling the wicked cheap scent, I was fucking her in my mind, and I swear to God it was almost as good as the real thing. Hurrah for Holyoake, a voice was intoning inside my head. Then the music stopped and the misery started.

As we circulated, Vinnie had caught sight of two girls, evidently known to her, who were dancing together. When the music stopped and everybody drifted to the edges of the floor, these two came up. Vinnie's circle didn't go in for formal introductions, but I gathered that the girls were friends of hers and that their names were something like Maureen and Doreen. That was the kind of name you had to get used to in those days. If this had been the nineteen-eighties we would have been in a disco and the girls would have been called Sharon and Kelly-Ann, but since it was the 'thirties we were in a dance-hall and they were called Doreen and Maureen, or words to that effect.

The two of them looked at me with momentary half-interest and turned back to their conversation with Vinnie. I then became aware that there was a youth of about my own age who was obviously trying to attach himself to Maureen/Doreen. Whether they had been doing their two-girl dance to try to exclude him or whether the object was to turn him on and get him to make a move, I didn't know and I didn't care. But he was giving me a hostile stare, as if regarding me as possible competition. I wasn't flattered. He was a skinny lout with an unnaturally small mouth, and a hair-line that started about a millimetre above his eyebrows.

In the hope of detaching Vinnie from this group I asked her if she would like something to drink, but all that happened was that we all drifted towards the refreshment counter and stood vaguely beside it. Vinnie was too busy talking to Doreen/Maureen about how she hated the under-manager at work, or something equally enthralling, to make up her mind what she wanted. This other chap – I gathered his name was Stan – stood near to the girls but without speaking.

The band must have been having an interval or something – after all, we had got there half an hour into the evening – and that left us all with nothing to do. If running into these two girl-friends of Vinnie's had been my first piece of bad luck, this was my second. If I could just have got Vinnie on to the dance-floor and into motion, I might have saved something of the evening. As it was, all five of us stood there, and once Vinnie had finished with the topic of the under-manager we started some sort of aimless general sub-conversation. Stan said very little; perhaps his organs of speech were not fully developed. He kept looking from Maureen to Doreen and back again as if trying to decide which of them looked the more likely prospect. But he pricked up his nasty little ears when it came out, from something Vinnie said, that I was at College. As soon as he heard that his nasty little mouth stretched, as much as it could stretch, into a spiteful grin across his nasty little narrow face.

'A College man, eh?' he said. Then, swaying his body about in a way meant to suggest a mincing walk, he began heavily imitating what he thought of as an upper-class accent. Actually, of course, my accent was much the same as his.

'Eau, bai Jove, a Cawlidge man,' he brayed. 'Ai sai, doncherknow.'

'Chuck it,' I said. I saw out of the corner of my eye that the girls looked bored. Even Maureen/Doreen didn't find this old routine any funnier than I did. But Stan was on to what he thought of as a winning streak and it would take more than boredom to shut him up.

'What you doing in a place like this?' he demanded, dropping the accent for a moment and staring into my face aggressively. 'Your lot have got their own dances. I've heard about 'em. Twenty quid each for tickets and stand about drinking champagne.'

'I should have thought it's fairly obvious what I'm doing here,' I said, nodding towards Vinnie and giving him the best I could manage in the way of a comradely smile. But if I hoped to disarm his hostility by appealing to our common maleness and our common aims, I was hopelessly mistaken.

'Ai should have thought it was obvious,' he bayed out in that music-hall toff's voice again. 'Bai jove, when are they going to serve the champagne? Ai'm not used to being kept waiting.'

To make a diversion I asked Vinnie again if she would like something to drink, and this time she said yes. We went up to the refreshment bar and for a second I hoped we might get away and be by ourselves. But Maureen/Doreen drifted, like seaweed on an invisible tide, over towards us, and Stan of course came and stood right beside me, keeping it up about the champagne. I bought a glass of sticky liquid for Vinnie and one for myself, and, the two glasses in my hands, turned away from the bar, but he pushed so close up to me that one of them spilled over and made a sugary blob on my trousers.

'Look, lay off, Stan,' I said. 'Push off and leave me alone.'

'Oh, I've got to keep you company,' he said with another smirk. 'It wouldn't do for a College gentleman like you to be all alone among a crowd of nasty rough common people.'

I realized, now, that he wasn't going to go away, that my evening with Vinnie had been ruined, that it had all been for nothing. And such an icy well of rage rose up inside me that I knew there was only one thing that would stop me from going insane. I had to smash my fist into Stan's face, trample him, bang his head against a wall.

Moving very slowly and precisely, I handed Vinnie her drink, and put my own glass back on the counter. My original impulse had been to set about Stan there and then, but mercifully I had just one scrap of sanity left, somewhere in the cauliflower-shape of my brain, and that scrap was enough to remind me that if I started anything in here the chucker-out and the manager would get drawn in and word would inevitably get back to Episcopus. So I said, holding my voice steady, 'Come outside with me.'

He pretended to fan himself. 'Outside. Phew. Must get some fresh ayah. Can't stand the smell of all these low-class boundahs!'

'I'm going to give you a good hiding,' I said, loud enough for the people standing round to hear me. Several turned and looked in my direction. 'Not in here. Outside, nice and quiet. If you don't come, you're a bloody little coward and everybody'll know it. And I'll wait for you outside anyway.'

His face turned ugly then, and without a word he turned and slouched off towards the exit. I followed him with that cold anger still freezing everything out of my soul except the wish, at whatever cost, to hurt him as much as possible. Very strange, all of it, and very foreign to my character. I am now, and I was then, repelled by violence, and most of the time more than half a coward, to use the word with which I had just taunted this Stan. But the stronger power always drives out the less. Put me down anywhere near Vinnie and my normal character – thoughtful, hesitant, rather timorous – melted away and revealed the sabre-toothed tiger that we all nourish within ourselves.

The box-office would issue tickets, called 'pass-outs', to people who wanted to leave the place for a while – to get a drink at a nearby pub, for instance – without paying the admission fee again when they came back. We got two pass-outs, without mentioning to the woman that our reason for going out was to see which of us could half-kill the other. Personally I hardly cared how the fight came out, as long as I could leave my mark on him. He didn't look strongly built, anyway, and I didn't anticipate that he would give me much trouble, unless he had a knife or something.

As it turned out, my theory was never put to the test. Extraordinary coincidences do sometimes happen in real life, and one happened at that moment. Precisely when Stan and I, pass-outs in hand, turned away from the box-office window, three young men came up to it. The first two I didn't recognize. They looked some years older than I, smartly dressed, very much on pleasure bent. The third one was Brian.

When he saw me he stopped dead. 'What the –' he began, but speech failed him. 'You!' was all he could manage.

'It's all right, Brian,' I said. 'You haven't seen a ghost.'

'I wouldn't mind if it was a ghost,' he said, giving me a nasty look. 'What you doing here, anyway?'

'Same as you, I expect,' I said.

All I intended by that last remark was to turn aside his hostile question and perhaps to make a faint appeal to the things that united us. After all, no one came to a dump like this except under the lash of the old familiar mating drive. Otherwise what? The music wasn't worth listening to, there was hardly a brilliant level of conversation, and there was nothing to drink. I meant no harm by my reply, but for some reason it seemed to irritate Brian still further.

'Leave me out of it,' he snarled. 'Never mind what I'm doing here. What I do is my business.'

'Okay, okay,' I said. Then I remembered what I had been on the way out for. And I saw Stan, standing over near the door and looking at me expressionlessly. My anger had been punctured by this sudden encounter with Brian, suddenly let out like air from a tyre. I no longer felt the slightest impulse to punch Stan. But I supposed I was stuck with it now. A great weariness took hold of my limbs.

'Who's your friend?' said Brian, still nastily, following the line of my eyes.

'I don't know who he is,' I said. 'His name's Stan. He keeps insulting me and I asked him to come outside.'

‘Come *outside*? For a fight, you mean?’

Brian’s tone was incredulous and I remembered that I was supposed to be the effeminate one.

‘You’d understand,’ I said, ‘if you’d seen the way he was needling me.’

‘Listen,’ said Brian, putting his face close to mine. One of the two fellows he had come in with was trying to attract his attention, but he held up one hand in a delaying gesture that said, ‘Just a minute till I’ve dealt with this nuisance.’ To me he said, ‘If you don’t want to be needled, stay away from places like this. Go back where you belong.’

I think I can say without self-pity that that moment was one of the worst of my life. To be told by my own brother to go back where I belonged, with the clear implication that I didn’t belong anywhere near him, went through my vitals like a cold knife.

And yet even in the instant in which his words reached my eardrums I knew that this was something I ought to have expected. For years I had been bending over books, listening to instruction, taking examination after examination, just in order to enter a sphere different from that of my brother. Or, to put it with more philosophical precision, I had done these things in the knowledge that they would have that result, and the knowledge had not hindered me from doing them. It was not so much a matter of intention, working to bring it about, as acquiescence, knowing that it would inevitably come about and doing nothing about that knowledge.

‘You were just on your way out, go,’ Brian said pitilessly. ‘You come in here making disturbances, wanting to fight people, there’s bound to be trouble and it spoils it for me. You’ve got your own life, go to it.’

‘I wasn’t going home,’ I said tonelessly. ‘The fighting part doesn’t matter. I’ll let it go. But I’m not in a position to go home. I’m with somebody.’

‘With somebody? A girl?’

Brian’s tone was totally incredulous, as if the thought that I might have anything to do with a girl had never crossed his mind. Who had placed this enormous, unnatural gulf between us? Some malevolent spirit? Or just the goddess History in her blind impartiality?

I turned away, despairingly. I wasn’t going outside with Stan. If he chose to come back and nag at me again, he would just have to. I felt that the evening had slipped away out of my hands. All I could do was suffer it passively, and hope that fate would not add to my misfortune by the crowning disaster of bringing the Proctors in and getting me reported to Episcopus, for frequenting a low, proletarian haunt where I was in danger of meeting female bipeds of my own species, sexually cloven after the fashion of their kind, and doubtless ripe for mischief.

I stood on the fringe of the floor, where the dancing figures were marked off from the standing ones, and looked round for Vinnie. I couldn't see her anywhere. But after a while, when I stopped looking at the standers and let my eye wander among the dancers, I saw her moving round with the throng, doing a slow fox-trot. Her partner was another girl, either Maureen or Doreen. At least, I thought dumbly, it was something that, straight after my disappearance from her immediate field of vision, she hadn't got herself picked up by another man. But perhaps she was going on display with that end in view.

She came past quite close to me now, and I managed to catch her eye. She gave me a little nod and shrug combined, which conveyed that she saw I was there waiting for her but couldn't very well stop in the middle of a number. So I stood and waited. I saw that I was standing near the two who had come in with Brian. They were somewhat similar, though not so much alike as to be brothers; it was more that they had a similarity of style. They belonged to the same type. They were not youths like Brian and me but grown men, in their middle twenties at least, rather heavily built. Both had dark hair, well oiled. One had sideburns, carefully razored to a shape, and the other a little hairline moustache. Both were evidently cultivating the same style of good looks – that dark, sultry, swarthy, over-pomaded style with which Rudolph Valentino had swept the world, and which in the early 'thirties had not quite died out. (It was soon to die for twenty years and then to be revived by Elvis Presley, and to this day when I see a picture of Elvis Presley I think of these two bucks in the Holyoake Hall.)

As Vinnie came by, one of them looked attentively at her, as if suddenly recognizing her. He nudged the other and said something. The other gave a greasy leer. Immediately my mind flashed up about seventy-five different theories as to how this man came to know Vinnie, what kind of relationship it was, and what he had said to his friend. Each of the seventy-five was more poisonous than the last. I turned away so as not to look at their faces. At that moment the music stopped and Vinnie and the other girl walked off the floor. They were at the other end. Before going down to claim Vinnie I turned to have one last look towards Brian. He was turning away from me, saying something to Stan. What it was I don't know, but Stan gave me no more trouble that evening. I had enough troubles already.

It wasn't that anything particularly disastrous actually happened. It was just that the sparkle had gone out of the evening. I managed to prise Vinnie loose from her friends and dance with her for the rest of the evening, but it was a lack-lustre performance on both sides. I couldn't tell whether she was bored with me or whether my general depression had communicated itself to her, but I just couldn't muster the energy to cheer up and try to jolly her along. We shuffled round the floor like two sick dromedaries. I couldn't think of anything to say, and Vinnie evidently wasn't going to try. The whole atmosphere of the place was against me, weighing me down. I felt that even the air was trying to poison me as it went into my lungs. I had promised myself the excitement of being physically close to Vinnie, but it was as if a crowd of enemies had pushed in between us. I avoided Brian, but every now and then I saw his tense, closed face and I knew that he just didn't want me within his orbit. Add to that the unpleasantness with Stan and the sheer damp weight of Maureen/Doreen, plus the generally alien atmosphere and the underlying drum-beat of anxiety lest the confounded Proctors should suddenly appear, and it all amounted to a huge, stinking load of misery.

The band tootled on till eleven o'clock, then suddenly stood up and went into a few bars of the National Anthem: God Save the King. I had a sudden vision of the old gentleman, George the Fifth, with his air of polite reserve and his pointed little iron-grey beard. Nobody took the slightest notice of the Anthem, of course – they simply walked off the floor and went to collect their overcoats. In those days it acted as a useful signal that the entertainment was over and you were to go home. It was like 'I won't keep you.'

Vinnie and I went out. It was a very cold night, but not clear or exhilarating in any way. It was still January, or perhaps just into February, I don't remember, but certainly very much the depths of winter. The sky was overcast as if there was a weight of snow up there in the darkness, getting ready to fall on us, and there was a light but icy wind. The patrons of Holyoake Hall were dispersing rapidly; a few had cars, and they were slamming the doors and revving up, but most people either just walked away or clustered round the bus-stops. I felt my spirits sink even lower, something I would not have thought possible. Our wretched evening was over, we were a couple of miles from either of our homes, and the thought of a long wait at a freezing bus-stop threatened a stretch of such boredom that it would probably finish our relationship for good. I would never dare to ask Vinnie out again.

Then I had the only piece of good luck that evening. A taxi came by, cruising, with its sign lit up. Oxford taxis, then as now, very rarely cruised about picking up passengers. They went from point to point and back again and purposefully as bees. But this one was cruising, and one of the two pounds I had borrowed from Dad was still in my wallet, not broken into.

I hailed the taxi, gave Vinnie's address, and there we were, comfortable, warm, bowling along. I breathed a great sigh of pure relief. Chance, yes, nothing else but pure chance, had saved me. I was still there in Vinnie's life, even if only on the fringe of it, and still with a hope, however slender, of repeating the performance of the other Sunday afternoon, which was something I needed as I needed oxygen.

'That was lucky,' she said. And she gave me a smile, as if congratulating me on being the kind of person to whom lucky things happened.

Seizing the moment, I put my arm round her in the same way as I had done on the dance floor, and pulled her gently towards me. She let her body topple against mine as the taxi swung round a curve, and went into a long kiss that sent the blood hissing round my veins like boiling steam. My swollen rod started pushing against its close-buttoned flannel barrier as if determined at all costs to get out. As we turned into Cornmarket Street and started to trundle towards Jericho, she brushed her hand lightly over my fly. For one delirious instant I thought she was going to take my plunger out, give it a taste of freedom, in that deft way of hers. I hoped so. Never mind the cab-driver. Let him mind his own blasted business. But she went no further than that gentle, mesmerizing stroking movement.

When we got to Canal street she made me stop the taxi. She didn't want to draw up right at the door. And when I started to get out with her, she gently pushed me back. 'Don't come with me,' she said. 'They'll be watching out. Take the taxi on. Go back to College.'

'When shall I see you?' I demanded in a hoarse, shivering whisper.

'Soon,' she said cheerfully and was gone.

I told the taxi-driver to take me to Episcopus. It took about five minutes to get there. Under normal circumstances I would have spent that time worrying about how much I ought to tip the man. It was the first time I had ever been in a taxi. Would ten per cent be enough? What was usual? It was the kind of small problem that, in those days, had the power to worry me. But not tonight. My thoughts were on quite other things.

*

At the end of that term it was time for the big springtime event for rowing men, the series of races known quaintly as 'Torpids'. It would not be true to say that I looked forward to this event with mixed feelings. My feelings were not mixed. They were purely negative. Though not a rowing man and with not the slightest intention of going anywhere near the river during the three days in question, I nevertheless thought of the approach of Torpids with distaste, anxiety and apprehension.

The Collegiate boat races at Oxford are not started by lining the boats up in a straight line and firing a signal. The river, though wide, is not wide enough for that. The boats are arranged in line ahead, they start at timed intervals, and the object of the race is to close the gap between your boat and the one in front until your bow makes contact with its stern, however lightly. This is a Bump, and the next time the race is held, be it the next day or the next year, the two boats change places. By bumping enough boats, through the years, you can move up to be Head of the River. When a crew achieves a Bump, everybody goes back to College for a Bump Supper, at which drinks flow freely, hearts are high, and the usual restraints are largely relaxed.

The two or three hours after a Bump Supper are the sweetest hours of life for people like Dick Kent, the hours in which their bad qualities can briefly be passed off as good: when their pack-hunting need to Join In can move easily into aggression against individuals who, for one reason and another, stand out as not Joining In with sufficient enthusiasm.

This I knew, and therefore wished ill success to the Episcopus eight, though the actual rowers who composed it were, as far as I knew, decent men enough.

In spite of, or perhaps because of, my bad wishes the Episcopus crew did well that year. They managed to bump Hertford or some equally faceless outfit, and hold on to their advantage during the other two days, thus giving the Dick Kent brigade the joy of a Bump Supper. I would normally have stayed away, but I was so spent up that I could not afford to eat if I didn't go into Hall, and that one taste of hunger had made me careful to avoid a second. I went in and tried to find a place as far as possible from the nearest knot of hearties, which was difficult because they were more in evidence, and more spread out through the general mass, than usual. This, after all, was their hour.

Dinner took a long time because of all the toasts that had to be drunk. The dons had wisely hived off and were having dinner in their Common Room, and High Table was occupied by the rowing eight, plus the coach and the cox. Every member of the eight was toasted, and it was done by shouting out the letters of his name, so that Joe Bloggs came out as JAY

OH EE BEE ELL OH GEE GEE ESS. Some of them had names like Featherstonehaugh, which didn't help matters. But of course the hearties, determined to wring every drop of juice out of the occasion, loved every minute of it. I remember catching a glimpse of Kent's flushed face, his mouth wide-open in mid-guffaw. He looked half drunk already, and we were barely a third of the way through the meal.

As soon as I decently could I got away and went up to my room to read. Wilmot dropped in and we made some coffee and sat talking, shaking our heads in disapproval now and then as a particularly loud whoop, or the crash of something being broken, reached our ears. Fairly early – about ten – Wilmot said he would be getting back. He didn't say so in so many words, but I knew he meant he would go across to his rooms before the quad became definitely unsafe to walk about in.

I don't know what possessed me – some kind of bravado, I think – but I said I would come across with him and pick up a book he had been talking about and had offered to lend me. It sounded an interesting book and I thought it might do very well to engross me for the hour or so before I wanted to go to bed. Partly I did genuinely want the book, but there was also a tiny grain of resentful stubbornness that I recognized as part of my character. I had taken a lot of trouble to become a member of this college, and I was damned if I was going to be imprisoned in one hole in it, like a rat, just because a few hearties wanted to re-live their days at Public School. If I wanted to go across to Wilmot's place and borrow a book, by God I was going to.

We went into the quad, trying to keep up some sort of small-talk, as if this were a normal evening with a normal atmosphere. We must have resembled two young subalterns whose duties required them to cross No Man's Land and who were trying not to show fear. There was, as a matter of fact, not much noise about at that moment – just a steady drumming of feet as louts clumped up and down staircases, and in the distance a burst of drunken singing followed by a crash of something falling over; it sounded like a cupboard.

I took the book, thanked Wilmot, and set off through the relative safety of his quad, aiming at the passageway and then the relative danger of my quad – of which, however, I only had to traverse a corner. But, as luck would have it, I emerged from the narrow archway just in time to see a knot of men, among whom I recognized Kent, appear at the foot of a staircase over to my left.

'Ah, there's Leonard,' I heard Kent say. 'We ought not to neglect him. He's another of that type.'

What type? I tried hard not to quicken my pace too obviously.

'Oh, well, there's plenty of time,' said another voice. 'Let's attend to the Urquhart swine first. He's the one who's really been asking for it.'

Gerard Urquhart's rooms were on the ground floor of the staircase next to where these men were gathered. As I moved away, thankful at least to have time to get up to my room and sport the oak before they remembered me again, I heard them banging on his door and shouting to him, with a variety of insults, to come out. There was a brief silence and then Kent's voice floated clearly over to me: 'The swine must be out.'

'It's like him,' came another voice, 'to be out of College on a night when he ought to be here, celebrating the Bump. Let's go in and leave him a few signs of what we think of him.'

I waited to hear no more. If those arrogant vandals were going to wreck Gerard's rooms, going to pull his pictures down from the walls, scatter his books and papers about, rip down his curtains and all the rest of it, I simply did not want to be in earshot. I wanted to forget that they and I were in the same College, at the same University, or even belonged to the same species.

I got up to my room, went in and sported the oak. In theory I was now perfectly safe. To smash down an oak door is a very difficult job, calling for strength, determination, and skill, not to say adequate tools. There was virtually no possibility that this mob, even if they remembered my existence as 'another of that type', even if they came surging up the staircase yelling for my blood, would actually be able to get at me.

I knew that, and yet I didn't *feel* safe. I felt as if Episcopus College had suddenly become a totally hostile place, a place where I was not wanted and which held out no promise except of trouble. Once again, this was not objectively true. Objectively, I knew that this gang of expensively-educated hooligans was a minority in the College. They represented, it was true, the Public School tradition that was in the majority, but only one part of that tradition. They were the ones who had not been able to make the transition from school to university. After all those years spent adjusting to a purely physical aristocracy, a society where the only thing that mattered was to be big and strong and loud, they had been unable to make the crossing to a society like Oxford, where other values, for the most part, obtained. They had an underlying nostalgia for that simple barbarism where might was right and Rugger boots and boxing gloves were the symbols of power, and at licensed moments of Saturnalia they retreated back into it.

But why, I wondered, did they lump me with Gerard? Me, of all people? What had I, so bread-and butter, so commonplace, so unredeemably West Oxford, have in common with a brilliant man from a brilliant background?

That question was to resolve itself in due course. At the moment, I had no energy to spare for speculation. I went into my bedroom and sat on the edge of the bed, fully clothed, with a fast-beating heart. What were they doing in Gerard's rooms? Where was he? Was he coming back tonight? If so, would he confront them in the middle of their work of destruction – and then, what? I had a very clear vision, suddenly, of Gerard with his scarlet corduroys and his intent, serious, self-forgetful face. It was like Lamont's face except that it was intent where Lamont was dreamy. Why, for that matter, did these thugs not go after Lamont? God forbid that they should, but why didn't they? Was Lamont not 'another of the same type'?

I sat there, lonely and frightened, unable to think of going to bed. All I could hope for was that the pack would be so far gone in drunken disorganization that for me to be out of sight would be out of mind. If only their riotous aggressiveness would spend itself and die down before they remembered about me... In short, I had the old ignoble wish that nearly every victim has had in his heart since the world began: O God, please make them pick on someone else, and not me.

My prayer, unspoken and perhaps not even fully formulated, but there as a strong wish at the centre of my being, was in vain. I heard shouts in the quad, then more shouts. Soon – and pure terror gripped me – I heard heavy feet on the twisting wooden stairs. They had remembered. They were coming for me. No, no, it must be somebody lower down. It must be somebody on the floor below. No. It was me.

When the pounding of fists and toe-caps on my oak began, I tried for a moment or two to hold down my rising panic. They can't get in, I said to myself. That's what oaks are for. They won't be able to get in and they'll go away. But the noise was so terrifying that my mind could take no consolation from such reasonableness. It had never happened to me before, and thank God it has never happened to me since, to be on one side of a single door, no matter how strong, with a hostile mob on the other, and to hear them beating on its uncomplaining surface. And suddenly I knew I could stand it no longer.

I know how some people will despise that admission. All right, I was losing self-command. A man of action, used to keeping cool in tight corners, would have taken this one in his stride. But I was not, nor am I now, a man of action. Historians speculate as to the reasons for decisions; they do not take them. My mind was suddenly flooded with horrible, unnerving images. In a flash I remembered all those stories of lynch mobs breaking into lock-ups in the Southern United States and dragging prisoners out from the cells. We have all heard these stories, and though we manage to forget about them for long periods they never really go away.

The shocks against the door had settled down to a steady rhythm, as if three or four of them were getting their shoulders to it. I heard Kent's voice say, 'The little swine's in there, that's one thing – we've cornered him.'

I got to my feet. My bedroom had one small window, rather high up. By standing on a chair I could easily put my hands on its sill, then swing up and clamber out under the night sky. Between the window and the horrifying drop to the ground was a row of battlements, and between the battlements and the steeply sloping roof was a narrow gully, just possible to walk along. I wriggled through the window, stood up and, steadying myself against the nearest stonework, moved along towards the right-angle corner. A couple of other bedroom windows looked out on that side like mine, but they were dark and closed. I was alone with the hugeness of the medieval roof. Below me I could hear voices in the quad, but I seemed a long way above them; they had no connection with me, they were not the voices of people I knew or would ever know. I was as alone under the cloudy night sky as an owl perching on the roof of a barn.

So far, so good. But I was a terribly long way from the ground. I had no head for heights, and would never have gone climbing about the roof at night if the greater fear had not driven out the less. Suppose those louts were successful, finally, in breaking down that door and trampling in to my room? Flushed with success, half drunk and lusting for violence, they would soon realize where I had gone. Sick terror seized me again as I pictured half-a-dozen of them, perhaps led by that swine Kent, scrambling out through my window and coming after me along that narrow gully. Alcohol would have made their movements imprecise: a scuffle as they collared me, a few clumsy movements, and one or other of them would be over the edge and falling, falling, to be crushed and smashed in the quad. Them I didn't care about, but whoever fell would refuse to let go his hold on me, he would clutch at me first in aggressiveness and then in panic... no. Overwhelmed by vertigo, I sank down with my hand over my eyes, hungrily spreading the fingers of my other hand to feel the solidity of the roof-tiles I was leaning my back against.

But, thank God, my oak must have resisted them. No one came after me. Slowly, very slowly, my fear subsided. I could hear, but distantly, the beating on my oak door; they were not giving up yet, or perhaps the beating was seen as an end in itself, a way of terrifying me. The emptiness of the night, the quietness of the sky over the roof, calmed me. I was near the chapel clock, and now it began to strike the hour: eleven.

All was silent now. They had gone. I was beginning to shiver in the night air, and the shivering broke my mood of peace. As I wriggled back through my bedroom window I decided that if I were ever again to be living in College on the occasion of a Bump Supper, I would go down to the Bargeman's and spend the night there.

I fell asleep straight away, and stayed asleep till, in the thin morning sunlight, there was again a knocking at my oak, insistent enough to wake me. But this was a very different knocking – querulous, but not threatening – made by one pair of gnarled old knuckles. Arthur had come to bring me my hot water and light the fire.

I got up, breakfasted, and went down the stairs and out into the garden in the springtime freshness of the air. I felt light and easy, as if having survived last night had been to pass some kind of test, a hurdle that had to be got over so that I could go on to the next stage of life. Term ended today and I was free to pack up and go at any time. Life seemed, at that moment, relaxed and pleasant. If only I had felt more confidence about seeing Vinnie again and getting what I wanted from her, I think I would actually have been happy.

The clamour of birdsong, and the delicate, bud-opening loveliness of the garden, had made me forget the more distasteful episodes of the last twelve hours, but of course I could not forget them for long. As I came back across the quad I saw two figures standing near the lodge. They were Kent and Lamont. Kent seemed to be listening and Lamont to be talking, but he was not raising his voice and I could not catch what he was saying without going right up to them. This I determined to do. Lamont's opinion of Kent would be well worth hearing. As I approached, Knowlton came out of the lodge and he, too, was drawn by what was going on. He halted beside Lamont, his long, loose-knit body canted over slightly as he listened. I got right up to them and stood there, frankly taking it in.

Lamont was pale with anger. He was speaking quietly but with an intensity that gave his voice a cutting edge I had not known him capable of.

'It's men like you,' he was saying to Kent, 'who bring this College down to your own dead level. If anybody has any mind or any distinction, you want to drag them down.'

Kent stood his ground. His glasses made his eyes look fish-like, and he trained them on Lamont's face with dispassionate insolence.

'That's not how I see it, of course,' he said. 'I think I'm more representative of College opinion than you are, and I see a number of little squits around the place who need bringing up, not down.'

'Who and what were you bringing up last night?' Knowlton put in. 'Doing that damage in Urquhart's rooms, that was a bad show.'

'He's just the type I'm talking about,' Kent snapped. 'He's not wanted here. He makes no effort to fit in.'

'Fit in?' Lamont's voice was incredulous. 'Fit in with a gang of louts whose idea of fun is to drink a few pots of beer and then look for something to smash up?'

'I say again, he's not wanted here. He doesn't join in anything. And he's a womanizer.'

'What nonsense! You simply have no idea what you're –'

'Once a college gets full of womanizers,' Kent interrupted in a high, steady tone that indicated his belief that he was winning the argument, 'the whole tone goes down. You get a lot of little squits who think chasing girls is the thing to do. I see Leonard's standing here listening. Ask him if you don't believe me. He's a little squit of a womanizer. He takes town shopgirls up to his room. Turns the place into a whore-house.'

If only it were true, I thought.

'You're pushing it too far, Kent,' Knowlton said in his calm way. 'If a man doesn't make a nuisance of himself to other people, why not leave him alone? What your lot did to Urquhart's stuff was a bad show, there's no other way of looking at it.'

'Look, Knowlton,' Kent rounded on him, 'you're in your second term here and I'm in my fourth year.'

'What of it? You're a medical.'

'What of it is that I'm not going to stand here and be told by you what's a bad show and what isn't.'

'What I hope,' said Lamont, 'is that you and those other vandals will get sent down for what happened last night. But I suppose that's too much to hope for. It'll be a fine and a mild wigging. Boys will be boys, won't they? But since you're in your fourth year, the time can't be far away when we'll see the back of you. I'm living for that.'

'Don't pin any hopes on it,' Kent said composedly. 'There'll be plenty more like me coming along. You can't turn the place into a nest of cranks and guttersnipes and womanizers in five minutes.'

'And you can't keep it for ever as an imitation of a third-rate

Rugger-playing Public School. Your type had their day, Kent, when King Edward was on the throne.'

'We seem to be doing all right under King George.' But Kent's retort was addressed to Lamont's back. He had turned on his heel and was striding away.

'I think you ought to draw it mild, Kent,' Knowlton said equably, looking down from his giraffe-height. 'I mean, there are quite a lot of people who think that last night –'

'Knowlton, if you tell me once more that last night was a bad show, I'm going to hit you right in the face.'

'I don't think you'd better,' Knowlton said gently. 'I'm pretty big, you know. If I fell on you I might hurt you.'

Kent, after a final cold glare, took himself off. I went too, in a different direction. As I went I heard Knowlton saying to himself, regretfully, 'Bad show. A very poor show.'

As I climbed the stairs to my room I reflected that one thing that had been baffling me had now become clear, at any rate. I had wondered what on earth could have led Kent to say that Gerard and I were 'the same type'. Now I saw it all. In his eyes we were both womanizers. The love that flowed so naturally, so reciprocally, so luminously between Gerard and Annabel was, from where Kent was standing, no different from my sated but shamefaced scurry across the quad with Vinnie, trying to get her out unnoticed.

That was the end of my second term as a member of Oxford University, vintage 1930-31. It was also, incidentally, the end of Gerard's attempt to find a relationship with the place. I learnt later that he had come back to College just before midnight to find his rooms wrecked, his books scattered about, his papers torn up, a pile of gramophone records broken and the gramophone itself knocked off its stand, and a lot of grinning louts hanging about to see his discomfiture. He showed none. He simply turned and walked over to the lodge and asked Frank to let him out. Frank refused, pointing out that after ten o'clock he was allowed to open the gate only for ingress, not for egress. So Gerard walked coolly to one of the recognized climbing-out places, swung himself over the wall, and vanished into the night. Where he went to, no one ever heard. Perhaps he went down to the station and sat on a bench till the first train to London left at dawn. But wherever he went that night, he never came to Episcopus again.

I said that was the end of my term, but there were still two hours to go.

The ugly scene with Kent had left an unpleasant taste in my mind. I didn't want my second term, which on the whole had been fairly successful, to end in such a damp spirit: and suddenly I knew what would raise my spirits. A magnificent act of improvident folly. I was supposed to be an historian, wasn't I? A man committed to study and learning? Well, a learned man needs books as he needs air and food. I owned far too few books; I relied on the College library and a few battered volumes picked up cheaply and usually just about falling to pieces when I got them. Well, this morning I was going to go to a bookshop, a big, famous-name, fabulously-stocked bookshop, and Lash Out. So I marched round to the shop and straight into the history section. The excitement! I can still feel it. All those books, some tall, some squat, some in dust jackets, some proudly showing their gilt lettering without such trumpery – books, books, of every kind, and I could have any I wanted, and I deserved to because I was a scholar and a dedicated historian, Leonard of Episcopus, you probably know his monograph on... his monograph on...

In the end I woke from my dream enough to choose one book and carry it away – and what a book – *The Cambridge Modern History Atlas*, a good clean second-hand copy, not much used. I couldn't imagine, as I stood there leafing through it, fingering the lovely thick paper, why it hadn't been much used. I was positively salivating at all those maps with coloured patches that showed you at a glance how some social force, or political decision, or military campaign, affected what regions of which countries – all with delicate, elegant colour printing that was a delight to the eye, and neat little colour keys in the top right-hand corner. And then, the economy! A map could show you the situation at a glance where pages of writing would only leave you confused. I was particularly delighted by Numbers 113 and 114, 'England and Wales: Parliamentary Representation in 1832 *before* the Reform Bill,' and ditto '*after* the Reform Bill'. Then again, the great colourful sweep of Number 3, a two-page spread of 'The Ottoman Advance in Europe and Asia Minor'. I had intended when I went into the shop to buy a new book for once, but this was far better than your ordinary new book; it was luxury, connoisseurship, bibliophily as well as scholarly information. It was a copy of the printing of 1912, a good period of book production when paper and materials were cheap and so was craftsmanship. Even so, they were asking the princely sum of four pounds for it. *Four pounds!* And I paid it, or rather bound myself to pay it one day, without a murmur. As I did so I reflected on the irony of its being exactly twice the sum I had chiselled out of my father with that lying story about needing to buy academic books, when my actual motive had been to keep up the long-drawn-out effort to home in on my obsessional target, to wit,

Vinnie's little white knickers. Evidently the lie I had told my father had not, at a deep level, been much of a lie after all. My need for scholarly books was a real need.

I carried the stately volume back to College and installed it proudly on the best shelf. It wasn't to stay there, of course; after lunch it was coming to the Bargeman's, to irradiate the vac. for me. That reminded me; I needed to get my ration of books from the library for those weeks (we were allowed, I think, five). I set off to the library staircase. Halfway across the quad I saw a figure moving steadily on a collision course with mine, a tall, thin figure; looking at me; evidently intending to address some kind of remark to me. I slowed down, stopped, waited. It was the Senior Tutor, Gadsby. I had almost forgotten his existence. All through these two terms he had simply been part of the remote frieze of don-figures that moved slowly and majestically across the end wall of my life. Gadsby! It was his doing, not intentionally but by a direct chain of causation, that I had taken that look at Vinnie's bird's nest in the shower-room that morning, that long, obsessional ogle at her crotch that had turned me there and then into a sexual maniac. Gadsby! I thought. You have a lot to answer for!

Gadsby had a way of moving his mouth as if he were chewing. He was not actually chewing anything, just masticating his own saliva. He also had a habit, when he looked at you, of taking his glasses off, and then putting them back on and looking at you again, and sometimes taking them off and replacing them three or four times during a conversation, as if he could not decide whether it was preferable to see your face dimly or clearly. Each alternative had, no doubt, something to be said for it. He was looking at me now, chewing and taking off his glasses; attentively; with manifest recognition; and benevolently.

'Ah, Leonard,' he said. He knew my name too. 'Leonard. I trust you've had... a fruitful term.'

Fruitful? I thought. I've read a lot of books, had one multiple fuck, and on one evening had to hide on the roof like a frightened cat. Vocally I said, 'Yes, thank you, Mr Gadsby.'

'I'm glad,' he said. 'Glad to hear it.' He stood there with the spring sunshine shining on his thinning hair and bringing out the dark red of his neatly arranged bow tie. He looked like a casting director's dream of the Distinguished Oxford Don, saliva-chewing and all. I, slight, fair-haired and respectful, must have looked like the equivalent image of the Good Student.

'I hope,' Gadsby pursued, 'I hope your interest in historical study is...'

He seemed at a loss for a word. Is what? Flourishing? Declining? Being killed by surfeit? Revealing itself as a transient phase? '...burgeoning,' he finally brought out.

'Oh, yes,' I said. I nodded to show how thoroughly it was burgeoning.

'I'm glad to hear it,' he said again. 'There is... so much to be quarried.' He seemed to be trying to tell me something. 'Historical materials exist in abundance. Young minds...' He put his glasses on, stared at me, took them off and said, 'keen minds... if an interest could be kept alive...'

He gave me another benevolent look and moved away without finishing the sentence he appeared to have begun. I went on up the stairs to the library. I had no idea what Gadsby was trying to convey to me, but it was evident that he wished me well, and that was good enough for the present.

I did what I had to do in the library and then it was nearly time to dump my suitcase in the lodge and pedal off down to the Bargeman's, a free man, the second term of my undergraduate life safely under my belt. One down and seven to go. The nature of my life in those seven would depend, of course, on whether I had done well enough in the Honours Moderations exams to be accepted in the Honours School, but I felt that it would probably be all right and it was too late to worry anyway. The exams had not been too difficult, and I had done my best, though I knew I could have done a lot better if my sexual frustration had not been tying me up in knots and my throbbing prick drawing all the blood away from my brain.

I took my suitcase into the lodge and asked Frank if it could stay there for an hour or two, receiving no verbal answer but a simple, stately inclination of the head: down once, back up once, and the matter was disposed of. As I came out I saw Fred Armitage and young McFarlane, outside on the pavement, having an argument with a taxi-driver. I stood and took it all in like any street-corner idler. The situation was that they both wanted to go to Oxford station, the train that was to take Armitage back to Yorkshire being the same that would then carry McFarlane back to Scotland; they each had some heavy luggage, and they each had a bicycle. Their simple plan had been to load their luggage into the taxi, send it on to the station, and themselves follow on their bicycles, arriving at the same time or a couple of minutes later. The driver, snorting at the ridiculousness of the idea, was telling them he was licensed to carry passengers, not freight, and that they had brought him out for nothing, an action which would cost them one shilling and sixpence.

‘One and six, that is. Now let’s be ’avin’ it and let me get off and earn a real fare. I’ve lost my place on the rank over this wild-goose chase. I’m surprised you didn’t know better.’

The two of them looked miserably comical as they stood there, bowing to the wind of the cabman’s rebuke, Armitage tall and raw-boned, his knobby wrists poking out of his tweed jacket as if his arms had grown longer since his careful parents had supplied him with it in September or the first days of October – and perhaps, with all his rowing, they had – and McFarlane pink and round-faced, with a haircut like a little boy’s and that air of pre-pubescent harmlessness he always wore.

‘One and six,’ the man repeated. ‘And I ’aven’t got all day.’

Something about his ill-temper rubbed me up the wrong way and I stepped forward and offered to ride one of the bicycles to the station. That way, Armitage or McFarlane could go in the taxi and count as a normal passenger with a slightly abnormal amount of luggage.

The driver accepted this; reluctantly, as if it hurt him to relinquish a legitimate cause of annoyance. He wanted to find these two undergraduates an absurd nuisance so that he could go away and talk about what an absurd nuisance they had been. But in the end, having had a satisfying grumble, he decided to do business.

So it came about that I was riding McFarlane’s bicycle while Armitage rode his own and McFarlane travelled in the taxi, looking exactly like a schoolboy going home for the holidays, which was, essentially, what he was. When we arrived, the taxi had been there long enough for the luggage to be unloaded and the driver to be standing by his vehicle trying to look like a man who had been kept waiting. I propped McFarlane’s bike on one pedal against the kerb and stood there for a moment while they settled the fare, and as I did so another cab drew up and Annabel Graveney got out. She looked incredibly beautiful with the hard fresh sunlight bringing out the lustre of her hair, and also rather pale and withdrawn, very much as if she did not want to be spoken to.

‘Will you give me a hand with these?’ I couldn’t help overhearing her words to her taxi-driver; she was standing within about five feet of me. Indeed, I could not tell whether she had seen me or not, and if she had whether she knew who I was. She ignored me, not in the purposeful way that goes with cutting someone dead, but rather as if her thoughts were turned so entirely inward that the people about her simply did not impinge on her attention. Or was there something else? Did I suggest Episcopus to her, and did she now hate Episcopus for Gerard’s sake?

The driver, grunting with effort, lifted out two very large suitcases, each secured by a leather strap, and a soft bag which probably held shoes, and a tightly-crammed briefcase which looked to be full of books. It seemed a great deal of stuff to be taking away for a five-week vacation. Was Annabel shaking the dust of Oxford off her feet? I didn't, of course, know for certain at that point that Gerard was not coming back, but I felt it was a strong possibility. Was she going to join him? If so, where? And would I ever see her again?

She told the driver she wanted a porter, and he went off to find one. (That kind of thing happened in those days.) While she waited, holding her cloak about her as if keeping her whole being secret and apart, not sharing it with anyone till she got to Gerard again, Annabel stood looking unswervingly ahead of her. I could only think, How straight her back is. No other coherent thought formed itself.

A voice at my elbow was thanking me and inviting me to have a glass of beer. It was Fred Armitage. At least he broke the spell that was keeping me standing there, gawking at Annabel. We entered the station and went into the refreshment room. To do this meant equipping me with a platform ticket, price one penny. Armitage regally provided it.

The two of them thanked me again and we made some desultory conversation, but they had to attend to various matters concerning bicycle tickets and what-not, and they drank up and left me with half my beer still in the glass. I drank slowly, looking about me, wondering if Annabel would come in, but she must have gone straight through to the platform.

I did, however, see Lamont. He was sitting in a corner of the refreshment room with a drink at his elbow and his suitcase beside him, obviously waiting for a train. His eyes were intent on a paper-covered book (they were rarer, in those pre-Penguin days, and usually indicated Continental origin), and that single lock of hair had fallen across his wide brow. The expression of his face was totally concentrated; I had time to study it and to notice his mouth; how sensitive it seemed, the lower lip rather full but not so much as to disturb the austerity of his face by any infusion of commonplace sensuality. After a while the mere fact that I was looking at him made him raise his eyes from the book. He recognized me and gave a friendly but non-encouraging smile. Then he took a sip from his glass, set it down and went on reading.

I was embarrassed to have him look up and find me staring at him, just as a few minutes before I had been staring at Annabel Graveney. Was that all I did with myself when I was not studying history, just stare at people who were more intelligent and beautiful and generally worth-staring-at than I?

I drank up and moved out of the refreshment room. As I passed close to Lamont I glanced, compulsively, at the title of the book that was claiming his attention so totally. It was *Opere di Leopardi*. How narrow my world still was; how these gifted, creative, instructed people wandered freely in realm after realm that I was hardly beginning to guess at, for all my large ambitions and my strong resolves. What went on, what actually did go on, in the mind of a man like Lamont? And come to that, who the hell was Leopardi?

Chapter 10

I needed money. So did a lot of people, in 1931. They mostly needed it for survival, just to have a roof over their heads and food on the table. I needed it to try to make some kind of approach to Vinnie, which in its own way was also a matter of survival. Lying in bed one spring morning not long after my arrival back at the Bargeman's Arms, with the energetic cawing of the rooks coming into the room from the budding trees in somebody's garden, I stopped, for once, fantasizing about what I would do with Vinnie if I could only get close to her in a willing mood, and switched to hard, concrete practical thoughts about ways and means. Clearly there was no point in approaching her, even reminding her of my existence, until I was in a position to take her out and give her a good time, at least once and preferably more than once so that she would begin to associate me with good times.

But money? There was damned little of it about. Wages were very low even if you were in work, and as for the unemployed, the dole they got was just about calculated to keep them alive; indeed, young, active working men often spent most of the day in bed because if they got up they would go out, and if they went out they would walk about, and if they walked about they would work up an appetite which they couldn't afford to buy enough food to satisfy. 'No going back to the nineteen-thirties' is a slogan one hears very often, nowadays, in Socialist oratory. Most of the people who utter this slogan have no knowledge of what the nineteen-thirties were like and couldn't even imagine them.

Our family, being in small trade and in all seriousness thinking of ourselves as middle class, when we thought of the matter at all, were of course aristocrats compared with the really underprivileged. Even so, there was never a penny to spare. My parents never had any help in running the pub, which meant of course that they never had any time off from one year's end to another, simply because they couldn't afford it. The only help they ever got was from me. I could see well enough that even if I increased the number of hours I put in behind the bar there would be no point in my asking the old man to pay me anything. Quite apart from everything else, there wasn't the work to do. In those days, the working man couldn't afford to go to the pub every evening. He went on Saturday, after getting his wage packet at midday, and if he had any money left over he went again on Sunday morning. The enormous beer-gut so commonly seen on the working man of our day is not, as the middle classes believe, a deformity. It is a trophy, the proud sign that a social and political battle has been fought and won.

There was no point, then, in asking Dad for this much-needed subvention. On the other hand, I could always do what he himself did to eke out his income: see if there was anything to do at the brewery. There were some drawbacks to this, the chief one being that if we were both working at the same place I might run into him one day, and he might ask me what I was doing there, and when I said I was earning money on the side he would expect me to give some to Mother. But I decided to cross that bridge when I came to it. There was, as I saw it, no real alternative to the brewery. Morris Motors would never take me on part-time for a few weeks, nor would the railway; the colleges were out of the question. As a guide to sightseers you had, I vaguely believed, to be licensed by the City, and they were unlikely to license me. As a last resort I toyed with the notion of picking the pockets of wealthy tourists as they stood gazing raptly at the beauty of Oxford's architecture, but I had enough self-knowledge to admit that I had neither the skill nor the nerve for such an enterprise. It would have to be the brewery.

Tingling with resolve, I got out of bed, dressed, breakfasted and by a quarter to nine I was at the gates of the brewery yard. A middle-aged man in blue overalls was sitting on an upturned barrow, reading a single sheet of newspaper, just the fold containing the front and back pages. Where the rest of the paper was I didn't know. I told him I had been sent to enquire if there were any temporary jobs going and asked where I should ask. The bit about being 'sent to enquire' was just camouflage, to make it a little less embarrassing to ask the question.

He showed no surprise, merely jerking his head over to an unpainted wooden door in the corner of the yard and saying, 'You want Ken. He's in there.'

I thanked him and went over and knocked at the door. Ken came out and looked me up and down. He was a fat, youngish man who looked as if he sweated a lot. His face, and what you could see of his neck, looked as if he had had a surgical operation to remove most of the flesh and pump in lard instead.

'You want what?' he said.

'Just to know about casual work,' I said. 'I could fit in with any time.' I was going to add 'for the next four weeks', but I didn't. I had an inhibition about letting him know I was a student at the University. I thought it might go against me.

I needn't have worried. So many things were going against me that one more would have made no difference. He surveyed my thin, unmuscular form as I stood there in the thin April sunshine.

'We don't need no casual work in the office,' he said.

'I meant outside,' I said.

'Outside?' Ken echoed. '*Outside*?'

'Yes,' I said. 'Outside. In the open air. Like, not inside.'

'Listen, sonny,' he said pityingly, 'the only outside work we do here is loading.'

'I know.'

'No, you don't know. You can't know, since you wouldn't come here askin' about it and wastin' my time. It's *loadin'*. It's work for a strong bloke.'

'I can try,' I said. 'I can roll barrels about.'

'A monkey eighteen inches high can roll a barrel,' Ken said. 'A lot of this is liftin'. Crates of bottles. Liftin' 'em up on to lorries. Stackin' 'em up high, liftin' 'em above your 'ead. You wouldn't live a day, sonny. The first one you tried to lift'd bring you out in a rupture.'

'Give me a chance,' I was going to say, but I only got as far as 'Give me' before he interrupted me with, 'Do me a favour, laddie. Run away and play marbles.'

He went back into the office. I stood there looking at the door after he had closed it behind him and all of a sudden, out of sheer nervous reaction, I felt cold and began to shiver. There were a couple of youths standing about in the yard, smoking, and I wondered if they had heard Ken brush me off so contemptuously. He despised me because he could tell from looking at me that I hadn't what he would have called a man's strength.

I mooched out of the yard. The day loomed ahead of me like a mountain I had to scale before nightfall; and another the next day, and another the next. My books were waiting at home, but my books were always waiting, and for the present they would just have to wait. I couldn't settle to anything. My mind, that trained mind that already made Ken's look simian, was no use to me today. All my plotting and scheming was aimed at getting one thing, and I had as much chance of getting it as of being crowned King of England.

I needed to put my body in motion, but where to? The brewery was in the tangle of streets, waterways and bridges that used to lie – and, in a chopped-up and reduced form, still does lie – between the railway goods yards and the solitary remaining tower of Oxford Castle. I walked up to Fisher Row. I went through Paradise Square – slums then, a meaningless blank space now. I looked at the oblong tower of the Castle, with its curiously Provençal air, as if it had strayed into the wrong country; I looked at the high, blank wall of Oxford prison behind it, with the barbed wire on top and the little iron-grilled windows and the stink of misery coming out of it day and night; I threaded my way up Castle Street and towards Carfax: and suddenly I realized where my feet were taking me.

Yes, to the shoe-shop. What had I better to do than hang about in Cornmarket Street, all morning if necessary, on the off-chance of catching a glimpse of Vinnie? But no, it wasn't as consciously formed as that, it was simply a compulsion, a mindless need to get myself into a space that was somewhere near the space she occupied.

Here was the shoe-shop. I walked past, slowly. No sign of Vinnie in the restricted part of the interior that I could see from outside. I turned and walked past slowly again. Same non-result. I didn't dare open the door and look in, much less go in. I had no clear idea of what was Vinnie's attitude to me, but if that attitude contained any streak of resentment or irritation I would only make everything worse by intruding into the shop and embarrassing her, possibly even drawing down on her the displeasure of the people who ran the place.

I repeated the walking-to-and-fro manoeuvre about six times, then stationed myself outside the window of the shop next door and kept an eye on the door of the shoe-shop in case Vinnie, for any reason, came out. But why should she come out? It was barely nine o'clock. After a while I crossed the road and watched the shop window from an inconspicuous distance. But people kept getting in the way, people and buses and cars and bicycles, and once I could almost have sworn that I saw Vinnie in the window, a slender graceful figure in that regulation blue-and-white overall, but my view was blocked again and when I next saw the window clearly, Vinnie-or-whoever had gone. This was torture, and self-torture at that, but to walk away and go somewhere else and try to think different thoughts would have been an even worse torture, and this was at least honest; it was doing what I wanted, or at any rate felt compelled, to do.

Thinking this, feeling disconcerted, I walked across the road and stood directly in front of the shoe-shop window. What use was concealment? I felt desperate, light-headed; everything seemed unreal.

And at that very moment, when I seemed to have crossed into a dream-dimension, Vinnie came out of the interior of the shop and stepped into the window. The sunlight fell on her face, and brought out the lustre of her brown hair, as she stood there, adjusting a display-stand, separated from me only by a sheet of plate-glass that I could have shattered with a brick.

I was mesmerized, I stood utterly still; a woman carrying a heavy shopping bag brushed rapidly past me, allowing the bag to cannon into my ribs – I noticed it no more than a fly landing on my shoulder. Vinnie was there, so demonaically attractive, utterly unreachable and yet so close to me in space. But for the glass I could have touched her. I stood there, oblivious of the people trying to get past, oblivious even of whether she knew I was there or not. Staring at her now, it struck me that I had never noticed before how beautiful her hands and feet were: small, perfectly shaped, neat. She had on little black slippers, like ballet shoes, and she seemed instinctively to put her feet into graceful attitudes as an animal does, while her incredibly erotic little hands did delicate things to expensive shoes.

I must have looked like a mental patient, or perhaps a person about to lose consciousness through an abrupt fall in blood-pressure (syncope). Since there are so many medical men in Oxford, it surprises me, looking back, that one of them did not notice my condition and lay me down on my right side, knees drawn up, till an ambulance could be summoned. Instead, what happened was this. Vinnie slowly turned her head, looked straight into my face through the plate-glass, and – briefly, but without haste, and beyond all possibility of error – closed one eye in a wink.

I even remember which eye it was: the left. She was facing south, which meant that her right-hand quarter-profile would be visible from the interior of the shop. She could wink with the left eye in perfect confidence, and wink with it she did.

I gaped, I gave a wide, foolish grin, and then she was gone. The window was empty. I strode off towards Carfax, my mind and body on fire. There was room in my being for only one thought: *money, money, money*. I was going to get hold of some money, somewhere, somehow, and when I had my pockets stuffed with it I was going to go and confront Vinnie and invite her out to do whatever high, wide and handsome thing she had a mind to, anything, anything, so long as I ended up between her legs.

Mesmerized by these thoughts, I walked aimlessly as far as Folly Bridge and leaned on the stone parapet, looking down at the sweeping, swirling surface of the river, now gathered to its spring fullness. (Like me, I reflected; but the river had the ever-receptive sea to flow towards.) Then, my gaze shifting a little, I noticed a long punt turned bottom upwards on a wooden landing-stage directly below me. Someone was bent over it in the chill sunshine, working away with a pot of paint and a brush. I couldn't see his face, but something about his stance and movements made me think that I knew this person. I continued to look down at him until, in that strange way that people seem to feel your eyes on them if you stare hard enough, he looked up and I saw it was my old mate from school, Tupper Boardman. Since, as I now recalled, his father owned this business and he was in fact standing just under a large sign that said BOARDMAN. BOATS FOR HIRE. DAY OR HOUR, I can't say I was surprised; but it broke unexpectedly into my train of thought to see him, not having thought about him since the day I left school.

He looked up now, recognized me, grinned, and said, 'Hey, boy.'

'Hullo there,' I said.

Tupper laid his paintbrush across the can, as if glad to stop work for a moment, and straightened up. 'They let you out sometimes, then?'

'Quite a lot,' I said. 'About half the year, for a start.'

'Cor,' he said. 'What d'you do when they let you out?'

'Nothing much. Read a lot. Walk around a lot. I suppose it's just chance that I haven't seen you.'

'Well, come down and talk to me while I paint this bugger. Got to finish 'er by dinnertime.'

I went down and joined him on the boards. It was pleasant down at river-level. The sun shone more warmly than on the windy bridge and the traffic noise reached us only as a gentler *swish, swish-swish, swish*. I looked at Tupper, his good-natured round face and beefy arms in rolled-up sleeves.

'And what do you do with yourself, boy?' I asked, relaxing, easy in his company.

'Work on bloody boats,' he said. 'And in between, keep a watch out for chances of getting my end away.'

This last phrase, as I knew well enough, was a demotic expression signifying the deed of procreation.

I had nothing I wanted to do that morning, except try to stop thinking about Vinnie, and I knew it would rest me to be with Tupper. On the other hand I couldn't just stand about and watch him work.

'Got another brush?' I asked. 'I'll help you, then we'll soon get it done.'

'Good,' he said. 'I'm off duty for an hour when this is finished. We could go for a drink.'

So we painted the boat together and then went and sat in the cosy little pub a few yards up the road, and laughed and joked and boasted a little and started on the job of getting to know each other again. Only a few months ago we had seen each other every day, but both our lives had changed since then and he needed to know if the mysterious influence of 'College' had changed me into a different kind of animal. The quickest way to convince him that it hadn't, that I was still the Peter Leonard with whom he had trudged off to the tennis courts on all those summer evenings hoping to Get to Know Girls, was to dive back into that great and abiding subject.

To hear Tupper tell it, he had enjoyed a good deal of *bonne fortune* in the few short months since his life had passed from my daily observation. I listened appreciatively but with not much conviction that I was hearing historical truth. He always was a terrible romancer. When he fell silent and asked me to tell him how I had been getting on in the chase, I could of course have told him about my insanely ecstatic afternoon with Vinnie that Sunday. But for some reason, I couldn't. The details, though they were vividly present to my mind, just wouldn't get as far as my tongue. Part of it, I think, was due to a feeling that Tupper, having told me what I privately considered a pack of lies, didn't deserve the privilege of hearing the beautiful, knee-loosening, shattering truth I could have told him about my gambols with Vinnie on the mattress in front of that glowing fire, but beneath the bare recital there was something more sombre: an edge of suffering, of tragic foreboding. Vinnie had brought me that bliss – *once.* Was I confident, did I even half-expect, that it would ever happen again? And if it were to be a unique, once-and-for-all memory, then I must keep it wrapped up in the secrecy of my mind, not gabble it out in a pub to amuse a former school friend.

So I gave him the Vinnie business in mere outline; said I had something promising set up with a girl who was town, not gown, and that I was working on it. I didn't tell him Vinnie's name or give him any clue that would lead him to where she worked or lived. But I did give him to understand that my plans, if they were to be carried through, would need money and that I was currently looking for a vacation job.

I mentioned this merely in the spirit of friendly conversation, and was rather surprised when he promptly took me up on it. The firm could use an extra pair of hands for a few weeks just then; it was always a rush to get the boats ready for the season, and the office work kept his father chained up day after day, ordering new equipment and seeing to insurance for the boats and all the rest of it. I could work alongside

Tupper and he would show me the ropes. It would be fun; it would be like old times.

'And then in the evenings, when we get a bit of free time,' he said, 'we can relax and enjoy ourselves a bit. Go out on the town. P'raps I'll get to meet this, er, new hobby of yours,' and he dug me in the ribs.

Yes, I thought, when hell freezes over you'll meet Vinnie. I could see exactly what anybody as sharp and alert as she would think of anyone as shambling and blowsy-witted as Tupper. He was good-natured, of course; in that respect, I had to admit, he was a better human being than she was. But the reason I was desperate with longing for Vinnie was not because I mistook her for a good human being. It was because she maddened my senses and inflamed my emotions and unseated my reason.

Tupper presented me to his father as soon as work resumed after lunch, and his father took me on, there and then. My wages would be thirty shillings a week, which was good for unskilled labour, but against that I should have to work six and a half days: Sunday morning would be my only free time, and evenings after seven. I settled for it. The vac. had five weeks to run. Five thirties were a hundred and fifty. I would have seven pounds ten shillings to spend on taking Vinnie out. That ought to be good enough to earn me a few evenings when we were together but didn't go anywhere. And those would be the good ones.

*

It troubles my conscience, now, to recall that I said nothing at home about the job I was doing for old man Boardman. As a loving son – and I did, genuinely, love my mother – I ought to have made her burden easier for a few weeks by giving her a regular few shillings towards the cost of satisfying my young appetite. But the needs of another and equally imperious appetite interposed themselves. Until I could lay to rest that thick truncheon I was carrying around inside my trousers, I was simply not a human being. In short, I was a typical product of Oxford University as it was run then – not (needless to say) as it is run now.

As for Brian, he could hardly have been described as a typical product of British industry. Not for him the slow, monochrome, plodding life of an assembly-line worker, clocking in, clocking out, with his union endlessly haggling on his behalf about a little overtime here, five minutes extra on a tea-break there, and the resulting tiny victories or defeats providing the only events in his working life. Brian's working life was more like that of a member of some highly-strung opera company, forever driving themselves to the brink of collapse in the effort to mount one brilliantly creative production after another, battling it out with obtuse critics, an indifferent public, rival companies, all under the threat of bankruptcy. M.G. was his team, his world, his club, his religion. It enshrined his ideals, gathered in his interests. He wanted nothing in the world but to work on those stubby little racing cars, to look at them, sit in them, wheel them around, start their engines, smell their fuel. When he was not actually in the presence of these sacred machines he was reading or talking about them. On his days off, he wore a tie on which that octagonal badge was repeated on a background of dark Oxford blue. Whenever he changed his jacket he religiously transferred from one inner pocket to another his photograph of 'Old Number One', as he and his circle called that strange 1923 contraption.

Now, in the spring of 1931, he was happy. I would have said, perfectly happy, except that his happiness was not quite perfect. It had, lurking within it, a little sharp grain of uncertainty. Everyone in that dedicated *chapelle*, of which he was doubtless the least important member but obviously one of the most devoted, was poised for one of those decisive surges of effort that happen in the lives of men and of companies. M.G. were launched into racing, but the resplendent successes were still in the future. They had one season behind them, that of 1930, and it had brought plenty of valuable experience but nothing much in the way of triumphant publicity. As far as I could judge, Brian's mood during that Easter was exactly that of Henry V on the eve of Agincourt, as Shakespeare portrays it; full of spirit, eager for the fighting to start, but well aware of not being a bookies' favourite.

In particular, the words 'Double Twelve' contained some kind of mysterious irritant. I never got much beyond hoisting in that it was inadvisable to utter these words in Brian's presence. Across such a gulf of years, I can't remember exactly what the Double Twelve was, except that it was a race at Brooklands. M.G. had been represented at it in 1930, but apparently it was more than your life was worth to ask Brian how they got on.

For instance: one evening at six o'clock, having done all the reading and note-taking I could manage, I was frankly idling in the bar. As a matter of fact I was playing shove-ha'penny against myself, taking alternate shoves and calling myself Episcopus and Balliol. We had a nice smooth shove-ha'penny board but since there was a lot of demand for it among the customers, and the strict rule was that Family must Hold Back, I seldom got a chance to play. Old Trundle and his circle of gossips never bothered with shove-ha'penny, so I was having a quiet one-man game thinking of it as Episcopus versus Balliol. My father was behind the bar, leaning his shirt-sleeved elbows on the counter and enjoying this half-hour of sociability as he always did. Then I heard Brian's motor-bike thunder into the yard and the engine come to a stop. Unexpectedly, he came into the bar like a customer and ordered a glass of stout. After being served he leaned up against the bar, looking tired.

'Hard day?' said his father sympathetically, handing over the stout.

'They're all hard days, just now,' Brian said. He took a draught of the dark liquid and came away with a moustache of froth.

'At least you're home in time to eat,' Dad said. 'You wouldn't believe,' he said to Trundle and the others, 'the hours he works sometimes. Goes off at eight in the morning and comes back after nine, ten at night.'

'Got a lot to do just now. Pre-race. Busy time,' said Brian. He obviously did not want to get into a general discussion.

'I got a mate,' said the youngest member of the circle, Ted, 'as works at Cowley. He reckons they're all daft, that lot over at M.G.'

My father looked across at him warningly, but he was either too stupid to notice or mischievous enough to want to annoy Brian.

Brian ignored the remark, but narrow-faced Peake said, 'How's 'e make that out, then?'

'The overtime they does,' Ted said. 'They works all round the clock sometimes and they just gets their ordinary wage-packet. They don't get no overtime. Tell me if that en't daft.'

Brian put down his glass with a sharp sound that echoed through the quiet bar. 'It'd be daft if you did it,' he said. 'But not when we do it, 'cause we do it for a reason. We believe in it.'

'You believes in working for nothing, then?' Ted asked challengingly.

'We believe in working for M.G. We think it's daft to just clock on and be bored for seven hours for a wage-packet. The M.G. racing car's on its way. It's going to be famous all over the world.'

'Yes?' Ted sneered. 'You sure about that?'

'Talk about something else,' said my father. 'You, Ted, talk about something else.'

Ted ignored him and said, his voice loaded with spite, 'They'll have to do better'n they did last year, then.'

There was a short silence. Nobody really wanted to take up the proffered subject. Old Trundle, who had not moved into the age of the motor-car, was frankly immersed in his own thoughts. Another moment, and the subject would have flickered out and a new one would have started up; but someone said, half indifferently, 'What happened last year, then?'

'Talk about something *else*,' my father said.

'They went in for a big race,' Peake supplied, 'and got beat.'

'*They did not get beat*,' said Brian loudly. 'The whole race was a preparation exercise. It was to gather experience.'

'Not get beat!' Ted echoed in mock amazement. 'How can you stand there and say that? They puts a car in and it only run two hours!'

'I can stand here and say that,' said Brian, his knuckles white, 'because I can stand here and say anything I bloody well like.'

'Now look here, Brian,' his father interposed. 'I'll give you another bottle of stout, on the house, and you take it through and drink it in the kitchen. Go along, now,' he said sternly when Brian did not move. 'I want you back in that kitchen, boy. Here's your bottle.' He jerked the cap off and handed it across the bar. 'I can see this turning into an argument.'

It was already an argument; what he meant was that he could see it turning into a fight. Brian took the bottle and walked out of the bar. I went back to my shove-ha'penny. Balliol were winning.

'These racin' cars and that,' said old Trundle. 'The only racin' I sees any sense in is a good 'orse gallop. A real sight to see, with the jockeys in their silks and that.'

He went into a long reminiscence about some local man called Dick Squibb or Phil Tripp or some name like that, who had risen to become a famous jockey. He recalled wonderful afternoons at Newbury or Stratford-on-Avon, when he was young and he and his friends took the excursion trains with crates of bottled beer and were happy under the azure skies of pre-1914 summers. 'Who'd go an' watch a lot of motor-cars,' he concluded rhetorically, 'when they could be judgin' a nice bit of horse-flesh and flutterin' a bob or two each way?'

To get the full flavour you have to hear his voice with the Oxford burr in 'carrs' and ' 'orrse-flesh.' There was general agreement in the bar. Ted sat silent, content with his pin-prick victory.

*

In the next few weeks I became, along with the other benefits of the job, an expert punter: an accomplishment which, if you live in Oxford, is worth acquiring early in life, like learning to swim or ride a bicycle. Every time I walked the length of a punt, stepping down from the polished platform to the well of the boat and up the slatted incline at the other end, feeling it pitch and settle on the water, my mind's eyes showed me Vinnie's slender form reclining temptingly among the cushions. Sometimes I got so lost in these visions that I had difficulty in remembering where I was at that actual moment, and once I nearly got the sack because old man Boardman had to bawl an order at me about three times from a nearby position on the bank.

We happened to be having a good spell of weather during that Easter vacation, and we got the boats on the water in time to pick up a lot of business from visitors, day-trippers mostly. I am sorry to say that in my youthful arrogance I rather despised these people. Unlike the members of the University, their vanity was not involved in the correct handling of a punt, and many of them, on being offered the pole, declined it and asked for paddles instead. They would then sit in pairs on the platform end, what I loftily called 'the Cambridge end', which was in my opinion not the stern of the boat anyway, and placidly splash off at the speed of an asthmatic duck. I look back now with fondness on these harmless people, enjoying a day out and taking a look at the Oxford that they had heard so much about. But in that intoxicating April, from the height of my new-found membership of the real punting class of gondoliers, I thought of them very much as a gourmet would think of people who went into a restaurant and ordered a lunchburger with chips and mayonnaise, and I only hope I didn't show it too much.

The spell of fine weather went on and on, I worked with the boats every afternoon and on Saturdays and Sundays all day, and most of the time I was in sunshine. I became healthy and tanned, and this did wonders for my confidence. Back at the Bargeman's, there was no longer such an obvious difference between me, pale and stooped, and Brian's friends, cheerful, loud-voiced, and permanently wind-burnt from riding motor-bikes. By appearance alone you could not have picked me out from among them; we were all young fellows together.

Better still, I became useful and relied-on at the boatyard. It took me no time at all to get on top of the simpler parts of the job, and I was skilful with the boats. An outdoor life, something I had never considered for a moment, suddenly seemed within my range of possibilities. I was not very strong, but I had a good sense of balance, which is more important in a boat than muscular strength, which in any case soon develops in the places you need it. After a couple of weeks I could steer a punt nonchalantly into the exact punt-sized space that awaited it among a row of others, allowing for the current and the general slowness of response that is punt-nature; and then, as it glided in, I could walk smoothly up from stern to bow and be ready with the painter in my hand to make fast as soon as we came up to the little iron ring set into the woodwork. It was satisfying, it was graceful, and it was done to the accompaniment of the gentle plashing of the river and the wink of sunlight off the ripples. Of course my motive in all this was purely sexual. I wanted, and needed, to get at Vinnie. But with all that, I had the canny patience not to rush it. Until I had pulled in three weeks' wages I made no attempt to get in touch with her. I kept away from the shoe-shop and in fact from Cornmarket Street altogether, and never went near the area in Jericho where she lived. I had an objective, I had something to live for, and I could wait.

Curiously enough, one incidental benefit I got from these three happy weeks was that it warmed and awakened my love of Oxford – just my physical love for it, as a place. The river with its little waves dancing in the sunlight, the first of the early summer flowers making their shy appearance in the grass along the banks, the early blossoms drawn out by that clear spring sunlight, and the glimpses of classic buildings seen through trees that were just coming into leaf, all went deeply into my being. The thought had never occurred to me before that I was lucky to live in Oxford – to me, the Bargeman's Arms was just the Bargeman's Arms – but now I knew it. In the mornings, before I reported for work at the landing-stage beside Folly Bridge, I used to wander about the place, seeing it for the first time, and since by now I was beginning to get some grip on English history I saw, also for the first time, that history was not just something you read about in books, it was life, lived out by real people in real places, and an extraordinary amount of it had happened in these lanes and buildings and fields, by this river, under these trees.

So I walked about, morning after morning, and the chimes from the assorted clock-towers found me at some different point each day, staring up at this building or that, poking around alleys and field paths, identifying a boundary-wall here or the foundations of a demolished abbey there. Cornmarket Street, as I said, was out of bounds, so I couldn't go and look at the Anglo-Saxon tower of St Michael's at the North Gate. To stand just there would have been to catch a strong whiff of Vinnie, and that would have been goodbye to any kind of historical reverie; so I imagined the tower instead. remembered it from all the times I had more or less carelessly looked at it, and I let it speak to me of the world that had been overthrown by William and his Normans. I looked at the one surviving tower of Oxford Castle and thought of that winter day in 1142 when the Empress Matilda escaped from the vigilance of King Stephen's troops by having herself let down over the wall and setting off, in a white cloak to take advantage of the snow, down the frozen Thames to Wallingford. I stood at Carfax beside the spot that used to be the site of the Swindlestock Tavern, where that vicious three-day riot started on St Scholastica's Day in 1355. I looked at buildings that had reared themselves on the downfall of the monastic houses in Henry VIII's day. I listened in my mind to the jingle of spurs as the horsemen gathered to form a troop of cavalry for the King in his war against the Parliament, and chose dark blue as their colour; I learnt why North Parade is south of South Parade; I heard the rumble of carts carrying away silver from the colleges to be melted down for the King's exchequer. I saw port-wine complexions under full-bottomed eighteenth-century wigs. I saw Victorian young men in high-buttoned jackets and mutton-chop whiskers, disputing as to whether after all there might still be a God. I paused outside the Science Museum and fancied that I heard the moment of shocked silence and then the applause that greeted T.H.Huxley's resounding snub to Bishop Wilberforce in their debate on evolution. My notion of history was very simple; it was merely a string of picturesque or dramatic episodes that had happened in the past; but during those heady days as the bright month of May came in, walking about Oxford, I looked for that picturesqueness, I listened for that drama, and I was rewarded because they came to meet me.

What I had absolutely none of – it would have been too much to expect it, at that age – was a sense of the moment in history that I was actually living through. The industrial world was sliding into slump, recession and crisis; rival ideologies were preparing for the armed test of strength that was coming. The brief illusion, sustained by most people throughout the 'twenties, that the War to End War had actually done anything for humanity was finally dispelled. Capitalist democracy, lurching from boom to bust, seemed more ramshackle and unworkable than ever, and the various totalitarianisms that confronted it seemed more and more ruthless and menacing. In only eight more years, the war in which my father and his generation had served would be back to engulf us in a scarcely altered form. But of all this I, at nineteen, was as oblivious as a bird along a hedge. My attention was taken up by the sunshine on the water, the greenness of the new leaves, the immense shapes of history which were finally breaking clear of the childish fog in my mind; and, beneath and in a sense driving them all, that intense, tireless need that focused itself, for the time being, on one slender girl with a fringe of brown hair, who spent her days selling shoes in Cornmarket Street.

Chapter 11

As soon as term began Bax sent for me and told me that I had done well in Mods. He had not been among the examiners, and he referred to that body as 'they', which had the effect of slightly distancing the whole thing. 'They evidently thought quite well of your papers, Leonard,' he said, as if to carry the suggestion, 'but then I have no means of knowing whether they're just being stupid.' He added that I had, in consequence, been admitted to the Final Honour School of Medieval and Modern History and that I would now be reading with him. 'Reading with', in the Oxford parlance of those days, meant that he would be my tutor. He did not tell me this as if he were glad of it, or sorry; it was simply information. His eyes behind those round lenses were entirely without expression, except of course that to be without expression when saying things of that kind is itself an expression.

So I was a pupil of Bax, official, and a member of the History School, official. The first hurdle, getting into the University at all, had been surmounted; so had the second; all that remained was the third, to get some kind of degree and I had seven terms to do it in. Beyond that, I did not trouble myself to think.

Not all of us in that set of freshmen who had met outside Bax's rooms that morning had done well enough to get into the Honours School, though oddly enough Knowlton had. Either he was more intelligent than he seemed, or, in his invariable practice of doing the minimum of work to get by, he was clever at picking the right minimum. It came, I suppose, to much the same thing in the end. Carshalton, that strange uncommunicative creature, had also got into the Honours School, though one could not imagine him taking any kind of interest in history; still, it might be a means to some self-centred end. But a real surprise to me was that Lamont was not accepted to read for Honours. He was going to read for a Pass Degree, which was still done in those days by quite a lot of people, but hardly the more able ones. Lamont, indifferent as ever to the world, showed no surprise and certainly no chagrin;

Intellectually, he appeared to me not to need the University, except as a place where he could get plenty of books and meet like-minded people; he read and thought incessantly, but he quietly and firmly retained the right to be the best judge of what he should be reading or thinking about at any given time. I met him in the garden on that first day of the summer term. We strolled together for a few minutes, and when he asked me how I had fared in Mods and I told him I had been accepted to read for Honours he congratulated me; but I saw at once that it would be entirely out of place for me to commiserate with him for not having been. The officially prescribed course of study hardly concerned him. 'An Honours degree is nothing unless it's a First,' he said as we moved beside a great bed of peonies, 'and a First is meaningless unless you either want to be a don or go into the Civil Service, and I'm not going to do either.' I asked him what he was writing (I was learning how to talk to people like him, and had even taken the trouble to find out who Leopardi was), and he said that he had spent the vacation trying to get started on a poem based on the life of Euhemerus, but it hadn't gone right and he had abandoned it. I had never heard of Euhemerus, but it was typical of him to assume, apparently in all good faith, that I must have. I just said 'Ah,' and left him pacing in his luminous cloud. I felt glad that such a man existed and that I knew him, and the thought cheered me as I went off on my eternal errand – to collect a load of books from the library; where, of course, the first thing I did was to look up Euhemerus.

All this concern with books and papers and essays and examinations and work in general was of course important to me, but, equally of course, it was nothing like so important as the One Great Preoccupation, and at five-thirty on that first Monday afternoon I was stationed where I could watch the door of the shoe-shop. It was closed to customers; it stayed dormant for a few minutes; then it opened to admit the staff on their way home. Vinnie appeared; she lingered on the pavement for a moment with a couple of other girls; then they took their way and she took hers, northwards towards Walton Street and Jericho. I let her get clear of the most crowded pavements before I put on a spurt and caught her up. I felt terribly tense in case she was in a difficult mood, but for once everything was absolutely plain sailing. She checked her step at the sound of my voice and said, 'Hello, Peter.' I don't remember that she had ever called me by my name before, and it sent a shiver of pleasure and excitement down my spine. I fell into step beside her, and without wasting time issued my invitation. Would she like to go on the river? In a punt? Well, yes, she would. Nobody had ever suggested that to her before, and she had seen people floating along, and it looked fun... It was like the sensation of going up to a heavy door that one has been told is locked and barred, ramming determinedly at it with one's shoulder, and finding that it simply swung open on well-oiled hinges. Surprising, disconcerting even. But in the most delightful way.

She made only one condition: it had to be on a Thursday afternoon, which was perfectly reasonable, and that afternoon must be a fine one. She didn't see any point in going punting in the pouring rain. She had seen people do that too, and it looked *miserable*. She shook her neat head as she said 'miserable'. One could tell she would be no friend of misery in any of its forms.

'That's fixed, then,' I said. 'I'll meet you from work next Thursday. One o'clock, when the shop closes.'

'No, not from work. I need to go home and eat before I come out.'

'We'll take a picnic.' This was to be the classic outing of my dreams, complete with wine-bottle and hamper. But Vinnie still shook her head.

'It sounds nice, but I want to change into different clothes. I don't want to go on the river in the clothes I have to wear for work.'

'You look fine in the clothes you wear for work,' I said fervently.

'Maybe,' she said, 'but I don't *feel* fine in them. No, we'll meet at Carfax. Two o'clock.'

I settled for that. What delighted me most was the quick, businesslike, direct way she agreed to it and set it up. No demurring, no pretending to think it over, no putting difficulties in the way. The outing sounded like fun, she said so and she agreed to it and fixed the details before we had walked fifty yards. I couldn't help wondering what had put her in this co-operative mood. Looking back on it now, I think I know the answer. Those weeks of working for Tupper Boardman had given me a tan and hardened my muscles so that I carried myself better. I was, in short, more attractive to her. And it is a comment on my youthful modesty and insecurity that the thought did not, at the time, cross my mind. I was so totally brain-washed into the belief that I was the pursuer and Vinnie the pursued, that I was the suppliant and she the goddess who gave or didn't give according to her inviolable will. And who had brain-washed me into that? As Desdemona says, 'Nobody; I myself.'

I made the usual offer to escort Vinnie all the way home, she made the usual answer that I must turn back before we got into gossip-range, and I turned back and walked to Episcopus four feet above the pavement. I had done it. She was coming out on the river! The very next Thursday that had fine weather!

Monday night, Tuesday, Wednesday, and Thursday morning, of

course, were not real time at all, simply a bad, restless dream. Just about the only thing I did was look at the sky. I suppose the radio (we called it 'the wireless') had started putting out weather forecasts by then, but I hadn't got a wireless and didn't know anyone who had. I just looked at the sky, tried to remember all the bits of weather lore I had ever heard, and fantasized. There was not even any planning to do. I had done it all weeks before. We were going to hire a punt at Magdalen Bridge and go up the Cherwell. There wasn't, in those days, anywhere in North Oxford where you could hire a punt, which meant that I would have to pole our craft a deuce of a long way before we reached a quiet enough stretch to moor and get some privacy. On the other hand, if I had to start from Magdalen Bridge, so would everybody else, and I didn't imagine there would be anyone else on the Cherwell that day who would be both as good at punting and as highly motivated as I was. And again, the open country began much sooner than it does now. The ring-road had not been built, nor the vast housing estates of Cutteslowe and New Marston, and very soon after emerging from the leafy confines of North Oxford you were into quiet farming country which, on a weekday afternoon, ought to provide just what I wanted. I knew the very stretch I would be making for, even the clump of willows that hung over the water and made a canopy. I didn't anticipate our getting out of the boat. There would be too much risk of being trodden on by a cow, or prodded by an inquisitive farmer. No, our delicious union was going to be strictly inboard.

How I got through that intervening time without actually going mad I shall never know. It was worse even than the time last winter when I had been waiting for Vinnie to turn up at my rooms. I have only one memory of that half-week, but it is a particularly vivid one. I was in the front quad one day just after lunch, chatting with someone or other before going up to my room to try to read, when I noticed my companion looking fixedly over my shoulder. Evidently he had seen something extraordinary, and when I turned and followed the line of his gaze I had the same reaction.

Carshalton was walking with a measured, deliberate stride across the quad to the College gate. He wearing a midnight-blue blazer with very highly polished silver buttons, a white shirt, a tie with what seemed to be some regimental or club pattern on it, startlingly white trousers and slender tan shoes. When I say that his trousers were white I completely fail to convey their effect. They were not just off-white or creamy, but vehemently white, almost hurting one's eyes. As for the crease down each leg, I can only say that it is a pity that 'knife-edge' is such a *cliché* when describing meticulous creases. Carshalton's looked capable of actually drawing blood if you had run your hand against them. Even his snowy shirt, though the sunlight flashed off its rigid collar, could not compete with the white of his trousers.

Normally, Carshalton wore the same kind of clothes as the rest of us – tweed jackets, flannel bags, that kind of thing, somewhat thicker in the winter and somewhat thinner in the summer. He dressed rather carefully, but so far the carefulness had been directed towards the end of looking like everybody else. This outfit was something very different. It made him look non-human, as if he ought to be standing in a shop window rather than walking across the quad, an impression heightened by the fact that the stiffness of his trousers made him walk in that mechanical way. The wild thought crossed my mind that there was some criminal inspiration behind all this. Perhaps Carshalton was involved in an attempt to carry out a daring robbery at a big department store, and his particular role was to pass himself off as a tailor's dummy and stand absolutely motionless among the other dummies in the window till the hours of darknesss allowed him to steal out from among them, open the back entrance and admit the rest of the gang. But the thought, as I say, was wild and it did not stay long. Carshalton was not the type to go in for robberies – not, at any rate, the ordinary straightforward robbery that landed you in the police court.

The man I was talking to – his name, after all these years, has gone – was a garrulous, good-natured youth who was not above showing common human curiosity. As Carshalton moved past us as if sleep-walking, this man followed him through the lodge and out into the street, returning a moment or two later with the information that Carshalton had got into a taxi.

'Must be going to London,' I hazarded.

'London, nothing. I heard him give the address to the driver. Out in the country somewhere. Must be going to cost him a packet.'

If Carshalton was going out to the country, there was no reason why, in the normal course of events, he should not have gone on a bicycle. But of course this would not do. It was a warm afternoon, and he might have sweated, and discoloured his crisp shirt; and his trousers would have bagged out a little at the knees and perhaps even collected a spot of oil from the chain. He was going somewhere where he wanted to impress people, and part of the impressing was to arrive in a taxi.

Well, I thought, there's one thing certain, he's not going to meet anyone like Vinnie. The thought of her, as usual, came snapping back like elastic. I went up to my room and sat there reading the same sentence over and over again in Reginald Lane Poole's *Medieval*

Reckonings of Time; a book Bax had told me to read, without of course knowing that he had chosen a week to do so in which the measurement of time was a subject that awoke my deepest emotions.

Wednesday was fine and warm. Helpless in the grip of my obsession, I was almost inclined to resent this, my reasoning being that since the English weather is so changeable the mathematical odds are always more or less in favour of tomorrow's being different from today. However, flouting the probabilities, Thursday rose bright and the fine weather showed no sign of breaking, and I moved about that morning with a sense that things might be, at last, going my way. Throwing away all pretence of thinking about anything else, I prepared for the outing with Vinnie by going out shopping for provisions. I hadn't a picnic hamper, so I just put everything into a knapsack: some fruit (the first cherries, I remember, were just coming in from Southern Europe, though the English ones were still a month away; I lashed out and got a good big supply), a bottle of white wine, and two glasses wrapped very carefully in tissue paper. After that I couldn't think of anything else to do, so I sat and watched the hands of the clock until it was time to go and meet Vinnie at Carfax. Whether I went into Hall and toyed with some lunch, I have entirely forgotten; if I did so, I did it in a dream.

At ten minutes to two I was standing at the Carfax crossroads. People moved around me, some walking with a springy step, some waddling, some limping, some stamping as if on a parade-ground, all going about their unguessable business. I looked at them with an unseeing eye. Only now and then, when a girl who passed seemed to have something of the look of Vinnie – to be slender and pale and have levelled-off dark brown hair – did I look attentively, and then it was not that particular human being I was looking at, it was my own vision of Vinnie.

Even so, completely psychologically prepared as I was, the sight of her, when she appeared punctually at two o'clock, nearly put me on the floor. She had on an outfit I had never seen before. (But then, why should I have seen all her wardrobe? I had been with her so few times, after all, and never yet in fine weather.) I'm no good at describing women's clothes – the garments have technical names which I just don't know – but I immediately thought of her style this time as 'gipsy'. She wore a loose-fitting skirt, bell-like towards the hem, with a white petticoat under it that showed an edge of lace. The skirt was orange in colour, and she wore a top half that was white, frilly, and buttoned rather tightly up the centre in contrast with the flaring, flowing looseness of the skirt; I suppose you would call it a kind of bodice.

All I could think of to say was, 'You're very punctual.' She smiled briefly and said, 'What's in the bag?'

'Just a bit of refreshment,' I said. 'We don't want to have to come in too soon just because we get hungry.' Such inane chatter is often the spume that blows off from our deepest and most churning emotions. I felt that the hammering of my heart must be audible above the traffic.

We walked down High Street to Magdalen Bridge to get a punt. On the way I saw several men I knew from Episcopus. One of them was Kent. He was standing on the pavement staring fixedly into the window of a men's outfitter's. Perhaps he was making up his mind to go in and get a blazer that would rival Carshalton's. The thought made me laugh out loud. At that moment all the Kents in the world were nothing more than walk-on comedy parts.

We got the punt, I paid the deposit, I settled Vinnie gracefully down among the cushions, I grasped the pole, and we fairly shot away. The steel claw of the pole bit fiercely into the gravelly floor of the river. I brought into play all the skill and muscle that the weeks of working at Boardman's had endowed me with, and I can still remember the look of faint surprise on the faces of some of the punters we overtook as they slowly wallowed along. Vinnie complimented me on my handling of the boat. I silently swelled to bursting-point with pride. We started out among a crowd of other punts and a few rowing-boats, but we had left nearly all of them behind by the time we had finished with the lower stretch and got as far as the rollers. Ahead stretched the broad, unfrequented Cherwell in its natural width before it is broken into two on either side of the meadows known as Mesopotamia: a country river, with gentle breezes and silences and chewing cows and skimming swallows. I longed to be there, to have done with people and buildings and civilization. As I pushed the punt over the rollers, *bump-bump, bump-bump*, the sound was music in my ears. Vinnie helped me. I noticed how lissom her body was, as she bent double to reach down to the boat, and swayed from side to side as it moved along. Her skirt was not at all revealing, but since it was so free-flowing, it was marvellous for suggesting the grace of her limbs. Odd, that a seventeenth-century clergyman should be the only poet who has been completely successful in putting into words for us that particular effect of a young woman's dress –

O, then methinks how sweetly flows
The liquefaction of her clothes!

I hadn't, at that time, read those lines; but I never read them now, or think of them, without remembering Vinnie on that Cherwell afternoon.

We got through the Parks, houses thinned out, people walking on the river-bank became fewer and finally disappeared altogether. We were north of the point where the ring-road now runs, which means that we were well into the country. Even so I kept going, without slackening pace at all, as if I were in a neck-and-neck race with a crew from Cambridge or somewhere. I was aiming to get to a particular cluster of willows with their green overhang. And then at last we came round a curve and saw it. Half-a-dozen more thrusts put us in among them; and, still as if I were competing in a timed event, I was out of the boat, tying her up, then back in again, driving the pole firmly into the river-bed to keep her from swinging out towards midstream. For a moment, before getting down into the boat, I stood and looked round, surveying my achievement. Surely, now, I had it made.

Vinnie laid herself back among the willows. The sunlight struck through the canopy of willow leaves in a gently dancing pattern of green. The punt was moored as solidly as a rock. At last, at last my moment had come: as I slithered down beside her I saw for the first time (could it really have been for the first time?) that her mouth was perfectly shaped for the expression of love: without being heavy or fleshy, it was very clearly defined, with a Cupid's bow above and a slightly fuller lip below. That mouth, if studied knowledgeably, yielded up the secret of Vinnie, why she was a restless explorer of sexuality, why she was always on *qui vive* to try whatsoever male elixir came along, why it was that after ten minutes' acquaintance she had decided to sample Chucker's barrel-chested virility (had he forgotten her by now?) and why, for that matter, she had so unconcernedly displayed her fan-vaulted pubic hair to me that morning in the shower room. The unmitigated, unalloyed sexual encounter of male and female was Vinnie's territory, where she lived and where she held sway.

I contemplated Vinnie's perfect mouth for no more than a few seconds – that was all the delay I could stand before planting my own mouth full upon it. Immediately the excitement flowed downwards, and my prick became so swollen and rigid that I had to give it its freedom or be crippled for life. As I wrenched at the buttons and struggled to free the crazed animal that was trapped down there, I became aware of a smaller, defter hand helping me. In no time at all Vinnie had my colossal cock out and was gently kneading it in the cool summer air. Her mouth was still moulded to mine and her tongue was sliding around my lips. I knew at once that only one problem remained for me – how to get it deep inside her before I went berserk. Delicious as her hand was, it was her moist little cleft that I wanted. Breathing hard, I slid my hand up her gipsy skirt. Her crotch was naked, as I had known it would be, and as my fingers found their target she gave a long gasp that drove me demented. *This is it, Vinnie*, I thought. And as I formulated the notion she pulled her skirt up to her hips and took me between her thighs.

What followed in the next couple of seconds was just about the most shattering experience of my life. Even after all the years that have gone by, I can scarcely bear to recall it, so piercing is the anguish that clings about it in my memory. Whereas my entire nervous system was keyed up for the most blissful moment I had ever known, what it got was the most disappointing, the most embarrassing, the most seismically disruptive.

I'll put it down in as few words as possible, to get it over. The punt, securely fastened as it was, began to rock violently from side to side, and at the same instant a heavy shower of water-drops fell on Vinnie and myself.

My first intensely startled thought was that a big dog was trying to scramble aboard, but as the grip of Vinnie's thighs loosened and I rolled off her, I twisted round and saw a large, round, grinning face peering up at me from water-level.

'Don't moind me, mate!' This face now shouted at me in a hoarsely triumphant voice and with a strong Oxfordshire accent. 'You carry on with it, as long as y' don't moind me watching!' At which the face dissolved into such gales of laughter that it drew in water and disappeared for a moment. Coming up and spluttering, the face turned back over what I now saw was a powerful shoulder and shouted to some invisible company, 'Over 'ere, lads, over 'ere, if you're not afraid to see What the Butler Saw!'

Answering cries greeted this invitation and in no time at all our small willowy haven was invaded by splashing, shouting, guffawing bodies. Vinnie, having twitched down her skirt, sank back and covered her eyes. I got to my hands and knees, rigid with shock and hatred, not knowing whether to try to stand up and lash out at them with the one paddle we carried, or to follow Vinnie's example of simply trying to blot them out from consciousness. Obviously our arrival had coincided with that of some party of local youths who were enjoying a summer-afternoon swim. From their point of view, catching the pair of us *in flagrante delicto* was simply one more, and the most glorious, bit of fun in their afternoon. I must say they milked it for all it was worth. They swam round us like heavy white porpoises, and every time one of them thought of a particularly excruciating witticism he bawled it out, causing the others to become convulsed with mirth so that they swallowed river-water in, I was sorry to note, slightly less than lethal amounts. One of them kept diving beneath our craft and banging on its hull with his fist. Another persistently offered his services to Vinnie, mentioning the dimensions of his virility. And amid all this, there was nothing I could do. There were four of them, they were strong fully-grown youths, and it would have been the work of a moment for them to keep me quiet by submerging me in the river.

Finally the main body withdrew to a spot on the other side of the river and about fifty yards upstream, where we could still hear their talk and laughter and the occasional splash as one of their bulky bodies hit the river; but for what seemed a long time after that there seemed always to be one or other of them swimming near us, rearing up out of the water with plastered hair and beady, watchful eyes, as if hoping that the show would recommence. Finally, even these tired of the game, and a dense afternoon hush came down on the ruin of our excursion.

I lay in the bottom of the boat, close to Vinnie but not daring to touch her, wondering what I could possibly say. Should I try to make light of the interruption, offer to pole on to an even more remote place? But, she could justly reply, gangs of youths went swimming in the whole length of the Cherwell; where could we find peace? I was mute. The disaster had stopped me. I could think of no remedy.

After a few minutes of this – or was it a few hours? – Vinnie first sat up, then got to her feet: slowly, and yet with a slowness that was studied, deliberate, showing her mind to be fully made up. Without speaking to me or looking towards me, she put one hand on a willow-branch to steady herself and stepped off the punt and out of my life.

Once she was on the bank she turned and looked at me one more time.

'Don't go, Vinnie,' I said.

'Go is all there is to do,' she said. 'You're bad luck. You must have a jinx on you or whatever they call it. Well, you can stop trying to wish it on me.'

And she walked away across the wide meadow, heading for the road that would take her down to Marston Ferry and back home to Jericho.

After she had gone I sat in the punt for a long time. I could still hear the shouting and laughing from the other bank, but I felt nothing towards the fellows there. If anything, I think, I was glad that somebody was happy. At least it meant that this warm sunny afternoon, so obviously designed for happiness, was not being wasted. Finally I untied the rope and pulled out the pole I had so skilfully jammed in to the river bed. I stood up and began punting away. The chaps took no notice of me now. I was just an undergraduate poling an empty punt.

I went much more slowly downstream than I had come upstream, though the going was so much easier. When I reached the point where I had to get out of the punt and move it over the rollers I stood for a moment on the bank, looking back. This was the point where I said goodbye to the wide, country stretch. It seemed a good point to off-load what had come to seem the unnecessary luggage of the journey, the luggage of an outing that never was. I threw the paper bags of fruit on to the surface of the water. The bags soaked and broke open, and the fruit drifted down the stream like rubbish. The bottle of wine I threw in a long arc. It landed in the middle of the river with a splash that I can still hear. I pictured it going zig-zag down into the cold depths and lying, tilted over, on the bottom. I wondered how long it would be before the cork rotted and the wine I had bought for Vinnie and myself to drink seeped out into the indifferent river-water. However long it took, H_2O and mud would win in the end.

Then I pushed the boat over the rollers, took it back to base, and collected the unexpired portion of my deposit money. Walking back to College, I saw no one I knew. But perhaps I would not have recognized them.

*

When I got back I went up and sat in my room with the oak shut. I didn't want to speak to anyone and I tried as far as possible to keep from thinking about anything, anything at all. When dinnertime came I still sat there and let it go by. I wasn't in the least hungry and I wanted to be left alone. Towards midnight I got into bed and fell asleep, but I woke about half-past three feeling ravenous. There was no way I could get anything to eat until the College kitchen started serving breakfast at eight. I thought longingly of the fruit I had thrown in the river; I kept picturing it floating away, further and further out of reach. I fell into an uneasy sleep and dreamed I was running along the bank of the Cherwell with a long net, trying to scoop up from the surface not the fruit I had tipped in but, oddly enough, dozens of eggs that were floating on the surface instead of sinking. I tried and tried to gather some of these eggs, and finally my foot slipped on the muddy bank and I fell in. My legs felt very cold in the dream as they stood there in the water, and when I woke

I found my fretful motion had caused the bedclothes to slip nearly off and that my legs were in fact naked to the fresh breeze of early summer that was coming in through the window.

I rearranged sheet and blankets and lay there waiting for Arthur to come up with my hot water at seven forty-five. There was no point in getting up and moving about; it would make me even hungrier. I looked up at the ceiling for what must have been two hours, trying to cultivate a Yoga-like discipline of emptying my mind, my memory, my emotions, my desires. It was a wretched failure. At eight I went down and ate an enormous breakfast.

It was Friday. There was no point in trying to do any work, so I just walked around aimlessly and came in to College for meals. Saturday, the same. On Sunday I went for a really long walk on Otmoor. The idea was to see and hear as few other human beings as possible, and Otmoor was always a desolate place. I walked miles and miles. It was a long way to get there – I went out through Summertown and Water Eaton and thence to Noke – and once I was there I kept on walking hour after hour. When I finally got back to College, just about in time for dinner, my feet were sore and I had that general, all-over fatigue that expresses itself by an ache in the shoulders. Sinking into mindless tiredness, eating a good meal, drinking a big tankard of beer, I felt almost contented, though I knew it couldn't last. Once I was not tired any more, once I was not hungry or thirsty any more, I knew my other hungers, my other distresses, would come to the surface.

After the meal I was walking slowly across the quad heading for my room (there seemed to be nowhere else to go and nothing else to do in the universe except just sit there behind that oak) when Fred Armitage, friendly and helpful as ever, came up to me and mentioned that Frank Penney in the lodge had been asking whether I was in College because there was a message for me. I went into the lodge and the wooden-faced old potentate handed me a folded piece of paper. My name was written on it in what I saw immediately was my father's hand. What had happened? He must have come round and delivered it himself, something he never did before or again.

The note was brief. 'Peter, Come down tonight if you can and join in the Big Celebration. This is Brian's big moment. Join in if you can. Any time, we are all here. It was on the wireless. – Dad.'

Success? Celebration? Brian's big moment? It would be something about M.G., what else? They must have pulled something off. My bones ached, my feet were reluctant to be set to the ground; but I might as well get down to the Bargeman's. If there really was a celebration for this big moment of Brian's life, whatever it was, I ought to show up, and I had nothing better to do, unless it was 'better' to sit in my room and grieve over the loss of Vinnie. I borrowed a bike from someone (I had sold my own when I was so hard up in the spring) and pedalled down to the pub.

As soon as I got to the end of our street I could see the place was jumping. The lights were blazing out and people were spilling out on to the pavement, clutching glasses, talking and laughing. They wouldn't be doing all that for nothing. Then, when I was still a hundred yards from the place, a figure dressed in a grey suit and trilby hat came out of the pub by the main entrance, and a burst of cheering came with him. He was surrounded by a mass of struggling figures – all male, and all shouting delightedly – who seemed to be fighting for a chance to slap him on the back or shake his hand or just simply to touch him. I stood still and watched. What tremendous celebrity, what royal or quasi-royal personage, had visited our side-street pub? The grey-suited, trilby-hatted man, nodding and waving as best he could, got into a car that stood at the kerb, settled down behind the wheel (so he didn't have a chauffeur – he couldn't have been *all* that posh), and started the engine. At first it seemed that the crowd seething round the car would make it impossible for him to get into gear and move off, but after a moment the space in front of the radiator thinned, then emptied, and people were standing back to let the car go, bending down to smile and wave and call in at the windows. Then it was gone, and the crowd of men drifted back into the bar.

I approached, and entered with them. The place was jam-packed. There were a few wives and girl-friends, but the overwhelming impression was of maleness: men, men, everywhere, standing so solidly shoulder to shoulder that they had difficulty in raising pint glasses to their mouths, grinning, laughing, talking loudly. It so happened that I had recently been reading some medieval Italian history, and one of the things I had learnt was that the reason why Italian cathedrals were built with large, stately baptisteries, standing separately from the main structure, was because in addition to the bishop's annual mass baptism they were used for important civil ceremonies, and one of these was the welcoming home of victorious armies. That image came back to me now – soldiers, triumphant in victory, rejoicing in their strength and success, knowing themselves the heroes of the hour, relaxing and laughing and shouting to one another: surely that was what I was looking at.

But whose soldiers were these? Where had their battle been fought?

A hand suddenly gripped my elbow. I turned and saw Brian, laughing straight into my face. I had been looking round for him, but he had seen me first and pushed his way to my side. He had a full pint glass of beer in his hand, as I turned to him he held it out; it was for me.

'Glad you got the message,' he shouted in my ear.

'Thanks,' I shouted back, taking the beer. 'It was a pretty short message – it just said Come to the celebration.'

'Well, you came,' he said and laughed again, as if he had made a joke.

I drank from my glass, waiting for him to give me some information, unwilling to speak in case I said something wrong that would annoy or disappoint him and take the edge off his pleasure.

'Did you see the guv'nor?' he asked me, shouting into my ear as another tide of noise welled up around us.

For a brief instant I wondered if the man who had just driven away was Billy Morris. But no, he was always called 'the Old Man', and in any case Brian would not have cared one way or the other about a visit from Billy Morris. No, there was only one person it could have been, and I took my courage in both hands and shouted enquiringly, 'Cecil Kimber?'

'Cecil Kimber!' he shouted back, his face lighting up as he named his hero. 'Pity you couldn't get down sooner. He was here half an hour. But he said he had about five or six parties to get round. Nothing formal, just where they'd asked him to go and show his face. We shall be having a proper big celebration next Saturday night with everybody there, the drivers and all, but of course that'll be at Abingdon.'

'Terrific!' I yelled. If we had been alone, I would have asked him to spell out exactly what tremendous achievement they were celebrating, but the noise was too daunting and I knew the details would reach me soon enough. I could look at *The Times* in the Junior Common Room tomorrow, or just ask around. Then the words 'Double Twelve' popped into my head. Of course, of course – this was the weekend, and they had tried their luck again, and this time they must have done well.

'When did you get back?' I bellowed.

'Not long,' he shouted. 'The race wasn't over till eight and then we had to wait to get the official results confirmed. But we knew it was in our pocket from about midday.'

The effort of shouting all this was obviously skinning his throat. I offered him my glass, which was still about a third full, and he accepted it with a grateful nod and drained it quickly. Then he slapped me on the shoulder and moved off. I could relax; I had not disgraced myself; I was part of the gathering.

I looked over towards the bar and saw that our father, shirt-sleeved and with a shiny red face, was serving on his own. I went up to him and he told me above the racket that Mother was in the kitchen making sandwiches, which were going to be distributed free of charge as soon as she had made enough. I saw at once what I had to do; without even volunteering in words, I took off my jacket and hung it up, ran my eye down the price list on display behind the bar to remind myself of what everything cost, and began pulling beer and handing it out. The revellers took on the aspect of so many gaping throats, voracious, insatiable, good-humouredly impatient. I heard my own name called out, 'Over here, Peter,' 'This end, Pete,' first in the voices of men I more or less recognized as regulars who would expect to know me, but soon from just anyone as it became generally accepted that the fair-haired young chap slaving away beside the licensee was called Pete or Peter.

The pub would have to close by ten. At about ten minutes to, my mother appeared with two large trenchers piled with sandwiches. She handed round one and the other was just put down on the bar for people to help themselves. My father uttered the ritual cries: 'Last orders,' 'Empty your glasses, please,' and finally 'Time, ladies and gentlemen.' He had to shout 'Time' again and again before the throng reluctantly began to thin, but finally only a few hardened lingerers remained, these were shoo'd out and we had the place to ourselves.

Then for the first time I learnt that the Brooklands Double Twelve of 1931 had been won outright by an M.G. supercharged C-Type driven by the Earl of March and C.W. Staniland, and not only that but the first five places in the race had gone to M.G.s, so that not unnaturally they had also won the Team Prize. Of forty-eight starters only twenty-four had managed to thrash round for the full gruelling distance, and of these seven had been M.G.s. It was a huge, unbelievable, fantastic, glittering triumph that had touched Brian's life and turned it, for a few hours or a few days, into a fairy-tale. Some of the magic had splashed off on to Dad and even to Mother – I say 'even' because motor-cars never meant much to her, even ordinary common-sense ones that were likely to take her to places where she wanted to go, and as for the stark, bare-wheeled, exoskeleton monsters that howled and thundered and pursued each other in a strange far-off arena called Brooklands, she always distrusted them as part of the unaccountable lunacy of the masculine world: what kind of creature but a man would *want* to be involved in such dangerous nonsense? What was it all *for*? I can see her bent head now, as we sat at the table that evening, having cocoa and biscuits, winding down, with Brian and Dad doing most of the talking. But she poured no cold water on their enthusiasm; she knew that, if men were nothing but big children, they had to be humoured like children.

I can't say the M.G. magic touched my life that night, but it was good to see Brian so happy. Quite apart from his being my brother, it would have done my heart good to see anyone, provided it wasn't someone like Kent whom I actively disliked or Carshalton whom I distrusted, as happy as that. It made one think more highly of the possibilities of human life. Joy, real joy, glowed in his face and sang in his voice, and after all there was a certain selflessness in it; the racing success of M.G. was not going to make a celebrity of *him*, not going to make *him* rich.

At half-past eleven I thought of the walk back to Episcopus and the gate that would be closed at midnight, and was quite glad of them because it made it easy to get up from the table and say I had to go. I was under discipline, it was not my choice, and I congratulated Brian once again, and shook his hand, and wished my parents a good-night. And then I was outside in the dark, fragrant summer night, wheeling my borrowed bike because it had no lights, listening to my own footsteps and the sound of all the clock-towers debating the exact moment when it would be a quarter to midnight, and no one was walking by my side, and Vinnie had said I was bad luck and I must have a jinx on me, and perhaps it was true, perhaps it was true.

Chapter 12

The next event in my life was that I bought a bicycle: a good one, fit to go for long rides on. I spent on it most of the money I had earned working with the boats, and which I had intended for a very different purpose. There was nothing for it, I decided, but sublimation. I had somehow to last out for two years and two months before I could sit for my degree and move out of Oxford into the wider world, where presumably I should find the means of assuaging my dire sexual frustration.

All this is bound to seem pretty funny to anyone who looks at it with the eyes of Now rather than Then. Having made a mess of it with Vinnie, why didn't I try my luck at Somerville and Lady Margaret Hall, at St Hilda's and St Hugh's?

The fact is, it was not on. And the reason why it was not on was, like most reasons, historical. In those days we were still not out of the long, long period when the professions were not really open to women. A girl who worked hard and got to the University knew that the only job she could count on getting was schoolteaching. As embryo schoolmistresses, they wore shapeless skirts and fuzzy cardigans. They had their own motives for being at Oxford, and those motives most definitely did not include enjoying themselves in the way in which Vinnie enjoyed herself. That frank surrender to her own impulses, that completely untroubled assumption that sex was for fun and the more fun you had the better, had been brain-washed out of these young ladies before it even got into them.

Now and again, I admit, one saw an Annabel Graveney type, a girl from the upper reaches who had somehow been imbued, before she got to Oxford, with style and vitality and a hedonism that, in its more delicate way, probably rivalled Vinnie's. But such girls were so rare that, statistically, they did not count. Nor was I such a fool as to imagine that they would be interested in the likes of me. Annabel Graveney, to stick to that example, had come into Oxford from the wider world, as Gerard had: neither he nor she had really settled down in it; and when he went, she went. I never saw her again after that morning at the railway station. Doubtless they were together in London now, or in Paris. That was not my world; such girls were not for me. And if I took to searching among shopgirls, that would involve hanging around awful places like Holyoake Hall, with the constant threat of getting into trouble with the Proctors, and the certainty of being victimized as a 'womanizer' if I did succeed in finding a girl and was seen about with her. It all seemed so hopeless that I just gave up, postponed the whole business of sexual satisfaction till my University days, or at any rate my undergraduate days, were over.

As if to underline the inevitability of this decision, I had, at about this time, a revealing little brush with Dick Kent, who represented, if ever a man did, the socially and psychologically reactionary type who in those days still managed to keep the ascendancy in undergraduate circles, making life difficult for aesthetes (Gerard Urquhart) or people of a solitary and reclusive nature (Walters/Waters) or those who evinced, or would have liked to evince, an interest in the sexuality of young women (me). It happened like this.

One of the quaint little customs of our J.C.R. was that on Sunday evenings from 6.45 to 7.15, i.e. the half-hour before dinner, a scout called Tom officiated in a tiny pantry and served, over a flap that came down to form a small counter, glasses of sherry. It was, I suppose, something to do with making Sunday dinner-time a little bit special: the food was slightly more elaborate than usual, and you were encouraged to bring in guests.

On one particular Sunday night, fairly early in the summer term, I was standing at Tom's flap-counter waiting my turn for a sherry. There were two or three in front of me, and just before serving me Tom had to go into the back of his lair and get out a fresh sherry-bottle. I was just standing there when Kent came into the room. He had two guests with him, they were talking, and he broke off his sentence to say, 'Sit down over there, chaps, and I'll collect some sherry for us.' He arrived at the flap just as Tom came back with the new bottle.

'Three sherries, Tom,' Kent said. I had noticed before that the word 'please' did not exist in his vocabulary.

'It's my turn,' I said.

Kent took absolutely no notice of me. I might have been an insect that had alighted at that second on a corner of the bar. Tom, a slow-moving man who kept his own counsel, put down the bottle on the counter and started carefully working out the cork. When it was out he looked up and said, 'Now, gentlemen.'

'Three sherries,' Kent said again.

'Just one for me,' I said, 'and I'll have it first, please, as I was here first.'

'You'll have what you're given, Leonard,' Kent said crisply. 'Don't come in here throwing your weight about. Not, of course, that you've *got* any weight. Don't be all night, Tom,' he said to the scout.

At this moment, a man who was sitting in an armchair near to Tom's counter, reading a newspaper, looked up and said in a cool, matter-of-fact voice, 'I see you haven't changed, Kent.'

'Changed?' Kent's tone was loaded with an ugly annoyance. 'Why the hell should I have changed? What are you talking about?'

'I used to think when we were at school,' said the other man, 'that you had the worst manners of anyone in the place. And now you have the worst manners of anyone at this college.'

Kent went very rigid, like a dog just before a fight, and said, 'Don't you start telling me what kind of manners I have.'

'I've no intention of telling you anything,' the other man said. 'I was merely remarking that you hadn't changed.' And he dropped his eyes to his newspaper again.

In the silence that followed, Tom poured out a glass of sherry and pushed it towards me across the polished wood. The sound it made was an almost inaudible scraping, but I think the whole room heard it. Kent's two guests were looking into the fireplace as if estimating its measurements.

I went and sat down with my sherry in a different part of the room, pretending I was alone. I felt grateful to the man who had intervened, but I knew it was out of the question to express that gratitude in any way. The way to deal with a lout like Kent was to squelch him and then proceed as if absolutely nothing had happened.

The man reading a newspaper was an undergraduate senior to me whom I knew by sight and name, but had never had a conversation with. His name was Norbert. He was a Public School barker – from the same barker-factory as Kent, it now transpired – but I had already noticed that he was one of the more civil and humane of the breed. He was stocky, with a broad face and a shock of reddish hair, and I knew he was reading Greats. If there were more like him, I reflected, it would be easier and more pleasant living in a college dominated by Public School men.

Not that Episcopus life was notably *un*pleasant; on the whole the atmosphere was reasonably humane, and if Kent and the very small number of his cronies who approached him in arrogance had been removed, it could fairly have been said that the undergraduate body contained no one it was not perfectly easy to get along with. The dons, for their part, I tended to see as a frieze of emblematic figures, always adopting the same attitudes, rather than as a group of human beings. They were supposed, corporately, to know our individual names and faces and to have some notion of how we were progressing, and for this reason Episcopus, like every other college, observed the custom of 'Collections' on the last morning of every term, when the Fellows assembled at High Table and each undergraduate, gowned and in academic dress, was summoned in turn from the body of the Hall to listen, under their judging eyes, to his tutor's report on the term's work. My work was adequate to keep me out of trouble, my interviews at Collections rarely took more than two or three minutes, and the dons remained a benign frieze with no individual characteristics. I knew Bax and Gadsby, of course, but for the rest I hardly knew any of their names, though I had dutifully attended the customary sherry party at which freshmen were supposed to get to know the aged President, Salterton, a venerable dotard whose heyday had been in the age of Gladstone and Disraeli.

Bax himself was an individual to me, obviously, since I spent an hour alone with him every week, but his manner was habitually so impersonal that I sometimes wondered whether he saw me as a human being at all. It was therefore the more surprising, and gratifying, when he made a sudden move towards establishing a relationship. At the close of one of our tutorials, instead of dismissing me in his usual off-hand way, a way that struck me as being just within the bounds of ordinary politeness, he suddenly looked across at me and said, 'May I ask if you've made any plans for the summer vac., Leonard?'

The question took me completely by surprise, and the only thing I could think was that the Oxford and Poplar Boys' Club was rearing its ugly head again. After all, it was with just that question that Gadsby had introduced the matter the year before. I decided to take evasive action.

'My plans are not – er – quite fixed at the moment,' I said.

'The immediate point of my enquiry,' Bax went on, as if answering the question I had not put into words, 'was to find out whether you might be interested in joining a reading party.'

A reading party? What was that?

'The college takes a house in the Lake District for the month of September every year. Actually it's the house belonging to Wentworth Aniseed,' or some name like that, 'whose reputation as an archaeologist you may have come across, though it's a bit faded compared with what it was in the 'twenties. He was a Fellow here for years and years, and he's still a Fellow Emeritus of course, though he very rarely gets down to visit us. But he spends every September in Greece, picking over archaeological sites that probably yielded up everything they had to tell us years ago. The college rents it from him for that month. It sleeps about ten, and there's a local woman who comes in to cook and clean. We do a certain amount of walking, and we read, and we discuss what we've been reading. I think a lot of the men find it helpful. If they've been trying to work on their own through the long vac., they're often getting stale by September, and for that last month before term they appreciate an atmosphere that's a little like College – people around to bounce their ideas off – and a little like being on holiday. Think about it, anyway, won't you, Leonard?'

I didn't have to think about it. I knew I wanted to go. I assumed the board and lodging at this place would be free, and I would get there if I had to ride my bike all the way. It sounded wondrously better than mooching round Oxford, avoiding Vinnie.

On the other hand, I couldn't say now, this moment, that I would be glad to join in, because I had put up that smoke-screen about my plans not being fixed. Just because I didn't, and quite justifiably, want another basinful of the Oxford and Poplar.

'I really like the idea of coming along on this reading party, sir,' I said to Bax. 'I'll have to... er... just put my arrangements in order... write a few letters... might take a few days...' I was pretty sure he could see right into my mind and knew I was just floundering to cover up for not having accepted straight away. But I was committed to it now. 'I'm sure I can let you know within a week,' I said. 'Many thanks for inviting me.' And I rushed out of the room.

The next move, of course, was to go and wander about in the garden for a while, which I always did when I felt agitated. It was a truly calming place. I strolled about the paths, seeing and not seeing the head gardener and his assistants at their clipping and trowelling, the other undergraduates sitting or wandering about. Finally, lost in thought, I sank down on a bench for a few minutes. When I stood up to go, I found myself facing four people who were coming towards me. At their head stalked a very tall and very patrician lady, wearing the clothes that in those days marked out such ladies in the summer months: a broad-brimmed sun-hat and a cool, shapeless linen dress. Round her august neck she wore, if I remember it rightly, a rope of pearls. She had the archetypal aristocratic face, long and rather horse-like, perfect for looking down the nose at lesser breeds. In her wake came two young people, obviously brother and sister and equally obviously the offspring of this beldame. The young man was dressed with casual elegance; a silk scarf was loosely knotted round his neck and he wore fashionable shoes, which at that date were just beginning to come in. His sister was beautiful in that long-faced way; her cheekbones were pronounced and her hair, which was of a rich chestnut brown, was gathered up behind with an effect of carelessness which had probably taken her, or her maid, an hour to achieve. I remember noticing that her feet, in open sandals, were narrow and perfectly shaped.

Behind them came Carshalton. He was wearing the tailor's-dummy outfit which had startled me a few afternoons before. Rigid with self-consciousness, he was walking like a clumsily-made clockwork toy. He wore an expression suggesting that he was about to speak, but no sound came out, perhaps because he was unwilling to interrupt the conversation going on among his three guests, for such they evidently were. Carshalton was doing the honours, showing them round the College gardens. As they passed the older lady was laying down the law, in the kind of penetrating tones that come naturally to people who have never had to lower their voices for fear of being overheard, on some question of horticultural history.

'Flowering grasses,' she was trumpeting. 'If I get an opportunity to talk with your gardenah, or whoever it is who decides what to plant in this corner and that one over there by the wall, I shall try to steer him towards flowering grasses.'

'We don't all share your obsession with them, Mama,' the young man observed pleasantly.

'It is not an obsession, Robin. I am thinking of the varieties that shine out with a particularly brilliant green. Invaluable for brightening those areas of a garden that are shaded for one reason or another and tend to look drab. *Mibora minima* would be suitable here, or *milium effusum* if he wants something larger. If I don't see him, perhaps you could pass on...'

The *cortège* took a turn to the right and went to look at the rockery, bending over to inspect individual plants, while Carshalton stood by with feet slightly apart, like a soldier who has been told to stand at ease but not dismissed from parade. I walked straight ahead and left the garden, but since they had only gone a few paces as yet, this involved me in passing within ten yards or so, and in the clear summer air every word they said was audible to me. The old lady's would have been in any case, because she was accustomd to trumpeting like a cow elephant, but I also heard Carshalton's answers.

'What kind of garden do you have at home?'

‘A Chinese garden.’

‘A *Chinese* garden?’ (Somewhat in the tone of ‘A *handbag*?’)

‘Yes,’ came Carshalton’s flavourless robot-voice, though now it seemed to me slightly flavoured by a cadence imitated from the party he was shepherding. ‘My parents live in Shanghai.’

Curious, I thought. I had never heard before that Carshalton’s parents lived in Shanghai. Not that it mattered to me. I had no fellow-feeling for Carshalton, who seemed in some odd way to have opted out of the human race, and therefore felt no curiosity about him. All the same, I was mildly interested in the elaborate efforts he was making, quite clearly, to get in with this family. Why was it so important to him? Was I witnessing, on the hoof, something I had been told about often enough but never yet seen, that there were men who regarded three years at Oxford as a once-and-for-all opportunity to do some social climbing? Well, let him climb if that was what he wanted.

I went through the archway into the quad and there I met Wilmot.

‘What on earth is Carshalton up to?’ I asked him. ‘I’ve just seen him going round the garden with some extraordinary stuffed-shirt types.’

‘Oh, they’re the Acheson-Fiskes,’ he said.

‘The who?’

‘These people he’s always dancing attendance on. They live in some stately home at the top of Headington Hill and they have a country place out in the Chilterns somewhere. They’ve got handles to their names of some kind, The Honourable This and Milady That, I’m sure *I* don’t know. But Carshalton knows who they’re related to as far as the tenth remove. Hell, he *talks* enough about it.’

This last remark rather surprised me. It so happened that I had very seldom heard Carshalton talk about anything. Although, for the first couple of terms, we had both been in Bax’s history set, I had hardly so much as heard his voice. Certainly it was impossible to imagine him engaging me in conversation about anything. And yet there were people, Wilmot for instance, to whom Carshalton talked: expatiated, even. Perhaps these were people among whom he felt no need to be on his guard. In my presence, he was usually silent.

It was now getting on for noon. All of a sudden I knew that I would do no more work that day. What with one thing and another – the thoughts of success and ambition suggested by the conversation with Bax, the sight of the tailor’s-dummy Carshalton at his social climbing, and perhaps the neuro-physical stimulus of the alternation of bright sunlight and shadow – I felt restless, unsettled. I knew that if I went and sat down in front of a book I would not be able to concentrate. My attention would start wandering, and of course that meant only one thing. Thoughts of Vinnie, thoughts of youthful femininity in general, grief and rage over my state of enforced sexual deprivation, would take over and move me one more step in the direction of becoming totally unhinged.

There was only one thing for it – the bike, and the beckoning lanes and fields and woods that lay outside the city. Should I hang around and have lunch first? No, no – it was still an hour away, and in that hour I could be away in a smiling landscape, contentedly staying my stomach with bread and cheese and beer in a village pub. Within five minutes of making the decision I was in the saddle and away.

It was wonderfully easy, in those days, to get into the country from Oxford. The activities of Billy Morris, to be sure, had already sealed in the city to the east; but on the other three sides the rural landscape came right up to its boundaries. The ring-roads were not there, the vast housing estates of the 1950s were not even dreamt of, and after a pleasant ten minutes of pedalling along mostly quiet town roads one was out into country lanes. The Witney road, for instance, was not yet built; to get out of Oxford to the west, you simply meandered from village to village, Eynsham, Ducklington, South Leigh, High Cogges, all the way to Witney itself. It was a sunny afternoon; the cloud-patches had blown away and everything was radiant. I cycled without haste, but with the tireless thrust of youth, and by about two in the afternoon I was somewhere in the neighbourhood of High Cogges. There, deciding it would be nice to feel grass under my feet, I leaned the bike against a fence and started out for a stroll.

The field that particularly attracted me was wide and sloping, reaching up at the top to the border of a small wood of mature trees, mainly oak and beech. At the bottom end a few cows lay about chewing the cud. I went up to where the field bordered on the wood and then walked slowly along with trees on my left hand and grass sloping away on my right. The weather was perfect; we were just into June. The grass was young and shone with the fullness of the juice it contained; in the wood the leaves had reached their full growth but were still silky and translucent. I came to a five-barred wooden gate and stood leaning idly against it and looking round. Below me, more fields, more trees, a stream, and – I now noticed – a medium-sized farmhouse with its outbuildings. On the other side of the gate, leading off to my right through the wood, was a track, not just a footpath but a passage wide enough for a farm cart. Along this track a girl came riding a glossy chestnut horse. I had been so sunk in my own thoughts, so oblivious of the existence of any other people in the world, that the arrival of another human being came as a real surprise.

The horse seemed rather a large one, but the girl sat on it with perfect ease. That was the first thing I noticed about her and the second was her hair. It was fair; when she was a child it must have been ash-blonde, but already (she seemed about my age) it had begun to darken slightly. She wore it drawn back and gathered in some sort of fastening from which a long sheaf descended to about half-way between her shoulder-blades, though of course I didn't see that detail in those first moments because she was facing me. What I did see was that it was drawn back from her forehead, which was high and unlined. Its skin, like that of her face generally, was of the kind that naturally has an ivory pallor, but exposure to sun and wind had bronzed it delicately. Her eyes, which were regarding me steadily and held a certain challenge, were light blue.

The horse came steadily on, trotting towards the gate. The girl reined him in and was evidently about to get off and open it.

'I'll open the gate,' I said on an impulse and started fiddling with the latch. It was a heavy, old-fashioned thing.

'It's a bit awkward,' the girl said. 'You have to lift it up.' I thought her voice sounded very musical. Low, but full-toned and clear.

I got my hand under the bar and lifted the gate with all my strength. Like most old gates, it had sagged so that its weight was resting on the metal shaft of the latch. I heaved and managed to free it. The thought occurred to me that if she was used to opening it herself she must have pretty sturdy musculature for a girl.

She said 'Thanks' and came through. That was when I got a look at her back view and saw the sheaf of honey-coloured hair hanging down. I also took in that she wasn't wearing the standard young ladies' riding get-up. She had on a check shirt and corduroy trousers that had probably been originally worn by a boy.

I shut the gate, being careful to hoist it up on to its latch again, doing it right because I could feel her eyes on me. The horse's hoofs were silent and I knew she had reined in. I turned to face her.

'I ought,' she said in a considering tone of voice,' to tell you that you're trespassing.'

'Oh,' I said. I was looking carefully at her eyes, so as to remember their exact colour.

'Yes,' she said. 'My father's instructions. He farms these fields and he told me when I met anybody walking about in them I was just to tell them they were trespassing.'

‘Oh,’ I said again. Feeling that this was not quite enough I added, ‘Well, you’ve done what he said. You’ve told me.’

‘That’s all I have to do,’ she agreed, keeping those blue eyes on me, wary but not hostile. ‘Then if they keep on doing it, they’ve been told once, and if they meet my father or my brother they’ll just be sent packing.’

‘Seems a complicated business,’ I said. ‘I mean, if I’m a nuisance here, why don’t *you* send me packing?’

‘That’s not my part of the job,’ she said. ‘I’m a girl. They’re big strong men.’

‘Is that your horse?’ I asked, to change the subject.

‘As a matter of fact, no. A girl who lives in the town,’ I presumed she meant Oxford, ‘keeps him here and comes out at weekends and rides him. I have to exercise him during the week. If he never goes out he’ll get fat and out of condition, and then she’ll take him away.’

The horse flapped his ears as if he knew we were talking about him.

‘And that would be bad?’ I said.

‘She pays us something for stabling him. This is a bad time for farmers. Every little helps.’

‘D’you like riding?’ I asked, just to hold her there a few moments longer.

‘So-so. I like lots of things just as much.’

‘So you do it to help your father.’

‘Every farmer needs help,’ she said. ‘All of them are in trouble, more or less.’

‘Why are they?’

‘Cheap food coming in from the Empire,’ she said, with a dismissive shrug, as if she didn’t care to get involved in discussing it with me. ‘Well, I can’t hang about here all day making conversation. I’ve got things to do.’

‘I’ve got things to do, too,’ I said. ‘But I like talking to you. You’re enlightening me.’

She laughed and said, ‘Now I know.’

‘Now you know what?’

‘I was wondering whether you were a student from the University. And why, if you weren’t, you had time to be roaming round our fields in the middle of the afternoon. Now I know.’

‘How?’

‘Only students say things like, “You’re enlightening me”,’ she said, laughed again, and was gone. The horse’s great hoofs thudded away down the slope. I stood and watched horse and girl getting smaller as they went down the long slope, going away from me. Her laugh was still sounding in my head. It was a very musical laugh, or seemed so to me.

The ride back to Oxford was very pleasant. I ought to have been starting to feel tired, but for some reason I wasn't. No, to hell with 'for some reason'. The reason, and I was perfectly clear about it, was that meeting the blue-eyed girl, exchanging a few remarks with her, experiencing her blend of down-to-earth straightforwardness with friendliness, and behind that again a certain reserve, had given me a lift. It was like having sat for weeks in a heavily curtained room, and suddenly having the curtains drawn wide for a moment, long enough to take a good look out and see that there really was a world out there, a world that one day could be explored and enjoyed. I felt a surge of energy; I pedalled easily. When I got to Eynsham I decided to go down to Oxford along the river towpath, rather than by the road. It was gravelly and bumpy, and one had to lose time stopping to open gates and pushing through clustering herds of cattle, but it was worth it for the quiet, and the beauty of the sky and the river, with the water shining in the afternoon light, and the swifts and swallows coming in low over it to grab their share of flies, the same flies that were causing the fish to rise and make expanding circles, here and there, on the broad smooth surface.

I reached the City of Oxford by the Botley Road bridge, and though of course I could have turned left as soon as I came up on the pavement, gone under the railway bridge and carried on along Park End Street or Hythe Bridge Street straight into town, I didn't. I crossed over and stood for a moment leaning on the stone parapet of the bridge, looking downstream. There, on the left bank, was the ornate Edwardian architecture of the Oxford Electric Light Company. On the other bank, were the ruler-straight streets of Oseney Town, laid out according to the points of the compass. Suddenly I wanted, very much indeed, to be stepping into the quiet unpretentious bar of the Bargeman's Arms, seeing my father behind the dark wooden counter as of old, taking a pint of his good beer, sinking down on a plain but comfortable bench, answering a few routine questions and then just listening to the talk of the regulars. It would round off perfectly my day of escape from the life of Episcopus and the preoccupations of the University. And, by a happy chance, my watch showed me that it was barely five past six: my father would only just have opened the place. Ah, those years upon years when Brian and I had panted home and scrambled through the door to be sitting down to our meal at just this time!

So I went down our little street and went in at the door of the pub. My father was behind the bar. Old Trundle was ensconced in the wooden armchair, with a pint pot beside him from which he had evidently drunk only a few mouthfuls. Peake was there. So was the young chap, Ted, and the rest of the regulars. My father greeted me.

'Hello, Peter,' he said. 'Surprise visit, eh? You're usually too busy to come and see us while term's on.'

'Well,' I said, 'they do keep us at it pretty well.' I was anxious,as usual, to dispel any suggestion that my non-appearance at the pub during the term was anything to do with the social distance between town and gown.

'Well, it's good to see you anyway. Looking well too,' my father said. He drew me a pint. 'It's on the house. No, go on, take it.'

I took the glass. At the same instant a voice beside my ear said, 'I don't know whether it's true what the young gen'lman says, that they keeps 'em at it, but one thing I does know is, they keeps *us* at it.'

This came from a character with foxy eyes and a purple nose, who was sitting on a bar stool immediately beside me. 'So I'll have to drink up, Jack, and get along to my work.' He lifted, and drained, his glass of cream-frilled black stout.

'Well, it's not for much longer, Corky,' my father said. 'In fact it beats me why you didn't retire when you had your birthday last week. You could 'a done. Sixty-five.'

'Oh, I could of, I could of,' this Corky said. 'But they asked me to stay on for a few weeks, just to see the term out. And I didn't like to disoblige them. It'll make a difference to the whip-round they has for me in a month's time, when I do sling me 'ook at last.'

'Ay, Corky,' said Old Trundle judicially. 'They'll notice a difference wi' you gone.'

'Reckon so,' said Corky, his face expressionless. 'Well, cheer-o, Jack. Cheer-o, lads.' And he went out into the summer air, and an evening's work.

Trundle let him get out of earshot before turning to the others and saying, 'And we knows what difference it is they'll be noticin'.'

Peake grinned sardonically, but Ted, really wanting to know, asked, 'What difference'll that be, then?'

'The brandy bottles,' said Trundle, weighing his words impressively. 'For the first time since Corky went to work there, they'll be full of brandy. Moind you, whether they'll *notice*... they never 'ave yet.'

'Why,' Ted persisted, 'what are they full of now?'

'Brandy and water,' Old Trundle said and laughed himself into a coughing-fit that shook the pub.

'Yes,' my father said when the wheezing finally died away. 'There's one ex-serviceman the Army can be proud of.'

'He didn't waste his time, that's true,' said Peake.

'Army? Waste his time? I thought we was talkin' about brandy,' Ted complained to the room in general.

'What we're a-talkin' about,' Old Trundle said, 'is *corks*.'

'Well, I'm listening,' said Ted. 'Is that somethin' to do with why he's called Corky? I always thought his name must be Corcorcan or somethin' like that.'

'His name's John Lovegrove,' Peake supplied.

'The reason 'e's called Corky,' Trundle, by right, took up the story, 'is because corks is 'is special loine.'

'Learnt about 'em in the Army, did he?' said Ted sarcastically.

'He was in the R.A.M.C. A medical orderly he was, right through from 'fourteen to 'eighteen. Naturally, at his age, he'd 'a been too old for service. He must 'a been, oh...' A long calculation ensued. 'Forty-eight, aye, forty-eight, when the war started. But 'e wanted to do something, wanted to go overseas. I remember him sayin' he wanted to get out of his rut. Get away from 'is wife, more like.' Another slowly spreading laugh. 'They took 'im because he 'ad a bit of first-aid training, could do bandages, splints, them kind o'things. Anyway, one o' the things he done during his service in the Medical Corps was handle them 'ypydermatic needles. Them that they uses for injeckerlating stuff into your veins.'

All nodded sagely and Peake said, 'The dentist I go to, he's got three or four of 'em.'

'You've all seen 'em,' said Trundle. 'They got like a thumbpiece on 'em. You presses down with your thumb,' he made the gesture in the air, 'once you got the point in the man's vein, and it drives out the stuff you've got to put in him. Right. Then you pulls it out, without pulling the plunger back out. But if you *was* to pull it out,' he looked round impressively from face to face, lingering especially on Ted and myself, 'you'd take out the same amount as what you put in. You'd take out that much of the man's blood. Only you doesn't, 'cause it wouldn't be no use to you.'

'Right,' said my father promptingly.

'But brandy,' Trundle said, leaning forward, 'fine old Napoleon brandy, that's a different story. That's some use to you, or to anybody.'

'It's to be hoped,' said Peake, 'that when old Corky retires they don't send someone round to look in his cupboard and sniff what he's got in them bottles.'

'Cupboard!' said Trundle. 'It must be more'n a cupboard by this time. Must be a right bloody cellar.'

'What'd he do then?' Ted asked. 'Draw the brandy out with a hypodermic?'

'That's what he done. Drawed it out and squirted it into a glass he had standin' by.'

'What about the level goin' down?'

'Filled it up wi' clean water,' said Trundle.

'Well, what about the hole in the cork?'

'Cork heals up like flesh. The 'ole closes and you can't see as there ever was one.'

Ted looked round, uncertain whether his leg was being pulled. 'No, he really done that? He got away with it?'

'Got away with it for years,' said Peake. 'He went to work at this college, whichever it was, when he came back in 'nineteen. And he's retirin' in a month's time. And unless they catches him in the next month, he'll 'ave got away with it right along. More'n ten years of free brandy – and the best, too.'

'But this brandy. Where was they keeping it?'

'In the Senior Common Room. They always has a bottle on the go.'

'Napoleon brandy,' said Old Trundle. 'And if they takes water with it, they has brandy and water and water.'

The conversation concluded amid splutters of laughter. I finished my pint of free beer, thanked my father and went through to the kitchen to see my mother. She was doing something at the sink. I noticed that though the table was laid, only one place was set out: my father's.

'Aren't you going to eat anything?' I asked her.

'Later, I expect,' she said. 'Dad needs his tea before starting the evening's bar work, but I don't do a two-stage meal like I used to. Brian's always late home from work and when he gets in he's too tired to eat. We usually have a little something after ten.'

How hard they all work, I thought. And it suddenly struck me that if I did turn out to be one of Bax's more promising students, well, so I damn well ought to be. Hard work, attention to detail, doing one's job adequately, putting work before one's own trivial comforts, ought not to be a virtue in my eyes. With my background, it ought to be second nature.

I gave my mother a kiss before I went. And for a moment, as I took lightly in my arms the body out of which my body had emerged into life, I felt very close to my roots.

Lying in bed that night, before drifting off to sleep, I thought drowsily and with satisfaction over the day I had spent. My country excursion had been relaxing and pleasant, a reminder that some sources of happiness were always reliably there; and my brief visit home had been strengthening.

Why, then, did I wake up next morning as restless and unsettled as before? Why did I spend that day – it was a Thursday – starting one small task, dropping it, going on to another and abandoning that? And why, on the Friday morning, without consciously forming any plans, without justification, almost without volition, did I wheel out my bicycle after breakfast and pedal off; and why northward and then westward; and why, at every fork in the road, did the handlebars always seem to turn themselves in the direction that would take me at last to High Cogges?

Chapter 13

The field was the same as I remembered it. In two whole days the wood at the top of the slope had not been cut down, nor the farmhouse at the bottom destroyed by an earthquake. The grass was still shiny, the leaves still tender and joyous with sap. Even the cows seemed to be dotted about in much the same places as before. To my no doubt disordered imagination, the place had the air of a stage set, waiting for the resumption of some action that had been begun and then abruptly halted.

Proceeding exactly as before, I propped up the bike, got through the hedge, and walked along by the fence dividing the field from the wood. A few birds were singing away in its green shade, though fitfully; the dawn chorus was long since finished, and soon it would be time for the midday hush while the birds rested their voices ready for the evening concert. I looked down at the farmhouse. It looked asleep. There was no one about in the yard and no sound of pail-clattering or tractor-chugging. Tractors had just about become universal on farms by then, though they were smaller than the ones you see today, and cheaper, because they had to be.

I reached the five-barred gate, paused a moment, then opened it and went through into the wood. If, as I now admitted to myself, the whole object of coming here was to see if I could meet the fair-haired girl again, it made sense to station myself in the only place where I had ever seen her before. It was a wobbly enough basis for action, but it would have to serve until I got a firmer one, if I ever did.

I went along the cart-track for about fifty yards, then sat down with my back against an oak. Since the bracken and general undergrowth were fairly tall at that spot, the effect was to hide me from anyone who was not standing close by. This was purely accidental; I chose to sit there because the tree-trunk was at an inviting angle, not because I was hiding. But my invisibility did, in fact, have a bearing on what happened next.

I leaned back against the tree and half closed my eyes, thinking. What the hell was I up to? If I did happen to waylay the girl, what then? I couldn't seriously be thinking of starting anything up, could I? No, I admitted, no. It was just that she... did me good, somehow. Just by existing, she raised my spirits. It was mainly that she was so different from everything else in my experience, while remaining true to one central strand that obsessed me, namely being a girl. She was utterly remote from the stress and competitiveness of college life, from Carshalton, from Kent, from Bax; she was also utterly unlike anything in Brian's world of pistons and tyres and oil and compression-ratios and superchargers. No racing driver, hauling on his wheel and sliding his car round a hairpin bend, would ever be as graceful as she was on that springy chestnut horse that she was exercising for someone else.

Yes, I decided, this girl gave me a lift just by existing, and that was all I was here for: another lift. Where was the harm in that?

In the same instant that the thought came to me, a sudden shattering explosion rent, as they say, the air; and what was worse, the air about ten feet away from where I was sitting. Chill fear gripped me. Some stupid bastard was blazing away with a gun, and doing it where he had a very good chance of hitting me. I scrambled up as if impelled by the bite of an adder. There, standing in the middle of the cart-track and looking up into the trees, was a young man. The girl had spoken of a brother, and I could see at a glance that this was he. The family resemblance was very marked. I judged him to be about four or five years older than myself; not that I had much mental energy to spare, at that moment, for arithmetic.

His feet, solidly planted about eighteen inches apart, were clad in stout boots. He wore twill trousers and a flannel shirt, the sleeves rolled up to show solidly muscular arms, under one of which he held a gun of some kind. I don't know anything about guns. It had two barrels and looked very businesslike. The gun's owner was staring at me in an entirely unwelcoming fashion. His hair was the same colour as his sister's; so, I conjectured, were his eyes, but it seemed hardly the moment just then to gaze into them.

'What the hell are you doing here?' he demanded.

'Sitting down,' I said, 'leaning against a tree. At least, I was till you –'

He interrupted me with, 'Well, you'd better go and sit down somewhere where you've damn' well got a right to sit down. Go on, start moving. Don't argue, I'm not in the mood for it.' He had a baritone voice that would normally have been quite attractive, but at the moment it had a harsh edge of anger.

'I'm sorry to hear that,' I said. 'Something disagreeing with you, is there? Got out of bed on the wrong side this morning?'

I spoke sarcastically because I too was angry. No doubt I was trespassing and that put me mildly in the wrong, but I didn't see that I had to put up with being spoken to like that by a chap of my own age. His reaction was predictable.

'If you want a clout on the jaw,' he said, taking a brisk step towards me, 'you're going the right way to get one.'

I had no intention of slugging it out with him. Not only am I not very good at slugging it out, but the contest would have been hopelessly unequal. He was about my height, but, broad-shouldered and stocky, he would have made two of me.

'All right, I'm trespassing,' I said with what dignity I could muster. 'That puts me in the wrong. And if you're the owner of this land or his representative –'

'Cut the cackle,' he said.

' – that puts you in the right,' I went on with feeble persistence. 'But if you assault me we change places. You're in the wrong then. Trespassing isn't a crime unless you can prove –'

'Oh, I shan't assault you,' he said. His annoyance seemed to have drained away and he spoke calmly and easily. His voice, I noticed, carried the lilt of the local accent, but not very heavily; about as much as mine did. 'I shall just fetch you a clout on the jaw and if you go to the police station and show them the bruise I'll just say I saw you fall off your bike and land on your chin on the road.'

The best I could come back with was, 'How d'you know I came on a bike?'

'You've still got your clips on,' he said indifferently.

We stood there looking at each other for another moment. I knew I was handling this all wrong, but I didn't know what else to do. It was important to me to be able to hang around in this bit of territory, and here I was already becoming a marked man, somebody just asking to be run off the place whenever he was spotted in the distance. I wondered if this beefy farmer's son had a better nature I could appeal to.

'Look here,' I said, 'I'm a harmless type. I'm not going to damage anything. I just happen to like walking in the country, and if you –'

'Well, go and walk in some other bit of it. If you're asking me to give you permission to wander about on our grazing land, the answer's no, so take it and get out.'

'Why is it no? What's so bad about –'

'It's no because I say it's no.' His annoyance was evidently returning.

'I've got enough to do without bothering with the likes of you. We've got enough on our minds without your type pestering about and getting under our feet. You get back where you belong.'

'And where might that be?'

'In a College, I suppose. You look like a College type. And they're a nuisance wherever they go. That's enough. Now get moving. I've brought this gun out to get some rabbits or enough rooks to put in a pie. But I've got a few pellets of shot to spare for you if you don't get out of range while the going's good.'

'So now you're threatening to *shoot* me,' I said bitterly.

'Yes, I am. Move and keep moving.'

There was nothing for it, so I walked back down the cart-track to the gate and went through it. I went back towards the place where I had left my bike and got into the field; then I stopped and waited. I thought it might still be possible to hang around long enough to catch a glimpse of the girl, and perhaps even to scrape a conversation with her. But a moment or two later the brother's head and shoulders appeared over the gate. He had come to make sure that I had really cleared off, and when he saw that I hadn't he shook his fist angrily and shouted, 'If you don't get off the place in the next two minutes I'll be down there to see to you!'

Cursing, I moved down to the hedge that bordered the road, feeling his eyes boring into my back as I walked. When I got to the spot where my bike was I started to squeeze through a thin patch in the hedge, which was how I had come in, but his voice followed me again.

'Not there, damn you! Go out by the gate!'

I walked along by the hedge and found the gate. There were cows clustered about it and I practically had to shove my way through them to get to it and climb over. I didn't unlatch it because the cows would probably have come out with me, and that would have enraged him still further. Then I walked back along the dusty lane and got my bike and stood there, considering.

The best thing to do, I decided, was to cycle around the lanes for a bit. I couldn't bear the thought of going back to Oxford with my tail between my legs, and in any case there was always a chance, however faint, that as long as I stayed in the neighbourhood I might see the girl. So I pedalled about, aimlessly enough but taking care to keep within a radius of half a mile or so of the farm (it was called Jasmine Farm, I noticed as I rode past the gate) and to keep an eye on the likely points in the village, the general shop and post office, things like that. She wasn't there. She wasn't anywhere to be seen.

About noon, thirsty and beginning to be hungry, I went for a drink in the local pub. There wasn't, and isn't now, a pub in the hamlet of High Cogges. The nearest one is in the immediately contingent village of South Leigh, which also has a medieval church. I visited the church first. It had very faded old wall-paintings that I could only just make out. I studied them for a long time, then I went and sat in the pub and rather gloomily began drinking a pint of beer. It seemed to me that my motives, and my situation generally, were as lacking in clarity as the wall-paintings in the church. The nature of my problems was clear enough, but just how was I going to remedy them by messing about in this neck of the woods, just because I had once seen a graceful girl on a horse and exchanged a few words with her? It was too ridiculous. Apart from everything else, all this was a colossal waste of time. I thought of the books on my desk back at College. If I were sitting there instead of here, I could put in a nice quiet hour's work and then go down to Hall for lunch, all as cosy and reassuring as could be. Yet here I was, miles away, with only enough money for a snack of bread and cheese instead of the sustaining lunch that I would have to pay for anyway, and no work done... I didn't go on to ask myself rhetorically 'And what's it all for?' because I knew damn well what it was for, but the it that it was for seemed more unattainable than ever.

Up to now, I had had the pub to myself, with only the landlord sitting reading a newspaper behind the bar, but now two local men came in, and for the next few minutes I divided my attention between my own thoughts and occasional snatches of their conversation which happened to impinge. 'Always a sore point with the old man,' I heard, and 'It's just a stage he's going through.' 'Well, the old man's got a point. What does he want meddling with them things?' 'Well, but you can see what he wants. He wants to get taken on one day and do it for a living.' 'He's daft, then. It costs money to get trained.' 'It wouldn't be if he joined the Service. Get trained for nothin' then, and paid a wage for it.' 'Ay, but that's just what old Burrell's afraid of, en't it? How'd he manage if the boy wen' off and joined the Service?'

Their talk wandered to other things. I idly wondered what Service they meant, and who was thinking of joining it and what for, but my curiosity was so faint that the least competition could drive it from my mind, and soon I started thinking about the girl again, and wondering where she was, and if she remembered meeting me, and what her name was. Then hunger took over, and I counted out my change and bought myself some bread and cheese, and while I ate it I wished myself back at College.

When I did get back, later that afternoon, I determined to settle down and make a real effort to get into the swing of things. Episcopus had a little Essay Society, to which people read papers. It was a traditional, rather formal affair; after the paper, a loving-cup of mulled claret was passed round before the discussion began, each member rising and taking the cup from the one who had just drunk from it and the pair of them exchanging stiff little bows. Pompous enough, and I daresay laughable enough among a lot of fresh-faced boys, and yet I could see the reason for it then as clearly as I can see it now. The loving-cup, taken before the cut and thrust of discussion began, signified that we were friends who had met to exchange ideas and opinions in a civilized setting, that we were intent on seeking for truth in a constructive way and not just wrangling. The discussions, of course, never lived up to the tradition represented by the loving-cup and the polite bowing, but these things lingered in the atmosphere none the less.

I went because the paper was being given by Lamont. He had chosen the topic 'Symbolism and the Artist's Impulse'. I have forgotten everything he said, and indeed he lost me from about the middle of the first sentence, but his face remains very vivid in my memory, and the easy but alert way he sat in his chair by the fire, one hand at his left temple, the other holding the mass of notes in a cardboard folder on his knee. His face was as serious and other-worldly as ever. He was so totally wrapped up in what he was saying that it was not boring to listen to him, as it usually is when one is not understanding what is said. As far as I could see, the only other person in the room who understood it, apart from Lamont himself, was our Senior Member. It was then, as it is now, the custom for such undergraduate societies to have one don as figurehead, attending the meetings out of benevolence and occasionally contributing to the discussion. Our Senior Member at that time was a Fellow of the College I had never had any contact with because he was a scientist. He was well along in his career and must have been about sixty, which meant of course that to us he seemed like Methuselah, but he must have been in full intellectual vigour, because a few years later he won the Nobel Prize for whatever kind of science it was that he did, and soon after that was knighted, one of the last to be dubbed by George V. His name was Weatherby and he was a long, leathery man with a huge skull that seemed more huge every year as his hairline went back. He had a deep, gentle voice and large eyes which looked naked and innocent until he needed to read something and put on a pair of heavy, thick-framed spectacles which made them almost disappear. His hair had been startlingly bright yellow and was even now only just turning from yellow to white – the colour of old teeth or piano keys. He was a very nice man, as self-forgetful and idealistic as Lamont; the forty extra years he had spent on this tarnished planet had not diminished his innocence. When the loving-cup had gone round and the discussion period began, it was Lamont and Weatherby who sustained it, moving immediately on to a plane of philosophical and metaphysical speculation that left me hopelessly behind. Most people there were as tongue-tied as I was, though inevitably there were one or two oafs who, missing the point of everything and not seeing any of the complexities, rushed in with shovelfuls of sheer garbage from time to time, or stubbornly maintained some foolish position because they had heard somewhere that the intellectual life was founded on disputation and they took this to mean mere wrangling.

Another thing that has stayed with me from that evening was the atmosphere of perfect equality between Lamont and Weatherby. They both gave their full attention to the matters under discussion and had nothing left over for self-consciousness. The result, on a personal level, was perfect courtesy. Lamont treated Weatherby, for all his years and his distinction, as a fellow explorer in these important regions; Weatherby treated Lamont, for all his youth, as a possible source of insight and guidance.

It was all very impressive, and yet it left me, as so often, with a feeling of being in between, not solidly based anywhere. I knew I should never be a Lamont and I very much doubted whether even a lifetime of devotion to my subject would make me into a Weatherby. On the other hand I despised the boneheads who now and then interrupted the discussion with their juvenile arguments. Most of them had been at Public Schools and therefore made the tranquil assumption that their opinions must be correct, if not intellectually then at any rate socially, which was probably the more important. I despised them all the more for it; but I felt isolated, below one level and above the other.

Afterwards I went back to my rooms and was just getting ready for bed when Wilmot knocked on the door and asked if I would care to go on the river with him the next day, in one of the College punts. Anyone else coming? No, just he and I. He seemed to want my company and I was feeling lonely, so I was glad to accept.

The College punts were down by Magdalen Bridge, and after lunch the next day Wilmot and I went down there and took one out. We went upstream, following the winding of the Cherwell between its banks of yellow, pebbly Oxford clay. The sun splashed on to the river, and on to us, through the interstices of the long green willow-leaves, and everything was very calm and idyllic: too much so for me, because the beauty and tranquillity of the setting only served to emphasize the fact that it was all a colossal wasted opportunity. The punt glided along, the cushions were soft, the river chuckled and murmured pleasantly, the willows clustered overhead, and it was the perfect setting for... what? For love, of course. At our time of life, and with good healthy normal instincts, Wilmot and I ought each to have been taking a girl on the river, not just punting one another along. This thought cast such a shadow of discontent over my mind that the gentle warmth of the sun, and the pleasantness of our surroundings, seemed like insults.

Wilmot asked if he could take a turn at poling us along, and turned out not to be very good at it. It wasn't his first time in a punt, but it can't have been more than his second or third; his steering was erratic and he wasted a lot of energy. I took his instruction in hand and in the course of half an hour he had already made good progress. We went over the rollers and got into the upper Cherwell, and went quite a long way upstream before deciding that we ought to get back. I worked Wilmot pretty hard, to give him the experience; his honest round face glistened and the stiff spikes of hair that stood out from his head were bedewed with sweat, as he dug the steel end of the punt-pole, with its small double prong, into the gravelly bed of the steadily flowing Cherwell and used his weight to heave the boat forward, trimming it towards right or left by leaning hard on his upper hand (to go right) and then equally hard on his lower (to go left), concentrating like mad, staring ahead through his big circular glasses, working as if this were the eighteenth century, not the twentieth, and he were a waterman with a hungry family to maintain. For my part, as I lay on the cushions in the well of the boat I felt all over again how frustrating it was to be lying there by myself. Our trip had taken us almost up to the point where I had planned to pull it off with Vinnie, and as I remembered that episode my mind boiled over with pure rage at those yobbos whose guffawing presence had sent Vinnie striding away, across the fields and out of my life. Curse them, I thought, curse them.

'What's biting you?' Wilmot asked. My face must have looked extraordinarily grim and tense, because he stopped pushing at the pole and stood there, holding it out of the water, peering down at me.

'Oh, nothing,' I said. 'I'm all right.'

'You look pretty fed up for someone who's all right,' Wilmot said. 'I must say, old lad, if you've got something worrying you, I think it'd be a good idea to talk about it if you can. You know me well enough, after all.'

'I give you my solemn assurance, Wilmot,' I said with the pomposity of eighteen years, 'that there's nothing wrong that isn't perfectly obvious. There's nothing I'm hiding.'

'Well, if it's perfectly obvious, forgive my stupidity, but what is it?'

I gestured round in an inclusive way that took it all in – the river, the trees, the soft blue sky, the meadows, the punt, him, myself.

'Look at it,' I said. 'Just look at what's in front of your eyes. Here are the two of us in a punt, taking turns to pole the damn thing along. And that's exactly what's wrong. Two blokes in a punt. Punts are for *couples*. Punts are for taking *girls* out. Instead of being in one punt together,' I spelt it out, 'we ought each to be in a punt with a passenger and the passenger ought to be a girl.'

'Oh,' he said and gave the boat a clumsy push forward. 'Oh, well, if that's all...'

'All? It's just about the sum total of –'

'All right, old lad,' Wilmot said soothingly. 'I see just what you mean and as a matter of fact I agree with you.'

'Well, that makes me feel much better,' I said savagely. I felt so sorrowful and frustrated that I was really taking it out on harmless old Wilmot – I despised myself for it but I couldn't help it. 'I mean, it's just great to be agreed with, but the question is, what the hell are we going to –'

'As a matter of fact,' said Wilmot, keeping his temper and speaking gently but with some dignity – thoroughly shaming me, in fact – 'as a matter of fact, I'm working on it. I have a date to take a girl on the river in two days' time.'

Suddenly I saw it all. The step-by-step approach. Some girl had agreed to go on the river with him, he knew me to be a good punter, and he had suggested our going out together so as to get some practice and some useful hints, not to make a fool of himself in front of the girl. 'You're a deep one, Wilmot,' I said.

'I don't see why. Surely there's no harm in trying to go into any situation as well prepared as you can. I'm pretty much of a duffer at punting, and I thought a trip out with you would bring me on a bit.'

He was so candid, so honest and unironical, that however mean and twisted I felt I couldn't dredge up anything that resembled a grievance. Why shouldn't I pass on a few tips to help his punting, enjoying his company the while? Wasn't that what friends were for?

'Where did you meet this dame?' I asked.

'Play-reading circle. Molière,' said Wilmot, swinging on the pole in an effort to keep us on a straight course. I remembered that he was reading French.

'Did she read well? Good actress, is she?'

'Not specially,' said Wilmot. 'Look, if the pole dips itself into this very sticky clay, is it better to pull at it like mad or let it go?'

'Let it go. And use the paddle to turn the punt round and come back for it. There's no hurry. It's better to take a bit of time when –'

'You see, I don't want to end up clinging to the pole in mid-stream and watching the punt move away, like those cartoons in old numbers of *Punch*.'

'No,' I said. 'What's her name?'

'Grace,' Wilmot said. He stopped poling and straightened his back. 'You wouldn't like to take over for a bit, would you? I'm feeling a bit creased, to tell you the truth.'

*

A few days later I saw Grace. I think it was in the early evening of the day when he took her on the river. The two of them were walking across the quad, not quite hand in hand but close together, and Wilmot was hovering protectively and, I thought, a trifle possessively. Grace was a sturdy girl, rather thick in the waist. She wore her hair wound round her head in plaits. Very much the embryo schoolmarm. But the fact remained that Wilmot had a girl to take on the river and I hadn't. Quiet, persistent, undemonstrative and totally unspectacular, he had at least got as far as the crease, while I was still sitting in the pavilion.

*

The summer term was now more than half over. The weather was glorious. If only it had been wet and chilly, the kind of English summer that is like a green winter, I would have been able to bear my girl-lessness better. But to be lonely and unfulfilled amid such a feast of beauty and fecundity was more than I could bear. Indeed I made no effort to bear it. I abandoned all pretence of carrying on as usual, of continuing somehow to function although I knew I was unhappy. I moped. I idled. Everything that happened, everything that came within my cognisance, either depressed me or put me into a temper. If I saw a young man and a girl together, obviously finding joy in each other's company, I would willingly have boiled the pair of them in oil. When I took a stroll round Episcopus garden after breakfast, the joyous carolling of the birds fell on my ear as pure mockery, and I longed for a rifle and a can of bird-shot.

Obviously this could not go on. I was neglecting my work – Bax's manner towards me, which at the end of the previous term had begun to thaw and become almost human, was now frostier and more distant after each skimped, halting essay I read to him. I felt he was preparing some really punitive measure against me, some intellectual headsman's axe that he was sharpening week by week till he had it ready to finish me at one deadly blow. But neglecting my work was only part of it. I was rapidly becoming unfit to live a normal life at all.

Needless to say it was not long before I was in the saddle again and heading for High Cogges. I hung about several afternoons, but the horse-riding girl might have ceased to exist for all I saw of her, and in moods of semi-delirium I sometimes wondered whether I had hallucinated the whole thing. I really think I might have come to that conclusion but for the fact that the brother, confound him, was real enough. I hadn't dreamt *him*, and the family resemblance between them seemed to indicate that the girl, too, existed in the tangible world.

I saw him again one lunchtime. I was in the village pub, sitting down at the end of the long bar because I didn't want to get drawn into conversation with anyone – not that there seemed to be much danger of it – when I heard his voice, recognizing it immediately. He had come in with someone else. After a time, having kept my face turned away from them till I judged they were settled, I swivelled warily and eyed them. They didn't notice me – not at first, anyway – and I got a good look at the pair of them. The other man was considerably older and had much the same facial bone structure: the father, obviously. The farmer himself. The owner, or in those days more probably the tenant, of Jasmine Farm. Pretty soon the pair of them had spotted me and Sonny Boy was indicating me with a motion of his head – I wasn't worth the trouble of moving his hands for – and saying something in a low voice. Quite obviously he was telling his father that he had caught me hanging about on their land and promised me a good hiding if I didn't take myself off. The fact that I was hanging about again, not exactly on their land but in the pub that they probably regarded as an extension of it, clearly brought me one step closer to the said good hiding.

Well, so what? I was sunk in such despair that it hardly mattered. Given that I seemed to be such a hopeless loser, what did it matter what these two yokels thought of me? For a moment I almost summoned up enough spirit to give them a cheerful wave across the room, or raise my glass as if saluting them. But something in the young one's eyes, as they rested briefly on my face, stopped me short. The lines of his face suggested determination – he had a strong chin, which, now I came to think of it, his sister also had – and one of the things he was evidently determined on was to dislike me.

I wanted to go up to the bar and get something to eat, but I didn't want to approach this pair any more nearly, so I sat tight and eyed the remaining two inches of amber fluid in my pint glass (I couldn't afford a refill and bread and cheese as well). Fortunately at that moment they finished their drinks, stood up and moved off, without looking at me. I got a clear view of the father as they went across my field of vision. He was tubby, shortish – at least six inches shorter than the son – and his face, though obviously from the same genetic stock, was rounder and more bucolic, with a muddy complexion and a balding pate. Whereas the son had something of a craggy-jawed, Empire-building look, the dad looked like what he was – a small, unambitious tenant farmer in North Oxfordshire, typical of what farmers were like in the inter-war years, when the era of the big hand-outs was not yet dreamt of, and the agricultural depression of the late nineteenth century, which brought country people time and time again to the verge of starvation, was still a powerful folk-memory. Farmers in my boyhood were still peasants, set in their ways, thrifty, cunning, suspicious. As this one went out of the pub he clapped on to his head an old battered hat of the kind they used to call a pork-pie. It was a sensible enough hat for one who had to do the bulk of his work out of doors and didn't need to waste money on dressing up, but it set the seal on his rustic appearance, crowning the simplicity of his round face with a circular halo of the bucolic. He looked like a man competing in a fancy dress competition who had chosen the role of Farmer Giles. The son, by comparison, looked striding and confident and positively loaded with Officer-Like Qualities.

They went, I had my frugal lunch, a last melancholy patrol of the neighbourhood revealed no trace of the person I was longing for a sight of, and I pedalled back to Oxford along the flat alluvial plain of the Thames, a long, boring, featureless ride to Eynsham and then under the southern end of Wytham hill. At least I was developing good leg muscles. And the job with Tupper Boardman had given me good arm muscles. Perhaps that was the secret. Get enough sexual frustration and you'll develop into a superman. You Too Can Have a Body Like Mine, as the ads used to say. Even if it's in a coffin. Cause of death at autopsy: arteries solidified by excess production of unused semen.

*

About the only part of my work that I did keep ticking over was that I went to lectures now and then – if, that is, they didn't clash with my excursions to High Cogges. I went to them partly because although I couldn't concentrate on a book I could at least slump in a chair and listen to someone's voice droning on, possibly taking in a thought or a fact now and again.

One series of the lectures I listlessly followed took place in the Hall at Magdalen. It was always, even amid my tensions and sufferings, a mild treat to go to that lovely place. To get to the Hall one had to traverse the calm shade of the cloisters, and afterwards I used to go out for a few minutes into the grassy open space between the eighteenth-century New Building and the deer park. To sit on one of the benches, or lean over the stone bridge that crossed the little cut they had made from the Cherwell, always calmed me down, and I was grateful though I knew it couldn't last.

The lectures I attended were from 11 a.m. till noon, and after one of them – in the fifth or sixth week of term – I was moving slowly across the grass in front of the New Building when I saw a figure emerging from one of the staircase entrances. When you see someone, however familiar, in a setting totally different from their normal one it is often a second or two before you recognize them, and in this case I experienced a brief double-take before fully registering that the man I was looking at was my own brother, Brian.

I was so surprised that my feet stopped walking of their own accord and I just stood and stared at him. It was a working day, and I had had no word that Brian was ill or had lost his job, which meant that he ought to have been attending to the interests of the M.G.Car Company. Well, perhaps he was attending to them. But why, in that case, was he not in Abingdon, why in Oxford and above all why in a college? I could see that something special was afoot because he was wearing his suit. I knew that suit well. It was the real tailor's-dummy double-breasted job that people wore in the 'thirties and it was chocolate-brown with faint pinstripes. He wore it for things like weddings and funerals. In those days, even in our station in life, every young man had a suit. No, we must give it a capital. He had a Suit. And when he wore it he was sending a signal, just as the mating plumage of birds, or colour change in fishes, are signals. But what he was signalling now was more than I could tell. With a sudden surge of relief I let slip my burden of misery and gave myself over to the simple emotion of younger-brother curiosity.

'Brian,' I said. 'Hello!'

He hadn't seen me, and now, looking confused, stopped dead in his turn.

'Peter,' he said. 'This isn't the college you're at.'

'I come to lectures here,' I said. 'What's the matter, you hoping to avoid me?'

At that he grinned and relaxed and said, 'Just got a bit of business here. Chap who lives up there.' He jerked his head to indicate the staircase he had just come out of.

'M.G. business?' I said incredulously.

'What other kind do I do? Look, now I've run into you, let's go and have a drink. I've got to get back to Abingdon before one, but that won't take many minutes.'

We went to a quiet little pub on the Plain. As we walked over Magdalen Bridge together I felt happy for a few minutes. This was the first time Brian had ever suggested that he and I should have a drink together, should spend time together just for sociability. It made a difference to the whole way I felt about him.

'Now,' he said when we were settled down with our beer. 'Have you ever met a bloke called the Honourable Fergus Kingswood?'

'Good God, no,' I said. 'That type doesn't exist in my circle. I don't think there's anyone in Episcopus with a handle to his name. If there is he must be a Socialist.'

'Why a Socialist?'

'Keeps quiet about having a title. Sweeps it under the carpet. No, this Kingswood chap sounds more the type you get at Christ Church or here at Magdalen. Where the Royal Family go. Anyway, tell me about him. Friend of yours?'

'In a way, yes,' Brian said, sharing the joke. 'He drives one of our cars, so he's got to be.'

'And you look after him? I'm surprised you have time to take on stray customers. I always thought you were terribly busy.'

'So we are terribly busy,' Brian said. 'There'd be plenty to do if we never came off the place at all, just slept on the floor every night. But that's all part of the way it is at our place. We only exist on sufferance. Billy Morris doesn't want us and he won't finance us properly. So we pick up a few bob wherever we can find it. Looking after private owners is one of the things we do.'

'I see. This Honourable Who'sit has bought a racing car from you.'

'Yes, and not just any old racing car. He's bought one of the latest jobs, the C-type. They don't come cheap, especially if you add what we charge for all the modifications he wants, things like down-draught carburettors and special gear ratios. He must be quite serious. He's planning to enter it in the B.R.D.C. Five Hundred. That's why I was asking if you knew him. I'm just wondering what kind of a show he'll put up. It's not going to look good if he's going to take one of our cars out and just drive it round looking pretty with a silk scarf flapping over his shoulder.'

'Well, I suppose you can't stop him.'

'Too damn' right. We can't stop anybody buying an M.G. if they turn up at Abingdon with the money in their pocket. And he's got that all right. Anyway, I've been put in charge of getting him started. I just nipped over here with some papers for him to sign and some technical literature about the car. And I advised him what spares he'll need for a season's racing. The next time I come I'll bring the spares and get really working on the car. I shan't be wearing this then.' He glanced down at his suit.

'Where is the car?' I asked. 'Surely they don't let him keep it at Magdalen?'

'Course not. He garages it in Alfred Lane. We fixed that too.'

We looked at each other in an amused, friendly way. Our worlds had touched at last. The fact that out of the thousands of young men at the University there was one who had bought an M.G. and was planning to go racing in it seemed to have brought the entire University within Brian's ken, whereas hitherto he had made rather a point of not being aware that it existed.

'When he races this car at Brooklands,' I said, 'will he drive it down there?'

'Heck, no. It won't be in road trim. No, he'll have to take it on a trailer. That's one of the things I came over for today, to find out if he wants us to hire him one.'

'Can't he go down with you? Put it on your lorry or something?'

'We're not going. It's too soon after Ulster. We couldn't turn round and go out again in the time, not on the shoestring we're on. No, it's up to private owners to show the flag there. That's why we don't want a lot of pansy amateurs.'

I was going to ask him what he meant about Ulster, but he looked at his watch, drank up and said he had to get back to Abingdon. We parted cheerfully, and as I walked back to College I felt a curious sense of relief. The fact that Brian had for years so completely rejected me, had regarded me as someone who lived in a kind of grey, cerebral hinterland rather than in the real world where men were men, must have been oppressive to me at some deep level that my consciousness had not plumbed. I had accepted it as a fact of life, and rather regretted that it should be so, but I had never consciously worried about it. Now, it became clear to me, if only because of this unexpected surge of relief, that it had been a trouble. I felt as if life had suddenly given me a present: a brother I had not known about before.

As it happened, sheer chance was soon to put me in the way of knowing a little more about the Honourable Fergus Kingswood. A couple of afternoons later I went to get my hair cut. I must have chosen my time badly because the barber's shop was very full, and while I waited I read my way through a pile of magazines of various kinds, united only in being ones I would never normally look at. Among them was one of the shiny-paper kind where you can read all about people who are rich and have country estates. The Kingswoods, it seemed, were rich and had a country estate. They were a respectable old family with bits of title breaking out on them here and there, like eczema, and they had stayed afloat financially by astutely arranged marriages with heiresses. A number of long, bony faces looked out at me from the glossy pages and most of them were framed by other long bony faces that belonged to horses, but when it got to Fergus, the youngest of the family, it showed him doing other things. There was one picture that showed him sitting on a bobsleigh getting ready to go down the Cresta Run, and another standing beside a racing car, whether his own car or not it didn't say. Evidently Fergus had decided that Speed was his thing. In terms of Oxford life he fitted into a ready-made slot: he was one of those young bloods with a taste for reckless sports and enough money to indulge in the more expensive ones. In the eighteenth century he would doubtless have had a string of hunters. In Victorian times he might have gone ballooning. In the 1930s, it was Brooklands and an M.G. (C-Type).

I decided I didn't mind Fergus. The face that looked out at me from the photographs was quite good-natured, with a lop-sided, boyish grin. Anyway, I would never meet him; but I was disposed to like him because his wild hobby had forged an unexpected link between Brian and me.

*

Meanwhile, racing cars and young bloods were all very well, but what about my own situation? I could see clearly enough that if I didn't get my needs satisfied I would never be able to concentrate on work. Having started by winning golden opinions, I would 'go off' as promising freshmen so often did; become a mediocrity; scrape a weak Second or a Third, and have to be content with some very ordinary job. Perhaps what lay ahead of me was the life of a schoolmaster, such as Grayson. And all for lack of a good healthy outlet for energies that, so far from being culpable, had been implanted in me by the Creator. Self-pity and gnawing anxiety forced me into the saddle and out to High Cogges again.

I suppose the plain truth is that I was out of my mind. I was no longer capable of behaving rationally or sitting down to think up a plan of action. With no more volition than a piece of iron ore jumping towards a magnet, I cycled full pelt all the way to High Cogges and didn't pull up till I reached the gate of Jasmine Farm. What I expected to await me there I didn't know – or, rather, my mind contained nothing so coherent as an expectation.

However, my blind, iron-ore instinct had in fact put me within reach of a small change in the situation. Small? It was infinitesimal. But I was ready to seize any shred of opportunity.

As I approached the gate I saw that somebody had tacked up a notice on one of the posts. It was neatly lettered in black ink and it was on an oblong of shiny cardboard, probably the top of a shoe-box. It read: PEDIGREE GOLDEN LABRADOR PUPS FOR SALE. BOTH SIRE AND DAM AWARD-WINNERS. DOCUMENTS CAN BE INSPECTED.

What I can see now, looking back, is that such a notice conveyed a slight hint of desperation. Or, if that is too strong a word, a very definite need to explore any possible source of income. The road past the farm was a cul-de-sac. You took a turn to the left from the road that ran through High Cogges, leaving it just before it mounted a slope and turned into the main road to Witney. When you got to the end of this left turn it was a T-junction. Jasmine Farm was on one side and another, larger farm on the other. Immediately facing the T-junction was a cottage, obviously occupied by the family of someone who worked on one of the farms. That was all: they were the only three buildings in the area. The number of people coming past the gateway of Jasmine Farm, and pausing to read that carefully written notice, must have been very small. On most days, nil.

I, of course, was not interested in reading signs. Not those signs, anyway. All that mattered to me was having the resolution to walk up to that farmhouse door and knock on it. No hesitation. If I faltered now I would never go through with it. They had put a notice on the farm gate which amounted to an invitation to any passer-by to enter the place and go and knock on the door. I opened the gate, went in, closed and latched the gate behind me and started across the farmyard.

It was a windy day with big clouds moving rapidly across the sky, by turns shutting off the sun and revealing it. As I started to move towards the farmhouse, the clouds parted and strong sunlight flooded down on to the scene like some kind of stage-effect. Our hero's life emerges from the shadows. Or perhaps it just meant: No place to hide.

I knocked on the door. When I heard someone coming towards it from the other side I nearly turned and ran, but there would have been no point. I just stood quite still and listened to the hammering of my pulse. *They can't eat me*, I thought. *I want a Golden Labrador puppy. I've always wanted a Golden Labr –*

The door opened and a woman stood there. I could see at once that this was my magnet's mother. If she got her rounded jawline from her father, it was her mother who contributed the blonde complexion and the light blue eyes. She wore her wheat-coloured hair neatly plaited. Her hands were dusted with flour, and she was wiping them on a kitchen towel, rough-textured but clean.

'Good morning,' she said. 'Or, I suppose, afternoon now.' The grandfather clock in the passage behind her showed 12.15. 'Is it eggs you want?'

'No,' I said and immediately realized that it might have been better to say I did want eggs. So much easier to handle than pedigree puppies. But there was no going back. 'It's the notice on the gate,' I said. 'Pedigree –'

'Oh, the Labradors. You're quick off the mark. I only put that notice up an hour ago. Well, that does give you first choice.'

Christ. She expected me to take one of them away there and then!

'I'd just like to –' I started off.

'Well, of course you'll want to see them,' she said reasonably, though in a businesslike, bargain-driving tone. Her voice was more middle class than I had expected, with only a light trace of the Oxfordshire burr. She didn't seem quite the same social class as her husband with his round peasant face and battered pork-pie hat. But then of course the daughter's was the same. Where was the daughter? Would I see her?

'If you'll just go round the side of the house,' Mrs Farmer's Wife said to me, 'I'll come through to the back. They're outside in the stable. We don't believe in keeping dogs in the house, naturally.'

I felt like assuring her that if there was one kind of human being I had always found it impossible to get on with, it was the kind who kept dogs in the house. Actually I ducked my head wordlessly and started moving off round the side of the house.

She popped out of the back door as I came round the corner of the house, and led the way across a cobbled farmyard to the stable. It was empty of horses, but in its cool shadowy interior the pups were lying next to their mother in a big wicker basket.

'How old are they?' I asked, bending down to look at naked rounded bellies and little soft, worried-looking faces.

'Five days,' she said. 'Of course we shan't be letting them go till they're weaned. But we can earmark one for you.'

'That would be nice,' I said in a dead voice.

'Is there one you fancy? Take your time, look them over. We've got all the documents inside about their ancestry and a list of prizes as long as your arm. Have you had Labradors before?'

I was, if anything, even more thrown by the way she said 'Labradors' and not just 'a Labrador'. 'No,' I said. 'But there's always a first time.'

'You'd be wanting to breed from it, I suppose. Will you want a dog or a bitch?'

'Either,' I said. 'It's the pedigree that matters.'

She shot me a look as if she were trying to size me up and said, 'Well, it all depends whether you just want a pet or whether you're thinking of breeding.'

I let that one go. If I had to be revealed sooner or later as a phony who didn't know one end of a dog from another and had no intention whatever of buying a Golden Labrador pup, let it be later.

'I like the look of this one here,' I said, looking down at one of the little round bellies. 'He... she... looks a nice...' I bent down to pat the creature, but the maternal bitch snarled and showed her teeth.

'I'm afraid she won't let you touch them,' Mrs Farmer's Wife said. 'She'll just about tolerate me picking them up. Is this the one you want to look at?'

She deftly gathered up the little animal and held it in both hands. I wasn't sure whether I was supposed to take it, or whether its mother would bite me in the leg if I did. So I compromised by bending forward slightly from the hips and staring intently at the pup as if trying to judge its finer points. As a matter of fact I was trying to guess its gender, but I got no further with that than with any other part of the encounter. (It isn't as easy as you might think, with a new-born pup.) I stared, feeling Mrs Farmer's Wife's eyes on me, thinking she must have me down by now as an impostor, not knowing what to say or do.

'Have you found a customer already, Mother? I always said you were a quick worker.'

The voice came from the doorway behind me. It made me spin round convulsively, and of course even as I did so, even as my muscles obeyed my brain signals and whisked my body round, I knew who it belonged to. It was her – She – the daughter. And I was caught unawares, with no idea how to cope, and in a foolish situation!

'Oh,' the mother said, 'I expect we shall have a procession of people.' Including non-starters like this one, her tone conveyed. 'In fact I'm quite sure we shall have more would-be buyers than there are puppies.'

'Is that what generally happens?' I asked, snatching at what seemed to be a chance to show an intelligent interest.

'It's her first litter.' Once again her tone conveyed that had I known anything about dogs I would have seen at a glance that this bitch was too young to have had pups before.

'At that rate,' the daughter said, 'we'll have to vet all the people who want to buy one. Have them go through a character test, to make sure they'll provide a good home.'

I could tell from the amused way she was looking at me that she recognized me as the trespasser who had opened the gate for her, the one she had twigged as 'a student from the University'. She and her brother both. They had my number. And though I had no idea *how* she knew, I also felt quite certain that she knew why I was there. The ploy about seeing the pups didn't take her in, and it wasn't going to take her mother in for much longer, either.

The mother now said to me, 'If you're certain that this is the one you want, the best thing would be to put down a deposit. They're five pounds each. If you put down one pound, we'll return it if in the end the dog doesn't come your way.'

I forced myself to look straight at her face for an instant. It really was very like her daughter's, except that, since she was fortyish, it was a little more heavily fleshed. That dimple in the centre of the chin, which in the daughter's case was merely hinted, in the mother's was quite pronounced. Not unattractive, though. And her eyebrows had the same shape. Two perfect arches.

'Er, yes, of course,' I said. 'The only snag is, I've come out without my cheque-book. You see, when I set out for a bike ride this morning, I didn't know I'd be –'

She bent down and put the puppy back in the basket. 'Well, when you *have* got your cheque-book, we can talk business.'

It sounded very much like the chop.

'Of course,' I said, 'I can easily pop over – I mean it's not very far and I –'

'Where do you live?' she asked indifferently, already thinking of other things.

'In Oxford,' I said.

'What part of Oxford? I drive in at least once a week, and I dare say I could bring the pup in with me if you do decide to buy it.'

'I live in College,' I said. 'Episcopus.'

She looked at me as if suddenly deciding to take me in more carefully. Up to that point she had been, I'm certain, simply bringing the interview to a polite close. But the information that I was a member of the University seemed to be important to her.

'In college?' she said. 'Well, that's interesting. We don't get many

Varsity men coming through our village.'

In all my life up to that point I had never heard anyone refer to Oxford University as 'the Varsity'. I knew it as a piece of Victorian slang, but I never expected to meet it on the hoof, so to speak.

'I don't know why not,' I said. 'I think the country's very nice round here. In fact it's something of a hobby of mine to –'

'Where do your people live?' she asked. 'I mean, where are you when you're not at college?'

'Oh, my home is in Oxford too,' I said. 'It's all very convenient. Otherwise I don't think I could think of having a dog. You see, the College –'

'So you'd kennel him at home,' she said, 'and go along and exercise him in the afternoons, and weekends, that kind of thing.' (So it had been a male I picked. Must remember that.) 'Is it far? Is your home near the College?'

'Not far at all,' I said. 'Quite handy.' I let it go at that. Everything about this woman told me that while Episcopus was a good card to play with her, the Bargeman's Arms was very definitely not.

Was I being snobbish in concealing where my home was? Certainly. Young people act snobbishly when they find themselves having to deal with older people whom they correctly assess as snobs. It was important to me to build some kind of bridge to Mrs Farmer's Wife, and I saw no point in building one and kicking it to pieces in the same instant.

The girl, still with an air of amusement, now asked me, 'Are you used to dogs?'

'Very,' I said. After all, everyone is used to dogs. There are so many of them. One sees them in every street. Who the hell isn't used to dogs?

'Had them before, have you?' she pursued maliciously. Obviously she was out to get her bit of fun out of me and the false position I was in.

'Yes,' I said firmly.

'What breed?'

It so happened that in my childhood we had had as a family pet an old, toothless fox-terrier bitch called Mavis. Why Mavis I don't know, it must be the least suitable canine name one could think of, but that was what we called her. Mavis was older than I was by many a long year. When I was six, she was run over one day as she tried to waddle across the Abingdon Road, and, never having taken much notice of her while she lived, I cried myself to sleep that night. It was my first recognition of death, as often happens with children and pet animals. Naturally I wasn't going to go into all that, so I just said crisply, 'Fox-terriers,' hoping that poor defunct Mavis would forgive me for making her plural.

'Win any prizes with them?' the girl probed pitilessly.

'I didn't enter them,' I parried. 'Of course it would be different if I had a pedigree animal.'

'I'll show you the papers,' the mother said. It seemed as if all of a sudden nothing was too much trouble. Did the word 'College' really carry that much magic? 'If you'll just come into the house.'

'I'm taking Punch out, Mother.' The girl had now finished having her fun and turned back to the realities of her life. 'He's had no exercise since early yesterday morning. I'll saddle him now and –'

'Oh, Heather,' said the mother wearily, 'can't you do it after lunch? I was hoping you'd help me to –'

'I'm going to Banbury after lunch, about that trailer. You can't have forgotten. No, sorry, I'll have to do it now.'

She was gone. Heather. Her name was Heather.

I followed the mother into the house, wiping my feet very carefully on the large doormat that was placed where you couldn't miss it. She led the way through the kitchen and into what was evidently the family sitting-room. The documents were in a bureau in the corner, and while she got them out I took stock of the room. Farmers in those days didn't invest their surplus cash in thousands of pounds' worth of antique furniture and have the interiors of their carefully styled houses photographed in glossy magazines, but in its simpler way the room was elegant and certainly everything was very clean and tidy; the brass fireside stuff – bellows, poker, toasting-fork, all that – were polished till they shone brilliantly, and there were bowls of flowers. You could see that appearances mattered very much to this lady.

She now flourished a sheaf of papers at me in which I might read, if I chose, the genetic history that lay behind Bessie, the Labrador bitch, and the mate they had hired for her. It all rather swam before my eyes. The situation was getting more out of hand with every turn of the spiral. Did I really strike this shrewd-looking woman as the type who would be very concerned about pedigrees or, for that matter, the type who had money to throw away on a dog when it was perfectly easy to get a puppy for nothing? It was the word 'College' that had done it. But what kind of fantastic image did she have of 'Varsity men', as she called them? Had she ever met any?

Deciding that the only thing to do now was to cut and run, I said, 'Well, that's certainly all the information I need. I'll put a cheque for the deposit in the post when I get back.' Like hell I will, I thought. 'What name shall I make it payable to?'

'Burrell,' she said. 'J.G. and A. Burrell. My husband and I have a joint account. It's so much more convenient.'

Burrell, shouted a voice in my head. Miss Heather Burrell, Jasmine

Farm, High Cogges, Oxfordshire. Something solid there. A name and address!

I gibbered something to Mrs Burrell and got away, crossing the farmyard almost at a run. She was trying to detain me with some rigmarole about being able to deliver the puppy to my home rather than to College, if she had the address. Amid all my haste and tension I nearly laughed out loud as I had a sudden vision of her driving up to the Bargeman's Arms with it.

'I don't know your name!' she called after me from the doorstep.

'Leonard,' I said, 'Peter Leonard,' but I spoke over my shoulder without ceasing to walk ahead. By now I seriously wanted to get away. I felt my nerve had gone and I had lost my grip on the situation; if I talked any more I was sure to say something that would blow the whole thing. Even so, I reflected, I had probably made a mistake in telling her my real name. I ought to have said I was Dick Kent.

My head was spinning with everything that had been happening to me in the last half-hour, but all I had to do was get away on my own and get things together, so I walked as nonchalantly as possible across the yard to the gate, taking care not to look back or show any sign of hesitation or second thoughts. But as I did so I had a strange sensation.

One of the few pieces of concrete evidence for telepathy to be met with in everyday life is that if somebody stares hard at you, even from a point outside your angle of vision, you often seem to feel it and look round towards him. I don't know why this should be, but it does happen now and again and it happened now. The farmyard, flanked by the appropriate outbuildings, lay behind the house; what you traversed to get from the lane to the front door was Mrs Burrell's neat garden. But one of the farm buildings was out in front. It was an ancient stone barn, as handsome in its way as the farmhouse, and it stood thirty or forty yards down the lane, right beside the roadway. In the last few yards before I reached the garden gate and got into the lane I had the distinct sensation of a pair of eyes boring into my face from somewhere to the left. I abruptly snapped my head in that direction and was in time to catch sight of a face peering round at me from the other side of this barn. The face abruptly disappeared as I turned, but not before I had an impression, as clear as a photograph, of a battered mackintosh hat with a long bony face under it. The hat, though it was ragged and dirty now, had clearly once been a good hat; probably it had been the cast-off of some well-dressed gentleman with a taste for country weekends. But the face under it, as even that brief glimpse was sufficient to reveal, could never have been a good face. It was long and bony, but not in the dignified, equine way of, say, the Acheson-Fiske face. It was more like the face of a crocodile, except that the eyes, instead of being hard and bright like a reptile's, were furtive and rheumy. The nose, long and slightly spatulate at the end, looked the kind that, in cold weather, drips as steadily as a tap with a leaking washer.

All this I saw before the head whipped out of sight again. I didn't, in the least, like what I saw, and the unpleasant feeling of being watched did not go away with the disappearance of the rheumy eyes. I came out past the notice that advertised the puppies for sale, and picked up my bike. For a moment I stood holding it, giving no sign as to which direction I was going to turn it in before moving off. Then, deliberately, I pointed it away from the farm gate, mounted and started to pedal away, but almost immediately whirled round in a tight half-circle that abruptly brought me facing the gateway, and for an instant I saw him again, peering round from the shelter of the barn wall, obviously to watch me go.

What with one thing and another I needed a pint of beer, but I avoided the pub down the road because I felt if I ran into Tom, or even the old man, after all that it really would just be too much, so I kept on going and had my beer-stop in a pub further along the road to Oxford; so much further, indeed, that I only just made it before afternoon closing time.

Chapter 14

Dear Miss Burrell,
Dear Heather Burrell,
Dear Miss Heather,

I wrote, sitting at the desk where I ought to have been working on an essay for Bax about the reasons for the excommunication of the Emperor Frederick II by Pope Gregory IX on Palm Sunday 1239,

You will be surprised at hearing from me...

Perhaps it will surprise you to get...

It is always something of a surprise to get a letter from a total...

I am a stranger to you, by name, but not quite in person, since we have met a couple of times, and I hope you will not be too surprised at getting a letter from me. Of course it is possible that your mother may have mentioned my name to you, since I gave it to her on my visit earlier today. It is Peter Leonard. I am the man who was enquiring about the Golden Labrador puppies. I have a confession to make. I...

...Golden Labrador puppies. Mrs Burrell was so kind as to say she would keep one for me if I would send £5 deposit. The fact is, to make a clean breast...

...Golden Labrador puppies. The trouble is that I was being less than strictly honest here, and this worries me. You see, I would like to begin as I mean to go on. Begin what? you will naturally...

...Golden Labrador puppies. And before that it was I who opened the gate for you one morning when you were out on that chestnut horse. You looked very...

...Golden Labrador puppies. I suppose Mrs Burrell accepted me at face value as a potential customer, but I rather wondered whether you did. Something about the way you looked at me, when you joined us in the stable, seemed to convey that you recognized me. I opened the gate for you one morning, a week or two ago, when you were out riding. We talked for a few moments, and something I said made you say I must be a University student, which is true. I am. I want to be perfectly honest with you, Miss Burrell. Our few minutes' talk together on that morning left me feeling that I would like to...

Would you mind if I were perfectly honest with you, Miss Burrell? After we talked together on that morning, I went away and...

Heather – it seems wrong to call you anything else, the name suits you so perfectly – I want to be perfectly honest with you...

At this point Arthur came thumping in, with his apron and his permanently disgruntled expression. That meant it was about five o'clock. Scouts used to go round the rooms at that time, to see if you wanted anything fetched from the kitchen or buttery, and to fill your coal-scuttle and things like that. God, it seems a million years ago that undergraduates were so waited on, and yet it was only in my own lifetime.

His interruption broke my mood, but I was glad to leave off struggling with the letter anyway. I wasn't by any means sure that writing to her was the best way to take the next step, it was just that I had an uncontrollable need to be doing *something* about her, and couldn't think of anything. If I really tried I might get my mind on to other matters for a few hours, and when I came back to the letter the problem might have solved itself. Either I might have thought of the exact words that would get a response from her, or I would see clearly that the whole notion of writing a letter was a wash-out.

I went downstairs and, for something to do, entered the lodge and had a look in the pigeon-hole I shared with everyone else whose name began with L. To my surprise there was something for me: an At Home card from Bax, for a couple of days later. At the bottom he had written in his sharp, neat hand the word 'Sherry'. Why had Bax invited me to take sherry with him? Some mechanical piece of protocol? Dons were supposed to entertain their pupils informally now and then, in fact they got an entertainment allowance for it – all part of that Oxford tradition of getting to know people personally and conducting everything on a face-to-face level. Thinking ahead to it, I felt a gentle boredom stealing over me in anticipation.

I put the card in my pocket and my feet carried me on out into the street. There seemed to be nothing, nothing, absolutely nothing that I felt inclined, or fit, or ready, to do. Work was out of the question. There was nobody I wanted to go and see. I had no 'social life' and no hobbies. Worse still, it suddenly struck me, although I had been in my new life for the best part of a year, I didn't seem to have many close friendships. There were plenty of people I liked and got along with, but I hadn't a Best Pal as one used to have at school, in whom I could confide.

The fact was, I thought as I waited for a gap in the traffic to cross over St Giles's Street, that the pursuit of sexual fulfilment had taken up the energies that would have gone into forming friendships. If I could have got *that* problem licked from the beginning, I would have expanded into the field of companionable male relationships. But first I was too occupied running after Vinnie and then in brooding over the doubtless unreachable Heather. My vitality was simply being emptied into a soak-away, and by now it had begun to take a toll of my intellectual life as well. My God, I thought, if Bax wanted to get some better work out of me and probably not only me, it wouldn't be a reading party he would organize in the Lake District, it would be a fucking party. I stood still in the middle of St Giles's Street, with the cars grazing past me, and laughed aloud at the thought of his face if I put the suggestion formally to him.

The traffic ceased for a moment and I went on across the road. I had no motive for crossing it, no thought-out reason for doing anything. I vaguely felt, when I got to the pavement on the other side, that it might be pleasant to go and look at some paintings in the Ashmolean. A painless way of filling the time, anyway. I went up to the door and found it closed. The Museum hours were 9 till 4. When I grew up and knew more about things I realized that this was just one more result of their chronic shortage of funds – they couldn't afford to pay the staff to stay on duty any longer. But at the time, of course, I just put it down to bloody-mindedness. A way of keeping out the common herd who had to wait till half-past five and go to museums in the evenings. Ah, well, for them there was always the cosy scrum of Sunday afternoon – two hours with six people standing in front of every painting. If England wasn't hostile to art it wouldn't be England.

I came slowly down the steps, and stood on the pavement with my back to them. My eyes were resting absently on the front door of the Randolph Hotel, and as I looked something unexpected caught my eye. A knot of young men, obviously undergraduates, came out through the swing doors and stood on the pavement for a few moments, evidently before going their separate ways. Even looking at them from the other side of the street I could tell that those chaps – there were some half-dozen of them – were something of a posh crowd. Their clothes looked expensive and they had that way of holding themselves, especially the set of the head on the shoulders, that seems to belong to people who have always known complete economic security. As I idly stared at these patricians, the face of one of them caught my eye and set me puzzling. It was a face I remembered having seen before, but I couldn't place it.

Who was the man? Had I ever known his name, or was he just a face to me? He was tall, with curly brown hair... then he grinned, and his grin was lop-sided, and suddenly it came to me that I had seen, not his face, but a photograph of his face. Of course. In the magazine at the barber's. So this was the amateur racing driver from Magdalen, the sporting young aristocrat whom Brian was nursing along for M.G. This was the Honourable Fergus Kingswood.

I looked across at him with a momentary interest. I must tell Brian I had seen him. And in that instant I noticed something else. The man standing next to him on the pavement, square-built and broad-shouldered, looking up at him and saying whatever it was that was making him grin, was Norbert, the man who had coolly intervened to rebuke Kent that Sunday evening in the J.C.R.

So that was the kind of circle Norbert moved in. I might have known. It certainly explained why I never seemed to run into him except in College. Well, good luck to him. It must certainly be more fun hanging around with Kingswood and his ilk than with the kind of Rugger-playing bonehead who would be prepared to tolerate Kent.

*

When, a couple of evenings later, I duly turned up at Bax's sherry party, I found that it had a more definite purpose than mere socializing, namely to set up the details of his reading party in the Lake District. With all the obsessive thoughts that had been filling my mind lately I had completely forgotten about the matter, and now that I was reminded of it I couldn't work up much enthusiasm. Fed up as I was with being forced into a single-sex life, I hardly relished the notion of being cooped up in a house among rain-swept mountains with a gang of blokes; on the other hand it was no worse than the alternative, which (presumably) was mooning about at the Bargeman's Arms. So I gave ear while Bax outlined the arrangements.

In fact I got a glimpse of a different side of Bax at that party. He was still as precise and contained as ever, his clothes and his movements and his words were just as neat and well chosen, but his manner was decidedly more genial and his eyes behind those round lenses were not quite as fish-like. He made a few little jokes; I've forgotten what they were, but I do remember that they were jokes because I can still feel the surprise with which I heard him utter them.

I have no doubt, with hindsight, that the whole exercise was as carefully controlled as the actions of an engineer who opens one valve on a dam a little, and closes another down a little, according to his calculations. But however conscious and calculated this relaxation was, it interested me, at the time, to see that Bax was capable of it. He was encouraging us, up to a point, to think of the trip as a holiday as well as a burst of work. He mentioned one or two of the places we might walk to, since after all we couldn't be reading all the time, and even mentioned that the local pub had a reputation for good beer. I drank my sherry – Bax was quite good about circulating the room and keeping one's glass filled – and listened to the chatter and made a note of the information about trains, and looked out of the window at the early evening sunlight falling on lawns and flower-beds and graceful old buildings, and reflected not for the first time that the University of Oxford was a strange mixture. It drilled you into a certain kind of life and punished you heavily if you tried to break out, but, as long as you stayed within those laid-down limits, nothing was too much trouble. It was a strange feeling, being spoilt and deprived at the same time. Well, I would give Bax's reading party a go, *faute de mieux*, but my God I could have done with a spot of *mieux*.

Something of this more humane approach lingered on, after the party, in Bax's ordinary teaching. As well as one-to-one tutorials, he got us all – those who were reading the Honours School of Modern History – together every Monday for a class, so that he could force-feed elementary information into us without having to repeat it all over again to each individual pupil. In about the sixth week of term he gave his class as usual and, at the end, instead of indicating a topic for the next week, he looked round at us with a casual half-smile and said, 'This class won't meet next week, gentlemen. In a fortnight's time we can pick up the threads of this discussion.'

'It's cancelled, is it, sir?' someone asked; the unspoken question being 'Why?'

'I've found through the years,' said Bax, 'that there is never any point in expecting my pupils to be alert, or to have read anything I put before them to read, or even to be in a condition to follow a simple argument, on the Monday following a Commem. Ball. It's simpler to cancel it until the disruption of life, whether alcoholic, metabolic or emotional, or some interesting blend of the three, has righted itself. That will be all, gentlemen, I needn't keep you.'

We trooped out, eight or ten of us, down the broad wooden staircase and into the sunshine. I found myself going down step by step with a burly young man with a boxer's flattened face. I knew him as one of those Public School men who, while totally enclosed within the conventions of their caste, were perfectly affable according to their notions of affability. His name was Dobbs.

'What's a Commem. Ball like?' I asked him.

'It's a night when they throw the College open to women and have dancing all night and everybody gets pissed on champers,' Dobbs said.

'You mean they scrub all that stuff about women having to be out by seven?'

'They scrub every kind of disciplinary stuff. Women can go up to the rooms at three o'clock in the morning if they want to. There's breakfast laid on for anybody who's still walking. It's the Big Night. You mean to say you didn't –'

'No, I didn't,' I said. 'I've led a sheltered life. I thought the entire disciplinary machinery of the University was designed to stop us from getting close to women.'

'So it is,' Dobbs agreed, 'for three hundred and sixty-four nights a year, and three hundred and sixty-five if it happens to be a Leap Year. But when there's a Commem. on, nobody gives a damn. Of course the College does not have one every year. More like every three or four. They're so expensive and they take so much setting up.'

'Are you going?' I asked.

'No,' he said. 'I'm a bit short this term. I haven't got five guineas to throw around.'

'Five *guineas*?'

'That's what a double ticket costs, sonny. It's typical of bourgeois puritanism, see? You can bring a girl in and get up to anything you like, so long as the girl is agreeable to it, but only if you've got money.'

'Five...' I stood there stunned as Dobbs prepared to stride off. 'One more question,' I said dully. 'Why is it called a Commem.?'

'Search me. Probably you're supposed to look back on it for the rest of your life and commemorate the one and only time during your Oxford career when they gave you a chance to get your end away.'

I saw what he meant. My mind was churning as I stood there watching him move off. The words of an old joke suddenly went through my mind: 'If we had some ham we could have some ham and eggs, if we had some eggs.' If I had five guineas I could bring a girl to this Commem. Ball and get some privacy with her, if I had a girl.

Five guineas! Five pounds and five shillings, at a time when a working man was expected to bring up a family on two pounds a week! Of course champagne was expensive, ten and six a bottle or thereabouts. But I knew, at the same time, that Dobbs was right. It was the freedom that cost you money, not the tipple.

Well, but if discipline were relaxed on that night, why not bring in a girl and never mind the Commem.? To the credit of my common sense be it said that this notion had got itself barely a quarter of the way to being formulated in my consciousness before I saw how ridiculous it was. Bring a girl in and say to her, 'There's a ball going on but it's not for you. There's a band playing and people all dressed up and champagne being served, but none of it's for you. You're coming up to my room with me to spend the night attending to my needs.' Who was I going to bring? Did I happen to know a nymphomaniac Cinderella?

And though I was certain in my own mind that if that fantasy were to come true, what happened on my bed would be much more *fun*, for both of us, than prancing about on a dance-floor in evening dress and drinking champagne, I didn't believe that any girl existed who would think so too. And in the 1930s I was probably right. I would have had to look ahead thirty years to envisage a decade when that kind of opinion really took root among girls.

I determined, as I paced slowly back to my room, that on the night of this Commem. business I would go down to the Bargeman's and sleep in my own bed there. I declined, just flatly refused, to add the torment of envy to the torment of frustration. I wasn't sure how much credence to give to Dobbs's ribald account of what went on at a Commem., but I supposed there was *some* foundation for it. Most of the men I knew were as far from having a flourishing sexual life as I was myself, I was sure of that, but if there were, in the entire college, as many as half-a-dozen couples getting it together during that night, it would be half-a-dozen too many for me. If I were not allowed on pain of death to eat grapes, at least I would have the sense to keep out of the vineyard.

These thoughts pushed me down into despair, and the same black, inert morass had no difficulty in swallowing up any faint impulse I might have had to follow up the business of the Golden Labrador puppies from Jasmine Farm. What a bloody mess it all was, I thought savagely. There seemed to be nothing I could say to Mrs Farmer's Wife if I tried to communicate with her. I didn't want a puppy, I couldn't have afforded one if I did want one, I had nowhere to keep one if I wanted it and could afford it. If we had some ham we could have some ham and eggs if we had some eggs.

Several times, in the week or so that followed the episode of the puppies, I took out the letter to Heather and dully read it over, wondering whether I ought to revise and polish it, or start it again in a completely different vein, or just throw it away and give up on the whole business. Usually I ended by deciding to give up and just forget Heather

Burrell, but the trouble was that my mind, like some sort of rubber toy, just wouldn't stay in the shape into which I pressed it. I would retreat from the topic and start thinking about other things, or trying to, and as soon as I wasn't looking my emotions would rally again and start demanding some plan of action that would get me into contact with that fresh, smooth face with its candid expression, those light blue eyes, and the cascade of honey-coloured hair. But what plan of action? What on earth could I possibly do?

And there, I suppose, I might just have let the whole thing moulder slowly away. The fact that things turned out differently was, in a way, due to Vinnie.

I had been down on the footpath beside Folly Bridge, having an afternoon walk by the river. I liked that area, upstream of Folly Bridge to about Oseney Lock. It was a no-man's-land between my University world and my home world, with some vibrations from each. My shortest way back to Episcopus led through St Aldate's and Cornmarket Street. But I never went along Cornmarket Street because I was afraid of meeting Vinnie. Even if I walked on the other side of the road from the shoe-shop there was always the chance that she might come out into the street for a moment, or worse still, suddenly appear in the window. Worse, because it would recall to my mind the image of her long, slender fingers holding that elegantly narrow golden shoe, an image that, whenever it returned, immediately caused my fertile member to extend itself in seemingly limitless fashion like a surreal telescope; and, in any case, even to be in the neighbourhood of the shop reminded me of Vinnie's existence, with the inevitable result that I started picturing the fan-vault shape of her pubic hair and sleep was banished for about three nights. No, thanks. My reason was hanging by a thread as things were, without making it all worse.

I therefore navigated back by a devious route, threading through the little tumbledown streets of St Ebbe's, a district that no longer exists, and thence along New Inn Hall Street and turning right into George Street.

There was, and is, a large department store with a frontage taking in the corner of George Street and Magdalen Street. This store was in those days, and for many years afterwards, known as Elliston and Cavell's. Until some of the big London stores put up branches in Oxford, it was more or less without rival.

Elliston and Cavell's was not a place I ever went into. I was, and am, depressed and frightened by big department stores for the exact reason why some people are hypnotized and exhilarated by them. That plethora, that abundance, that enormous over-supply of material things, seems to choke my spirit. Even the fact that I was walking past the George Street entrance to the store was slightly unusual and resulted, as I say, from my dread of meeting Vinnie or even encountering her in my thoughts.

But there I was, and the glass door opened, and out came Mrs Farmer's Wife, looking as keen and alert, as single-mindedly devoted to a clear objective, as if she were a Golden Labrador herself. I found myself looking full into her face, and, lacking the presence of mind to murmur something polite and pass by, I stopped dead. In the same instant I saw over her shoulder that Heather was with her. She was wearing a blue dress with a white collar, and over it a light mackintosh. I could see that much although she was carrying such a load of bags and boxes that she was nearly hidden behind them. The mother was pretty well laden too. The shop door swung to behind her, and there were the three of us standing on the pavement.

I could see they both recognized me, which was intelligent of them. The mother was even struggling to recall my name. She wrinkled her brow as we stood there and said, 'It's Mr...' then stopped.

'Peter Leonard,' I supplied.

'Oh, yes. Mr Leonard. You remember, Heather, with the puppies the other day.'

Heather, understandably, looked as if she would rather be on her way than make small-talk on the pavement. She gave me a glance that was neither friendly nor unfriendly, just preoccupied.

Clearly my cue was to say something about those puppies, to explain why I had never written or sent a deposit. But I just couldn't go back into all that mess of falsities and evasions. And fortunately I had the perfect excuse for not getting into it. They were both loaded to the gunwales. Obviously they had to transport all this stuff to some waiting form of transport.

'Lucky running into you just at this moment, Mrs Burrell,' I said brightly. To make sure that my remembering her name impinged on her consciousness, I pronounced it very distinctly. 'It's quite clear you could do with a little help. Do let me carry some of those things for you.'

'We can manage, thanks,' Heather said with a hint of impatience. 'We're quite used to carrying our own –' But before she had got that far, her mother was already handing over several bags and unwieldy rectangular boxes. Nowadays the pair of them would have been festooned with plastic shopping bags in garish colours, but all this was before the invention of plastics, when you got your shopping in stout brown-paper carriers or just boxes with more brown paper round them. In a trice Mrs Burrell had off-loaded almost her entire lot on to me. Then she reached out and took over one of Heather's bigger parcels to make it all more fairly distributed.

'Why refuse a little help, dear?' she said reasonably. 'I'm sure Mr Leonard meant his offer to be accepted.'

'Certainly I did,' I said. 'Where are you taking them?'

It occurred to me, as soon as the words were out, that it would have been a neater touch to say 'we' instead of 'you'. 'Where are we taking them?' would have conveyed that I was staking out a claim – however small, however modest, and however deferentially expressed – to be one of the party. Too late now.

'Just to the car,' said Heather shortly.

'And that is...'

'St Giles,' she said even more shortly.

So to St Giles we went. It took us about three minutes to get there. The car was about half-way along, so that was another three. During the whole six minutes I couldn't think of a single thing to say. All the opening gambits that rose in my mind were on the level of 'Been shopping, I see,' or 'Use the Oxford shops a good deal, do you?' Fortunately the mother seemed to be in a sunny mood. She looked about her with a pleased, interested air, almost as if she had made a long journey to get here and were saying, 'So this is Oxford.' Heather walked in silence, but not, so far as I could judge, a bad-tempered silence. It was just that her thoughts were not with us. To begin with I was walking between them, but when we encountered a cluster of pavement-standers we had to shift about and change places, which put me over to one side. From this position I could, by rapid glances rather than by staring, take in the subtle interplay of likeness and difference between mother and daughter. They were pretty much alike, though obviously the mother's figure had broadened and her hair grown darker. Apart from that the resemblance was broken only by two things. One was that the mother's chin was more prominent than the daughter's. She had a thrust-out, fighter's chin that made me, suddenly, remember her son's face; she had passed on that pugilistic spirit to him. Heather's jawline was softer; her facial structure was a more delicate version of her father's, rounded like his though not, like his, comically football-shaped. The other difference was in the way they walked. Mrs Burrell marched. She forged ahead like a soldier moving in to take up an attacking position. Heather walked like a racehorse being led round a paddock. She flowed over the ground in the same totally effortless way.

We got to the car. It was a Ford. I don't know enough about the history of Fords to say what model it was, but it wasn't new and it wasn't very big. Clearly the resources of Jasmine Farm could just about be coaxed into reaching as far as one car, probably second-hand, certainly all-purpose and used by everyone in the family. Heather opened the boot and I put my bags and boxes down in it very, very carefully. Some had to go on the back seat. I did that too.

'There you are,' I said, standing back.

'Thank you very much,' the mother said. 'It's so nice to come to Oxford. One meets *gentlemen*.'

It struck me, standing there, how easy it was after all to get yourself taken for a gentleman. All you had to do was carry a few parcels for a woman whose daughter you fancied.

'It's nothing, really,' I said.

Heather, who was evidently doing the driving, settled herself in behind the wheel, but Mrs Burrell didn't seem to be in any hurry. She stood there beside the car and looked round as if photographing the scene on her mind.

'Oxford is so lovely,' she said. 'All those wonderful old buildings. It's got *style*, hasn't it? You're lucky to be up at the Varsity.'

That Varsity business again. I was afraid if she repeated the word I would burst out laughing and spoil everything.

'Well, you live not far away,' I said, 'and that's lucky too, I suppose.'

'Ah,' she said, 'but it's not the same as having the run of the place. Being able to go in and out wherever you please. It's a great privilege, you know, to *belong* here, and not be just a visitor.'

Suddenly I saw my next move with blinding clarity. If the Golden Labrador puppies had been the first opening, this was the second, and altogether bigger and better. Tension and excitement surged inside me; it seemed to me that I could hear my pulse hammering as I said:

'Look, Mrs Burrell, I don't want to be – forward or intrusive or anything, or force my company on you, but – well –'

They were both staring at me now. I made a supreme effort to stop babbling, to speak calmly and clearly, and make my suggestion like a man in his right mind. 'When I met you,' I said in an unnaturally calm voice, as if reading the words from a typewritten sheet, 'I was just on the way home to put the kettle on and make some tea.'

'Home?' Mrs Burrell put in.

'College,' I said. 'Not my actual home. My College rooms, where I live in term time. I wondered if you and your – Miss Burrell would like – if you're not too busy and don't have to get back straight away, which of course I realize you might have to, because there must be so many things to see to on a farm, what with all the –'

I was starting to gibber again, but Mrs Burrell saved me by intervening in her clear, decisive middle-class manner. 'Are you inviting us to have some tea with you, Mr Leonard? In College?'

'Yes,' I said. It was the only word I could form. My energies had spent themselves in that one wild surge of resolution.

'We've had tea, Mother,' said Heather from the driving seat. 'How many times do you need to break off and drink tea?'

'As many times as I get nice, kind, interesting invitations,' Mrs Burrell returned stoutly. 'Of course we'll come, Mr Leonard. We're not pushed for half an hour, are we, Heather?'

'Half an *hour*? We've got to call and pick up that saddle, and that means going round by –'

'I'm sure the saddle won't run away. I don't know how often it happens to you to be asked to tea in an Oxford College, but it's never happened to *me* before, and I'm going to accept.' She turned to me. 'Which college is it you're at? Is it far?'

'Very near,' I said. 'Just over there.' And I pointed to Episcopus.

'Oh, how exciting!' And she trotted along determinedly by my side, with Heather resignedly bringing up the rear.

We bumped up the twisting wooden staircase to my rooms and I opened the door for them. I had never thought of the place as exciting, but that was the word Mrs Burrell kept using, and as we went in I tried to see the place with her eyes. With its bookshelves and its lumpy *chaise longue* and armchair, its fireplace blank and empty for the summer, its print of Tintern Abbey on the wall, it seemed to me to look exactly the room of a student, and what was more, a student of my kind and from my background. There was no *chic* about the place, and certainly no evidence of money. There were no fine bindings on the bookshelves, and no objects that I had picked up on my travels because I hadn't had any travels. When I went to the Lake District in a few weeks' time, it would be the longest journey I had made in my eighteen years. In short, it seemed to me that by taking them up to my habitat I was overtly declaring that I was a very ordinary young fellow, not at all the kind of person it was an adventure to go to tea with. Yet Mrs Burrell seemed to get some kind of stimulation out of pretending that it was one. For surely it was a pretence? Or were there elements in the situation, visible to her but invisible to me, that really were worth getting excited about?

Well, whatever the hidden reason, I had got them as far as accepting my hospitality. For the first few minutes my attention was wholly absorbed by procedures – get them sitting down, fetch this, fetch that, boil the water, find the milk. I installed Mrs Burrell in the armchair and Heather perched, in a detached way, on the end of the *chaise longue*. At last, with a cup of tea in everyone's hand, I felt I must get some sort of conversation launched: about anything, so long as it stayed off puppies.

'Do you regularly shop at Elliston's?' I asked, feeling as I uttered the question that its falsity must be ringing out like a cracked gong. Surely it must be obvious that I couldn't conceivably give a damn where they shopped.

But Mrs Burrell, in keeping with what seemed to be her general policy, seemed ready to make even this a matter of importance. 'Well, we quite often go there,' she said, 'but this particular shopping trip was rather special, wasn't it, Heather?'

'If you say so, Mother,' the girl replied indifferently.

'I should think I do say so!' the mother exploded. 'Your first Hunt Ball!'

Heather seemed almost on the point of stifling a yawn. 'Really, you know, the way you say "My first Hunt Ball", as if it's the first rung on some terrific ladder that's going to lead me to heaven or something....'

'Heather, don't be silly,' said her mother calmly. 'I was never asked to a Hunt Ball when I was young and now I never shall be.'

'So you want me to –'

'I want you to have a more interesting life than I had when I was young, is that so unnatural? But I'm sure,' she turned her attention back to me, 'that we're boring Mr Leonard dreadfully.'

And her gaze, which had swivelled round the room on its way to meet mine, came to rest as she looked full into my face for an instant with an expression that said, 'Don't hesitate to tell me I'm being a tiresome, fussy woman at a tiresome, fussy time of life – but only if you want to be branded for ever as another bull-necked male oaf who simply doesn't understand how women feel about things.'

I had the presence of mind to assure her that she wasn't boring me in the least, and the statement was true as far as it went. A not very pleasant mixture of sensations was going through me, but boredom wasn't one of them.

'I expect you're one of these terribly high-powered Oxford intellectuals,' she said, 'who look down on hunting people and think they're all a lot of brainless Philippines.'

I was fairly sure she meant Philistines, but let it pass. 'No, not at all,' I said. 'There've got to be... I mean, foxes would become extinct...'

'He's just being polite, Mother,' Heather put in, her voice coolly ruthless. 'If he were to be honest he'd tell you that he thinks anyone who even knows how to sit on a horse must have their brains in the wrong place.'

'*Heather*!' Mrs Burrell remonstrated. 'There's no need to be *indelicate*.'

'Why not? Horses are very indelicate, and that's just what people like Mr Leonard have got against them.'

'Unfair,' I said. 'To begin with I'm not people like me, I'm me. And to go on with –'

'There's no need to go on,' she said. 'Why bother to be fair to people when it doesn't matter one way or the other?'

'Fairness is always worth having,' I said stubbornly.

'Well, all I was going to say,' Mrs Burrell said with the air of one determined to drag the conversation on to a more interesting level, 'is that our shopping trip this afternoon was rather special because we were buying Heather's outfit for the Royal Bicester Hunt Ball, which she's going to next month.'

'Is that the hunt you belong to?' I asked, for something to say.

'Oh, no,' she laughed, making a dismissive gesture. 'Goodness, I couldn't look you in the face and tell you we *belonged* to it. Tenant farmers and their families don't belong to hunts. You have to have expensive horses and the right clothes and time off in the hunting season. All good things, but we don't happen to have them, Mr Leonard.'

'Peter,' I said.

'Well... if you really insist.'

'I do insist. If you can sit in my room and drink tea with me, you can call me Peter.'

'Why does it matter?' Heather asked. She certainly seemed to be in an evil mood. She hated this waste of time and she was going to take her annoyance out on me.

'It matters,' I said, 'because it pleases me and it doesn't hurt you.' *And you can stop being such a sulky bitch*, I added silently.

'So we came shopping, Peter,' Mrs Burrell said, voicing the name deliberately, handling it as if with tongs, 'to get what Heather needs for the Hunt Ball.'

'What I *need*? You know we're making the dress ourselves. All we're getting is –'

'We're making the dress ourselves,' Mrs Burrell continued, still speaking firmly to me, 'but the accessories, the evening bag and the matching shoes and the gloves and ornaments, all the other little things that make up the total effect, we came in today and –'

'Mother, why don't you let Mr Leonard off the hook? It's quite obvious just from looking at him, just from looking at his room and his books and papers and what-not, that the thought of a Hunt Ball with a lot of horsey people togged up in evening dress, with pink jackets and all the rest of it, must make him just about kill himself laughing.'

'Not quite true there either,' I said. I was beginning quite to enjoy sparring with Heather, crossing even these wooden swords with her. It seemed the nearest I was ever likely to get to a relationship, so why not? 'Number one, I think horses are beautiful animals and I sympathize with people who like to keep them. Number two, if people want to get together in a spirit of friendliness to dance with each other and have a good time, I'm not going to despise them for it.' I was talking in a torrent now, driven by nervous tension and by irritation at Heather's near-hostile coolness. And even as I talked, a new element came into play – a wild inspiration, a sudden idea that manifested itself first as a rainbow glow in the back of my mind, a premonition that something miraculous was on the way, and the next instant formed itself concretely.

'May I be inquisitive,' I said, facing Heather and addressing her directly, probing at her defences, ignoring the mother's watching and listening presence, 'and ask you when this Hunt Ball is to be?'

She gave me a slightly surprised, almost mind-your-own-business look and said, 'Next week. Saturday.'

'Well, I never,' I said. 'Exactly one week before the very similar one here.'

'Similar...?' from Mrs Burrell.

'A Commem. Ball,' I said. 'The big event of the year. Champagne, two bands, a marquee in the garden, everybody giving themselves up to revelry till morning.' I felt I was selling it too hard and added, 'I've no plans for going to it, actually. Or at least, I hadn't. But I must say, the coincidence of meeting you just when you're on this shopping trip to get ready for the Hunt Ball does make me wonder if...'

'Wonder if what?' Heather demanded. She was sitting up straight and staring at me almost threateningly. But at least she was giving me her whole attention.

'Well, if you enjoy balls,' I said, *Oops*, 'and if you've taken trouble to get an outfit together to go to one, why not stretch the outfit to two before it goes back into moth-balls?' Balls again. I must have them on the brain. 'I mean, since they're on successive weekends.'

'This one you're talking about, Mr Leonard – Peter,' said Mrs Burrell, 'it would be here? In College?'

'Yes,' I said. 'In the Hall. And in a marquee in the gardens. And in the public rooms generally.' Not to mention the private rooms, I thought. Well, why not give it a try? What had I got to lose? I looked defiantly at the two of them and said, 'More tea, anyone?'

There was a brief pause and then Mrs Burrell, ignoring the business about the tea, looked over at her daughter and said, 'Well, Heather, that strikes me as a very kind offer.'

Kind? I thought. *Kind*? Can the woman really be so foolish as to think kindness has anything to do with this?

Heather said nothing and Mrs Burrell sounded almost coaxing as she went on, 'After all, it's not everyone who gets a chance to go to an Oxford Commem. Ball.' She came out with the phrase as if she had been using it all her life, and yet I would have taken a bet that she had never heard it till two minutes before. That was how fast she picked things up. There must be some tremendous motivation, I thought, behind such a drive. She wanted to belong, to get inside, to be one of the chosen. On whose behalf? Heather's, or her own? Or had they, in her mind, become fused into one?

Heather had still not spoken, in fact she hardly seemed to be listening. I could tell she was trying to stand well back from her mother's eagerness, which must have seemed to her undignified and threatening to drag her down. To make it a little easier for her I decided to put the whole thing on a much more casual footing, to represent it as a triviality. 'Of course,' I said, 'I realize it may strike you as a lot of effort for not very much. I'm afraid I couldn't chauffeur you into Oxford. I don't get the use of the family car in term-time.' A good touch that, as if I had the use of the faithful old chugger at any time, or would have known what to do with it if I had. 'You'd have to get yourself here, and I can quite see that that would make problems.'

I looked across at Heather with what I hoped was an expression of relaxed, comradely enquiry, giving her a chance to accept my invitation with the same *insouciance*; but it was Mrs Burrell who answered.

'Oh, I don't think there should be any problems, do you, dear? When is it, a week on Saturday? I'm sure there's nothing special on that night that we need the car for. Daddy or I could drive you in and come back for you when it's time to go home.'

'No,' Heather said levelly. She didn't raise her voice, she didn't bother to turn round and look straight at her mother, she just said No, and the unstressed coolness of her tone made the refusal even more total.

'What on earth d'you mean, dear, no?'

'You surely know what No means,' the girl said in the same cool, deadly voice.

'But what...?'

'No to Daddy or you driving me in and then coming back for me. Delivering me like a bundle of washing and picking me up when the job's done.'

'But don't make so much of it, dear. It's no trouble. After all, Richard will be driving you this weekend.'

Richard? I thought. Who is this Richard? The brother, perhaps? But why should the brother drive her to the Hunt Ball? Much more likely it was the bastard she was going to the ball *with*, curse him.

Heather snapped her head round to look straight at her mother and said, 'Look, Mother, forget it, please. Just forget it. We're late as it is. Let's go and collect the saddle. I don't want to be driven in to this Oxford dance by Daddy or anybody else and then picked up at what you think is a suitable time. That's what used to happen at children's parties at the Village Hall and it's just not going to happen any more. It's not on, so please don't keep talking about it.'

There was a short silence and then I said, 'That looks like it, then. Sorry if I spoke out of turn.'

Heather turned her cool blue eyes on me and said in a gentler voice than she had yet used, 'You didn't speak out of turn. The idea's a perfectly reasonable one, and it's kind of you, especially as you weren't thinking of going. It's just that I won't be driven here and collected. If I come, I drive myself, *by* myself, and park the car, where *I* decide to park it, and come back when I'm ready to come back. In other words, I want the car till I've quite finished with it. And I just can't see the family agreeing to that. We've had enough rows about it and I just can't stand one more.'

I dimly began to see what was going on. I had stumbled on one of those long-running, incurable family disputes that bring out the worst in everybody. This was – I guessed – one of those families that spent about eight hours out of every twenty-four arguing about who was going to have the car. The social side of it was nothing, the evening out was nothing, going to a ball with a chap she had only just met and took no interest in was nothing, compared with the struggle to win the next point in the car power-game.

The mother now said something that was almost enough to make me believe that she was working on my side and, with the cunning of a Machiavelli and the strategy of a Clausewitz, steering the daughter into a position of having, ineluctably, to accept my invitation – if I could have credited the woman with that much intelligence. Assuming a calm, thoughtful expression that indicated a willingness to be scrupulously fair to all parties, she said, 'No, honestly, Heather, I don't think either Daddy or I will make any difficulties about that. I don't know quite why it's so important to you to drive yourself rather than be driven, but it's just as conventient from our point of view because I expect the ball will go on pretty late.'

'Early, you mean. It'll be the next morning before I set out for home. If you knew anything about Commems. you'd know that everybody dances all night and then has breakfast.'

'All right,' said the mother benignly. 'So the only thing to settle when we get back is whether Tom's arranged something that he'll need the car for.'

That was the magic touch, the Machiavelli-cum-Clausewitz. I could almost hear the box lid snap shut on Heather – and yet I'm sure the mother was just being her ordinary unthinking, habit-ridden self. Heather said 'Tom!' and got up from the *chaise longue* in a single convulsive movement. You could see, in that sudden rising, how springy her thighs were and how little weight she carried above the waist. '*Tom!*' she repeated. 'Am I never going to hear anything else but how *Tom* must have the car whenever he wants it, how *Tom* must drive all over the country whenever the mood takes him, how I have to be stuck at home whenever it suits *Tom* to...'

'There's no need to get so excited, dear. I'm sure if Tom's going somewhere that night and needs the car he won't mind dropping you off here on the way, and –'

'No!' Heather almost shouted. 'I thought we'd had all this out once and for all. I'm just damned well not going to sit down under it any longer. You and Daddy have just got to start being *fair*.' As she stood in the middle of the room, the sunlight from the window lit her dramatically; the flush of anger made her colour even more beautiful; blood flamed in her face, but not so as to turn her into the red of a brick or a beetroot like an ordinary mortal. Vivid as her colouring was, it was still delicate. I didn't do what is called falling in love with her, but at that moment I wanted to take her in my arms and, for that matter, I wanted to dance with her, and, for good measure, I wanted a lot of people to see me dancing with her: all those Episcopus blokes, for a start, and then Brian and Brian's friends, yes, and Tupper Boardman and even Trundle and Peake. And this Richard bastard, whoever he was.

'Look, dear,' said Mrs Burrell, her voice soft and placating. 'I don't know whether Tom has any plans for using the car that night, but I'm sure he can change them if we explain to him that it's important.'

'It doesn't matter a damn whether it's important or not,' Heather said venomously. 'If I want the car and I take fair shares with him, it doesn't have to be important. It can be the least little thing in the world, my God it can be completely *meaningless* if it wants to, if I choose to take the car and drive it into the middle of a field and sit there and read detective stories, I'll –'

'Yes, Heather, all right, dear. There's really no need to go on like this in front of Mr Leonard.'

'Peter,' I said.

How far we might have gone with this washing of dirty linen in public I don't know – Heather's temper was up and she was in no mood to leave the subject alone, Peter Leonard or no Peter Leonard – but, perhaps fortunately, Arthur chose that moment to rap splenetically on the door and bang into the room in the peculiarly deafening way he always affected, drumming his boot-soles on the floor as if determined to loosen the boards.

'Oh,' he said, stopping dead as if struck with amazement. 'Didn't know you 'ad company, sir.' This was his usual technique for making me feel bad about giving him a few extra cups and saucers to wash up.

'I didn't know I had to give you prior notice,' I said in a thin, hostile voice. I had recently decided to start hitting back at Arthur.

'You doesn't,' he said. 'Nobody doesn't need to tell me nothing. That's why it's such a bleedin' bed of roses. Pardon my French, milady,' he said to Mrs Burrell as if he had just noticed that she was not one of my fellow undergraduates.

'We haven't finished tea, Arthur,' I said.

'Speaking for myself, I've quite finished,' said Heather. 'I really think we must get back, Mother.'

Get back? But what about the Commem.? Had we reached a decision, or hadn't we? I felt completely disorientated, especially as Arthur, not knowing what was going on but sensing with an infallible instinct that it was in his power to do me some damage, began clumping round the room, picking up cups and saucers and rattling them with a practised intensity that must have been audible down in the quadrangle.

To my dismay the two women left the room in silence, save for Mrs Burrell's hastily murmured thanks for the tea. We went across the quad to the lodge in the same tongue-tied state, as if the curmudgeonly dotard had put a curse on our organs of speech. I was walking behind Heather and I distinctly remember looking with great care at her shapely bum, in case I should never again be that close to it. Despair flooded me like a sudden Dartmoor mist. But as we went through the lodge and were just about to step out into the great impersonal world, everything changed. Mrs Burrell halted in front of a poster advertising the ball.

'H'm,' she said. 'I see it starts at eight. That's a time you could manage all right, isn't it, dear?'

'Yes,' Heather said simply. Perhaps she was beginning to regret her outburst, because she turned to me and gave me a sudden, very pleasant smile.

'It'll be fun. Thanks. I'm glad you had the idea.'

'So am I,' I said truthfully.

'I'll park the car somewhere nearby – just about where it is now, I expect – and come and find you. Where? In your room?'

'Better meet here,' I said. 'Here, in the lodge.'

'What time?'

I had no idea, but in order not to dither I said decisively, 'Seven-thirty.'

She nodded, smiled again, the mother burbled something, and they were gone. I walked back across the quad on cushions of air.

I was intending to go back to my room, to sit quietly and think things over, but when I was almost at the top of the stairs a thought struck me that made me turn back immediately and hurry to the lodge. I must make sure of that ticket, now, right away. The Ball was not very far off and there couldn't be an unlimited number of them. How awful to have to write to Heather and say that, after all... I was panting as I galloped into the lodge and asked Frank Penney for a ticket. He said he had just a few left. I breathed again. I told him I would have the five guineas charged to my battels rather than pay it there and then. I had no idea where I was to get the money from, but the problem could be put off till the end of term. My various bits and bobs of grants and scholarships were so finely stretched that an extra sum of this size would sink my finances altogether, and, since I was not of age, if I failed to meet them the matter would be referred to my father. How on God's earth I would explain to *him* that I had blued five guineas for one night's dancing I had no vestige of an idea, especially since there was no way of conveying to him that the whole thing was a desperate gamble, a sprat to catch a mackerel who had shown no sign at all of wanting to be caught.

Well, the struggle to raise some cash would at least give me something to occupy my thoughts during the ten days or so that lay between me and the big gamble. I would certainly need an object to focus on if I were not simply to fret myself to death. Work had completely gone for a Burton. I simply could not settle my attention on it. My essay for Bax on Gregory IX's motives for excommunicating Frederick II was a laughably thin piece of rubbish. It didn't even approach the subject in the right way by drawing a distinction between the Pope's ostensible motives and his hidden ones, though it was obvious to any donkey that that was what Bax was after in setting the subject. I had floundered through it, under his pitying gaze, and he had wearily dismissed me ('I needn't keep you') before the hour was up. As for trying to do better in the week that lay ahead, it was obvious that I was going to do even worse.

*

Somehow the ten days went by, and during them I sold *everything*. This, I recognized, was a crisis, a watershed. Later, perhaps, if I ever settled down in a state resembling contentment, other things would take their turn, but for the moment nothing mattered but the struggle to make some sort of break-through on the girl front. What sort? I repressed the question and went on fund-raising.

One of the first things to go was the Cambridge Historical Atlas I had bought with such pride, and such a glow of high ambition, only at the end of last term. For a few brief weeks it had been the pride of my bookshelves, but what was pride, what was ownership, what was knowledge itself, compared with a chance, however remote, of release from this prison of frustration? Round it went to the shop where I had bought it, and on the very first day of selling-up at that. The problem of how to finance the adventure simply blotted everything out. Five guineas, I soon came to see, was not going to cover it. I would have to hire evening dress. And it would obviously be necessary to have a bottle of something in my room, in addition to the champagne we would be getting on our tickets. Heather must be offered a polite glass of something on arriving. Sherry would be the safe thing, the great Oxford stand-by. Must do everything right. No slip-ups now. I could get a bottle from the buttery and have it charged to battels. Ah, those battels! The perfect machinery for building up unmanageable debts! There were times when I had a sudden unnerving vision of myself handcuffed to a policeman and with another one following behind, being taken off to the Marshalsea.

The price I got for the Cambridge Historical Atlas, by the way, was my first lesson in the methods of academic booksellers. I took it to the very shop I had bought it from, hoping for half price at any rate, but all I could wring out of them was a mere fraction of what I had paid. More, much more, was needed. During my schooldays I had had bouts of collecting stamps, and my album with quite a few in it, neatly mounted on hinges, was down at the Bargeman's. I went and got it, took it to the appropriate shop and got a few shillings, again nowhere near its resale value. While I was at home, I scooped up my cheap box camera and sold that too. Still not enough. What else? Clothes?

Well, yes, but I had only about enough of these to get by; what could I spare? Then I thought of my winter overcoat, a good thick one which my parents had given me to set me up for going off to College last year. It was summer now, and fine weather. I wouldn't be needing an overcoat for months, and when I did, well, that problem, like all the rest, would have to be solved when its turn came. For the moment, nothing mattered except...

Getting the coat meant going down to the Bargeman's again, and a tweed overcoat would take a lot more smuggling out of the house than a stamp album or a box camera. In theory I had a perfect right to take any of my belongings to College, but my parents would certainly smell a rat if I took a winter overcoat there in the middle of a spell of warm weather, and at a time when I was due to come home in a couple of weeks anyway. I was going to have to play this cleverly – get the coat down from my room and out of the house while Mother and Dad were both busy with other things.

In the end I settled on a Sunday morning, timing my arrival for midday when Dad would be just opening the bar and Mother working in the kitchen. I combined the raid with a social visit, going back into the living-quarters and chatting with Mother for a bit while she peeled potatoes. After catching up with the domestic scene and reassuring her that I was eating enough in College and not wearing myself away to a shadow by over working my brain, I went through into the pub and there was Brian, leaning against the bar and chatting with Dad. He really was coming out these days. The adventurous life at M.G., now that they were out in the world and having successes, had made him expansive. He was wearing a check tweed cap, and thrown loosely over his shoulders was a leather overcoat. *Très sportif.*

He nodded to me and said, 'Have a drink. You bought me one last time.'

It was true that I had paid for our beer in the little pub on the Plain, but I had not expected him to remember. I accepted, basking in his good humour, and said, 'Nice coat you've bought yourself.'

'I need it,' he said. 'It gets pretty cold on the Irish Sea at night.'

'The Irish...?'

'We're going across to Ulster for the T.T.,' he said. So that was what he had meant when he talked about Ulster. 'Another big push. If we pull this one off we've really made it. And we're going to pull it off. Nobody's taking any chances. We've prepared three cars absolutely *perfect*. After the successes we've had, people are looking to us to stay on top. We're going for a class win, and if the handicappers get it right that should give us an outright race win as well.'

'Oh,' I said.

A couple of customers came in and Dad went along to the other end of the bar to serve them. Then he came back and drew me the pint of beer Brian was standing me. During the couple of minutes he was away, Brian and I did not speak, just stood there companionably. Looking at him now, attentively and at close quarters, I could see that under his jauntiness he was rather pale, and that there were bruises of fatigue under his eyes. I knew he was working fanatically hard. I wasn't worried about his health – yet; he was young, and the adrenalin of success would keep him going in any case; but if success should dry up?

'Have you got it in your pocket?' I said to him.

'Got what in my pocket? The race?'

'No,' I said. 'The photo.'

At that, his grin came back and he reached slowly into his jacket pocket and brought out the photograph of Old Number One.

'There she is, the little beauty,' he said, holding it out.

I looked at the little beauty, for the first time doing so with real interest and attention. To me she seemed nothing more exciting than a highly polished metal shape like an inverted bath-tub with wheels sticking out at the corners, her sleek lines broken only by the outside handbrake which looked like something from an obsolete printing-press. And yet there must be more to her than that, if one looked at her with a lover's eye. She represented a force, powerful and mysterious, which did not touch me personally but had the power to take over men's lives.

'She's lovely, isn't she?' I said.

Brian put the photograph back in his pocket before answering, and when he did answer he looked at me with an expression I had not seen before.

'You're coming on, young 'un,' he said.

My mother wanted me to stay and have Sunday dinner, but I gently excluded myself, saying that I had a lot to do back at college and my day was already set up. These late, protracted Sunday dinners were for the vac., not for term. She grumbled a bit, of course.

'They must be driving you hard,' she said, 'if you haven't got time to yourself on a Sunday.'

'Well, you haven't got time to yourself on a Sunday either, Mum,' I countered.

She shrugged. 'Oh, you know why that is. There's no time off in a licensee's life.'

'No, and there isn't any in an historian's, either.'

I felt a cad telling her I was working in view of what I was actually giving my energies to; but not too much of one, since (I reasoned) if all this effort actually achieved any results I would be much better able to get on with some work, so that, by only a slight degree of sophistry, I might be said to be attending to my work by trying to get something set up with Heather.

That point settled to my own satisfaction, I said my farewells and got out out on to the towpath. In twenty minutes' time I would be able to get lunch at College, and it struck me that a pleasant use of that twenty minutes would be to walk down-river to Folly Bridge, cut through the nearer end of Christ Church Meadow, and get over to High Street, *en route* to Episcopus, through one of the narrow alley-ways that came out opposite St Mary's. I set off briskly, but had barely got to Oseney Lock before I was halted by the sight of a familiar figure. It was Lamont. He was standing near the lock cottage with a thick book in his hand, alternately looking down at the book and round him at the river-bank and the buildings.

'In search of something, Lamont?' I said, going up to him.

'Oh, hello. Yes. Oseney Abbey was just about here, wasn't it? I'm trying to see if there's anything still to be seen of it.'

'What's the book?'

He held it out. Hurst's *Oxford Topography*, a solid Victorian job.

'I can't tell much from this, actually,' Lamont said. 'Even which side of the river it was on.'

'It was on both sides. The lands were very extensive, with orchards and gardens. The most magnificent bit was the church, and that was over there, on the side we're standing on.' I pointed behind him. 'It's under that cemetery.'

'Good Lord,' he said, looking. 'All that splendour under such a featureless plot. But that's the story of the Reformation, I suppose.'

'It didn't happen all at once,' I said. 'There were still masses being said in that church in the 1570s. And there were buildings standing for a couple of centuries. Probably the worst effacement was when the fields were ploughed up in 1718.'

'I still can't picture where it was all grouped,' Lamont said. 'Where was the mill?'

'Where it is now. But you have to start by realizing that the pattern of the water-courses was different. The Thames is very varicose round here, even now. It has one main channel, true, but the subsidiary channels are a very complex pattern and they've been altered through the centuries by virtually ceaseless engineering, to try to make them fewer and deeper.'

'They've all got individual names, haven't they? The Bulstake Stream is one I seem to remember.'

'Yes, the Bulstake Stream is still there, and if you walk on from here in the direction you're going you'll have to cross it to get to the Botley Road. But there was another, just as important, that seems to have been called the Elde. It was to the west of here, and an important boundary. It's gone now, swallowed up in other streams.'

Lamont looked at me with an unusual closeness of attention. 'You know a lot about it, don't you? D'you know this much about everything historical?'

I laughed. 'Far from it. I just know about this part of the world because I live here.'

'I thought you lived in College.'

'No, I mean I live here when I'm not in College. It's my home. I was born here.'

'Really? You live in Oseney? What marvellous continuity!'

'I don't see that it's so marvellous. Oxford isn't a very old city, but every district of it has been continuously inhabited for a thousand years at least.'

'Yes, but –' Lamont gave one of his rare laughs. 'It's so Chaucerian.'

I was aware, of course, that Chaucer's 'Miller's Tale' introduces a young scholar by the name of Nicholas, who has lodgings in Oseney at the house of a carpenter and his pretty young wife, and that the academic rapscallion has his will with the said p.y.w. while the carpenter is out at his work, 'at Oseney', by which Chaucer must mean that he is one of the army of craftsmen employed at the Abbey. But being a native of Oseney did not seem to me so amusing as it did to Lamont.

'Are you trying to say,' I said, 'that because I live in Oseney I shall let a room one day to a student and be cuckolded by him?'

'Not necessarily. You might be the one who does the cuckolding.'

'All the same,' I said, my mind still running on Chaucer's carpenter, 'if it was my destiny to be cuckolded while I was out at work I'd rather that work consisted of craftsmanship with wood in Oseney Abbey, that I could get some creative satisfaction out of, than standing by a production line at Cowley.'

'What d'you think the man himself would decide? If you brought him back to life and showed him the two jobs?'

'Impossible to say. You'd have to show him the whole surrounding life in each case. Job for job I'm sure he'd rather be a carpenter.'

'I would,' Lamont said, 'and you would. But some people like motor-cars.'

Yes, I thought, and there's one drinking beer fifty yards behind me, my own brother, who loves cars and wouldn't be a carpenter at any price. But then I thought, even Brian can't love assembly lines. The M.G. is a hand-built job. Craftsmanship. The spirit of Oseney Abbey.

Lamont was still peering about, still clutching Hurst. 'Is there nothing at all to see?' he asked.

'You're over a century too late. There's a drawing that dates from 1815, just before the mill was knocked down and rebuilt, that shows a lot of medieval structures. And about thirty-five years ago the owner of the mill built a new turbine stream to the west of the mill, and while they were digging it out they found part of a stone arch sticking out of a wall, and a paving floor, in masonry different from the surrounding stone. But of course they went on with the work and covered it up again.'

'So there's *nothing*?' he said wistfully.

'There are a few fragments of a stone gateway, and some bits that may or may not be part of ruined medieval buildings. But even to see those you'd have to cross the river just here, and get onto a bit of private ground. You have to get the lock-keeper's permission.'

'Will he give it me easily?'

'No. He's a surly bastard.'

'Oh, well,' Lamont said, 'I shan't bother. It's just too sad anyway. Better to imagine the Abbey as it was. You know,' he went on, his tone changing, 'that's a real question, what that fourteenth-century carpenter would decide to do if you called him back and offered him a job at Morris Motors today or his old job back at Oseney Abbey. Which d'you think you'd choose?'

'If I were him,' I said, 'the first thing I'd do would be to get a different lodger. Then I'd think about the job. Being me, I'd probably go for the Abbey.'

'Being me, I certainly would. I find machines stop me from writing poetry. It's something about the non-organic rhythms. I'm quite reconciled to the fact that I shall never be able to make a living by writing poetry and I'll have to do something else for most hours of most days, but I've discovered already that being anywhere near machines is no good. They're all very well in their way, but it's not the way of poetry.

That's where Mayakovsky made such a mistake. He wanted so much to identify –'

Lamont then talked for several minutes about Mayakovsky, who thus joined Leopardi among the phalanx of names which I first looked up because of Lamont. By the time he had finished I realized that it was too late to walk back to Episcopus via Christ Church Meadow, and we must take the shortest route or even, if possible, catch a bus from the neighbourhood of the station.

Lamont agreed to this plan, and we set off together, he carrying Hurst's *Oxford Topography* under his arm.

'How extraordinary', he mused as we strode along, 'that an achievement like Oseney, one of the glories of medieval civilization, should have been so utterly obliterated when a monument to material comfort like the Roman remains at Bath should be so well preserved.'

'There's a poem there.'

'There are poems in everything. And speaking of that, there's every reason why all the poets in the world should make pilgrimages to Oseney just to look at the blank space where the Abbey was.'

I waited for him to go on, but he didn't and I said, 'Why? You mean the bell?'

'What bell?' It was his turn to be puzzled.

'Thomas of Oseney. Reputed to be the biggest bell, or the equal of the biggest, in England. Taken down when the Church was destroyed, and then after many adventures hung in Wren's tower at Christ Church and renamed Great Tom.'

'No! Really? The bell we hear every night of our lives, is that from Oseney?'

'That's Thomas of Oseney.' I felt as proud as if I had personally cast the great bell, personally tuned it and hung it.

'You do tell me some things, Leonard. You're a very interesting man'.

'Nobody's ever called me that before.'

'Well, you certainly are one. But of course when I said that about poets I was speaking of the *Chanson de Roland*.'

We walked for a few paces and then I said, 'Go on, fill me in.'

'The *manuscript*,' he said patiently.

'Of the *Chanson de Roland*? You mean there was one at Oseney?'

'Not just one. *The* one. It survived here.'

'*What?* Are you telling me –'

'I'm telling you,' Lamont said, 'that although copies were naturally multiplied in the later Middle Ages, the oldest and best manuscript of the *Chanson de Roland* existed and was treasured and cared for in the library of Oseney Abbey and all modern editions have to start from it.'

I was silent all the way back to Episcopus. The greatest imaginative expression of the ideals of chivalry had been preserved for the world in a monastic library, on the bank of my own river, within a few yards of the humble beer-house that was my own home. The carpenters and binders and glaziers and plasterers who looked after that library, who made shelving and ladders and staircases for it, who saw to the ceilings and the guttering and the tiling, and leaded in the window-panes, when they finished their day's work, did they come to the Bargeman's, or to some inn just like it, for a pot of my father's good beer, or for a pot of beer just like it from someone just like him, and was I, or someone just like me, growing up in the house, watching the river flow past from my upstairs window?

As we got to Episcopus Lamont, who had obviously been immersed in his own thoughts as I was in mine, broke the silence by asking me, 'What's the first recorded mention of Oseney Abbey?'

'I forget what the first one is,' I said, 'but the first authoritative description's in Dugdale, *Monasticum Anglicanum*.'

'Thanks,' he said.

We parted, thoughtfully, in the lodge.

*

By the time the Saturday of the ball arrived, I had scraped together £8 in all – not enough, of course, in view of the fact that the confounded soup-and-fish outfit I had to hire cost me a sum I could have lived on for a week, but enough to enable me to bundle the whole problem into the back of my mind during those last hours while I dressed up, tied my white tie about a thousand times, calmed the fluttering in my stomach with a glass or two from the pristine bottle of sherry I had bought to offer on Heather's arrival, and generally paced about half-crazed. And finally it was time. No, not quite time. Yes, nearly time. I stared fixedly at the minute-hand of my watch, driving it doggedly over the last five little lines.

With a last vicious yank at the drooping wings of my dress-tie, I closed the door behind me and went down the twisting wooden stairs. As I went I could not help thinking what a world of difference there was between this occasion and the last time when I had waited for a girl to visit me in College. That had been the Sunday afternoon work-out with Vinnie. This was something altogether more complex, even though I didn't disguise from myself the fact that the ultimate target remained the same.

On that Sunday afternoon I had simply been an enormous throbbing prick, with an insignificant and characterless youth anchored somewhere behind it, hoping to get it some work to do. Now, though the prick was certainly there as before, the person behind it was not quite so callow and featureless; he had learnt a thing or two about life and about himself; and in any case the occasion was entirely different, as different as the one girl was from the other. It was legitimate and above-board, in that her parents knew she was coming to the dance and with whom; and there were huge question marks over the whole enterprise, whereas with Vinnie there had just been one big exclamation mark.

Punctually at seven-thirty Heather came into the lodge. She had been successful in borrowing the car without the services of Tom as policeman-chauffeur, and had had no difficulty in parking it in St Giles, but she wanted me to take the keys and stow them safely in a drawer or somewhere, because her evening bag was flimsy and she didn't want to lug them around all evening, especially on the dance floor. In her calm way she got these practical details attended to first, as we stood there in the lodge. She had some kind of lacy black cloak over her shoulders and as she stood under the electric light in the lodge – it was not dark but the light was switched on as if ready to indicate that it would burn on relentlessly till morning – her hair shone out as brilliant as a gorse-bush on a hillside.

I invited her to come up to my rooms and leave her things. Then we would go in search of a drink and start dancing. We walked together across the quad. I noticed once again what a well-grown girl she was, almost exactly the same height as myself, and with such a spring in her step. She'll dance me into the ground, I thought. Well, here goes for whatever happens.

We didn't stay long in my rooms. I had already drunk about half the sherry – it was rather a shock to discover that – but Heather seemed quite content to drink one glass and move along. I was counting, in any case, on having plenty to drink once we joined the merry throng. Surely, I argued, the fantastic price would entitle us to as much champagne, and anything else that was going, as we could absorb without sliding into a coma. I certainly had every intention of drinking five guineas' worth of wine single-handed, or single-throated.

Heather took off her dark cloak and revealed a long dress in some silvery material that swished when she moved. It must have been constructed with whalebone or something, because it ceased just above her breasts and revealed a shining expanse of smooth bare skin and firm rich flesh. On each ear-lobe she wore a little flashing star. I wanted to put my mouth on her neck and feel its warmth and smoothness. But of course I didn't. I just made some remark like, 'Well, shall we go down and see if it's all started?' and we went down to see if it had.

It was certainly a slap-up affair. The Hall had been cleared of furniture and some big-name London dance band was already tuning up on the dais. In the garden an enormous marquee had been erected, on the lawn, and this had been provided with a wooden floor, about half of which was roped off as a space for dancing – to a smaller band – with the other half being left for drinking and socializing generally. Scouts in white jackets, many of them recruited from other colleges, were on hand to open bottles and hand round trays of glasses and concoct various kinds of fruit punch and claret cup. It all seemed like a colossal expenditure of effort, thought, time and money just so that a hundred or so people could enjoy themselves for a few hours. Not that I cared a damn about the Commem. one way or another. It was simply a device for getting a foot in the door with Heather. I would have attended any *Walpurgisnacht* as long as she came with me.

We went into the Hall first. The floor was beginning to fill up with couples, standing around, but the band had not yet gone into their opening number. Someone mentioned that drinks were being served in the minstrels' gallery at the kitchen end of the Hall, so we went up the stairs. Sure enough, it was already full of people standing about drinking champagne, and scouts handing the stuff out. I noticed a number of people, both men and girls, shooting glances at Heather, and I began to feel proud of myself. Certainly, as I looked round, I saw girls of all shapes and sizes, but none more handsome.

I ploughed in and got us each a glass of champagne. Heather held up her glass, before drinking from it, and looked at the bubbles. Her eyes were bright with enjoyment, but she was cautious about what it might do to her and made a good-humoured joke of her caution.

'This'll be the first glass of champagne I've ever had,' she said, looking at me past the bubbling liquid. 'Will it come down my nose? It won't make me *drunk*, will it?'

I liked her openness. She had her feet so firmly planted on her own ground that one couldn't imagine her being embarrassed or upstaged. I had never drunk champagne before either, it was my first glass as much as it was hers, but nothing would have made me admit it. After all, I had, unlike her, a role to play. I was the insider, the sophisticated one, who had been for almost a year in the great world, the one who was going to show her Life.

'It may come down your nose a bit,' I said, 'but it won't make you drunk. If you feel yourself getting a bit wobbly, dancing's the cure for it. Well, cheers, and I'm very glad you could come.'

Our eyes met for an instant. 'Cheers,' she said. 'I'm enjoying it very much already. I'm so glad you asked me.'

That was about the limit of our amatory exchange during the next four hours. Heather seemed to want nothing but to give herself up to dancing, occasionally eating and drinking, and in between times observing the scene. She was totally without fatigue, and perfectly happy. As for me, I wanted nothing but for her to have what suited her. It was important for her to want to go on knowing me, and I was prepared to regard the whole fantastic extravaganza as bait. Viciously expensive bait, but bait all the same.

On the dance floor, I found my rudimentary knowledge of ballroom dancing, as practised in 1931, was just about good enough. I knew the few simple steps that made up the two or three standard dances, and could get by with them, especially on a crowded floor where there wasn't room to do much apart from shuffle round. Heather danced well, not showily but with a perfect natural sense of rhythm and with an enjoyment in moving her body that was contagious. It made me feel what a miracle it was to have limbs and to be able to put them into controlled movement; and after all, though I wasn't as fit as she was I was light on my feet, and young, and active, like her. I held her in a light but firm grip, and now and then, under cover of having to execute some manoeuvre, pulled her as close to me as I dared, so that for a moment our bodies, from the waist up, were plastered together. It was a wonderful feeling, but I was quite glad it wasn't prolonged more than a few seconds, or it would have given me an erection that would have come between us as awkwardly as a bag of golf-clubs.

There were a lot of people there that I recognized and a lot more that I didn't, mostly quite predictable. One thing that did surprise me, though, was, in a crowded corner of the floor, suddenly coming face to face with Fred Armitage. I saw his partner first, a girl I had never seen before with pale fair hair and a rather long nose, and then they pivoted round in some kind of spin turn and there was Fred. Somehow I had not associated him with Commem. Balls, and yet, I reflected, why not? Probably no one here would get quite so much out of it, the champagne, the dressing-up, the famous band, the posh occasion. It would all go into his mental photograph album. This is me at the Commem. Ball at Episcopus in 1931. My first year. I supposed it was his girl-friend from back home who was with him, invited down to be duly impressed. Well, after all, he was only doing, in a slightly more honest and straightforward way, what I was doing myself.

The other person I remember is Carshalton. I didn't notice him till about midnight. Heather and I had been out to the marquee in the garden to drink some wine and try dancing to the quartet out there. It was quite fun, more informal and uninhibited, and we put a bit more zest and inventiveness into our dancing. When the band took an interval, we joined the throng who were trying to get glasses of champagne, but there were too many of them, so I led the way back to the Hall and up to the minstrels' gallery. It wasn't so thick there, partly because the main band happened to be playing and most people were dancing. Then I saw Carshalton. He was squiring the sister of that aristocratic brother-and-sister pair he was working so hard to get in with... what was their name? Oh yes, Acheson-Fiske. Well, he had got this far anyway. We were standing quite close to them and I took a good look at her. Quite attractive, I decided, and certainly her dress, a pale green affair, had been made by a good designer and sat well on her. She had the regulation long-boned face that makes all the upper class look rather horse-like, but on the other hand I was feeling warm and tolerant towards horses because Heather liked them and clasped her delectable thighs around them, a fact which immediately put them on a different level in the scale of creation from, say, pigs or tapirs or crocodiles. I decided the Honourable Lady Acheson-Fiske was probably all right. Carshalton, on the other hand, was quite manifestly not all right. His face, I saw with interest, was a strange colour, a kind of dead matt white such as one sees on cloakroom walls, his eyes were set in a fixed stare and he moved stiffly as if his joints were fashioned from clumsily-hewn chunks of wood. Jammed into a corner of his mouth he had a cigar roughly the size of a policeman's truncheon, which gave off sullen firework-fumes. He had two empty champagne glasses in his left hand and was poking them out awkwardly towards the scout who was at that moment opening a fresh bottle; his right arm formed a stiff triangle through which the young lady was supposed to loop her arm. She had in fact withdrawn her arm and let it fall limply to her side. but Carshalton continued to hold the triangle in readiness.

Two large, broad-shouldered fellows now approached the table to replenish glasses and, I am sure without particularly meaning to, jostled Carshalton slightly so that he lurched to one side. Only then did I realize how drunk he was. The prolonged nervous effort of trying to live up to Lady Whatever must have driven him to fortify himself too liberally and for too long. Having begun to side-step, he went on doing so until he fetched up short by a table on which stood a large silver bowl of mulled wine, with orange peel and various related *débris* bobbing around in it. A scout had just brought in this bowl and had in fact barely set it down before Carshalton arrested his tottering progress by knocking against the table. He clutched wildly at the rim of the claret-bowl, letting go the glasses he was holding in order to do so. One glass went into the wine and disappeared, the other had its stem snapped neatly in two against the edge of the table. At the same time Carshalton brought up his other arm, the one that had been forming the triangle, and took the cigar out of his mouth. Straightening up and holding himself unnaturally erect, he stared for a moment at the long ash that had formed on it. The cigar must have been of excellent quality because the ash was about three inches long and so firm in texture that I could plainly see, from where I stood, the shape of the rolled leaves with their central spines. Looking carefully at this ash as if estimating its weight, and moving with the deliberation of a man poised on the brink of nervous collapse, Carshalton tapped the cigar with his forefinger, a sharp and decisive tap that caused the ash to fall off. Some instinct for tidiness and order made him do this over the bowl of mulled wine. With a short hiss, the ash disappeared into the previously appetising refreshment.

Several bystanders exclaimed at the sight, and the scout in charge of the mulled wine began an angry expostulation. Carshalton, swiftly coming out of his trance-like state and realizing that he had done something disastrous, backed away from the table with a sudden reverse lunge, which brought him into abrupt contact with another scout carrying a tray of newly filled glasses. Tray and glasses flew wildly, the scout staggered, and Carshalton halted, his face a glazed mask of horror.

That was the only time I ever saw Carshalton make a fool of himself and appear in a bad light in a public place. Normally he was as sure-footed as a cat, because he was as watchful and as self-centred as a cat.

And of course it was no accident that the occasion on which he fell on his face should be that particular one. He was trying too hard, it all mattered too much to him; there was something sweaty about his desperate wish to be accepted by real, dyed-in-the-wool, copper-bottomed members of the governing class. That sweat greased his feet and hands like butter on a cat's paws.

I managed to commandeer a couple more glasses of champagne – for myself, not for Heather; she was drinking much more slowly than I was – before taking to the dance floor again. The ball was really getting into its stride now, between midnight and one am, and of course there was the usual sprinkling of louts whose loutishness had come to the surface with the aid of a few glasses of bubbly, and who were shouting things to one another across the dance-floor and cutting various capers. Two factions had got hold of an emptied bowl of fruit punch and scooped out the orange and lemon peel and cucumber rind, which they were intermittently trying to shove down one another's necks. Yells and guffaws rose above the music.

Their foolishness didn't seem to impinge on Heather. She was floating along tirelessly, her strong legs moving her lissom body about as if it had been a feather, and looking around her with a rather dreamy expression of happy acceptance, as if she liked and approved of everything and everybody she saw. I thought how insulted she would have been if I had invited her to come dancing with me at Holyoake Hall, and yet in all essentials the two were the same thing. Then I thought how much nicer it would be if, instead of bumping around among this boring crowd, we were just strolling in Episcopus garden, among the dark groves and flower-beds, enjoying each other's company in quiet. But for that she would have had to come on some other evening, when there was no silly squawking Commem. going on and no meaningless crush of people everywhere – and then she would not be allowed in College after seven o'clock. What a tissue of absurdities, I thought, and for a moment I felt something close to a patronizing irritation with her for liking this foolishness, this non-occasion of a Commem., so much.

And then, of course, I felt ashamed of myself, remembering that she was a farmer's daughter and lived a long way out in the country, and mostly had just her parents and her brother and the animals for company, and must so seldom get to any bright lights or dressing-up festivities, and as for champagne... and at the thought I tightened the arm I had round her waist amd drew her close to me for an instant in a gentle squeeze. My motive was not sexual, merely a wordless apology to her for an unworthy thought she didn't even know I had had; but she went along with it, allowing her body to be pressed against me without making any attempt to pull away.

Then the music stopped, and suddenly it was like getting off some galloping-horses merry-go-round, and while it was nice to rest for a while, to stop exerting oneself and just stand still, there was that slight sense of let-down. With the solid wall of sound from the band suddenly not there, there was just the sound of people's conversations and their voices, in the surrounding night silence, came to my ears as scrappy, hesitant, disjointed. It was a moment of hiatus, of pause, of 'Where do we go from here?' and Heather stepped straight into it and took over the leadership.

'I'm just beginning to realize,' she said, turning her lovely eyes full on my face and giving me her whole attention, 'how hot and tired I'm getting. Do let's sit in the garden for a bit and enjoy the cool night.'

I was glad of this and said eagerly, 'Yes, of course. Right. Come along and we'll find a...' Then it occurred to me that perhaps I wasn't looking after her properly, letting her go and sit in the chill night air when she was hot from dancing, and I said, 'Er... your shawl's up in my room... I could go and get it...'

'Never mind. If I need it I'll go and get it myself.' And we went outside into the garden, Heather's hand lightly on my arm, and started wandering about among the dark lawns and pathways, under the dark trees.

It wasn't cold, and there was a moon about two-thirds at the full, casting a silvery light over everything which was very beautiful once our eyes had got rid of the dazzle of the electric bulbs. We kept clear of the marquee, where the quartet was cheerfully tooting away, and sought out the quieter places, where thick bushes screened out the sounds and one could almost forget, for a minute or two at a time, that there was a big social gathering in full swing. People were sitting on benches or walking slowly about the shadowy paths, but in every case they were couples, obviously welcoming a few minutes of each other's undiluted company. We found a wooden seat that had another couple on it; there was plenty of room, and Heather sat down firmly and indicated that I should sit beside her. After a few minutes the other couple got up and walked on. Heather turned her head to look at me, and as she did so I saw the moonlight glitter in the little bright ornaments she wore in her ears.

'I hope it's all... I hope you're having a good time, Heather,' I said.

She looked at me, not smiling, but with an air of softness and gentleness, and said, 'It's quite, quite different from how I imagined it.'

'How did you imagine it?'

'Like the Hunt Ball,' she said.

'And that was...?' I prodded gently.

'Oh, loud and brassy and quite jolly once you got into the mood. You just had to forget everything except making a noise and laughing a lot and having vast amounts to eat and drink and having a Good Time.' I could hear the capital letters on the last two words.

It didn't sound as if this bugger Richard, whoever he was, had managed to sweep her off her feet and make a magical experience of the whole thing; but just to get a bit more reassurance I deliberately set up the comparison.

'Whereas this...' I prompted.

'Oh, this is a good time all right, Peter.' She had never, as far as I remembered, used my name before, and to hear the word, my special identifying syllables, come out of her mouth, especially in that tone of voice she was using – quiet, but vibrant with meaning – gave me a tremendous jolt. I think she must have heard me gasp. Certainly I drew in my breath sharply. 'But it's quite different,' she finished.

'How is it different? There's plenty of noise here, and plenty of people drinking and chattering, and those louts throwing orange peel at one another – it seems to me pretty much the –'

'I don't know why, but it's different.'

I took my courage in both hands and pressed on. 'Different and better, or different and worse?'

She gave a toss of the head, almost defiantly, as if to convey All right, if you want plain speaking! And with her gaze locked into mine she said, not in the same soft tone but almost off-handedly, 'Different and better. And it's not true that I don't know why. It's being with you. You're someone rather special.'

I wondered if the champagne had really made me drunk and if I were mishearing her, imagining things. The whole situation seemed suddenly to have left the bounds of the normal and expected. Especially when she stood up and said, 'I'm cold.'

'You're cold?'

'Yes. I need my shawl after all. I'll go and get it from your room, but I need you to come with me in case I get lost.'

Dazedly, I hoisted in that the two of us were going up to my room, not as a result of any cunning trap or sweaty persistence on my part, but at her suggestion, now, without ceremony, immediately.

So we went. I was still so much in the grip of College discipline that as we entered the dark well of my staircase I glanced about nervously, wondering if anyone in authority was registering the fact that I was taking a girl up to my room in the middle of the night. But of course they weren't. This was Saturnalia, the licensed occasion. My glancing round was a purely nervous reaction.

We went up the stairs, Heather first. When we got to the top landing she stood aside to let me open the door, and as I brushed very close by her I got a faint but heady scent composed of whatever perfume she was using and, beneath and around it, some wholesome, healthy body-sweat from all those hours of dancing. Neither was at all pronounced – she wasn't the kind of girl to drench herself in scent and she didn't sweat heavily – but the two together blended into a kind of musk that, for an instant, excited me so much that I nearly fainted.

I pushed open the door and had my hand on the light-switch when Heather, reaching from behind, put her hand on my wrist and said, 'No light. It'll spoil it. We want to see the night.'

So we went into the unlit room. Actually it was fairly well lit, because the moonlight slanted in through the windows. Even someone not accustomed to the room could see perfectly well enough to steer round the furniture.

I opened the window on the side that looked down into the street, threw it wide, and together we leaned out. The sky was everything we could have wanted it to be and it did everything for us that we could have wanted it to do. We leaned out, and looked up, and then down at the trees to one side of us, and I put my arm round her shoulders and she let it stay there.

But then a lorry came noisily along the road, even at that time in the dead of night, and barely had its sound died away when a car came along and drew up right underneath us and there was a great slamming of doors and raising of voices in cheery farewells that seemed set to go on for half-an-hour together.

This wouldn't do. I had a better idea. 'Come across here,' I said to Heather, 'and I'll show you something.' Our eyes were accustomed to the soft light now and we moved easily across the room and into my tiny cell of a bedroom. The window was high up and the way to peer out through it was to stand on the bed. On the other hand, if you did get as far as peering out you could easily go one better and clamber through it altogether and come out on to the same ledge on which I had crouched like a hunted animal while Kent and his mob bayed outside my oak on that early spring evening that now seemed years distant. I hadn't climbed on to it in all the intervening months. Why should I? I had had no occasion to. Now I had an occasion. I wanted to be alone with Heather, close to her, close to the stars. I wanted to kiss her.

I stood on the bed and said to her, 'If we just get out of the window there's a perfect place for enjoying a night like this. *The* ultimately perfect place. I'll show you. You just have to get up on the bed, like this, and put your hands on the outside window-sill, like this,' and I did it, 'and swing yourself up, like this,' and I did it, 'and draw your legs up after you and you're out.' I did it, and I was there, under the stars. The medieval roof and chimneys around me were unearthly, fantastical, in their beauty. The Thames Valley night was pure velvet, and the moon, beginning to sink now behind the trees, made it almost too much. I looked round. I breathed. *I am happy*, I thought. *Already, before Heather has joined me up here, I am happy just to be here, and to know that she will soon...*

She will soon what? I was standing there ready to help her up; obviously it was my place to do so, and it seemed more polite to do it by going up first and demonstrating how to climb to the sill, then lean down through the window ready to take her hand and pull her up, than to get behind and push her by shoving at her bottom. But when I bent forward and looked back into the room, hand outstretched, I saw to my surprise that she was lying on her back on my bed and smiling composedly at me.

'I –' I began, and stopped.

'I don't think I'll bother getting out through the window,' she said. 'I can see the moonlight from here, shining very brightly on some little white clouds, and your bed's very comfortable.'

I knew for a fact that my bed wasn't comfortable, but to stretch out on it might well be relaxing after all those hours of dancing. Or was it something else, and better? Did she feel like stretching out on my bed for a more welcome reason than just being a little weary in the limbs?

Perhaps I was on a completely wrong hunch, but standing there in the moonlight I decided to risk it. What had I got to lose anyway? I had never even kissed her. It seemed to me that if I acted with sufficient promptness now I could at least put that right. In a flash I was inside the window-frame, on the sill, on the bed, lying beside Heather. There was just comfortably room for our two heads on my moon-flooded pillow.

We kissed then, and everything about Heather's kiss told me it was no accident that we had come up to my room. She had engineered it for just this purpose. For a long time we didn't say anything. We just got our mouths together and let them do the talking, wordlessly.

Finally, though, the first great wave of ecstacy spent itself and I began to be aware of various discomforts. I was still dressed with complete formality in the absurd outfit that one was supposed to wear for these functions, starched shirt-front, dress tie with stiff collar, tight-fitting jacket and all. I hadn't paused to shed any of it, not even to take off my jacket or un-knot my tie, and the whole ensemble buckled and creased and dug in to me until it finally drew attention to itself. I paused for a moment in my ministrations and began clawing at my tie.

'You must be terribly uncomfortable,' Heather said softly, and with one smooth, skilful hand she popped my collar away from its moorings and began to work her way down my shirt-front, pulling out the little imitation-pearl studs. My shirt now resembled the wing-case of a beetle when it parts ready for flight, except that it was white and was in front rather than behind. My chest appeared, clad in its prosaic singlet.

'What a funny little vest,' she said, but not mockingly. 'D'you always wear this kind?'

I was perfectly willing to enter into a discussion of my preferences in underwear if this was what she was interested in. 'Yes,' I said flatly.

'I think you'd look nicer without it,' she murmured. 'Those singlets always make me think of people in a gym.'

I sat up and slipped off everything above the waist, then lay down close to her again. It all felt wonderful. The cool night air caressed my skin, I didn't feel in the least chill in the beautiful summer darkness, and to add to my bliss Heather joined in and began running her hand over my chest in a caress as delicate as the air's. Her wonderfully supple body moulded itself to the shape of mine as she lay on my narrow iron bed.

I say 'everything felt wonderful,' but after another few moments I became aware that not quite everything did. From the waist down I was still wearing the silly shiny trousers with their bit of braid down the side of each leg, and the patent leather shoes. Heather's form-fitting silvery dress didn't seem to be giving her any trouble, but that was a damn sight more than I could say for those accursed trousers. I had not taken the precaution of positioning my *membrum virile* so that it could telescope upwards if need be, and Heather's kisses and caresses had caused it to buckle into an agonizing hoop, a shape from which it was now striving to free itself by convulsions so seismic as to put me in mind of a full-grown rhinoceros that had somehow managed to get itself trapped inside a drainage pipe. Heather must have been aware of my spasms, because she said in a cool, amused voice, 'Wouldn't you be more comfortable with all your clothes off?'

'That may be,' I mumbled, 'but I'd feel pretty silly being completely undressed with you completely dressed.'

She put her mouth close to my ear and said, still softly but very distinctly, 'Who said anything about me being completely dressed?'

Then, with a quick, gliding movement, she was at the foot of the bed, standing up, and I heard the almost imperceptible sound of garments dropped on my bedroom floor of hard, cold linoleum. Light garments, but perhaps with hooks or fastenings of some kind, or little buttons, because I could hear a tiny scratching or clicking sound, as if something weightless but resistant had hit the floor.

I dragged wildly at my dress trousers, my shoes, my socks. My underpants, which for some reason had skilfully formed themselves into a tourniquet that was cutting off the blood supply to my legs and threatening me with the rapid onset of total numbness, gave me more trouble than the rest put together, but at last, naked, I dived into the bed and lay there, my head deep in the pillow, my eyes tight closed, shutting out everything in the world until the moment Heather was with me.

Then she was beside me and we were utterly naked to one another, and the effect on me was twofold, with both parts seeming to pull different ways. Partly the realization that she was there, that we were together with no barriers at all, was calming because it meant an end of that fevered tension of longing and uncertainty; and partly it was insanely stimulating. But then I have noticed all through my life that the really big experiences often seem to have this paradoxical, centrifugal quality, as if any centre that could be imagined is too cramped and limited to contain their strength and richness. It was the same when as a boy I won the Essay Prize and suddenly saw the beatific vision of what it would be like to spend one's life trying to understand the past – how the sombre mystery of the timeless drew me and the bright, shifting, dramatic surface of the quotidien held me, both simultaneously. So now holding Heather in my arms in what had been my lonely bed, I experienced a widening of my consciousness that both strengthened it and threatened to blow it apart.

And beneath, or within, that widening, there was bafflement – yes, even at that moment. Why was Heather doing this? Was it just an impulse? She seemed a girl of such solidity of character: would she give way to a mere impulse, in such an important matter? It didn't seem like her. Yet it seemed even less like her to have planned it from the beginning. But what was she like? I still hardly knew her. And here I was... here I was...

And then the thought came, well, she is a farmer's daughter, accustomed to animals, with an earthy, practical streak no doubt, not some over-refined boarding-school Missy. And also a horsewoman, inured to taking jumps, and knowing well enough that the essence of taking a jump is to go for it, determinedly and at full speed, that hesitation and slowing down can bring only disaster and injury. She's going for the jump, I thought.

So we went for it together.

Chapter 15

When I woke it was already bright daylight and I had slept so deeply that for a moment or two I couldn't imagine why there was another person in my bed. Then it all came flooding back and I lay looking up at the ceiling, which was brilliantly outlined in sunshine because my bedroom window faced east and the morning sun was flooding in so strongly that it might have been saying to me, 'This is a new dawn, a new creation; everything starts from here.' I heard a voice from down in the quadrangle, somebody walking across and talking as he went, and I remember distinctly catching the words, 'Get them tables back in.' The College servants were about, and that reminded me that it must be time, now or soon, for Arthur to come clumping up the stairs and into the room. The thought, which under other circumstances would have filled me with panic, now seemed to me merely hilarious, so that I almost burst out laughing as I imagined his narrow, puckered face coming round the edge of the door. Fuck Arthur, I thought. Let him report me, let him tell anybody he cares to. I felt so rich, so strong, having Heather lying there beside me, not merely beside me but touching me at half a dozen points because of the narrowness of the bed, I put my hand on the small of her back and rubbed it gently to and fro. Let them create hell, let them send me down if they wanted to. I wasn't going to put the clock back now. Having broken out of my tense, lonely, anxious state of frustration to this golden mood of well-being and fulfilment, I wasn't going back, and if they wanted to send me down, let them. As long as Heather was in my life, all other problems would solve themselves. I'd go and get any old job, tinker, tailor, soldier, sailor. No, not soldier or sailor. That would mean going away from Heather. Rag-picker, petrol-pump attendant. Perhaps Episcopus would take me on in the kitchen.

Heather was lying very still. My bladder was getting pretty fractious by now and I decided to put my dressing-gown on and get down to the lavatories, which were about half a mile across the quad. As I got out of bed, and looked round for my dressing-gown, I hoped she wouldn't wake. I wanted her to stay asleep so that I could come back and slide in beside her and let her come to consciousness gently, in my arms. But she must have been awake all the time because she opened her eyes and said, 'Where are you off to?'

'Call of nature,' I said. 'I'll be back in a couple of minutes.'

'I wouldn't mind going myself,' she said in that easy, natural way she said everything. 'But I suppose you've only got one dressing-gown, so you go first.'

Well, that was fair enough, but it did rather bring me up with a bump against the realities of the situation. The morning after a Commem. might of course be nothing like a normal morning; the whole circus had been going all night, for one thing, and I supposed that even now the weary revellers were eating breakfast, those who had stayed the course, in the marquee. Heather's being around in College raised no problems at all (as for Arthur, I was prepared simply to kick him downstairs if I had any trouble with him), but to have her wandering across the quad in a dressing-gown was really a bit much. It would look like coat-trailing, deliberately drawing attention to what had been happening, and while I wasn't prepared to be browbeaten by the College authorities I thought it was hardly sensible to provoke them deliberately. So I thought for a second or two and then said,' Well, by all means, of course, but as it involves going out in the quad I wonder if you'd mind just slipping your dress on – the one you wore last night.'

Obviously it would be the one she wore last night; she hadn't any others with her. What that inane phrase showed was that I was getting nervous, beginning to babble. Heather rescued me at once.

'Of course. There's no reason why they should all poke their noses into our private business. I'll even wrap my shawl round me and it'll look as if we'd been on the river or something. I've heard people sometimes do that. Dawn on the Cherwell, you know. Romantic.'

We both laughed; not because she had said anything funny, but because we were happy, and pleased with ourselves; and, in my case, a little bit because I was relieved to know that this wonderful episode, this most magnificently blissful thing that had ever happened to me, was not, repeat not, going to be followed by punishment.

Heather got out of bed and the strong morning sun gleamed on her lovely skin as the moonlight had glimmered on it palely the night before. I didn't know which was the more beautiful, but this one was more physical, more frankly fleshly and of this world, and as she went past me to gather up her dress from the chair, my lustful member stirred uneasily, as if trying to raise its bald head to stare at her.

But she slid her dress on – that *swish, swish* again – and I pulled on my clothes too, and we opened the door and started down the stairs. As we did so we met Arthur coming up. He said nothing, but he gave me a look that said it all. I could see he was cursing his luck that he hadn't come up five minutes earlier and caught us in bed. As it was, there was nothing he could be unpleasant about and nothing he could pin on me. That Heather should have stayed all night was not in itself a breach of College discipline, on that one night of the year; we might, as she rightly said, have been on the river to see the dawn from a punt.

Then, as we went round the corner of the staircase, I remembered that she had not bothered with her underclothes, but had simply pulled her ball dress on over her naked limbs and left the skimpy odds and ends on the floor under the chair. And at that I really did burst out laughing. Because of course I didn't give a damn whether Arthur, as Arthur, knew what had been going on or not. And obviously he wasn't going to go to the Dean with a pair of stockings over his arm and a spider's web of knickers in his hand, and say he found them in my bedroom. Not on the morning after a Commem. He would have looked ridiculous, and the Dean would have sent him about his business.

As we walked towards the bath-house I realized that I had not prepared this part of the exercise very well. I was playing it by ear and I was far from certain what my ear was going to tell me. For one thing, I was fairly sure that if I were seen going into the bath-house with a girl there would be trouble of one kind or another. It was bound to be against some College regulation, if not specific then general. Well, the hell with that. It would be very uncivilized to let someone stay overnight, and a very active night at that, and deny them a bath in the morning. It was a matter of ordinary human comfort. But I still wondered if I ought to be careful; and if so, how careful should I be?

Heather seemed to have no such thoughts in her mind. She simply walked into the bath-house with me as if it were the most usual thing in the world, and fortunately I don't think anyone saw us. Once inside, we were in a stone-floored passage between two rows of green doors, about six or eight on either side. Some of the doors were closed and the sounds of splashing and tap-trickling came from behind them. One hearty youth was singing as he scrubbed himself. The song he had chosen was 'I Want to Be Happy'. I wanted to be happy too, but I had the feeling that it would be easier to be happy when I had got over this slightly tricky patch, in which lurked distinct possibilities of trouble.

I forgot all about the trickiness and the lurking in a moment, because Heather drew me with her into an empty cubicle, and as soon as the door was bolted behind us she turned on the bath taps and slipped off her dress. I was still not quite prepared for her deciding to share a bath with me rather than go into a separate cubicle. But it seemed that things were happening to me whether I was prepared for them or not. For the second time that morning, she was naked and she was standing close to me. Another moment or two and we were horizontal, twined together with the warm water swirling around us.

When you are in a bath with someone to whom you feel irresistibly attracted, it must be very difficult to refrain from getting at them with the soap. I say 'must be' as a matter of conjecture, because I have never,on the rare occasions when it has happened to me, made any attempt to refrain. This was the first time, and the best of all. I gave Heather a thoroughly good lathering, concentrating mainly on those areas of her that protruded above water-level, but by no means neglecting the more mysterious subaqueous regions. Needless to say, after a few minutes of this I had a gigantic erection. From then on I had only one ambition – to wriggle her into a convenient position – but just as I was working on the problem (no easy matter in a well-filled bath, no matter what they tell you) the youth three or four doors down sent up such a baying of

Life's really wo-orth living
When you are mi-irth giving
Why can't I give some to you?

that Heather collapsed into a fit of giggles; which, of course, blew it, since, as Lord Chesterfield says in one of his letters, 'No passion is so serious as lust.' She sank back, cramming one hand into her mouth to keep from giggling too loudly and attracting attention, while with the other she hung on to my prick as if it was a lifebuoy. 'It's all right,' she whispered in my ear, 'don't be impatient – wait a bit for the next one, you'll appreciate it all the more.'

How cool, how matter-of-fact she is, I thought. It must be the farmer's daughter coming out. We listened in a tranquil silence while the chap who was singing got through the middle eight and came back to the main melody with the final

I want to bee happy
But I can't bee happy
Till I've made yooo
Hap-py Too-oo!

during which he was evidently towelling himself; then his door banged open and he took himself off. By that time my erection had declined from resembling a lighthouse to resembling a wind-sock in a force six; the immediate crisis was over. We let out the bath water, dried ourselves as well as two people can with one towel, and went back to my rooms.

When we got there we could find no sign of Heather's under-garments. We turned the place upside down, but they were not there. The only possible explanation was that Arthur had stolen, or, as he probably thought of it, impounded them. He knew I wasn't in a position to make a scene and demand them back, and it was just his way of giving me a dig, the old sod. And also, of course, there was the possibility that to have them in his possession, to contemplate and handle them, afforded him some kind of senile sexual enjoyment.

Heather was completely unconcerned at the loss. 'It's a lovely warm day,' she pointed out, 'so it doesn't matter whether I've got anything on under my dress or not. I'd rather not actually. It's so nice and fresh. And when I get home, well, the first thing I'll have to do is take my Cinderella dress off and get into scruffy old working clothes anyway, so I can start from scratch.'

She was right, it was a lovely warm day, sunny and lyrical, exactly fitting my mood; all the same, that mention of getting home recalled me to the prosaic realities of life, and I asked, 'When are they expecting you home?'

'When they see me,' she said indifferently. 'I told them I'd take my own time for once. Still, as it's Saturday I shall have to be there from about midday because the girl who owns the horses wants to come and talk over a few things.'

That seemed to be that, so we got dressed, and a strange sartorial contrast we must have made because I, of course, put on my normal workaday clothes while Heather had no choice but to stay in resplendent full fig. Not that it seemed to phase her at all. She even fell in readily enough with my suggestion that we should go and have breakfast in the town somewhere, rather than take advantage of the breakfast in the marquee that our ticket would have entitled us to. I thought it would probably be all a bit tail-endish and lowering, and in any case I was determined not to have the magic of my time with Heather ruined by some garrulous fool coming and sitting next to us and making inane conversation. I must wring every drop of juice out of every minute, now, till she got into her car and headed back to High Cogges; because how could I tell when I would see her again? No, no, keep that thought off.

I kept it off successfully for another hour or more, while we went and got breakfast at a café in the market. Ordinary foods like bacon and egg and toast and coffee can never have tasted so good as they did to us, or at any rate to me, on that bright sunlit morning when the world was new and nothing was impossible. I remember looking at Heather's arm as it lay carelessly across the table, how smooth and firm and strong it was, how exquisite in its gradations of colour – the ivory pallor of the inside, the hint of a sun-warmed brown on the outside, the faint down that one only saw when a beam of sunlight happened to pick it out, the hint of delicate blue in the veins of her wrist – and thinking that all her body was as perfect as this limb and that I, Peter Leonard from the Bargeman's Arms, South Oxford, insignificant first-year undergraduate, knew how lovely her body was because I had been permitted to adore it and devour it and wander over it and pasture on it.

When we got to her car and she unlocked it I knew, simply *knew* beyond all argument, that I couldn't just peel off there, that I had to be with her a little longer. So I asked if I could get in with her and come a little of the way. 'Just out into the country,' I urged. 'I feel like being on my own for a bit, and if I hang around Oxford I'm bound to run into somebody who'll want to talk.'

Heather seemed to take this as quite natural – but then I was beginning to wonder if anything really surprised her, ever. She merely said, 'Well, I'm only sorry I can't come for a country walk with you, but I've got so many things to do at home.' She started the engine and we drove off.

Down the Botley Road we went, under the railway bridge and then over the big river bridge and the one, two, three little bridges, leaving the skating rink on your right, turning on to the Eynsham road, all the way I usually slogged on my bike, and this time I had to walk back every step of the way, but I didn't care, I wanted Heather beside me, close to me, where I could steal glances at the lovely composed face in profile... Why *steal*? Why had I suddenly become timid, stealthy, oblique? Where did it come from, this feeling that I had no rights in her, no place to stand? By Jupiter, the very hand with which she was now lightly but firmly gripping the gear-lever had, not two hours ago, been lightly but firmly gripping my dick. And yet here I was, feeling like a chance acquaintance to whom she had politely offered a lift in her car, feeling as if I had only just met her!

And yet – the thought came – and yet, dammit, I *had* only just met her. Before last night, I had spent a total of about forty minutes in her company, and not a single second of that had been *tête-à-tête*. Even our conversation by the gate at the top of the field, even *that*, I had had to share with a horse.

But last night. She was certainly alone with me last night. Wasn't she? Admit it!

Before I had time to admit anything, though, or generally to carry on this dialogue between the two halves of my mind, Heather turned to me and said, 'I've been thinking, Peter.'

Thinking! I didn't like the sound of that. What was she going to say next? 'It would be better if we didn't see each other again,' or 'Don't let's spoil it all, let's leave it a beautiful memory – don't you think it's perfect as it is?' or perhaps, 'I expect my father would like a talk with you.' What she actually said was, 'If I drop you off at Eynsham, just by the toll bridge, you can get on to the towpath and walk down the river to Oxford and you should make it by lunchtime.'

You could have knocked me down with an engagement ring. I managed to say 'Yes, that sounds a good idea,' keeping up the casual-acquaintance role, but behind that my mind was whirling with questions. 'I've been thinking' – and then this stuff about the towpath. Was that really all she had been thinking about? Nothing at all about how this new dimension was going to change our lives, where we were to go from here, was it going to last or not last? And what about that business about not taking precautions? Certainly I hadn't. Could it be that *she* had? Was there – my inexperienced mind stumbled uncertainly here – the possibility that she had it all taken care of, with some contraption deep inside her before our night out began? I had always assumed that that was what Vinnie did; but Vinnie was that kind of girl, she would go out for an evening knowing perfectly well that she would get fucked before she came home that night. And surely Heather wasn't... I mean, she didn't *seem*... everything I knew about her seemed to indicate that... and yet, just what the hell *did* I know about her? My bewilderment began to translate itself into a kind of panic, which I felt rising up my throat and beginning to choke me, and I wanted to shout out at the top of my voice, 'Stop the car! Stop the car and pull off on the side of the road and tell me, *tell me* what's really going on!'

All that happened, prosaically enough, was that she braked and slowed down long enough to hand over the toll at Eynsham Bridge, a penny, or was it a ha'penny in those days, and drive about a hundred yards further before braking again, slowing, stopping the engine, and coming to rest on the grass verge. Suddenly it was very quiet. The broad shining ribbon of the Thames was just behind us; so too were the towpath stretching away downstream from Eynsham Lock to King's Lock, and the gentle rise of the slope that was the beginning of the wooded hill of Wytham, covered with hawthorn bushes newly dressed in the rich white lace of their blossom.

In that magical quiet Heather turned her face towards me and kissed me unhurriedly. I grew dizzy in the strong grip of my need for her. 'I love you,' I said.

Instead of answering she opened the door on her side and got out. Standing beside the car, she bent over and put her head inside and said, 'There's no need for me to drive on this minute. I'll start you on your way.'

We locked the car and went down to the towpath. The fact that Heather was still in her ball-dress made the scene surreal, like a scene in a dream. Not that there seemed to be anyone except myself to witness it. In those days the entire populace worked until lunchtime on Saturdays and the weekend was a day and a half, not two days. Saturday morning was as quiet as a weekday; you didn't meet many people in the countryside till the afternoon.

We walked along the towpath until a bend hid us from the road. Above us, to our right, was the thick screen of hawthorn bushes, and the fields to our left, across the river, were deserted. There were no boats going up or down. We had the world to ourselves. The sun shone warmly, as it climbed towards its meridian, almost too warmly.

'Let's cool off,' Heather said. 'A swim's what we need.' No sooner were the words out than she was unhooking and pulling at her ball-dress and off it came, for the third time since she had met me in the College lodge the previous evening, centuries ago now. I simply couldn't remember a time when I wasn't watching her taking it off and putting it back on again – my whole psychology had changed. 'Come on, slow coach,' she said and walked towards the grassy river-bank.

I liked that. 'Come on, slow coach' is the sort of thing girls of about twelve say to their brothers when they do things like climbing trees. It made me feel I was being accepted into her life. Not that I wanted to be close to her in a brotherly way; especially *that* brother.

I got quickly out of my own clothes, chucked them down next to Heather's gown and her handbag, and followed her into the water. The Thames is still pretty cold in May, and it crossed my mind to wonder, as I slid in from the smooth rich grass into the chilling stream, whether she was doing it as a test, to see if I were the kind of man she could respect. If so, it was a test I passed easily. My new-found happiness made me so strong that a moment of physical discomfort was nothing; and, after all, once one was in it was very pleasant. The sun sparkled deliciously on the ripples in the water, and we gambolled like two young seals. Heather was a good swimmer; I was beginning to realize that she was a good everything.

A man walked by while we were in the water; he looked like an Oxford don out for a determined country walk, and I wondered how I would have reacted if it had been Bax. I decided I would probably have swallowed a gallon of water and had a choking fit, through uncontrollable laughter. Anyway the man passed on steadily, looking neither right nor left. I watched him as he went past our clothes and it was impossible to tell whether or not he had noticed them. No one else came along. We swam around for a long time and then Heather glided over to the bank and lay on her back in the water, holding on to a clump of grass-stems with one hand, so that she looked like an elegant moored boat. All aboard! I thought. Any more for the Skylark?

I swam over and joined her, but the cold was beginning to get to me and I pulled myself out and sat with just my legs in the water.

'Feeling cold?' she asked me with a grin: the twelve-year-old again.

'Women can always stay in swimming longer than men,' I retorted loftily. 'They have an extra layer of subcutaneous fat.'

'What does subcutaneous mean?'

'Under the skin.'

'Well, dash it, *all* fat's under the skin. There's nowhere else it –'

'No, but *immediately* under.'

'How d'you know about it? You don't study medicine, do you?'

'No,' I said. 'I study women.'

She kicked her legs up and splashed me for that, and for a moment we were two children playing beside the river. Then Heather seemed to decide it was time we became grown-up again, and she put her hands on the bank and pulled herself out as easily as an acrobat. God, she was physically perfect.

We stood together on the bank, and before moving off Heather turned and paused for a moment looking at the river as it flowed past – whether in a silent act of gratitude to it for the pleasure it had just given her, or just seeing if she could spot fish or identify aquatic plants, I had and have no idea. I walked on ahead and started up the slope to where we had left our clothes, to check that nothing was missing. When I had satisfied myself about this, I turned to see her walking up towards me, shining with health and the joy of living, beautiful beyond imagination. The cold kiss of the river had brought out her nipples, and the water was running down the smooth drum of her belly and moulding her sexual hair, as it poured away, into the shape of an inverted coxcomb. I knew I would never again see anything so beautiful as she was at that moment. She was like some untamed naiad of the river, perpetually youthful, perpetually hospitable to the desires of love. She came straight towards me: obviously her mind was made up as to what was going to happen next, and as she got close up to me I saw in her eyes that it was exactly what I wanted to happen. There and then, on the soft green grass, between the great drifts of hawthorn blossom, she sank to the ground and pulled me down with her. What brought me straight to fever-pitch was the contrast, maddening to my young senses, between the coldness of her octopus-wet limbs and the heat I knew that smouldered in the little thatched oven she kept alight between her legs. One kiss – I could taste the river water on her mouth – and we were away, driving at one another as urgently as if neither of us had known release for a year.

Only minutes later she was on her feet, pulling her elaborate dress round her, hooking it up, hiding her magnificent breasts as she settled it demurely into place; and I was lying there on the grass, the hot sun making my wet body steam – or was it the effort, the sexual heat? – and Heather was smiling down at me with that Vicarage-tea-party calm.

'I must get back to ordinary life. Peter, thank you for my treat. It was wonderful. It was better than wonderful.'

She was going, no, I couldn't believe it, she was actually *going*.

'Heather,' I croaked desperately. 'Heather... when do I see you next?'

'D'you want to?' she asked with the same composed smile.

'Do I *want* to? Are you asking me do I *want* to?' In my anguish I scrambled to my feet. 'Heather, can you possibly imagine I –'

'All right, next Tuesday,' she said.

'Morning or afternoon?'

'Afternoon, probably. I'm likely to be busy till after lunch. But I'll telephone. I'll ring College and leave a message telling you what time to get there.'

'You wouldn't rather I rang you?'

'No.' She kissed me, lightly. 'Look after yourself. Dear Peter.' Then her straight back was receding; the fair hair, falling between her shoulders, was already drying in the sun.

I staggered about like a drunk as I got into my clothes; I felt woozy, and no wonder. But I somehow managed the long march down the towpath to Oxford. With hunger tightening its grip on my belly despite that good breakfast, I hurried past Binsey, crossed the iron bridge at Medley, then the wooden one, trudged over to Walton Well Road and through North Oxford to Episcopus, arriving only about ten minutes after the beginning of lunch. And how I needed that meal! I slumped down at the long table and began fiercely shovelling it in, feeling the gnawing in my belly gradually fading into contentment with each swallow, and until it had appreciably faded I had no attention to spare for anything else and hardly lifted my eyes from my plate. When at last I did so, I became aware that some sort of altercation seemed to be going on down at the far end of the next table. Carshalton, looking pale and tense (anger? or just exhaustion?), and still in full evening dress, was standing there confronting tall, bony Fred Armitage and short, puppy-fat McFarlane. They were explaining something and smiling as if expecting him to enter into a joke, but there was no answering smile on Carshalton's face, just unremitting grimness and accusation, and as I watched the smiles faded from their faces too and were replaced by expressions of earnestness (Armitage) and bland defiance (McFarlane). Some of the undergraduates sitting nearby started to join in the discussion, whatever it was, but Carshalton took no notice of them and strode out of the hall. The other two sat down and evidently started to give an explanation of the matter to anyone who would listen. I noticed Wilmot attending in grave silence, and Kent staring through his fish-eye lenses as if they were a pack of urchins who had come in off the street and started a brawl in the quad.

What was it all about? I wondered idly. What was eating Carshalton? And why was he still wearing last night's costume, absurd among all those flannel bags and rumpled jackets. He had passed quite close to me on his way out, and something about his face – its clamped rigidity, the hardness in his eyes as he stared straight ahead of him – suggested a man who would never, in a million years, forgive an injury; especially, I felt, one that took the form of making him look a bit ridiculous. No, he would not be able to stand that.

But there was a date pudding to come, and cheese after that if I wanted it, and I did want it; and after eating my fill I went out into the garden, the day having turned very warm, and sat down with my back against a tree, and listened to the whisper of its leaves above my head in the almost imperceptible breeze of that perfect summer day; and went gently to sleep.

*

When I woke, the sun was still shining, though beginning to slope to the west. I felt a bit stiff in the joints – leaning one's back against a tree isn't the ideal position for going heavily to sleep – but as far as my mind was concerned I felt well rested and very buoyant. It had happened, well and truly happened; the door of my cell had been burst open and I had walked out into the free air that was the birthright of every normally constituted person. No more frustration, misery, tension, nightmares, low spirits, loss of concentration. And funnily enough all my anxieties and questionings about Heather and our relationship seemed to matter no longer. Somehow or other, that last coupling on the river-bank seemed to have blown them away. I felt that it was natural for the two of us to be together and to love each other; and, sooner or later, what is natural will happen.

I went and made myself a cup of tea and then, as the workaday world came back into focus, I remembered that Bax had told all his Honours pupils to catch him in his rooms during the latter part of Saturday. Even the ones who were going to be at the Commem., his tone had implied, and couldn't be expected to have functioning brains the next day, ought at least to be able to hold up for a few minutes' instruction on what work to do during the last week of term. So I went along about five, knocked, and caught him by himself.

Clearly the sight of me did nothing for his spirits. After the rubbish I had been turning in lately, he must have written me off as a dolt who had managed to make a good early impression by a series of flukes but now stood revealed as a lazy numbskull, one whom it had been a mistake to admit into the Honours School at all and a double mistake to invite along on the reading party. He knew he was stuck with me, but his manner made it plain that he wasn't going to invest much unnecessary effort in the job. We had been working that term on the Middle Ages, and as Bax mechanically searched his mind for an essay subject within that period he looked out of the window as if afraid he might die of boredom if he actually caught sight of my face. 'We'll make it an easy one,' he said insultingly. 'Take the arraignments brought by the Good Parliament in 1376 and see how far they're traceable to the military defeats in Normandy and Brittany in '75.' And his eyes behind their lenses flickered back to me as if in dismissal. All right, Bax, I thought as I went down the stairs. You've asked for it and you'll get it. I had that date to see Heather on Tuesday, a prospect that seemed to energize rather than distract me, and until Thursday, which was the day I had my weekly tutorial with Bax, nothing else to do at all. I was free to work, and the thought of work was a joyful one to me. To gather information, to weigh evidence and ponder questions, were natural activities to me; they had become impossible lately, but only because the whole frame of my natural being had been sprained, jarred, capsized, by that crucial dislocation at the centre. Heather had taken care of that, and now – watch out, Bax, and watch out all the world!

There and then, with two hours to go before dinner, I settled down to work like a joyful madman. I was already familiar with the general account of the Good Parliament in the second volume of Stubbs's *Constitutional History of England*, but after boiling that down into three or four pages I plunged into the discussion of particular problems. How guilty was Latimer? Weren't the charges against him to some extent a smoke screen? Why the complete failure of John of Gaunt to establish common military objectives with John IV de Montfort, Duke of Brittany? – and didn't that failure, rather than the bribing of any individual, lead to the defeats at Bécherel and St Sauveur? The more I got into it, the more the game started springing up. Sunday and Monday passed in a delightful dream. I surrendered myself completely – in a youthful, half-fledged way, of course, but with total dedication and self-forgetfulness – to the scholar's passion, the historian's devouring need to *know*, to make the past get up from its grave and march past, and this time to see everything for what it was and to recognize everyone's motives and every link in the inexorable chain of causation.

I was happy. The study of history was making me happy. But it was Heather who had enabled the study of history to make me happy; and I took a little time on the Sunday to lean out of my window in the middle of the morning and send a wordless message of love floating on the fragrant summer air, across the fields from Oxford to High Cogges: no words, just vibrations of love, love, love, gratitude, gratitude, gratitude.

*

On that Sunday something happened that was unusual enough to perform the rare feat of taking my attention away from my own affairs, if only briefly. When Arthur made his rounds about five, he delivered to my room a typewritten slip about a J.C.R. meeting on the following evening. Apparently this was the big once-a-term meeting where the accounts were discussed and officers elected for the following autumn and God knows what, and it seemed that everybody but me knew about it and had made a note of the date. I am not – and I say it not complacently but with a certain contrition – a good community member, whether that community be minuscule or majuscule, when it comes to things like attending meetings and volunteering for office and reading reports, that kind of thing. I skip-read circulated documents that I ought to go through carefully, I shirk meetings whenever I think I can get away with it, and when I can't get away with it I draw pictures of comic animals on the scratch-pad so thoughtfully provided when I ought to be attending to the chairman's weighty remarks. And I was no different as an undergraduate. In theory I would have admitted that it was an excellent idea for the undergraduates of Episcopus to have their own self-governing Junior Common Room and that this involved having a President and a Secretary and minutes and accounts and a Treasurer; but in practice I took no more interest in these things than if they were on another planet; I never went to meetings and had not even registered that this one was happening. And now, here was this slip, placed on my desk by Arthur, saying that some VERY SPECIAL BUSINESS would be transacted at this meeting and that it was hoped everyone would attend. MATTERS HAVE ARISEN WHICH COULD DAMAGE THE REPUTATION OF THE COLLEGE AND THEREFORE OF ALL ITS INDIVIDUAL MEMBERS, it read. What on earth could they be?

At dinner, I asked Wilmot, but he just shook his head and said, 'Something about Carshalton,' without going any further, and somehow that name weighed the conversation down until it sank. I felt that anything 'about Carshalton' must, in the nature of things, be (a) tedious and (b) distasteful in some way. I looked round for the man; he was not there. Armitage and McFarlane were sitting together, but they did not seem to be talking much. Whenever I looked over at them they were just eating silently, and as soon as the meal was over they left the hall, still silent, still together.

I went back to the Good Parliament and, except for dream-flashes of Heather, thought about nothing else till the following evening; but then, though I would willingly have carried on reading and note-taking, there seemed nothing for it but to turn up for the big meeting, so I went along. The J.C.R. was packed out by the time I got there. Not only the usual organization men were there, the bureaucrats-in-the-making who actually *liked* J.C.R. meetings, but, owing to the unprecedented three-line whip delivered to our rooms, even the waifs and strays like me were gathered in. I looked about me curiously as we all settled into our seats, the first arrivals taking the armchairs and sofas, the later ones the plain wooden chairs, and finally the last-comers perching on window-sills or sitting on the floor. I had not even known, so befogged was I about the whole J.C.R. business, that Norbert was the President. He sat in a wooden armchair beside the small table that had been brought in for the minute-books and what-not: square-cut, solid, filling his chair and looking as if nothing short of a tank would push him over. Somebody switched the lights on in the gathering dusk, and the one directly above him lit up that shock of wiry red-brown hair.

We went doggedly through the ordinary business, with proposings and secondings and shows of hands and *nem. cons.* and all the usual drill. Evidently Norbert and the other office-holders had decided that if they dealt with the special business first, whatever it was, people would begin to slip away. Remembering Wilmot's words, 'It's something to do with

Carshalton,' I looked over at him as he sat in a front seat just to one side of the committee's table. His face had its usual strange waxen, doll-like look, his eyes deep-set, the fringe of dark hair looking like a wig. It was so unlike an ordinary human face that one wasn't, after all, surprised at its total lack of expression; it would have been more surprising to see any animation on a set of features that seemed to have been mocked up by a pastrycook. Thinking back to his altercation with Armitage and McFarlane, I twisted round in my seat till I saw the two of them, sitting together, quiet and watchful.

It was a hot evening, and the minutes dragged by in the stuffy room, but finally we got to the point where the secretary closed the minute-book and said, 'The rest of this meeting is off the record.' He looked towards Norbert, who was obviously going to handle the next bit. An expectant hush descended, and Norbert spoke in his strong baritone voice, which carried to every corner of the room without being raised.

'It's not been a particularly well-kept secret, so I expect most people know something about it already, but we wanted everybody here so that we can all start fair and that we can have precise information without a lot of rumours flying about. Something happened on the night of the Commem., that is, last Friday night, that's led to a lot of unpleasantness. And the unpleasantness is only just beginning. What we need to do is decide on a course of action, *tonight*, that'll put a stop to it and keep it within these walls.'

He looked round briefly, then went on, 'The outline is quite simple. Carshalton here –' he nodded in Carshalton's direction – 'claims to have been robbed, and of one object only, no money or anything else. He claims to have lost one gold watch and he's named to me the two chaps he accuses of taking it.' It was obvious, from the way heads turned, that the two in question were Armitage and McFarlane. Armitage half rose in his chair and said in a hoarse, emotional voice, 'It's completely untrue. Anyone's welcome to –'

'Just a minute, Armitage,' Norbert quelled him. 'This isn't a court of law, but we might as well run it like one to the extent of taking statements from people one at a time rather than all together. I promise you can give your version of it and so can McFarlane if he wants to, all right?'

Armitage sat down and looked over at Carshalton. 'You'd better go ahead,' he said.

'There's not much to tell,' Carshalton said. He kept his eyes on Norbert but his voice, with its curiously denatured intonation, was pitched for the whole room. 'A lot of clothes were taken out of the wardrobe in my bedroom while I was at the Commem. It was part of some silly joke, or at least that's what I was told by the two who took them. The next day they brought the clothes back. The first thing I did was to look for a gold watch that had been in a small inner pocket in one of the jackets. It wasn't there and I want it back. It's valuable and it's a family heirloom. That's all there is to it. I want my watch back, and I'm sure it's somewhere in this College unless the thieves have already sold it or taken it to an agreed hiding-place outside.'

'Before you start throwing words like *thieves* around the room,' said Norbert, 'I think we'd all like to feel more certain that your watch was actually stolen rather than mislaid.'

'What was the idea,' someone asked, 'taking his clothes away in the first place?' I couldn't see the man who had spoken, but I recognized Knowlton's voice.

Everyone looked at Armitage, expecting him to speak, but he seemed to be struggling for utterance, and after a second or two it was McFarlane, with his round, innocent face, who got to his feet and said with his soft Scottish accent, 'We did it for a wee joke. A praank.'

'Not much of a joke, I'd say,' said Norbert.

'We live on the same staircase,' said the guileless lad, 'and we'd both been finding Carshalton pretty irritating all through this tairm. Of course he didn't do us any harm, you know, but he was getting on our nairves.'

The gentle cherub did not look as if he had any nairves to be got on, but his account of the matter seemed to be commanding general attention, which encouraged him to go on.

'I think it was the way he looked right through us whenever we met on the staircase or anywhere, as if we didn't exist. We both know we're not important people but after all we are his neighbours and we are at the same College.'

'So you took my watch,' Carshalton said, jabbing the words in like a short-arm punch.

'We never saw any watch from start to finish,' McFarlane insisted calmly. 'I suppose it was a silly idea and not a very funny joke, but we were sitting there having a few bottles of beer while the Commem. went on in the distance, and I suppose you might say there was a general spirit of foolishness in the air. But harmless foolishness, I think.'

I had not known the stripling was so articulate. We all listened, our interest caught.

'So we suddenly came up with the idea, and I really couldn't say which of us thought of it fairst, that it might take Carshalton down a peg if we just quietly removed all his ordinary clothes from his warrd-robb and put them where he wouldn't find them for a few hours. Och, I know it was silly, but we didn't mean him any harm. We just had this vision of him walking about the next morning, still in full fig, asking people where his clothes were. And of course we planned to return them by about lunchtime. One of us was going to watch till the coast was clear and then the other was going to nip in with the clothes and hang them up just where they'd been originally. We thought he might look a bit of a loon over it. People'd think he must have been drunk when he thought his warrd-robb was empty. And we didn't mind him looking a bit of a loon, not for long and not in front of the whole world, just in his own College. We thought it would do him good.'

As he said the words 'do him good' McFarlane, who had been looking towards Norbert and addressing his words to him, brought his face round in a quarter-circle so that his eyes came to rest full on Carshalton's face. It wasn't done as a trick of oratory, I was sure of that, but it was very telling in its effect of mild-mannered accusation. *Carshalton*, it said, *you are a lout and an arrogant snob. You are the kind that attracts the attention of people in the mood for a practical joke.*

Carshalton said furiously, 'I can only repeat that that watch was fourteen-carat gold, it was a family heirloom, and it was in the small inner pocket of that jacket when these two –' he seemed about to utter some word like 'thieves,' checked himself with a small but perceptible pause, and went on '– men removed it from my room with the rest of the clothes. And not when they brought it back.'

Norbert said to the meeting, 'I persuaded Carshalton not to go to the Dean over the matter. The Dean would have had no alternative but to get the police in. And we know what that would mean. Half the Oxfordshire force'd be swarming round the College, conducting searches here, there and everywhere. Not a chance of keeping it quiet. And probably the newspapers getting in on the act too. You know how they love that sort of thing. *College Scandal of Stolen Heirloom. Was it an inside job?* Can't you just see it?'

'That may be,' said Carshalton, his clenched fists thrust into his jacket pockets, 'but they might have got me my watch back. I wish now I hadn't listened to you, Norbert, to tell you the truth. We've let the scent go cold and if we do bring the police in now, it'll be a pretty hopeless job and they'll ask us why we held off so long.'

'They won't,' said Norbert levelly. 'They'll know why we held off. If we made the whole thing public we'd be opening a very unpleasant can of worms and even then we might not find the watch.'

McFarlane was still standing, but Armitage had been sitting down, holding himself almost unnaturally still, his eyes downcast. Now, he began to get slowly to his feet. His face was white and drawn. His mouth opened, but no words came out. To see him at that moment was to understand something of the terrible strain he was under. He stood there with his face turning from side to side; the naked electric light picked out its bone structure and the hollowness round his eyes. If Armitage had anything to say, nobody was going to interrupt him. But no words came out, and after a moment it was McFarlane's soft voice that sounded in the listening room.

'It's a funny thing,' he said as if thinking aloud, 'but I've never actually seen this famous watch that's worth so much.'

For an instant I thought Carshalton was going to hurl himself across the room to get at McFarlane. Norbert must have had the same thought, because he looked up from his chair as if ready to grab him as he went past. In the event he merely stood there, glaring murderously.

'I mean,' McFarlane went on, 'we live pretty much on top of each other in College, especially when we're on the same staircase. I suppose I've seen Carshalton for some part of every day since we all came up last autumn, every day of tairm that is, and I've never seen him with a gold watch.'

'I suppose you've got X-ray eyes,' Carshalton said in a thin, jarring voice, 'that can see into my pockets.'

'No,' said McFarlane equably, 'but a man who has a watch usually takes it out now and again to see the time.'

'I have a wristwatch for that,' said Carshalton, holding up his wrist in demonstration that he was in fact wearing one. 'The gold watch is more a matter of association. Family feeling, that kind of thing. This is a clumsy attempt to make me out a liar and it only convinces me even more strongly that you're a th –'

'Keep it calm, Carshalton,' Norbert interrupted commandingly. 'This is just what happens when people start throwing accusations around. The chaps who are accused start making counter-accusations till the mud flies all over everything. I don't see why you shouldn't put it beyond doubt that you do in fact own a watch of that kind. If you're going to go about saying it was stolen, you shouldn't mind a few enquiries. Was there insurance on it?'

'No. I didn't think there was need of any. It was perfectly safe in the pocket of that jacket, hanging up in my wardrobe, till these two took it into their heads to –'

'Yes, all right. Well, it would be perfectly simple to clear it up. I suppose it was a gift from your people, was it? Your parents?'

'I don't know about a gift. It's the property of the whole family. Didn't I say it was an heirloom?'

'Well, then, you could easily get your father, say, to write a short statement saying that you had this watch in your possession. That you came up to College with it.'

'No,' said Carshalton. He shook his head with finality. 'Not easy. In fact out of the question, in a matter like this that won't wait for ever. It would take weeks. My people live in Shanghai.'

'Oh. Well, I suppose it would take a fair time for letters to go back and forth.' (Air mail was on a very small scale in those days, and went about twice a week.) 'We shall have to let that one go.'

'I don't see why you shouldn't take my word for it.'

'Neither do I, but then I don't see why I shouldn't take the word of Armitage and McFarlane that they aren't thieves. Even if I didn't believe in their honesty, and there's absolutely no reason *not* to believe in it, they'd have to be of subnormal intelligence to do anything as loony as take a watch that would immediately, on their own statement, be traced to them. An action like that just isn't consistent with having any kind of intelligence. They're not a pair of village idiots, you know. The thing's incredible.'

'That's probably what they're relying on,' Carshalton said offensively.

Armitage suddenly said in a loud, unsteady voice, 'Every man in this room is welcome to come across the quad to my room and search it. Every drawer, every cupboard, all my pockets, the mattress... pull the floorboards up...' He seemed in danger of choking.

'Easy, Armitage, old man,' Norbert said. 'Nobody's going to search your room or McFarlane's. We must just find some way round this, that's all.'

At this point a man with a thin face and dark hair, whom I only knew very slightly, spoke up from where he was lounging in an armchair with his long, spidery legs thrust out. I had hardly even heard his voice till now. He had a slow, languid manner.

'Look here, I don't know what everybody else feels about all this, but I'm beginning to get bored with it. If our friend here has lost a watch and wants to make a song and dance about it and keep us here all night, why don't we just have a whip-round? We could collect enough for him to buy another one just as good. Pretty well everybody's here and we could soon do it. I don't mind starting the ball rolling with, say, twenty quid.'

Twenty quid! I thought. A working man's income for two months!

'I don't see Carshalton agreeing to that,' said Norbert. 'A new watch isn't the same as an heirloom.'

'Well, it doesn't have to be a new one,' the thin-faced man said. 'He could buy himself a nice antique one. It'll have been in somebody's family even if it wasn't his. I daresay one family's very like another.'

There was a general mild laugh. Everybody looked at Carshalton, who paused as if in thought and then said, 'I agree to a whip-round for the sake of not making any more unpleasantness.'

'We'll make a list,' said the J.C.R. treasurer in a practical manner. 'Everybody can say what they'll be good for and then they can hand it in later if they haven't got the cash on them. And,' he added, fixing an attentive stare on Carshalton, 'if your watch turns up there can be a refund.'

'Of course,' said Carshalton blandly.

The secretary, an owlish youth who obviously loved little bits of procedure, now produced a pad of paper and wrote at the head of the top sheet CARSHALTON WATCH SUB LIST. He filled in the languid man's name for him and put '£5' beside it, then started the pad on its journey round the room. As name after name was put down, each with its promised sum beside it, I began to feel a mixture of alarm and curiosity. Cleaned out as I was, I couldn't possibly promise more than a pound (alarm: was I going to look conspicuously mean? Or conspicuously poor?), and I was devouringly interested in what everyone else would come up with (curiosity about their circumstances and their degree of motivation). When the list finally got to me it was nearly completed, and I held on to it as long as I dared, letting my eye race over the names and figures. Nobody had come anywhere near the £5 put down by the careless Croesus who had started it all off; there was a fair number at 10/- and £1, and one crotchety rebel had written firmly, REFUSE TO CONTRIBUTE. Kent had put down for £2. Wilmot, by whom I tended to pace myself, had put down £1, so I followed suit. Before handing it on – the man next to me was growing restive – I noticed that Lamont had written in neat, firm letters the words 'One Guinea'.

The treasurer than counted it all up and said that the collection totalled seventy-eight pounds. With that, Carshalton could buy a watch good enough to last him the rest of his life; or, for that matter, he could have gone to the South of France for the entire summer. It was decided that the promised sums would be collected by the J.C.R. treasurer, and given to Carshalton on the last day of term.

As the meeting broke up Armitage walked past me, his face pale and expressionless; I watched him go across the quad and out through the lodge gate, as if he were sick of the place and needed the outside world for a while. It took a lot to make Fred Armitage sick of Episcopus College, a place he had been so delighted by and felt such joy in belonging to, but Carshalton had pulled off that trick as he would doubtless pull off many others. I was thinking how much I distrusted and disliked Carshalton as I walked slowly over to the lodge gate, not to follow Armitage but with the idea of going to the pub across the street and having a soothing pint of beer after the stressful scene I had witnessed. It was a modest little place and the Proctors very rarely bothered with it, any more than they bothered with the Bargeman's Arms, so I felt quite secure. I was just heading towards the friendly little snug, feeling in my pocket to make sure I had the necessary four pence, when someone walking a little faster caught me up from behind and then slowed to keep pace with me. I half turned. It was a man who had been at the meeting, another of the ones I hardly knew, even after three terms of living in the same College. People formed clusters and the clusters tended to stay apart. Here and there, of course, there were men I scarcely expected to get to know at all, because of the immense gulf between their background and mine, such as the unimaginably rich one who had spoken so carelessly of getting the list started with twenty quid. What must it feel like to have absolutely no money worries and no prospect of having any, ever? I just couldn't imagine it. But the man who fell into step with me now was someone I hadn't bothered to get to know because, frankly, he hadn't interested me. He had slicked-back hair and wore a neat and slightly shiny blue suit. He was doggedly reading some subject like Modern Languages, and no doubt one day he would be a clerk in a Whitehall office, translating official documents and filing them away and writing little reports. He had a sub-cockney accent and seemed to me to sum up everything I understood by words like 'average' and 'undistinguished'. He was the Little Man, in person. In short, I was a bit of a snob about him. I didn't deceive myself that I was very interesting, but I know I was more interesting than he was. His name was Perkins or something like that. I daresay he was all right really. But he was Perkins by name and, if it doesn't sound an insufferable remark, Perkins by nature.

'Going for a drink?' he asked. 'Mind if I join you?'

'Yes,' I answered to the first part of his question and, as there seemed no way out of it, 'No' to the second, though I would rather have said Yes to both if I had had the nerve.

We went in and got our beer, going Dutch, and as soon as we were sitting down Perkins started up immediately, as if he had something he badly needed to talk about.

'That was all rather horrible, didn't you find? The meeting? All that stuff about the watch?'

'Storm in a teacup,' I said. 'I'm sure they didn't steal it.'

'Yes,' he said, 'but it's a pretty big teacup that you can put your hand in and take out seventy-eight pounds.'

'What are you suggesting? That Carshalton's a liar?'

He pushed his snout into his beer-glass and looked at me, sideways, over the rim of it. He didn't answer my question in words, but the knowingness of his expression said it all. I decided that perhaps I had been wrong: he would go far in the Civil Service.

'I didn't like Carshalton before this happened and somehow or other I like him even less now,' I said. 'But it's over and we can stop thinking about it, and that's the main thing.' Personally I wanted to be left in peace to think about Heather. In particular I wanted to spend a good long time thinking about her nipples as she came out of the river.

Perkins took the beer-glass away from his face and, still looking sideways at me, said, 'He made one statement at that meeting that I'm in a position to know was a thundering lie, for a start.'

'Oh? What was that?'

'The guff about his parents living in Shanghai.' Perkins gave a short, mirthless laugh. 'Shanghai my arse. They live in Hounslow.'

'You're in a position to know that, are you?'

'Course I am. I live there myself.'

'You know him at home then?'

'I don't exactly *know* him. I mean we're not *friends* or anything. We didn't go to the same school. But I've seen him about in Hounslow all my life, and as it happens my old man knows his old man. They have some kind of business dealing. My old man runs a furniture shop and his is manager of a warehouse or something. When I mentioned that he was at Episcopus, my dad said 'Ah, that'd be Bert Carshalton's boy.' And the next time the matter came up he said they'd met at the golf club or somewhere and he'd confirmed it.'

While Perkins was telling me this I was listening to his accent, and realizing that this was how Carshalton would talk if he had not denatured his speech to that utterly flavourless robot-voice. I much preferred the London way Perkins talked. It suggested bus-stops and long wet streets with shops selling bottled sweets and cheap papers and sticky varnished furniture, and ordinary people going cheerfully about their unremarkable business. But of course it would never have done for Carshalton. It did not occur to me to doubt the truth of what Perkins was telling me. The whole thing was so inherently probable.

Only one thing puzzled me. 'Why are you telling me all this?' I asked Perkins.

'I just wanted to tell somebody,' he said simply.

'You didn't think of blowing the gaff there and then, at the meeting?'

He shook his head. 'I'm a man of peace. The way I look at it, life's rough enough without making enemies. Carshalton must know I know he's telling a pack of lies; he's relying on me to keep my mouth shut, and if I don't he'll watch and wait till the day finally comes when he can do something really hideous to me. You can see it in his face. You can call me a coward if you like.'

'I wouldn't,' I said. 'I think you're right.'

'Thanks,' Perkins said. He suddenly looked helpless, vulnerable. All at once I saw how it is that completely ruthless people can bend ordinary inoffensive people to their will, sometimes in surprising numbers, sometimes to the extent of coming to absolute power in huge countries. That moment helped me as an historian. Perkins put down his empty beer-glass and stared straight in front of him. He seemed to want to say something, to make some statement important to him, but nothing came out. I waited. Finally he spoke, in a flat, unemphatic voice.

'People like that... They can make a lot of trouble.'

'True,' I said.

'Wherever they go they make trouble,' he said. 'It's best...'

'Yes?'

'It's best...' he said and paused a long time. Then he said, 'It's best not to tangle with them if you can avoid it.'

And without another word he got up and walked out. He wanted to leave me. I think he was suddenly ashamed that I knew his secret.

*

On Monday evening there was a note in my pigeon-hole, written in Frank Penney's crabbed scrawl. 'Message from High Cogs, 6.45.' He spelt the name of the hamlet as it is pronounced. 'Meet Tuesday Stanton Harcourt churchyard 3.0.'

All right, I thought, she wants to meet somewhere near home but not right on top of it. The distance between Stanton Harcourt and High Cogges must be about a mile. So I got myself out there after lunch. The route was the same until you got to where the narrow lane to High Cogges branches away to the right; then you kept on curving round in a wide sweep to the left, turning right again as you passed the Fox Inn and came in sight of the church tower and, next to it, the tower of the manor house with its heraldic flag flying. I went into the churchyard and messed about for half an hour or so, reading the dates on tombstones. I wanted to go inside the church and see what the plaques and things on the walls would tell me about the history of the place, but it was three o'clock and I was afraid Heather would come and, not finding me in the churchyard, go away again. I felt confident about her, but not confident enough to take any chances. Which is just a way of saying that, about a millimetre down, I didn't feel confident.

Then she came into view, unexpectedly mounted on a bike, and a skimpy, dropped-handlebar, man's racing bike at that. I was startled. I hadn't, somehow, imagined her on a bicycle, especially that kind. In my daydreams of her, she was always riding a horse when she wasn't driving the car.

'Hello,' I said, advancing to meet her as she came up to the churchyard entrance. 'Amazing bike.' And as she got off it I went to kiss her.

'It's Tom's,' she said, turning away and avoiding my kiss. 'I hate the damned thing. But I had to use it. I was late already without walking all the way down here. And of course it's not my turn to have the car. So I took this bloody awful bike. Where's yours? You did come on it, didn't you?'

'Just inside the gate here,' I said, showing her. 'Where it can't be seen from the road. You could put yours with it. I'm sure they'll be pretty –'

'Oh, no, get yours and we'll move on a bit,' she said impatiently. 'I'm not hanging about in the bloody churchyard, I've got enough to depress me as it is. Come on, bring it out and we'll go on a bit further.'

'All right,' I said, getting the bike, 'but you *said* meet in the –'

'That was just to give you a place that you'd find easily. And something simple enough to drive into the head of that old moron of a porter.' She was certainly in a sour mood. Her face seemed pinched, pulled together at the centre by the tension of the muscles. I was almost sorry it wasn't raining, to fit in better with the disgruntlement I could feel radiating from her.

'Well,' I said pacifically, 'if you know a better place –'

'I know a million better places than this. Just follow me and we'll talk when we get there.' And she whizzed off on the racing bike.

It was all I could do to keep her in sight, but the horrible bike at least had the merit of holding that trim rear end of hers up in the air, and it was so well worth looking at that I pedalled like a madman just to keep my eyes on it. We swerved off to the left a little way past the manor house and went down a lane past some cottages. Presently the cottages came to an end, the lane became simply a rough footpath beside a thick hedge, and, at a spot where the hedge was especially thick, we stopped, dismounted and leaned our backs against a grassy bank. This was more like it.

For quite a while neither of us spoke, just lay back and stared up at the thick green tangle of the hedge as it curved forward over us. Heather peered up at it so intently that she might have been examining it for birds' nests, but I knew she was only thinking. She had on her working clothes, old corduroy trousers and an open-necked, short-sleeved white shirt that looked as if it had originally been part of a tennis outfit. The only fancy touch was that her shoes, flat-heeled and outdoor, were made of soft red leather and didn't look as if she wore them to do the mucking-out. I silently looked down at her as she lay back, and, serious and compassionate though my mood was, the old familiar straining forward at the crotch began to afflict me. When she moved her arms up to put her clasped hands behind her head, her breasts under the thin shirt moved with them and I was afraid for a moment that my *membrum virile*, which was trapped in a tangle of shirt and underpants, was going to rupture itself rather than give up the attempt to rear up for a better view. Silently I cursed its disobedience. But the wave of desire ran out into the sand very quickly when Heather abruptly sat up, gave me a challenging look straight into my eyes, and said, 'Yes. This is what it's going to be like.'

'What what's going to be like?'

'This is what I'm like when I'm in a bad temper. And I'm bound to be in a bad temper sometimes.'

'Oh, yes, well,' I said, 'perhaps I'll be able to make a difference to that.'

'Perhaps you will and perhaps you won't. But keep trying, Peter. Unless you feel you've got something better to do with your time.'

'Good God, no. I can't imagine how you could *possibly* imagine for a single *second* that I had, or ever could have, a –'

'If I were a completely free agent,' she interrupted me, speaking half to me and half to herself, 'if I could decide from one day to the next, from one hour to the next, what I want to do, I could pick up the telephone when I really felt like seeing you and say "Peter, are you busy just now? Would you like to come over and see me?" And then, supposing you were –'

'No supposing about it. I'd be free always, any time.'

'I could always be in a sunny mood, always welcoming. I suppose there are people who live like that. People who are absolutely free to do just what they like.'

'I suppose so.'

'But I have to plan my week, and argue with my horrible family to get time off, and when the time comes I have to take it then or not at all.'

'Most people's lives are like that.'

'I know that of course, but most people's lives aren't as bloody awful as mine. I have days when I'm just about b.t.a.'

'Just about what?'

'Oh, that's just an expression we used to use at school, b.t.a. It means back teeth awash. Ready to throw up.'

'Oh.'

'And today's been like that. I've been b.t.a. ever since I got out of bed this morning. Everybody's been annoying and stupid and bloody inconsiderate and insensitive and I could feel myself getting more and more.... oh, I don't know, more and more closed in on myself. Tight, shut in, nothing to give anybody.'

'I understand, Heather. You don't have to worry about me.'

'I didn't say I was worried about you.'

'No, you didn't, but I expect it was part of what you meant. It can't be pleasant being with someone, especially someone who loves you, and not being able to respond to them at all.'

She was silent for a moment and then looked down at the ground and said 'Do you?'

'Do I what? Love you? Of course.'

'You don't have to say that just because we've been to bed, you know.'

Since she was evidently in a mood of bleak honesty, I searched within myself for a few grains of bleak honesty to chip in on my own behalf. But if this meant finding that I didn't love her, I had to report non-success. Sitting there tense and unhappy, her beautiful face disconsolate, her lovely light blue eyes looking close to tears of discouragement, her perfectly arched brows pulled together in a fretful little scowl, she seemed to me immensely lovable, all the more so for being, suddenly, vulnerable.

'Heather,' I said gently, 'I'm not pretending that our... going to bed together didn't make a difference to me. It lit me so that I'm one blazing torch, blazing from head to foot. So perhaps you could twist it round and say I'm just telling you I love you because we've been to bed. But it wouldn't be true. When we made love, we started something. In me anyway.'

Heather stood up and looked down at me for a moment, appraisingly, and yet with something gentle in her face.

'That's a nice speech, Peter,' she said. 'I could make a speech too. But I'll do something better. I said I felt as if I had nothing to give to anyone. But I am going to give you something. I'm going to show you a secret.'

'A secret?'

Without answering she moved over to where our bicycles lay together in the hedge, gathered up hers and swung on to the awkward narrow saddle. 'Come on,' she called over her shoulder. 'I'll show you.'

I toiled after her as she whirred down a field path, through a gate, over another field by a path that was only just perceptible among the rich grass, clover and daisies; then we lifted our bikes over a stile and to my surprise we were on the river towpath. I have never had a strong sense of direction, and had completely lost orientation, but I surmised that we were somewhere in the neighbourhood of Bablockhythe, though I could not see any buildings nearby; we seemed to be in deep country.

Heather led the way again and we bounced along the sparse gravel – the towpath along these upper reaches of the Thames was never very well-kept even in those days, when it was so much more used – and in a few minutes we came round a bend shaded by a clump of fine trees. Just to the other side of the trees was a small, amateurishly built landing-stage, rather in need of repair, with a couple of iron rings for tying boats to, but no boats. On the bank, just back from the landing-stage and with the gravel path running between, was a hut of the kind one sees on beaches or by the river. It had a small verandah in front, a couple of steps up, a double door and that was about it. Heather stopped and leaned her bike up against the side of this hut, so I did the same, looking the place over a bit more as I did so. It needed a coat of paint; the planks of the steps were loosening; the glass of the two small window-frames in the double door, and there was no other, was dirty and one pane was cracked. Heather produced a key and opened the door. 'Welcome to Riverside Lodge,' she said.

I looked in. Almost the whole floor space was taken up by a punt, exactly the kind I had been employed to service and hire out in the spring when I was working for old man Boardman. In the dim, dusty light it looked rather eerie, almost coffin-like. There was nothing else except a couple of deck-chairs, folded and stowed against the wall, a primus stove, and various odds and ends of junk, coils of rope and what-not. On a wooden shelf covered with worn oilcloth stood a kettle and teapot, but there was no water laid on. But Heather seemed contented enough to be there, and so of course I was too.

'What's the time?' she asked. 'I haven't got a watch on me, and I've got to be back home by six.'

'Well, it's nearly five now.'

'H'm. I knew we wouldn't have much time. But I wanted to bring you down and show you this place.'

I didn't know what to say, so I just stood there. She came close up to me and stood, with her hands lightly on my shoulders, looking up into my face. I was only just taller than she was, so she only had to tilt her head back a little. Her eyes had a lovely gleam in them and when she spoke it was in a much softer voice.

'I wanted you to see this place, Peter. I know it's just a shack, but it's... got possibilities.'

Well, I could see it had a lock on the door, and that was possibilities enough for me.

'Is it yours?' I asked.

'No. I just look after it for some friends. A girl whose horses I used to stable. She and her chap use it when they want to go on the river. It's their punt and their everything. All I do is keep an eye on it, see that the local hooligans don't smash it up – there's not much I can do about that, but if they do a bit of damage now and then I can arrange to have it put right. And in exchange I can take the punt out, not that I ever do.'

'Don't you? It might be quite fun.'

'Well, if you'd like to we'll do it one day, but I've heard the river's not much good for punting round here. Too deep. I've never tried it myself. The most I ever do is sit in the deck chairs. But it's a place where I can come and get away from my family, and at the present stage of my life that's everything. I'm sure you understand.'

'I certainly do.'

She nodded, brisk and efficient now. 'Good. Well, we're wasting time. I reckon we've got half an hour here at the most. Here –' and she rummaged on the shelf, found what she was looking for, and handed it to me. It was a box of drawing pins.

'What am I –'

'I'll show you.' Bending swiftly, she took up a pile of newspapers from the shadowy corner behind the punt. 'Get some of these pinned up. We don't want any idle curiosity.'

'Idle...?'

'People looking in at the window. Now get on with it!'

Immediately all became clear, and I turned and got those sheets of newspaper up against the panes, and secured them with plenty of drawing-pins, as fast as my fingers could move. I could hear a soft swishing and thumping noise from behind me and when I turned round Heather had arranged the punt cushions comfortably in the well of the craft and was standing beside it, unbuttoning her neat white tennis-shirt. In the strange pale light that filtered in through the newspaper she looked hallucinatory, like something in an underwater film, but to me she was the realest thing in the world.

'Now,' she said, her eyes holding mine with an expression of command, 'take everything off but keep your watch on and don't forget to look at it. Remember we've got exactly half an hour.'

'I'll keep it on,' I said, 'but I can't guarantee to look at it.'

'Hold it where I can see it, then,' she said and giggled softly. That giggle went straight to my balls, charging them with a raw energy so concentrated that it would have killed me but for the prospect of an immediate outlet.

Which outlet it duly found.

And so it came about that I had, at last, the experience of making love in a punt, something I had wanted to do ever since I realized that punts existed and that girls could be invited into them. I had daydreamed about it while I was working for Tupper Boardman's father. I had tried to bring it off with Vinnie and been frustrated by those river-diving yobbos. And now here it was, happening – but, in the funny way things work out in life, in a punt resting solidly on a board floor and enclosed in a building. The gentle rocking motion of the craft on the water, which had been part of my daydream, had to remain a missing ingredient. But the newspapers over the window, the privacy, the pale dream-like translucency that gave it the flavour of an erotic fantasy, more than made up for that.

Just before we had to get out of the punt and dress, Heather held me close and said softly, 'You do me good in every way, Peter. Not just... this. You know?'

'Likewise,' I said. 'I'm not going to make any speeches. Just, likewise.'

We kissed, and that was the sweetest kiss of all. Then we dressed and got out into the sunshine, and the towpath was lined with cow-parsley, and the willows reflected the silvery undersides of their leaves in the water, and the world was so beautiful, so beautiful.

When we got to the turning where Heather went off towards High Cogges and my way lay straight on towards Eynsham and Oxford, I made as if to accompany her, but she smiled and said, 'I'll go on alone from here, Peter. It's easier if I keep things as simple as I can at home.'

'All right,' I said. 'When's the next time?'

She thought for a moment. 'Monday afternoon's the next time I'll be free.'

'*Monday*? But that's ages. Nothing this weekend?'

'I'm sorry, I really am,' Heather said, 'but when you're in the sort of line I am, looking after people's horses and what-not, weekends are often the busiest time. Things should have calmed down by Monday. Anyway, I'm sure you've got a lot to do.'

'Well, I have at the moment, but it'll all be over by the end of this week, because it's the end of term and I'll be going home.' As I spoke I realized that I hadn't yet got round to telling her where I lived. Well, all that could wait. Everything could wait, except setting up a re-play of what we had just done, and then another, and then another.

'Well, I'm sorry, but Monday it is. I can be away from the farm by about two. Let's meet down here.' She nodded towards the river-bank. 'We can take the boat out if you'd like to.'

'All right, Monday,' I said. 'And meanwhile, however difficult it is, I won't communicate, right?'

'Right,' she said. 'Thank you for being so understanding. My blasted family are so nosy about letters and I can't always intercept the post. So no writing. Line of least resistance and all that.'

'Till Monday, my love,' I said, kissing her, 'and here's to the line of least resistance.'

*

I had signed off dinner that evening and I couldn't afford a restaurant meal, so I deadened my hunger as best I could with a packet of fish and chips in Botley on my way back to College. I felt dreamy and light-headed; happy, in a lyrical, absent-minded way. Spending the evening alone immediately after being with Heather and getting so close to her, I would have expected to be thinking about her, and about our relationship, very intensely. But in the event I couldn't think of anything very intensely. Every time my mind got on to a subject, even that subject, it slid off it again.

Next morning, the release and happiness inside me translated itself into energy, and energy meant work, and work meant going on with this essay for Bax, the one that I was going to paralyse him with. At least, paralyzing Bax had been an important part of the original intention, but never quite the whole of it, and the sheer joy of historical enquiry had largely occupied the foreground since. I hardly gave Bax a thought until about eleven o'clock on the evening before I was to go to him, when, after days of reading and note-taking, I sat back and looked at the haystack of material I had accumulated. The main lines of my analysis were clear to me, but they would hardly have been clear to anyone else. If Bax and I had been going through a good phase, if there had been anything like sympathetic *rapport* between us as teacher and pupil, I would just have taken that mass of material along in the morning and thrown it at him, knowing that the two of us would enjoy spending the rest of the hour putting it into some sort of coherent shape. But I also knew that we were too much at odds for that. If I took an undigested mass of facts to him, he would trample me down remorselessly. So, feeling such freshness rising in me that I hardly needed rest (God bless Heather), I stayed up till five in the morning writing it all out afresh and making a neat job of it, arriving at conclusions which in some cases I clearly labelled 'provisional' so that he would not be able to shoot arrows in through the slits in the building. Then I went to sleep for three hours, as peacefully as if Heather's arms had been round me, and woke at breakfast time as fresh as a daisy.

The sudden improvement in my performance evidently startled Bax, and for a moment or two after I had finished reading the essay he sat looking at me through his thick lenses as if he had never seen me before. Then he pulled himself together and started to discuss the events of 1375 and '76 in all their ramifications, pulling books off the shelves to consult them and leaving them in a heap on the table rather than neatly replacing each one in turn – a pattern of behaviour that seemed to indicate unusual interest and absorption. It was not in Bax's nature to congratulate a pupil, in so many words, on having written a good essay; you gathered the degree of his approval from the amount of involvement he showed in the discussion afterwards. By that test, his reaction this time was very favourable. And when the hour struck, and we had spent a few extra minutes, because this was the last tutorial of the term, talking about what I was going to do in the autumn, he sat back, gave what passed with him for an amiable smile, and said, 'Well, I shall be looking forward to seeing you in August.'

Christ! I thought. The last few days had been so jam-packed, first with the developments in my personal life and then at that fantastic slog at the essay, that I had completely forgotten about the Lake District reading party and how impossible it was for me, now, to go to it. I had meant to call and see Bax and explain that my plans had changed, but since it was manifestly impossible to tell him the real reason and I had not had time to think of a convincing alibi, I had put it off. Clearly the decent thing to do was to tell him now, while everybody was still around and he had a chance to find someone to fill my place. I stood there, trying to find the words, but nothing came out. I absolutely could not speak. We had had such a pleasant talk, the whole hour had been so enjoyable and Bax had really come out with some quite interesting historical ideas that had suddenly made me see him as a man who had some right to be where he was, rather than a remote and slightly supercilious martinet – and to go and spoil it all in the last few seconds, leaving him with a disappointed impression of me: no, it was impossible. So I said, 'Yes, that will be... that is, thank... August... I shall be looking forward.' I didn't tell him what it was I would be looking forward to. Something very different from a reading party in the Lake District.

Still, it couldn't be put off for ever. Bax couldn't eat me for not going on his reading party, but he would have grounds for very real annoyance if I pulled out without giving him reasonable notice. Term ended on the Saturday, two days from now; in the afternoon we were expected to go down, though technically we had the right to stay in College one more night on sufferance; but on the Saturday morning we had to put on academic dress and turn up for the march-past of Collections. I determined, with a leaden feeling in my stomach, to go and see him after Collections and *tell him*.

The actual Collections would have been quite a pleasant experience, if I hadn't been so uneasily aware of the ordeal that was so shortly to follow. When my turn came to go up for my statutory five minutes, Bax was remarkably pleasant; he even allowed a slight smile to play over his features while he informed the assembled dons (among whom I recognized the benign face of Nobel-Prize-Winning Weatherby, peering shrewdly over a pair of half-glasses) that, after a slight stagger about two-thirds of the way through the term, I had continued to fulfil the promise I had shown since my admission to the College in the autumn. There was a general response of pleased condescension, and Gadsby in particular seemed to find satisfaction in the knowledge that my hat was still in the ring. He made some remark to the effect that when I reached my third year, he 'hoped to have the pleasure of reading with me'. Evidently they had some arrangement that Gadsby, close to retirement, only took the third-year men. He made his chewing motions with his bony jaws in between speaking, and looked thin and papery and rather ill. Since I knew him for a good historian I hoped he wouldn't pop off before my third year arrived, though I wouldn't have cared to take a bet on it.

I really must have made a good impression, because the President, old Salterton, was stirred from his usual immobility. Salterton was immensely aged. He had been a Fellow of Episcopus since 1887 – Life Fellowships, of course, in those days – and had been elected President in about the year I was born. He had little black button-eyes and the dome of his head was still covered with a thin layer of beautiful white hair. Usually he sat absolutely still, with his eyes fixed on you, like a lizard. On this occasion he stirred slightly and opened his mouth and some words came out. The words were, 'I'm glad to hear you are settling down well to your work, Mr Leonard.' He always called everyone Mister.

All that was fine as far as it went, but it didn't help the immediate situation. I had to bite the bullet and get it over with Bax, so, before leaving the daïs and while they were all still looking at me with mild approval or glancing down at their notes to see who the next victim was, I leaned across and asked Bax if I might call in and have a word with him later on.

'By all means,' he said pleasantly. 'Come about midday.'

I went away with a heavy step. It may seem a small thing to have been upset about, looking back across half a century so full of enormous catastrophes and incalculable suffering for mankind, but I can remember my anxiety and depression quite clearly. Bax had shown me a mark of approval and encouragement – to be invited to join in a reading party didn't come the way of everybody – and, though I had spent hours trying to think up a plausible story, I had come up with precisely nothing. My family were going on holiday in Italy and wanted me to go with them? – He knew I didn't have that kind of family. I had been invited to join a party that was going to explore the head waters of the Amazon? – He knew I wasn't that kind of chap. I had been invited to act in a film version of Scott's *The Talisman*, which would involve spending the summer in the Holy Land? – He would want to see the film. I was going into hospital for a long series of operations? – He would arrange for me to be visited with grapes.

How quaint all this kind of thing must seem to the young of today, who (I suppose) would simply march up to their tutor and say, 'By the way, I shan't be coming on the reading party because I've got a new girl-friend who lives near here, and I'm having such a good time with her that I don't want to leave the district, even for two weeks.' All the same, now is now and then was then; and when I rapped on Bax's door at midday I knew the next quarter of an hour was going to be bad, damned bad.

The suffering began straight away, because he greeted me genially, which made me feel even worse. There was a decanter of sherry on the table and two glasses ready – another bit of Bax's procedure for congratulating me on working hard and producing a spectacular essay without actually saying so. The sun shone brilliantly in through his Jacobean windows and lit up the crowded bookshelves and the polished dark wood of the table. I felt like a trespasser. I took the glass of sherry he offered me, took a mighty gulp of it to give myself a bit of courage, and blurted out that I had changed my mind and wasn't coming to the Lake District.

'Oh,' Bax said and carefully put his glass down as if, suddenly, he didn't feel like drinking sherry. Then, keeping his voice casual, he said, 'Any special reason?'

'Oh,' I said, struggling to catch the same tone, 'it's just that I've had to... rearrange things a bit. Change my plans in response to...' I cleared my throat heavily. 'Various things have cropped up.'

'Like a chance to get a regular fuck.' said a voice inside my head, so loudly that I was astounded that Bax showed no sign of hearing it.

'In other words,' Bax said, 'you're not saying what your reasons are, which is of course your right. The scheme is and always was purely voluntary.'

'Yes.'

'It just seemed to me that you would have enjoyed it. That you would have found benefit in it, benefit to your historical studies, is a matter not of opinion but of fact.'

'Yes.'

'I conduct these reading parties every year and I don't think anyone has come on one and then wished afterwards that he hadn't.'

'No,' I said. 'I'm sure not.'

There was a silence.

'However,' Bax said, 'if your mind is made up...'

He was giving me a chance to change my mind again and we both knew it. For an instant I wavered, but in that instant I had a vision of Heather's shoulders, naked and perfect in their creamy smoothness, and the strands of her shining hair lying across them like flakes of sunlight.

'I can't change my mind,' I said. 'I would if I could because I was looking forward to the reading party. I just hope I haven't caused any...'

'Don't worry about that. It isn't the inconvenience to me I'm thinking of, it's the loss to you.' Bax's face had gone hard. 'I shall probably be holding another one of these reading parties next summer, but I find it's more useful for men at the end of their first year. And in any case, if you're the type who's given to changing his mind for incommunicable reasons at the last moment...' he shrugged.

The interview was over. There was nothing to do but go. I think I managed some kind of 'Good morning' or something, but it may have been just a wordless cry. When I found myself outside the door I was sweating. I really hated doing this to Bax; well, never mind Bax, I hated doing it to myself. But then the vision of Heather came again. I couldn't leave her, for a whole fourteen days. Anything might happen. She might Meet Somebody! I cringed at the thought. No, Heather came first; and, as far as I could see, she always would. I went on down the broad, graceful staircase and out into the summer air.

Chapter 16

I was entitled to lunch in Hall that day, the last such entitlement I would have till October, but I knew I wasn't going to be able to face it. The unpleasant scene with Bax had put me right down on the floor. I expected, with any luck, to get back on my feet within an hour or two, but for the moment it was too soon to put on a social mask. I took a turn in the garden to restore minimal calm, and went back across the quad. Ignoring the men going across in twos and threes towards Hall, and the cheerful clatter of dishes that could be heard from in there, I climbed determinedly up to my rooms to stow the last odds and ends in my suitcase and grip and bring them down to the lodge. My father would bring me round some time in the afternoon to pick them up in the car, and meanwhile all I wanted from Episcopus College was that we should leave each other alone for a while. Overall, I was reasonably satisfied with my first academic year, especially since that burst of glorious sunshine, called Heather, had made the future seem so much more inviting; but enough had happened to me for the time being, and I wanted a spell of non-event.

I got my bike and rode across town, calmly and casually bridging that gulf from one life to another. As I came down our familiar street with the good old Bargeman's Arms sign hanging out in front of our dwelling, I saw a Morris van parked outside. Nothing special, just a well-used ten-horse-power job, but it attracted my eye. It was very dusty and mud-spattered, and had a 'G.B.' sign on it. Somebody had been travelling. I leaned my bike against the pub wall and went over to the van. Now that I approached it from the side I saw that it had the octagonal M.G. emblem painted there and underneath the words, RACING DEPARTMENT.

I went into the bar and sure enough Brian was there, standing against the wooden counter with a pint glass in his hand. With him, also holding a pint, was another man, of his own age or a little older. The two were so dissimilar that it was difficult to compare them. The newcomer was tall and bony; his face was of the kind that gets called 'rugged', with prominent cheekbones and a forward-jutting jaw. His eyes, under a mop of curly hair that looked as springy as wire, seemed extraordinarily alert and watchful. Brian, standing beside him, looked more than ever what he was, compact, strongly built, close-knit – rather like, when one came to think of it, a human version of the M.G. Evidently they were deep in discussion; Brian, I could tell, had a good deal of respect for this fellow, whoever he was, and listened very carefully to every word that proceeded from him.

'You must have had to keep pushing for over seven thou.,' the man was saying as I went in, 'and then bring her right down for those hairpins.'

'Twice every lap,' Brian assented. 'Twice up and twice down, and the race is two hundred laps. You can imagine what it does to the torque. And there's not much you can do to –'

'Well, look who's here,' said my father suddenly, recognizing me as I came up behind them. He was serving in the bar at lunchtime because it was a Saturday, when he did not go to his job at the brewery. 'Look who's here. Let you out a bit early, have they?'

'I escaped,' I said, grinning. 'Hello, Brian. What's the van, then? Been travelling?'

Brian ignored the question and spoke to his companion instead. 'Doug, this is my brother Peter. He doesn't... know the score very well. He's away at College most of the time.'

'Pleased to meet you,' this Doug said, giving me a brief, painful handshake. I now got a closer look at him; he had, it struck me, something of a gipsy look, with penetrating dark-brown eyes and dark hair that, though it was cut short, still clustered in curls on a head as neat as a snake's. Everything about him suggested extreme alertness and wiry strength. He was a man who, but for his stature, could have been a jockey; but for the spareness of his frame, a wrestler; but for the fact that his long, slender nose was not flattened and his ears not cauliflowered, a boxer.

'Doug Ravenscroft,' Brian said as if I ought to jump to attention at the name; but having never heard it I could only mutter, 'Pleased to meet you' in my turn.

Brian was obviously not going to answer my question about his travelling. Evidently it was beneath his notice or offensive in some way. With a gesture that seemed suddenly heavy and weary, he picked up his glass and took a deep draught. Looking at him attentively now, I could see that his face was rather drawn and his eyes a little red-rimmed:

nothing serious, just the marks of too little sleep and too many hours behind the wheel.

My father now ducked swiftly back into the living-quarters and returned immediately with a copy of the *Oxford Mail*, folded open at the appropriate page.

'Here,' he said, and handed it to me. 'Do your homework.'

'Certainly.' I said. 'While I read this may I have a pint of beer at family discount? Cost price?'

'Nothing doing,' my father said. 'You'll pay for it like anyone else. But the first one, to welcome you home, you have on the house.' And he drew it with a practised hand; a full, amber pint with exactly the right mound of froth on top. I took a long draught and set the glass down contentedly. 'Thanks, Dad,' I said. 'The best glass of beer in Oxford.'

'Flattery will get you nowhere,' he said, pleased.

'No, I mean it,' I said and turned away to sit down and read whatever it was in the *Oxford Mail*. As I did so three men came in and ordered drinks and started talking in loud, excited tones about football, though it was not the football season. They must have been living for it to start. Through interstices in their babble, I heard the occasional snatch of the talk Brian was having with Doug Ravenscroft, whoever he was.

'You have to work hard to keep from blowing up,' I heard Brian say once. 'Up to peak revs, down again, up again. Up torque, down torque, twice in every lap.'

'An engine doesn't blow up if you know your business,' Ravenscroft returned crisply. 'After all it's pretty predictable compared with road-circuit racing.'

The braying about football started again and I turned my eyes to the paper. 'M.G. Success,' I read. 'German Race Win.' And 'International Prestige.' The news story said that the German Grand Prix had been held the week before and that M.G. had won it. No, that was a first impression and as I read more attentively I sorted it out. There had been a 750 c.c race as a curtain-raiser to the big event and it was this that M.G. had won. Well, I thought, you can't ask for more than that. Winning a race in which everyone starts fair. There were pictures: Cecil Kimber looking pleased; a man with a linen helmet and goggle-marks who was evidently the driver; and a more blurred photograph of the car making a pit stop, in which I thought I recognized Brian as one of the figures huddled round the car, changing its rear wheels and putting in fuel.

Doug now took himself off, and as the football maniacs settled down to a quieter phase of their discussion, I was able to get Brian into talk.

'Congratulations,' I said, going over to him. 'Well done, eh? You must be pleased.'

'Well, naturally I'm pleased,' he said. 'You go to a race and you win it, what is there to feel but pleased?'

He seemed almost offended. Yet I didn't see how I could have expressed myself any differently.

'I think it's great,' I said.

'Hardly much in your line, is it?' he shouldered me off, as if I were guilty of offensive insincerity by talking of the matter at all.

'Well, no, I'm not going to pretend it's in my line,' I said, 'but if my brother goes into something, whatever it is, I'd rather he did well at it than did badly. That's my attitude and I hope it's yours too.'

He looked more cheerful at that and said, 'Fair enough. Come to that, it is my attitude. Forgive me for being a bit short. They've found me a lot to do in the last few days.'

Mention of a 'few days' caused me to look at the date on the paper. It was Monday's edition. The race had been last Sunday. Where had Brian been? It didn't take a week to get home from Germany, did it? Then the thought came, Where had I been, for that matter? Brian had obviously enjoyed a great triumph – or M.G. had, which to him was the same thing. The triumph had been six days ago and I could still walk into the pub knowing nothing about it. No wonder he saw me as almost a stranger. I was so totally cocooned in my life and it was so totally out of contact with his. Of course that was only part of the explanation. He couldn't know about the cataclysmic events that had been taking place in my life, cocooned or not. I was so deeply immersed in the business with Heather that hardly anything short of war or revolution would have reached my ears.

'Look, I'm sorry I got so behind with the news,' I said. 'The last week of term's a bit hectic, you know. What with one thing and another, I've hardly –'

'That's all right,' he said, cutting me short, not wanting to hear a lot of excuses.

'When did you get back?' I asked.

'Half an hour before you came in.'

'Really? Did it take that long to –'

Mother appeared in the little doorway behind the bar and said, 'Brian, your meal's ready.' Then she caught sight of me and said guiltily, 'Oh, Peter. I didn't get anything for you. I thought you wouldn't be along till later.'

'That's quite all right, Mum,' I said. 'I could have stayed for lunch in

College, but I chose to come down straight away.'

'There are sandwiches,' she said.

Didn't I know there were sandwiches. It occurred to me for the first time that she must have had to make them herself ever since last October. 'That'll be fine,' I said. 'It'll be fine, really.'

Brian stood up and was obviously on the point of going to the kitchen to eat his meal, after which he would probably fall asleep for hours. He was grey with exhaustion. But this was the last moment I would have to speak to him, probably, till tomorrow, and I wanted to begin right away showing a more intelligent interest in his life.

'Before you go, Brian, who's your friend?' I asked.

'Friend?'

'Yes, this Doug Ravenscroft, who is he?'

Brian had begun to walk across the room, but he stopped for an instant, looked across at our father and said, 'Dad.'

'Yes, Brian?'

'Tell Peter who Doug Ravenscroft is, will you?' Brian said in detached, patient tones, like a teacher in a school for educationally sub-normal children who was going off duty and wished to pass on to the next teacher a particularly obtuse child.

'More homework to do, Dad, it seems,' I said.

'Don't let it bother you, Peter,' he said, taking the damp cloth off a couple of rounds of sandwiches and putting the plate on the bar. 'Pickled onions? You know how Brian is about these things.'

'Just one onion,' I said. 'They're rather big. Thanks. Well, who is this Doug Ravenscroft?'

'I don't know as I'd have known myself, if Brian hadn't mentioned him so much. But it's true his name's in the papers quite often, specially the Oxford ones 'cause he's a local boy made good, see? He's a motor-cycle racer. He goes in for these races like the T.T. – the motor-bike one, not the car one that Brian's concerned with – and let's face it, it's the motor-bike one that draws the big crowds. That's the popular one.'

'Does he win it?'

My father shook his head. 'According to what Brian tells me, it's only factory teams that win these big races. Private owners can't compete, like. All the stuff they need, and the spare bikes and the mechanics and the race tactics, sending one rider out to force the pace and never mind if he blows up his engine as long as he makes the competition do the same – a private owner can't do all that. No, when Doug goes in for it he's racing for a replica.'

‘A replica?’

‘Yes, that’s something else I wouldn’t have known about if Brian hadn’t told me. If you finish the T.T. in eleven-tenths of the winner’s time, you get a replica of the winner’s trophy, exactly the same but smaller. It’s yours to keep, and Brian says Doug’s got the sideboard covered with them at his house. Says you can hardly move for fear of knocking one on to the floor. Exaggerating, of course. But he does admire him, I know that.’

‘Well, after all, it’s Brian I’m interested in, really,’ I said. I took a bite of cheese sandwich and said through it, ‘I only asked about Doug Ravenscroft because I don’t want Brian to despise me for not knowing who his hot-shot friends are. But let’s talk about Brian, now that he’s not here. Fill me in, Dad.’

Dad filled me in. It seemed that after the German race, which had been held at the Avus track in Berlin, the main party had come home, and Brian had been left to make his own way back because they wanted him to route himself through France and make an information-gathering visit to the Montlhéry circuit near Paris. He was to take the second racing car with him, the one that had been used to back up the car that actually won the race, and look over the facilities and arrangements at Montlhéry; also to take the car round the circuit for a few laps and see if, in his opinion, it was a track on which M.G. could expect to do well.

The story opened my eyes to the distance Brian had come in the few short years since he had gone to work at Morris Motors and managed to get across the barrier line into M.G. Obviously they recognized him as a skilled judge of these matters. The company was going to risk money or not, and individual drivers were going to risk their necks or not, on the basis of his assessment of whether Montlhéry was a suitable proving-ground for their kind of car. Not to mention the fact that they trusted him to set off by himself, in a foreign country and with another foreign country to go through, driving a van containing an expensive racing car. Altogether, Cecil Kimber (for surely the decision must have been Cecil Kimber’s) had clearly developed a solid trust in his young lieutenant.

Would I be capable of doing what Brian had done? Obviously not. Not one corner of his programme could I have fulfilled. I went outside to where the travel-stained van stood demurely in the afternoon sunlight. Opening the doors at the back, I leaned inside and looked at the chunky little racing car, its dull green colour making it hard to see in the deep shadow of the van’s interior. It had a racing number painted in a white disc on either side of the tail. I peered at the driving seat. A pair of string-backed gloves lay carelessly in its deep recess. Brian had worn those gloves, holding that taped-over steering-wheel, sitting behind that little rounded windscreeen as the car roared and pounded round this Montlhéry, wherever and whatever it was. Brian had certainly arrived. He was, at last, unquestionably a part of the world he wanted most to belong to.

*

After I had had my beer and sandwiches I waited about, feeling very unsettled, till it suited my father to drive me over to College to pick up my possessions. At first I tried to tell myself that I would settle down all right once I had got my suitcase up to my room, hung up clothes and put books on shelves and papers into drawers. But I didn't really believe it. Underneath the pretence I knew it was Heather I was feeling disturbed about. The still unanswered questions were beginning to needle me again.

It took Dad till about three to get ready and drive me over to Episcopus, and all the time the feeling was growing on me that what I needed was a long, solitary walk. So when I had carried out my suitcase and grip and a few other things in a cardboard box, I asked him if he would mind driving home without me. I said I had a few calls to make in that part of town and didn't want to keep him waiting.

He nodded and said, 'I'll just leave the stuff in the car and you can unpack it and take it upstairs when you get back.'

'Of course, Dad, of course,' I said, above the drumming of the engine. I was very, very careful, at this period of my life, not to give my parents any occasion to think that because in College I had a servant to do things for me I expected the same treatment at home. Not that the surly attentions of Arthur were ever likely to make me feel like a pampered scion of the governing class.

My father drove off and I started to walk north along the Woodstock Road. I went all the way through the Victorian academic suburbs, through the undistinguished middle-class housing that starts about Bainton Road, till I reached the point where the city ran out into open country. Then I turned left down Godstow Road, went over Wolvercote Bridge and through the long, straggling village until it, too, ceased and open country stretched before me. I went over Godstow Bridge, pausing to stare briefly down into the dark glass of the Thames, and along to Wytham Village. The woods, up there on the skyline, looked thick and green and inviting, so I went and trespassed in them and sprawled at ease among trees, bushes and wild flowers, listening to the industrious hum of insects and watching the shadows of tree-trunks move slowly along on the mossy ground.

And as I lay there, I thought of Heather, of course, and worried about her a little, of course, because she was so opaque to me. I had no experience of women to measure her by (a Venus Fly-trap like Vinnie hardly counted as 'women'), but intuitively I felt that a normally constituted woman, like a normally constituted man, would show her feelings more openly than Heather seemed to be showing hers to me. It was her motives that I found unguessable. I went over our history step by step. First, why had she accepted my invitation to the Commem. Ball? Because her mother had been keen for her to go, would have nagged her if she hadn't, and because her life was pretty dull anyway and an evening out would make a change. Clear so far. But why, once we got up to my room, had she stripped off and got into bed as casually as she might have accepted a glass of champagne? She seemed to enjoy it all right, yes, but then she didn't seem, in any other respect, to resemble a girl like Vinnie who would be simply out for pleasure. There seemed to be more depth to her character than that, more range. But where was this depth, this range? Where did they extend to?

And what about my own feelings? Did I love her? She was beautiful, yes, and she was willing to go to bed with me, and in my state of desperate privation that would be enough to make me need her so fiercely that I might easily *believe* I loved her. A deep need could seem the same thing as love. Well, wasn't it the same thing? If you needed somebody deeply, didn't that mean you loved them?

Working away at this problem of exactly how I felt about Heather, I came up with an interim answer. My body needed her as a source of release. That was obvious, undeniable, and perfectly natural. My mind... no, my spirit... wait a moment, my *brain* needed her because I felt an intense discomfort in the presence of the enigma she posed. I felt enough of a devouring interest in her as an individual, as a separate person, Heather Burrell, to desire with the utmost keenness to understand more about her. *Why* did she do what she did? *What*, at bottom, was her attitude to me? And to life generally? I hated, passionately hated, this state of being very close to her in one way, the closest it was possible to get, and infinitely remote in every other. And as I reached that conclusion, a great wave of longing simply to see Heather, simply to meet with her and talk together, washed through me with an overwhelming force I felt hardly able to bear. But I bore it after all, because the peace and solitude, and the beauty of the place, worked their magic, and I felt rested when, after an hour or two, I came down to the village and got on to the road at the point where it runs past the Abbey gateway. From there I walked along to where the city began at the end of the Botley Road. There was a bus service along that road and I hoped I might get one as far as the Thames bridge, but none came, so I walked all the way down the Botley Road to the bridge at Oseney Town. Then I walked along East Street, so small-scale, so domestic, so calm, it confirmed the peace that had, however temporarily, come down on me. Altogether the walk had taken me three hours. It was six now and Dad was just opening up. I took my luggage upstairs and came down to the bar for a pint of much-needed refreshment.

I had time to drink it fairly slowly; with Brian working and me away, our evening meal was no longer rigidly timed for six o'clock. Hardly had I settled down to it than Old Trundle and his *cénacle* came in and began their evening deliberations. It seemed that the German motor race, and our local participation in it, was occupying their thoughts. I did not know whether they had been talking about it all week or whether (what was more likely) the appearance of Brian's van outside for a couple of hours that day had freshened up the topic. But at the point where I picked up the conversation, long, thin Peake had the floor, and his narrow face was dark with indignation.

'I'd motor-race 'em,' he was saying venomously. 'I'd motor-race 'em.'

'Meaning what?' asked young Ted.

'Meaning,' Peake said in a hard, dry voice, 'that if I 'ad my way with the bloody Germans they wouldn't have no time to stand about watchin' cars rushin' round a track. They'd be at work, payin' off what they owes to the rest of the world.'

'That's all over and done with,' said Ted dismissively. 'Can't go on for ever with all that stuff.'

'You're wrong. That's just what I'd do. Go on for ever. That's just what we ought to'a done. We ought to'a gone on for ever. We was too soft, letting 'em get up.'

'You've got to let 'em get up some time,' Ted urged. 'Got to let 'em build up, else they'll be a drag on everybody all round. You don't want to have to feed and clothe 'em for ever, I suppose?'

'I wouldn't do too much of that,' Peake said. 'Bare rations it'd be, and enough clothes so they could live through the winter. No finery. From what you read in the papers now, they're a damn sight too well off. And even their Army and Navy and that, they've got money to fit 'em out again. I wouldn't have none of that.'

'Well, what would you do, then?'

'Quite simple,' Peake said, looking round the circle. 'After the last lot, Germany ought to'a become a colony of England. We ought to 'a ruled 'em the way we rule these Indians and Africans and that.'

'That won't go on for ever, seemingly,' another man put in. 'These Indians are talking about getting shut of us. You know, that little chap in the bath towel and glasses.'

'I'll take more notice of 'im,' said Trundle, who up to this point had appeared not be listening, 'when he can afford a pair of trousers.'

'Ah, that's just 'is cunning. He's got plenty of pairs of trousers back home in the wardrobe. He just puts on all this native stuff because that's the lark he's on, see? Gets their support when he goes about looking just like the rest of 'em. He's a clever man. A lawyer. Don't tell me he hasn't got a pair –'

'Yes, but the *Germans*,' Peake interrupted fiercely. 'What I'm telling you is that it's a mistake to let 'em get up. They ought to be a colony of England and that's it.'

'How you going to get these Frenchies to swallow that?' my father asked judicially. 'They fought in the war too. They had worse losses than we had. If you'd declared Germany a colony of England, they'd have wanted to know why it wasn't a colony of France, and before you knew where you was they'd have been at each other's throats again.'

'Look, Jack,' said Peake. 'You knows what I'm saying. You served in the last lot.'

'I did, by God,' my father said.

'Well,' said Peake, 'don't you sometimes wonder what you done it for?'

'I wondered at the time. I used to think, Why in God's name did I let 'em bring me out here? But when it was all over and I was still alive, and then we got back and was demobbed, and then we heard all that stuff about the German money being worth nothing and a wheelbarrow full of thousand-mark notes to buy food for a couple of days, I began to think we might have done it for a reason after all.'

'What reason?' said young Ted. 'So that the Germans would have to take a wheelbarrow full of –'

'No,' my father interrupted commandingly, not caring to be involved in a disputation with any whippersnapper. 'So that we wouldn't. Look, lad, whoever loses a war goes down. I mean *down*. Right down. And then everybody else jumps on 'em.'

'That's just what I means,' Peake came in excitedly. 'We *didn't* jump on 'em. We was too easy. We let 'em get up and they ought to 'a stayed down for good. A man can't attack you when he's layin' on the floor.'

Brian had come into the bar, quietly, and was listening unobserved. At this point he said, 'A man who's lying on the ground can't do anything. He can't work, nor feed himself neither. You can't keep a whole country like that, a big country in the middle of Europe, lying down for ever. In the end it holds everybody back.'

'I remember the last lot,' said Peake stubbornly. 'I was out there by 'fifteen. My best pal was with me, Ginger Corcoran from Bridge Street, Oseney. They shot half his chest away the first day he got to the front line. It took him six hours to die and I had to watch him do it. Bloody Germans. Don't tell me. They should 'a become a colony. A *colony*.' His face was what I believe is called 'working'.

'I don't underrate that,' Brian said. 'Believe me I don't belittle all that suffering you blokes went through in the last lot. It's just that –'

'If you lets 'em get on their feet again,' Peake said, 'all I says is you *are* belittling it. We went through all that to stop 'em and now you're lettin' 'em get started again.'

'Look, I've just *been* there,' said Brian. 'I don't know what you call getting started, but what I've seen with my own eyes is that they've just about started working again. They've got twelve harvests in since the war and they've got some of their factories going. They're eating, just about, without having to go to soup kitchens. But there's still a lot of unemployment. They're not well off – they've not even as well off as we are and I don't think anybody'd say we're doing very well. But it's working they've started, not fighting. They won't be doing any fighting. They don't want to. They learnt their lesson last time.'

'Well, you *know*, you've been there,' said our father decisively. 'You must know how their minds are working.'

'I don't know all that much about it,' said Brian. 'I wasn't there for long and I don't speak the lingo. But if ever I saw a country that doesn't want to fight, they're it. They just want to build up a bit of prosperity and have a bit of a good time when they can afford it and get stuck into the beer and sausages. Yes, and watch a bit of motor-racing. The Avus track, where we were, it's right in the middle of Berlin. There's no motor-racing track in the middle of London. The Germans have woken up to it, that's more than our lot have. I mean, M.G.s are brilliant but they're still not Mercedes.'

'Beer and sossidges,' said old Trundle. They seemed to be the only words that had caught his attention. 'Ah. You can't beat the German for them. Mind you, the sossidges en't like ours. But they're all right. And the old German knows how to brew a good pot of beer. You ever tasted it?' he asked Peake.

'I wouldn't spit in it.'

'Ah, well, it's understandable. It's the war 'as turned you sour. A lot of you young chaps.'

'You'd 'a been sour,' Peake said, 'if you'd 'a seen some of the things I had to see. Lucky for you you was too old.'

'I served my Queen and country,' said old Trundle with dignity, 'at the time of that dust-up with them Boors. Ay, them Boors was a right lot of bloody hard cases.'

'You served in South Africa, Mr Trundle?' I asked, the historian in me taking over and precipitating me into the conversation against my better judgement. From the corner of my eye I saw my father frown warningly.

'I served,' said Trundle with massive dignity, 'in Southampton. Ay. Southampton Docks. That was where I served my Queen and country in the year nineteen hundred.'

'Workin' for the recruiting sergeant,' said Peake, *sotto voce*. 'Drivin' the bloody swaddies up the gangplank with a pitchfork.'

'What I was doing,' said Trundle, who had heard the remark perfectly well, 'was loading horses on shipboard. Horses. For the cavalry. You can't chase Brother Boor over the bloody karoo on your own two feet. Horses they needed and horses they got. And let me tell you it was dangerous work. They used to kick like mad things when they got on that gangway. Yes, and bite. More than once I've seen one go right over into the water, yes, down between the ship and the dock where you couldn't get 'em out. It was pitiful to see. We lost some horses that way and we lost some men. And casualties! We 'ad any number of men lamed.' He drank from his tankard and said, 'Ay. There's many a man drawing a pension today, walking round with a bad limp, or a wooden leg, some of 'em, ever since nineteen hundred.'

'Don't,' said Peake. 'I can't stand it. Makes Vimy Ridge sound like the bloody Vicarage tea-party.'

'Brother Boor,' Trundle continued, 'was a nasty sharp character. He could shoot straight and he knew all the tricks. In them days we never 'eard much about the Germans. In fact we had the idea they was pretty all right. That Kayser, now.'

'Don't talk to me about the Kayser,' said Peake warningly. 'A colony, that's what they ought to –'

'Now I believe I'm right in saying,' old Trundle majestically continued, 'as he was the nephew of Queen Victoria.'

'The more fool her,' said Peake.

'The way we looked at it in them days,' Trundle said, 'there couldn't be much wrong with a country as was ruled over by a nephew of the Widow of Windsor.'

'Widow of Windsor, my bollocks,' said Peake. 'She was a bloody German. All that lot were bloody Germans. Look at bloody Albert.'

'I don't remember Albert,' Trundle conceded. 'But the Widow of Windsor was as English as you and me, and if she hadn't 'a been I wouldn't a spent the year nineteen hundred risking my life and limb gettin' them 'orses on to the ships at Southampton Docks.'

As his peroration came to a close, Trundle picked up his tankard, drained the last few drops that lurked in it, and set it down with a thump of finality. Everyone was silent. He looked round the company, glad to have re-established his ascendancy as the doyen of the circle; and, after all, one could not grudge it to him.

*

The next morning my restlessness, temporarily driven away by the three-hour walk and a deep night's sleep, was back in full force. That imperious need to see Heather, to take my knowledge of her mind at any rate a few steps further, simply would not let me rest. I bore it during a long aimless morning; after all, the day was Sunday, and to absent myself from 'Sunday dinner' on the very first occasion when I should have been at home to share in it, was unthinkable. But by midday I knew that the afternoon would see me in the saddle, pedalling doggedly in the direction of High Cogges. Against Heather's instructions. Against my own better judgement. Against everything except that dull ache inside me.

The expedition was what it deserved to be – a frost, a farce, a fiasco. At first I had some vague notion of knocking on the door of Jasmine Farm and asking in a cheery, socially-acceptable, I-was-just-passing tone if Heather was at home. But as the miles laboriously unrolled under my wheels I came to see that that was out. I knew I had to become a caller at the farm – an official visitor, so to speak; I was serious about wanting to go on seeing Heather, on any terms, and if the parents proved to be reasonably welcoming, or even not hostile, I was perfectly willing to cultivate them like mad. But I also knew that the first time over the doorstep would be a bit nerve-racking and I would need Heather as an armed escort. Women were supposed to have Intuition. They were supposed to Know What You Were Thinking, like animals. And if I found myself sitting in that chintzy parlour with Mrs Burrell's bright and beady eyes on me, I knew I would start feeling that she must know what I was thinking, and what I was thinking would be to wonder what she was thinking and whether she could tell intuitively that I had been to bed with Heather. I brushed the thought away as if it were a dangerous hornet, actually physically brushed it away with my hand.

So there I was. Heather had given me a perfectly clear directive: come on Monday. But leave it to me, I was on my way out there, uninvited, on Sunday. And without even the nerve to go and knock on the door, so there was always the nagging little uncertainty – perhaps she *was* at home, doing some chore, perhaps she *would* have time to talk to me for just a few minutes and make my day?

But then, how much of a day would it make to have her talk to me if I thrust myself on her, uninvited, when she was in the middle of mucking out stables or plucking chickens or whatever it was? Or perhaps her mother had commandeered her to spend the afternoon darning socks or something. What girl wants to break off and talk to a lover, particularly a *gauche*, awkward lover like me, in the middle of darning a pile of socks?

So I turned away before I reached the farm gate, went to the top of the hill and, settling myself in a thick part of the hedge where I wouldn't attract attention, spent the long hours till sunset just watching the farm buildings, hoping for a glimpse of Heather. If she had gone out she must surely come back some time; if she were messing about the farm, doing jobs, surely I would see her crossing the yard or opening a gate. But she must have been away somewhere, because she never appeared at all. Mr Burrell rattled up in an old van and got out. With him was a figure I thought I recognized as the man who had stared at me in a lurking, secretive way on the day I had made my dummy enquiry about the Golden Labrador puppies. (I wondered, briefly, if they were all sold by now, launched on their little canine lives.) I recognized him partly by the stooping, secretive way he held himself, and partly by the mackintosh hat he had pulled down over his eyes, a hat that even from this distance looked terminally worn and frayed. He and Mr Burrell unloaded some sacks from the van and then Mr Burrell got into the van again and drove off, while the lurking man slowly carried the sacks one at a time into a barn.

That was all that happened in the hours I lay on the grass, propped on one elbow or the other, watching; except of course that the life of nature went on. Birds wheeled in the sky or flapped raggedly across it, according to their species; insects hummed and danced in the warm slanting sunbeams; I glimpsed the white scuts of hurrying rabbits; and I, part of nature myself, a young male whose veins pounded with fertility, longed for a sight of Heather.

Finally, when the shadows grew long and took on a touch of purple, I decided to give up and go to the village pub to drown my sorrows. I had three or four shillings on me, enough to buy an ample amount of beer and some simple food if they had any going, and I picked up my bike, coasted down the hill past the farm, and pedalled along to the pub. It was called 'The Green Man', and the thought came to me that I had shown myself a pretty green man to waste an afternoon in that way.

The pub was quiet and restful and full of old wood and shadowy corners; just to be there made me feel more peaceful. I drank, and ate a little, and stretched my legs out under the table and leaned back, almost contentedly. I was just working up the will-power to face the long slog back to Oxford when the door was energetically pushed open and two men entered. One was a lean, dried-up-looking character in a three-quarter-length leather coat. The other was Tom. Tom Burrell.

They went over to the bar without noticing me, greeted the three or four men who were there already and chatted to them for a moment, then, still standing at the bar, hived off to a clear space and resumed some evidently serious discussion they were in the middle of.

I could hear every word perfectly. 'I can't give a decision myself,' the leathery man started off. 'I can only put it to the Committee.'

'Oh, come on, Frank.' Tom Burrell's voice was rough with impatience. 'You know you could push it through if you really got behind it.'

'You're wrong there, my boy. They're quite apt to dig their heels in good and deep if it's anything that means spending money.'

'But this engine's a *snip*. It's spending money to *save* money, anyone can see that. It's factory reconditioned, not some backyard job, and they can get it for a piddling one seventy-five.'

The leathery man drank from his glass, set it down, and shook his head. 'How are you going to get types like the Major and Ted Logarithm,' some name like that, 'to regard a hundred and seventy-five pounds as a piddling sum when they look twice at every five shillings and go over the accounts with a microscope?'

Tom Burrell blew out his breath in a gale of frustrated energy. His strong shoulders, inside that old check tweed jacket, jerked as if he would like to punch somebody. 'Look, Frank, if that's going to be the attitude, I really think it's time to stop pretending to run a gliding club. Three times this season, *three times*, I've hauled my kite over to the field and never got up in the air. I wait my turn, I'm a good boy, I play by all the rules, and then Phut! when it gets to the chap next but one, or next but two or three, the word goes out: *No more launching today. Mechanical failure*. And back home I go without having got off the ground. What's the use of that to me? I'm in the club to get flying experience and if all they can field is a Gipsy Moth held together with string and sticking plaster, with a leaky engine that won't run smoothly for a four-hour session, who's getting anything out of it?'

The leathery man said reflectively, 'If we say one seventy-five for the engine, there'll be the installation costs on top of that.'

'I'll install it. It won't cost anybody a penny. I know a couple of blokes from Cranfield who'll give me a hand.'

'Willoughby'll never stand for that,' said the leathery man, shaking his head. 'You know what he is. He'll say that if he's going to go up in it he'll want to have it installed by qualified –'

'Willoughby!' Tom Burrell exploded. 'When did Willoughby ever take a risk? He handles that thing like a flying bath-chair. Refuses to take off if there's enough wind to blow a match out. I tell you, Frank, if they let slip this offer I'll –'

His eyes were roving across the room as he spoke and at that instant he caught sight of me. My being there must have surprised him because he abruptly stopped speaking; that the surprise was not a pleasant one was clear from his expression, which registered an incredulity first infiltrated and finally replaced by outrage.

I was frankly hoping he would content himself with glaring at me, but after a moment he came over and stood in front of me, his hands thrust into his trouser pockets. Lowering his voice, which during the latter part of his tirade to Frank had risen to a volume that dominated the pub, he said for my ears alone, 'What the hell are you doing here?'

'What do people usually do in pubs?' I countered, making my tone casual in the hope of keeping the situation fairly low-key. 'I've just drunk a pint of –'

'You're hanging round my sister, aren't you?' he demanded, bending forward to thrust his face close to mine.

'Look, this is getting impossible,' I said. 'If I can't go into a pub without –'

'Yes, you're right, it is impossible, damned impossible. You leave her alone, that's all I've got to say to you. Keep your sweaty little hands off her.'

I half rose, but sank back in my seat as Frank came over and said from behind Tom's shoulder, 'I'll be off, Tom. I'm expected at home, and I think we've discussed everything we had to.'

'Sorry, Frank,' Tom said without turning round. 'If you've got to go you've got to. I was hoping to talk a bit longer, but I find I've got to deal with this skunk.'

Frank moved on, through the door and out, and I said, 'I suppose I ought to be interested in why it is that you call me a skunk.'

'A skunk stinks. A skunk comes into an environment and stinks it up. That's what you're doing.'

'You're being too ridiculous.'

'Ridiculous, am I? Look, laddie, don't push me too far. I'm very conscious of a wish to knock your teeth down your throat, so don't make it worse by talking back to me.'

Still hoping to be reasonable, I said, 'But what is it I'm doing wrong in your eyes?'

'Don't give me that. You know damn well. Hanging round Heather.'

'If Heather chooses to –'

'Look, it's as simple as this. If you're just fooling with her, trying to grab yourself a bit of fun, forget it, go away, find somebody else because she's simply not available for that kind of thing.'

'And if I'm not fooling?'

'If you're not fooling that makes it all the worse. If, God forbid, you were to take it into your head to suggest marriage to her and she was fool enough to go along with it, that'd be a complete, total skunk-up.'

'Why, may I ask?'

'Because you'd be taking her out of the farming community where she belongs.'

'I suppose,' I said carefully, 'she belongs where she wants to belong.'

'Rubbish. Don't give me any more of your damned rubbish. Girls don't know their own minds, they have to be shown what to do by the men they live among. Then they accept it and they're happy. Heather may get fool ideas at times – all the more reason why she should be helped, yes, helped, to have a bit of sense and steer clear of skunks like you. She'll find her natural partner with someone who's in the world she's grown up in, the world she's used to.'

On an impulse I said, 'Someone like Richard?'

He tensed for an instant, looked at me narrowly, and said, 'Richard?'

'The one she went to the Hunt Ball with.'

'Oh,' he said, still staring at me. 'You know about that then?'

'Why shouldn't I? She told me.'

'What d'you mean, she told you?'

'For God's sake,' I said. 'She told me she was going to the Hunt Ball.

Royal Bicester. She and her mother talked about it when they were having tea with me in Oxford.'

'And she told you she was going with Richard, I suppose,' he said, nodding.

'I can't remember whether it was she or her mother who actually mentioned the name. What can it possibly matter?'

'If it doesn't matter,' he said slowly, 'why did you bring it up?'

'I might do a bit of asking why,' I said bitterly. 'I might ask you why you think you have a right to come up to me when I'm sitting quietly in a pub and insult me. I might ask you –'

'It's perfectly clear why I do and you know it. Now that's enough talk. Just leave my sister alone, keep away from her. Keep away from me, don't show your face in this neighbourhood. Is that clear, skunk?'

He stepped back to the bar, picked up his half-empty beer-mug and drained it, turning his back on me. I hated his wide shoulders, his thick neck, his dark blond hair neatly cut about the ears. Fear tried to restrain me in my seat, but rage drove me to get up. I wasn't going to let matters stay there. But before I could get round from my side of the table he had banged down his empty mug and walked rapidly and viciously over to the door and out. I had the impression that if anyone had happened to be coming in at exactly that moment, Tom Burrell would have marched straight into them and knocked them flat. He didn't so much go through the doorway as shoulder his way through the space between the lintels.

Obviously he was angry. But then so was I. Angry with him, angry with life, angry with the dusky chilly evening that seemed to mock my bright visions of warmth and satisfaction. I felt intolerably cheated: had I slogged my way out here, pushing those damned pedals round thousands and thousands of times, and at the end of it not only no Heather but a flaming row and a packet of insults? Well, he wasn't going to get away with it. Barely had he got through the door when I was after him. How dare he rant at me like that and then simply sweep out? I had a thing or two still to say to him, by God.

What exactly I was going to say I don't remember now and I don't believe I really knew then. I just wanted to confront him for a little longer and throw some of the aggression back at him. But it was too late. He was walking rapidly across the pub yard. The family car, the Ford, was parked over on the other side.

'Just a minute,' I called to him. 'Don't think you can just –'

He answered me with a curt 'Piss off,' delivered over his shoulder as he yanked the car door open. Then he was inside, the engine started and revved up, and the headlights stabbed out into the gloom.

Still too possessed by anger to think what I was doing, I went after him, and as he swung the car round in a tight, angry semi-circle I was for an instant almost directly in his path. He didn't alter course by a millimetre, as if to indicate that while he wouldn't actually run me down neither would he take the smallest trouble to avoid me. I stood my ground, raising one fist in readiness to shake it at him, and the car almost grazed me as it shot away towards the yard entrance. Tom drove through that entrance in the same way as he had lunged through the door – ready to smash headlong into anything that got in the way. Mercifully nothing did. The high, climbing note of the engine as he thrashed it up through the gears – even Tom couldn't make a well-used old Ford more like a Maserati – gradually died away and the depressed silence of the pointless, aimless evening wrapped itself round me like a soiled towel.

It was really deep dusk by now. Rain wasn't actually falling, but the cloud cover was so heavy that hardly any light seemed to be reaching the earth from the soggy sky. Long before I reached Oxford I would need lights on the bike, and several days ago some bastard had stolen the front one. It was just on a bracket in front of the handlebars, and whoever it was had simply helped himself to it, leaving the back one alone because (presumably) it was fastened on with nuts and bolts and would have taken a bit more trouble. Oh, well, what the hell. I had the back one, and there was always more danger of being hit from behind than in front. But the theft was one more example of the annoyingness of things in general.

My bike was round at the front of the pub; I had propped it where I could see it from the window, which was about as much anti-thief security as you needed in those innocent days. Had it not been for chasing after Tom I would not have been in the pub rear yard at all. It was an old-fashioned place, a traditional inn yard not yet fully transformed into a modern car park, and one side of it, the side furthest from the building and adjacent to the open field beyond, was mostly taken up by a one-storey brick structure, its tiled roof beginning to sag, that had doubtless once been a set of stables and was now full of junk, crates of empties and various paraphernalia. As I turned to cross the yard and go round the side of the pub, I had that curious sense that someone was watching me, the same that I had had on the morning of that farce about the Labrador puppies. Yes, there he was, standing in the field on the other side of the fence, at the exact point where the stable-building ended. It was the same lurking creature I had glimpsed on my first visit, and he was peering at me in exactly the same way, squinting way from under the brim of that old mackintosh hat. He was not exactly hidden, just well shielded. Anyone looking from the further end of the stable would not have seen him at all, because he was back behind the line of its wall. His chest was against the top rail of the fence. He seemed to be one of those animals that have a rooted objection to getting into a clear space where they will offer a good target. He hugged the wall for its reassuring solidity as a cat does in a farmyard.

I kept quite still, looked at him, and said nothing. At first I thought he would be content to stand there and look at me all night, in perfect silence. But suddenly he startled me with a rasping, wheezing laugh.

'What's funny?' I said. I felt the same impulse to challenge him, to provoke some reply, as one might with a ghost if one were trying to control one's rising panic.

'He got his dander up, Mr Tom done.' He jerked his head towards the gate of the yard. 'You done that.'

'I don't know about his dander, but he certainly behaved like a –'

'He've got a terrible dander, Mr Tom have. But I never takes no notice. His blood's too 'ot, see? 'Ot blood, he 'ave. I never makes no matter of it.'

'You work with him, do you?'

At the direct question, simple and obvious though it was, he ducked his head so that the hat-brim came down over his eyes. And he said nothing.

'Has Miss Heather got hot blood?' I threw the question at him suddenly, to see if it would startle him into any kind of statement.

He stood motionless, and looked at me for a long time while the dusk gathered about him as if it were his shapeless figure, in its nondescript clothes, that was exuding it.

'I seen 'em,' he said at last. 'I was lookin' to me traps.'

I waited. He leaned forward slightly from the hips, and said, as if this were the most important thing to communicate, 'I traps all kinds.'

'Yes?' I said.

'I traps anythin' as moves. 'Ceptin' snakes. I doesn't trap 'em cuz it don't hold 'em. Thass all right. Nobody wants snakes.' He pronounced the verb in the Oxfordshire way, 'waunts'. 'You waunts snakes?'

'No. Not trapped ones anyway.'

'There you are then. Everythink else I traps. Rabbits, 'ares, squirrels. I even gets 'edgehogs. But moles is the best. Thass what I goes for most, moles. Them's the best.'

'A good price for moleskin,' I said to keep him going. Not that I cared about his blasted traps. But I thought if I let him go on I might learn something one way or another. It was clear enough that he worked at Jasmine Farm. Perhaps he was the entire hired labour force. He must know things I didn't.

He suddenly broke into a wide grin of pleasure, revealing several broken teeth. 'Moles,' he said. 'Them's the best.'

'Ah,' I said.

'When you moves your 'and acrost 'em. The little soft fur. It don't have no right way nor wrong way. It don't have no way that it waunts to go be its nature. When you moves your 'and, *it* moves the way your 'and moves.' He mimed, in the air, the action of stroking back and forth. 'It don't 'ave no way of its own. It agrees with your 'and.'

By this time I had got him typed as a mental defective, probably a deviant who derived sexual pleasure from stroking the pelts of dead animals. How such an unfortunate could make himself useful on a farm I could not see, but after all he was sturdily built and quite young – less than ten years older than I, at a guess, though his broken teeth and overall degeneracy put years on his appearance. Bands of spittle had formed at the corners of his mouth as he talked about the amenability of moles' fur; I had, probably, been right about the sexual excitement. If this was the kind of company Heather had around the farm, no wonder she was willing to accept social engagements.

'I was lookin' to me traps,' he said suddenly. 'It worn't no more 'n five o'clock. I gets to 'em at first light. You can lose 'em if you doesn't get to 'em when light comes up. Crows has 'em. They pecks 'em,' he said with relish, 'all to rags.'

'Ah.'

'But thass no good to Phil. The creeters in them traps is for Phil, not for the crows.'

Phil?

'I gets out at first light an' I keeps the crows off of 'em. So I was down by the corner of the 'edge and I see 'em.'

'You see who? Saw who?'

'I see 'em,' he said softly. The bands of spittle were thicker now. 'They stops the car.'

'*Who* did?'

'Stops the car, they does, and sits there a bit. I steps back into the 'edge where it's thick. Waitin', see.'

'What for?'

'See if they gets out of the car.'

He seemed to regard his story as finished. I waited, then said, 'And did they?'

'On the way 'ome they was. The missis sittin' up for 'er an' all. She never went to bed till her daughter come 'ome.' He wheezed gently with what seemed to be laughter. 'She should'a been with Phil, down in the 'edge. Seen what Phil see.'

'Well,' I said, longing to beat his evil brains out, 'what did you see?'

I knew this was what he wanted – to draw me into questioning him so that he could enjoy his power, and feel the relish of torturing me. But though I saw clearly enough that I was playing his game, I couldn't help it. If she was on her way home, with a chap in a car, at first light, that must have been the accursed Hunt Ball. The man with her would have been the accursed Richard. It was a chance to *know*, at last, whether he was a contender.

The horrible spectre in front of me preserved its silence, so I said, forcing myself to adopt a lighter tone, 'Sounds as if you saw something interesting. What was it, if I'm not being too inquisitive?'

Standing there in the cold dusk, he tilted the hat-brim up to look at me, then bent his head forward to bring it down over his eyes. 'I see what I see,' he said softly. 'I don't know as I got no call to tell you what 'twas.'

'All right,' I said, my frail patience snapping. 'Keep it to yourself.'

'I was there. Seein' after me traps.'

'You were there, and you saw Miss Heather, with somebody in a car, and they were on their way home, and they stopped, and her mother was waiting up for her, and you start telling me about it and then you suddenly stop.'

'Ass right,' he said contentedly.

'Well, if you were going to stop half-way why did you start on the story at all?'

' 'T en't no story. 'S the truth.'

'*What* is, for God's sake?' I was almost shouting now.

He shot me another crafty look and said, 'You very keen to know, mister. Asking I a main lot o' questions.'

'Only because you started –'

'I don't see no reason for you to come pokin' round 'ere askin' a lot o' questions of I.'

'Oh, forget it,' I said. 'I'm going.'

I was turning on my heel when he suddenly spoke again, more loudly, as if to arrest me.

'If you doesn't believe me you oughter been here and seen what I seen.'

I turned and faced him, certain now that his motive was to torment me, though why he should have such a motive I had no idea. All I knew was that I must bring this grisly scene, shaded by evening and brooded over by rain-clouds, to an abrupt end if I valued my sanity.

'Look, Phil or whatever your name is,' I said.

'Urr. Phil. Ass my name, Phil.'

'Right, well, get this, Phil. I don't care a fuck what you saw or didn't see when you were looking after your traps and hanging about the corner of the hedge. Is that clear?'

'Aaaaargh. A fuck.' And he burst into a loud bellow of laughter.

That sudden yell of mockery brought home to me, as his words had not yet done, the truth that the situation was one I could not cope with. All I could do was escape from it, as fast as possible. This creature calling itself Phil was not a human being but a fiend, despatched from some festering pit of hell to persecute me, to cause me terror and anxiety, to unseat my reason.

As I walked away across the yard, with my back resolutely turned to the shadowy figure of nightmare standing there on the other side of the fence, I half expected to hear the cracking of wood as the zombie moved blindly forward, pursuing me, splintering its way through the fence, reaching out to seize me in a superhumanly tight grip and hold me while another flood of sick suggestion was poured into my ears. Rounding the corner of the building, I had to restrain myself from breaking into a run. And as I grabbed my bike, clicked on the rear light and pedalled away with no front one, I relied on that single, staring red eye, glowing out behind me, as the men of the Middle Ages hoped that the grimacing gargoyle-faces they carved on their churches would scare off the swarming devils who issued from Satan's kingdom.

Physical realities – fatigue, drizzle, the need to dismount for a moment whenever a car came towards me on the narrow road – drove away these fancies before I had gone a mile. But nothing very cheerful came in their place, and I was glad to get back at last, after an unimaginably weary ride, to the Bargeman's and climb to the sanctuary of my bedroom. I heard my mother call to me as I went upstairs.

'I'm going to bed, Mum, sorry,' I called without ceasing to mount the stairs. 'A bit tired.'

'I've kept something warm for you,' she called protestingly.

'I'm sorry,' I said and shut the door behind me.

Chapter 17

When I woke up the next morning, in my narrow little bed in my narrow little room at the Bargeman's, I was aware, even before coming to full consciousness, of being in pain. It was not a physical pain, and yet it was so sharp, so concrete, so localized, that it might just as well have been. But as a phenomenon it was mental. As I opened my eyes and looked at the familiar contours of the room, the reproductions on the walls, the books on the shelves, the clear summer light that peered in round the edges of the blue curtains, I heard a voice inside my head say severely and distinctly, 'This is jealousy. You fool, you are jealous.'

'Why is that foolish?' I said. I spoke the words aloud; it seemed to make them more real. 'Why isn't it perfectly natural that I should be jealous? Rational, even.'

'Jealousy over another person's sexual choices,' the voice said coldly, 'is always foolish.'

'Look,' I said, 'I want that girl, she has come to me, she has come to my bed and I have fucked her, I have also fucked her on the bank of the Thames a little downstream of Eynsham lock, and I consider that makes her mine, at least until I get notice to the contrary. But last night, as you damned well know, I got strong hints that someone else is getting inside her little –'

'Are you all right, Peter?' said my mother's voice through the door.

I was silent for a moment, trying to collect myself, and she said again, this time rapping gently on the door panel, 'Peter, are you awake?'

'No,' I said. 'I'm asleep.'

At that she opened the door and stood looking at me from the threshold, with a worried expression. I realized it must have shaken her when I refused food the night before.

'You're sitting up,' she said. 'You look awake to me.'

'I've just woken up, Mum,' I said, recovering my natural cunning. 'I was having a dream and it must have been a disturbing one because I sat up before I –'

'Oh,' she said. 'Well, I'm glad I've got you home where I can look after you for a bit. You seem like a bag of nerves to me. I suppose you've been working too hard at all that studying. I sometimes wonder what's the point of it all, to tell you the truth. Filling your head with all that stuff from days gone by.'

She moved away and I lay back, willing to let study take the blame though I knew it was not study's fault. But once I was left alone the twisting jealousy-pain, exactly like a blade turning in my vitals, started up anew.

Desperately, feebly, I tried to soothe it with the utterly unconvincing hypothesis that it was only I who had made it and not Richard, that he was a mere casual acquaintance, that she loved me and it was natural for her to show it in that way, whereas... I couldn't even be bothered to formulate it to the end. It was such obvious rubbish. The testimony of Tom's 'You know about that, do you?' and Phil's drooling 'Aaaaargh – a fuck,' converging as they did on the same point from two such totally different launching sites, was rock-solid; and besides... besides.. I struggled to formulate what was in my mind, and after a moment succeeded in focusing it. Little experienced sexually as I was, Heather had not seemed to me, at our first encounter on that moonlit bed, to make love as a virgin would. Without taking it in any way too lightly or casually, she had not seemed to be as deeply stirred up as a girl would naturally be the first time out. At the time, I had put this down to the matter-of-factness of a farmer's daughter who was always around animals, but in retrospect I was less confident of this interpretation. Heather was not, of course, and never would be, a girl like Vinnie whose legs automatically went round the nearest personable male when she happened to have nothing better to do, but there was a wide area between being like that and being virginal, and Heather was somewhere within that area. But *where*? And above all, what about this bugger Richard?

I was still turning these questions over in my mind as I cycled out to Stanton Harcourt and down the field path to the river. I got to the boathouse a little before Heather and sat leaning against its unpainted blank wall, enjoying the sunshine; at least, I would have been enjoying it but for the turmoil inside me. Then I saw Heather coming, bending forward over the handlebars as she pedalled her bike – no, Tom's – vigorously along the towpath. Hurrying. Hurrying towards me. She was in her working outfit, the old corduroy trousers and the man's short-sleeve shirt, as if as soon as she had finished her jobs about the farm she had simply splashed her face with cold water to get rid of the sweat, run a comb through her hair, and come straight out of the house instead of taking the time to change her clothes and primp herself up. The sunlight caught the gold in her hair and made it shine out. My heart should have leapt up at the sight of her beauty. But it didn't; it was leaden with jealousy.

'Sorry if I'm a bit late,' she said as she braked to a standstill. She dismounted and gave me a kiss, then leaned the bike against the wall next to mine and fastened the two of them together with a bit of chain and a padlock. 'Now,' she said, businesslike, 'I'm free for a couple of hours. D'you want to take the boat out?'

I hesitated. 'Can't quite think,' I said. 'What would be the best use of two hours?'

Heather laughed. 'You're pretty transparent, aren't you?' she said, her eyes bright with the amusement of a shared joke. 'If I could make a guess at what you're thinking, you're wondering whether putting the boat actually on the water will stop us from using it for what we used it for last time. Well, you can set your mind at rest. If the mood takes us,' and she gave me a mock-demure look from under the lashes, 'there are plenty of places where trees come down over the water.'

'Yes,' I said. 'And I bet you know all of them.'

I hadn't meant to say that. The words just jumped out of their own accord, propelled by the pain and bitterness inside me. As I emitted them they didn't feel like words at all – more like a sudden stream of boiling urine. The sort of stream a horse would shoot out if it were hit by a train at a level-crossing. A death-stream.

Heather stood very still looking at me composedly and holding my eyes. 'I suppose you don't mind telling me what you meant by that remark?'

'I'm sorry,' I said, feeling weak and indecisive after that mad lash-out. 'I shouldn't have put it that way.'

'Shouldn't have put *what*?'

'Look, forget it, please,' I said. 'I was just feeling a bit tense and –'

'Forget it?' Heather's voice was cold and she stood there with her back very straight. 'You call me a whore and then you tell me to forget it? What were you doing, just making conversation?'

'Oh, come on,' I said. 'I didn't call you a whore or anything like it.'

'That's exactly what you did. You called me something just like a whore. You called me the kind of girl who when she goes out in a punt with a man knows where all the sheltered spots are where they can get up to things. Well, if that's what you think of me, get lost. Go back to your College and make love to a bookshelf.'

'Now look, Heather,' I said, seriously frightened, 'I said a very silly thing just now and I'm determined to make you believe I'm really sorry for it.'

'Being sorry doesn't alter anything. You wouldn't have said a thing like that if you didn't feel it, somewhere inside yourself.' She turned to unlock her bicycle. 'I'm going.'

'For Christ's sake,' I said.

Heather bent down and clicked open the padlock, then straightened up. Facing away from me, she said, 'I came here to meet you because I thought we were going to enjoy this lovely afternoon and give each other a bit of happiness. And the first thing you do when I get here is tell me you think I'm the kind of girl who spends her time unbuttoning men's trousers in punts. *I hate you.*' As she said the last three words she turned to face me and I saw that her eyes were brimming.

'I don't blame you,' I said. 'I hate myself. I'd hate anyone who could say anything so mean and cruel, especially to someone as sweet and good and loving as you are. I swear to God if you go back home now I'll kill myself.'

'I can't help that. I just can't stay here with you, it's impossible. I don't know what horrible thing you'll say next.' She sniffed, blinked back her tears, and said, 'Damn, I haven't got a handkerchief.'

'Have mine,' I said, holding it out. 'Go on, it won't contaminate you.'

'I don't want to touch anything of yours. I'm going to finish with you.'

'No, you're not, *Heather*. You're going to listen to me for just a little while. You've just told me you've got two hours to spare, well, give me just two minutes and let me try to explain. I said that stupid, bad, wrong thing because I was in a state. Can't I at least tell you what kind of state it was?'

She stood there holding her bike, ready to move off, but she didn't get on it, so I continued.

'I love you, Heather,' I said. 'And when you love somebody, it makes you very vulnerable.'

'So you go after them with a knife,' she said. 'Funny. The way I'd always heard it, when you love somebody you try to be *nice* to them.'

'Oh, I want to be nice to you. I want to be really, really nice to you absolutely all the time. It's my present ambition; it's the one thing I truly want to do all my life.'

'Looks like it, doesn't it, when you start calling me –'

'Look, Heather, for Christ's sake, I'm *jealous*.'

The word silenced her. It seemed to come as a real surprise. She opened her eyes wide, paused, and said, 'Say that again, will you? You're what?'

'I'm jealous,' I said. 'I know it's sick, and mad, and unbalanced, but that's what I am.'

'But who *of*?'

'Richard,' I said flatly.

'Richard who?'

'I don't know his other name,' I said. 'The chap who took you to the Hunt Ball.'

'But why on earth him?'

'He's the only man in your life I know about,' I said. 'I'd be jealous of anyone who took you out, but he's the only one I know about.'

'But *what* d'you know about him? You've never met him, have you?'

'No,' I said. 'I wouldn't know it was him if he passed me in the street. I don't know anything about him. I just know his name's Richard and that he took you to the Hunt Ball.'

Heather leaned her bike back against the wall, came to me and put her hands on my shoulders. 'Poor old Peter, you *are* in a state, aren't you?'

'Yes,' I said.

'But, however much of a state you're in, you must still be able to reckon time. You must still know that May comes before June and June comes before July and that kind of thing.'

'So?'

'So you must know that my going to the Hunt Ball with Richard happened before our... thing started up.'

'That's true,' I said.

'You surely don't think I'm seeing anyone else at the same time as you? Seeing them in that kind of way, I mean?'

'Look, I know it's irrational,' I said. 'It just hurts to think of anybody getting close to you.'

'Getting *close* to me? What's that supposed to mean? After all, damn it, if he's going to dance with me he's bound to put his arm –'

Suddenly, and I swear it happened without volition and completely to my surprise, I heard my voice saying, 'Phil saw him taking you home.'

There was a deep pool of silence that seemed to spread out around us and into this pool Heather said, very quietly and very precisely, 'Just say that again, will you?'

I've ruined everything, I thought. I've blown it all away like a puff of smoke. Not knowing how it was that the words I had just uttered had even formed themselves in my mind, let alone issued from my mouth, I croaked miserably, 'I met Phil last night.'

'And had a nice cosy talk with him, I'm sure.'

'Heather, don't be like that. I couldn't bear him. He made me want to vomit. There's a kind of – oh, I don't know – spiritual stink that comes off him.'

'You seem to take a certain amount of notice of what he says about me, whatever you thought of him.'

'I *don't*. I wasn't even *talking* to him, in any ordinary sense. He just, well, suddenly materialized in front of me. Drooling something about his traps, and mole fur and stuff. A person like that seems to infect the surrounding air. He puts poison into it.'

'And you took in this poison of his and now you're sicking it up all over me. Well, thanks. Now I really am going home.'

'Heather, *please*. I'm just trying to explain why I'm in a sick state.'

'Yes. You've been bitten by a poisonous animal, Phil. Well, don't come whining to me. Go to a hospital.'

'Look,' I almost shouted. 'Before I could stop him, Phil poured out a lot of sick rubbish into my ears about being in the lane, hiding in a deep hedge, about dawn, and seeing you and this Richard bloke in his car parked by the hedge.'

'And you believed him, of course.'

'It isn't a question of believing or not believing. It's just that it makes me –'

'Yes, it is. That's exactly what it is a question of. You come lurking round here on a day when I haven't invited you and you run into Tom and put his back up –'

'Oh, you know about that, do you?'

'Yes, I know about that, and then you hang about some more and Phil spots you and sees a chance to enjoy himself. You're right that Phil's sick, anyone can tell that a mile off, it doesn't need a clever-clever genius like you, and one of the ways he's sick is in his sexual thoughts. I suppose you've never stopped to think what it's been like for me, having to grow up with him around. He's worked for us since I was about twelve, which means he came on the scene just as I was beginning to change from a child to a woman. My behind was getting rounder and my breasts were starting to grow. And my God, didn't he make me conscious of it all, and in the worst way, the very worst way.'

'I'm terribly sorry. I ought to have thought –'

'One day when I was about fourteen he exposed himself to me. I came round the corner of the stables and there he was, waiting for me, with this big dark red thing in his hand. For a second or two I couldn't think what it was. I mean, growing up with animals and everything, I knew perfectly well what male creatures had, but I suppose the whole situation took me by surprise – my first thought was that he was offering me a stick of rhubarb or something, till I saw it was coming out of his trousers. And of course, being an innocent girl and not thinking about these things very much, I hadn't realized that when a human male gets an erection it stands up in the air, whereas four-footed animals let it down towards the ground.'

'How shattering for you. I'm terribly –'

'No, shattering it wasn't. If I'm to be honest, it didn't affect me much at all. Phil's such a sub-human creature anyway, I won't call him an animal because he's not nice enough to be an animal and it's a slander on them to call him one, but he's sub-human. I didn't think to myself afterwards, I've seen a man's prick and that's what they're like. I just thought, Phil had to go and wag that thing about in front of me, what a dreg he is. It wasn't any more to me than seeing a donkey let it down.'

'Did he do it again? Did he make a habit of it?'

'He would have done, I'm sure, but the next time he did it, a few days later, Tom came round the corner and saw him at it. Tom was about, oh, fifteen then, and big and strong already. Phil was a bit older but he was no match. Tom beat him pretty well senseless. I thought he was going to kill him. I ran away, and as I ran I could hear Tom's fists pounding into Phil's body. It upset me more than having to look at his thing.'

During this recital of the tale of Phil, some of Heather's anger had died away as her mind busied itself with reminiscence rather than with her indignation at me. But now she snapped back into the present moment.

'So there it is. Phil's been afraid to expose himself to me ever since that time, but he still gets his kicks out of having dirty fantasies about me, and of course fantasies like that are more fun if you can find someone to tell them to, someone who'll believe them. Well, he's waited a long time but at last you've come along. You're the answer to Phil's prayer. He can make up anything about me and you'll believe him, won't you? He probably told you he'd seen me doing it with animals.'

'Now, Heather, for God's sake listen to me.' I made a real effort to pull myself together because I knew it was now or never. 'I'm quite sure you're not interested in what loathsome Phil said about you, but for what it's worth I'll just mention that it was nothing specific. He didn't actually say he'd *seen* you do anything. He just said he saw you and this bloke in the car and then he grinned evilly and dribbled. There wasn't anything to believe or disbelieve. What he did was *upset* me.' I was talking faster and faster in an effort to head her off from interrupting me.

'That's not how I'd put it. If he'd really upset you you'd feel sorry for me, having to live where I have to set eyes on him every day. Instead of that, one hint from him and you immediately get as bad as he is. "*I* bet you know all the places to make love in a punt" – that's just the sort of thing Phil'd say.'

'No, it isn't. He couldn't string enough words together to come out with a sentence like that. His mental processes are those of an idiot.'

'So are yours. You're obviously not normal on the subject of me and men.'

'Guilty,' I said. 'I've already admitted that. But being unbalanced about you doesn't make me into Phil. He has sexual fantasies about you because he's sick and twisted in his mind. I just have terribly strong desires towards you because I've got the sense to see how beautiful you are, and how wonderful, and how totally unique and Heatherish and precious, and I love you and that's a kind of madness in itself.'

When I had finished saying this, we stood quite still and looked at one another, and after a moment the rigid lines of Heather's body relaxed, and in the same instant her face broke into a grin and she said, 'You're a chump.'

'Yes,' I said. 'And with good reason.'

'Shall I decide to like you after all?' she said in a considering voice.

'Well,' I said, 'you couldn't like anybody who'd appreciate it more.'

She gave a delicious laugh and said, 'Let's go punting.'

So we opened the boathouse doors and slid the punt out and into the water, and I poled it upstream while Heather lolled in classic fashion on the cushions, and she did indeed know a place where the thick-leaved branches curved down till they almost touched the water and we were in a green, translucent canopy with the boat tied firmly to a gnarled root that projected from the clay bank. And there, everything happened that should happen. Heather's long, elegant thighs emerged from her old corduroy trousers and she settled back wearing only her shirt, and then I unbuttoned the shirt.

Afterwards, her trousers back on, lying peacefully and looking up through the clustered leaves, Heather said, 'No wonder you were in a tizzy earlier on. I mean, if you had all that thrashing around inside you.'

'Yes,' I said. 'It's pretty hard to keep things in perspective sometimes.'

'Well,' she said, 'would it make you feel happier if I said that from now on I don't think you'll need to worry?'

We kissed, and the punt swayed gently beneath us, a foot or two away a water-vole plopped peacefully into the water, and at that moment I was very happy. And yet I knew, lying there with my lovely girl beside me, and the languor of having made love spreading gently through my body and mind, that there were unanswered questions still hovering in the air above us; that I was no nearer to understanding what really motivated Heather when it came to the choice of a man. But I knew that the questions would just have to wait.

My relationship with Heather was in fact settling down to a pattern, and it was a pattern I was beginning to recognize. Each visit I made to her had four stages: the anticipation, a matter of intense mixed emotions; the meeting, with its first delighted shock of realizing about her beauty and femininity; the bliss of sexual release; then the tranquil afterglow. It was this afterglow that always seemed to fade into a stale twilight of depression and insecurity in which the questions and anxieties surfaced over again.

On that particular afternoon, Dad was just opening the bar when I got home, and I treated myself to a pint of beer and sat in a corner like a customer. Trundle and the others drifted in one by one and started some meaningless discussion in which they all said the same thing over and over again, but I didn't bother to listen. I was thinking.

I looked round the familiar bar: the dark wood, the linoleum floor, the open grate (empty and swept out now, on this warm summer evening), the scrubbed wooden tables, the bottles on their shelves behind the bar, the little door where my parents went in and out, hundreds of times a week, like ants threading the passages of their constricted labyrinth. This place was my home, I had been brought up here; its values of sociability, attention to the details of small business, and regular hard work were bred into my bones and made me the person I was. If I spent the rest of my life with princes and maharajahs and millionaires, with ambassadors and tycoons and pontiffs, I would always be the son of the couple who kept the Bargeman's Arms in South Oxford. And Heather knew nothing of this. She had never asked me where I lived when I was not in College, nor anything about my parents, nor even whether I had any brothers and sisters. She seemed to be content to have me appear in her life, perform certain functions (companionship, sex, Making a Change) and then dematerialize again till the next time. I wondered if she would have consented to stable a horse for someone she knew as little about as she knew about me.

I gave up. It was time to go and eat my high tea. My mother was pleased that I came to the table punctually and seemed to have a good appetite. She said she had been worried about me lately.

*

The following Sunday, when we were all having our ritual family dinner at about half-past-two, chewing away contentedly and drinking bottled light ale, Brian suddenly threw a grenade into the somnolent calm of the Sabbath. Pushing back his chair a little as a signal that he had a statement to make – and I can still hear its little squeak on the tiled floor of our quiet kitchen – he looked at our mother, sitting opposite him, and our father at the head of the table, and said, in a rather challenging tone, 'Another Sunday dinner at home. Wonder how many we've had.'

'Hundreds,' said Dad placidly. 'Nice, I reckon. Sort of a fixed point in the week. Give us a chance to catch up with a bit of family life.'

'I wouldn't have said,' Brian went on in the same tone, 'that family life was something we were short on, would you?'

'Well, I don't know about that. I don't know about that. What with Peter going away to College, and you being out all hours and never quite knowing when you're –'

'Yes, yes, we know all that. But there's always good old Sunday and we're always here and we always eat together.'

'Is there something wrong with that, Brian?' Mother asked.

'Look out of the window,' said Brian.

'Don't tell me to look out of the window when I've just asked you a question. I said is there something wrong with us having Sunday dinner together every week as a family. A lot of families'd be glad –'

'Look, Mum, I wasn't trying to be rude or interrupt you or anything. Asking you to look out of the window *was* the answer. Look out and what d'you see?'

'What should I see? It's a nice day, the sun's shining, those geraniums I potted out are doing well although your father told me it wasn't a suitable place for them and they'd never do any good there.'

'Don't let's have all *that* again,' said our father. 'I'm ready to carve if anybody wants a bit more beef.'

'Yes, please,' I said.

'The sun's shining,' Brian said. 'It's a lovely day in July. We've got a car standing out in the yard.'

'Why don't you tell us something we don't know?' said our father, whacking down a slice of beef on to my plate in a manner that bordered on the irritable.

'I'll tell you something you don't *seem* to know,' Brian said, leaning forward. 'It's a damn sight too long since you and Mum had a holiday.'

'A holiday? Don't be daft, lad. You don't have holidays in our business.'

'Yes, but to let year after year go by and never take a break –'

'In case you hadn't noticed,' Dad said heavily, 'licensed premises open twice in every twenty-four hours. And seeing as we're in England and not Wales, they open seven days a week. So where's the holiday going to come from?'

'Get help in while you're away, of course.'

'Oh, you mean like a doctor? With whatever it is they calls it, a locust?'

'Locum,' I said, but nobody took any notice.

'Something else you may not have slowed down long enough to notice, Brian,' Dad went on, 'is that doctors earn a lot more money than public house licensees in a small way of trade.'

'Look, Dad, don't get steamed up. I was just –'

'I'll get steamed up if I think fit. Lectured at my own table!'

'It's all right, Jack,' my mother said.

'Just listen to me, that's all, just listen and keep calm,' Brian almost shouted. 'I see the pair of you working day after day, week after week, never getting a chance to go anywhere and see anything different. I'm not talking about taking off for a fortnight, or even a week. I never remember you leaving this place even for a *day*.'

It was true, I reflected silently. I never remembered any such thing either. But it had never struck me as odd, let alone a matter for indignation as it now seemed to be striking Brian. That was because I had always seen my parents not as human beings but simply as part of the fittings of the pub. There was the bar and there was my father behind the bar. There was the kitchen and there was my mother in the kitchen. There was the cellar and there was my father bumping about mysteriously in the cellar.

'I work as hard as hell,' Brian was saying, 'but at least I get Sundays off.'

'I'm glad you do,' said Dad reasonably. 'It's nice to see something of you.'

'Yes, but what I'm trying to say is, if you could once get a day off, we could do something all together one Sunday. Take the car and drive somewhere.'

'Well, we can't get a day off so there's no point –'

'Do you remember,' Brian broke in excitedly, 'that first Bullnose we had? When I first got the job at Cowley? And Mr Prothero bringing it over?'

'Course I do, we all went up to Cumnor.'

'Well, I remember something you said to Mum and I remember what she answered. I do, I remember the actual words. You said, "This'll make nothing of going to the seaside. Just chuck everything in and off we go." And Mum didn't say, "We can't go, we never get the time." She just came up with something about the reliability of the car. "As long as it doesn't break down," she said, or something like that. Well, what's changed?'

'Nothing's changed,' Dad said. 'I just can't have been thinking what I was saying on that evening. There was a lot happening all at once and I just wasn't stopping to think very carefully, that's all it was.'

'I don't believe that's all it was,' Brian said. 'You know what I think? I think that at that moment you saw a door opening in your life and later on, when the excitement wore off and you went back to your ordinary habits, you found you just hadn't got the nerve to walk through that door and you let it gradually creep shut.'

'Don't be daft, lad. Finish your dinner and talk about something else. You're just being daft now. I find the car very useful and I'm glad we got one when we did, but all this talk about door opening...'

He trailed off into grumbling silence and I stole a glance at my mother to see if she was showing any sign of how all this was affecting her. She was looking very attentively at Dad's face and I thought I saw, for a moment, an expression in her eyes that I could almost call yearning. But it faded as quickly as a light being switched off, and her face resumed the watchful calm that was its habitual mask.

'We could be down on the coast today,' said Brian, returning unexpectedly to the attack. 'We could be on a beach now, this minute. Tell me this, how long is it since you saw the sea?'

Dad laid down his knife and fork, put his hands on his knees, and turned full-face to Brian, which I knew was the sign that he was ready for an all-out shouting match. But before he could begin, Brian had nimbly continued.

'So I've been thinking it over and I want to make an offer. It's Mum's birthday on July the 18th. That's a Saturday, so next day, Sunday, I'll take you out for the day. We'll drive somewhere nice. And don't say what about the pub, because we'll pay somebody to come in and serve and keep everything ticking over while you're away.'

'Pay? *Pay*? Where d'you think at a time like this I'm going to get the –'

'Sorry,' Brian grinned. 'That was a, what d'you call it, slip of the tongue. I haven't got the gift of the gab like Young Hopeful here, and sometimes the wrong words come out. I didn't mean *we*'ll pay somebody, I meant *I*'ll pay somebody. It'll be my present to Mum.'

'Well, I'll see. I'll have to think about it.'

'No, Dad, you won't see,' said Brian calmly. 'You'll say yes, now, and you'll do it for Mum's sake. You won't stop her from having a nice day out as a birthday present.'

'Look, lad, *I* won't stop her, but it might be difficult –'

'If there are any difficulties we'll overcome them. We'll do what we do at M.G. when things seem to be going wrong. Find out where the trouble is, hit it hard, and keep on hitting it. You're talking to a man that works with Cecil Kimber.'

He breathed the name with reverence.

'Well,' Dad conceded, 'I suppose it must be having that approach to difficulties that's put Billy Morris where he is.'

'Billy *Morris*? He's never had a difficulty to face in his life. He's been riding the crest of a wave, building cheaper and cheaper cars at a time when the industry would have expanded whether he was in it or not. It's in racing that you meet the really tough....'

They went off into an enjoyable wrangle, which at least averted the danger of a quarrel. Looking back, I believe now that our father introduced the name of Billy Morris for precisely that reason. He wanted to avoid losing face by agreeing too quickly to Brian's daringly radical suggestion, but he had to find a way of getting off the subject without simply invoking parental authority and shutting him up. He was a much wiser man than I took him for, and now that it is too late to tell him so I realize it and reproach myself for my shallowness, but that is unjust too because it was the shallowness of youth and I meant no harm.

*

We had a July heat-wave that year; it went on, as I remember, for most of the month. Because the earth of Oxfordshire is so heavily saturated, to the point of being waterlogged, for seven months of every year, the first effect of summer heat is to draw a lot of moisture out of it, and a thin white mist hung about the thick vegetation in the morning and evening. But by about ten o'clock it had burnt away, the light was very bright and sharp, the sky was dark blue, and the colours were incredible. I used often to take a book and go and sit and read in the garden at Episcopus, and it used to seem to me that the beauty that surrounded me, as I sat there on a wooden bench with some staid historical tome open on my knee, was almost unbearable; I *needed* the staidness, the stodge, of some good solid collection of constitutional documents, with plenty of footnotes and appendices, to anchor my mind and calm my emotions.

Not all of Episcopus was beautiful, of course. The fifteenth-century quad, where I lived, was a plain, rather forbidding structure, originally built as a barracks for housing as many young monks as possible as economically as possible, so that they could get the intellectual benefit of Oxford and be sent where they could do some good for their Order; and the Victorian bit was just Victorian. But the seventeenth-century part, which overlooks the garden and which I saw, on those long golden mornings, every time I raised my eyes, had what every beautiful garden needs to set it off – style, and harmony, and a grace like that of baroque music, and yet, a touch of ironic self-mockery, as if the culture had reached a pitch of ripeness at which it could afford not to take itself with deadly seriousness: the same self-parodying excess that one sees in the clothes of Charles I's court, or some of the stage sets of the time. Sir Herbert Grierson's *Metaphysical Poems and Lyrics of the Seventeenth Century* was a standard book at that time, and sometimes during that summer I would sit reading it in the garden, looking up from time to time at that building, and I could quite see why the poetry of that epoch had to go all the way from the intensely conscious plainness of Herbert to the wild, almost surreal nimiety of Crashaw.

I owed the repose of mind that set me free for general reflections like this to the fact that sexual satisfaction was coming my way regularly, for we usually managed an afternoon at Riverside Villa at least three times a week. I might as well face it, I owe my education partly to Oxford University and partly to Riverside Villa. All the good teaching, the famous libraries, the beautiful surroundings in the world would have gone for nothing if Heather had not been willing to part with her knickers on a regular basis. I would simply have pulled up stakes and gone. It was one thing to house me in a fifteenth-century monk's cell, but the fact remained that I was not a monk and no power on earth could transform me into one.

I sometimes wonder, looking back, whether I was more highly sexed than my contemporaries, most of whom seemed no better catered for than I had been during my first year. But I simply haven't the information to come up with an answer to that. The nature of the problem, and the nature of the solution, must have varied so much from case to case. Of the undergraduates at Episcopus in my time, the ones I saw every day, some had girl-friends; a few were homosexual, which of course the Public School/Oxbridge tradition saw as far less of a threat than anything involving women; others may have been able to get something going in the vacation at home; and a good many were just plain late developers, whose sexual needs would not become strong until they were into their twenties. Or, perhaps more accurately, they would not *know* that their needs were strong until then.

'What's going to happen in the winter?' I asked Heather once, as we lay clasped together in the immobile punt in its shadowy hut. 'I mean, there's no heating in this place.'

'Oh, no, it won't do in the winter,' she agreed cheerfully. 'I'll come to your rooms in College once you go back in the autumn.'

'Will you be able to manage that?'

'I'll get the car sometimes. And I'll bike sometimes. And I'll take the bus sometimes. I'll keep coming, don't worry. But it's true I shan't be able to manage it as often as I do just now, with you doing the travelling and me only having to take the, well, essential time away from work.'

'*How* often? Make a guess.'

'No. I refuse to. I'm just going to take each week as it comes. Anyway, greedy thing,' she kissed me, 'you won't need so much in the cold weather.'

That was typical of her approach. The young of the human species, like the young of any other, needed to couple up less often in the winter, when their hormones were less active and they had to expend more energy on keeping warm. A couple of times a week was good enough when the snow was on the ground. When the sun shone warmly and the air was soft on one's skin, it had to be more, much more. She spent a lot of time looking after animals, and she looked after me as if I were one more animal, and, after all, what else was I?

And she was an animal too, a beautiful, strong, healthy animal, honest about her needs and proud of her perfections. That, in the end – and the thought came to me more than once, about this time – was where she differed from Vinnie. Vinnie's attitude to sexual pleasure was not animal, it was human. Human beings are corrupt, animals are innocent. Human beings are not content with simple and natural satisfactions: they devise perversions and dream up pornographic fantasies. Who can imagine an animal doing these things?

*

The next Sunday, when my mother, with a little inefficient help from me, got the dinner out of the oven and on to the table, I could feel that the atmosphere was nothing like the usual Sunday truce with life. Brian, I was sure, would return to the subject of our parents' day of liberty, and sure enough we were barely five minutes into the meal when he opened up.

'Wonderful how this fine weather keeps up,' he began with an air of innocence that deceived nobody. 'Must be lovely down on the Sussex coast. Or some of those places even nearer – you know, that bit of coastline between Southampton and say, for instance, Hayling Island.'

'How did I know you was going to start talking about that as soon as I took the weight off my feet?' Dad asked in a mock-querulous tone. I was glad about the mock part of it, somewhat uneasy about the querulous part. I hated, and always have hated, disagreeable scenes at the table. They give you ulcers.

'It's like being pestered by an insurance salesman,' Brian grinned. 'All you have to do is sign on the dotted line and he goes away.'

'Yes, and then you find you've signed something that was a mistake, and you're going to have a lot of cause to –'

'Dad! How can taking *one* day off be a mistake? Damn it, by the evening you'll be back and you can start putting it all right, whatever they've done wrong.'

'I have to be off to the brewery on Monday morning. It's your mother it'll all fall on.'

'I don't mind, Jack,' she said quickly.

'Look,' said Brian. 'Mum's birthday is on Saturday. So, say she works all Saturday. Say we just give her a card or two and a five-bob present and apart from that we let her birthday go. Just take no notice of it. All the more reason for Sunday to be a day out for her. Yes, and for you. She won't enjoy it unless you go.'

'I'd like us all to go,' Mother said. 'I'd like Peter to come too.'

Someone's mentioned me, I thought. I was beginning to think I wasn't here.

'Oh, Peter can come if he wants to,' said Brian indifferently. His tone was exactly what he would have used if we had been discussing whether to put the car's side-screens up or leave them off to enjoy the wind in our faces. Ham or cheese in your sandwiches? Shall Peter come or shall we have meat paste?

'Hold on a minute,' Dad said, 'we haven't said we're going yet.'

'Course we're going, Dad. You're not going to turn your back on a birthday trip out for Mum, in the lovely summer time, just once in a year.'

'You mean you're planning to do this *every year*?'

Brian exploded into laughter, though it was laughter that seemed to me to have an edge of anger in it. 'Oh, Christ,' he said, wiping his eyes. 'Oh, Christ. We shall have to watch out, shan't we? Otherwise in the next thirty years we'll be going out for a trip *thirty times*! Hold on to your chair! The world's tipping over sideways!'

'All right, Brian,' said Dad with dignity. 'You've grown your wings in the last few years and you've soared a long way, you're mixing with all this smart motor-racing crowd, the Honourable This and the Honourable That, and driving around in these foreign countries, but we're plain stay-at-home people who do our jobs and –'

'Jail-rot, that's what you've got, Dad,' Brian hissed. 'You're just like these old convicts who've been in the nick so long that when they open the cell door and tell 'em they're free to go, they can't walk out. They wouldn't know what to do with freedom if they had it. Being in a cell's all they understand –'

'Now you listen to me, Brian, I've had enough of your –'

The inevitable quarrel developed, and it was a bad one. Voices became louder and louder, arguments dropped all pretence of logic and became mere assertion, the table was thumped. Mother and I were profoundly uncomfortable. We had, however, slightly different reasons for being uncomfortable; she because she had a natural hatred of family discord, and because, perhaps, whenever her husband seemed to be winning, and fending off the prospect of a day trip, she saw her one chance of a few hours' change and relaxation disappearing over the hill; I, for those reasons but also for another. I hated being so totally ignored, left out of account, never appealed to or consulted over any aspect of the matter. But what could I expect? In terms of the household, I was a passenger, a house-guest for part of each year, contributing no resources; in terms of the family, the junior, the kid brother, with no vote and no influence. I began to appreciate how women have been made to feel all through the centuries, and why so much silent bitterness has accumulated in their souls.

It was Brian, in the end, who won the argument. He won it because he was the younger, the fiercer, the one with the greater reserves of energy. He would keep on bringing up the subject, mining every Sunday dinner, until summer passed into autumn and thence to winter, and sometime in the following summer, by mere attrition, he would get his way, so why not now? His offer was on the table: to pay the wages of a competent person to look after the pub for the two sessions, midday till two and seven till ten, for which it would be open.

'There's not going to be that much to it,' he said. 'All they've got to do is serve the beer and take the money, and that's the easy part of running a pub. You often say that yourself. Well, you can fix it all up and whoever comes in can just –'

'Yes, but you talk as if just anybody can come in and take over for a day, anybody off the street corner. It's got to be someone with experience. I mean, look, you start pulling off beer. Right. Everything's going fine, then suddenly the beer runs out. You've got to the end of the barrel and you've got to go down in the cellar and put a new one on. It's not everybody that knows enough to do that.'

'Oh, rubbish, Dad. You're just making difficulties. Anybody can do it.'

But at this point I intervened. I had suddenly seen a chance to count for something, to be a person in my own right in what was, after all, my home.

'Dad's right, Brian,' I said. 'Changing a barrel, making sure the new one's all right, pulling off the first pint and knowing what to look for in it – they're all things that call for a bit of experience.'

Brian turned on me like a dog, engaged in fighting another dog, who suddenly finds himself attacked by a third. There was a really canine snarl in his voice, he was so irritated with me.

'You stay out of this. It's hard enough to get them to see sense without you poking your snout in.'

'Don't be unkind, Brian,' said Mother.

'Unkind doesn't come into it. He's interfering where he's got no business. I expect he's just afraid you'll go off for the day because then he won't get his cooked dinner.'

Here was my chance to show lofty moral superiority, which in any family quarrel is the heaviest club to knock your opponent down with. That's why it is so commonly used by the least scrupulous people. I was dimly aware of this moral truth, even in my green youth, but Brian had given me an opening I couldn't resist taking.

'What I was going on to say, Brian,' I said, 'and what I am still going on to say however much you insult me, is that I could solve this little problem very easily by spending the day here myself, while the rest of you take your trip, and helping out whoever you get in to run the place. I can do simple bar work, I can put on a new barrel, and I know where most things are kept.'

There was a brief silence while my offer sank in, and then a contented smile began to dawn on our father's face.

'Now that's what I call sense,' he said, looking round the table at everyone in turn. 'That'll put my mind right at rest, that will. Well, lads, you've got together to make it a good old birthday present for your Mum, and I'm sure she's pleased.'

Mother said nothing. I think at that moment she could not speak. But she gave Brian, and then me, a radiant smile in which one could see, in the faded handsomeness of her face, what she had been like as a pretty young girl.

'There's only one thing, and then I'll stop worrying,' Dad said. 'I want Mrs Warmley to come in. I'll step round and see her myself, later today. If Mrs Warmley'll do it it'll be done right.'

Mrs Warmley, it emerged, was a woman of our parents' generation and an old friend, who had had vast experience of bar work through years of on-and-off employment in numerous Oxford pubs. Bringing up a vast family had prevented her from taking a regular position, but she had 'helped out' here and there for years. She was one of nature's helpers-out, and our father had confidence in her.

With all this settled, Brian left the table without saying anything more. But later in the afternoon, I happened to be crossing the yard and he was there, tinkering as usual with some component of the family car. As I went past, he straightened up.

'Peter,' he said.

'Yes,' I said. I stopped walking, but remained very much poised to move forward.

'That idea of yours,' he said. 'Staying behind to help out while we go off.'

'What about it?'

'It's a good one,' he said. 'Good thinking there.'

He bent to his task again and I walked on. This was, I knew, the nearest he could get to making amends for his contemptuous treatment of me; and, having always had a reasonably forgiving disposition, I was content with it.

*

A couple of afternoons later I had a real surprise. I ran into Tom Burrell, not in the country around High Cogges but in the centre of Oxford. He was coming out of a big ironmonger's shop in the St Ebbe's district and as he stepped on to the pavement we almost bumped into each other. In spite of the fact that we were looking straight into each other's faces, I was quite prepared to keep up the polite fiction that we didn't know each other – after all, a shower of threats and insults hardly counts as an introduction – but he evidently wasn't. A smile appeared on his healthy face, causing me to reflect once more that his features were very like Heather's except that his eyes were narrower; or, more accurately, that having a more suspicious nature he kept them narrowed.

'Well, well,' he said. 'Mr College Boy. I've been rather hoping to run into you.'

'What on earth for?' I asked stiffly.

‘To congratulate you, that’s all, old chap,’ he said. ‘To say I’m glad for your sake that you’ve got some sense into your head.’

‘Oh,’ I said.

‘Yes. I told you to keep out of our neighbourhood and as far as I know you’ve not been seen there since. I told you to keep away from my sister and to the best of my knowledge you haven’t been sniffing around her, either, from that day to this. No more Commem. Balls, eh?’

The best of your knowledge can’t be very good then, mate, I thought with a spasm of inner laughter that nearly blasted its way out of my lungs. Fortunately, I maintained iron control and just looked at him, as impassive as a Red Indian.

‘Well, keep it up, sonny,’ he said, enjoying what he imagined was his triumph. ‘You’ve shown that you’ve got the sense to heed a plain warning when you get one and not everybody’s got that much.’ And, grinning maliciously, he strode off. The bag containing his purchases swung jauntily against the leg of his twill trousers.

‘Keep it up, farmer,’ I said gently to his receding back. ‘Enjoy thinking you’ve scored. And one of these days I’ll tell you exactly what it feels like to fuck your sister up to the neck.’

Whether because of the extra zest added by this thought I don’t know, but my next assignation with Heather out at Riverside Villa turned out to be one of the most delicious. She surprised me by appearing not in her old corduroy trousers and working shirt, but in a sweetly summery dress. I’m no good at describing women’s clothes, but it was about knee-length, was a light lyrical blue, and had a wide white open collar at the top which spread out along her shoulders and down to about four inches above her navel. The space directly over her navel was occupied by a large white bow, tying up a belt which emerged from two slits at her waist and was, at the rear, contained within the dress. The effect was all blue and white, like many of the most beautiful wild flowers of the hedgerow. It caught my eye so much that I commented on it immediately – which was, as it turned out, what I was meant to do.

‘I’m very pleased with it,’ she said. ‘I got it in a summer sale and it was only one pound.’

It seemed rather a lot to me, but she was evidently pleased to have found a bargain.

‘It means I don’t have to be terribly fussy about looking after it and making it last,’ she said. ‘I can wear it for everyday things and give my spirits a lift.’

‘Even such everyday things as messing about in the countryside with peasants like me?’ I couldn’t help asking.

'I put it on for you because I thought you'd *like* it, duffer.'

'I do like it,' I said fervently. 'You were right. I do fantastically like it.' As I looked at the lovely dress with lovely Heather inside it, I felt the old familiar sensation of surging and swelling, and wondered how soon we would be getting down to business.

Not long, as it happened. Heather proposed that this time we should leave the punt alone and go for a stroll through the fields. The hedges were thicker in those days and there were more of them. They were also much more beautiful, rich with wild flowers and delicately scented. People who only know the English countryside as it is today, after decades of insult and impoverishment and degradation at the hands of agri-business and the highway-planners and developers, will just have to take my word for it that fifty years ago it was very, very beautiful. We settled ourselves in the lee of a wonderful hedge. I think the beauty of my surroundings must have affected me subliminally, for I didn't bother to get Heather out of her dress, just lifted up her pretty skirt and we made love there and then, amid the clover and buttercups and vetch and tall seeded grasses and the lovely big cranesbill that had seeded itself along that hedgerow by the hundred, a fine stately flower as blue as Heather's dress. Dog-roses nodded among the hawthorn branches above us, honeysuckle gave out its intoxicating scent. It was easy to believe that all nature approved of what we were doing.

Chapter 18

'Just come down to the cellar with me for a few minutes, Peter,' my father said, one afternoon that week. He had come back from his brewery job at about five-thirty, and as usual he was spending the last half-hour before opening time in lining everything up for the evening's trade.

I followed him down the stone steps, remembering my childhood. The cellar was shadowy and cool and whitewashed and primeval. It was my father's kingdom, my mother never went there, so, although it was so clean, it was clean in a man's fashion, not a woman's. My father kept the floor well swept and the brass taps polished and the shelves dusted, but he did not trouble to chase up the odd cobweb high in a corner of the ceiling, and I am sure a fair-sized population of arachnids lived prosperously down there that would have been relentlessly chivvied out on the upper levels.

With each downward step you took the temperature dropped a little, until it was perfect for beer: English beer, that is, brewed to be drunk in long, slow swallows from pint glasses, not sipped from frosted tumblers that get lost in the hand. As a young boy, anything from three to about seven, I had often tried my father's patience by dogging him at the heels when he came down into the cellar to set up the barrels and wash the pipes and generally keep everything in order. I had never tired of watching him deftly tip a large barrel over on its side on the two wooden beams raised about six inches from the floor, the stillage, and settle it on the chocks, shaped pieces of wood that supported it in a stable position, the one at the top end slightly lower than the one at the bottom end. Then, the best moment of all, he would skilfully tap out the bung and, with light, accurate blows of the same mallet, drive in a wooden peg. And finally the mallet was used to tap the barrel, – drive in at the appropriate place the brass tap with the pipes running from it that had been taken from the empty barrel now being replaced. And suddenly, not having thought of him for years, I remembered Charlie.

Charlie was a drayman employed by the brewery when I was a small boy, a huge, broad man with arms that seemed to my wondering childish eyes to be as thick and muscular as the hind legs of a Shire horse. He used to call at the pub once a week to deliver fresh barrels and take away the empties. In those pre-school years I was always at home and I used to wait for Charlie. He would trundle the full barrels down a wooden chute from a trap-door in the pavement in front of the pub, using a noosed rope, then, using the same rope, he would hoist up the empties. This was the bit I was waiting for. All agog, saucer-eyed, I used to stand on the pavement and watch as he picked up each barrel in turn, hoisted it up to put it on his horse-drawn cart, and, as he got it to mouth-level, pause for a moment with his head tilted back, to drink any remnants that still lurked in it. Needless to say, in those days of natural brewing methods, it wasn't only beer that lurked in there. The last four or five inches of any barrel, the ullage that didn't get served to customers, were as much vegetation as beverage. They were at least half composed of fragments of yeast, bits of hop-leaf, stalks of this and shreds of that, all fermented into a porridge that would not have disgraced the witches' cauldron in *Macbeth*. As Charlie lifted each barrel in his colossal arms and held the bung to his capacious mouth, I would vibrate with pure joy. I specially liked it when, after swallowing the liquid, he chewed meditatively on the mulch that remained in his mouth before turning his attention to the next barrel.

'Don't you mind all that stuff, Mr Charlie?' I once plucked up courage to ask him, round about my fifth birthday. 'All that stuff like tea-leaves and that that's in the beer?'

He looked at me benignly, wiping his mouth with the back of his hand, and I shall never forget his answer. 'That's where the goodness is, my boy... That's where the goodness is!'

I heard that rich bass voice, forgotten for more than a decade, ring in my head now as my father moved about the cellar, purposeful, light on his feet for all his chunky build, deft in his movements. 'Make sure you knock it in flush... pull a pint and hold it up to the light before you serve it to anybody... if it's still cloudy after three or four, take it off and put another one on, and if you do that, roll the cloudy one over to the end after you've closed it off, and put a chalk mark on it.'

Finally he straightened up and looked at me intensely and said, 'Think you've got all that?'

'Dad,' I said, 'I'd got it when I was about four years old. I used to come down here and stand and watch every movement you made till I could have counted them off in my sleep.'

It was true. And I don't think I was unusual. I think most boys enjoy watching their father exercising a skill. They feel, obscurely, that it's something to go on the credit side in that on the whole boring, meaningless and time-wasting procedure, growing up.

*

A day or two before the big Sunday trip, Dad drove the Morris round one teatime before opening the pub and fetched Mrs Warmley round, 'to show her the ropes'. She turned out to be the sort of woman to whom one compulsively applies words like 'motherly' and 'reassuring'. Give her the right colour of skin and the right 'Ise-gwyne' accent and she would have been the coal-black mammy of Southern lore, saying things like 'Lawd bless you, chile' and shaking with affectionate laughter. As it was, her complexion was Anglo-Saxon and her accent Thames Valley. I took to her immediately, and as for showing her the ropes, she knew it all as well as my father did, and whenever he let fall the name of one of our regular customers, it always seemed to be someone she knew by his first name. About forty-five, energetic, ample-bosomed, not fat but getting there, she fitted that slot behind the bar (dared I think it?) more naturally than my watchful father or my pale, sensitive-faced mother. I could see this Sunday's work, for which I was going to earn so many moral good points, was going to be a breeze.

After Dad left to take her home I sat idly in the bar, which was still not due to open for another few minutes, turning over the pages of a book I had brought home from the public library, a large illustrated tome on railway history. In the 1930s there was as yet no equivalent of the present-day nostalgia for the great age of railways, with loving photographs and paintings of giant steam locomotives and all the rest of it, because we were still living in that era. Electric trains existed, but they were genteel toy-like things, used on commuter services that were for ever stopping and starting, hardly trains at all, more like multi-unit trams. The long runs, the high speeds, were still in the care of the vast boiling kettles, festooned with bubbling pipes, hissing from mysterious outlets and brandishing huge oiled pistons. Every country had its distinctive styles of these, though the ones used in India, Latin America and most of Africa seemed generally to be made in England, and I took a low-powered but pleasurable interest in reading about them and looking at their majestic outlines; it made me think of travel, and enormous mileages, and the size and variety of the earth, and the richness of the life that might be mine one day. So I sat on the bench by the window in our bar, leafing through this book, and hardly noticed that Brian came and stood nearby and looked down at it too. But when he spoke, his voice was disapproving.

'Trains?' he said. 'You reading a book about *trains*?'

'I'm a student,' I said. 'I reserve the right to read a book about anything. People have gone to the stake for that kind of issue.'

'If you're going to tell me that you're reading a book about trains because you study history, I can just about understand that. They belong to the past all right, they're *history*.' He pronounced the last word as if it were something shameful.

'The early motor-cars are history too,' I said. 'Everything that happened in the past is history. Old Number One's history.'

'Yes, but cars are different. I should have thought you could see that. Old cars are history with a *future*. Old Number One led to the M.G.s of *today*.'

'And you don't think railways have a future?'

'Course they don't,' he snorted. 'They're dead and gone already. Nobody builds railways now. These foreigners, they're cleverer than we are and they don't stick their heads in the sand – they don't build railways, wasting their money. They build good long straight roads where a car can really get moving. I've driven on 'em and I know.'

Some imp of mischief prompted me to say, 'Some of the Continental express trains are pretty good too, by all accounts.'

His face closed and he snapped, 'All right, argue. You'd argue the hind leg off a donkey. I suppose that's what they teach you.'

It surprised me that an abstract issue such as the motor-car versus the railway train should arouse such passion in him. But of course to him it wasn't an abstract issue. He was a lover, a worshipper, of the motor-car. If every train had been scrapped, every inch of track torn up, every station dynamited, Brian would have felt a sense of relief that the lingering opposition was gone and that henceforth all resources would be poured into roads, petrol, tyres and (doubtless) race-tracks.

I closed the book and took it up to my room. I didn't want to oppose him. I was not, at that time, particularly hostile to the motor-car. I had no crystal ball into which I could look and see what a killer and polluter it was destined to be within the next half-century. It was merely that I had a slight sentimenal fondness for trains and would have been sorry to see them disappear. But I realized that I must keep that fondness to myself in Brian's presence. To him, a puff of steam from a railway engine was a smoke-signal from the enemy.

Well, I was in no mood to make trouble over it. If Brian was having a love affair with the motor-car, it was turning out to be a happy one. Our well-used family Morris must have seemed an impossibly staid old bath-chair to him after the M.G.s among which he lived his working life, but for all that he was cheerfully willing to get behind the wheel and do the bulk of the driving on this famous day out – all of it, if the old man wanted to take a day's complete rest and just watch the scenery go by. Brian had determined on Brighton as the objective, going down via Farnborough and Guildford. When they said it seemed a long way to go there and back, he pointed out briskly that Oxford was a long way from the coast in any direction, and that was about the best, and had good roads going to it. There was no arguing with him. He was absolute master.

The Sunday after 18 July dawned still and bright. Already by eight o'clock in the morning the haze was clearing from the sky and there was not a cloud to be seen. Brian, of course, accepted this as proof that the Almighty had inspected his plan and seen that it was good. He had everybody out of bed early and loaded the hamper for the roadside picnic into the car with his own hands. Breakfast was a hurried affair. No one dared chew slowly or ask for another cup of tea under Brian's accusing eye. The open road beckoned imperiously.

Our father, for his part, looked with some misgivings at the signs of a climbing temperature. For him, it did not necessarily signal divine approval. It could also mean that the beer would not stay at the correct temperature and, by the evening, might begin to taste sour. After breakfast he beckoned me to accompany him down to the cellar and dragged out a pile of hessian sacks.

'Now, Peter, I'm going to trust you to see to this,' he said anxiously, casting a nervous eye at the cellar steps as if expecting his elder son to come bounding down them and drag him up to street-level by the scruff of the neck. 'Get these good and wet under the tap out in the yard. Run the tap till it comes out really cold and soak them properly. Then put them over the barrels. It'll hold the coolness in. Now, you won't forget, will you, lad?'

I assured him earnestly that even my limited intelligence was capable of remembering this one extra item, and to make him feel more secure I bundled the sacks under my arm and took them out to the tap there and then. Comforted, my father settled himself into the car with the other two, Brian revved up, honked the bulb horn, and they rolled out into the street and away. Silence descended. At first it was delicious, as it always is to get a house to oneself that is normally full of people: the peace, the emptiness, the freedom to do as one likes. But then, as is probably inevitable with a male at that time of life, my thoughts began to turn to sex. What a waste this was. If only I had organized it properly, it might have been possible for Heather to be here now. It was barely nine o'clock, and Mrs Warmley was coming at eleven-thirty. What a chance to be undisturbed and unhindered. We could have got into bed, a rare treat, a welcome change from the narrow, boxed-in punt or the lumpiness of the hedgerow. Not that I seriously minded those venues, but a chance of bed would have been marvellous.

My father had told me that Mrs Warmley would be coming by car, driven by one of her sons. 'You know him, I think,' he added vaguely, 'friend of Brian's'. The name had rung no bell, and the more was my astonishment when, loafing about in the empty bar at half-past eleven, I heard in the street outside the drumming and crackling of a high-compression Anzani engine and looking out, saw, of all things, Ivan's Morgan, the one in which he had given me that delightful ride to Cropredy, drawing up at the kerb. Hastening to the window, I took in every detail. Ivan stopped the engine, the low-slung contraption ceased its St Vitus shaking, and he got out and went to the other side. A prolonged struggle followed; finally a generous pair of female buttocks were perched triumphantly on the tail-end of the skimpy racer, causing me to expect the front to rear up in the air; then, smiling in relief, the passenger was on her feet.

So Mrs Warmley was Ivan's mother. I had never even known his name was Ivan Warmley. The fact of their relationship was, I realized, no more incredible or unlikely than any other everyday fact; but still, when my father said she was coming round 'by car' I would have guessed for ever before guessing that the 'car' in question would be that cheerfully mad little green grasshopper, not so much running along like a wheeled vehicle as jumping in a series of bounds. As an example of the unexpectedness of ordinary life it would do well enough.

She proved wonderfully easy to work with. The day went by very pleasantly. She had brought a cold lunch for the two of us – slices of roast beef and some salad fresh out of the ground. She also had some excellent new potatoes, which she deftly scraped and put into a saucepan of water before we opened the pub, so that we could put them on to boil as soon as we shut and they would be ready when we had finished tidying the bar.

Mrs Warmley served every Friday and Saturday night in a big pub in central Oxford, the kind that on busy nights needs half a dozen staff behind the bar. That week had been particularly busy because she had found herself having to train two new barmaids.

'We don't usually get girls who've never done bar work before,' she said. 'Mr Anstruther doesn't take them straight from school, and most of the girls we get have got some experience in. But these two, their background's retailing. They did shop work and they've got good references. They weren't sacked or anything like that, it was just that the shop closed down.'

I was only half attending to this – it seemed to have no conceivable interest for me – but out of politeness I asked Mrs Warmley what shop it was that had employed these girls and was now no more.

'It was that shoe-shop in Cornmarket Street,' she said. 'Seems they got branches all over the country and they're shutting down the Oxford one, for some reason.'

The shoe-shop in Cornmarket Street... I searched my mind for the leading question that would elicit the information: was one of these two girls Vinnie?

'I, er, knew one or two of the people who worked at that shop, slightly,' I said, trying to sound casual. 'I had a friend at school called... Bill Wiggins who became a shopwalker in the men's department.' (I hoped to God there wasn't a real person called Bill Wiggins who worked there and was a friend of Ivan's or something.) 'I... er... went to a cricket match once when their shop played Blackwell's Reserves.' I felt I was babbling wildly, an old fault of mine when telling a pack of lies, but I had to know, I had to know. 'Is one of these new girls you're training – is she slim built with brown hair that she wears in a fringe? You'd recognize her, I think – she's rather a pretty – rather a –'

In a word, no. When Mrs Warmley described these girls it became clear that neither was Vinnie or anything like her. She talked calmly on to another subject, and I sank back in my chair with a sense of relief. At least, I thought at first it was relief. It certainly *ought* to have been relief. After all, it would have been very unsettling to know exactly where Vinnie was, to know moreover that, at any time from eleven a.m. to two-thirty p.m. and six till ten (weekdays) or twelve till two and seven till ten (Sundays) I could go and order a glass of beer and stand there and look into her eyes and watch the shine of the lights on her hair and the movements of her body as she went to and fro behind the bar, now bending down, now reaching up... that wouldn't have done *at all*. I wouldn't have wanted to do it, of course, but still it would have been unsettling to know that, at any time I chose, I *could* do it. That feeling inside my chest, a feeling which had now turned curiously leaden and had almost begun to resemble disappointment, must be seized and yanked back to its proper moorings and firmly labelled 'RELIEF'.

After all, if I had wanted for some fantastic reason to see her, I could always have hung around the shoe-shop. The shoe-shop, with Vinnie in her neat little salesgirl's smock, simply represented defeat and humiliation. I was never tempted to go in there. And now at least I could take to walking along Cornmarket Street again. I was getting definitely sick of skulking round the side roads. Though that, come to think of it, was how I had bumped into Heather and her mother that day and taken them off to tea at Episcopus.

So I owed Heather to Vinnie! Well, why not?

'She finished up having to have it out,' said Mrs Warmley, evidently concluding some story of which I had not heard a word. 'And they said it was one of the worst they'd ever seen.'

'Good grief,' I said.

'Well,' she said, getting up from the table, 'there's some things it's better not to dwell on.'

'Yes,' I agreed. 'There's some things it's better not to dwell on.'

We worked steadily through the evening session, in the course of which I successfully tapped a new barrel, and had the place swept out and in perfect order by the time the family got back at about ten-thirty. My parents had had a wonderful day and Brian was grinning with quiet satisfaction. My mother had brought me a present: a straw hat, not some piece of half-crown fairground rubbish but quite a good one, well made and with a linen band inside the brim, quite a find on a Sunday with all the shops shut and only stalls to buy from. She knew my size and had chosen one she thought would look well on me, and it did. I was really glad to have it; it lasted for years and was known in the family as 'Peter's Brighton hat'.

*

I put in a good solid spell of reading on the Monday and Tuesday. I was due to see Heather again on the Wednesday, so there was no dreary stretch of time ahead of me, lowering my spirits, just a nice clear run at the work before the next bit of wonderful play. The reading absorbed my entire attention for the two days, and by the late afternoon of Tuesday I was glad to close my books and take a walk along the river-bank to stretch my legs and breathe the cool air.

I came into the Bargeman's just after six, intending to drink a pint of beer and then eat with Dad. Brian was not coming home till later, so one of our parents would have to eat alone anyway, and I had chosen to keep my father company as I wanted to discuss a few small matters with him. I mention the circumstance because it explains why I came in through the bar like a customer, instead of entering the house through the back door and going straight to the kitchen table as in my boyhood.

At least, I was *going* to enter the bar like a customer when I was hit amidships by a tremendous surprise. As I opened the door, even before I had taken a step into the interior, I saw standing at the counter a figure so unexpected that at first I could not force my brain into recognition.

But yes, it was. Mr Burrell the farmer. Heather's father. And in the same instant I saw Heather, sitting on the long bench that ran along the length of the room, under the windows.

I backed out again. I couldn't handle this. What were they doing here? Was it pure chance? But surely this was the kind of chance that simply can't happen. Someone must have intended it. But who? Heather or her father? Had the old man got wind of our relationship? Had he come here to make trouble?

I got out on to the pavement before old Burrell saw me. My own father didn't see me either; his head was down to the job of pulling a pint of beer. The usual locals were sitting about, but they showed no interest. The one who did see me was Heather; she must have been on the watch. As I retreated along the street, taking care not to be visible from the windows, she came out briskly and joined me.

'It's all right,' she said. 'Don't run away.'

'I was just...' I said. 'It's all so...'

'So unexpected, yes,' she said. 'Such a surprise.' Her eyes were doing what they call in books 'dancing with mirth'. I felt mine must be gavotting with apprehension. Rumba-ing with panic, even.

'I did it for a joke, I admit it,' she said, laying a hand placatingly on my sleeve. 'Don't be upset.'

'I'm not. Not necessarily, anyway. You did *what* for a joke? I mean, how did you know? How much does he know?'

'How much does who know?'

'Your father, of course, who the hell else?' I noticed she was not going to tell me how she knew where I lived – not yet, anyway.

She flashed a mocking little smile. 'Well, how much does *your* father know, if it comes to that?'

'Nothing. Absolutely not a thing.'

'Well,' she conceded. 'mine does at least know you're on this earth. He knows you by sight and he knows I went to a ball with you in Oxford.'

'Does he know we're still seeing each other?'

'No. Neither he nor my mother do. In any case, she'd be interested and he wouldn't. He really never thinks of anything but crops and animals and the tractor and stuff.'

'But why on earth have you brought him here?'

'I wanted to see the place,' she said simply, 'and it seemed a chance.'

'A chance?'

'Daddy and I were in Oxford. I was helping him to shop for some anti-infestation dip he needs for the cattle. He's very confused about all the new drugs and I know a bit about it. Then I thought, let's have a drink at Peter's family's pub before we go back.'

'But I never even knew you –'

'Look,' she said, 'I've got to go back in. He'll think it's very funny me coming out here and talking to you in the street when we could perfectly well be sitting in the bar. Daddy's getting me a drink. If I'm not there to drink it he'll come out and look for me.'

'All right, I'll come in,' I said. 'But tell me one thing first, quickly. Does he know I live here? I mean, does he expect to see me here?'

'No. I just said I knew a nice little pub and he asked me how I knew it was nice and I said I knew someone who lived there. He didn't ask any questions and I don't suppose he was a bit interested. Come *in*.'

She entered the bar and I followed close behind, instinctively staying near her for safety. Although this was my home territory, my stamping-ground, Heather had invaded and taken it over, all in a few minutes, by superior confidence. Old Burrell had a glass of light ale in his hand and was looking round in a bemused fashion, as if Heather had suddenly been snatched through the window by a passing boa-constrictor. My father, seeing the two of us come in together, took on his watchful mien.

'Daddy, this is Peter Leonard. You remember I said I wanted to come here for a drink because I know someone who lives here, well, this is the somebody. We met when he came to the farm to buy puppies and later on we went to that College ball in Oxford together.'

I liked the cool effrontery of 'to buy puppies'. I saw my father store that one away.

'Oh, yes,' old Burrell said. He looked at me with almost, but not quite, total non-recognition. His weather-beaten, muddy-complexioned face was without expression, but his little rhinoceros eyes were watchful, and I saw something resembling a thought come into them. 'Seen you before, I think,' he said. 'In our local. Out where I live.'

'Yes,' I said. 'You were with your son and he pointed me out. I wasn't sitting near enough to hear what he said but I noticed him pointing to me and saying something. I don't think it was anything I'd have liked if I'd heard it. I've an idea he doesn't like me.'

'Why would that be, Peter?' asked my father, dead-pan. 'Why would anybody not like you?'

'I can't speak for Tom,' old Burrell said, moving his shoulders in a gesture that was half-way to a shrug. 'He's got his own likes and dislikes, same as anybody else.'

He said this with finality; it is obvious that what he was really saying was 'Leave me out of your quarrels, and for good measure leave me alone altogether.' He turned firmly to my father, one sensible middle-aged man talking to another and letting the flighty young people get on with it. They resumed a conversation they had evidently struck up while Heather and I were having our rapid confabulation on the pavement. It was about barley. I listened for a moment or two; just long enough to get them safely launched on the tide of their talk, so that I could go over to the other side of the room with Heather and be effectively alone with her; but during that brief time I actually learnt something about barley, namely that it is what malt is made of. I had never known before that malt is barley that has been allowed to sprout and then dried. We never know the moment when the mind may be enriched with new knowledge.

Only subsequently, however, did I realize that this information was of value. At the time, all I wanted was to get across the room with Heather. In another moment it was accomplished. I had no drink, but that was a detail. I didn't want to break into my father's attention with the risk of bringing it back to myself.

'So,' I said as she demurely sipped her light ale and her eyes kept up that dancing-with-laughter business that I found partly very attractive and partly very irritating, 'what's going on?'

'Going on? Don't you want me to take an interest in where you live and what you do and who you are?'

Floored again. That was exactly how I had expressed the matter in the innumerable silent dialogues I had had with her, when I had accused her of egotism, of making use of me without really seeing me or wanting to see me. And now she had answered my reproaches without even having heard them. Unless, of course, she had heard them in some recess of her being which did not depend on the usual transmission of information to the brain via ear or eye. Was her vagina, I wondered, wired up to the lobes of her brain in some way?

Before I had lived another ten years I was to learn that every vagina is so wired up, but at this time I was still short of twenty years old and very lacking in experience.

'But you didn't *ask* me,' I said. 'If you'd wanted to know about my background, you could have asked me at any –'

'And you didn't tell me. You'd been to where I live, you'd seen my parents and my brother, you knew all about that, and you never opened your mouth about yours. I began to wonder if there was something mysterious about it.'

'Quite simply, I was waiting for you to ask. To show any kind of interest.'

'And I was waiting for you to tell me.'

'You seemed to me,' I said, 'not to show ordinary curiosity about someone you were close to.'

'And you seemed to me,' Heather said, 'not to show ordinary openness with someone you were close to.'

And suddenly we were both laughing.

'We were both right, I suppose,' I said.

'No. We were both wrong. Why don't you get yourself a drink?'

'I will,' I said. 'And will you have a refill?'

She shook her head. 'One's enough. I'm always a very good girl when either of my parents is around. And if they were *both* here, I'd probably have a lemonade or something.'

We laughed again at the small joke, just because we were happy and relieved and glad to see each other. I went behind the bar and drew myself a pint and put the full price for it into the till under Dad's watchful eye. Old Burrell had had another glass and was saying a bit more about barley, or perhaps it was oats by now. Over in the corner, Trundle was giving his opinions about the Gold Standard. I had not suspected that he even knew of the existence of the Gold Standard, let alone had any views about it. I was a bit hazy about what it was myself, but one heard a lot about it at that time because England had done something called Going Off it, which was either a notably good thing or a notably bad one according to one's economic views in general. I sat down beside Heather. She was a notably good thing from any viewpoint I could imagine.

'I love you,' I said quietly.

'I'm pretty keen on you too. And I like your pub. It's nice. I'd a damn sight rather have grown up here than at the farm. There must be such a lot going on.'

'To be fair,' I said, 'I think you'd find a certain sameness about it. Mostly it's the roll-call of regulars coming in and airing their views about things they don't know much about.' Behind me I heard Peake say 'Wall Street.'

'Oh, but it's bound to be better than the farm. Stuck out there, you go for weeks without seeing *anybody*. I mean, here, that door's open on the street, with the whole world going by, and you never know who might come in.'

'Yes,' I said. 'I never knew you were coming in this evening, for instance.' And we both laughed again. Then a thought struck me and I said, 'But wait a minute. Just how did you find out my address?'

'No,' she said. 'I got it from Episcopus.'

I was considerably surprised at that, for several reasons, but I kept the surprise out of my face and said, 'Went round there, did you?'

'No. I telephoned. While my father was discussing worm tablets or something I went out and found a box on the street corner and rang up the lodge at Episcopus and said I wanted your home address.'

'And the porter gave it to you? Just like that?' It didn't sound like Frank Penney to be so accommodating.

'I made him give it me,' she said demurely.

'How?'

She laughed softly. 'I told him I had some letters for you and wanted to deliver them.'

'Letters?'

'Yes. I said you'd been staying with us in the country and these letters had arrived after you'd left and I wanted to deliver them.'

'So you managed to get him to believe,' I said, 'that I know you and your family well enough to have been staying at your house and you didn't know my home address?'

'Don't be so nit-picking. I'm sure he wasn't interested in all those details. We might have been running a bed-and-breakfast place or something.'

'So now I'm the type who has his mail sent to a bed-and-breakfast place. Frank Penney's going to think I'm a pretty rum character.'

'No, he isn't,' she said decisively. 'He isn't going to think about it one way or another.'

Which was very probably true. All my cross-questioning revealed was that I had already developed the historian's instinct for examining evidence; an inconvenient habit when carried into everyday life, but then we all have our *déformations professionelles*.

So I made amends by saying, 'You're right, of course. And the important thing is that it worked and you're here and I'm looking at you.'

'Heather,' her father called over from the bar. 'We must get off.'

'Coming, Daddy.' And to me she said softly, 'Tomorrow. At the Villa.'

As she got up from the table she trod gently on my foot, making it look like an accident. A thrill ran all the way through my body. Then she was gone.

Later my father said to me, drily, 'Seems like a nice young lady you've got to know there, Peter.'

'She rides horses,' I said.

'Is that something you're interested in?'

'No,' I said. 'I was just out in the country one day and she came along on a horse and I opened a gate for her. Then we chatted a bit.'

He digested this and then said, 'D'you go out in the country very often?'

'Just on the bike,' I said. 'Just when I feel my brain needs a rest. I find I can't work all the time.'

'Well,' he said, 'a bit of fresh air never hurt anybody.' And we dropped the subject.

*

July had moved into August and we had entered the period of 'the Wakes', when whole industries stopped for a week, mills ceasing to roll, furnaces cooling, and entire towns went on holiday together. Places like Oldham and Blackburn stood almost deserted, while places like Blackpool and Rhyl suddenly bulged. To this circumstance, I suppose, I owe it that, walking along Broad Street one morning, I saw Fred Armitage, in company with a middle-aged couple who were obviously his parents. They were standing outside Trinity, looking through the wrought-iron gates at the classical figures on the roof of the chapel, and he was evidently explaining something to them.

I had still time to take immediate evasive action and for a split second it crossed my mind to do so. If I had, my motive would have been pure benevolence. I knew that Armitage's father was a miner, and in those days of frank (not to say ruthless) class distinction, the unassuming lad could not have been blamed if he had wanted to give his parents the pleasure of a guided tour of Oxford while at the same time avoiding the strain of trying to mix them socially with his fellow-undergraduates, who were all at any rate potentially of the governing class.

That I decided in fact to confront them was also motivated by benevolence, and of a superior kind. I wanted Armitage to know that he had at any rate one fellow-student who respected a miner as much as he respected a brain surgeon or bank manager. And I wanted the parents to go home with the knowledge that they had met one of Fred's college-mates and got along with him very easily.

Accordingly, my 'Hello, Fred!' was conspicuously affable, and the handshake I gave to his father's square, hard palm as hard as I could make it. Since my normal manner was quiet and rather contained, Fred Armitage looked rather startled at my impetus, but also, after a moment, relieved and pleased. I chatted determinedly. I took an interest in everything. I got out of them all the details of their holiday, where they were staying (a bed-and-breakfast place in the Iffley Road) and for how long (five days). As I talked I sized them up. The father had a tough, stocky body; the mother had similar measurements, with the addition of a swaying bosom, but her flesh looked soft and waxy where his looked hard and compact. No doubt she worked as hard as he did, but his work was all muscle-building, and besides she probably spent the family budget on first-class protein for him while she lived on tea and white bread and margarine. Neither of them gave any clue as to where Fred's tall, rather gangling physique came from.

The couple were different in attitude too. The father, walking round Oxford, was thrilled with it all as Fred was. To him, it was a magic wand, waved for his son, that had produced a magic city. The mother was more wary, more judging, not at all swept off her feet. Her expressionless face but watchful eyes seemed to be saying that she was, as yet, by no means convinced that any tangible good would come out of it all, these fancy buildings and these odd people with their strange talk about *matriculation* and *undergraduate* and *Bachelor of Arts* which apparently you could still be if you were married; not to speak of Christ Church that wasn't a church and the Camera that wasn't, it seemed, a camera that took pictures, and progs and bullers and God knows what-all. She hadn't decided yet, and she was going to take her time about deciding, whether it wasn't all a put-up job, some kind of a conspiracy for robbing her of her son, filling his head with a lot of daft ideas, taking him away from her world, making him different.

'D'you know Oxford well, Mr Armitage?' I asked the dad, feeling damn sure he wouldn't.

'Never been 'ere in me puff. Never entered my 'ead as I might do, till Fred come 'ere to study.'

He cast a sidelong glance at his son in which I caught the lingering glow of that surprise he must have felt at having fathered such a prodigy.

'Is it what you expected?' I couldn't help asking.

'Well,' he said, 'I knew what the buildings was like, the Colleges and that, because Fred gave a us a book of fortygraphs of them for our Christmas box last year. So I knew the shape of 'em, like.'

I thought of him sitting by the kitchen range with the book open on his knees, gazing at Merton and Magdalen and the Bodleian while the clogs rang on the pavement outside and the shawled women went back and forth to the little shops, and the pit-wheels revolved endlessly, taking his mates, and ready to take him in a few hours, down in the cage to lie on his side for seven hours and hack away at a two-foot-six seam of coal. What did he make of it all?

'But the place, really, it isn't quite what I thought to find,' he went on. 'It's busier. More crowded in the streets and a lot more motors.'

I guessed the book Fred had given him was one of those serene-beauty jobs, where the photographer gets up at five on a midsummer morning in the hope of catching the streets empty of cars. Dreaming spires... whispering from her towers the last enchantments of the Middle Ages. You could still get away with it in those days, if you were willing to get out of bed at dawn.

Fred Armitage now addressed me. 'You're the first familiar face I've seen,' he grinned. 'Quite a surprise. What brings you up in the vac.?'

Had I really not told him that I lived in Oxford? Quite possibly not. I was pretty close-mouthed about my background.

'Oh, I'm local,' I said. 'My parents are in business in Oxford.' I didn't tell him what business. My deep-seated aversion to mixing my two worlds held good even with harmless Fred Armitage. Especially with him, perhaps. He would fit in so smoothly in that little public bar; he would enjoy going in for a pint or two, chatting with my father, even listening to the likes of old Trundle. Pretty soon he would be so cosy down there he would be practically taking it over, enjoying a joke with my Uncle Ernest from Pembroke, taking his mates, such as McFarlane, with him, artlessly gossipping about it all back at College, till I would become Leonard of the Bargeman's Arms all over Episcopus. And in a social *milieu* that had changed hardly at all since Edwardian times, I winced at the thought of some of the people who would use that against me.

As I bade the trio a courteous good-day and moved on, I reflected that Heather, at any rate, did not hold it against me that I came from a side-street pub. Her mother would, of course. But while I was considering that subject, what about the brother? He didn't strike me as the type to be an ordinary shallow snob. A bad-tempered oaf he might be, but he would have too much contact with the real world to live in that kind of fantasy. On what, then, was his deep hostility to me based? I determined to ask Heather, the very next time I saw her, if she could help me with this puzzle.

When the next time actually came round, it was one of those chill, rainy days that even a good English summer is apt to come up with now and again. Any activity *al fresco* was out of the question, and the interior of the boat-house, dark and damp-smelling, seemed not in the least villa-like. But Heather, equal to this or any other occasion, had brought a thick, warm blanket, and as we settled down in the well of the punt with the cushions under us and the blanket tucked round us it was very like being in bed, that state so keenly desiderated in my spell of fantasizing as I waited for Mrs Warmley.

She was in her working outfit today, corduroy trousers and shirt – elegant summer dresses are not for rainy, mud-splashing days – but before getting under the blanket she slid out of everything except the shirt, and I was as happy as a sandboy and as busy as a beaver. When at last I could spare the energy to talk I brought up the subject of Tom, first sharing with her the joke of his stopping me in the street in the middle of Oxford and congratulating me on having the sense to keep away from her. 'God, if only he *knew*,' she murmured delightedly, and the punt shook and creaked with her silent laughter. Lying close to her, holding her, I loved to feel the vibration of it running all through her body. When it had subsided I asked, 'But why is it, d'you know? Why should he have a special dislike of me?'

'Oh, he hasn't,' she said. 'He's the same about anybody.'

'Anybody who comes after you, you mean?'

'Yes. Always tries to drive them away with a pitchfork.'

'Surely he's not one of those neurotics you read about who...' I decided to pick my words carefully. 'I mean, he's not in love with you himself or something crazy like that, is he?'

'Far from it,' she said wryly. 'Most of the time he doesn't know I'm there, and when he does it's just to register me as a nuisance. No, it's all to do with the one thing he really cares about. Flying.'

'You mean.. he hates me because he's interested in flying? How does he think I'm going to stop –'

'He wants to reserve me for Richard,' she said flatly.

'Oh,' I said.

'Richard's got money, he's bored, and he doesn't know what to do with himself half the time. His father's got a big farm with a lot of land and one day Richard'll be running it, but he doesn't feel any particular thrill about that. He doesn't care about agriculture; it's just the most convenient thing to do so he'll do it. He's been and done a course at Cirencester or somewhere and I believe he scraped through all right. But he's bored, and anyway his father's going to live for hundreds of years yet. So he's hanging about, and Tom's trying to interest him in buying an aeroplane.'

'Buying one for Tom, I suppose?'

'Well, the way Tom puts it, the two of them would buy it. Richard'd be the owner and Tom'd be the pilot and navigator – the world's best, of course. He wants to get his pilot's license and then take Richard on all sorts of wonderful trips, to France and Ireland and the Lord knows where. And teach him to fly, of course.'

'And how does Richard see all this?'

'Well, his mind's so *blank*, it's easy enough to put anything into it. You just have to wait and see if it *stays* there.'

I began for the first time to have a mental picture of this Richard. I saw him with an essentially vacuous face, slightly buck teeth, sandy hair beginning to recede at the temples; tall and weedy; light blue eyes, the pupils so light in colour that they were even lighter than Heather's, giving them a colourless, washed-out look; expensive clothes, especially a good tweed hacking jacket with two slits tailored into the back, and hand-made brogues.

Had Heather, this lovely, vibrant, healthy girl, really given herself to this odious creature? I could quite imagine her doing so, that was the trouble, at any rate in the days before she had met me. She had been so bored, so frustrated, so charged with a vitality for which there was no adequate channel; I could just see her allowing herself to be taken up by this equally bored young oaf with money and horses and motor-cars, and letting him have his way just because she saw no good reason why he should not.

While we had been making love, the rain stopped, and with the capricious rapidity that one associates with English summer weather the sky cleared to a vivid blue, dotted here and there with freshly laundered clouds too small to be anything but decorative. The boathouse was anything but well off for windows, having only the small panes roughly carpentered into the doors which no one ever bothered to clean, but since these faced more or less westward the sun, declining now on that side, sent such a golden radiance into our shadowy retreat that I felt personally proud, as if my sexual efforts had switched on a huge parade of cosmic rejoicing. Pulling back the blanket, I got up and peered through the smeared glass. The sunlight was gleaming and flashing on every twig and leaf, every stalk of grass, every droplet of water in the whole soaking landscape. It was as if, having been relentlessly drenched with water, Oxfordshire was now bathed in fire: but a golden, benedictory fire that would never singe the fur of a rabbit or the feather of a hedge-sparrow.

'Get up,' I said to Heather. 'This is probably the one and only time you'll ever hear me suggest that you get up and come outside when you could be lying with me in something like a bed, but I mean it. You mustn't miss this.'

'You're all soul, aren't you?' she grinned at me over the blanket. 'That's because for the time being you haven't got any bodily needs left.'

'All right,' I said. 'You know it, I know it. And if you're feeling smug about it, go ahead, because you've a perfect right to. You've given me my soul back just as you've given me my mind back. I owe everything in life to you. And now that we've got that cleared up, put some clothes on and step outside this hut. I want you to see the world looking so beautiful. Beautiful enough to deserve having you in it.'

'All right,' she said. 'I've got a soul too, you may be surprised to hear.' And in a moment she was dressed and beside me on the towpath.

The scene around us was perfectly ordinary, in the sense that anyone who has lived through a summer in the Thames Valley will have known those evenings when, after a day of heavy rain, the sun comes out and bathes the landscape in that abundance of golden light and golden warmth. Anyone who hasn't, won't. To neither group is it worth attempting a detailed description. The first group knows it already, the second group could probably not be helped to it by words alone. Effects like that are better left to the great painters. Or, possibly, the great composers. The after-the-storm passage in Beethoven's Pastoral Symphony has most of the right feeling to it.

We locked up the boathouse and started back to the road and the point where we would have to part, wheeling our bikes so as to be able to go slowly and enjoy each other's presence and the beauty around us. At that moment I would have been hard put to it to find serious fault with life. I was content, I was with the person who had given me that contentment, and the landscape through which we moved was paradisaical. Which was, of course, the signal for *homo sapiens*, always the serpent-invader of every paradise, to introduce a disruptive note. We were walking along one side of a tall, thick hedge. From the other side of it, some fifty yards further along, there came through the clear, tranquil air that most horrible of all sounds – the bang of a gun going off.

'Damn whoever that is,' I said. 'I'd like to get him in a court of law. Loosing off a thing like that in the peaceful countryside.'

'I'm afraid you can't,' Heather said. 'The local farmers round here take guns out into the fields and have a go at rabbits and rooks and pigeons whenever the fancy takes them. Try telling the men in our household that it's against the law.'

We had reached a thin patch in the hedge, and I cautiously parted a few branches of hawthorn and got my head far enough through to see where this pest was. My main reason was to know whether he was going away or coming towards us. If the latter, we ought to show ourselves to avoid being shot by accident. It all brought back nasty memories of the time Tom had driven me off the meagre bailiwick of Jasmine Farm by threatening me with his confounded shotgun.

I turned my head and looked towards where the sound had come from. What I saw brought me back with a quick movement of sheer surprise. The wet twigs showered golden drops as I released them abruptly.

'Well, my God,' I said.

'What is it?'

'I don't believe this.'

'*What*? Let me look.'

She peered in the same direction, but came back looking merely puzzled. 'All right, a chap with a double-barrelled sporting gun. What's the big –'

'Didn't you get a look at his face?'

She tried again. 'Well, he's coming this way, and I got his face pretty clearly that time, but I can't say I recognize him.'

I decided not to poke my head out again, but to freeze and let him come past. If the marksman was who I thought he was, if that first hasty glance had not been an illusion, there was no point in staging the empty charade of a genial meeting among friends.

'Is it someone you –'

'Hush a minute,' I said. 'Let him get past.'

The man was coming along at a reasonably good pace now, with only the hedge between us. Heather and I stood quite still, and as he went by, looking down at his gun and fiddling with it, I saw his face in profile, hardly at all obscured by the hedge, and not six feet away.

There was no longer any doubt. It was Carshalton.

Heather and I resumed wheeling our bikes along the path and I said, 'Did you really not recognize that chap?'

'Never saw him in my life as far as I know.'

'Well, he's called Carshalton. He's an Episcopus man. He was at the ball, in fact he was the one who made a bit of an exhibition of himself, dropping his cigar-ash into the claret cup and then scattering that tray of glasses. He's usually engaged in getting the better of somebody. That's why it interests me to see him walking round the fields with a gun. I'd be willing to bet it isn't harmless recreation. More likely something to do with his –'

As if on purpose to interrupt my analysis, Carshalton's gun now went off again, some distance away. He must have solved whatever technical problem was troubling him as he frowned down at his weapon when walking past us and thus failed to turn his head and see us, because for the rest of the time he was within earshot we heard fairly regular bangs, as if he were getting in a concentrated spell of practice.

I wondered what cold-hearted little scheme he was pushing. But I didn't care much. My chief thought was that if the weather improved, and Heather and I took to making love in the open air again, I must be slightly more watchful than before. How unthinkably awful to be just in the act of scaling the heights of bliss and to feel oneself peppered with buckshot: injurious enough from any source, but especially invidious if the trigger had been pressed by the robot-finger of horrible Carshalton!

Chapter 19

So it was October again, and time to climb up that twisting staircase at Episcopus and settle into the two rooms where I could move and have my being. What a difference twelve months had made! In October 1930 I was a shrinking, insecure newcomer, glancing nervously around to know if anything I happened to do or say would transgress some unwritten law; in October 1931 I was a second-year man, established, knowing the ropes, greeting friends, steering clear of people I had learned to distrust, and ready with a kindly word of advice for timid freshmen. The sight of all those young, well-washed, frightened faces, clustering in the lodge or round notice boards, made me feel seasoned, rooted, solid. Also, I knew I was on top of the work. As soon as we settled into the swing of term, I started to turn in good essays for Bax; I knew they were good and I knew he knew I knew. It seemed to take him very little time to get over his annoyance with me for dropping out of his reading party, though his manner was always rather distant whether he was cross with you or not, and he was not a man who would like to show that his composure had been ruffled.

The key to my situation, of course, was that my energies were no longer being deflected by my sexual needs. Heather usually managed to get over a couple of times a week, and even in bad weeks it never fell below one. I used to sport the oak, get a blazing fire going, and then for three or four hours it was continuous merry-making. In between bouts we used to toast muffins at the fireside, so when we were not enjoying ourselves in one way we were enjoying ourselves in another. And then, after she had gone and the dark, foggy autumn-into-winter night came down, I would sit contentedly by my fire, reading, reading, always reading, the restlessness taken out of my youthful body, my strong young mind ready to devour facts and ideas, my fresh eyes not daunted by acre after acre of print. It was a good season. No part of my life has been better.

'May you live in interesting times,' says the old Chinese curse.

Precisely because my second undergraduate year was happy and tranquil, it isn't interesting to talk about. I often wish my whole life had been as uninteresting as those nine months. They were like the nine months I spent in the womb; all I did in them was grow.

The sort of thing that passed for an 'event' in that calm stretch was that I joined a History Discussion Club, which used to meet once a week in various colleges. Sometimes a big-name historian would condescend to lead a discussion, or more rarely a journalist or politician who had an interest in some historical issue would come and parade his prejudices, but most often it was members only. Bax told me of its existence; he had been instrumental in founding it, and quite often came to meetings, though he rarely said much. I met two people there who were memorable in their different ways. The first was a girl named Geraldine. Since the club was University-wide it had some girls in it, and though I was not feeling the need to break new ground I naturally took an interest in them, girls having such rarity value in my life. I knew so few of the mysterious creatures that even now, when I knew one specimen in total detail, I still found it fascinating to watch and listen to them and try to get some idea of how their minds worked.

I knew Geraldine's name because she was Secretary or Treasurer or something of the club, so that her name was on the membership card. Also, she had to get up and make brief announcements now and then, about the next meeting and suchlike. She used to make these announcements in a hard, matter-of-fact little voice, standing there with her shoulders hunched and her hands thrust deep into her pockets, like a schoolboy. She wore a kind of loose knitted jacket, like a cardigan but thicker and heavier, and she used to jam her hands down into the pockets so that the whole garment dragged down over her hips, which were barely noticeable anyway, her figure was so boy-like. She always wore narrow black trousers and her jacket was dark red. Above the outfit was a white collar, always startlingly white, and then her pale, intense little face with a mop of black hair. As a rule she wore a defiant expression, as if she were going through life saying to the world, 'Just you try to pick a fight with *me*!', but if something amused her she would give a sudden wide grin and then her face looked like a cheeky schoolboy's.

As a matter of fact, whatever the expression on her face, anyone would have known at first glance that Geraldine had a defiant, combative streak in her nature from the mere fact that she wore trousers. In the 1930s, these were socially respectable only as working clothes. It was all right for a girl like Heather, who exercised horses and cleaned out stables, to wear old corduroy trousers, but for any other occasion they were regarded as 'fast'. Certainly the young ladies of Oxford University were not supposed to be fast, and one knew, without having to be told, that Geraldine would have had to fight like a cat for the right of wearing what she chose to wear – fight not against any definite rule, since the University did not have sumptuary laws in the twentieth century as it had done in the seventeenth when Archbishop Laud was Chancellor, but against freezing disapproval and many a good talking-to. They couldn't actually send her down for wearing trousers, but they could (and, as I found out when I got to know her better, most certainly did) make her feel that she was the kind of girl who really *ought* to be sent down. But she had them in a cleft stick, because she was a good student: clever, always eager to know more, her mind unresting in the way it moved from one judgment to the next, trying always to get nearer the heart of the matter, whatever matter it was that concerned her. She must have been a real thorn in the flesh of the authorities. She was undocile without being merely unruly; radical and enquiring without belonging to the dervish Left, always suspicious of authority but not exactly along predictable lines. An uncomfortable young woman! And very much the type that, when the University first opened its doors to women, they must have half hoped to attract (because she was clever and energetic) and half hoped they wouldn't (because she was a handful.) She did me good; I was grateful for her.

I got to know Geraldine step by step. The first conversation I ever had with her was in public. We tangled during the discussion at one of the history meetings; we were talking to each other, but in a roomful of other people, mostly strangers to us. She had, I remember, annoyed me by applying some hard-boiled socio-economic theory a bit too literally. She was clever, but a shade predictable, always brushing aside any kind of idealism, giving to the Crusades, for instance, a purely economic motivation.

On this occasion the speaker had been talking about some aspect of the feudal system, and Geraldine had been quick to pounce with statistics about land tenure and the cash-nexus. I weighed in on the other side, with stuff about the spirit of feudal allegiance and Eleanor of Aquitaine, and God knows what. I'm sure all our arguments were very thin and amateurish, but we were trying our wings. I noticed Bax listening expressionlessly, his eyes narrowed to slits behind his pebble glasses. I couldn't tell whether he was bored or not. He didn't intervene in the discussion, which could have been a good sign, because he usually did if you were talking utter tripe.

When the meeting broke up – it was in a featureless room on one of those interminable corridors in Keble – I carried on talking with Geraldine and we went down the staircase together. She marched keenly over to the bike-stands, still talking, whipped her machine out of one of them and began wheeling it towards the lodge.

'You have to go back straight away?' I hazarded.

'You just bet I do. It's twenty past ten now, and you simply can't form any idea, unless you've seen it, how hysterical they get at St Hilda's if you come in after half-past ten.'

'Half-past ten? I though midnight was the standard –'

'Technically you're right, but they watch you like a hawk at my beloved Alma Mater, and they know I belong to a Club that has men among its members, and that makes them as nervous as hell. My moral tutor's probably sitting on the edge of her bed at this moment with curling-papers in her hair, afraid to go to sleep till she knows I've come in. She probably thinks I'm getting myself seduced or something.'

'Oh,' I said. I found all this slightly surprising. In those days it was not at all usual for well-brought-up girls at Oxford Colleges to make remarks about 'being seduced' to young men. From some girls, I might have regarded it as a come-on. But I knew Geraldine's way.

'Well, see you around,' she said when we got to the street, and swinging her leg over the saddle, schoolboy fashion, pedalled rapidly off down Parks Road. I called 'Good-night,' but the darkness had already closed over her. It was always like that – interesting, vivacious, irreverent conversation, then the unceremonious farewell and the whisking off.

The other person I got to know through the History Discussion Club was a man named Harry Goodenough. Like me, he was a second-year undergraduate, but not reading history, and not from Episcopus. I had never met him till he came to a meeting to read a paper on 'The Evolution of the Tudor Stage'. It wasn't the kind of subject we usually discussed and not many people turned up. Harry Goodenough was a large, rather fleshy young man with a great bush of wiry sand-coloured hair through which he ran his fingers when he got excited, which he soon did in a discussion that interested him. To interest him, a discussion had only to have some bearing on Shakespeare.

He was a Warwickshire lad, this Goodenough, and my theory was that he must have been bitten, as a child, by the descendant of a dog that had once been patted by William Shakespeare in some quiet back lane in Stratford-on-Avon. Certainly something had got into his blood and its effect was to make him obsessed with the Bard. He was reading English, but he seemed to be doing so because that was the only discipline within which the University would permit him to spend at least some of his time soaking up information about Shakespeare with their official blessing. He seemed to take very little notice of the other things he was supposed to read, from *Beowulf* to Byron. Anything, however, that could point in the direction of Shakespeare was fair game.

His paper, for which he had prepared far too much material, and to which most of the sparse audience listened with glazed eyes, took us all the way from the medieval inn-yard to the Fortune and Globe theatres. It was all about the craftsmen's guilds and the Court and the Lord Chamberlain's Men and about Henslowe's diaries, and surviving account books, and what parts of the stage spectators were and weren't allowed to sit on, and the fact that the Globe had a tower twenty-six feet high, or was it thirty-six feet? I forget the details, and whether the actors could make use of it for exits and entrances... It all came pouring out in a torrent, badly arranged, and all that came over was that this was a devouring passion. Goodenough's large, round, rather meaty face glistened in the electric light as he turned page after page, hastening on towards no particular conclusion, unloading his treasure, serving Shakespeare.

Geraldine was there, and she tangled him up in discussion in the brief time that was left after he had finished. She asked him what was the subject-matter of the plays that were put on in medieval inn-yards; they must have been, she said, an important part of the people's recreation, and the subject-matter would be an indication of which way their thoughts were running. Goodenough, obviously not wanting to go down that particular alley, said that at the beginning of the period he was covering the plays were mainly Bible stories. Geraldine said that sounded as if the whole thing was an off-shoot of the Church, which was part of the apparatus by which the common people were kept in order, and it didn't sound to her as if they had a popular art that questioned the nature of authority. No, said Goodenough, that came later. How much later? He began to try to head her off, saying that dramatists like Kyd had started a vogue for plays dealing with scandalous goings-on at wicked foreign courts, and she said that sounded escapist and hadn't the playwrights ever criticized Tudor authoritarianism? At this point Bax, unexpectedly, struck in and with a few decisive sentences managed to shut Geraldine up and leave Goodenough in peace to tail off with a few more remarks about stage areas and instructions to carpenters. Bax reminded her that Walsingham had run an effective police state in Elizabethan England, so that criticism had to be in code, and as for the medieval side of things, advised her to look at Karl Young's *The Drama of the Mediaeval Church* and also read a few of the mystery plays. Having fired this off, he relapsed into the silence that usually enwrapped him at these meetings; it was as if he came along to see fair play rather than to take an active part.

I made an attempt, when the meeting broke up, to have a few minutes' talk with Geraldine, but I had also found Goodenough sympathetic and wanted to get to know him, and since she scampered down the stairs quickly and he lumbered down slowly, leaving me hovering somewhere in between, I lost her. Goodenough and I strolled along the street together. I warmed to him as we talked. There was something gentle and clumsy about him that was lovable, and besides I admired the selflessness of his devotion to Shakespeare. It was like my interest in history but more fanatical and more self-forgetful. After all, though I studied history for its own sake, I also had fairly firm expectations of using it to make some kind of a living, either teaching, or working for a publishing house, or something of that kind; whereas I wouldn't have minded betting that Goodenough never considered such matters at all. After taking his degree, I supposed, he would head for some theatre where Shakespeare was performed and hang about till they gave him a job shifting scenery or sweeping up after hours, just so that he could be within the life-giving aura.

He developed some of his ideas as we walked along, making me secretly ashamed that I didn't even own a copy of Shakespeare, only the two or three dog-eared texts of individual plays we had had to study during our schooldays; and I found it interesting enough to ask him in for a drink when we fetched up outside Episcopus. The previous evening, expecting to be host to a few people, I had laid in a dozen pint bottles of beer, and because of a change of plan they were still unconsumed, so I re-lit my fire and Goodenough and I settled down and started opening them.

'I say, that girl was a bit sharp, wasn't she?' he said, leaning back with a full glass and ready to chat in a more relaxed way about our evening. 'You know, the little tomboy one who started off about escapism. With trousers. Christ, she's the only one I've seen with –'

'Geraldine,' I said. 'She's all right really. Rather fun, actually. But she does like to get an argument going, and I suppose stage dimensions and account books didn't give her much of an opening.'

'I thought for a moment she was going to turn out to be one of these people I seem to get every time I start talking about Shakespeare, who ask me why he wasn't a Marxist. They're the ones who always say the only productions of Shakespeare worth seeing are the ones in Moscow and it always turns out that they've never *seen* these productions, it's just a line they hand out.'

'No, Geraldine isn't a Communist. We get enough of them, goodness knows, at meetings, and always with the answer to everything. That's what puts me off them, actually – the assumption that there aren't any complexities in anything, that party dogma's settled everything and if you see any question from a different angle, whether it's to do with politics, history, art, philosophy, anything – that's just because you want to be awkward or because you're a reactionary and you hate the working people or something.'

'I know,' Goodenough sighed, 'I get it all the time. Mind you, Shakespeare had some pretty definite attitudes on all those questions. If you take the two tribunes in *Coriolanus*, for instance... Now, what are their names... Menenius and Sicinius, that's it... Well, if you take them....'

Long before he had talked himself out and before we had despatched that dozen of bottled beer, the hands of the cheap clock on my desk stood at 1.15. The College gate was finally closed, for egress as well as ingress, at midnight; indeed, as the chimes of twelve had floated towards us through the frosty air (for the season was midwinter) it had crossed my mind that I ought to interrupt his flow, but I hadn't the heart to do it. So now, he would have to climb out of Episcopus, with my help, walk to his own rather distant College and, once there, climb in. It all sounds a lot of trouble, but in the Oxford of those days scores of young men carried out these routines every night.

There were a number of recognized climbing-in and -out routes at Episcopus; the one I favoured myself made use of a magnificent old chestnut tree which grew beside the wall bordering an unfrequented lane. To this tree I conducted Goodenough through the labyrinths of the silent, slumbering College. There was a silvery half-moon, and roofs and walls glistened with a faint rime of frost.

Getting Goodenough up into the tree proved to be difficult. I, of slight build and active, had never found it anything but childishly easy, since the trunk was rough-barked and thick, with frequent holds for hand and foot; but he, heavily built and rather clumsy, was further handicapped by wearing a bulky overcoat with several buttons missing, so that it tended to bunch up and billow out at inconvenient points, and by his refusal to let go of the bulky file containing the notes for his paper. At last, however, I coaxed him to a height sufficient to make it possible for him to move out along the branch that crossed the wall into public space. He was, however, facing the wrong way.

'Look, turn round,' I said in a low voice, designed not to carry across the quad. 'Get your back to the trunk and you'll see a –'

We swayed about for a moment as if wrestling; finally I had his bulk facing out along the branch.

'Forward,' I hissed. 'You're there now.'

He reached out for a branch that would do to steady himself against while he took the two or three steps along the broad branch that were all he needed. Really it was no more of a balancing feat than walking down a garden path. But he was, of course, more than slightly drunk. The hand with which he reached out for the branch was the one in which he gripped the file of notes. His fingers skidded on the bark, which was probably a little iced. Suddenly and disastrously, his weight tilted sideways. There was a confused snapping sound as his falling body broke off several minor branches, then a soft thud as he landed, on all fours, on the ground. It was not a long fall – as I looked down, appalled, he seemed to be only just below me – but a cataclysmic one. Peering down through the branches, I saw that as he clambered unsteadily to his feet he was not alone. Standing motionless in the faint light from that metallic half-moon was a figure smaller and slighter than my own, and, compared with the ox-like Goodenough, positively elfin. This figure was regarding Goodenough, who had suddenly appeared in the trajectory of its walk, with an air both thoughtful and bemused.

Up there in the branches, I froze into immobility. It was the venerable scientist, Weatherby. Goodenough slowly climbed to his feet and stood rubbing one knee and blinking at Weatherby.

'You're not hurt, I hope?' Weatherby asked courteously.

'My knee,' Goodenough mumbled, 'but not broken, I think.'

Weatherby nodded, and, seeming to sink back into his own thoughts, continued his walk round the quad. I waited until he disappeared through a dimly lit archway before dropping down to join Goodenough and offer my sympathy.

'We'll soon have you over,' I said. 'Just scramble up that tree again and in two shakes you'll –'

'Nothing doing,' said Goodenough shortly. 'I'm doing no more climbing. I just don't feel up to it. I'll sleep on your *chaise longue*, if you don't mind.'

'Well, of course I don't mind,' I said, 'but number one, I don't think you'll be very comfortable, and number two, what about your College when you stay out all night?'

'I'll get up in the morning before anybody's about and just walk in before breakfast. Ten to one nobody'll notice me and if they do, to hell with them. It's better than breaking your neck.'

So Goodenough slept on my *chaise longue* and when I woke the next morning he was gone. I daresay the cold woke him very early, huddled as he was in a fireless room with only his overcoat for covering. It was a trivial incident, the small change of undergraduate life, but I expect Harry Goodenough thought back to it now and then in the years that followed. It was, after all, his first meeting with one of the foremost scientists of the twentieth century.

*

Of such picayune coinage were the 'incidents' made up, in my uneventful second year. But hold on, there was one small episode that had a little edge of drama. It provided a nine days' wonder when it happened, and a pleasant memory to look back on for many years afterwards.

It happened during the same reach of the winter as Goodenough's involuntary meeting with Professor Weatherby; during the same lengthy spell of frosty cold, in fact. I had mislaid a notebook which was, at that stage, crucial to my studies, being full of notes I had made during a concentrated spell of reading during the summer. After scouring my room at Episcopus without avail, I decided it must be at home somewhere, and I went down to the Bargeman's in search of it at the first opportunity, which happened to be late the next afternoon. It was there all right – it had fallen behind other books on a tightly-wedged shelf – and, feeling relieved, I decided to treat myself to a glass of beer in the bar, which was just opening. It meant listening to the usual bovine chorus from Trundle and his mates, but after so many years I had grown used to that, and indeed found myself missing it now and again in my new, intellectually more rigorous existence.

This evening, by sheer chance, proved to be one of the rare occasions when the two halves of my existence merged as one. The conversation in the bar concerned a report in a local paper – not the *Oxford Mail*, but a smudgily printed sheet covering a cluster of outlying villages, which had somehow found its way into the possession of Peake. He came in brandishing it. And the story, as it happened, concerned an undergraduate at my own college.

This did not immediately emerge; indeed, Peake, Trundle, Bob and the rest, who took no notice of me as I sat over in a corner, slowly absorbing my pint of beer and with it the story, never realized that I was acquainted with one of the actors in the drama. At first, as Peake read out the headline and sub-heading, I paid only slight attention, but presently I began to see where the tale was heading.

' "ACCIDENT MARS SHOOTING PARTY," ' Peake intoned. "HEIR TO LOCAL ESTATE INJURED." And then underneath, "Motor Dash to Oxford Hospital." '

To sum up in a few words the information that emerged in a more tangled, gradual and crabwise manner, the injured party was the Honourable Robin Acheson-Fiske, the elegantly-dressed young man with the aristocratic face whom I had seen in the garden at Episcopus, in company with his sister, she of the equally long-boned face and the narrow elegant sandalled feet, and the trumpeting cow-elephant pearl-roped mother, all being shepherded along the trim leaf-shaded and flower-bedecked path by sweatily anxious Carshalton as he soaked up the matriarch's information about flowering grasses and told her about his parents' garden in Shanghai (also known, it seems, as Hounslow). And now that same Carshalton, no doubt still sweatily anxious but now with his anxiety focused on a definite end, that of appearing a gun-toting sportsman to the manner born, had clumsily discharged his weapon – the same, no doubt, with which Heather and I had seen him blazing away along that sun-flooded August hedgerow – and lodged a few pellets in the patrician anatomy of his junior host. There followed a thrilling description of the dash by motor-car to the Radcliffe Infirmary; evidently the party had decided neither to trust the local Cottage Hospital nor to wait till the ambulance service could get to them. Doctors had pronounced the wounds not serious; no charges for criminal negligence were to be brought; forgive and forget was to be the watchword. But the unfortunate blunderer was punished there and then in the columns of a local newspaper by having his name and address announced to the world. Mr Donald Carshalton, a student at Episcopus College, could (one assumed) quietly close the book on any ambitions he might have had for a busy social season revolving round the sporting weekend, the hide and the game-bag, let alone the grouse moor. He was, as the paper didn't trouble to say, in outer darkness, and it would take him ten years to work his way back, if he ever managed it at all. It all sounded to me like a one-way ticket to Hounslow.

The inevitable inside story came to the Trundle *cénacle* via some character called Old Ern or Old Vern or such, who worked in some capacity at the Acheson-Fiske stately home, which it appeared was called Mulberry Park and lay somewhere in the west of the county towards Gloucestershire. He had been helping out as a beater when the calamity happened. It was this character who had found out (from the housekeeper) the name of the luckless marksman, and communicated it, along with the rest of the story, to the local weekly news-sheet, doubtless in return for the price of a couple of pints. The Acheson-Fiske family, disliking publicity of any kind and certainly in such a ludicrous misadventure as this, had managed to keep it out of any more prominent paper; had it not been for the vigilance of Old Varmint, Carshalton might have reasonably hoped that his *débâcle* would never reach the ears of anyone outside the gates of the stately home. But now it had reached the Bargeman's, it would, inevitably, percolate into the network of College servants and, in no long time, arrive at Episcopus. So I reflected as I listened to the long susurrus of conversation between Old Trundle and his mates, as they worked over this topic at their infinite leisure and in their pleasantly burring Oxfordshire voices. 'Arr, 'twouldn't'a happened years agone,' Trundle led off. 'When I was a lad and Queen Victoria was on the throne, the undergrads were gennlemen. You never heard nothin' about *them* blazin' away at the wrong time and pointin' their guns the wrong way. They was bred to 'em. They was brought up with guns.'

'Sure it worn't bows an' arrows?' young Ted put in facetiously.

'Arr, you can larrf, but they was gennlemen. Mischiefs they done in plenty, but never that kind o' mischief. Pepperin' innocent people like that.'

'It's true enough,' Peake assented, 'but that's a long time ago. The undergrads that used to come here in your young days, they was raised to it, like you says. Shooting parties and that. Going up to Scotland for the Twelfth of August and all that. India and Africa, too, I shouldn't wonder, some of 'em.'

'Don't get that type now,' said Old Trundle, shaking his head ponderously.

'No, and why not?' Peake pursued his advantage. ' 'Cause they don't exist no more, that's the long and short of it. That kind of young chap, that had all the money and the spare time and could shoot well and ride to 'ounds and all that, they've gone. Twenty years ago they was there, in their country houses, or in their Colleges. Fifteen years ago they wasn't. You knows where they are as well as I does.'

'Yes, I knows.'

'Laying dead,' Peake said. He pointed, with the full stretch of his arm, in what we had to assume was the direction of Flanders. 'Laying dead out there, in the mud. Quarrel between a lot of foreigners, and we has to get mixed up in it. Serbia! Who the 'ell cares what happens in Serbia?'

A meaningless wrangle ensued; switching off my attention, I drank up my beer and took my notebook back to Episcopus.

It was dinner-time when I got there, and as I took my place at one of the long benches and waited to be served I looked around for Carshalton. I was interested to see if his experience at Mulberry Park had left any mark on him. But, externally at least, it hadn't. His face, with those deep-set watchful eyes, was as expressionless as ever, and he entered the Hall and moved towards a vacant place with the impersonal, programmed movements that were habitual to him. He was sitting fairly near to me, and I noticed that no one said anything to him that related in any way to his misadventure. The explanation, of course, was that the undergraduate body was, just as it has largely remained, inward-looking and impervious to local news. The story would filter in by degrees, from casual remarks dropped by scouts leaning on their brooms and porters gossiping in quiet moments in the lodge. They were the people who knew the local news, just as the customers at the Bargeman's knew it; I would not have known it myself, but for the accident of my having gone home for half an hour that evening. Carshalton may have been hoping to get away with it, to let his discomfiture sink into oblivion, unknown to any of his contemporaries; as I went to bed that night, I reflected on this and wondered whether it would be worth the trouble to blow the gaff on him. And then I remembered the words of the otherwise unmemorable Perkins, as we sat in that humble pub in the Giler. He'll watch and wait till 'he can do something really hideous to me. You can see it in his face.'

Perkins had been afraid of Carshalton. *People* like that can make a lot of trouble. I, for my part, was not afraid. Why not? Because I was brave? No. Not brave. Because I was a fool then? But if so, what was I a fool *about*? What large, important truths were visible to mankind in general but invisible to me? If Carshalton was dangerous, what was the danger and why didn't I feel threatened by it?

Because, I decided as I drifted to sleep, because I was not ambitious. I was not in competition with the thrusting, grabbing people of the world. Did that mean that I didn't want any kind of worldly success? Because if you did go for any kind of worldly success, any kind *at all*, you came into competition with ambitious people who hated you and set out to harm you. Well, I just wanted to be a good historian. Would that be success? Would that make people hate me? Only if I took jobs and positions they might have liked. But surely they wouldn't... surely *success*, and *the world*, were far, far apart from anything I cared about? The grabbers and thrusters would never want what I... and then I almost sat bolt upright in bed as I saw Carshalton's matt-pale, fanatic's face, those little deep-buried eyes that were looking ahead for only one thing – success, success, success – and I knew that he, and people like him, would never forgive anyone else for being good at *anything*, for showing excellence or even promise in any field whether they personally were competing in it or not. Safer by far, more comfortable, preferable in every way, to live in a world where everyone but yourself was a mediocrity and a failure. Yes, for Carshalton, the rise of anyone meant the possibility, somewhere and somehow, of a fall for him, and if he could do anything to prevent it he would.

Having got this point clear in my mind, I dismissed it from my thoughts and went to sleep. Normal life resumed its tidal sway, and for a week or two I gave no thought to Carshalton or his foolish escapade. But one evening not long before the end of term, ten or a dozen of us were lounging about in the J.C.R., and Carshalton was sitting by himself in an armchair, looking at a newspaper, when another man suddenly called to him across the width of the room, 'Hey, there, Carshalton!'

'What?' Carshalton asked coldly, lowering the newspaper an inch or two.

'Been firing off any guns lately?'

There was a general laugh; I gathered the matter had been a topic of conversation before Carshalton or I had entered.

Carshalton went, if possible, slightly paler than his usual lifeless white, and said, 'Is that supposed to be funny?'

'Deadly serious, old man, deadly serious. Just a friendly enquiry. I mean, hang it all, if you're going to go round peppering people with buckshot and putting them in hospital, you're hardly the kind of man I'm going to pick a quarrel with, now are you?'

The undergraduate teasing Carshalton was an oafish fellow enough, very much one of the ruck of undifferentiated Public School men – I have forgotten his name now and am not sure that I knew it even then – but at this moment, with the sense of the meeting clearly on his side, he was enjoying a rare chance to show off and seem witty.

'Come to think of it,' he pursued, 'I've got an uncle who gets up shooting parties in Norfolk. I must get him to invite you. I've never got on with him at all well, and it would suit me down to the ground if he had a good long spell in hospital. I'd go and stay down there and borrow his car.'

Carshalton folded the newspaper carefully, laid it down on the table beside his armchair and, without haste, got up and walked from the room. Presently we all went in to dinner and Carshalton, presumably hoping that the joking he had just endured would be an isolated incident, came in among the rest. He sat, as it happened, opposite me. I said nothing to him across the table, but I heard the man sitting to one side of him asking him some fairly harmless questions about the matter, not in an aggressive or derisive tone, merely as if taking an interest. Had the newspaper report been accurate?

'There wasn't much they could get wrong,' Carshalton said, 'short of making up a complete story from scratch. But they did make one damn silly mistake.'

'Yes?'

'Yes. They got my first name wrong. Put me down as Donald. I don't know where they got that from. It isn't Donald and it never has been.'

'What is it?'

'Dominic,' said Carshalton.

My own reaction on hearing this detail was that 'Dominic' did not sound a very likely Christian name for Carshalton; I almost wondered whether it was one of his touches of fiction, to bring his personal style more into line with the social ambitions and the Shanghai parents domiciled in Hounslow. But I was so little interested in the creature that I again dismissed the matter from my mind, not even troubling to ask the honest Perkins, who would surely have known.

It proved, however, impossible to remain completely oblivious of Carshalton. In the last week of term there was a J.C.R. meeting, which as usual I didn't attend; but on going in to lunch the next day I found Wilmot grinning about something as he helped himself to mashed potatoes.

'What's funny?' I asked, sitting down beside him.

'You weren't at the meeting last night, were you?' he said and grinned even more broadly at the fresh recollection. 'They gave old Carshalton a good roasting. Of course he wasn't there, but it'll all go down in the minutes. He won't like that.'

'No,' I agreed. 'He doesn't like to lose face, especially if it's going to go on the record. What happened?'

'Well, Norbert was in the chair, and we'd just about got through everything when he announced an extra item that he'd slipped in since the agenda was pinned up. Said it wouldn't take a moment. He'd already got somebody to second it. Then, very solemn and serious and official, you know how Norbert can be when he wants to, just like a Cabinet Minister, he reads out this motion: 'that in future all members of the J.C.R. who intend to handle lethal weapons should submit themselves beforehand to instruction by a qualified person before discharging the said weapons in the company of other human beings.' A very shrewd dig under the ribs, I thought it. Carshalton quite obviously just took up shooting as a way of getting into the right social circles and it's damn lucky he didn't kill somebody in the process.'

'It went through all right, I imagine,' I said.

'*Nem. con.* But that wasn't the best of it. Norbert's just about to close the meeting when Knowlton gets up from the armchair he's been deep in, over in the far corner. He says he has a motion to put that he's just thought of, but he hopes it'll seem agreeable. And then – you know that casual, easy-going, nothing-matters-a-damn way Knowlton has – he moves that Lamont, as the College poet, should be asked, by the collective invitation of the J.C.R., to write a cautionary poem with some title like, now let me get it right,' Wilmot's brow wrinkled with the effort of memory, 'On the Recent Narrow Escape by a Member of Episcopus College from the Perpetration of Criminally Negligent Homicide.' God, he really rolled it all round his tongue, and it sounded all the more, what shall I say, satirical, in that drawling, half-awake voice the man has.'

'Good going,' I said, and we both chuckled. While we talked I had been looking round for Carshalton, but he was not there. During those last days of term he must have taken all his meals out. But I saw Lamont, sitting over on the other side of the Hall. The man next to him was talking steadily, evidently explaining something. Lamont was keeping up a façade of listening, his head bent over courteously towards the other man, but I could see from the abstracted expression on his face, even at this distance, that most of his mind was elsewhere.

'Lamont won't take up that business about a cautionary joke-poem,' I said to Wilmot. 'It's not the kind of thing he writes.'

'Of course not,' Wilmot said. 'It'd be too ordinary for him. He'd only write a poem about something if it was... completely up in the air.'

He spoke tolerantly and yet it was obvious that his attitude was not as reverential as mine. I admired Lamont more than anyone I had yet encountered at Oxford. I admired him too much to think of trying to make a friend of him; I did not aim so high. To Wilmot, as I now saw, Lamont was simply an amiable eccentric; Oxford, and for that matter the world, would get on perfectly well without him.

I looked across again at Lamont. He was still keeping up the polite appearance of listening as this bore droned on, and still, I could see, voyaging among his own thoughts. What kind of thoughts were they? I could never imagine that. I had no idea of the reach of Lamont's mind; it was beyond me. But, sitting beside Wilmot now and suddenly seeing him through Wilmot's eyes as well as my own, I realized that his was the usual view of Lamont and mine very much the exception.

*

I didn't work at the Boardman boat business that Easter vac. I lacked the special motive that had, a year before, impelled me to sign on for the money-earning and muscle-hardening work. All through the long hours of work I had been sustained by that single-minded vision of Vinnie's knickers, and in the end it had all come to nothing. But now, with Heather in charge of that department, I was all right, thank God, and free to get on with some work. And work I did. I read a lot of basic documents, the kind you have to go through carefully, notebook at hand and commentaries beside you. There just isn't time for that kind of reading in term-time, when you want to see something of your friends and in any case are constantly interrupted by essays and tutorials and clubs and discussion groups and what-not. That's why the present-day student attitude, which divides the year into two parts – term, when they do a bit of studying, and vac., when they go off and get paid jobs – is such a disaster, turning them out at the end of three years with a B.A. but no real grip on their subject.

Well, I worked solidly that vac. and, for recreation, wrote a paper to deliver to the Discussion Club. I thought it best not to talk about anything specialized, because frankly most of the members were pretty amateurish, so I chose, as a good general subject that had plenty of colour and action in it, the St Scholastica's Day Massacre of February 1355. Everybody who came would at least know what that was: the worst and bloodiest of all the medieval outbreaks of violence between City and University, and in some respects the culminating one, because the full power of Church and State was brought in, afterwards, on the University's side, and the City lost a lot of privileges.

I didn't, however, want to give my whole time to just *describing* the massacre: how it had started on a Tuesday with a brawl in a tavern at Carfax, developed into widespread town-and-gown rioting by nightfall but ended inconclusively, and would doubtless have died away if the townsmen had not brought in reinforcements from the surrounding villages, who poured in the next morning as soon as the town gates were opened and set about the scholars, who were now outnumbered. During Wednesday and Thursday the mob broke into the houses and halls where the students lived; very few of the colleges in their later form had yet been built, so only a handful of the University could take refuge behind thick walls and oaken gates, and for those who could not it was a time of terror. They were hauled from their habitations, or from churches where they had gone for sanctuary, beaten, injured, in some cases tortured by having the skin flayed from their tonsured scalps, and, in six cases, murdered. After three days the sated townsmen withdrew, leaving Oxford emptied of scholars except for those few who could find safety in very strong buildings. A dismayed silence fell; people must have wondered whether it was worth going on with the effort to set up an international university in a place where it was so much hated.

All this, my hearers knew before they came in. I had decided to concentrate on the social and economic consequences of the massacre rather than its mere occurrence. My title was 'Five Centuries in the Corner: the Retribution for St Scholastica's Day, 1355-1825.' I reminded, or informed, my hearers that the City had been forced to pay £50, an enormous sum in an age when a farthing bought a pound of meat, for damage caused to University property; that the Mayor and his chief associates were sent to prison; that a new charter, later in that year, was granted to the University which gave its Chancellor sweeping powers over the trade and general management of the city; and that in general Town, for nearly five hundred years, had had to bow the knee in penitence to Gown. Every year there was a service in St Mary's Church in which mass was said for the souls of the scholars killed in the rioting, and the Mayor, Bailiffs and sixty burgesses had to attend and hand over a silver penny apiece to the University in token that they were ashamed and sorry; and this went on until 1825.

At a rapid canter I then outlined the probable reasons for that outburst of resentment among the townsmen. Xenophobia would be part of it; the medieval universities were more international than modern ones, and many of those early students were foreigners, which would be enough on its own to get them disliked. Anti-clerical feeling was another strand; most medieval students were candidates for the priesthood, and by the fourteenth century the ordinary man had had enough of Mother Church. Again, the medieval student was usually poor, so that he did nothing to enrich the local tradesmen; often unruly; certainly too numerous, so that Oxford, then as now, suffered a housing problem. All this added up to a barrel of dynamite. But the tremendous and horrifying bang when that barrel finally went up was, I laboured to show, ultimately to the University's advantage, bringing in Higher Authority on its side. I cited the picturesque exaggerations in Antony Wood's account of the massacre, with its suggestion of an enormous death-toll without actually giving figures, and its general tone of outrage ('a numberless multitude, desiring to heap mischief on mischief, and to perfect by a more terrible conclusion that wicked enterprise which they had begun'), especially important in view of Wood's own position in history, after the overthrow of the Commonwealth and the restoration of the monarchy. Wood's account, even more lurid than the truth, suggests that what really appalled him was that the lower orders should have dared to lay their horny hands on the sacred persons of the clerisy, and this, I maintained, was increasingly how the episode had been viewed. For this, like disobedient children, the townspeople of Oxford had been stood in a corner for nearly five hundred years: four hundred and seventy, to be precise.

The usual discussion followed. It's not surprising that, after so many years, I can't remember much about it, but a few things stand out. One was that the talk drifted to town-and-gown relations in general, through history, bringing up such issues as, To what extent did the actual populace of Oxford share the Royalist sentiment that led the city to become the King's headquarters in the terrible events of the 1640s? I remember a Scottish student remarking that in Edinburgh, people were proud of their University, and if a visitor asked the way to it they took pleasure in showing the way; they felt it was a feather in their cap to have a famous University in their city, like having Holyrood Palace or Arthur's Seat; but he had found a very different attitude among the local people in Oxford, who felt threatened and diminished by the University.

That set me thinking of those town butchers and bakers and tanners and stall-holders who had turned with such savagery on the students seven hundred years ago. I remember staring out of the window. The meeting was being held in the rooms of some history don at Merton, which meant that we were in the Fellows' Quad, a place of dream-like beauty and order if ever one existed on this earth, and as I gazed out I wondered if there would ever again be an invasion of the multitude, if those who saw the University and its concerns as an excrescence, something not needed in wholesome everyday life, an intrusion that bred disturbance and disproportion, would crowd in here again with axes and crowbars... No, I thought, not in that form, not with axes and crowbars, but with what then? For the underlying quarrel had never been healed, I knew that.

These thoughts went through my head while our host, the rather dim Merton don whose name and face I have forgotten, was explaining some minute point about the early statutes of the University – something, doubtless, that it would have done me good to attend to. But my attention was drawn irresistibly towards that velvety summer evening, that green lawn with its colour only just beginning to darken in the twilight, that architecture full of grace and composure; most of which, of course, the terrified students who were chased through the streets hereabout never set eyes on – they lived too early, as I perhaps was living too late, to see the fine flower of what Oxford gave to civilization...

A question, fired rather irritably by Bax (and, his tone suggested, not for the first time) brought me back to that time and that place, and I mumbled something. We limped on to the end of the evening and the conventional vote of thanks delivered in the conventional monotone. Geraldine was present, and I wondered, as we all stood up and gathered our bits and pieces ready to leave, why she had said nothing in the discussion. The reason, when it transpired, was rather flattering to me.

'I had a few points I wanted to make,' she said in a quiet voice as we emerged into the perfect summer evening, 'but they were... oh, I don't know, a bit personal to bring out in front of a miscellaneous crowd like that. I wish we could go somewhere and talk.'

'Well, come back to my –' I was beginning, when I remembered that I couldn't take Geraldine in to Episcopus because she was a girl, a girl, a girl, and That Would Never Do. God! I thought. Are we criminals that we should be put under lock and key in this way?

'Walk me back to St Hilda's,' said Geraldine. 'I'll push my bike.'

So we walked and her bike whirred and ticked its way beside us, and for a while she said nothing, as if she were revolving some matter in her mind and wasn't quite sure how to come at it.

'Come on, Geraldine, out with it,' I said at last. 'Are you going to tell me my paper was rubbish, or what?'

'Oh, no,' she said quickly. 'Nothing like that. Your paper certainly wasn't rubbish. But then, what I have to say... isn't really about your paper at all. Not strictly, I mean.'

'Well, what on God's earth is it about?' I asked, really intrigued now. Intrigued, but also anxious. Was she going to bring up some topic I wouldn't know how to handle? Was it – I suddenly wondered – something about Heather?

'It isn't anything really. I mean it isn't anything to do with the content of your paper. It was just... well, something that caught my attention about the *tone* of it.'

I relaxed. If it wasn't about Heather I felt I could handle it all right.

We had reached Magdalen Bridge by now, the dark flow of the Cherwell moving endlessly under us as it had moved in 1355. That thought steadied me. Geraldine said, 'I couldn't get rid of the feeling that there was something behind what you were saying. I could feel that the subject was an emotional one to you.'

'Well, it's a pretty emotional subject, isn't it? People having their throats cut and their –'

'Yes, I know, but the emotion it brought out in you was... well, undirected somehow. You seemed to be stirred up by it and yet not to know quite in which direction to go. It's as if you were standing there in a cloak of invisibility, watching it all happen, and you didn't want the townsmen to succeed and scare the students away and go back to the days before there was a University, because you think the people who wanted to set up a big international university here, at this point in the country and at that point in time, were right. But you also felt so much for the townspeople. You understood their resentment, being pushed around by a lot of clerics and having their town taken over by a lot of people who were protected by the Church, and often were foreigners, which made it worse, and talked to each other in Latin even when they weren't foreigners, and generally threw their weight about.'

'I think I covered all that,' I said. But I knew what she meant, and I knew she was on to something real.

'I kept wondering as I listened,' she went on, 'if your own background is Oxford town.'

I hesitated, not out of any embarrassment – that had been left behind with my first year's nervous inhibitions – but from surprise at her perspicacity. Then I said. 'Well, yes, my parents keep a pub here.'

'Do know anything about what your family were doing in the fourteenth century?' Typically she showed no surprise, or interest, in the present – only in the flow of history.

'You must be joking. Families like mine never trace themselves back more than fifty to a hundred years.'

'Well, I thought so, which means that you don't know, any more than most people, where your ancestors were. They might have come to Oxford in quite recent times. But if they *were* here, they were presumably the type who had a grudge against the scholars.'

'Yes. They were probably out in the streets with clubs and meat-cleavers.'

'I didn't say that. But what is clear is that, compared with the Church with all its wealth and privileges – and they didn't make any distinction between the University and the Church, they saw them as one – they were the Have-nots rather than the Haves.'

'So were most of the students, in origin. The only ladder a bright boy from a poor family could get up was into the Church.'

'Yes, precisely, the students were Have-nots too, but they'd have crossed a barrier, and that's what made the resentment so bitter. That's why they behaved so brutally to them and skinned off their tonsures and all that.'

I was silent. Geraldine, as usual, had landed exactly on target. She didn't know of the existence of Brian, but as she spoke my memory flashed up a quick picture of his face as I had seen it that night at Holyoake Hall, scowling with pure dislike, telling me to get back where I belonged. There were so many thoughts forming in my mind, so many feelings gathering about my heart, there were so many things I knew I was going to want to say, and Geraldine was the person I was going to want to say them to. But we had reached St Hilda's, and halted. The bike had ceased its whirring. Our short journey, that had brought us for a little while together, was over.

I stood there on the pavement with the calm summer sky above me, the promise of the young summer night all about me, and my brain teeming with ideas, and she was going through that wicket gate to sit in her skimpy little bed-sitter. 'Geraldine,' I said, 'at this moment I disapprove of the University of Oxford so totally that I just can't find words to reject it strongly enough. Because of its foolish discipline, we have to break off our talk together just when there are so many things we've started that I'd –' It was a physical feeling, like choking. I knew Geraldine's mind was important to my mind, that in some important respects she had thought her way through questions that I was still only fumbling with, and to talk to her might have been crucial to my development, there, that evening, without any thought of what they, the stupid bigoted authorities, would think of as misbehaving.... Curse them! It was they, not I, who were hypnotized by the fact that Geraldine was equipped with a vagina. They let that well-concealed little cunt of hers dominate their thinking, and that meant that it had to dominate my thinking too, and shut off my intellectual and personal development, which was what the whole damned University was advertised to promote. Oh, to hell with it!

'Well,' I said lamely, 'let's take it up sometime.'

'Yes, let's,' she said. 'Good-night.'

I turned away without saying good-night. It was rude of me, but the polite formula would have choked me. The fact is, I *needed* Geraldine at that moment; needed her not as a woman, but as a person, a fellow human being. Yet Oxford's inflexible machinery ensured that discussions like the one I would have been having now with Geraldine were being snapped off and choked, at this moment, all over Oxford. How long? I thought as I walked back along Holywell Street. I was walking, as I thought this, along by the side of that meanly ugly Victorian building with which New College decided, in the 1890s, to despoil the charm of Holywell. There it stood, a great graceless cliff of a structure, frowning down on the street, taking on itself the authority of something from a venerable age though it was in fact, on that evening, less than half a century old. And I remembered reading an account of the original fourteenth-century statutes of New College, particularly those relating to the personal discipline of the scholars. They had to walk out in pairs, never alone, which would make it the more difficult for them to pick up the local girls. No female servants, however old and scrawny, were allowed within the college walls, and – a sentence that had jumped out at me – 'even male laundresses were preferred'. Male laundresses! Bishop William of Wykeham and his associates, in their sacred wisdom, had taken full cognisance of the fact that the discipline their rules imposed would tense up these youths to such a pitch of sexual erethism that even a clapped-out old laundress, with wrinkled hands and steam-bloated face, would not be safe from their crazed pursuit. *Male laundresses*! Patient Christ, what suffering has been inflicted in your name! How much longer, I wondered as I walked, could this foolishness go on? And the gaunt, prison-like building to my left seemed to throw back at me the sardonic answer, *Long enough to see you out, young man, long enough to see you out.*

*

Bax was my tutor, which meant that he was supposed to keep an eye on everything that concerned my academic life. My moral tutor, supposed to keep an eye on my life as a human being, was the Junior Dean, Hungerford, a man who appeared to have no character whatsoever. He was simply a large, pallid mass which – one supposed – got out of bed in the morning and poured itself into a tweed suit, after which it moved about and consumed meals and took part in conversations and attended to duties of one kind and another. I remember very little about Hungerford; later on, in my third year he left Episcopus to take a more senior post at another College, and I used occasionally to see him in the street, floating vaguely along, as anonymous and flavourless as ever. The only duty he ever attended to in respect of my well-being (not that I minded; I was glad to be left alone) was to send for me towards the middle of that second summer term and remind me that in the following autumn I should have to move out of College and find myself lodgings in the town. 'They'll have to be licensed lodgings, of course,' he said tonelessly. 'The delegacy has a list; either you can work from that, or you may know someone who's going down and you can arrange to inherit his lodgings. The College will want to know where you are, of course. Just leave word at the Bursary.'

As I went down the stairs from his room, two thoughts were jostling for supremacy in my mind. One concerned Heather, naturally. If I had to leave the relative impersonality of College – and I did have to; even in those days there were too many of us for everyone to spend his whole three years in College, and it was felt that third-year men would have settled their circle of friends and should in any case be quietly settling down to work – it would mean being plunged into a lodging-house world where some sharp-nosed landlady knew exactly who came in and went out and how long they stayed. People who kept licensed lodgings were expected to enforce exactly the same disciplinary procedures as the colleges, even down to locking the door to stop anyone going out after ten at night, and if any hint of slackness came to the ears of the authorities, they were struck off the list. It was the old story over again – a little drunkenness was all right, a little smashing of the furniture was fine as long as it was followed by an apology and the settling of a bill, but there must be no bed-hopping among the Oxford young – not, at any rate, among the privileged young, the ones who were having the good education, the ones who were going to run the country! In exactly what ways three years of closely-invigilated sexual frustration were going to make them better able to run the country was never set down in words, though I always hoped one day to come across the great work in which this doctrine was proved. How on earth could Heather and I satisfy one another's needs with a busybody of a landlady, or perhaps even a husband-and-wife team, perpetually on staircase patrol? It would be all right in the summer when we could use Riverside Villa, but next winter... I switched my mind off that topic and allowed the second thought to bubble up, which it did immediately: my parents! Very soon I would cease to have a room in College where I could make them welcome, even on a simple tea-time visit, and if I didn't act promptly the chance would be gone for ever. There would be no point in having them to visit me in digs. Where would be the interest, for a born-and-bred Oxford couple, of consuming tea and toast in somebody's parlour in St John Street or down the Iffley Road?

It was, of course, they who had hung back. During the time I had been in College – my God! Nineteen months now! – I'd suggested it several times, but never with much energy, never as if it mattered to me. 'Why don't you drop in one Sunday afternoon and let me give you tea?' – that had been about the level. And of course they hadn't really wanted to.

Their own life was real to them, mine wasn't, and to step from one framework into another, from reality to unreality, was something they were unwilling to do. Not deeply unwilling, but just slightly unwilling, just enough to make them parry the invitation with gentle evasions: 'Oh, it would be very nice some time, we must come, yes, but this next Sunday's a bit awkward what with one thing and another and Old So-and-So coming over.' Old So-and-So always chose to come over on days when I remembered to ask my parents to tea, and of course Sunday, when the Bargeman's did not have to open till seven, was the only afternoon that would do anyway.

At this rate, I could see, my parents would never set eyes on my College rooms, never see where I had hung my print of Tintern Abbey or how I had arranged the crockery in my cupboard, never peer into the little bedroom that was so much more bleak and Spartan than the room I slept in in their house, though what went on there was, thank God, so frequently Cyrenaic and Sybaritic. And all these 'nevers', though I could not pretend that they weighed on me much at present, I could imagine becoming, as the years went by, rich sources of self-accusation. No! I would not endure that plague in some unfocused future time! That same evening I hastened to the Bargeman's Arms and extorted from my parents a firm promise to come to tea at four-thirty the very next Sunday.

And come they did. I'm not going to say that occasion went badly; nor, for that matter, that it specifically went well. It didn't, strictly speaking, 'go' at all. They seemed quietly determined to make it a non-event. A cup of tea, they seemed to be saying, was just a cup of tea, whether one drank it in a room that was part of a fifteenth-century building, put up originally to house studious young monks, or in the back room of a pub built in the later days of Queen Victoria. And of course they were right, as far as that goes; and for the life of me I didn't see how I could push it into going any further. A teapot, milk, hot water, buttered scones which my mother couldn't force down ('No, really, Peter, it's too soon after dinner'), these things were in the foreground as being small realities we could all share, wherever we were, and we were all very willing to keep them in the foreground. Anything new, anything strange, was played right down. Were my parents fending off this unfamiliar world that was in the process of swallowing their younger son? Did they, somewhere deep inside, feel grief at my going? I couldn't tell, they were so matter-of-fact.

'Is Bert Farley still the cellar man here, Peter?' my father asked, settling back in his chair.

'I don't know,' I said. 'I didn't even know there was a cellar man. And if there is, he'll be working for the dons, not us.'

'Why, aren't you allowed to buy wine from the College cellar?'

I racked my brains for things I had overheard people say about such matters. 'I believe there's a J.C.R. cellar and an S.C.R. one. I'll leave you guess which is the better.'

'No prizes,' my father said. 'But if Bert Farley's still here, it'll be him that looks after it.'

'Bert Farley must have retired, Jack,' said my mother. 'He must be at least –'

'Well,' I said, tired of the topic, 'I've had precisely one bottle of wine since I got here and that was last Christmas. And I got it from the buttery.'

'Who runs your buttery, then? Is it a fellow called,' he wrinkled his brow, 'Geoff Parsons? Tall, sandy-haired?'

'No,' I said. 'It's a little tubby chap with a red face and he's called Dudley, but I don't know whether Dudley's his Christian name or his surname.'

'It'll be his Christian name, of course,' my father said.

I could see well enough what he was doing; domesticating my changed world along his own lines, assimilating it to his own. Through Ernest, and through contacts naturally arising in his own trade, he knew the world of College food and drink and domestic arrangements as well as I was coming to know the world of lecture-rooms and libraries. It was his way of holding his ground, and I respected him for it, but at the same time it filled me with a certain hopelessness. If I had ever had any thoughts of sharing my new life, in any way and from any angle, with my father, those thoughts flickered out as he sat there in my armchair, cup and saucer in hand, asking me about Geoff Parsons. He had taken up a defensive position and driven me into the opposite one; we were looking at each other through slits. Patiently, tolerantly, without any hint of antagonism, but through slits.

As for my mother, she simply drank her tea and gently refused her scone and sat waiting to go. She had no family connection with the world of scouts and butlers and stewards. Her father had worked in a sawmill all his life, and was now the foreman. He would soon be retiring. There was no mystique attached to his job. He just sawed wood.

Before they went home I walked them round the garden. It was a beautiful afternoon, the place was looking its best, and my mother picked up in vivacity as she identified flowers and shrubs that pleased her. She even said, slightly to my surprise, that she had quite often come to Episcopus garden as a girl. 'I used to come in, when it was open, and sit for a while looking at the flower-beds and trees and everything. That's a long time ago. I never seem to do it now. You have to do things while you're young, Peter.'

'Yes,' I said, thinking of Riverside Villa.

'Somehow, when you get older, you never seem to get the time.'

'Well, you're here now,' my father said rather testily. 'How many gardeners do they employ, Peter?'

Once again I had to say I didn't know, but having asked a sensible question had evidently made him feel one-up and cheerful, and we walked back across the quad to the lodge gate in good spirits. I knew, though, that the high spirits came mostly on their part, and even a little on my part, from the sense of having fulfilled a duty, accomplished a slightly awkward task that could now be crossed off the worry list.

I should have been able to dismiss the matter from my mind; having done my best I ought to have been able to let it go at that. But the sense of disquiet remained inside me, the feeling that something in my life ought to be better adjusted and that somehow or other it was my fault. After seeing them bowl off in the Morris (and the sigh of relief they gave was almost as visible in the air as the exhaust fumes), I went back through the lodge entrance and stood irresolutely in the quad. I didn't know what to do in the ninety minutes that still remained before dinner. I didn't feel like working; my mind was too unsettled. I felt I needed someone to talk to.

Barely had I formed that wish than it was fulfilled. Geraldine came striding in her lean-legged, purposeful way from the inner quadrangle, obviously making for the lodge and the outside world. She was wearing her usual outfit, those black trousers that hugged her slender legs, that chunky red woollen jacket, and above them the white collar and the mop of jet-black hair. Style! I thought. Why do some people have it and some don't? I knew I was one of the ones who didn't.

It would be nice to talk to Geraldine at this moment. Her no-nonsense approach to life was just what I wanted, and besides I would have liked to continue the discussion we had had to break off.

'Hello,' I said. 'Come and have a cup of tea.'

'I've had tea, thanks,' she said. 'Your tutor's just given me some.'

So she had been to see Bax on Discussion Club business, doubtless. 'Well, come and sit in the garden with me for a bit,' I said.

'Glad to,' she said, turning to come along. 'Might as well soak up a bit of the beauty of these privileged precincts before we all disperse to whatever industrial suburbs we're going to spend the rest of our lives in.'

That was Geraldine all over. A good healthy douche of social reality to bring you out of your self-pitying reverie.

'Why is it so certain,' I said, plumping myself down on a bench and making room for her beside me, 'that we shall be spending our lives in industrial suburbs?'

'Because the whole world will be given over to them,' she replied, burrowing in her pockets for cigarettes and matches. For Geraldine, to sit down was to light up a fag.

'The whole world?' I said. 'Including Oxford? Will that be an industrial suburb too?'

Geraldine laughed shortly. 'It's one already. Or haven't you noticed what's happening at Cowley? It's more or less doubled in size even in the short time I've been here.'

'Well, that's partly what I wanted to ask you about,' I said. 'Your attitude to... all that sort of thing.'

'All what sort of thing?'

'Oh, the nature of the society... competition between groups. If the University of Oxford is going to become a small island of study and meditations in the middle of a sea of industry, how long will the industry tolerate it?'

She thought for a moment, inhaling smoke, then spoke, exhaling it brokenly through her words. 'As long as the industry's prosperous it'll tolerate the University perfectly well because it won't notice it. The Cowley works and the housing estates will expand outwards, they'll eat up agricultural land, they won't expand into the city where land's expensive. The workers won't know the University's there and the bosses will have a working relationship with it because they'll want to have their children educated there, as a social advantage. And perhaps they'll get some help with research and development from some specialized parts of the University, though obviously most dons won't ever know which end of a motor-car is which.'

'So,' I said, 'they'll tolerate us.'

'They'll tolerate the University – I'm afraid I don't think of it as 'us', I don't identify with it as much as you do – as long as they're doing all right and there's money in their pockets. But if there should be a slump –' she shrugged.

'Then what?'

'Well, what do you think? Unemployment, poverty, very large numbers of dispossessed, resentful people with a lot of time on their hands, and there in the middle of their town, right where they've suddenly got time to stand and look at it, a concentrated little island of privilege.'

'It sounds,' I said, 'like the perfect recipe for another St Scholastica's Day.'

'Well, your guess is as good as mine. But a slump does seem to be coming. The economic system's falling apart, anybody can see that.'

In my head I suddenly heard Peake's voice saying 'Wall Street'.

'All right,' I said, 'there's going to be a slump, and economic chaos, and the maddened workers with empty bellies are going to come swarming over the College walls and break windows and get in.'

'I didn't exactly say that. Obviously it won't take that form. What'll happen is that some form of crisis government will take over, probably very far Left, who'll take over the Colleges and turn them into training centres for people they feel are really needed, like engineers or aircraft mechanics or something. It'll be goodbye to the old standards of leisure and excellence. There won't be people sitting in graceful surroundings cultivating scholarship to very high standards of accuracy for its own sake.'

'I can't make out from your tone,' I said, 'whether you'll be sorry or glad when that happens.'

'That's because I don't know myself. In any case I don't think it's an historian's business to be glad or sorry. All we have to do is say what happened.'

'Well, I dare say, but can you really keep that up? Don't historical events move your emotions at all? You were talking the other night about my attitude to the St Scholastica's Day massacre; well, what's yours? Don't you feel sorry for the victims?'

'All I'm saying is that it doesn't matter whether I feel sorry or not, the main thing is that it happened. What I have to do is to say what happened without getting the facts wrong, and then be as clear-headed as possible about the reasons. Of course some kind of outbreak of popular resentment was inevitable, with a big university growing as quickly as that when nobody had asked them if they wanted it.'

'And according to you,' I said, 'if I, personally, have any feelings about it they must be pretty mixed ones.' She laughed, not dismissively this time but with genuine amusement. 'Does it worry you? That I said that?'

'Not that you said it. What does worry me, somewhat, is that I think it's true. I don't really know what my loyalties ought to attach themselves to. After all, history looks pretty different according to whether you see it from above or below. For the haves, the story of Europe, and particularly of England, is one of achievement. For the have-nots, it's a never-ending recital of hunger and drudgery and injustice. What's the Victorian age? Is it Gladstone in the House of Commons, Jowett at Balliol and the Apostles at Cambridge, or is it little boys being sent up chimneys? The sort of gruesome things you read about in the 'Working Day' chapter of *Das Kapital*?'

'Somewhere in all that,' she said, 'I sense a spurious involvement. You're trying to force yourself into the middle of the picture somehow, instead of standing back and looking at it and describing it. Is it because that's how you see yourself – as the little boy who was sent up the chimney? Or do you feel guilty exactly because you weren't? Were you not made to suffer enough?'

'Why d'you feel that about me? That I want to be made to suffer?'

'I just do. I don't know why you should, but I feel you do. I think you feel a need to be punished for the St Scholastica's Day massacre. Perhaps an ancestor of yours really did kill a few students. Either that or your ancestor *was* a student, someone who'd done what you've done, and you feel he's haunting you, telling you to do something, to bear witness in some way to what he suffered.'

'Now you're getting all feminine and intuitive,' I said. 'What happened to that objectivity? I thought all we had to do was to say what happened.'

She tensed up, was silent for a moment, and then said, 'That's unjust and uncalled-for. It wasn't me that was getting into a state, it was you. To try to explain your state, to help you with it, I have to talk about subjective things. And then you tell me I've abandoned objectivity.'

'I'm sorry.'

'I think you'd better get yourself straightened out, I really do.'

'Geraldine, I really am terribly –'

'Feminine and intuitive, is that what I seem to you? Hardly worth discussing anything, then, is it?'

'Look, I'm a bit off balance, that's the truth of the matter. I wouldn't have said anything as silly as that if I'd been thinking clearly.'

'You're damn right you wouldn't.'

'The fact is,' I said, 'when I met you just now I'd been seeing my parents off.'

'Seeing them off where to? China?'

'To East Street, Oseney. I told you they keep a pub down there. What's more, my father has an elder brother who's a college servant at Pembroke. So you see – in coming to the University I had to climb over a social fence.'

'What d'you expect me to do, cry about it?'

'No, but you could show a bit of ordinary understanding.'

'Yes, I could be feminine and intuitive and let you pat me on the head and say "There, there, little woman."'

'Oh, for Christ's sake, Geraldine. Just because you're a woman, you don't have to keep trying to think like a man.'

'I've got news for you. There isn't thinking like a woman and thinking like a man, there's just one kind, and it's called thinking, and I do it.'

'All right, now that's settled, tell me one personal thing. What does your father do? For a living, I mean?'

'He's a solicitor.'

'Well then. There you are.'

'Where? What are you talking about?'

'When you came up here, you didn't have to make any adjustment. You simply stayed inside the middle class.'

'And that's my fault too, is it?'

'Geraldine, what's got into you? I'm trying to confide a difficulty to you, something I'm having to come to terms with. I thought we were friends.'

'We are friends.' As she said it she looked me straight in the eyes for an instant, with no animosity. But then, immediately, she stood up. 'I've got things to do. I'll see you around.'

'You're not – cross about anything, are you? Look, if I annoyed you with that stuff about –'

'I'm not cross,' she said. 'Just take it absolutely straight that I'm not cross. I've got things to do, that's all.'

I stood up to go with her as far as the lodge.

'Don't see me out,' she said. 'I can find my way. Women have as good a sense of direction as men.' And she walked off.

Holy God! I thought. Why did she get on her high horse like that? When I said she was being feminine and intuitive, it seemed to have flicked her on the raw. But what was so insulting about it? Women, in those days, didn't generally mind having it said that they thought like women, so long as it was agreed that they thought effectively. Oh, well. Geraldine, I realized, must be in a state about something; but what it was, and what kind of a state she was in, I had no idea.

Altogether, I was in a bad way. I had a tutorial with Bax next day, but for once I couldn't whip up any enthusiasm for historical discussion. We were talking about the economic and social effects of Henry VIII's devaluation of the currency, and I knew perfectly well that before I started I ought to have got the facts and figures sorted out and in particular established whether the worst price rises came before or after recoinage. I hadn't got it straight at all, with the result that my essay was a dog's breakfast. I could feel Bax getting impatient as I read it out; and yet, a small, persistent voice inside me kept saying, 'What does it matter? It's all over and done with.' I knew that wasn't true, of course; I knew that history is never over and done with, that the same issues always return again and again to plague and bewilder mankind. But I couldn't silence that peevish little voice. The tutorial ended on a chilly note.

What I needed, I told myself as I went down the stairs, was a shot of the sterling old remedy that never failed to work: I needed to plug into that good healthy sexual relationship with Heather. A couple of hours with her would straighten me out. And tomorrow was the day. We had our customary date at Riverside Villa. I went to bed and slept fitfully, telling myself that tomorrow everything would be all right.

When tomorrow came, though, it turned out to be a painful disappointment. Heather didn't show up. I went to the boathouse and waited. First I leaned my back against the wall and sat there patiently, telling myself some last-minute job had held her up. Then I stood up and paced back and forth along the towpath, wondering if I had come on the wrong day. (But I knew I hadn't.) Then I slumped down against the wall again and started to imagine horrible catastrophes. After an hour and a half, I got on my bike and went along to where the road to High Cogges joined the larger road. She would have had to come that way, if she came from Jasmine Farm. I waited there another half-hour, then went slowly back to Oxford.

I didn't see her. But what I actually did see was a lot worse than just seeing nobody. I saw that horrible creature Phil. He was about fifty yards down the lane, leaning against a fence-post with his hands in his pockets and his noisome old mackintosh hat pulled down over his eyes. Bright, beady, inquisitive little eyes I knew them to be, though at that distance I couldn't see them under the shadow of his hat. What was the bastard hanging about for? I was full of restless anxiety as I cycled home.

I couldn't telephone to ask what had happened, since I was officially supposed not to exist, and for the same reason I was under orders not to write letters to her in case her family intercepted them. I just had to go back to Episcopus and sit about in patient misery. It was the next day but one, Thursday, before I found a letter in Heather's hand waiting for me in the lodge after breakfast. It was brief:

Love,

Crikey! What a mess-up! Horrible doings here. Am coming in to town on day you get this. See you in College. Probably round 3. Hang on till I come anyway. Will tell you all. – Kisses. H.

I had to be content with that. She didn't arrive at three, nor at four, but at nearly half-past four, and I found the waiting very hard. My nerves were stretched, I was full of dry foreboding. What was it that had kept her from coming to be with me, that she couldn't tell me about it in a letter?

When I finally did hear her footstep on the stairs – unmistakably light, rapid, decided – I whipped the door open. I was going to greet her rapturously, to sweep her into an embrace, but something in her face stopped me. I let my arms fall to my sides and said, 'Glad you're here. Come in.'

She kissed me, not as if she particularly wanted to but as if it were part of an expected routine, and sat down on the *chaise longue*. She was wearing her working outfit, corduroy trousers and shirt, and the one concession she had made to dressing up for a visit to town was a pretty blue scarf round her neck. It matched the blue of her eyes. As usual, she looked shiningly healthy, but her face, this time, did not strike me as beautiful. It was rigid: it seemed to have composed itself into straight lines. And when those blue eyes rested on me, they seemed to be going through me and looking at something on the other side.

'Well, talk, my darling,' I said.

After a short silence, in which she seemed to be considering how to come at the topic, Heather asked, 'What did you think when I didn't turn up the other day?'

'I didn't know what to think. I thought that was what you'd come over for now, to tell me.'

'It is.'

I waited.

Suddenly it seemed monstrous to me that we two, who usually rushed into each other's arms and got straight on with the joyous business of being wonderful lovers, should be looking at each other as if my well-worn carpet were a thousand miles of frozen tundra. 'For God's sake, darling,' I said, holding out my hands to her. 'We're talking like strangers. Aren't we going to get close together? Can't we talk about this in bed, whatever it is?'

Not taking my hands, she said, 'It isn't the kind of thing we can talk about in bed.'

I didn't like the sound of that at all. Not one little bit.

'Well, let's talk about it sitting here, then,' I said, a mood of grimness beginning to come down over me. 'Whatever it is, let's get it out in the open, for God's sake.'

'All right, here it is. I didn't come because I was being followed.'

'Followed? Who by?'

'Tom. He was keeping me under observation.'

'Keeping you under... but you were on your bike, weren't you?'

'*His* bike. Yes. But he followed me along the road in the car, and when I went down the lane he came after me. I knew if I lifted the bike over the stile and came down the field path to the river he'd know I was going to the boathouse. So I had to go straight on and he followed me till the lane ran out, and then got out of the car and hung about. I came back a couple of times and he was still there, just waiting to see where I went.'

'So what did you tell him in the end?'

'Well, there's a meadow further down that lane that we rent for grazing. We had two or three horses in it yesterday and I had to tell him I thought one of them had gone lame and I was going down to have a look. It was pretty thin – I mean, we were all together at lunch and if I was going to do anything like that I'd have said so. He didn't believe me, obviously, but I couldn't think of anything better. Oh, it's all so awful – so *awful*!' Her face crumpled into lines of pain and I thought she was going to have a fit of crying, but she managed to pull herself together. 'I went straight back home, after telling him what I was supposed to have been doing. I didn't ask him why he was spying on me, didn't show a spark of spirit.'

'Why not, I wonder?' I said carefully.

She gave a gesture of hopelessness. 'Oh – there are times when you keep up a pretence and it gets thinner and thinner, and in the end you're just playing it like some boring game that nobody wants to play any more, but they can't stop the game because nobody can think how to end it. Like when you play draughts and one person has hopelessly lost the game but won't admit it, they just keep moving their pieces to and fro rather than saying "I've lost, let's do something else" because they don't want to lose that bit of face. I'm like that. Tom knows I'm doing something I can't talk about at home, he knows I'm seeing somebody when I go off by myself in the afternoon, and he just thought he'd take a look. I'm surprised he didn't come down to the hut, for that matter.'

It chilled and saddened me that our bower, our 'Riverside Villa', had suddenly and bleakly become 'the hut'.

'Well, he didn't,' I said. 'Though I did get a glimpse of that horrible creature who works for you, Phil.'

'Phil? My God! Where?'

'Not at the Villa,' I said. 'Nearer your place. Where the road forks off. Perhaps Tom sent him out to spy out the territory.'

She shook her head vigorously. 'Tom wouldn't. Tom's awful but he wouldn't sink to that. He'd rather not know something than hear it from Phil.'

'Is there anybody in your family who does like Phil?'

'Look, never mind Phil. We've got real things to talk about, not a village idiot like him. It's Tom who's the problem.'

'You don't have to tell me he's a problem. He's one hell of a problem. He could wreck everything. Does he still want you to marry this character Whatsisname... Richard?'

'Yes.'

'Oh, God.' I groaned softly. 'It's so long since you mentioned his name that I was beginning to hope he'd rolled away.'

'Well, he hasn't. I haven't mentioned his name because I haven't mentioned any of the horrible things that have been happening at home. I've wanted you to be happy and I knew if I gave you anything like a complete picture of how things are, you'd worry.'

I moaned again. 'So you've been letting me live in a fool's paradise.'

'I'm afraid that would be one way of putting it, yes.'

'Well, my beloved,' I said, 'before any more of my world comes crashing down, on this last moment while I still have my sanity, let me at least tell you that it *has* been a paradise. No other word would do for it. With or without the fool bit.'

She gave me a weak, discouraged smile.

'But on your side,' I said, 'it's been a noble pretence.'

'Not noble. Just a pretence. I haven't really wanted to bring miseries with me when I came to see you. Being with you has always lifted me up. It's afterwards, when I've got back to all that mess,' she gestured in the general direction of High Cogges, 'that I've come zooming down.'

I thought a bit and then said, 'So what's the situation? How would you sum it up?'

Heather looked away for a moment, as if trying to see something out of the window, and when she looked at me again her face was harder, more determined. 'I'd sum it up quite simply. We can't go on as we are.'

I said nothing. I didn't know what to say.

'It's all gone too far. It's too God-awful,I just can't stand any more of it.' And her eyes accused me as if it were I who had been tormenting her, not her overbearing brute of a brother.

'I think you ought to stand up to Tom,' I said. 'Tell him to mind his own business. Suppose you *are* seeing somebody, what the hell is it to do with –'

'Oh, don't waste my time with fool advice, Peter,' she burst out. 'I *ought* to stand up to him – what d'you think I've been trying to do? But he's worn me down, that's all there is to it. I'm so *alone*. I can't tell anybody what's in my mind, not *anybody* in the whole world.'

'Except me.'

'Not even you. I try to keep a good face on things when I'm with you.'

'Well, honestly, there's no need –'

'Oh, yes, you feel protective *now*, at this moment. No, don't touch me.' I had made as if to put my arms round her. 'Just let me get this said. I'll weaken if you take hold of me. I'm sure you feel protective now, because it's news to you that everything's been so horrible for me for so long and you're quite a kind person at heart. But you're like everybody else, you're playing your own game, you're out for the things *you* want. My function in your life is to go to bed with you and take the jumps out of you so you can settle down to some serious work when you come back here to your desk and your bookshelves. And generally to be a ray of sunshine in your life. We have picnics and bike rides and we go on the river and it's all wonderful *fun*, isn't it?' She spat out the word 'fun' as if it were some hideous obscenity. 'Well, I've had enough bloody fun. I want some real life. If I'm going to have a man I'm going to get some of the benefits of having one.'

'Like what?' I asked.

'Being looked after. Being protected. Having someone to stand up for me. Not much, just a little bit. I'm not a shrinking violet, and I'm not a weak person. A man who wanted to look after me and make me feel secure wouldn't have to work like hell at it. All he'd have to do would be to get up out of the ditch, stand up and show himself and say *I'm here*.'

'You mean...'

'I mean that I can't stand secrecy any more. I can't stand sneaking off to see you and not being able to say where I'm going and who I'm going to be with.'

'But,' I said, 'if Tom knows you're keeping company with me, he'll know you're never going to marry Richard and he'll be furious,'

'I've *told* him I'm never going to marry Richard. But he finds it so easy to knock me down on that one because I never put forward any alternative thing I want to do. Am I planning to leave home and have a career somewhere? No, how could I? Girls with no money and no decent education don't have careers.' She had stood up now and was pacing about the room. 'Am I going to get married to someone else? How do I know? The only man I ever get close to is you and you never mention such matters. It's not part of your plan of action, is it? One thing at a time, eh? All you want at this stage is a good fuck and back to your happy old history books.'

I was about to deny this indignantly, but before any words came out, something happened that kept me silent. The something that happened was that I perceived, in the echoing space of my own mind, that what she said was perfectly true. She had, in fact, summed up what I needed, and what up to that point I had been getting, as well as I could have done myself. She knew me; she understood me.

Was it an advantage to be known and understood? Did it make my position in any way easy or enviable? It did not.

'Heather,' I said, coming straight out with it, 'what do you want of me?'

'I want you to show that you love me. You're always saying you do, well, I want you to show it.'

'Yes, but how?'

She stopped pacing. This was it. 'By coming to my home and seeing my parents and telling them you want us to get married.'

'Married?' I repeated helplessly. It must have sounded as if I had never heard the word before, or was trying to pretend I hadn't.

'Well, engaged then. If you think it's too soon to talk about getting married, while you're still at College and all that, well, you can tell them you want to announce our engagement.'

'And what d'you think they're going to say to that? A fellow from nowhere, with no job, no career –'

'You'll have a career when the time comes. Anybody with an Oxford degree can do that. And as for what they'll say, that's easy. My father won't say anything, and if he does nobody'll hear him. He'll go out to the cowshed and say it to the cows. It's my mother who wears the trousers in our family, and she'll be delighted. Tom'll be annoyed but she'll tell him to shut up. A Varsity man, an Oxford graduate,' she parodied her mother's voice with deadly accuracy, 'can marry my daughter any day of the week.'

'And what,' I said carefully, 'does the daughter think about it?'

'Well, I don't feel very emotional at this moment, I feel dead and scaly and old and as if I'll never have any feelings again, at least not any happy ones. But going on what I *remember* of my feelings, well,' she shrugged, 'if I can fuck with you I suppose I can marry you.'

'That doesn't always follow.'

'It does with me. I must be old-fashioned or something.'

There was a silence in the room, a long silence. I didn't know what I was going to say. I didn't know what I ought to say, or to think, or to feel. The only thing I knew was that I was not, repeat not, going to go out to Jasmine Farm, High Cogges, and tell Mr and Mrs Burrell that I wanted to become engaged to their daughter Heather and would they please announce it in *The Times*.

Heather waited until it was clear that I was not going to speak and then she said, 'You're not going to do it, are you?'

'No.' I said.

She walked, with that lovely springy stride, over to the door. As I watched her going away from me, the thought flashed into my mind: *What a perfect body she has. Those legs. Like a racehorse.*

She turned with her hand on the door-knob and said, 'Am I allowed to ask why not?'

'I just don't feel ready,' I said.

'Well,' she said, 'when you do feel ready, I hope you meet a nice girl.'

She opened the door and was gone. I didn't get up from my chair and run after her. I didn't do anything. A few minutes later I heard Arthur clumping up the staircase, wheezing and grumbling under his breath. As he came through the door he was cursing the stairs. 'Be the death of me,' he said. 'The perishin' death, mark my words.' He was simply relieving his feelings, not speaking to me. Which was just as well, because I wasn't listening.

Chapter 20

I woke up the next morning with the words sounding in my head, 'The system has beaten me.' At first I thought they were just a fragment from some dream or other, but as I lay there coming awake and thinking it became clear to me that they were an altogether accurate, objective summary of my life-situation. Stage One: Oxford, with its monastic discipline, had tried to make me unhappy by thwarting my natural instincts: Stage Two: I had found a way to outwit the discipline and get my needs satisfied: Stage Three: I had run smack into a brick wall – the demand to sign on the dotted line of marriage – and, having recoiled from it, had tumbled straight back into the meshes of the monastic discipline. Back, in a word, into misery.

All right, I thought savagely as I got up and dressed. I was going to give up trying, that's all there was to it. In not much more than twelve months, now, I would graduate – because surely, even if my work went off disastrously from now on, I knew enough history by this time to get some sort of degree – and then I would be justified in leaving the University and shaking off its medieval superstitions. With an Oxford degree, if I took my chances, I could go pretty well anywhere. And I didn't much care where, as long as it was a good long way from these hallowed walls.

But what about my youthful admiration for Oxford, my reverence for its great traditions, my day-dreaming about all the great thoughts and great aspirations that had arisen out of these few streets, century after century? No more, I thought, chewing the half-congealed bacon that Arthur, dawdling up from the kitchen, had finally managed to place in front of me. No more, it's gone, goodbye to it. If noble thoughts and aspirations had to be bought at the price of turning generations of men into raving pederasts or causing their natural, instinctual lives to wither like last year's apricots forgotten on the tree, then some other way must be found.

I don't know, when I think back on it, whether the bitterness with which I turned against my Alma Mater was partly a camouflage for other emotions I was afraid to face. Losing Heather was a grievous blow. I had, in my fashion, loved her. It was not even impossible that if we had gone on making each other happy without strain, without threats and promises and time-limits, we might have become so necessary to one another that the idea of getting married, and staying together for life, would have flowered as naturally as hawthorn blossom, not planned, not regulated, just suddenly there one day. But marriage with a pistol at my head, marriage with Tom's clenched fist in the background, *no*.

And so Heather had gone. No more Riverside Villa, no more ecstasies behind the sported oak. Back to the millstone. All right, I thought. I'll toe the line for another twelve months, because it suits my purposes. But gratitude, veneration, reverence for a hallowed tradition – stuff it. Of all that side of Oxford I have had enough – enough and to spare.

And if I felt a disillusionment with the intellectual tradition of the University, how much more did I reject the trimmings that went with it – the social solidarity, the membership of a cosy middle class. Who cares? I thought. Show me one respect in which Episcopus College, as a human environment, is superior to the Bargeman's Arms, Oseney Town. Am I happier than Brian? Have I more self-respect than Brian? My life, now that I looked straight at it, seemed poor by comparison with his. He had an easy, natural relationship with our parents, which I had lost; and what had I put in its place? Education? And what the hell was that? A trained mind? Trained what for? To end up like Bax? To grow into an aged Gadsby?

This mood persisted as the summer spread its feast all round me and week followed glorious week. Heather had cut out in mid-May, and though for the first ten days or so I had occasional moods when I wondered if I could coax her back, if there was anything I could do, short of getting engaged, that would mollify her, I always came back to the bleak conclusion that there would be no Heather; and by about the last week in May I had settled down into a dour, resistant mood, getting by on the minimum of work, seeing very little of anyone, going down to the Bargeman's to drink beer in the evenings more and more often, as if I wanted to begin signalling that the whole business of becoming a 'College man' had been a mistake, a waste of time.

One thing was certain: in the summer vacation I firmly intended to go to work for Tupper Boardman and his father again. This resolve formed itself as soon as I began facing the prospect of those three-and-a-half months of being at a loose end in South Oxford. I knew Bax wouldn't invite me on the reading party a second time, after I had messed it up once, and I also knew that if he had done I would have refused. No, it was to be the boats for me. I would make some pocket money, and get tanned and healthy, and build up the muscles that had gone flabby, and perhaps meet some nice girls who wanted to be shown the river. There was, of course, more risk of Being Seen in the summer vac. than in the Easter one when I had originally done that kind of work; the Long Vacation was so inordinately long that quite a lot of University people had business that brought them to, or kept them in, Oxford for part of it. A fat lot I cared. All that class-distinction stuff was over. I didn't give a sod who knew I was working for a boat-hire business. In fact I relished the thought of giving offence to the kind of person who would see it as something to be ashamed of.

So, one Saturday afternoon when I knew the Boardman business would be working to capacity and everybody, from old man Boardman down to Tupper, would be on hand, I went down there to renew my contacts. As I walked in the direction of the river there seemed to be an awful lot of people going the same way; not only undergraduates, but people who looked like visitors up for the weekend. I had been getting so totally out of touch with University life lately, sunk in my gloom and hostility, that I hadn't even noticed it was Eights Week. But of course now I remembered that annual ritual. Going over Folly Bridge, I took it all in with a few glances – the crowds in their finery on the towpath, the crews getting ready to pull away, the College barges, moored in a long straggling line on the fringe of Christ Church Meadow, already swarming with a colourful mob of spectators. I went down the steps to where old Boardman, with his almost overwhelmed employees, struggled to find punts, rowing-boats, canoes, poles, paddles, oars, cushions and what-not for everyone who came to hire them, plus clocking them all in and out, arguing over the deposit money, adding up the amount due when a boat came in, giving advice to novices on how not to get drowned, and generally dissolving in a heap of grease under the brilliant afternoon sun. It took me no time at all to persuade him that he needed me, in fact he was disappointed that I wasn't prepared to lend a hand that very afternoon. But at that, I did draw the line. I thought I would certainly be disciplined if I were seen doing work of this kind during term-time; there was probably some statute against it, dating from the fourteenth century. And of course, on this of all days with everybody down by the river, I *would* have been seen.

'Term ends on Sunday, June 20, Mr Boardman,' I told him. 'That is, technically it ends then but most people go down on the Saturday. On the Sunday there's no work done and no compulsory attendance at anything. I'll be free then and I'll start right away.'

'Nine o'clock in the morning,' he said. 'Whatever the weather's like. But if it's warm and sunny, be par-ticklarly punckshal.' And he looked at me sternly, from under his bushy eyebrows, as if he had caught me working out a plan to swindle him. That was how he looked at everybody, and he meant no harm by it.

We had this conversation in the office, a single-storey wooden building that stood parallel with the landing-stage. To return to the outside world you had to walk along the landing-stage and go up a flight of steps to the street. As I came out through the office door, the place was crowded and becoming more so by the minute; I had to stand back to let people push past me, then walk a little, then stand aside again. As I did so for the second time I found myself close to a man whom I dimly remembered having seen before. He was thick-set, older than I, middle twenties, dark hair well greased, sideburns razored to a careful edge... in the micro-second that followed, my memory flashed up a picture of him standing with another man of much the same type, looking at some... yes, by God, looking at *Vinnie*, and here, instantly, she was, and here the other fellow was, as the knot of people in front of me parted and I saw them, one, two, three, four: these two blokes, and Vinnie, and another girl, a flaming redhead, making up the quartet.

They had come to take a boat and go out on the river. I stood motionless, my pulse hammering. Had Vinnie seen me? I honestly didn't know; she moved past, within six inches of me, looking straight ahead of her with that contained little smile she so often wore.

She was wearing the same orange-coloured bell skirt and the same tight, frilly white bodice as she had worn on the day I took her out for that ill-fated Cherwell excursion, the one that had ended with her walking out of my life. And of course she looked delicious. It must be her punting outfit, I thought bitterly. Punting and fucking.

The four of them were past me now and I put my head down and almost ran forward. I had to get out of there. The last time I had seen those two men, alike as they were in their slightly outmoded Rudolph Valentino style of *dandysme*, they had been standing among the fringe of onlookers round the dance floor at Holyoake Hall, and when Vinnie went past, dancing with that other girl, one of these two had looked at her with sudden recognition and said something to the other, something I was not near enough to hear, and I could still recall the hot pain of jealousy and insecurity that had stabbed through me: did he know something about her? Had she the kind of reputation that made cheap dance-hall types like him and his mate grin and pass remarks to one another? I wouldn't have cared, it wouldn't have mattered to me how much of a whore she was, it was just that having got hold of her, however tenuous a hold it was, I wanted to keep her – and what chance had I, a College boy hedged about by discipline and with no spending money, of keeping any kind of grip on a girl around whom men of that kind instinctively clustered?

Vinnie and that vacuous redhead were going out in a boat with these two Valentino types. A punt, I supposed. With paddles, doubtless. And cushions. As I walked blindly along my skull was like a cinema, all its rows of seats empty except for one solitary spectator, myself, and an endless blue film, featuring four performers capering on the screen. It was all a fantasy, of course, and miles away from anything likely to happen on the crowded river on the Saturday afternoon of Eights Week, however randy the men and however willing the girls. But I couldn't stop the film; it ran on and on. I even found myself shaking my head to try to dislodge the images that possessed my brain, but they flashed and writhed on and on.

I had climbed the stairs to the street, I had crossed the road, I was back on the towpath going downstream, and now I realized that I was right in the middle of the Oxford of Zuleika Dobson. Nobody, at that time, would have believed you if you had predicted that one day the college barges would be broken up for firewood and their place taken by functional concrete boathouses with strip lighting. People would have told you, indignantly, that it was unthinkable. The college barges were indispensable. They had a serious function, to be the headquarters of the crews for training, and a light-hearted social function, to dispense hospitality and applause on race days. Even when they were silent and deserted, their two functions still palpably brewed an atmosphere. The framed photographs of past crews spoke of innocent, non-mercenary athleticism, and their saloons were haunted by the popping of ghostly champagne corks.

Normally I would have kept clear of this kind of social occasion, distrusting the Mayfair side of the University which, tiny in proportion to its numbers, bulked suddenly large at such times. But now, with the burning fit of Vinnie-fever in full possession of my veins, I was glad of the diversion and the sanctuary. For another hour or more, while the crews competed, ordinary craft would be kept away from that stretch of the river, or at least made to moor and keep still. There was no danger that Vinnie's boat-load ('The barge she sat in, like a burnished throne, Burnt on the water') would come drifting past to sear my eyeballs while I sat helpless among the dolled-up spectators. And the mere presence of that chattering crowd, showing off their bright summer clothes, in frivolous mood, many of them laughing almost continuously, seemed to act as a layer of cool muslin between my tormented spirit and the harsh world of reality.

I stepped aboard the Episcopus barge. There was a solid crush. If you were a paid-up member of the Boat Club, you got a glass of champagne; if you weren't, you didn't, which seemed fair enough. The sun sparkled on the water and the girls looked pretty in their summer dresses and big hats; while those of the men who had dressed for the occasion in blazers, white flannels and straw boaters looked hardly more absurd than usual. I wondered if Carshalton was there. Surely he would not miss this kind of chance to invite people he wanted to impress, to play the Oxford card and further his social advancement. But I couldn't see him. Perhaps he had given up social advancement.

I did, however, see Dick Kent. He was right behind me, in the centre of a group of people most of whom I didn't recognize. Some of them were girls, but they didn't look like girls from the University; they had a Londony, Home Counties look. The fact that an unattractive, self-satisfied boor like Kent was acquainted with girls, even boring ones, that he knew them well enough to squire them about even to such non-events as Eights, made me dislike him even more.

He noticed me looking at him and his piscine eyes, behind those lenses, lit up with satisfaction, as if for some reason he were glad to see me. Indicating me with a nod of his head, he said to the man standing next to him, 'That's the man I was talking about, Geoffrey.'

This Geoffrey, a pudgy youth who, though stupid-looking, did not seem as unpleasant as Kent, merely nodded as if the subject did not particularly interest him.

'See what I mean about the resemblance, don't you?' Kent pursued. 'Blood's thicker than water, eh?'

'All right, Dick,' the man said. 'Hardly matters in any case, does it?'

'You'd probably think it did matter,' Kent said in a loud, carrying voice, obviously designed to attract attention, 'if the man was at your college and you found yourself having to mix with him.'

The attention-attracting ploy was clearly succeeding. Conversation died down among the party of which Kent and Geoffrey were members, and a few heads further off were turned to look in our direction.

'If you're talking about me, Kent,' I said, 'have the goodness to do it as if you knew I was present.'

'Oh, I know you're present. But that doesn't necessarily mean I'm very keen to talk to you.'

'If you can talk *about* me,' I said, a red mist of anger beginning to rise behind my eyes, 'you can talk *to* me, surely.' My voice would have sounded shaky if I hadn't made a supreme effort to hold it steady.

'It doesn't follow at all,' Kent said. 'I don't see why I shouldn't remark to my friend here, in the course of a private conversation, that I haven't been very pleased about some of the types we've been getting at Episcopus in the last two or three years. Not the kind to keep up the tone of a decent college, in my opinion.'

All at once I felt my anger draining away. The man was so ridiculous, just so plain bloody ridiculous, that he wasn't worth anger. I could see, too, that the man Geoffrey was slightly embarrassed at Kent's assumption that they shared the same viewpoint.

'Yes, it must be a disappointment to you, Kent,' I said. 'You've certainly done your best to keep up the tone at Episcopus. If you so much as suspected a man of having any original ideas in his head, or not being a standard machine-made Public School product, or being – what is it you call it? – a *womanizer*, you were already ready to assault him and smash up his belongings and scrub his arse with boot polish, weren't you? Public-spirited, that's you, isn't it, Kent? And how disappointed you must be that in spite of it all they kept coming.'

'I'm quite aware that types like you kept on coming. I wanted to deal with you, Leonard, at the very beginning, when you were a freshman. I could tell what was going to happen if you were encouraged in your slack ways.'

'Yes, you could smell me, couldn't you? The matutinal tub and all that. The lower orders have a distinctive body odour, don't they?'

Kent rocked forward slightly on his feet like a boxer coming in to deliver a knock-out punch. 'I don't know whether you stink, Leonard, because I've never got near enough to find out and I don't intend to. But I can certainly tell you that your ideas do. Your ideas and your attitudes generally.'

'Oh, come on, Dick,' said the Geoffrey man. 'Where's the point of spoiling a pleasant –'

'I shan't spoil anything. I'm just going to tell this scut in a few words what it is I find offensive about him. You don't appreciate what's been done for you, Leonard, that's your trouble.'

'Done for me? Who by?'

'That's just it, you don't see it, do you? You think it's all due to your own efforts. It doesn't seem to occur to you that fifty years ago, a man like you would never have got to the University. The nearest you'd have got to a college would have been working on a staircase like that uncle of yours at Pembroke.'

So that was it.

'Geoffrey here,' Kent continued in triumph, absolutely certain now that he had me in the sights of his hunting rifle, 'is a Pemmy man. I was round at his rooms the other day and his scout came in, to take away the tea things or whatever it was. The old chap's face seemed extraordinarily familiar but I just couldn't place it. So I asked him –'

'His name's Ernest Leonard,' I said, 'and he's my father's elder brother. Are you quite happy now, Kent?'

'I wouldn't say I was *happy*,' he returned comfortably, 'but I think I've made my point.'

It was one of the members of his own party, an elegantly dressed young man with the posture of a guardsman, who asked, 'And what point would that be, Dick?'

'Simply that once you admit just anyone to the University, without any discrimination, the rot's bound to set in.'

'By discrimination,' I said, 'I suppose you mean money?'

'I'm not going to discuss it any more.'

He turned resolutely away from his confrontation with me, and I had the impression that his party were glad of it; he had not carried them with him, though they had probably thought it would be bad form to intervene on my side; and in any case, most of them would doubtless have said, discussions like this were *boring*. Upper-class young people spent a lot of time and energy, in those days, in the ceaseless (and generally unavailing) effort not to be bored.

Thinking that if I withdrew now it might look as if I had been driven away by Kent, I stayed where I was till the racing finished, and then drifted away when everyone else did. As I walked I examined my feelings on this latest demonstration of Kentishness. So now it was known to him, and doubtless would shortly be known to as many people as he cared to pass the word to, that I had an uncle who was a college servant. Could I honestly say that I gave a fuck? I could not. Once, no doubt, when it had seemed to me necessary to put on the appearance of an entirely typical Episcopus undergraduate, taking the line of least resistance by being inconspicuous, I might have felt insecure at having my slightly unusual social origin pinpointed in this way. I would have resented that because I wanted to have a natural relationship with Oxford, to breathe freely there, to spread my wings and develop, to take ever longer and higher flights of the mind while always returning to that sheltering and sustaining environment, that all-providing eagle's nest.

That was then. This was now. That was when I had Heather and could look back indulgently on the miseries and tensions of adolescence. This was now, when I was chained up again in the monastic cell and had to watch girls like Vinnie walking past, without a glance in my direction.

No, not girls like Vinnie. Vinnie, herself, the one and only, the node of all demented fantasies, the everlastingly unattainable. And there at last, I realized, was a solid service Kent had performed for me. Swine though he was, I owed him my deepest gratitude. For quite a long time, something like half an hour, he had made me forget that I had seen Vinnie that very afternoon.

*

Meanwhile, life had to roll on somehow. I found, as the weeks went by, that there were some people whose company I could stand. They tended to be people who, although in Oxford, were not of it; individual souls who pursued some private vision or ideal, and on whom the trivial surface values and mannerisms of Oxford had no chance to rub off. Lamont would have been one such sustaining figure, had I not been too much in awe of him to try to approach him on terms of equality as a friend. But in the presence of his rarified mind, I felt humbled; and, though a person who makes you feel humbled can be good for you in a number of ways, being a friend is not one of them.

Harry Goodenough, by contrast, did not make me feel anything but affection, tinged with admiration and also with a certain slightly superior amusement at his total failure to deal with life on an ordinary day-to-day level. I enjoyed his company and had no compunction about inflicting myself on him, though he was very busy during that summer term. Busy, and happy. A fairly important dramatic society, one based on two or three colleges, had offered him a production, and he had decided to put on *Twelfth Night*. 'It's the comedies that give one a chance to show some critical intelligence,' he said to me. 'Any fool can make a raw emotional impact with a tragedy, but the comedies need *putting on*. And then all this nonsense of not having a theatre building, so typical of Oxford, and having to do them in the open air, in College gardens, no longer matters. If you put on a tragedy in the open air, the emptiness that surrounds the actors takes away all the concentration. But the comedies, because they have that kind of lyrical beauty, can actually come more alive in a garden. Provided, of course, that it doesn't bloody well rain.'

I was rather flattered by the way he confided his thoughts in me. It showed that we were becoming good friends. Certainly I felt friendly towards him; I liked his self-forgetfulness. Like all people who have found an object of burning interest in life, he spent very little time cooped up in the stifling confines of his own personality, and this kept his nature remarkably sweet and generous. He was a bore, of course, with his reluctance to talk about anything but Shakespeare, but there are worse things than being slightly boring. I was particularly interested when he told me he had persuaded Geraldine to act in the play and had cast her as Viola.

'I hadn't thought of her as an actressy type,' I said.

'I don't know what meaning you attach to "actressy",' he said, 'but she can project and she's got a good voice and that's all I need. What particularly made me choose her for Viola – well, I'm sure you can guess.'

I hadn't read the play, but I didn't want to admit it to him because it would be like admitting that I never washed my feet or something. So I just said, 'I'd still like to hear your reasons.'

'Well, damn it, she has to dress up as a boy and then she falls in love with this older man, who of course believes she's a boy so he's not interested in her sexually, and at the same time a woman falls in love with her, also thinking she's male. It's right up Geraldine's street.'

I wasn't quite sure just where he located this street of Geraldine's, so I said cautiously, 'Yes?'

'Well, of course.' He began to run his hands through his mop of sandy hair. 'You know what a *gamine* she is. That boyish figure, that grin like a cheeky third-former. Perfect fodder for the heroines of the comedies.'

I remembered vaguely being told, or reading somewhere, that in Shakespeare's own day there were no actresses and the women's parts were played by boys, so to keep my end up I said keenly, 'Why only the comedies? I thought all –'

'Well, of course, but I think it's fairly obvious that by the time he came to draw the mature heroines he was fed up to the back teeth with the convention. I mean, a clever boy who'd been well trained could just about play Juliet, but think of a boy trying to convey the wonderful rich warmth you get in Paulina. And Cleopatra – well, he says it himself.'

'Says it himself?' I asked, wondering if Harry had discovered a signed statement by Shakespeare in some dusty corner of the Bodleian.

'Yes, in that speech where she says she'd rather be dead than taken prisoner and led through Rome for the populace to stare at her in a triumph. You remember she says, it could all go on till one day I'd even have horrible little boys taking me off on stage – 'some squeaking Cleopatra boy my greatness in the posture of a whore.' There's such a savage anger in those words – *boy* my greatness, *squeaking*. He felt cheated. He needed a Sarah Bernhardt. And if it comes to that it was Bernhardt who turned the tables on the whole thing by being a smash hit as Hamlet.'

As usual, he was going too fast for me, but I saw the main point. 'So this Viola part,' I said, incautiously speaking of it in a way that revealed I didn't know it, 'is tailor-made for Geraldine?'

'She for it,' he said, 'and it for her.'

He was right, too. I went along to the dress rehearsal and had to admit it was a really heady effect. Geraldine dressed as the handsome youth Cesario seemed partly disguised and partly more vividly herself. Harry, who kept a tight hand on every detail of the production, had designed the costumes as well as everything else, and he had put Geraldine in the Elizabethan version of the outfit she habitually wore – black tights with a doublet the same red as her woollen jacket, and the white collar that set off her black hair. To cap it all, he had chosen a young man to play the Duke Orsino who either was, or at any rate seemed very like, a thorough-going homosexual. So that the dramatic situation one was watching in those scenes was: girl, pretending to be boy, loves man, and looks forward to having a chance to reveal herself as girl. And the para-dramatic situation, the one we were watching as an actual situation involving real people in front of us at that moment, was: girl, acting part which for reasons of stage history had originally caused a boy to pretend to be a girl pretending to be a boy, finally admits to being girl, whereas original boy would have had as the final stage to revert to the original pretence... It all seemed to involve a sardonic statement about gender and its amatory repercussions. And Geraldine, no mistake, was the right person to make that statement. Watching Harry Goodenough directing her at that all-important last rehearsal and talking to her in a corner afterwards, I realized, just from the way he looked at her, that he found her very attractive. He wants to fuck her! I thought. He probably thinks Shakespeare would have wanted to, so that makes it all right.

I slipped away without talking to anyone. I found it all rather disturbing, given my state of emotional privation which made me unstable to begin with. The certainty that Harry Goodenough was after Geraldine's crotch gave me the usual male reaction – if someone else wants her why don't I? – and I wondered, uneasily, if I had been too slow, let a good opportunity slip, in not trying to start something going with her. But what chances had I had? Our meetings had been strictly within the palings of the watchful College authorities; she was not, like Heather, a child of the fields and hedgerows, with a boathouse on the river-bank. And in any case, we seemed to have gone past it, somehow. I couldn't imagine starting anything of that kind with Geraldine now. Our relationship was too unemotional, too brother-and-sister. If Harry Goodenough could get something going, good luck to him.

And yet, and yet... It was, admittedly, all very *interesting*, mixing with these crazy creative types like Harry Goodenough, and these strange, off-beat, high-pressure intellectual types like Geraldine, but I longed sometimes – and the times grew more and more frequent – for the wholesome earth of 'everyday' life, or was I ceasing to be able to remember what ordinary life was like? Was Brian's life, for instance, an ordinary one? In some ways, obviously it was not, being glamorous, studded with famous names, a life of frenziedly hard work criss-crossed with travel and adventure. He was ceasing, just as I was ceasing, to resemble an ordinary West Oxford, Oseney Town type. But one big difference remained: big? It was overwhelming, all-deciding. Brian's life was devoted to something that, however exotic, was a competitive sport, and the ordinary man can always understand a sport. To get aboard anything, from a horse to a kangaroo, and race against other people similarly mounted, seems to be an activity that awakens an echo in every human breast. Every normal breast, that is; strange types like me, who tend to be most interested in what people do, and think about, and make, and project, when they are staying still in one place, are heavily outnumbered. Probably it has a biological basis; at some prehistoric period when the human being was nomadic, or perhaps even earlier when *homo sapiens* survived by hunting and had to be fleet of foot, there may have been a serious motive behind the urge for speed, speed, speed as there certainly was behind the urge for strength and aggressiveness. Whatever the reason, Brian's involvement with M.G. racing, however exotic the life-pattern it brought, put him within earshot of ordinary humanity, Bargeman's Arms division, as my historical studies equally firmly did not.

On the Sunday after I had been at the dress rehearsal of *Twelfth Night* and had those multi-dimensional perceptions about Geraldine as a bi-genderal sexual marionette, I was glad to slouch down to the Bargeman's for good old 'Sunday dinner', having taken the precaution of inviting myself by postcard a day or two earlier. I felt in need of an exposure to sanity and centrality. What I actually got was a meal-time discussion about a character named Nuvolari.

'Look, it's no good telling me you haven't heard of him,' Brian was saying, with controlled irritation, to Dad.

'Well, there it is, I haven't,' our parent responded, chewing a savoury slice of beef.

'The greatest racing driver in the world, bar none. Undisputed.'

'All right. I'm not arguing. But why should I have heard of him? There's no interest in motor-racing in this country. When is there anything about it in the papers, for instance?'

'When there's an accident and somebody's killed. Next question. We know the masses don't take any interest in –'

'You haven't got any Yorkshire pudding, Brian,' Mother intervened. 'Don't you like the look of it, or what?'

'No, of course I like the look of it, I just didn't notice. I don't come here on a Sunday just to get a square meal, like Peter. I've got other things on my mind.'

'Don't start on me,' I said. 'I know who Nuvolari is.'

'Who is he, then?' Brian challenged.

'The greatest racing driver in the world, bar none,' I said smoothly.

Brian looked at me narrowly. 'How long have you known that? Did you know it before you sat down at this table?'

'I'm a student,' I said. 'It's my business to learn things. What does it matter when I –'

'Oh, clever, aren't we? If you knew anything about motor-racing you'd have known years ago that Nuvolari –'

'Brian, have some *Yorkshire pudding*,' Mother hissed. 'I've taken a lot of trouble. Never mind all this nonsense.'

'Yes, please. Now look, Peter –'

'No, you look. I study history. I have a lot of ground to cover. Every day I have to take in a lot of facts. If I don't, I shan't get my degree and a lot of people will have wasted their time and money. So why should I take time out to read specialized books and magazines about motor-racing? Especially when I've got a brother who's an authority, who can give me the inside news any time I ask him?'

'He's got a point, Brian,' our father said.

'All right, he's got a point.' Brian looked round the table with an air of tolerant contempt. 'And don't think I'm going to cry myself to sleep if it turns out that none of you here has heard of Tazio Nuvolari. All over Europe they travel through the night and get to circuits before dawn to get a place near the railings to watch that man drive. He's a legend. He's completely fearless and he drives with the precision of a machine. He can race against men whose cars can do ten miles an hour more than his at top speed and still beat them, because he can always pull that extra something out of the bag – he can out-manoeuvre them, out-drive them, leave his braking a little bit later on the corners, take that extra risk because his reactions are faster than theirs.' He talked faster and faster as his excitement mounted. I had never seen him like this before.

'All right,' said our father. 'I can see you think he's great, now tell us why it should matter to us.'

'No reason. You go right on not knowing and not caring. But it so happens that it matters to me, and to all of us at Abingdon, because –'

'Don't tell me!' I cried. 'You've got him working for you.'

'Not yet. But we're after him. One of the directors has been over to Italy to talk things over with him. He's under pretty solid contract to Alfa-Romeo, but we might get him as long as it's not a race they're competing in. That's the big if. He comes expensive. We want to get him for the Ulster T.T. next year. We'll have a new Magnette out, and it's a fast enough car to make it worth getting a world-class driver.'

'What kind of money are we talking about?'

'Oh, I can't start talking figures. Only Cecil Kimber and maybe a couple of other people at M.G. know what he'd really cost and what's in the kitty to pay out. The rest of us, even people on the inside like me, only hear rumours. It wouldn't be fair to repeat them. And if we did know anything we've all sworn to keep our mouths shut. It mustn't get out.'

'Why not?' our father asked in a rather irritated way. 'What's so blooming secret about it?'

'If Billy Morris had goodwill towards us,' Brian said, a note of weariness creeping into his voice, 'we could take him along with us, step by step, and tell him our troubles. But we're not much better than a thorn in his side. We annoy him by just existing. The only way he'll tolerate M.G. is if we win every race we go in for, make a steady profit and never, never have any problems. The first whiff of any trouble, he's ready to say he never believed in racing at all, it's a lot of nonsense, close it down and put everybody to work on the ordinary assembly line turning out tinware.'

'Well, he's got a point, hasn't he? If I was Billy Morris –'

'Jack, *please*!' Mother said sharply. 'I'm not going to sit here and have another Sunday dinner spoilt by an argument between you and Brian. Leave him in peace with his M.G.s. He knows what he's doing.'

'If I leave him in peace,' Dad said heavily, 'it's because peace is a good thing, especially on a Sunday at dinner-time, and you're quite right, Katie, about that. It don't mean I agree with you that Brian knows what he's doing.'

'All right, *don't* agree, just be quiet. Men are all the same, they like to argue, argue, argue just for the sake of it. It's only women who value peace.'

To make a diversion I said, 'How's that chap from Magdalen getting on, Brian, that you deal with? Kingswood, isn't his name?'

'Oh, yes,' said Brian tolerantly. 'The Honourable Fergus. He's been showing a bit more keenness lately. Seems to have decided to put some ginger into it. That Cambridge bloke was beginning to show him up.'

'What Cambridge bloke?'

'You really don't read the papers, do you? There's an American chap at Cambridge, Straight his name is. Whitney Straight. He's more or less the opposite number of Kingswood, a private owner, just in it for fun, but the difference is that he seems to be pretty good. He only started last year but he's had some successes. A natural. That doesn't go down too well with our Fergus, of course. He'd love to show Straight the way round but he just isn't fast enough. So he's trying that bit harder.'

'D'you prepare Straight's car too?'

'If it's a big race we give him a hand. But we can't cosset him like we do Kingswood – he's too far away. Kingswood knows that and he's always nipping over to Abingdon to have his hand held. Came to ask us the other day what gear ratios he ought to put in his D-type for Shelsley. He's decided to try his luck there, and managed to qualify, which isn't easy, to be fair. Anyway, he's entered.'

'Entered what?' Dad asked, irritated again. 'Blow me if I can make head or tail of half your –'

'The British Racing Drivers' Club Speed Hill-Climb at Shelsley Walsh, Worcestershire, Dad,' Brian said slowly and loudly. 'The most important speed trial there is. You have to be good just to qualify for the starting line. Well,' he continued in a normal voice, 'Kingswood brings this D-type job in because even he knows that he'll need specialized gear ratios. We weren't all that busy at the time and me and another bloke took it on as a kind of private bit of fun. We didn't even charge him anything.'

'Bit daft, that. A chap with plenty of money.'

'Well, we thought if he did fairly well, it'd be good M.G. publicity, what with him and Whitney Straight both getting a bit of limelight, and that's what our jobs depend on, after all. So don't worry, Dad, we were looking out for ourselves too. Right, well, after we ran it around for a bit and thought over what he'd need for Shelsley, a thousand yards with an S-bend three-quarters of the way up to the top, we decided to fit him a one-in-ten.'

'Good idea,' I said, keeping my face expressionless.

'There was no room for it, of course, without taking one of the existing gears out. So we had to lose his reverse gear for him. He'd have to work at it a bit, of course, to re-educate his gear-changing hand, to go for the one-in-ten in the position where he normally went for reverse.'

'Did he drive it on the road?' our father asked.

'Well, he had to drive her back to Oxford from Abingdon. When he takes her to Shelsley, we'll come over to Oxford the day before and tune her up for him and put hard plugs in, then he'll tow her on a trailer. We'll strip her down for him, too – take the wings and lights off, make a real little sprint job of her.'

'Let me get this straight. You took his reverse gear out and then he drove the car nine miles to Oxford? That's against the law, you must know that. A car isn't allowed on the public highway without means of reversing.'

'No, Dad,' Brian said calmly. 'And forty years ago it wasn't allowed without a man walking in front waving a red flag. Considering that the D-type M.G. is a car you can push along with one hand, I don't think it'd be likely to cause many traffic congestion problems for lack of a reverse gear. Or are you telling me it wouldn't be good enough for Billy Morris to drive?'

'Now, then,' our mother said, 'which one of you boys is going to finish up these potatoes? What happened to the two hungry sons I used to have at this table?'

'We grew up, Mum,' Brian smiled. But we ate the potatoes all the same.

*

Rather to my surprise, Lamont did actually produce the cautionary poem it had been suggested he should write on Carshalton's wounding of Acheson-Fiske. He handed it to Norbert, who pinned it up on the notice-board in the J.C.R. Carshalton tore it down, but not before some industrious wag had copied it into the J.C.R. book, which Carshalton dared not interfere with. I read it with attention; what interested me about it was that Lamont, for all his visionary other-worldliness, seemed to see Carshalton very directly and to understand his horrible little mind as well as anyone. It was called 'The Tube', and began like this:

> Fashioned from ore that furnaces released
> to sound the clap of death for bird and beast,
> remember that this muzzle has no eyes.

It cannot choose its prey, nor feel surprise
nor guilt, nor awe, if the wrong blood wells out.
Ambition's minion, mind what you're about!
You thought to kill the unprotected, till
their gaping bodies stiffened to a hill
you saw yourself safe as a nested eagle.
But mangling living bodies is illegal
if they turn out to be of human kind.
Improve your aim, or leave your gun behind.
In reaching for the joys you're so prepared for,
shoot only at the innocent and uncared-for!

The poem then mounted to a metaphysical plane on which its main topic seemed to be the nature of innocence. Philistine that I was (and am), I took less notice of this part, which was about forty lines long and probably intended by Lamont to be the essential portion of the poem. I was only interested in the lines that diagnosed the behaviour of Carshalton.

Apart from such mini-events as these, my life had settled down into a long, dull grind as I tried without much success to pay attention to my work. Heather had brought joy and release into my life, and now that the joy and release had once again been replaced by misery and frustration, my brain had seized up; it was as simple as that. One particularly splendid morning – for the lovely burgeoning summer weather had arrived to mock my pent-up state – I was sitting hunched at my desk, dispiritedly trying to make some notes on the *Calendar of State Papers for 1681-5*, particularly as they bore on the legislation concerning the constitutional status of the Leeward Islands, when suddenly the impossibility of the whole enterprise struck me and I abruptly pushed back my chair, stood up and walked out of the room, down the staircase, into the quad and out. Ten minutes later I was in the Parks, walking along on the gravel path by the Cherwell, facing upstream.

Rapidly and restlessly walking on, I found that my feet had carried me out of the Parks, along leafy streets and lanes, to the boundaries of the Gryphon School, where about twenty months ago – God, was it so recently? – I had briefly represented the typical Oxford outlook amid a sea of boys from Poplar. What had been my state of mind? How could I have taken on such an assignment so carelessly? – for I didn't remember devoting five minutes of serious consideration to the complexities of what I was doing. Gadsby had suggested that I should go along, so I went along. What had I *thought* I was doing? Oh, I remembered that well enough. Having been accepted by Oxford University, even though I had not spent a single day as a student there, even though I was still your original untreated Oseney Town local boy, I thought of myself as that mystically transformed being, 'an Oxford man'; not as having climbed up the social ladder, but rather as having waved the social ladder aside as an irrelevance. I had thought of the University as a community of scholars, pursuing knowledge and understanding, and scholars, surely, belonged to no social class; they were born again into a new life, like religious neophytes. Religion! Hah! That was the trouble – the monastic Christian origins of Oxford University had survived into the modern epoch, into the centuries when the University, accepting that it was no longer an adjunct to the Church, had increasingly concerned itself with science, with history, with languages, with political and philosophical questions. In me, the University had had a novice willing to be as devoted as any monk – but not to that precise set of values, those practices.

There, getting nearer as I walked along, was the stately chestnut tree behind whose bulk I had lurked in fear of being seen by Chucker as he stood there with the girl I was to know as Vinnie. And before long, even more frightened, I had lain motionless in my bed while, a yard away, near enough to touch if I had stretched out my hand, the hearty ruffian had, time and time again, beguiled the watches of the night by impaling her lissom form on his enormous dick. I was level with the chestnut tree now, and I halted for a moment and touched the roughness of its bark, seeing in memory the hurrying figure of Robbo as he went out of the gate into that scented summer night on his own unstated business; and then other images crowded in on me, and suddenly I was seeing, with hallucinatory clearness, the fan-tracery of Vinnie's pubic hair as she stood naked in that shower cubicle. And at that I nearly fainted away. To hell with Oxford University! I wanted to shout with all the power of my lungs, sending the words in skirling flight over the quiet gardens and calm roof-tops. I want Vinnie! Vinnie! VINNIE!

Some little boys in blue corduroy shorts came out through the gate and I thought they were looking at me curiously. With an effort I controlled myself and walked on, wondering as I did so why my longing for Vinnie, now that it had come out of hiding and declared itself again to my consciousness, had so completely obliterated the need for Heather. And yet Heather was beautiful... Wasn't she? Yes, undeniably. And she had made me genuinely happy, in that boathouse, and in my narrow bed at Episcopus... hadn't she? Yes, undeniably. Then why was I, effectively, denying it?

In an effort not to think any more about either of them, I thought briefly of the Oxford and Poplar Boys' Club. A missed opportunity there. I had taken no real interest in those boys, so brain-washed had I been into the notion that they and I were of different species, that their preoccupations could never be the same as mine because I was now 'an Oxford Man'. Deluded stripling! What we had actually was a member of the upper working class from a background still semi-rural, an individual already bookish and headed for a life among the professional classes, set down amid a group of the hard, deprived, city working-class of his own age or slightly younger. A fine opportunity to get to know their minds. Why couldn't I have seen that? Wasn't it as plain as day that to understand how they saw the world would help me in due course to understand the Chartists – the Luddites, for that matter – and every comparable movement all the way back to Wat Tyler? I had begun my life as an historian by committing what every scholar knows is the one great sin against the light – I had been offered an increase of understanding and had turned away from it.

And why should I, a person with at any rate average intelligence, have shown this stupidity? Because – the answer came at once – I had swallowed the Oxford bolus, the magic compound that unsteadies the legs and blears the eye. Adorable dreamer, I thought bitterly. Whispering from her towers the last enchantments of the Middle Ages. Cut your balls off and hang a couple of cold potatoes there instead – how's that for an enchantment?

Turning my steps back towards Episcopus at last, because after all I was young and lunch was lunch, I amused myself satirically by constructing a portrait of the ideal Oxford undergraduate, 1930s vintage, the man who would be happiest and fit in most smoothly with the system. He would have a father who had been at the same College; be a reasonably good player of at least one game; Public School of course; mildly homosexual; not intensely lazy, because laziness in the end created more problems than it solved, but certainly with no strong intellectual interests; tolerant of religious belief to the extent that going to chapel seemed a natural thing to do, though not to the extent of thinking about religious (or any ultimate) topics outside the chapel walls; and with a prospect of unbroken economic security.

I completed this picture at just about the same time as I got back to Episcopus and went in at the lodge gate, realizing as I did so that I had given a reasonable working description of about two-thirds of the men I should be sitting among in that venerable Hall.

*

As for the Long Vacation, I remember it as a total blood-bath of boredom, a boredom that passed beyond mere *ennui* and became almost a metaphysical experience, as if I had been mummified and lowered into some stone chamber deep within a pyramid to lie there in silence and immobility for aeons. I worked on the boats, but the endless stream of people who walked along that landing-stage and hired punts, canoes and rowing-boats never included any girls who were out by themselves and looking for a gondolier; had I really expected them to? Nor did I ever see Vinnie again; her going on the river that afternoon, as part of a foursome, had probably been an exceptional occasion, and it was just a cruel stroke of fate that she had arrived just as I was leaving after a few minutes' visit. There was a little pocket-money in it, but no satisfaction; I couldn't even take the pleasure in seeing my skills as a boat-handler develop day by day, since I had gone over all that ground two Easters ago and they were already developed. And needless to say, I couldn't work. Work at history, that is. If I did sit down in front of a book, a parade of sexual images immediately started coming between me and the printed page. Perhaps if I had been, as I was sure some of my fellow-undergraduates were, a twenty-year-old virgin who simply didn't know what sexual satisfaction was like, I might have found deprivation easier. But I did know what it was like. Vinnie had started me off with a sharp plunge into the deep end, and subsequently Heather had allowed me to swim steadily and strongly in broad, sunlit waters. Now – just to round off the metaphor – I was like an eel thrashing in a dry ditch.

To make everything just that little bit worse, Brian's life seemed to be on an upward curve just as mine was on a downward. Nuvolari, it seemed, had agreed to drive for M.G. at the Ulster T.T. the following spring, and everybody was working in a fever of happy excitement to put together a car fast enough, and reliable enough, to be worthy of the wizard. They were developing the K3 Magnette. Even I, during that summer of 1932, could not help getting to know quite a lot about the K3 Magnette. It was bigger than the bathtub-sized racers they had been making up to now, a purposeful-looking car with determination built into its every line. Brian lived for K3, ate it, drank it, made love to it, dreamt about it at night. The big moment of his year came when he was allowed to take the prototype over to Ulster, with one mechanic to help him, and put the car through its paces on the circuit that would be used for the race.

'D'you mean,' said our father at the inevitable Sunday-dinner conclave, 'you're allowed to rush round the roads in this contraption?'

'At stated times, yes,' Brian told him. 'Not just any time.'

'What times?'

'When they're going to have a race, they close the roads they're going to use for the circuit. They close them on race day, of course, and for practice periods before that. About a week, usually, six to eight in the morning.'

'So these roads,' Dad said, 'are closed to ordinary traffic for two hours every day for a week, and then for a whole day while they have their race.'

'You've got it.'

'Well,' our father said, 'all I can say is I'm glad they don't do it round here. Must be a right damn nuisance.'

'Don't start a quarrel, Jack,' Mother said, as she said every Sunday.

'There's no question of them doing it here,' Brian said. 'The roads are too busy in a town like Oxford, too many people wanting to use them, too much business, even today when it's supposed to be in a slump. They'd never get away with closing the roads for motor-racing.'

'I should think not. Strikes me –'

'But they do in France, and they do in Italy, and in Spain, and in Monte Carlo. And they do in Northern Ireland because it's a poor country and there isn't much motor traffic anyway, and what there is doesn't mind keeping clear of the roads for a bit, two or three times a year, so that a big motor race can happen. A lot of people go to watch, English people and Continentals too, and they all spend money. Why d'you think the Isle of Man closes the roads to run the motor-bike T.T.? Because during that week you can't book a room anywhere on the island. The fans go in their thousands. Doug Ravenscroft –'

'Oh, yes, Doug Ravenscroft. We all know he goes rushing round the Isle of Man, trying to break his neck. He'll succeed, too, one of these days. I don't believe Doug Ravenscroft's a good influence on you, Brian.'

'You think that's how I live my life? By letting people influence me? All right, maybe I should be influenced by Billy Morris, then I'd be a millionaire, wouldn't I? Well, I'll tell you something. For all I care, Billy Morris can stuff his –'

'When do you go to Ulster, Brian?' I asked, partly to break it up and partly because while they had been talking an idea had come to me.

'In about three weeks, why?'

'Can I come with you?'

Brian put his knife and fork down and said slowly, 'Can you what?'

'Can I come with you? I'll pay my own way. I've got some money I earned on the boats. I could be very...' My voice trailed off under his unblinking stare.

'You could be very what?'

'Very useful,' I faltered. 'I could make myself useful in all sorts of ways. Just... you know... fetching and carrying things round.'

'Look, laddie,' said Brian kindly, 'motor-racing is a very specialized business. There's not much room in the pits, and everybody who's there is there for a very – definite – reason. Have you got that?'

'Well, yes. But surely you could use someone who was willing to do little things... like...'

'Making the tea? We take it with us in a thermos.'

I said no more, but I must still have looked mutinous, because he added in a tone of finality, 'If you come over to Ulster there'll be no task that could be assigned to you and no way you could be useful. You'd find yourself spending every day and evening wandering about on your own and you might just as well do that in Talbot Road.'

I lowered my eyes to my plate, but not before I had caught a glimpse of his face. It had on it the look it had worn when he had met me at Holyoake Hall and told me to go back where I belonged.

*

When October finally dragged round again – the third October of my undergraduate life, and the last, thank God – it was not a matter of going back to Episcopus and the tender mercies of Arthur, but to a three-storey terraced house way down the Iffley Road. In the last week or two of the summer term, I was in such a mood of lethargic misery that I could hardly bring myself to bother with anything; Bax must have noticed that my work fell away disastrously, but since he had seen it do so before and recover miraculously, he evidently wasn't worried and didn't refer to my recent poor performance when I went up for Collections. He merely remarked, a trifle frostily, that Mr Leonard 'continued to do good, sometimes outstanding, work'. The frostiness had never quite left his manner since my backing out of the reading party the summer before – an invitation, naturally, that hadn't been renewed. Old Gadsby chewed his saliva and smiled bonily, his long neck above the bow tie more stringy than ever though the tie itself had lost none of its neat elegance. 'Very glad to hear it, Mr Leonard,' he said. 'And when you come back after the Vacation, I shall have the pleasure of... ah... discussions with you.' So it was to be goodbye to Bax and a year's tutoring from Gadsby. Episcopus certainly did its best for us, in the matter of teaching. Pity I was not in a state to work up any interest in the whole thing.

In that mood I had gone along to the Delegacy of Lodgings, at more or less the last minute, and got a typewritten sheet containing the addresses of all the lodging-houses that were licensed; it was *verboten*, of course, to stay in any other kind. (How bloody silly, I reflected, that I couldn't just go back every night to my own bedroom at the Bargeman's. But then my own parents, not being licensed to have undergraduate lodgers, did not qualify as fit people to look after me.) The list turned out to be more or less useless; I was such a late starter in the field that nearly all the addresses in it had been snapped up already, which was why I finished up in a hole like that, so inconveniently far out. We were very spoilt in those days. The University was so small, by present-day standards, that everybody could be lodged quite comfortably in central Oxford, and to be a mile down the Iffley Road was regarded as a terrific time-waster. Fortunately this disadvantage was reflected in the price charged for the lodgings, which was very low, so I had plenty of beer money.

I needed it, too, because the place was such a dismal hole that I used to wonder whether even entertaining Heather would have made it seem much better. Not that there would have been much chance of getting away with that. The landlady, a brisk, sharp-faced little woman called Mrs Groundsel, was always dodging about the corridors and staircase. She had a way of shifting very rapidly from foot to foot, as if braced always to be able to avoid a blow or something thrown at her. Not that she was the persecuted, downtrodden type; rather cocky, if anything. Sharp in the face and sharp in the mind. If she had heard heavy breathing coming from behind a closed door in my sitting-room she would soon have knocked and pushed it open, on some pretext; and if I had had it locked, and it turned out that there was a female person in there with me, that would have been goodbye Charlie. As for the bedroom... Lodgings in those days had to be organized strictly on college lines, which meant that we couldn't have bed-sits. No, you had to have a separate bedroom, and while in college you did at least have one that opened out from your study, in digs the bedroom might be anywhere. Mine, in fact, was at the top of the house, a tiny and very cold attic room, while my sitting-room was on the ground floor. The thought of getting Heather up those linoleum-covered stairs without the ladlady dodging out and seeing us – the creak of the staircase would have brought her out instantly – and then trying to enjoy ourselves without making the bed-springs give us away with their rhythmical oscillation, another signal that would have brought her running, was obviously too silly to be entertained. Well, there was no Heather. We couldn't put it to the test.

I suppose it all just sounds like adolescent self-pity, but sometimes in that gaunt house in the Iffley Road I used to get into such moods of almost suicidal depression that for years afterwards it lowered my spirits to walk past the place; I used to cross the road to the opposite pavement. The house stood, by chance, just about opposite the gravelly path along which I had fled on that afternoon in 1926, clutching my brown-paper bag of fritillaries, with those yobbos behind me thirsting for my blood. Luck had saved me then. But what would it take to rescue me now, from this dank, lonely, frustrated existence? I felt I was living like a newt in a ditch, which was all right for newts, but not for a young, healthy, fertile, vibrant male of my species. The only solution, the only equivalent of that bus drawing up in the nick of time, was a complete change. I must get right away from Oxford, or at any rate from the University.

As if rehearsing already for this change, I began positively to avoid the more purely academic parts of Oxford. Living so far out from the centre, it was easy to spend three, four, five days at a time without going into a College or an academic building of any sort. When the unspeakably dreary winter began at last to yield to something like a pale watery spring, towards the middle of March, I took to walking the short distance to Iffley, crossing over the river at the Lock, getting on to the towpath and walking into the town centre that way, very often passing the evening at the Bargeman's, where I spent those spare shillings on beer that I saved by living in such a dreary place. It gave me malicious satisfaction, disaffected with the University as I was, to see the spare cash from my various grants and my Exhibition going into the till of my father's pub. I felt I was kicking on the right side for once.

These visits also served the purpose, of continual importance to an historian, of plugging me into *vox populi*. Particularly I timed my visits home to get there at six o'clock, when Trundle and his mates forgathered in the newly opened bar, I was assured of a running commentary on the events of the day. One sleeting February evening, glad to get into the bright, welcoming pub out of the awful weather, I was in time to hear one member of the *cénacle* throw the conversational ball into play by remarking, 'I see these undergrads 'aven't 'alf stirred up more trouble. A fair old row. In the noospapers 'n all.'

'Trouble, is it?' said Peake. He spoke tensely, as if anger was not far below the surface in him. 'If you asks me I think it was a bloody silly question to put to 'em.'

'Nobody did put it to 'em, like,' said young Ted. 'They picked it themselves, as the subject they was going to debate, like. Would we, or would we not, fight for King and Country?'

Several voices joined in, 'Who's asked 'em to? Who's attackin' their King and Country?' – 'Well, you never knows. The way things is shapin' up, some blighter might, one of these –' 'Well, time enough if they does.'

'The Fuzzy-Wuzzy,' Old Trundle suddenly said in a commanding voice. 'Now there was a fighter. Strong as a 'orse, and no fear of death. Many's the time a British regiment 'as 'ad to form a 'ollow square and fight to the laarst man.'

'That was a long time ago,' said Peake. 'It's the Germans we're talking about.'

'Have the Germans declared war on England?' my father put in from the seat of judgement. 'Have they said they're going to?'

'The Zulus,' Old Trundle said. 'Some of the finest soldiers in the British Army left their bones on the field of battle when those buckos got goin'. No quarter they gave, no surrender. Fight to the laarst man. Form a 'ollow –'

'Look,' said Peake in the tone of one whose patience has snapped, 'if there'd been five times as many Zulus as there is Frenchmen, they wouldn't've given the British Army as much trouble as one battalion of German infantry with artillery support. How many went west on the Somme? You've forgotten, Trundle. You were too old for service and when you looks back on wars, you misses one out.'

'That Kruger was enough of a bloody 'andful. I've seen men –'

'Yes, Kruger, but that were all over when I was about ten year old. When we talk about fighting for King and Country now, we don't mean Kruger, and still more we don't mean Fuzzy-Wuzzies and Zulus. Form a 'ollow square! What kind of 'ollow square could they have formed at Vimy Ridge?'

'It don't matter what kind of square, if you got fightin' spirit. It's fightin' spirit as pulls men through.'

'Well,' said Ted, 'it don't look as if these undergrads've got any of that, or want any. They voted as they *wouldn't* fight for King and Country.'

'Are you surprised?' Peake demanded. 'Would you expect 'em to say they would? Look, fifteen years ago the guns was still firin' in France.'

'Yes,' my father said. 'I was looking at the calendar the other day, reckoning it up. Eighteen to thirty-three, that's fifteen. The Armistice was fourteen years ago last November. Sounds a long time, but it only seems like yesterday to me.'

'Right,' said Peake. 'Fifteen years, it's still too soon to start tellin' about fighting again. The men that fought last time won't go again. They seen it and they knows too much. You need a new generation – young chaps that've never seen action and can't picture to themselves what it's like. They'll march off all right, they'll fall for all the big talk and the flag-waggin'. They'll get down into the trenches and when they wishes themselves out again it'll be too late.'

'What about these undergrads, then?' Ted asked. 'This Union Society or whatever they calls it. Do they remember it? Can they picture it?'

'It's like I say, they're too close to it still,' Peake insisted. 'If they're nineteen now, they was four when it ended last time. They'd be the ones that was born in 1914, just when it broke out. They could easy have 'ad their fathers and older brothers killed off. Grown up wonderin' what kind of men and what it was like when they died. People like that don't want to fight. And on top of that, they're ejjicated. They're clever. They looks around and they sees the country in a bloody mess, blokes thrown on the dole, factories closin' down, trouble 'ere, trouble there. And they says, my dad, my brother, my uncle, fought for King and Country and it don't seem as if King and Country's a blaarsted bit better off for it. They might as well be alive today, enjoyin' theirselves.'

'They wouldn't all be alive today if they'd 'ad to stand up to them Fuzzy-Wuzzies,' said Trundle. 'Them buckos could charge up a 'ill faarster than you or I could run down. And yellin' all the time, fit to freeze your blood. I talked with a feller in Cowley Barracks who'd lost a leg above the knee, tryin' to 'old 'em back.'

By general consent, no one contradicted him, and the Fuzzy-Wuzzies were, figuratively, left in possession of the field. But I was interested by this evidence that the celebrated resolution passed that term at the conclusion of a debate by the Oxford Union Society, 'That this House will in no circumstances fight for its King and Country', had made an impact on these men. I knew, of course, that it was being discussed in London, in Paris, in Berlin and in Geneva. But to get itself talked about in the Bargeman's Arms, barely a mile from the debating chamber but as a rule so totally impervious to what people from 'the colleges' thought about anything – this struck me as more of an achievement.

I spent, as I say, a good deal of time alone during that autumn and winter avoiding those parts of Oxford which in the minds of most people, and certainly of most visitors, are the 'real' Oxford, and hanging about side-streets and back lanes, the canal towpath, the long featureless stretches of the Iffley Road or the muddy allotments between it and the river. When I sought out company, it was either in the Bargeman's Arms – and then, mostly, the kind of company that consists of having other people physically close to you, packed into a warm, companionable atmosphere, rather than any meeting of minds or personalities – or it was a question of going and finding Harry Goodenough or Geraldine.

In fact, if I think back over the entire stretch of time from the autumn of 1932 to the early summer of 1933, I can only remember one conversation at Episcopus, and that was one I got dragged into against my will. It was one Sunday evening in the J.C.R., the lighted windows staring out on to a black January night, and people going through the usual pre-dinner ritual of getting one's glass of sherry from Tom, finding an armchair, and sinking down for a bit before Hall. I had spent the preceding three hours sitting glumly at my desk, listening to the spluttering of a badly-laid coal fire and reading the same five or six paragraphs over and over again in William A. Shaw's *Introduction to Volumes XI-XII of the Calendar of Treasury Books Preserved in the Public Record Office (1695-1702)*, trying to drive some information into my head if only for lack of anything better to do. But it hadn't worked. I knew no more about the fiscal deliberations of those years, whether they concerned the prosecution of the war with France or the permanent reinforcing of the Civil List, than I had when I sat down. I was in a downcast mood as I sipped my sherry and looked idly round the Common Room to see if there was anybody I felt the slightest wish to talk to. There wasn't, of course. McFarlane, who still looked no more than about sixteen, was leafing through an illustrated magazine a yard or so to my left; an equal distance to my right, Wilmot was leaning back in an armchair and looking up at a man who was standing beside the fireplace, one arm on the chimney-piece, and holding forth to him. This man was Dobbs, he who had first told me, as we emerged from Bax's rooms on that summer afternoon, what a Commem. Ball was like. I could hear his voice now. *Look back on it for the rest of your life. The one and only time in your Oxford career when they gave you a chance to get your end away.*

It was in a more discontented, querulous tone that Dobbs was now saying, to Wilmot and to anyone else who happened to be in earshot, 'God! I can't wait to get out of this place. Thank God it'll all be over in six months.'

'Haven't you enjoyed it?' Wilmot asked in his calm, balanced way.

'Oh, I don't say some things haven't been quite fun, but it's worn so damned *thin*. I mean, the whole thing goes on too long. Three *years* – it's too much to spend in a backwater like Oxford, cutting yourself off from life.'

'Is that how you see it? Cutting yourself off?'

'Well, of course it is, how else can anyone see it? I mean, what *happens* in Oxford? Just a lot of colleges with people reading books and having tutorials. And meanwhile, life's going on.'

Unobtrusively, I eyed Dobbs while he was saying this. He had struck me on first acquaintance as having the beaten-in face of a boxer, and indeed it had turned out that before coming to Oxford he had represented his Public School, some minor outfit which probably contented itself with turning out young men with plenty of muscle and the right social contacts, in the boxing ring. Doubtless he had traded punches boldly and even with a certain amount of skill, but at the University he had made no effort to get a boxing Blue. The training and dedication called for would have been foreign to his easy-going nature. He was a decent enough man, mediocre in every way, and in the 1930s every Oxford college could show types like him on every staircase. He now caught me looking at him and said, 'What do you think about it, Leonard? Have you enjoyed being here three years?'

'No,' I said. 'But I don't think my reasons are the same as yours.'

'Aren't you just about bursting to get out of all this' – he gestured around him – 'and start living?'

I countered with a question. 'What kind of living will you start?'

'Well, *earning* a living, for one thing. Getting my hands on a bit of income. I'm sick of existing on an allowance.'

'Have you got a job lined up?' Wilmot asked.

'Yes. I'm going into the City.'

'But,' I said, 'life in a City office isn't any less artificial than life at the University.'

'How on earth d'you make that out? Of course it's less artificial. The City's bang in the middle of London, for one thing.'

'What difference does that make?'

'Well, London's where things happen, isn't it? If people want to work and make money, they go to London. If they want to have fun and enjoy themselves, they go to London. Don't you want to do those things?'

'In my own way, yes.'

At this point another student entered, carrying his glass of sherry from Tom's counter and looking for somewhere to sit down. His name was Hunt. I had never registered him very much – he was in my year and was reading English or Modern Languages – except to feel a vague distaste for him. He had never done or said anything unpleasant to me, or to anyone else in my presence, yet there was something about him that I didn't care for. Tallish, fair-haired, he was always very well groomed, with never a trace of undergraduate scruffiness, and had the kind of good looks that consist of not having any positive defects. His nose was not too large or too small, his eyes were not too bulging or too deep-set or too close together, his forehead was not too low, his chin was not too weak or too strong, *ergo*, he was good-looking. Something I didn't know at the time, but got to know later, was the fact that two women out of five regard men like Hunt as irresistibly attractive, and the other three as repulsive. Not being a woman, I didn't care whether he was attractive or not, but I thought he looked about as interesting as a glass of milk.

Dobbs now appealed to him. 'Here, Hunt, you can settle this. I'm just saying how *bloody* glad I shall be to get finished with my degree and get out of Oxford. I've had enough waiting about on the sidelines, I want to get into life. Leonard here doesn't seem to take my point, but I should have thought it was pretty obvious.'

'It's obvious all right,' I said, 'provided one grants your initial premise – that Oxford, or any university, is the sidelines.'

'Well, if it isn't the sidelines, what is it?' Dobbs demanded. Like all people who are unused to thinking, he sounded hurt that his simple convictions could be held up to the light of scrutiny. Surely what he thought must be the obvious truth?

'What do you think, Hunt?' Wilmot asked in his pleasant way.

Hunt gave a slight shrug. One of the few things I had noticed about him was that he often prefaced what he had to say by this minimal shrug, which seemed to convey that it was more or less futile to discuss this, or any, subject since what would be, would be, whatever we thought about it. 'Can't say I've considered it much,' he said, 'but I suppose, since you ask me, that a man who isn't pretty keen to get out of Oxford, after spending three years here, can't have got much out of being *in* Oxford.' He raised his sherry to his lips and sipped, with the air of one who has discharged a duty.

'There you are,' said Dobbs triumphantly, to me. 'He thinks like I do.'

'Not quite. He doesn't use disparaging terms like 'backwater'. He says the function of Oxford is to make you eager to get out of Oxford, which is a different thing. A backwater doesn't make you eager for anything, it rots you.'

'You're splitting hairs now. You ought to be a bloody lawyer. You do think the same as me, don't you, Hunt?'

Hunt looked slightly weary and said, 'I think Oxford, by which I take it we all mean the University and not the town, is like the beginners' slopes at a ski resort. You're glad of them at first when the real slopes are too much for you to face, but when you've learnt the rudiments you want to move on.'

'I think that's fair enough,' Wilmot said. 'Oxford may not be real life but it's about real life. I mean, people have got to be *trained*, haven't they?'

Dobbs, unmollified, scowled and said, 'Yes, but there's no need to take so bloody long about it. To the extent that I'm trained now, I was trained after about my first year.'

Turning my head, I saw that McFarlane had put down his magazine and was unconcernedly listening. Quite clearly the issue of whether or not Oxford dealt in 'real life' had no meaning for him. I had a sudden vision of McFarlane's world. He was already nearly three years into the study of medicine; he must have been clever, an apt and promising pupil, to start at the University at such a tender age, since even allowing for his youthful appearance he was in fact younger than most of us. Ahead of him stretched more years of study, years in hospitals, in wards, in laboratories; then, success and eminence: Harley Street or a distinguished Chair; power of life and death over people, his fellow human beings deferring to him wherever he went. No wonder, I thought, that Carshalton had not been able to hurt McFarlane as he had clearly hurt Fred Armitage, a character otherwise rather similar in his simple directness. To Armitage, Oxford was a peak to which he had clambered painfully and where he would only be staying for a very short time, and during that time he desperately wanted it to be bathed in sunlight. To McFarlane, it was just another step on a long, assured road.

However, medical men live in a world of their own, like musicians, and though the subject of our conversation did not concern McFarlane, I thought it important enough to the rest of us to put in one last contribution. 'You're all talking,' I said, 'as if Oxford was a technical college, existing just to train people in a few skills. But it's an international centre of learning. If there were no undergraduates here at all it'd still have an important role.'

'It wouldn't,' Hunt said. His tone was casual, as if he took it for granted that I was not worth arguing with. 'It'd close down. The Government funds the University to train students, not to be an international centre of this and that.'

I looked at the man attentively for the first time. Yes, there really was something dislikable about him. What was it? His smoothness, his complacency? His conviction that he was absolutely right not to look beyond his own limited horizons?

'It's true,' I said, 'that after seven hundred years of getting along without any help from Whitehall, the University had to turn to them about fifteen years ago and ask for money, because the flood of chaps coming back from the War, and the need to teach expensive things like science, was getting too much. So your attitude, Hunt, is that the place changed in the twinkling of an eye, on whatever date that was, into a teaching mill?'

'I've already said what my attitude is. It's the beginners' slopes.'

'Well, for some people it is, and quite legitimately.' (Why hurt the feelings of honest Wilmot?) 'But there are people in every generation who stay here. Who commit their lives to scholarship. What about them?'

'Oh, them? They're the ski instructors.'

I struggled for utterance for a moment and then said, as calmly as I could, 'Well, that may be a fair enough comment on some of them, but it seems an odd description of a real scholar, a man who... who...' I stopped. What was the use?

'A ski-ing holiday,' Hunt said as if explaining something to a child, 'is a way of having fun while getting fit. You enjoy yourself and you also build yourself up for your real life that you'll go back to when the holiday's over. But the ski instructor doesn't go back to anything. He stays at the resort. He lives there. And when you go back for another holiday, he recognizes you and you feel flattered to be recognized, or he doesn't and you don't. But in between visits you don't think about him. He's away up on his mountain and you're down where life goes on.'

I could see that the others all agreed with this view, but some grain of stubbornness made me hang on, and I said, 'I don't quite see it that way. I don't see it as learning to ski. I think what the universities of the world do – not just Oxford but all of them, if they're any good – is to hand on a traditional body of knowledge to each new generation, like old birds teaching young birds to fly. Knowledge not just of facts but of how to handle facts, to relate them to one another, to get truth out of them. Imagine,' I said, warming to my theme, 'if every bird that had learnt to fly were suddenly obliterated and only the fledglings were left. The entire race of birds would be extinct in a week, because without the older ones to teach them they'd never –'

'Number one,' Hunt cut in, 'it'd be starvation they'd die of, not being unable to fly. The old birds *feed* the young birds. They fetch worms and things and put them in their beaks. As long as they keep that up, the young birds are all right whether they can fly or not. No one needs to work if they can survive without work. Number two, the whole example shows you as a case in point. It's fanciful – theoretical. It won't happen. It's not worth discussing, let alone using as the basis for a whole argument the way you're doing.' He stood up. 'What you're doing,

Leonard, is to demonstrate that you're a typical Oxford product, revolving a lot of empty concepts and calling it thinking. Perhaps it's time you left the nursery slopes and got to where the real action is.'

Holy Christ! I thought. Do I have to take this kind of talk from a nothing like Hunt? Committed as I was to a life of scholarship and reflection, I felt a primitive desire to knock his teeth down his throat. 'I don't think,' I said carefully, 'that my example of the bird generations is any more theoretical than yours of the ski slopes. Flying is *essential* for a bird, whereas ski-ing –'

'Oh, sod this,' said Dobbs, getting up in his turn. 'For the next half-hour I'm going to use my mouth for eating, not talking.'

He and Hunt moved off. I stood there lost in my thoughts, my mind sending up a fountain of unanswerable arguments which it was now too late to utter; and then Wilmot was at my elbow, giving me his gentle smile, saying, 'Come on, let's go and eat,' and I remembered how glad I had been to talk to him on my first lonely, timorous evening at Episcopus, and I willingly went down with him into Hall.

*

But speaking of men with a lifelong commitment to scholarship, the dreary, apathetic, half-baked work I turned in all through that academic year must have been a sore disappointment to old Gadsby, I could see that. He was too polite to ask me what the hell was the matter with me, but the silences between his courtly sentences grew longer, as if he were debating within himself whether it was worth going on with such a bird-brain as I was turning out to be. I used to feel sorry for him. He was getting near retirement age, and he had been looking forward to having perhaps one more interesting pupil, someone who might yet strike sparks from his mind, and whom he could inspire with a true love of history and an eye for its essential issues. He sat there in his Windsor chair – unlike more easy-going types he didn't slump in an armchair while he conducted a tutorial, but sat up straight as if he were at an international conference of distinguished historians and was anxious not to miss a word – looking at me with silent wonderment and reproach, and he was so old and tall and bony and frail and distinguished that I used to crawl away feeling like a cad, a ruffian who had desecrated a fine presence. But it was no good: I couldn't perform intellectually in my downcast state, not even to please an old man I would dearly have liked to please.

He must have confided all this to Bax, because one day Bax stopped me as I was going across the quad. It was March, with a stir of spring in the air, though streaks of snow still lay along the sides of walls where it had drifted. He stood firmly in my path and said, 'Are you doing anything particular for the next fifteen minutes?'

'The next...? No, sir.'

'Good. Let me have that much of your company.'

He led the way up the staircase to his room and I followed, wondering what was coming. Once inside he waved me to a chair, looked at me attentively for a moment, and started straight in.

'Mr Gadsby hasn't been very happy with your work, Leonard, these last two terms.'

'I know, sir. At Collections...'

'I'd rather built you up in his mind – well, in all the Fellows' minds, really, because some of the work you'd done for me was quite out of the ordinary. But you know that. And now it all seems to have come to nothing.'

I gestured helplessly. 'I haven't been working well.'

'That usually means,' Bax said evenly, 'that there's something the matter.'

I said nothing. What the hell was the use? But he pressed on.

'D'you mind my asking if it's... something personal?'

'It isn't anything I feel able to talk about, sir.'

'Well, there's no arguing with that, of course,' Bax said. 'Have a glass of sherry, anyway.'

Oh, yes, of course. A glass of sherry. The great Oxford answer to everything. The finest pale, dry, smoky *fino*. But I did realize, as he handed me my elegant little glass, that he was behaving decently according to his lights. He was not my tutor; that place was taken over, during my last year, by Gadsby, who was simply nonplussed by his failure to get any response from me. Strictly speaking the person who ought to have been trying to sort me out, to enquire if I had any disabling personal problems, was Hungerford. But doubtless Bax, living in the same college with Hungerford and seeing the man every day, knew what a nothing he was. Hungerford would never, in a million years, get off his arse and see if there was anything he could do to help me, which was just as well because there wasn't unless he had been able to fashion me a living, breathing, willing sexual partner out of empty air.

I sipped my excellent sherry and looked at Bax. I supposed this was the parting of the ways. First he, and then Gadsby, had tried to make a professional historian out of me, and it wasn't their fault, or history's fault, that they weren't going to succeed.

'I suspect, in fact, that you're getting very stale,' Bax was saying, though I was hardly any longer listening to him. 'You've been reading history pretty hard now for... well, two years at school and three up here, five years without a break.'

I didn't bother to tell him that as far as that went, I would have been quite happy, if my other needs had been met, to read history without a break for fifty years, let alone five.

'There are ways and ways of getting stale,' he went on as if he could read my thoughts. 'Quite possibly it's not a question of taking your attention away from history but of coming to history by another route. Approaching it via landscapes and buildings rather than by the printed page and the spoken word.' He glanced over at me, thoughtfully. 'You haven't had much opportunity to travel, have you, so far?'

'I've never been abroad at all.'

'Well, I think it would do you good.' Bax came over and filled my sherry-glass again, without waiting to know if I wanted any. 'I think it's the next step for you to take, whatever happens or doesn't happen. We're nearly at the Easter vac. now. Why don't you get across the Channel? Take a look at the great medieval buildings of Northern France? They'll suggest perspectives to you, I feel sure of it.'

'There isn't any cash to spare for that, sir,' I said.

'Oh, I wasn't suggesting you should dig into your own pocket for the cash. The College has bits and bobs of spare money that are earmarked for exactly this kind of thing. We don't enjoy seeing a promising man go off form, and perhaps deny himself an interesting career, for lack of a – what do people call it nowadays? – shot in the arm that could be provided for a few pounds.'

'Oh,' I said. 'Well, I won't deny I'd be very –'

'I've already spoken about it to Mr Gadsby, as a matter of fact. He agrees with me and so does Hungerford, who also thinks you're stale.'

What the hell does Hungerford know about it? I thought. Aloud I said, 'Well, sir, if Mr Gadsby and you, *and* Mr Hungerford' – I gave that *and* a slightly satirical tone – 'all think I deserve a little travel money from the College, I'll be glad to have it.'

'Oh, I didn't say you deserved it,' Bax said pleasantly. 'What I said was that we'd like to give it to you. As an historian you must always be careful about causation.'

I thanked him and went down the staircase in a more cheerful mood than when I had come up it. My stomach was glowing with his superb sherry, and my bank account would still be glowing with an infusion of money from the College, the only stipulation being that I spent it in

France. For a little while, I positively liked Episcopus College, and, as long as that mood lasted, even tolerated Oxford University.

A few days later, the money duly arrived, in the form of a cheque from the Bursar left in an envelope in my pigeon-hole. No fuss, no going cap in hand, no waiting in corridors; and it was for £30, which of course was a fortune in those days, when the pound bought an astronomical number of francs. I could go for two weeks and it would pay for everything from door to door, including fares.

It wasn't until I got busy with cross-Channel time-tables and French railway maps and what-not, and began to plan it concretely, that I began to imagine lonely evenings, silent days spent mooching around medieval towns with no one to share it all; and of course, over-arching everything else, the need for feminine solace. It took me no time at all to arrive at a decision; I would invite Geraldine along. We didn't, so far, know each other quite that well, and wouldn't, in the ordinary course of things, expect to see each other in the vacation after we had departed to our respective homes. But it wouldn't be a very long step to take. My suggesting it wouldn't give her much of a surprise. She was at exactly the same stage of her academic life as I was – third year, one more term to go, last vacation coming up – and to go to France and look at a few landscapes and buildings made just as good sense for her as it did for me.

Without giving myself a chance to hesitate, I marched up to her the very next time I saw her, which happened to be in the main Post Office in St Aldate's. She was sending off a parcel. I waited till she had finished, then said, 'Come and have a drink.'

'A *drink*? In the middle of the morning?'

'It's twelve o'clock. They've been open for an hour.'

'Well, thanks, but I don't drink in the middle of the day. It makes me sleepy.'

'Well, have a soft drink then. Just so that we can sit down while I talk to you.'

We went into one of the small pubs on that side of the street. As I got a pint of beer for myself and a lemonade for her I remembered with amusement that this was the pub where the landlord had suddenly shouted 'Everybody upstairs!' on that far-off evening when I had been out with Knowlton and his amiable friends. What a different person I had been in those days, when a trivial event like that had seemed a real event in my life.

Geraldine composedly sipped her lemonade while I rapidly outlined what I had in mind. At least, I gave it a broad outline. I wasn't quite sure, myself, what *exactly* it was that I had in mind. I left it entirely unclear whether I had any thought of our sharing a room in the hotels we went to, for instance. Needless to say, if she had shown any interest in sleeping with me, I would have jumped at the chance. Ever since Harry Goodenough's interest in her had triggered off mine, I saw her quite clearly as a girl with her own magnetic field of force, and it was a field I was perfectly willing to be drawn into, if I were so lucky as to get an invitation. But I avoided stating the matter openly. I thought a certain friendly vagueness would be the best strategy; and, after all, if she chose to come with me on brother-and-sister terms, that would be a lot better than nothing because I really liked her company.

But, as it turned out, she wasn't interested whatever the terms. 'I'm sorry, Peter,' she said gently, 'but I'm not free this vac.'

'Not free? You mean they want you at home?'

She gave me a level look and said, 'Home isn't the only place where one can be wanted, you know.'

I felt a fool. 'Sorry,' I mumbled. 'Of course I didn't mean to be inquisitive.. It's your own business if you...'

'I don't mind telling you what I'm doing, up to a point that is. I'm going to Italy. With someone who's... very central in my life and with whom I generally do go away in the vacations.'

'Oh.'

'I thought I'd mention it just in case this sort of idea comes into your head again at any time.'

'Oh. Right.' I felt curiously flat as I said the words.

She finished the glass of lemonade. 'That was very refreshing,' she said. 'Thank you for it. And I hope you have a good time in France.'

'Thanks. I expect to,' I said despondently. I drained my pint glass and followed her out. *Everybody* upstairs! The cry rang, ironically, in my memory. Well, that was one thing I wouldn't be doing: going upstairs with Geraldine.

*

In the end I went to France with Harry Goodenough. He wasn't doing anything in particular, and his people, being an ordinary middle-class business family, weren't so strapped for money as mine, so they had no difficulty in handing out the modest amount it cost him to come along with me. He made a good companion, being so self-forgetful, so entirely focused on whatever train of ideas was going through his head, that he paid hardly any attention to his comforts and conveniences. He never grumbled if an hotel gave us lumpy beds, or cold coffee at breakfast, or if we ran into a spell of bad weather and had to walk round the streets in driving rain. He even budged over slightly from his eternal topic of conversation, William Shakespeare. Not far, admittedly; but in deference to our being on French soil he was reading Montaigne. A copy of Montaigne's *Essays*, he pointed out, had come down to us with Shakespeare's signature in it. 'Of course,' he admitted scrupulously, 'not every book from that period with Shakespeare's name in it can be accepted as his. Some of those signatures are forgeries – sharp sale-room practice, to make the book worth more. But I reckon the Montaigne did belong to him. There are specific echoes in the plays, that show he read Montaigne, and if he didn't have the book himself he must have borrowed it from somebody else, and it's just as easy to believe he'd have his own copy.' Armed with this, he had brought Florio's translation of Montaigne along in a little three-volume edition, and in the evenings, resting after the day's wanderings, we used to sit around drinking cheap wine and getting our noses into these volumes, pointing out good passages to one another.

It was, of course, my first glimpse of life outside my own country, and Bax had certainly been right in predicting that I would find it stimulating. Some of the stimulation was of the kind he evidently had in mind; some, quite plainly, wasn't. Because we had to keep to a budget and because any part of France was new and exciting to me, the near as well as the far, I had planned a modest itinerary. Though I had already decided that, even in the unlikely event of my becoming a professional historian, it wasn't medieval history that was going to preoccupy me, I saw no harm in taking Bax's tip and looking at some of the medieval buildings of Northern France. We started straight away with Boulogne, getting off the boat and taking our first walk along the massive ramparts of the *haute ville*; and, perhaps because I was a clean slate for impressions, that walk has stayed with me as one of the utterly unforgettable experiences of my life. Then we meandered from town to town, not troubling to book ahead, using local trains and buses, and with just a few fixed points that were marked with a 'must'. We saw the Cathedral at Amiens. We wandered into the Cotentin Peninsula, glorious in its lyrical spring weather, and saw the Cathedral and the Tapestry at Bayeux. Finally we got to Paris, our furthest point from home, and had a couple of nights in a simple little hotel on the Left Bank, before taking the train and boat and coming home along the beaten track of tourism.

Everything I saw in France impressed and captivated me. The

countries of Europe were very different from one another in those days, before a cheap varnish of internationalism, made up of fast food, cut-rate travel, chain stores and pop music tended to make all Europe seem like one big sleazy airport; but no two were more sharply different than England and France. Simply by crossing those twenty-two miles of water you entered a world that was totally different from the largest matters down to the smallest. And in particular, of course, I noticed the Girls.

In those days, it was accepted as a universal article of faith that the young women of France were not only the most *chic* and stylish but also the sexiest to be found anywhere. This isn't just my opinion; everybody thought so and everybody said so. In the intervening decades these things have levelled out, and I realize that Paris is no longer the erotic capital of the world. But in those days it was, and I certainly held that belief as firmly as it was held by young Englishmen a hundred years before my day. The girls I saw on that trip in the spring of 1933 – and I can see them now, vivid in my memory, not perhaps as individuals but merging, as it were, into one archetypal French Girl – really did seem to have a lot of style and also to flow with an energy that was, quite obviously, sexual. It issued in all sorts of ways, mental, physical and sartorial, but its origin was between their legs.

To take a twenty-year old male, especially in the state of deprivation I was in at that time, and put him down in France, and particularly in Paris, was exactly like soaking a bunch of twigs in petrol and then holding it very close to a furnace. Goodness knows why I didn't simply shoot up to the sky in a ball of flame. Looking back on the couple of weeks Harry and I spent in France, it stays with me as a crazy pattern of contrasts: the solemn lofty emotion engendered by cathedrals, the intellectual excitement of tracing historical patterns, the connoisseurship of finding nuggets of wisdom in Montaigne, and all this spinning in a dark, fathomless maelstrom of unsatisfied sexual curiosity. I was swivelling my head to look at girls as they went across medieval courtyards, weaving erotic fantasies out of illuminated parchments, walking round solemn cloisters with a permanent erection.

Oddly enough I never got on to this perennial subject with Harry. I was quite sure he had normal needs like myself, and was probably going through much the same kind of ordeal, but there was a kind of other-worldliness about him that somehow kept us talking about the things of the mind rather than of the body. Very often I was on the point of steering our conversation on to that whole range of preoccupations that obsessed me so totally, but at the last second I always drew back.

The nearest I got to mentioning the subject of gender was to ask him if he had ever got anywhere with Geraldine. I didn't put it as baldly as that, of course; I thought it over carefully and formulated the question in some very discreet way: had he found his relationship with her showing any signs of turning into a deeper one?

'Not a chance,' he said, shaking his great mop-head. 'Never a bit of progress. I really tried to get to know her better. I find her very attractive – all that sparky energy and directness. And when I saw her as Viola I knew my estimate of her character had been right. She'd make a wonderful lover for somebody.'

'She would? You don't think she is already?'

He looked at me warily, as if wondering what he was getting himself into. 'Well... what do you think?'

'I think she's having an affair with somebody and she's absolutely determined to keep it under cover.'

He nodded and blew out his breath as if relieved. 'Well, now that I don't feel I'm being indiscreet... She actually *told* me as much.'

'Don't worry,' I said. 'She told me too.'

We both laughed.

'I might as well tell you,' I said, 'that you're on this trip because Geraldine refused to come along.'

'And I might as well tell you that I'm here because I wanted to have a holiday with Geraldine this Easter and she turned me down.'

'So she turned both of us down.'

'Looks like it.'

We sat in silence for a while after that, but it was a companionable silence. This mysterious love of Geraldine's obviously had the power to make her untemptable by either one of us; and that, in its way, was a bond.

That, as I say, was as near as I got to broaching with Harry the Great Explosive Subject. And I even managed to keep my thoughts off it myself, for some of the time, as long as we were in the quiet Norman towns or the cool green countryside. It was when we got to Paris that I nearly blew apart. Fascinating though I found the place, I was glad our stay was a short one, barely forty-eight hours. The place was too hot, too full of whirling sparks, for a petrol-soaked bundle of twigs. We had two evenings in that wonderful city, the Paris of the 1930's, the Paris of Valéry and Gide and Cocteau and James Joyce, of Breton and the Surrealists, of Georges Braque and Sacha Guitry and Josephine Baker and Django Reindhardt, and all I did was try to control the eagerness of my chopper. On the first evening, Harry dragged me to some far-out fringe theatre in the suburbs which was putting on an *avant-garde* production of *Hamlet*. In French, naturally. I kept on saying I knew where they could get a good English translation and I would understand it better that way, but Harry was adamant. He said he had read somewhere that this production had interesting changes of pace. I could see what he meant. Some of the scenes whipped by like demented rattlesnakes, others were just dumped on to the stage like a delivery of horse manure. I was bored and fatigued, and the journey back, by a mixture of bus and Métro, took about four hours. But it was all Paris, and when I look back I can find something to cherish even in that memory.

The next evening, we had split up for a while to do some separate shopping, our wants being not quite identical, and had arranged to meet for dinner at the little restaurant at the corner of the street where our hotel was. Seven was the time agreed, but when seven came, and half-past, and a quarter to eight, Harry was not there, and when he did show up, nearly an hour late, he had obviously drunk quite a lot. He was glassy-eyed and preoccupied, and the evening was not very cheerful. Only once, before we went back to the hotel to sleep, did he rouse himself to utter a few connected sentences, and to my surprise these turned out to be a request for a cash loan. I had thought him fairly well provided. But I split in half the little that remained to me, and we got by till we reached London, where he departed for his Warwickshire home and I came on to Oxford.

*

The long desert of the Iffley Road and the bleak lodgings seemed even more dreary after my French trip. My zest for history had indeed been freshened, but it was soon dulled again when I settled to the grey monotony of each day: a stodgy breakfast served by Mrs Groundsel, followed by a day spent mechanically turning over the pages of books and notebooks, dinner at Episcopus (for economy's sake) and afterwards a few glasses of beer in some out-of-the-way pub with one of my few regular companions, usually Harry but sometimes one or other of my generation of Episcopus men whom I had come to know well over the years. Or perhaps a cinema. I was growing to be a great film fan. We were getting the German Expressionist masterpieces, and a lot of French surrealism, at the minority cinemas and film clubs in Oxford. Harry Goodenough, who had picked up the surrealist bug while we were in Paris (he wanted to mount a surrealist *Timon of Athens* and assembled a bulky file of notes on exactly how he would do this, carrying the file under his arm wherever he went in case he suddenly had a fresh insight to add to it) made me accompany him to Cocteau's *Le Sang d'un Poète* no fewer than three times and Buñuel's *Un Chien Andalou* twice.

Apart from the inevitable pulsating of his theatrical obsessions, though, a lot of the sparkle seemed to have gone out of Harry: and nowhere else did my scrutiny of the horizon see any gleam of brightness. Life seemed totally leaden. Geraldine I scarcely saw; she was working very hard for her final examinations ('Schools', in Oxford parlance); I was supposed to be revising too, but it all seemed so remote. Gadsby had more or less given up on me. I was prepared to ship my oars and drift into the week of examination papers, relying on my ability to unload, however listlessly, the knowledge I had amassed during the time when historical study had been a joy to me, and a passion, and a liberation.

The early part of May, in England, is very often chilly and wet, with cold winds blowing across rain-soaked fields and fallen blossom lying in little sodden pads under the trees. So it was this time, or at least so my memory reports it. I felt that my years as an Oxford undergraduate were going to end up drowned in a pool of muddy rainwater. I paid a duty visit to Bax to tell him about the French trip, and as I described our itinerary and the places we had seen a flicker of the old excitement, the old involvement, came back into my brain, but it was all no use. It wasn't my interest in history that had been flagging; it was my life-energy in general. My instinctual nature, tired of being dammed up and frustrated, had taken its revenge by poisoning the irrigation channels of my mind. I could no more think creatively about history than a blind pit-pony could have danced in 'Swan Lake'.

Life trailed along in this stagnant fashion until the extraordinary, the never-to-be-forgotten morning, about midway through the second week of May, when I had two visitors in rapid succession. This in itself was exceptional. I disliked my lodgings so much, and my dislike extended so justifiably to Mrs Groundsel, that I had never, in the eight months since I moved in there, invited anyone to visit me. I always met people in the pub, or in College, or just ran into them in the street. But on this morning, chilly and rainy like the others, Mrs Groundsel had just taken away the breakfast dishes and I was just wearily getting out file, notebook, tome from the library, one or two reference books, and grouping them on the desk as I grouped them every morning, when there was an unaccustomed flurry in the hallway outside my door. I heard the rattle of the front door opening, then I heard Mrs Groundsel pouncing on the visitor. I had thought she was in the basement kitchen, but she had the gift of pouncing from any distance in the twinkling of an eye. She could materialize, instantaneously, anywhere and at any time if she thought there was something worth getting her snout into.

'Mr Leonard,' I heard the visitor's voice. It was Harry Goodenough. And Mrs Groundsel, disapprovingly: 'He's in there. But I don't think he's expecting –'

The next instant, Harry had given a quick knock on my door, opened it and was inside, grinning widely and with his hair standing out all round his head like a circus clown's. One glance showed me that he had changed, almost out of recognition, from the depressed, preoccupied Harry of the last week or two.

'Sorry to disturb you, Peter,' he began, but I cut him short.

'Harry, I'm glad to see you. I'm sorry this is such a hole, and I haven't even a gas-ring to make a cup of coffee to offer you. All I can say is, sit down and be welcome.'

'I won't keep you long. I just had to talk to somebody. Not just anybody, but a person I could confide in.'

'You've had good news. What is it?'

Harry burst out laughing, from sheer exuberance. 'You bet I've had good news. The best.'

'Well, what? Don't keep me –'

'I've just been to the doctor. Clean bill of health. I just couldn't keep it to myself.'

'Is that all?'

'*All*? I've been going out of my mind these last weeks.'

'I didn't know you'd been ill.'

'I haven't been, as it turns out. But I was absolutely shit scared that I might be.'

'What with?'

'Syph.'

I jumped up. 'Syph? *Syphilis*? What the hell made you think you'd...' I stopped and looked at him narrowly. 'Harry, did you get up to something in France?'

'Yes. You know when.'

'That evening in Paris, you mean.'

'Yes. You must have wondered where I went off to, and came back drunk and spent up.'

'Well, I did rather, but it wasn't any of my –'.

'I went to a knock-shop.'

'Good God!'

'Yes. I just had to. I felt I'd go raving mad if I didn't. It was all – you know – building up.'

'You don't have to tell me,' I said. 'I know the feeling.'

'How d'you cope with it?'

'I don't. I haven't coped. I've gone raving mad.'

'Oh.'

'Well, go on with the story, Harry. Don't just drop me there, on the whorehouse doorstep. How did you find the place, to begin with?'

'A tout handed me a card with the address on it.'

'And was that what decided you to do it?'

He shook his head. 'No. I knew I was going to do it when I told you I was going off shopping. Didn't you wonder, when I got back, why I hadn't bought anything?'

'No. I don't notice things like that. I'm too self-absorbed to look attentively at other people.'

'Well, I went to this address and I did it.'

'What d'you mean, you did it? I want more details than that. What's the procedure?'

'Well, assuming they're all the same as this one, you go in and the Madame receives you in a little parlour and offers you a drink. Then you go into a kind of foyer with benches round it, blokes sitting around on these benches, and the girls are there parading round in these filmy things... I don't know how you'd describe.. what's a *chemise*?'

'Look, skip all that, I can imagine what they wear. How many girls were there?'

'Well, seven or eight, but I suppose the others were hard at work upstairs. They have these little rooms... cubicles, really... well, you pick one and the Madame introduces you, kind of, tells you the girl's name, anyway, and you go back into the little office and you settle up. Cash down.'

'Oh, I see. Understandable, when you come to think of it.'

'Understandable, as you say. Well, I paid up and came out of the office and then the girl, she was called Claudette, was waiting and we went up to her cubicle and got on the bed and I screwed her. It didn't take long. When I got out into the street again I looked at my watch and realized I'd only been in the building for about fifteen minutes all told.'

'It took you long enough to get back and meet me.'

'That's because I went off and had a few drinks and started worrying. Then I got lost a couple of times getting back.'

'Worrying, eh?'

Harry's smile vanished as he went back into his mental turmoil, re-living it. 'God, Peter, I tell you I started worrying even as I was pulling my trousers back on.'

'Didn't the girl look healthy? Claudette?'

'You can't tell what they're like under all that powder and rouge and stuff. I knew I was in line for a dose of clap, that's pretty common, but what really worried me was the thought that I might have caught syph.'

'But those places are inspected by doctors.'

'Yes, but how many chaps had been banging away at her since the doctor last made his rounds? And how thorough are those examinations, anyway? I don't believe they give them a blood test.'

'Is that what you've had?'

He nodded and his beaming smile returned. 'I've just had the result of it. I'm in the clear.'

'So Claudette *was* healthy,' I said.

'Yes, bless her. I suppose I ought to be grateful to her for letting me shoot that load. But it's a very temporary solution to the problem. Twenty-four hours later and it's as bad as ever and meanwhile you've got this other problem of ghastly worry.' He shuddered. 'Syphilis isn't curable, you know. You end up paralyzed. G.P.I., they call it. General Paralysis of the Insane.'

'Yes. Baudelaire had it.'

'And Lenin. And God knows how many others. Practically half the people you've heard of in the last hundred years or so.'

'Your nose rots off, doesn't it?'

'Practically everything rots off if you live long enough. Christ, it must be awful.'

'Harry,' I said. 'It's none of my business and you don't have to tell me this, but was it...'

'My first time? No.'

'And the other times weren't over-the-counter stuff, were they?' Now that we had broken the silence barrier, I really wanted to talk it all out.

'It. Not they. There's only been one.'

'In Oxford?'

'No, not in Oxford. It was last summer when I went as Assistant Stage Manager with a little touring company. I worked for nothing just to get experience. There was a girl who wanted to get into the company, she'd done her training at RADA and all that, and she was working as Stage Manager on a tiny little salary. She was a lovely girl, too, Penny. I hope she makes it. A clear-headed, practical girl, able to manage people and situations. I cast her in my mind as Major Barbara. Or perhaps an Ibsen heroine – I can see her as –'

'Yes, yes,' I said, desperate to head him off before he got to Shakespeare. 'And you got it together with her, did you?'

'I did indeed. She took about three days to look me over and then she let me know that one of my jobs would be to release her tensions after a hard day's work.'

'Good for you.'

'Yes, it was lovely. But it only lasted about six weeks and then the tour ended and Penny went off to another job and I came back here. After six weeks of happiness with Penny, Oxford seemed more like a morgue than ever.'

'Well, sexually that's what it is. A morgue. Row upon row of dead bodies lying in cold storage.'

He sighed and then said philosophically, 'Well, at least I haven't got syph. I'll live to fight another day.'

'True,' I said, 'and it's not for long now.'

'Yes, and that reminds me of practical concerns.' Harry began to fumble through his pockets. 'I went to the bank the other day and checked on the exchange rate. I suppose you don't mind if I give you back that loan in English money?'

'I don't want it back.'

'What d'you mean? Of course you must have it back.'

'No, honestly, Harry. It wasn't my money, anyway. What I lent you was a slice, roughly half, of what I had left of the money Episcopus gave me for the trip. The fact that I shared a bit of it with you doesn't matter.'

'Well, that's very decent of you.'

'Not at all. It's purely selfish. I get a lot of pleasure from the thought that some of the money I got from Puritanical, monastic, killjoy old Episcopus College went on helping you get it out of sight.'

At that, we both burst out laughing, and in the middle of our laughter I noticed that the door was opening.

I do not wish to slander Mrs Groundsel and would be far from suggesting that she would stoop to throwing open a door without knocking first, merely in the hope of catching someone doing something she could disapprove of. On the other hand it is undeniable that she had exploited her natural quickness of movement to develop a curious technique, the like of which I have never met with in anyone else. She would give a staccato double knock on the door and, in the same instant, her hand would go flashing down to the handle, twist it, and push the door open. For all practical purposes the two actions were simultaneous.

'*Another* visitor, Mr Leonard,' she said, her cutting tone leaving me in no doubt that she thought me a waster, a socialite who frittered away his precious time for study in idle chatter. And there, coming through the door, was Heather.

Beyond all doubt Mrs Groundsel had heard my last remark as she whipped the door open, and this caused her to give Heather a very disinheriting look. If I was the kind of person who said things like *that*, what kind of young woman would it be who came visiting me all the way out here – and *in the morning*?

Heather, for her part, betrayed no consciousness that Mrs Groundsel was, or ever had been, on this earth. She came straight into the room with her eyes on my face, and as she did so I suddenly saw her as I had seen her that very first time, when I was standing by the gate and she approached on that big horse, sitting so skilfully and confidently on its enormous back. Her eyes, those wonderful light blue eyes, had been turned on me steadily, with a hint of challenge, on that summer day with the young sun in the sky, and that was just how they were now in my dingy lodging with the rain slanting down outside. I stood up. One does not receive a goddess in a sitting position.

'Hello, Heather,' I said. 'This is my friend Harry Goodenough. Harry, this is Heather Burrell.'

Mrs Groundsel hovered in the doorway to make sure of catching Heather's name. Then she closed the door and, for all I know, eavesdropped in the passage. At least I didn't have to look at her any more.

'Hello, glad to meet you,' Harry said to Heather. He, too, had got to his feet. 'It's a pity I'm just off.'

'I don't want to drive you away,' she said.

'Oh, you're not,' he assured her. 'It was just a flying visit. I was in this part of town and I just dropped in to tell Peter a piece of news. I haven't got –'

I thought for a fevered instant that he was going to say 'I haven't got syphilis after all,' but of course what he said was '...much time this morning – rather a lot of errands to do. Well, see you, Peter.' Then he had gone and Heather and I were alone.

She looked coolly amused and said, 'He got out pretty fast, didn't he?'

'He probably thought he'd be *de trop*,' I said.

'Well, he might just as well have stayed because all I'm here for is to issue an invitation.'

'What to?'

'A glider club rally.'

'A what?' We seemed to me to be starting at the wrong end. Surely after not having seen each other or had any communication for a year, there were things we ought to get said before we started talking about gliders. But, quite clearly, Heather was determined to play it this way. Matter-of-fact.

'Look, the basic facts are these. Next Saturday there's a rally of gliding clubs. About half-a-dozen of them are getting together for a big event. It's going to be held at Fish Hill, that big escarpment up above Broadway. I expect you know it.'

'I suppose Tom's taking part, is he?'

'Tom's taking part but he doesn't need the car. He and another glider fanatic have got the use of a long trailer and they're taking two gliders, packed up in those long boxes they have, towing it behind the other chap's car. So Tom's taken care of. And my parents are going to London, to Smithfield or somewhere. They're going by train so they don't need the car either. So I can have it. Dutiful daughter takes parents to Oxford station and collects them in the evening. Dutiful sister goes to glider rally to gaze open-mouthed at exploits of brother up in the sky. Duty all round.'

'And where do I come in?'

'I just thought if you felt like a day out in the country you might like to come along. I've got to go to the rally. I mean if I don't something's bound to happen that everybody talks about and if I don't know anything about it they'll know I took the car and went off on my own, and letting me have it was one of the things that decided my parents to go to London by train instead of driving. Etcetera, etcetera.' She gave a gesture of boredom and weariness. 'I'm sure you can imagine the kind of thing.'

I could imagine the kind of thing. I could also see that she was playing it cool. Was that because she *was* cool? Had her deeper feelings towards me died away, to the point where she could offer to drive me out for a day in the country, without any premonition that to do so might be dangerous?

I didn't know, I couldn't guess, and it wasn't worth speculating. I knew I was going to accept this invitation anyway. Even if it re-kindled my physical longing for Heather, what the hell? I couldn't be in a worse state than I was in already.

'Count me in,' I said, 'and thanks.'

'Saturday morning,' she said. 'Mummy and Daddy are getting a train at 9.10. The poor old chap'll have to be up at six, as usual, and do the milking and see to this and that. Then he'll go into the house and wash his neck and shave and put his best suit on, and I'll drive the pair of them to the station.'

'Sounds a long day for him. Couldn't Tom –'

'Tom? Mess about with cows on the morning when he's going to be the big star of a gliding display? You've forgotten what he's like.'

'I suppose I have,' I said. 'I haven't thought about him much, this past year.'

I wanted her to say 'Have you thought about *me* much?' I was giving her an opening, a chance to move the talk to a more personal level. But she didn't take it. She just said, 'Well, that's settled, then. I'll come and pick you up about twenty past nine on Saturday.'

'Are we taking a picnic?' I asked.

'Good idea. I'll see to it. You can bring a few things too if you like. But don't do it if you're busy. You've got exams soon, haven't you?'

'In theory, yes,' I said. 'But I can't get very worked up about them. I'll be glad to take the time to do a bit of shopping for the picnic.'

'As you like. Well, I must get off. I've left Mummy having her hair done and I think she must be just about coming out from under the drier by now. I'll have to buy one or two things to convince her I've spent the time usefully.'

You've done that all right, I thought as I watched her swing the old Ford round in a U-turn and accelerate away towards Magdalen bridge and the dreaming spires. Then I went back into my sitting-room and looked at the litter of books and papers on the desk. What on God's earth was I going to do till Saturday?

Chapter 21

I suppose it's just part of the general unpredictability of life that the person who did most to help me to survive over the aching void of the next few days was a person I had never met and knew that I never would meet. His name: Tazio Nuvolari.

Early on the evening of the day of Heather's visitation, I went down to the Bargeman's Arms. It had become my refuge against the worries and perplexities of adult life, the place where I could get back into the cosy, protected setting of my childhood and be surrounded by people whose preoccupations were entirely different from mine. And on this particular evening, my arrival couldn't have been better timed. It was, as I said, Wednesday, and Brian had arrived back from Ulster on the Tuesday evening. The Tourist Trophy race, in which M.G. had entered the K.3 Magnette with Nuvolari at the wheel, had been held on the previous Sunday. Sunk in my own discontent and frustration, I had completely forgotten about the matter, but mercifully I was sufficiently quick-witted to cover up my ignorance. Brian was the first person I met when I went into the house, and I knew from one look at him that something tremendously good had happened.

'Congratulations,' I said, at a venture. It was a calculated risk, and it came off.

'Did you read the Press reports?' he asked.

'Not quite all of them.'

'I've got them all there.' he said, nodding to a pile of newspapers on the table. I sat down and started to work through them; a glance at the first headline gave me the essential information I needed – that Nuvolari had won the race for M.G. – and after that it was just a matter of absorbing detail. I lingered particularly over the photographs – a blurred shape flashing past the downswept chequered flag, beaming faces at Abingdon including Cecil Kimber's, and a shot or two of the hero himself, a wiry little man like a jockey. His enormous dark brown eyes seemed to have a reserve of sadness behind them, though, since his life seemed to be one long series of glittering triumphs, the sadness must have come from further back – perhaps from the generations of back-breaking toil on the peasant farm from which he was the first member of his family to break away. He was to motor-racing what Caruso was to singing or Mohammed Ali to boxing: a human being perfectly adapted to a specialized purpose. The most daring driver who ever sat behind a steering wheel he yet lived to be an old man and died in his bed, because his fineness of judgement and timing saved him from ever making a disastrous mistake.

Nuvolari did not visit Oxford, or Abingdon; his racing time-table was too busy to allow time for hanging about in places where cars could not be driven on circuits. Having signed up to drive for M.G. on the strength of having seen M.G.s perform in the Mille Miglia and knowing they were good cars, he went straight to Ulster in a privately chartered aeroplane, sat in the car for the first time four days before the race, and had just that much time for practice. For the little wizard, it was enough. Once he got the hang of driving the Magnette, he made it sing round the Ulster circuit, beating the opposition with an ease that looked almost contemptuous. Brian watched him do it, and when he got back to Talbot Road afterwards he seemed to me to at least three inches taller. His eyes shone as he talked about the way the car had performed, the way the driver had performed, the way car and driver had performed as one, the way this, the way that...

Hearing his rhapsodies, I wondered if anything that could possibly happen within the context of my own life could possibly put me on such a crest. I couldn't think of anything: not, at any rate, without bringing my sexual fantasies into it. Working at the question, I decided that I might just feel as Brian did now if I were having a holiday in the South of France with Vinnie, renting a villa overlooking the blue Mediterranean, and if I were just undressing to get into bed with her for the fourth time that day when an express letter arrived from the Registrar of Oxford University, congratulating me on being elected to the Regius Chair of History, and at the same time the telephone rang and someone informed me that I had won the Pools (they were just getting going in those days) and was a millionaire. Yes, that might just do it. And the difference between Brian and myself was that my fantasies could not possibly come true, whereas his had been fulfilled down to the last detail... An important international win for M.G. – and Brian there to help to prepare the car, to watch the race, to cheer on the winner, and to share in the celebrations! It was a wonder that he hadn't died of joy.

'Did you get to meet Nuvolari?' I asked.

'Of course.'

'What's he like?'

'Well, to look at he's like his photographs, and you've seen them. Of course what the photographs don't show you is this terrific nervous force, this... electricity coming out of him. I can't tell you what he's like to talk to, because I don't speak Italian and he doesn't speak English, but we shook hands all round and he gave us all a big grin.'

I tried to imagine it. 'Did you get his autograph, at least?'

'As a matter of fact, I did. I wasn't going to at first, it seemed like a kid's game,but when everybody else got out autograph albums and he had the old fountain pen flashing away, he must be doing it all the time, I thought I wouldn't be the only one to come away without his signature. So I felt in my pockets for some paper. And I hadn't got any. No diary, no notebook, no old envelopes, nothing.'

'So what did you do?'

Brian grinned and reached into his inside pocket. Even before his hand reappeared I knew what it would be holding. The one thing he always carried in that pocket: the sacred photograph of Old Number One.

'This was the only thing I had that he could write on.' He turned it over. There, on the back, in a bold, flowing hand, I read: 'Amicizie – T. Nuvolari.' The shiny surface had made the pen slip a little, but it was legible.

'Phew,' I breathed. I knew I had touched greatness. Millions of Italians, at that time, gave at any rate mouth-homage to Mussolini, but just as many admired Nuvolari; and in the end they shot Mussolini and hung his body up by the heels, but Nuvolari they always loved.

*

Saturday was a day of miracles, and the first miracle that happened was that when I awoke the sun was shining out of a sky as clear and blue as Heather's eyes. I scrambled out of bed, washed, shaved, swallowed the gunge that Mrs Groundsel called 'breakfast' – stale poached eggs on soggy toast – and was sitting on the edge of my chair, clutching the bag with the few choice items I had bought for our picnic, for some time before I saw the Ford draw up outside. Heather gave a discreet toot on the horn, but even before she had done so I was heading for the front door.

Outside, the day was even more idyllic than it had looked through the window. The air was caressing to one's skin, and after so many days of rain everything sparkled now in the sun, as if this were the first sunny day since the waters receded from Ararat. As Heather leaned across and opened the passenger door for me, I saw with a sudden bound of my pulses that she was wearing The Dress, the lovely summery one she had been so proud of buying for £1, with the big collar and the bow at the waist. I had always loved her in that dress, and her putting it on had always heralded a very special good time. All at once I *knew*, with a complete and untroubled certainty, that this was going to be a day on which she wouldn't hold back. We both said Hello, we both made the odd casual remark, but as I settled into my seat and our drive began, we did not speak much. There was no need of words. Without needing to be told, without even needing to verbalize the matter in my head, I knew that Heather was just as keen to enjoy that day, to enjoy it to the full, as I was, and that before Oxford saw me again I would have got inside her knickers. And whether it was to be a one-off job or the beginning of a renewal of our relationship, I neither, at that moment, knew or cared.

We drove the twenty-eight miles or so to Fish Hill, and selected a nest near the top of that magnificent natural embankment. The venue for the gliding rally was somewhere among the fields above us, hidden from our sight by the crest of the ridge. Below us, a mile away, the picture-book Cotswold town of Broadway, beginning even then to be debauched by commercialism, but still magical at the right distance, displayed itself like a town in a fairy-tale.

We parked the car on the road verge, and climbed over a gate some distance away, so as to avoid planting any clue that might lead an inquisitive person to us. Once on the wide hillside, we searched for a long time to find the entirely ideal spot: but once we found it, we knew we had everything. Behind us was a high, impenetrable hedge; to one side, the trunk of a huge felled tree, so thick that we had to kneel up with straight backs to see over it; on the other side, a couple of self-seeded hawthorn bushes that were now freshly in full leaf; and at our feet, the steep slope up which we could easily hear anyone toiling.

True to the mood in which we had started our day, we put nothing into words. Once we had the spot picked out and everything we needed grouped around us, Heather lay back and held out her arms. I went down on to her and we kissed, a long and intricate kiss that said it all. We were away: nothing could stop us now.

The first gliders were just swooping out into the hazy blue of the sky overhead as we two young people, down there among the fragrant grasses, swooped into the first curves and loops of our ecstasy. Once again, Heather kept her dress on; there was always the possibility, however remote, that someone might happen along, and the whole situation would be much more awkward if she were stark naked. Besides, her wearing the dress did nothing to diminish our pleasure; it merely altered its nature somewhat.

When natural exhaustion caused us to untwine and sit up, leaning our backs in perfect comfort against the huge rampart of the tree-trunk, we started on the delicious picnic Heather had brought – thick brown sandwiches of home-cured ham and good cheese, with tomatoes and apples and a stone jar of rough cider which we drank out of paper cups. The gliders were taking off in rapid succession now, being launched from the crest of the hill above us and soaring out over the valley below us. When seen against the glare of the sky they all looked black, but when they dipped below the line of the horizon their colours became visible. There were often seven and eight in the sky at the same time, occasionally even more.

'Can you tell which is Tom?' I asked.

'I think so. He's using a glider with broad yellow bands on the wings, and where it isn't yellow it's green. Frog colours. And it's got a recognizable shape too. The wings are very broad. I haven't seen it yet.'

We finished our meal, lay back contentedly, and then Heather said, 'There he is. No mistaking it. Look at those yellow bands.' She leaned on one elbow, watching.

A glider answering to the right description had indeed come into view above us, climbing steeply, the pilot skilfully using the thermals that came off the hill as the day grew warmer; and now it was circling, at the furthest point of its spiral, and showed its colours clearly against distant hills and trees before turning to float across directly above us.

A sudden thought seized me, and I said, 'D'you think he can *see* us down here?'

She shook her head. 'I'm sure not. For one thing I don't think you can see the ground directly beneath you. There'd be no point in it. It's where you're heading for that you have to watch.'

The broad-winged glider circled again and again, becoming smaller as upward draughts lifted it, then larger again in colder air. For some reason the combination of brother and sister – Tom up in the sky, unconscious of us and powerless to intervene even if he had seen our every movement, and Heather here with me on the warm sweet grass of the hillside, sheltered and willing – excited me tremendously. I knew with complete precision what I wanted: to take possession of her there and then, with her would-be guardian, the brother, looping about in the sky above us. I began, immediately, making unambiguous approaches.

'Just a minute,' she said. 'You're so impatient... I'm spilling my cider.'

'Never mind your cider. Drink it.'

'No, I'll put it down carefully. I think I'm going to need something refreshing when you've finished with me.' She placed her half-full paper cup steadily on a level patch of ground.

If anything further was needed to excite me, it was there in the calm, off-hand way in which she spoke. That was one of the things I always found exciting about Heather – her matter-of-factness. It goaded me, somehow. A few seconds later I was sliding my weapon in up to the hilt, again and again, only regretting that I did not have eyes in the back of my head to look up in triumph at the brother wheeling about the sky like an absent-minded vulture as the two of us jockeyed on the ground. Sexually, it was one of the most intense bouts of my life, and for years afterwards I could never see a glider in the sky without fidgeting and growing restless.

After a cosmic fuck like that, there was really nothing to do but lie back and relax completely, and nibble the rest of the food and drink up the cider and feel the sun on our bodies, tempered by a gentle, caressing wind. It was one of those days when England really does seem like a paradise, a green and pleasant land with (on such days) the perfect climate. The air temperature, I would guess, was about 70 degrees Fahrenheit, the perfect temperature for the human body, everything we could see was beautful, and we were fully, generously, gloriously, lyrically satisfied.

As we lay there, with gliders hanging in the sky above us like toys in a shop window and the buttercups glowing in the grass beside us, I said to Heather, 'How've you been since I saw you last?'

'So-so,' she said. 'And you?'

'Bloody awful.'

'Awful how? In what ways?'

'Well, in a word,' I said, 'when you pulled out you left a big hole in the middle of my life, and I didn't find anything to put in it.'

'Any*thing*? Any*one*, you mean, don't you?'

'I didn't find anything *or* anyone. I've been living like a stalactite hanging from a cave roof. Drip, drip, drip of misery.'

'Poor you. I can't say I've had much fun either.'

'Life pretty monotonous at Jasmine Farm, eh?'

'Oh, I haven't been at Jasmine Farm. I've been on a training course.'

'Really? A training course? Training for what?'

She smiled lazily. 'It's all over now. It just didn't work. Catering and hotel management.'

'I can't imagine you –'

'Nor can I, as it turns out. But I was desperate to break out, and try something.'

'You couldn't go on as you were?'

'No. That would have been abject surrender. I would have given up any kind of independence and just sunk without trace into being a maid-of-all-work about the place, and in the end marrying some awful pompous bore who'd be Tom's idea of a suitable husband.'

'I see, of course,' I said. 'Sorry I was stupid.'

'So I went in with this idea that Mother hatched out. She's as fed up with that narrow, monotonous life as I am. She's longing to break out and her latest idea is to turn Jasmine Farm into a select little guest-house.'

'What? But there's hardly room for you all as it is.'

'Build an extra wing on. Make a speciality of really good cooking and have the dining-room open to non-residents. Just a select few, of course. Sky-high prices. It goes along with her social snobbery. I can just see her doing it, too. She'd got it all worked out, how to get the money with bank loans and God knows what. Never consulted Dad at all, of course. I could positively see him receding into the background before my very eyes. Every time she looked straight through him, he turned a little bit more transparent.'

'Well, is it going to happen?'

'No.'

'Why not?'

Heather's mouth set in a straight line. 'Because it all depended on me and in the end I jibbed.'

'Jibbed?'

'Yes. You don't ride horses or you'd know what it's like when a horse just *won't* take the next jump. He stops dead and rears his head up and down and nothing, nothing at all, will make him try it. You could stick a red-hot poker up his rear end if you wanted to – he just wouldn't do it. Well, that's the stage I reached, a couple of weeks ago. I've spent the last six months in Birmingham taking this bloody awful course. Catering and hotel management. God, I'd rather have been reading about history any day.'

'I bet you would.'

'But my mother would never have scraped up the money to pay fees for me to read about history. For this, she did. And now I've walked out on the course without finishing it and I've had to promise to pay her back, penny for penny, everything she spent having me trained. It'll take what I earn from looking after people's horses for about the next three years. But I suppose it's fair enough.'

'I suppose so.'

'There was the most God-almighty row, of course, when I turned up at home and said I'd chucked it. I've never seen any human being in such a rage as my mother was in. Her eyes actually stood out from her head, the way they do in cartoon drawings. All the frustration inside her, I suppose – the thought of being baulked. I'm amazed she didn't have a stroke there and then. Finally she said to me in this ice-cold voice, "I've brought you up for twenty-three years and at the end of it what am I left with? Just one useless lump of a girl." It was horrible – the dead, cold-mutton way she said *One useless lump of a girl.*'

'Don't upset yourself,' I said. 'Just because you don't fit in with her selfish schemes doesn't mean you're useless. If she had a decent angle of vision she'd be proud of having brought you up.'

Inwardly I thought, twenty-three, eh? Heather had never, I realized, mentioned her age. I had not known she was a couple of years older than I. Well, what of it? Nothing of it.

'So you got fed up with the course,' I said, picking up the thread of her story.

'I was fed up, yes, but that was only a small part of it. The real nightmare was that after finishing it I'd have to be a slave to my mother. Planning menus, producing fancy meals, smiling and smarming round a lot of greasy overfed people, and with *her* as the boss, working me to death. I must have been mad ever to consider it for a moment. I suppose I just wanted a change so much that even Birmingham sounded attractive.'

We sank into silence. The drowsy hum of insects in the warm afternoon air, the fragrance of the new grass and hedgerow flowers, and the delicious languor at the centre of my bones all merged to fill me with peace. I believe I slept for a while. When I next became aware of Heather, she was beginning to gather up our oddments towards moving off.

'Are we going?' I asked, raising myself on one elbow.

'Not exactly going,' she said, 'but I must put in an appearance at the rally. Mingle with the merry throng and all that, and make sure Tom sees me. That's my title to having the car, remember.'

We delayed a little longer, kissing, and I felt tempted to take another shot at her, but she sat up sternly and said, 'Come along, now. Practical things to attend to.'

'You sound like someone who's taken a course in management.'

'I feel like one.'

We went back to the car and she drove up to the crest of Fish Hill and we found the car park. Next to it was the immense paddock where the gliders were being unloaded and assembled and generally fussed over, and on the other side of that, the field at the crest of the ridge from which they were towed up into the sky by two light petrol-driven aircraft.

'I don't think it'd be quite tactful for me to appear in front of Tom in your company,' Heather said as she switched off the ignition. 'Tell you what, I'll go and find him and reassure him that I've been watching his exploits and you can wander about on your own and we'll meet back here in' – she glanced at her watch – 'it's nearly four now, shall we say half an hour?'

'Four-thirty it is,' I agreed and we separated. In the event I got no further than the car park. Gliders, on the ground, don't particularly interest me, and I could see the ones in the sky just as well from where I was; and there was more variety in the car park than elsewhere. People who went to air displays, in those days, were often the type who liked sports cars, and some that had turned up that day were what Brian would have called 'hairy', real sports-racing jobs with fold-flat windscreens and outside exhaust pipes; one or two looked almost as stark as Old Number One. I was just idling among these contraptions, looking them over with an uninformed half-interest that was at any rate keeping me from being entirely bored till Heather should return, when I came on one that I had surely seen before, a low green Morgan three-wheeler like Ivan Warmley's. Like it? It *was* it. I recognized a certain pattern of scratches on the edge of the cockpit that had been there when I rode in this same car three summers ago. I stood there, staring down at the worn leather of the two bucket seats, the stubby gear lever, then the speedometer and rev. counter on the dashboard... How it brought back my boyhood, not at all distant in time but impossibly remote in *timbre*!

And since then, I went on to reflect, this strange little car had become domesticated, connected with my home and family, by being used to ferry Mrs Warmley. Strange, how time was incessantly at work, stitching and weaving, stitching and weaving: with the result that even the most insignificant life did not simply have a duration like the life of a salt-cellar or an overcoat – it had a history. Ivan's Morgan was part of history, its own and mine, though to its own mind, if it had had a mind, it would seem only to have had duration. And suddenly I understood Shakespeare's lines

The summer's flower is to the summer sweet,
Though to itself it only live and die.

'He's lost in thought,' I heard a voice say behind me, followed by a girl's laugh. Brian! I knew it was his voice even as I turned to look at him. He was smiling – but then, since Nuvolari's great all-justifying victory he had been more or less permanently smiling. With him were three other people: Ivan, not surprisingly since his car was here; the craggy Doug Ravenscroft; and a girl, she whose laugh I had heard, whom I thought vaguely that I had seen before.

I had not, in fact, seen her before, and the reason why I had that impression was simply because she was Doug Ravenscroft's sister and bore a family resemblance to him. Brian introduced me. Her name was Primrose. As usual, Brian's tone when he introduced me was slightly apologetic, as if he were saying, 'This is my brother, but don't blame me; it's not my fault he turned out like that.'

'Hello,' Primrose said to me and gave me a quick smile. In the physical comparison between herself and her brother, the advantage was all on her side. Where he was tall and bony, she was fairly tall, for a girl, but slender and wand-like. Where his curly hair seemed to spring outward from his head like steel wool, hers was simply a mass of tight curls that covered her head snugly and looked as soft as a lamb's fleece. Where his chin and cheekbones jutted out like crags, hers were merely pronounced. The cheekbones in particular, set high, gave her face a wildness, a gipsy quality, a look of something untamed.

I thought she was very attractive, and as we stood there in the sunshine, chatting, it took me no time at all to realize that I was not the only one who thought so. From the way Brian looked at her – or, to be more precise, could not for an instant take his eyes off her – I could see how he was feeling. And from the fact that she stood close beside him and kept touching his arm as if reassuring herself that he was close by, I could see that things were shaping well. Good old Brian! First the T.T., now this!

Their talk drifted into arrangements for the journey back. Apparently, on the way out there, Primrose had ridden behind Doug on his motor-cycle; now, going back, she was going to have a turn with Ivan in the Morgan, and Brian would get up behind Doug. When I remembered my panic on that nightmare ride back from Cropredy, I understood afresh that with these people I was with a breed entirely different from myself, who had come into the world with no nerves. So be it; there was no point in trying to remake myself so as to resemble them. But it was interesting to note that the girl, Primrose, must have belonged to this breed. It would make her a very good partner for Brian, should their relationship take root and become lasting.

I kept glancing round, hoping that Heather would get back before they set off. Now that Brian had found himself a lovely girl-friend, I wanted to show him that I, too, had a lovely girl-friend, for this one day at least. (Or was it going to be for longer now? *What the hell was going on*?) But the half-hour wasn't quite up, and she didn't appear, and they drove away.

She got back in another few minutes and we set off in our turn. Tom, it seemed, was staying on to make one or two more flights while the tow aircraft was available. He never left any meeting as long as any facilities were still on hand, or anyone still there to whom he could talk and so perhaps learn something. Flying was becoming, day by day, more of an all-devouring passion with him. I asked about Richard, the man Tom was hoping to talk into buying an aeroplane. Was he there?

'Richard? No. Tom's washed his hands of him. He found out Richard wasn't serious about buying the 'plane so he didn't waste any more time on him. It was the 'plane he wanted, not Richard's friendship.'

'And yet he was quite willing to try to push you into marrying Richard, wasn't he?'

'Yes, when he thought he might get an aeroplane out of it.'

'Phew! Pretty single-minded!'

She shrugged. 'That's the way it goes.'

By this time we were driving along the main road, Heather keeping her eyes steadily to the front, driving fast and efficiently. Neither of us spoke for a while. I had no means of knowing the reason for her silence, but the reason for mine was simply that I couldn't think of anything to say. Everything was taking place against such a wall of silence. Heather had walked out of my life, left me alone for a year, suddenly reappeared, scooped me up, we had ecstatically enjoyed one another, now she was driving me back to Oxford: and all against a background of non-statement, non-explanation. That must be how she wanted it, but why did she want it that way?

As we drew near Oxford she said, her tone conversational and casual, 'How long does your term go on for?'

'Oh, the usual. Beginning of July. But I'm taking Schools, so I'll have to show up in the middle of July for my Viva.'

'So you'll be around till mid-July.'

'At least.'

She was silent again. Because we entered Oxford from the Witney side, we had to drive right through the city to get to the Iffley Road, and I offered to get out at the Plain and walk the rest of the way to save her time, but she said, 'Why bother? I'd only have to wait at the station.' We trundled along the Iffley Road, still in silence, and pulled up outside Mrs Groundsel's penitentiary. It was back to normal life for me. If anything in my life could be called normal, ever. The wheels stopped but the engine kept on running. This was it. Get out, Leonard, and for what you have received may the Lord make you truly thankful.

As I put my hand on the door-handle Heather said, 'Are you doing anything on Tuesday afternoon next week?'

'Nothing at all.'

'Could you find your way to Riverside Villa?'

'Well,' I said, 'I haven't forgotten the route.'

'Good,' she said. 'Three o'clock suit you?'

I said 'Perfectly,' and turned towards her thinking to kiss her lightly on the cheek as a comradely gesture on parting. But she turned her face to mine and kissed me full on the mouth. It went through me like an electric charge.

'Tuesday,' she said.

'Three o'clock,' I said and tumbled out on to the pavement.

*

I had no idea what was going on in Heather's mind, why she was back in my life and for how long and on what terms, but for the moment I didn't care. Happiness and release had come again and with them, energy. I suppose it must be a simple medical fact about myself when young that my cerebral cortex was in some fashion directly geared to my balls. When the latter were too full, the former was choked up likewise; it slowed down and stopped. When they were healthily emptied, intellection was free to begin. It began now.

Immediately, that very evening, I began thinking with real relish and interest about history. I also made the interesting discovery that during the last twelve months of inertia, when I had believed myself to be taking nothing in, I had in fact ingested quite a lot of information. It was just that my intellectual system hadn't known what to do with it. My mind had been like a disorganized warehouse, crates of material arriving and nowhere to put them. Everything had had to be piled in corners, not labelled, not listed, unopened, never used. Now, I opened and used all those crates. I assembled all the information I had been listlessly passing before my eyes, hooked it up here and there, established connections between various parts of it, turned it into a living system.

I had a tutorial with Gadsby on the Monday. The effect on the poor old dotard of finding he had a real student on his hands instead of a straw-filled effigy was comic and touching. When I first entered the room he greeted me with his invariable courtesy but with unmistakable weariness. Another interminable hour to spend with this bore, Leonard! How could Bax ever have thought that he... Why was this College ever so misguided as to... But right away, I fired off a couple of leading questions about topics I had been turning over in my mind all Sunday. After all, he was an internationally known scholar, even if he was over the hill, and it hadn't all washed away yet. He soon perked up, sat straight in his chair, began to speak in a less languid voice, and even, as I went faster and faster, to interrupt me and anticipate what he thought I was going to say next, and try to head me off if he expected it to be erroneous. We were having a *dispute*, by God, trying to arrive at truth by the clash of mind on mind, doing what the University had been set up to do seven hundred years before. And in spite of all the blinkered intellectual routine, the snobbery, the endlessly confusing way it had all got itself involved with money and property and social influence, that impulse to disputation and truth-seeking had never died, no, not in seven hundred pock-marked years, and here were Gadsby and I, across the huge gulf of our generations, carrying it on as freshly as ever, because it was what we wanted to do, the breath of our life, the blood of our veins. I saw, that afternoon, something of the depth and authority of Gadsby's learning, and I do not exaggerate when I say that I respected and feared it. Yes, *feared* – because that standard of comparison was something you had to measure up to with your whole being, and if you went down in the end, it was your whole being that went down.

That afternoon was wonderful. What came back to me during it was something as precious as life itself – my sense of a *métier*, of a purpose for which I had come into the world; and, incidentally, I recovered my love for Oxford University as a place where these good things could flower. I knew now, as I came away from Gadsby's rooms, that I loved Oxford as devotedly as Fred Armitage loved it: but for the right reasons. Show me the Carshalton who could spoil Oxford for *me*! I would tread on such vermin, I would pinch out their lives under my thumb like aphids!

In accordance with Oxford practice during one's Schools term, Gadsby and I had not been engaged in a weekly essay; we had been 'revising', which mainly involved going through collections of Schools papers and foreseeing what one might be asked. But I asked him if we might scrap this nonsense and spend a week or two breaking some fresh ground. I wanted to write an essay on Thomas of Aquino, and in particular on his effort to provide a fresh basis for Augustinian theology on Aristotelian philosophy. It was a subject I found fascinating but hard to get into, and I knew Gadsby could point me in the right direction if anybody could. He agreed readily enough, just uttering a routine warning 'not to neglect revision altogether'. I cheerfully reassured him and went on my way. I was back on course as an historian; and, come Tuesday, would be back to Riverside Villa and another ecstatic afternoon.

On the Tuesday morning, as it happened, I was in the library, exchanging a stack of books (I was burning them up at a prodigious rate) and I ran into Bax, who was in there to discuss some matter with the librarian. He saw me and came over. Speaking in an undertone, so as not to set a bad example by talking loudly in the library, he said, 'I hear from Mr Gadsby that your work has picked up a good deal lately.'

Lately! I thought. Exactly twenty-four hours ago! News certainly travels fast in a closed community. 'I think I've found a little fresh energy,' I said.

'Evidently the French trip had the effect I hoped for,' he said with what I thought a touch of smugness. I felt like telling him that it was Fish Hill, not France, that had got me started again. But what would have been the good? And at least, I reflected, Claudette had *not* given Harry Goodenough a dose of anything to ruin his health. The future of the English Shakespearean theatre was still in safe hands. The French trip had, at any rate, done no one any harm.

*

A few weeks, and it was time. I got out of bed one morning and put on, not my usual shapeless jacket and baggy flannel trousers, but full academic dress – black suit, white shirt and black tie, gown, the lot. As I ate Mrs Groundsel's awful breakfast I thought with each forkful, 'One down, not many more to go.' And then I got on my bike and pedalled down to the Plain, over the Cherwell bridge, to the Examination Schools.

The next few days have all fused in my memory into one. Bent backs, hunched shoulders, scribbling, scribbling, unloading the information, the thoughts, the *aperçus* original or stolen, that had gathered in everyone's head during three years at Oxford and at least two of intensive preparation before that. Five years, at a time of life when one year is the equivalent of seven or eight in middle age. Shafts of sunlight gleamed through tall windows. T.G. Jackson's Schools Building, horrible though it is in some ways, was at least put up at a time of confidence and wealth, when the University was not short of funds and never expected to be; the rooms are very large and the ceilings are very high; no one can ever have claimed that a bad result in an examination was caused by stuffy conditions or lack of suitable surroundings generally. Along with that, memory reports a few sharp, isolated impressions: the girl who burst into hysterical sobbing when the invigilator said 'Stop writing now, please,' at the end of one paper, having evidently been scrawling faster and faster in an effort to get whatever it was said in the time allowed; the friends outside, clustered on the steps, opening bottles of champagne at the end of the afternoon sessions; the general air of theatricality, with some faces wearing a conscious expression of *insouciance*, others a hang-dog defiance ('it's too late now anyway') and a few, probably my own among them, rather closed, contained and determined. I had gone past the stage of caring much whether I got a first class degree or not, but at least I was going to show these bastards that I knew something about history. They weren't going to patronize me. I'd been listening to them for three years, now, by God, they were going to listen to me.

Things went pretty well for me, I'll admit. There's probably no such thing as a candidate competent to answer *all* the questions in an examination. Even if you go into fantasy and imagine the papers being taken by a professional, a Bax or a Gadsby, he wouldn't do much better because professional historians tend to specialize and the chap would end up being stumped by perfectly routine questions in some area he hadn't thought about for years. So a well-prepared undergraduate, a good First Class candidate, remains the best runner, and by the mere laws of nature he isn't going to be able to tackle the whole spread of the subject – he just hasn't been on this earth for a sufficient number of years to read everything up. So luck is going to come into it at some point. And in my case, the luck was reasonably good. As soon as I went into the hall for the paper on 'Outlines of Constitutional History' and ran my eye down it, I knew I was on a winner when I saw Question 4, 'What signs are there that the centralization of feudal authority was carried too far by the first three Norman kings?' That happened to be something of a hobby-horse with me. I was strongly of the opinion that feudal authority was only an efficient and just form of government as long as it was not too centralized, and that this fact had been insufficiently realized in Norman times. So I off-loaded my opinions with a happy sense of having brought them to the right place.

I had one or two more questions of a fairly detailed nature like that one, that happened to be right where I lived, and what I needed after that was a question or two that allowed me to spread myself on some general topic concerning the English people and their attitude towards those who have power over them. What did people like Chucker and Alf, people like Old Trundle and Peake and Ted, people like my parents and Uncle Ernest and Brian and Ivan, think and feel about the big issues that were fought out with their help, often with their blood, but argued out over their heads? I wanted to talk about that aspect of history, I knew something about it and I cared about it, and all I needed was a concrete historical issue to which I could anchor some wide-ranging generalization in the manner of Macaulay. And I got it right in my lap when I sat down and ran through the paper on 'English Political History'. Question 10 simply jumped at me off the page. I felt I must be dreaming, it was so perfect. 'Which', it asked with a disarming directness, as if we were playing some party game round a log fire, 'has the more claim to be described as a popular movement, the Restoration or the Revolution of 1688?' Barely had I read the words when, pen in hand, I was accelerating like Nuvolari. I don't even remember what specific answer I gave to the question. Whether Tweedledee got the palm, or Tweedledum, doesn't matter. What I was talking about was the whole question of government with the consent of the governed – and as a matter of fact, *mutatis mutandis*, a lot of what I said could have gone as it stood into the answer on centralization of feudal power. After three years of living the life of a feudal serf, the whole question of authority coming down from the top was a very real one to me. It may seem quaint these days, but the life of a student in the 1930s – particularly a student like myself, committed both by temperament and by conscious decision to a life of scholarship and intellectual enquiry – was, as understood at Oxford, really not very unlike medieval vassalage. The toll that was exacted from us was not primarily fiscal; it was expressed in services and in symbolic observances. For what, after all, was the constant interference of the University with one's personal life, particularly in the field of sexual relations, but a kind of *droit de seigneur*? When I at last got a chance to take Vinnie joyfully to bed on the floor of my room, and the brief exultation was followed by humiliation and blackmail, what was that but the College's version of *jus primae noctis*? I don't say I wrote of these matters in my answers; what I do say is that the three years of subjection fuelled my speculation, and motivated my formulations, and I had things to get off my chest.

*

It was over, and the inevitable unclenching followed. I packed up and left Mrs Groundsel's, as soon as term was formally over. There was nothing to do but wait till mid-July when I had to put on academic dress again and go back into T.G. Jackson's building to be subjected to oral examination, the Viva. Presumably the examiners spent that month in reading the papers and making notes on what they were going to ask you during the Viva. It was a merciful system because all you could do was move yourself up, never down. If you were already sure of a Second but were hovering somewhere near the edge of a First, you could move yourself over into a First if you did well at your Viva, but if you did badly you couldn't plummet down into a Third. The written papers had the primacy.

About the only thing that happened, apart from my blissful regular visits to Riverside Villa, was that one evening I was invited to Gadsby's rooms 'to take wine', as his note put it. The wine turned out to be port, ready on the table in a cut-glass decanter that was probably seventeenth-century Venetian if I only knew. With it were two glasses and a silver dish containing a few dry biscuits. Gadsby unfolded his bony length from his armchair by the fire to greet me. Though the month was July, the evening was cool and rainy, and a fire, evidently newly lit, was struggling into some kind of flame in the polished grate. Evidently we were in for a cosy evening.

'Ah, come in, Leonard,' Gadsby said. 'I'm glad to have this opportunity of... ah... retarding the hasty passage of time for an hour or two so that we can sit together and drink a glass and... let our thoughts... clothe themselves in such words as may occur to us, without the pressure of other business.'

'I'm glad you thought of it, sir,' I said.

'It becomes... wearisome, yes, finally, wearisome, this practice of always meeting for a fixed length of time, in our case sixty minutes, so that the last ten or fifteen are always... to a certain degree constricted or overshadowed, one might say rendered monochrome, robbed of colour, by the impending... but do sit down, Leonard. I thought we'd be more comfortable at the table, to begin with at any rate.'

So we sat at the table and Gadsby put the decanter in front of me for me to help myself. I had never before tasted really good port. It rolled across the tongue and down the throat very, very smoothly. And once it was down inside, it made me feel that my blood, which previously had been flowing through my veins rather coldly and sluggishly, had become warmer and was also lit up by a deep, slow-burning fire. If I had happened to cut myself and any blood ran out, I would have expected to see it glowing with a rich ruby light, like the colour of the wine in our glasses as it reflected the firelight.

'I haven't asked anyone else,' Gadsby said. 'Not because I think you unsociable but because it seemed to me... ah... an advantage to let the talk go in any direction in which it seemed inclined to... point itself. So that if you felt any wish to speak of your... future... ah... plans, for instance...'

He allowed his voice to trail away, having given me the gentlest of nudges towards talking a bit of career shop, if I wanted to. That was his generation. The convention was that we were two cultivated gentlemen drinking our wine together and discussing books, ideas, travel, reminiscence; and that the world of job-competition and career-hunting was a million miles away. Such was the convention in which Gadsby was brought up, and it died with him. The modern world killed it. You might say, indeed, that social justice killed it, by opening these same jobs and careers to a much greater number of aspirants and making the going tougher with every year that passed. Oxford dons only a few years older than Gadsby had been elected as Fellows for life, utterly secure and unremovable except for 'immorality' (yes, that one again); his own position, as a modern don whose Fellowship theoretically came up for review every seven years, must have seemed to him precarious by comparison. To a younger man like Bax, he must have seemed like an old-fashioned uncle. To me, he seemed like a man from the age of Socrates.

So we sat and talked about history. Thank God, since Heather enabled me to straighten out and fly right, I had been enjoying my reading and thinking on historical topics, and the mere detail that I had finished with Schools didn't cause me to close up my books and lose interest. On the contrary, it was liberating. I didn't have to wrap the vast, illimitable subject up into little packets and get ready to throw them at a series of coconut-shies called 'the Papers'. My mind had been ranging rather widely during the couple of weeks since I took the last of these idiotic papers, and I threw quite a number of ideas at Gadsby; I wanted to test them against the man's quite unusual depth of scholarship. He responded very willingly, and years later I would catch myself coming across echoes of that conversation still sounding in my mind. To the impatient, heedless undergraduates of his day, Gadsby was often a figure of fun with his old-fashioned courtliness, his bow tie, his senile saliva-chewing, but I remember the man as he was at a deeper level, as I knew him that evening, as a true scholar with a scholar's passion: *Gladly wolde he lerne, and gladly teche.*

About half-way through the evening Gadsby's scout knocked on the door to know if we wanted anything before he went off duty, and after consulting me Gadsby said we would have some black coffee. I was beginning to need it by that time – we had drunk an enormous amount of that good port, in fact when I looked at the decanter I was startled to see how far the level had gone down. But port isn't like whisky, you don't get fighting drunk on it, nor does it send you to sleep like beer; it just loosens your tongue and makes you feel at peace with yourself and the world. A dangerous feeling to have, in some circumstances! But I was safe enough on this occasion, surrounded by goodwill.

I hadn't been noticing the time, but when the scout knocked it was about nine-thirty, and when he came back with the coffee I noticed that there were three cups on the tray. 'Mr Bax's compliments, sir,' he said to Gadsby, 'and he says he hopes you don't mind if he steps along and joins you for a few minutes. So I puts another cup on. I think that's him I can hear now, sir.' And there was Bax, his watchful, slightly sardonic face appearing round the door at that moment.

'Leonard'll begin to think I'm hounding him,' Bax said to Gadsby, after nodding at me in what was for him an affable fashion. 'But you did say earlier that you didn't think he'd mind.'

'Yes, I did. And I'm sure Leonard has no... ah... objection to your company, Bax. Be seated, my dear fellow.'

I began to feel they had cooked this up between them. What was coming? Were the two of them going to sound me out as to what I Intended To Do? And if so, was that because they knew something I didn't? Something good, or something bad? What the hell went on?

We drank coffee and I sobered up. Bax's arrival, predictably, switched the mood in the room. Up to then, it could have been the Oxford of 1850, or 1750 for that matter. (Not 1650, of course; it was not turbulent enough, nor 1550 either. 1450? Just possibly.) But Bax definitively shifted us to 1933. Before long he had actually broached the subject – which Gadsby, of course, had been far too delicate to get his tongue round – of how I felt I had done in Schools.

'Oh, not so badly, I think,' I said. 'My chief emotion is just being glad to have it over.'

'Some people might misunderstand that remark,' Bax said, giving me that quizzing look through his thick lenses, 'but I don't. It's not reading history that you've had enough of, it's just all that boring business of taking examination papers.'

'Well, of course,' I said.

'Mr Leonard,' Gadsby put in, 'is a dedicated historian by nature, and you and I know that, Bax.'

'I wouldn't dream of denying it, of course,' Bax said. 'The question in my mind is, what does a dedicated historian do in the year of our Lord nineteen thirty-three, if, like all of us here, he has no private income, wants to give his life to the effort to illuminate the inert facts of history, and has nothing to help him but an Oxford degree?'

'The first question that... ah... arises, must be... how will that degree be classified by the... to a greater or lesser extent conventional minds who... ah... find themselves entrusted...'

'Yes,' said Bax. 'What class d'you think you'll get, Leonard?'

'How do I know? They might not like some of my papers.'

'It's not their business to like or dislike your approach, as long as you don't make egregious mistakes of fact and as long as your historical perspectives are, shall we say, worth looking through. That's as much as anyone can expect of an historian twenty-one years old. Don't you agree, Gadsby?'

'A desideratum... fulfilled with sufficient rarity for its fulfilment to be... ah... noticeable.'

'Well, Leonard,' Bax turned to me, 'neither Mr Gadsby nor I are in the confidence of the examiners, and we have no more idea than you have what class you'll eventually emerge with. There's still your Viva to come, but of course there's nothing to be afraid of in that, as you know, since you can't pull yourself down.'

'So I gather.'

'Now, I know Mr Gadsby won't mind if I let out a piece of College information. He and I have talked about your situation before this evening and it would be disingenuous to pretend we haven't. We have a certain belief in you, Leonard. Your work has fluctuated during your three years, but some people are like that, including some of the very best. Only a mediocrity can be on form all the time. Now, you might as well know that there's a three-year Research Fellowship going here, starting next Michaelmas. Obviously you're in line for it. Would you take it if it were offered?'

'Yes,' I said simply. I didn't give him any bullshit about thinking it over. I knew fine and good I'd take it.

'If you turn out to have a First,' Bax said, 'I think you can take it that it's in your pocket. It's not much, just two-fifty a year and a room in College, but it'll get you started.'

'The room in College,' Gadsby said, 'is... important.'

'Yes. Not only would you find it much harder to manage on the stipend if you had to pay rent somewhere, but in fact residing in College is more or less part of the package. It isn't actually written into the terms of the Fellowship, but you can take it from me that if you weren't willing to move into College the job would simply be given to someone who was. However, that's just theoretical. Obviously you'll want to live in. It's free and it's comfortable.'

'Why is it so important?' I asked.

'Every College,' Bax said patiently, 'has to have a statutory number of Fellows who live in College. Their presence is needed. Quite apart from everything else, they're the ones who fill positions like being Junior Dean. You know, putting the drunks to bed and breaking up noisy gatherings.'

'Yes,' I said, thinking what a dead loss Hungerford had always been in that department.

'Well, as I say, all that's theoretical, because you won't be wanting to move out unless you get married, and who does that at twenty-one?'

Who indeed? I thought.

'So to come back to the main point,' Bax said, 'it'll be a big help if you turn out to have picked up a First. It probably wouldn't be impossible with a decent Second, since Gadsby and I are behind you, but some of our colleagues have men they want to back and there's some competition. A First would make it more of an open-and-shut case.'

'Well, I can't answer for –'

'No. We shall just have to wait.'

There seemed to be nothing much more to say. My head, still not quite clear in spite of the black coffee, was spinning with possibilities. And impossibilities. Peter Leonard, Research Fellow, Episcopus College, Oxford. That sounded good. Peter Leonard, married man, living in a two-room flat along the Cowley Road. That sounded bad. But keeping Heather in my life sounded good. Letting Heather drop out of my life sounded bad. But were there alternative Research Fellowships somewhere else? Who knew? And were there alternative Heathers somewhere else? Who knew that either?

It was late. I said good-night to Gadsby, with real gratitude and with the feeling that if I got to know him better I would become fond of him as a person. I never did. He was struck down by a cerebral thrombosis during that summer and never saw another autumn term. When I left those quiet panelled rooms of his, I was leaving his earthly life. Bax let me out of a side door with his own key, and I walked back through the dark and silent streets to the Bargeman's.

*

In the event, my Viva told me all I needed to know. It was, in fact, a formality. After a few questions, the examiners asked me if I intended to take up academic work, and they would hardly have asked me that if they had not given me a First. Etiquette did not allow them to tell any candidate what degree he or she had been awarded, but what they were signalling was clear enough in my case.

However, I kept my mouth shut. The official announcement of the results was not for three days yet. I spent those three days mostly on, or beside, the Thames. One afternoon, thank God, was spent with Heather at Riverside Villa. As usual, we had no talk about plans or intentions or large perspectives, but I did tell her I expected to be getting my Schools results and on what day.

When the day came, I went along to the Schools building in the morning about nine-thirty. The list would be pinned up, I knew, in the entrance hall. There it was. I walked over to it. In spite of my reasonably-based confidence, I felt a cold dread as I walked across that broad marble floor towards the notice-board. I decided to work from the bottom up, reading the names of the fourth-class graduates first, then the second, then the first, so that at least it would get better as I moved up.

My name was not among the fourth- or third-class names. It was not among the second class. It was among the first class.

The way to a professional career as an historian was clear. Just as long as I did nothing stupendously silly, there was no reason why, if I simply attended to my work and did what came easily, I should not live a life as natural and contented as Brian's life among his M.G.s. Oxford would take me on. And, once I was established in Oxford, I could go anywhere else that I chose. It had happened. I had done it.

A strange quiet settled on me. More than anything else I wanted space round me, quiet, solitude, a few hours to think although I was not conscious of any issue that burningly demanded to be thought *about*. I walked down by the side of the Schools to Merton Street, then into Christ Church Meadow, then on to the towpath. I went to Folly Bridge, across the road, back on to the towpath and home to the Bargeman's. My parents asked me how I had got on and I said I had got a First. They said that was very good and added they were proud of me.

I went up to my room and sat there for a while. My mother called up to know if I wanted anything to eat, so I went down and had sandwiches in the bar. Then I went up to my room again. I sat there for a long time, not really thinking, just letting everything revolve slowly in my mind. There was no need to think at high pressure. There was probably no need to do anything at high pressure, ever again, in my whole life.

About the middle of the afternoon, human curiosity broke in on my egocentric reverie to the point of making me want to see the Schools lists again. I had been so intent on locating my own name that I had not hoisted in how any of my friends and acquaintances had fared. Slowly (why should I, now, do anything *quickly*?), I cycled over to High Street, propped the bike against the kerb and went into the barn-like foyer where the lists were displayed. A quick check, the fighting down of a sudden spasm of nervous dread (had it, after all, been a hallucination? – had I only *thought* I saw my name among the First Class?) and I was calmly investigating how our Alma Mater had distributed her favours. Norbert was the only other person I could see who was listed as having a First, though there may have been some among the medicals, who did exams at strange times and in a different rhythm from the rest of us. (I hoped Kent had been ploughed.) Norbert had a First in Greats. I knew he already had a First in Mods, so that made him the proverbial Oxford success-figure, the man with a Double First. I didn't grudge it to him; I was glad. It seemed to me an excellent thing that someone like Norbert, so obviously decent and fair-minded, so obviously disposed to improve any situation he found himself in, should get a good start in whatever career he went into.

Geraldine and Harry Goodenough had Seconds; so had Wilmot, Armitage, and most of the run-of-the-mill Episcopus men; including, I was amused to see, big easy-going Knowlton, whose policy of doing just enough work to stay out of trouble had also kept him clear of the relatively conspicuous cropper of a Third. Perhaps, after all, his methods were more subtly thought out, or informed by a better natural intelligence, than he allowed one to suppose. And in any case there was the cover afforded by Oxford's practice of having an enormous Second class, taking in at one end those who just fell short of a First, and those who were lucky to keep one jump ahead of a Third.

Dobbs had a Third. So, I was sorry to see, did that honest toiler, Perkins, the one whose father knew Carshalton's. Carshalton himself had a Second. Lamont, who in an Honour School would have had to be given either a First or a Fourth, had, I saw, been awarded his unambitious Pass degree. What would he do now? But then, what had Lamont been doing all along, but build his own world? Had he got what he wanted from Leopardi, drawn whatever mysterious elixir he was after from the stanzas of that beautiful but hopeless lyricist? (For I, in the intervening years, had been driven to dip my nose into Leopardi, if only as a tiny knot-hole through which to glimpse Lamont.) Had he, for that matter, finished his poem on Euhemerus? Would I one day be able to say that I had been the fellow-student of a great poet? Or was Lamont, like so many strange and talented men who have drifted through Oxford, destined to disappear once these few congenial years of his youth had passed, and to be, like most of them, utterly unknown by the world outside and utterly forgotten in Oxford?

It seemed to me, standing there in the large empty hallway, that the Schools Building, at that moment, was like a hawser-hole in the hull of a sailing-ship: that many ropes came together there, briefly and for the last time, before branching out in widely divergent and, to the onlooker, unguessable directions. An immense melancholy settled on me. Young and unformed as I was, not yet equipped with any defensive skills, not yet having developed the habit of irony with which older people fend off the all-pervading sadness of life, I felt a swelling in my chest that would gladly have relieved itself in some stately piece of oratory, a lofty edifice of words built before the eyes and in the mind of an attentive audience, to live for ever in their consciousness. But my life was not cast in that mould. Standing there in the afternoon silence, I heard in my mind the opening words of that brief and moving statement of Socrates to his judges after they had condemned him to death. 'The hour of parting has come.' He had gone on, to be sure, in words yet more noble and more cognate, 'We go our separate ways, I to die and you to live. Which is better, only the gods know.' But at that moment my thoughts were not on anything so clear-cut as the choice between living and dying. Of course I, and the people I knew, would die; some quite soon, no doubt, and some after fifty years of habit-ridden existence, but what was important to me just then was that we had been together, we had composed a world, and suddenly that world was on the point of vanishing like a puff of smoke. People I disliked such as Kent and Carshalton, people I understood and sympathized with like Armitage, people I admired from afar like Lamont and Norbert, and the ordinary, easy-going background people like Wilmot and Knowlton, were all about to go their separate ways. Friends, those few I felt close to, like Harry Goodenough and Geraldine, I would probably keep in touch with, but the rest would disperse where I could never follow them, we would meet only on nostalgic occasions, gaudies and reunions, and at twenty-one I was not ready for that. 'Remember old So-an-so?' 'Remember how we used to...?' No, no, not that already, not for twenty years yet. The hour of parting has come! It struck me then, and the thought has often returned since, that the entrance hall of T.G. Jackson's Examination Schools must have been modelled on the great railway stations of the time. You go into the high, echoing marble vestibule and there, facing you, is a space that would do perfectly for an indicator of arrivals and departures. Beneath it, between the staircases, is the obvious place for a couple of ticket windows. On the right-hand side, where the porter has his cubby-hole, would be the enquiry office; and the sanitation is down a flight of stairs to the left. All that is needed is the trains, and they are only missing in the physical sense. Mentally and spritually they are all ready to go, since this is where everybody's career pulls out from.

All these thoughts – of sailing-ships and hawsers, of Socrates, of railway booking-halls, of individual names and faces and of the nothingness left behind by blown-away puffs of smoke, were slowly washing back and forth in my mind, showing no sign of coalescing into anything resembling a unity, as I pedalled gently back to the Bargeman's, went up to my room and sat quietly, letting my mind sink into emptiness. More time passed, largely unnoticed. It must have been about half-past five when I heard my mother's voice calling to me up the stairs. 'Peter. Peter, are you up there?'

I opened the door and called from the landing. 'Yes, what is it?'

'Someone to see you.'

To see me? Here? I went down the stairs and there, standing with my mother in the kitchen, was Heather. 'I've introduced myself,' she said when she saw me.

'Well, that saves me trouble,' I said.

My mother smiled gently at Heather and said, 'Stay as long as you like, dear, but if you'll excuse me I've got some things to do before we open.' To me she said, 'If you go out, Peter, don't be late for tea. If your friend wants to stay we'll be glad to have her.' Then she went out into the yard.

Heather said, 'I can't stay long. Come for a little walk by the river.'

'With pleasure.'

'What did you get in Schools?'

'A First.'

'Congratulations. It's what you wanted, isn't it?'

'It's what I hoped for.'

We went out and down the short street to the river towpath. It was a dull, calm evening and the surface of the river gave off a smooth pale light like clouded glass.

'Which way d'you want to walk?' I asked. 'Upstream or downstream?'

'Which should I choose?'

'Downstream. It's prettier. Upstream you've got all those gasworks and railway bridges and things.'

'We'll go upstream,' she said.

I made no comment. Whatever was her reason for coming to see me in this unexpected way, whatever her reason for wanting to walk in an industrial rather than a classic and gracious setting, I had a feeling I would find out before long.

We walked along the gravel path and looked at the ducks. There was a man getting ready to fish from the bank. He had a huge tin of fat wriggling maggots, and as we passed he was just threading one on to a hook. Some rain-clouds drifted slowly in the sky. It was a Thames Valley July evening like so many others I had known.

There were no benches to sit down on and the grass was too dirty and dog-encrusted to be inviting. We walked as far as the first railway bridge and Heather leaned her back against its wall and said, 'Let's rest a bit and then go back.'

'It won't be much of a walk.'

'I didn't want much of a walk. I just wanted us to be by ourselves for a few minutes.'

'Heather, if there's something you want to tell me, what is it?'

She stood there with her shoulders against the blackened bricks and said, 'I've missed two periods.'

'Two...?'

'Since that afternoon on Fish Hill, I've missed two periods in a row.'

'Oh.'

'Well, you know what that means, don't you? I'm pregnant.'

'I see,' I said.

'I need hardly say you're the only one who could possibly be the father.'

'I expect so.'

'What d'you mean, you *expect* so? It's true, damn it!'

'All right, it's true.'

A train went over our heads, rattling the bridge, filling our brains with noise. The rattling went on for a long time. In the silence after it had passed, two ducks landed on the water beside us with two soft splashes.

Heather said, 'Why don't you say something?'

'I'm thinking.'

Chapter 22

The Church of St James the Great at South Leigh, Oxfordshire, is a medieval building of considerable interest to the historian. Originally a Norman church, it has been restored and renovated many times, and during one of these renovations, in 1872, a number of medieval wall-paintings were discovered under a thick coating of whitewash. Most of these paintings are concerned with the Last Judgment. One, to one's right immediately on entering, shows the Archangel Michael, with a pair of what are evidently grocer's scales, weighing the souls of some recently deceased persons. Over the chancel arch is an even more dramatic representation of the same eventuality. Two archangels with trumpets are awakening the dead, those on the south side having charge of the Saved and those on the north of the Lost. The Saved, once awake, are being wafted upward and received by St Peter, the Lost dragged down towards the mouth of hell (which of course is blasting out flames) by exoskeletal bipeds, presumably devils and therefore at home in the everlasting bonfire. It would all be too horrible for words were it not that everyone is given a fair weigh-in before judgment is pronounced, rather as in T.G. Jackson's Examination Schools in High Street.

I rely for this somewhat cursory description on my memory because, though I am a professional historian with an interest in such matters, I have never brought myself to look attentively at these paintings since the sultry Saturday afternoon in August 1933 when Heather and I were married in this church. While waiting for the business part of the ceremony to be accomplished I had plenty of time to look at these murals, particularly the one that showed the damned being dragged away to eternal torment, bound together with a spiked band round their waists. The experience has put me off that particular building, and though I have sometimes had occasion to enter it since I have always done so for the briefest possible time.

During the ceremony I was in a trance-like state, hardly aware of the other presences around me, even Heather's. Old Nick with his gaping maw and filed teeth was more real to me than any of the human beings assembled in the place. The only person I noticed at all was Heather's mother, Mrs Burrell, because of the pang of pity I couldn't help feeling for her. When we all met at the church porch my first impression was that she was very heavily made up. She had been laying it on with a bricklayer's trowel, especially round the eyes. Then I realized she had been crying. No amount of patching up and smoothing over could hide the evidence: her eyes were so red and puffy that she must have been in a continuously tearful state for hours, perhaps days. I felt an impulse of genuine sympathy. She had, I realized, been robbed of one of the few things left in life that she might reasonably still have hoped for – and robbed in such an ironic way, as if fate were deliberately setting out to mock as well as deprive. A good marriage for Heather, enabling her, Mrs Burrell, to move in circles she considered fit for her breeding and accomplishments instead of being stuck out in a damp field with a tenant farmer – it would have given her a new lease of life. She wasn't choosy either. If Heather had managed to catch a young farmer from a prosperous background, heir to broad acres, that would have been fine, but so would a city gent who happened to fall under her blonde spell during a weekend in the fresh country air. And so would 'the Varsity'. I remembered how she had pricked up her ears, how her manner towards me had completely changed in a twinkling, when she discovered that I was at Episcopus. 'Where do your people live?' I wished now that I had answered straight away, 'At the Bargeman's Arms in West Oxford.' At least it would have spared her what she was going through now – the agony of knowing that what she wanted had been brought to her on a silver plate and then suddenly snatched off that plate before her fingers could close on it. Heather was indeed going to marry a Varsity man: a man, what was more, with his foot fairly solidly on the first rung of an academic career. Episcopus College, where she had been given that cup of tea and where she had encouraged Heather to go to the Commem. Ball at which this whole train of events had been set in motion, had come towards her beckoning and smiling and then – whisk! the elastic had been pulled back and Episcopus had, for her, ceased to exist. No wedding in the College chapel, no champagne and strawberries on that immaculate lawn with attentive scouts in white jackets, no photographs in the *Oxford Mail*, just the local church and ham sandwiches in the farmhouse with everyone wondering how soon they could decently get away.

Because, of course, it had all had to be kept a dead secret. Once I had netted my First that Junior Research Fellowship at Episcopus had been a certainty. A moral certainty, at any rate. The College was committed to electing me when everybody reassembled in October and they held the first meeting of the Governing Body. Committed, that is, unless I did something really stupid, something that would have been professional suicide. Such as what? Getting into a razor-fight outside a seamen's hostel? No, that would have been dismissed as harmless rowdyism. Being arrested for shop-lifting? It could have been brazened out as all a mistake. Indecent exposure at the gates of a girls' school? Easily rationalized as a simple need to urinate and a failure to realize my location: a defence, I recalled as an historian, that had been offered in apparent good faith in 1865 by George Corfield, 'a Vagrant', who when arrested on the testimony of a Mrs Philips for an offence of this kind in a side street during St Giles's Fair maintained that he 'did not see the prosecutrix, and simply went to obey a demand of nature'. Convincing enough! No, I failed to see how I could mess up my chances, with only the formality of election lying between me and a three-year-Fellowship, by any offence against the law short of murder, which I had no inclination to commit. But matrimony – now there was something else again, something absolutely certain to capsize my academic career immediately and finally. At the exact moment when I stood beside Heather at the altar in South Leigh church, hearing the parson ask her if she took me to be her lawful wedded husband, I could hear inside my head, much more clearly than Heather's quiet response, Bax's patient voice as he had explained the matter to me that evening in Gadsby's rooms. 'That's all theoretical ... you won't be wanting to move out unless you get married ... who does that at twenty-one?'

'I do,' I said to the vicar. And I thought, that's the kind of damn fool I am. Bax had given me his warning in July. And here it was, only August. I was standing before the altar, with the ring on Heather's finger, *for life*, and Old Nick on the wall swallowing misguided souls as if he had a headache and they were aspirins!

As we filed out of the church in ceremonial order I took a quick look at the few ghouls, as it were, who had bothered to come along to see me cannibalized. Most of them were dim second cousins and what-not whom I would meet for a few minutes back at the farmhouse and then never see again in my life except when somebody died. But, to my sudden horror, I saw in the back row, at the end furthest from the door, in deep shadow so that I nearly didn't see it at all, a face I recognized and would have been glad not to.

Phil. Phil was there, poisoning the solemn piety of the church with his horrible presence. A human, or half-human, equivalent of the most repulsive figures in the wall paintings.

Phil! Who the hell had let him in here? But then, how could he have been kept out? What law said that a church, a place of public worship set up in accordance with the statutes of the land, could be closed to *anybody*?

Certainly there would have been no chance of excluding Phil. He even seemed, as I stared at him for that brief second, seeing him clearly as my young eyes accustomed themselves to the shadows, to be dressed with something like an approach to respectability. The rustily dark garments he had on were, or had been, a suit. His shirt was buttoned approximately up to the neck and encircled by something resembling a tie. Why had he made this effort? He couldn't, surely, have been *invited*? Nor could he, equally obviously, have been a regular churchgoer, an habitual member of the congregation. Why then?

I knew why. I plumbed the horrors of it even as we emerged into the sudden sunlight outside the stone porch. Phil was there to stare at Heather dressed as a bride. I knew from experience that it gave him sexual pleasure to fantasize about her in erotic situations. The bridal outfit would be a gift to him, enriching his fantasies for years to come. And abruptly I had a vision of him on that morning of years ago, suddenly emerging round the corner of a shed, grinning and drooling and exhibiting his big jackass tumescence to her startled adolescent eyes. What a wedding guest!

Those thoughts were bad enough, but there was an even worse shock lurking just below the surface. As I moved to the door to go out, still looking across at Phil, it seemed to me that just for a moment he lifted his head and stared straight into my eyes. It was the first time I had ever seen him without his mackintosh hat on, which as a rule enabled him to give that sly duck of the head and not meet anyone's look directly. Did he, now, shoot me a direct look, or was it my own guilt that made me think so? I had only a split second to decide, and it was not enough. I moved out, blinking, into the sunlight.

The reason I felt guilty was because I had indeed, on the previous evening, the last evening of my bachelor life, done something wrong. Or at any rate something I would certainly need to keep a secret from everybody present here and now. My blood ran cold at the thought of any of them even suspecting it. I didn't, myself, regret what I had done – the stakes had been too high, the forces that came into play were too strong and too elemental, to be talked of in civilized tea-table terms of 'regretting' this and that: I had been simply engulfed. But, having set out with no other intention than to spend a blameless evening revisiting favourite scenes of my boyhood, now that the chapter of my boyhood was about to be closed, I had wound up in an entirely different situation, and it would have been disaster pure and simple if any of the people who now surrounded me had even guessed at that situation. With most of them, there was no danger of any such guess. But what about Phil? Phil the lurker, Phil the spy and watcher and eavesdropper? Or was I, like everyone who feels guilty, simply imagining things? I felt as if Old Nick had me fast already. With a tremendous effort I pulled myself together. It was time for Heather and me to go round to the vestry and sign our names. We did so. I was mildly surprised that we were not required to sign them in blood.

As Heather bent over the table to sign I noticed that her pregnancy, which had been duly confirmed by the doctor, had not yet begun to thicken her figure; she was as trim and lissom as ever; we were well in time. That, of course, had been one reason for rushing into it so quickly. Another, and even stronger, had been that August, as far as Oxford University is concerned, is the dead month, with most dons, and virtually all undergraduates, well clear of the place. A wedding in a country church, the marriage of a local farmer's daughter to an unnoticed young man who is possibly going to be, but isn't yet, a Fellow of his college, could be counted on to pass unnoticed at such a time. This was the agony of Heather's mother. She must have been crying for days out of sheer vexation.

If it came to that, this clandestine marriage was a bit of a let-down for me too. I had already seen the rooms I would occupy as a Junior Research Fellow, a study with tall windows looking out on flower-beds and a neat little bedroom, with a bathroom I shared with one other man. It was much more attractive than the two-room flat Heather and I had arranged to rent over a shop in North Parade, with someone else's sticky furniture and lumpy mattress, and a leaky bathroom shared by four or five other people. After being elected in October I would move into my two comfortable rooms and of course to make the act convincing I would have to spend a good deal of time there, in addition to the equally good deal of time I would have to spend reading in the Bodleian in connection with the D.Phil. thesis I was going to write (it was to be on 'Lord Stair's "Pragmatic Army" and the dream of a direct invasion of France, 1742'). Both in the later stages of her pregnancy and the first couple of years of motherhood, Heather was going to spend a lot of time in those two rooms over the shop in North Parade, and I very little.

All this ought perhaps to have made me feel guilty, but in fact it didn't. I just felt, as soldiers are said to feel during a war, that the whole disaster had been dumped on our lives by outside forces over which we had no influence, and all we could do was go on doggedly and put up with it, trusting that one day it would be over and that we would live to see that day. In the weeks before this fateful Saturday Heather had gone very much inside herself and I had not much idea what she was thinking or feeling about anything. Our families had had to be let into the whole thing, of course, and that on its own had been enough to take all our time and energy. But it was unavoidable, for every reason, not least because the three months' rent we had had to put down on the North Parade flat had been raised by borrowing half from each set of parents, to be faithfully paid back within six months out of my income of £200 a year. All this dickering and bargaining and promise-making and flat-hunting, not to speak of trying to calm her mother's state of continual hysteria and her brother's of smoulding resentment (thank God my family were so sane), had made a hell of the past six weeks compared with which the difficulties to come could hardly help seeming like a rest cure.

What made it even worse was that I couldn't, for some reason, bring myself to tell my parents that the reason Heather and I were getting married in such a hurry was that she was pregnant. I knew, of course, that I ought to tell them. If they were going to be horrified and scandalized, well, that was coming soon enough anyway, because the baby would be due after about six months of marriage. But I shied away from it. I just felt I had enough to cope with as things were, without facing the ordeal of making a clean breast of everything.

We now left the church and went back to Jasmine Farm, covering the half-mile journey in an assortment of vehicles that looked as if they were on their way to a used car auction. Heather and I went in the old Morris with Mother and Dad. My God, I thought. Two Mrs Leonards in one car now! I ought to have found the sudden transformation mildly funny, but I couldn't. Everything seemed so leaden. When we got back to the farmhouse and everybody stood around with glasses in their hands it was even worse. Mrs Burrell had worked at it, putting on some kind of show; in the main living-room there were two tables covered with snowy cloths, food *à la fourchette* and two village girls hired for the half-day to hand it round and wash up afterwards; but beyond that she just couldn't make herself go. The vast effort of falsification involved in pretending to be glad that she was now united by law with my parents, with Brian, and with my maternal grandparents, the old sawmill foreman and his timidly smiling old wife – all this was too much for her. She looked at them with a kind of helpless non-welcome that put me in mind of Heather's words,

'You don't ride horses or you'd know what it's like when a horse just won't take the next jump.' This was one gate, one brook, she was just not going to take. Her husband, meanwhile, stood about as if he honestly did not know what had hit him, and as for Tom, he made it plain from the outset that he simply was not part of the proceedings. He was disappointed and annoyed that Heather was getting married to me instead of to someone who might do something to improve the family's, and in particular his own, chances in life (notably by getting him nearer to ownership of an aeroplane), and he clearly regarded what she had done as a betrayal.

Standing nearby, I heard Brian make an attempt to get into conversation with him by bringing up the topic of the glider club rally at Fish Hill, but Tom's response was terse, discouraging and indeed barely within the range of common politeness. Brian gave up at once. Soon afterwards I heard the angry snarl of exhaust as Tom drove away, forcing his foot hard down on the accelerator of the old family Ford, trying to turn the simple act of driving out of the farm gate into a statement of rejection of me, my family, and the whole *mésalliance*.

So there we were. No one wanted this wedding. It was merely something we were stuck with because the alternatives were all so unthinkable. Heather, I thought, went through it with a good deal of dignity. My parents put on a creditable show; there were times when their gaiety seemed almost genuine. Brian, who had been forced by united family pressure into coming along as best man, carried it off good-humouredly enough. He had now definitely proposed to Primrose and been accepted, so she was also present as his *fiancée*. I was glad she was along. I liked her. That air of slight apartness, which conveyed no disdain or aloofness in the ordinary sense but merely a sense, conveyed in that slight contained amusement, that her real feelings and real interests were somewhere else and she was there just as a spectator, helped to keep me calm. And her face, which had the same wildness in repose as a panther's, made me feel that my life was very humdrum and bourgeois beside the one she would probably live if she got the chance, and was already beginning to live with Brian, the life of international racing circuit and superhuman effort and triumph and glory and sudden death.

Would Primrose, I found myself wondering briefly, have got herself into a situation like the one Heather and I were in? No, surely. She would never tolerate being walled in by disapproval and trapped among secrecies. She would simply turn her back on it and walk away, with her lean swinging stride, choosing rather to sleep under the open sky and drink rain-water than play somebody else's game. I felt ashamed in her presence, and yet I also knew that we were creatures of a different kind and that her needs were fierce and uncomplicated. I was playing my shabby, devious game to try to keep my balance on a tightrope which, if I could only succeed in walking along it, would lead me to the only kind of life I would find fulfilling. In the silence within my skull I framed my excuses as I looked across at Primrose; but even as I did so I saw her eyes rest for a moment on Heather, as she stood on the other side of the room, and I read pity in them. And then my shame came back.

Not that I had much time to think about Primrose. One of the absurdities of my wedding day was that it was virtually the first meeting between Heather and my parents. I say 'virtually' (*Oxford English Dictionary*, sense 4 of 'virtual': *That is so in essence or effect, although not formally or actually; admitting of being called by the name so far as the effect or result is concerned*) because she had, after all, spoken to my mother briefly on the afternoon when she came round to tell me she was pregnant, and she had been in the bar while her father chatted to mine. Also, during the run-up we had managed one brief visit. But they were still so shell-shocked from the sudden news, and the air so heavy with unspoken questions, that there was nothing we could do but circle round each other and keep the conversation down to practicalities. Now, happening to go into the kitchen of Jasmine Farm, I found my mother and Heather getting to know each other. There was a large solid-fuel range in there – an Aga, was it? – that gave the room a feeling of comfort and solid well-being, and my mother, doubtless as a lead-in but probably also from genuine interest, was asking Heather how it worked and how often it had to be filled and raked out and whether it heated the water, things like that. They were establishing some kind of common ground, inch by inch: 'I've always wanted one of these, but our kitchen isn't big enough.' 'Yes, that is one good point about these farmhouses, the kitchen's always a fair size.' *Und so weiter*. I stood there idly, glass in hand, not wanting to go back into the socially freezing living-room and also curious to know how they would get on; and, looking about me, I saw a basket in the corner with a tawny-coloured dog curled up in it, dog-napping but occasionally opening one slit of an eye to check on the proceedings. Of course! This would be the Golden Labrador bitch, the mother of the fatal puppies! By procreating just when she did, this animal had provided me with the occasion for getting over the doorstep into this house, introducing myself, making Heather's acquaintance – learning her name, to begin with. The whole sequence of events, already quite a long chain but stretching illimitably into the future, had been started in the moment when some dog induced this bitch to share his spasm of gratification. Highly appropriate, I thought, bending down to stroke the innocently culpable creature. You can't know this, girl, I said silently to her, but you've started something you'll never be able to stop.

'What shall I call you – mother-in-law?' Heather was asking. Her tone was light, but I knew it wasn't just fun, that she was feeling her way towards a serious relationship.

'You must call me what you feel comfortable with, dear. I expect you know my name's Katie, but then Katie's what people of my own age call me, my friends that I've known since I was young. The boys call me Mother or Mum, and Katie isn't the same sort of name as Mum. It makes me into a little bit of a different person.'

'Different how? You're the same person really, aren't you?'

'Well, deep down, of course, but it brings out a different side of you, somehow. If you're Mum you're just a working part of the household, not so much a person. 'Is tea ready, Mum?' – 'Can I have a clean shirt, Mum?' – you don't have to be a person to see to those things, just a kind of machine, though it's not as bad as that really because they're fond of you. But they're fond of what you do as much as what you are. More, really. I was Katie Webber when I was young. Then I was Katie Leonard. That was a change already. Katie Leonard was a married woman, with the job of making a home.'

'Was she very different from Katie Webber?'

My mother laughed like a young girl. 'Oh, yes. Katie Webber was flighty. I mean, I didn't go off the rails or anything, but I wasn't serious.'

I could see her. I could see Katie Webber tripping along the pavements of West Oxford, under the willow trees in a summer dress, pretty as a girl in an Edwardian advertisement.

'I hadn't had time to turn serious. I was nineteen when I married Jack.'

'Did that', Heather said, really wanting to know, 'make life better or worse?'

'Oh, better. Jack's always been a good man in my life. But it made it all – well, heavier, you know. Being a girl at home, there was nothing in it. You didn't have any rights in those days, a daughter at home, you were just a kind of servant in the house, but my parents were kind to me and I didn't have a bad life, only it wasn't a life that *meant* anything. I knew I was just waiting. That's how we were in those days. Everything's changed now. The nineteen-thirties! Goodness, it does sound strange. It was the nineteen-tens when we got married.'

'Not even nineteen-ten yet,' I said. 'Brian was born in that year.'

'I didn't know you were listening, Peter. No need to push dates down my throat and make me feel older than I am, even. I know you study history, but I'm not history.'

'We all are, Mum,' I said.

'To go back a bit,' said Heather. 'To go back to you saying your life as a girl was different from what it would be today. I don't think it was really. You might have been talking about my life. I was a servant. I had no rights. And I was waiting.'

'Well, I hope you were happy, dear,' my mother said gently, 'because I was.'

'No,' Heather said.

The one-word statement fell flatly into the quiet air of the kitchen; I couldn't think of anything to say, and neither it seemed could my mother. There was a short silence, broken after a moment or two by the entry of Heather's father. He stopped dead when he saw us.

'I wanted a big plate,' he said, addressing the room in general.

'How big, Dad?' Heather asked. 'If you mean one of the trenchers, the oval ones ....'

'Yes,' old Burrell said. His eyes wandered about helplessly, avoiding the eyes of anyone present.

'There aren't any. They're all being used for food, which means they're in the sitting-room. Ask one of the girls if you really need one for something.'

'The girls ...?'

'The two village girls Mother's got in for the day. They're called Betty and Hetty, something like that. Just move about and you'll see one of them. You'll know them because they're the ones with the aprons. Or will an ordinary dinner plate do? What's it for?'

Her father looked at her, then quickly looked away. I wondered if his wife had sent him for the plate, but it seemed likely that it was his own idea and that was why he was so bewildered and indecisive. You would have thought that instead of being in his own house he was in someone else's, someone who had not given him permission to be there. He stood silent for a moment, then moved stiffly out of the room. We watched him go and my mother said, 'We still haven't decided what's going to be my name.'

Heather smiled and said, 'We'll just let one grow. As I get to know you I'll know what it feels natural to call you.'

'That's a good idea. And you can make it more than one if you like. You can have one name you call me when you like me and one you call me when you don't like me. To me you'll be Heather, of course.

Welcome, Heather.' And she kissed her cheek.

'I'll always like you,' Heather said. 'You'll only have one name.'

Betty or Hetty now came into the kitchen with a tray of glasses which she began washing at the sink, splashing the taps noisily.

'D'you need to wash glasses?' Heather asked her mildly.

'Shouldn't be doin' it if I didn't need to,' replied the girl, banging them down on the draining board in rapid succession.

'I mean I thought we had enough.'

'We would 'ave enough, only they puts 'em down and wanders off, can't remember where they leaves 'em and then they 'as to get fresh ones. Some of 'em 'asn't got the sense they was born with.'

Heather silently left the kitchen. My mother turned to me and said, 'I've never been here before and I love looking round farms. You know the place quite well, I suppose, Peter?'

'Well enough.'

'Will you show me round? I love seeing the animals and everything.'

I hesitated. 'Oughtn't we to join the guests?'

She moved the flat of her hand forward as if pushing the guests away. 'Give me a bit of time first. I'm one of the guests, after all.'

'Katie Leonard,' I said penitently, 'you're the most important guest there is and of course you shall see round the farm.'

We went out. The sun was shining dully through a layer of haze. We looked at chickens and pigs, and peered into a cow-shed that turned out to be empty. Two well-groomed horses were in the stable. They looked like hunters. There was one remaining outhouse, but when I tried the door it was locked. No, it only seemed to be locked. I couldn't open it, but as I pulled it didn't have the solid, fixed feeling of a locked door. It was resistant, that was all. Was it stuck? I gave a sharp tug. It almost gave, then snapped shut. Someone was holding it fast from the inside. Whoever was in there was not going to let us in.

'It may be Phil,' I said, turning to my mother.

'Who's Phil?'

'That funny-looking chap who was at the back of the church. Did you see him?'

'Yes. At least I took one look and then I just had to keep my eyes off him. He gave me the creeps. I wondered what he was doing there. He looks like the village idiot.'

'I suppose you might say that's what he is.'

'Why would he be in that shed?' she asked, rather nervously, as if hating the thought that Phil was anywhere near her.

'He works here.'

'Here? At this farm? But why do they employ someone like that?'

'I don't know. It's not the kind of thing you can ask. I expect they get him cheap.'

I was relieved to come away from the closed door of the shed. If Phil really was in there, I had no wish to confront him. Another of those knowing glances, another triumphant leer, and I was going to feel that every dark corner of my life had been ransacked and the contents tipped out on the carpet, in front of everybody, and on my wedding-day too. Damn Phil!

'We'll go into the house,' my mother said. 'I just want to see these roses first.' She led the way round to the front and stood looking at Mrs Burrell's carefully-tended rose-beds; I knew she was just prolonging these precious few minutes of being alone with me. 'They're nice, aren't they?' I said as she pretended to examine the roses.

She looked up at me and said, quickly and lightly, 'I like Heather.'

'I'm so glad,' I said. 'Not that I thought you wouldn't.'

'You might so easily have chosen a girl I just couldn't talk to.'

'Oh? I don't see why you couldn't talk to anyone.'

'No, Peter. Heather doesn't live in books like you do. I don't mean I can't talk to you because, well, you're my son and everything, but you've got a life I can't follow you into. I don't *mind*, I don't want to follow you into it, it's best you should go on by yourelf into your new life, or at least not try to lug me and Jack along. The idea's too silly.' She laughed softly. 'But if you'd married a girl who was all books, the way you are, well ….' She gestured. 'Heather isn't. She's down to earth. I know the world she lives in and it's the same as mine.'

'Look, Mum, don't overdo this phobia about books. Books aren't anything in themselves. A book is just an instrument for getting to know something.'

She shook her head. 'If you understand a book it may be just an instrument. If you don't understand it, it's more like a steel spike right in your path. It's sharp and you daren't stumble against it.'

'Oh, come on, Mum.'

'Look, Peter, last spring you brought some books home for the holidays and when you went back to College for the new term, your last one, you left three of them in your room. They were there for a couple of months. I'll confess something. I kept going into your room and handling these books and looking at them. Trying to see what kind of thing it was you were giving your life to. Well, it might as well have been double-Dutch. I couldn't understand a word.'

'Well, I suppose specialized historical –'

'There was one called,' she repeated the strange words with a wrinkled brow, '*The Scottish Presbyterian Polity*. It's stuck in my head because I used to know old Mr. Finlay who kept a dry goods shop in St Thomas's, and he was a Presbyterian. What's polity? I thought it must be a mistake for policy, but it kept coming in.'

'That's Janet MacGregor's book you got hold of. It's very useful. About the sixteenth-century origins of –'

'I couldn't understand it. I couldn't make out what it was all about. And I'm not stupid.'

'Of course you're not.'

'I don't suppose Mr. Finlay even knew he had a polity. Whatever that is.'

'Look, Mum, don't bother your head about it.'

'I won't, only don't you see, that's why I feel happy with Heather. You can't see her writing a book like that.'

'Or reading one,' I said, laughing.

We went back into the house, but even while I took those few steps my mind was busy with problems. Was Heather's mental world, then, so different from mine? It must be, for my mother to see the difference so clearly, and in fact I had never, in this whole pell-mell relationship, stopped to consider whether it was a good thing to ally myself for life with someone to whom the kind of questions that preoccupied me were nothing but a blank. It was all right as far as my one-to-one relationship with Heather was concerned, because I had other ways of communicating with her, and other grounds of urgent concern. But would I, one day, find myself feeling lonely amid a family life that revolved round the immediate and the practical rather than round the harvests of knowledge and the towers of imagination? Would I find myself rearing a family of people to whom my life's work was at best a harmless eccentricity? Then I checked myself. No need to run on too fast, Leonard, I thought. One pregnant girl and you start thinking about 'a family life'. But then, the reflection came, every family life starts off with a pregnant girl.

On the doorstep something prompted me to look back one more time at the farmyard. It lay sleeping peacefully, but I knew that farm work never stops for long, and quite soon, when the guests had gone and the wedding was just another memory, the animals would have to be fed and the milking done. As I thought of this, just about to pull my attention back to the interior of the house, old Burrell came round the side wall. He was walking rapidly, for him, and holding a large plate (so he had found one), on which I could glimpse sandwiches and a pie. Sticking up from a side pocket he carried a bottle. Going over to the shed in the corner of the yard, he halted at the door and evidently said something. It opened and he disappeared inside. Food and drink for Phil: for surely it must be Phil. I supposed I ought to have felt glad he had not been forgotten.

I went back into the living-room and distributed my attention among the guests, trying to say the right things, feeling a slight ache in my limbs after standing up so long when I had not yet fully recovered from the heroic exertions of the evening before, which I was determined not to think about, not to admit any image or memory of them till I could lie down in the dark and think in peace. I was suddenly aware that my father was at my side, asking some questions about trains. 'Five thirty-two, I think,' I said.

'We'll give you a send-off,' he said. 'Then I'll have to get back, to open up.' And he looked at his watch. Obviously he was wishing as much as I was that five thirty-two would come quickly.

It dragged itself to us in the end, and everyone straggled down to South Leigh Station. (It has long gone now, but you can still see the embankment, and the place where the station buildings stood.) I had claimed the privilege of the honeymoon couple to depart for an undisclosed destination. In actual fact we were going back to Oxford, not having a wedding trip at all, simply getting on with life, but I had seen clearly enough that it would be discreditable to admit this, so we were going to begin by taking a train that left in the opposite direction, conveying the impression that we would be catching some big West-Country express and going down to Cornwall or somewhere appropriate. What we were really going to do was ride into Witney and have dinner at an hotel. I had booked a table by telephone, and that booked table was our one and only sign of celebration. Later in the evening we were going to take a train back into Oxford and get out to North Parade to begin our married life in that rented two-room flat.

We all stood about uneasily on the bare little platform, while the flat fields slumbered all around us in the dull August sunshine. No one had anything to say; I had hardly heard Heather's voice all day except when she said 'I do' and 'I will' to the parson. We had about nine minutes to wait and each one seemed like a fortnight. Finally Brian, perhaps driven by a desperate need to break the silence, looked round him and said, 'I'd forgotten these places still existed.'

'What places?' I asked. Bemused as I was, I had a vague notion that he meant medieval churches.

'Railway stations,' he said and gave a dry laugh. I realized how characteristic of me he must have thought it, to go off on my wedding trip by such an obsolete form of transport.

'Here it is anyway,' said my father as the engine clanked into view. Heather and I duly stepped aboard, the heavy doors were slammed; almost at once, the train began to pull forward, and our new life began. We waved mechanically. The figures on the little platform slid backwards and disappeared. I felt somehow that I ought to find this an emotional moment, but nothing happened inside me except a feeling of mild gladness that the worst part of the day was over.

We duly had our dinner at the one and only fairly posh hotel that Witney boasted in those days. It was chicken chasseur and a bottle of white wine. Why on earth I should remember across all these years that we ate chicken chasseur I have no idea, especially as I can remember nothing else, least of all what we talked about. What I do recall is a few details that stand out very clearly. The business with the suitcase, for instance. Though we had of course no need of a suitcase, we had obviously had to take one along when the wedding-party saw us off at South Leigh station so that we could keep up the fiction of being off on a trip. I had even put a few books in it so that it wouldn't feel obviously empty if anyone picked it up. At the Witney hotel, the desk clerk's eyes lit up with suspicious relish when he saw us come through the swing doors with a suitcase. I suppose we looked too young to be a regular married couple, and he assumed we were some pair of young scamps who wanted a room for the night. In those days (how everything has changed!) a lot of hotels kept up a 'This-is-a-respectable-house' attitude and while obviously they couldn't prevent a lot of couples from signing in as Mr and Mrs Smith, they enjoyed fending off the ones who didn't look the right type, especially if they hadn't booked ahead. I saw him zestfully draw in his breath ready to say they were full up, as I walked over to him with our suitcase and Heather demurely in tow, and it gave me pleasure to puncture him by merely asking casually where we might leave the suitcase to be out of the way while we had dinner, for which we had booked a table. It was one of those times when you really could say of someone's face that it 'fell'.

Another detail I remember was that I was tired. The ache in my bones had become more pronounced now; after all, it had been a long day, and it was by no means over yet. I suppose I made some kind of small talk with Heather because if there had been a prolonged silence I'd have remembered it, but what we said I don't know.

Not until we settled into the train for the journey back to Oxford did we have a conversation I can remember. Whether surprisingly or not, I can recall just about everything to do with the train ride. We got to Witney station about ten minutes early (bored at the dinner-table? impatient to get back to real life?) and stood on the almost deserted platform waiting for the little local train. It was only a branch line that went to Fairford or somewhere like that, and they used little chunky saddle-tank engines pulling three or four coaches. Darkness had fallen, the August days were shortening, and I can see now the clouds of white steam from the engine as it came in under the station lights. We were alone in a compartment, looking out at the dark fields and woods; it felt strange to halt at South Leigh, and I wondered fleetingly whether anyone who had been at the wedding would join the train there and ask us where we were going. But of course they didn't, why should they? It was after ten at night, and no one was going from the country into town; they were all coming the other way if they were not in bed already. Except for a few stray remarks, neither of us spoke until we were clear of South Leigh and headed for Eynsham and Oxford. Then Heather, leaning back in her corner and looking at me with an expression I couldn't read, said, 'How d'you think we're going to manage it all?'

'Manage all what? Our married life for the next fifty years, you mean?'

'No, of course not, who knows that? I mean the immediate situation, obviously. So far, so good, I expect you're thinking. You wanted to keep our marriage secret and it's been done.'

'Well,' I said carefully, 'I suppose it *was* me that wanted it, but it's just as much in your interest. A husband who's in work is probably a better bet than one who's tramping round looking for a job.'

'I don't know what I'm supposed to be betting on,' she said, 'but I'll take your word for it. Anyway, it's been done. Apart from your family, there wasn't anyone at all from central Oxford there today. And certainly no one from a newspaper, not even the woman who writes our Village Notes.'

'No, that's good, isn't it?'

She looked at me levelly. 'It's good as far as it goes. It means you've managed to conceal the crime for the time being.'

'Heather, I suppose you've got to talk like that. I was rather hoping that you'd –'

'How d'you expect me to talk?'

The train clacked sardonically on.

'Well, a bit more positively, I suppose. I thought you might have been willing to look on the bright side.'

She was sitting opposite me, and now she pulled back into her corner, as if to avoid even touching me foot to foot, and said, 'Congratulations. We've only been married about eight hours and you've come out with the Cliché of the Year already. Look on the bright side! As if marriage was some kind of disaster like infantile paralysis that just strikes people out of the blue. I suppose that is how you see it. All right, see it that way. But I hope that kind of remark isn't typical of the stuff you're going to throw at me across the breakfast table every morning.'

'Unfair. We're not at the breakfast table. We're in a train coming back from our wedding-day.'

'Skulking back would be more like it.'

'All right, we're skulking back, but whichever it is we're sitting on a train on the evening of the day we got married, and I thought you might be quite interested in getting things straightened out, taking an honest look at our situation so that we can stop worrying about it and go back to living.'

She moved over till she was directly facing me and looked hard into my face. 'All right, husband, if you're in a mood to straighten things out and take honest looks at them, I'll tell you something you don't seem to know, though why you don't know it is more than I can fathom, I should have thought it was obvious.'

'You'd have thought *what* was obvious?'

'This thing I'm going to tell you. This thing I think you ought to have bloody well seen for yourself, Professor Know-All Leonard.'

'Well, tell me what it is, only for God's sake stop talking as if you hate me.'

'I'm not going to wrap my feelings up. If I have moods when I hate you I'm going to let you know I'm having them.'

'When do they come? Is there any pattern to them?'

'Yes, they come whenever you don't seem to be taking a blind bit of notice of *me*, not seeing me as a person. I'm not your mother, I'm not part of the furniture. That's how you've seen it up to now, isn't it? Your mother's part of the furniture of the kitchen, and I'm part of the furniture of the bedroom. Well, I'm not, I'm me, me, me, I'm Heather Burrell.'

'You mean Heather Leonard.'

Her hand flew to her mouth. 'Oh, yes, my God! I've done it now, haven't I? I've even given away my name. It was the only thing I had left and I signed it away in that damned church vestry.'

'And even that was your father's name,' I said brutally.

'Why did you have to remind me of that?'

'Why should I sit here and let you kick me and not kick back?'

'Yes, but what a dirty way to kick back. Is that what you're going to do – every time we're at odds, hide behind the unfairness of the law?'

'That's exactly what you'd do if I ever really treated you badly. If I ever committed adultery or deserted you or anything like that, which obviously I shan't do but which if I *did*, you could walk out and invoke the law and the law would force me to keep you for the rest of your life, whether we ever met or not. As of today at mid day I support you till the day one of us dies, and if I didn't I'd go to prison.'

'Been thinking it all out, I see.'

'No, I haven't been thinking it all out, but that's the plain fact of the matter, and show me the man who gets married without that kind of thought at least crossing his mind.'

The train was slowing down. Heather said bitterly, 'It didn't cross your mind, though, did it? It bloody well pitched camp and stayed.'

'Look, let's get off all this rubbish about the law, I don't know how we ever started on it. I want to hear what this great truth is about you that I've been too stupid to see. This would be a good time to learn it.'

But we had almost stopped. The wheels were giving a last few clanks, despairingly. This was Eynsham Station.

'It's too late, people'll get in here and I shan't be able to talk about anything, and then it'll be too late, we'll have gone past it.'

'No, they won't. They won't get in. I'll stand and block the doorway and if anyone wants to get in they can just bugger off.'

We were standing still now. The little saddle-tank engine, a few coaches further up, sighed contentedly to itself as if pleased to have got this far. I heard it as I leaned out into the still air. There was no one on the platform. Two people left the train, but no one joined it. We pulled out and I settled back.

'Darling,' I said, 'you look so lonely on that long seat for six people, and you all by yourself.'

'Perhaps that's what marriage is. It's a long thing made for a lot of people and you're by yourself there.'

'Well, come and sit next to me and then at least there'll be two of us being lonely together.'

She smiled, but didn't move, so I moved over to her, but when I went to put my arm round her she held me off. 'Not just yet. I have to say this first. I can't feel close to you till I get it said.'

'Well, get it said, for God's sake. I'm listening, and I apologize ahead of time for not knowing it already. I'm just a stupid, insensitive fool, and you can help me to grow into something better.'

And a fool whose bones ache, a voice said inside my head. A fool who's as tired as a worked-out sheepdog.

She turned to look at me and said, 'This business about, We can go back to living.'

'Well, can't we?'

'That's just it.'

'Just what, Heather? What?'

She looked down at the floor and said, her voice almost inaudible, 'I never have lived.'

For a moment I thought I couldn't be hearing her properly above the thump of the train, but she didn't have to repeat the words. They sank in and I knew, all too well, what she had said.

I felt blank. All I could think of to say was, 'I find that so hard to believe.'

'Well, it's true.'

'But ....' I looked out of the window. The lights of the outlying districts of the city were beginning to appear. 'You've always seemed so alive.'

'In my body, yes.'

'Well, not just your body. I mean, well ... you're very physically vital and all that, but I always thought there was more to it.'

'I always hoped there would be myself. But there was always such a dead weight on me.'

I put my arm round her now and really squeezed her. 'Look, darling, don't tell me there haven't been times when you've been as totally alive as it's possible for a person to be.'

Not looking at me, her face against my chest, she murmured, 'When?'

'Well ... Fish Hill.'

At that she straightened up and looked me in the face and said, 'We made life at Fish Hill. But I wasn't alive.'

'I just don't believe it.'

'My body was alive, and you were full of sex and all that, and of course I responded to it and it was nice. But somewhere in the middle of it, where *I* ought to have been, there was a hole. A lead-lined hole. Like a box made of lead with no lid to open it by. Nothing inside it but stagnant air.'

'Heather, if you'd really been like that, it would have been noticeable from outside.'

'Well, it was sometimes, wasn't it?'

'But why? If you've been not alive all these years, why is it?'

'You've seen my life. You've been to Jasmine Farm. You know my background. That's why I thought you might have seen the state I was in and what it had done to me. All those years of not being a person. Nothing was ever planned round me. It wasn't just that I didn't have any rights, girls never do have any rights but at least they're sometimes treated as if they exist. My parents probably thought they were being kind to me but actually they weren't being anything to me, kind or unkind. They weren't seeing me. I was just a space with clothes on it. I functioned. I did things. And when I walked out of the catering course it was just as if I'd broken a law of nature. If you throw a stone into the air it falls back to the ground because that's the law of gravity. Well, I was a stone that was thrown into the air and just lay there and wouldn't come down. My mother was furious, but even more than furious she was just … just ….'

'Incredulous,' I helped out.

'Incredulous, that's it. She'd produced a stone that lay on a cloud instead of falling back down, a bucket of water that didn't flow down a trough, a match that wouldn't strike, a cork that wouldn't float, and she thought it must be a sign that God was cross with her.'

'Is she still furious?'

'Well, she's terribly hurt at the way we've done things, of course, robbing her of her moment of glory, but really I think she'll settle down now. When I told her I was going to have a baby she wasn't half as angry as when I told her I was leaving the catering. Sleeping with men and having babies is all part of what girls do, as she sees it. Of course I'm doing it wrong, doing it out of turn, but she's never expected anything else of me. I'm the ugly duckling.'

At that, I threw back my head and laughed. It was genuinely funny. 'Heather, you're so beautiful and you talk about being an ugly duckling. What you actually are is a very proud, very lovely young pen swan, at the point where she grows out of being a cygnet and gets her dazzling white plumage and is the loveliest sight on the river.'

She leaned closely against me as the train slowed again and said, 'What does that make you?'

'Oh, I'm the lustful cob swan following her shapely tail and watching out for a chance to get on the nest.'

'Well,' she murmured, 'I've got an egg inside me, I do know that.'

And after all that was true, and at that moment I was glad to hear her say it.

We took a taxi from Oxford station to North Parade. I had only a few pounds left in the world, and they had to last until I received the first instalment of my pay from Episcopus, which would not be till almost Christmas; but I felt I ought to lash out a little on this day of all days, and in any case I was in no shape to lug a suitcase a mile and a half. We drew up in style at the shop above which we were going to 'live', and let ourselves in at a side door and climbed up the steep stairs, covered with hard shiny linoleum, to our dump.

At least there was a bed in it, and I had reached the stage where sleep seemed to me the one really desirable thing in all the world. While Heather was fiddling about with something in the kitchen, I went along to the scruffy bathroom, cleaned my teeth and emptied my bladder in the minimum of time, and, coming back, undressed and dived into bed. It wasn't a very good mattress – it had the inevitable lumps and the usual trough down the middle – but a much worse one would have seemed like heaven to me at that moment. The ache at the centre of my bones had got steadily worse in the last couple of hours, and just to be resting was infinitely delicious.

The bedside light was on, and of course I did my best to stay awake, to welcome Heather to our bed on that first night as man and wife. but luck was against me. She went along to the bathroom and came back immediately and said, 'Damn, there's somebody in there. I hope it won't be like this all the time.'

'I don't suppose they'll be long,' I murmured and at that moment a huge wave of sleep rose up and tried to drag me down into fathomless unconsciousness. She said something in reply, but I didn't hear her properly, and after a few minutes she went along to the bathroom again and this time didn't return immediately. I settled down comfortably to wait for her and that was the last I knew. Fully aware as I was that to go dead asleep while waiting for my bride to join me in bed was hardly the tactful thing to do, hardly the way to convince her that I had genuine passion for her – and a few hours earlier I had solemnly assured her, as part of the marriage service, 'With my body I thee worship' – it just couldn't be helped. My whole being was crying out for sleep, and in a blissful moment sleep came.

How long I slept I don't know, but it must have been for a couple of hours at least. What woke me was the bed was shaking. Heather was lying beside me but not touching me. She was crying, great convulsive sobs that vibrated all through the bed, and it was this that had woken me.

'What is it, darling?' I said, moving over and touching her.

'What the hell d'you mean, what is it?' Her voice was strangled, her face thrust deeply into the wet pillow.

'I'm sorry I fell asleep, if that's what you're –'

'Leave me alone. Don't try to talk your way out of it. You can't even stay awake while I go and wash my face, that's how much you –' She went into another paroxysm of sobs. This was serious. I didn't know what the hell to do.

'Look, it's been a long day –' I began lamely.

'Don't give me that. You've come to bed with me before after longer days than this.'

That's what you think, I thought. You don't know about last night. And suddenly a great hopelessness descended on me. How was I going to cope with the crazy pattern of my life? How was I going to fit all these disjointed pieces into something resembling a whole?

'It's such a let-down,' Heather was saying through her tears. 'A let-down for you, a let-down for me. You're bored already. Our very first night and you're bored. I've just become a boring bloody wife.' She was quieter now, her voice was steadier. She just lay there softly weeping as if she would never stop.

I knew I ought to comfort her. After all, there were obvious things I could do to make her feel better, the most obvious of all being to make love to her. Well, why not? Go ahead and fuck her, I said to myself. But nothing happened inside me. I seemed incapable of ever feeling desire again. Not only Heather, but every woman in the world had become meaningless to me. Except one, confound her. And now, finally, I faced it. I rolled over on to my back, staring up into the darkness, with Heather weeping beside me, and gave myself up to thoughts of what had happened to me the previous evening.

Chapter 23

I had made absolutely no arrangements to fill that blank space of time. One or two people had asked me if I planned to go out 'on the tiles', or 'with the boys', or whatever formula seemed right to them, but I had simply shrugged off the notion. Of course not! There was, I knew, some kind of vague folklore about the last night of bachelor life; I had heard stories about packs of young men taking out the doomed member of their group who was about to lose his freedom, and doing self-consciously bachelor things like getting drunk in a group and, also in a group, watching what used to be called 'stag movies'. The thought left me paralytically bored. On the other hand, what was I going to do? Sit in my room at the Bargeman's and read? I couldn't even go to College because my wedding had been arranged – not accidentally – to fall during the fortnight when the kitchens were closed, the domestic staff given a holiday, and even the thin thread of life that was kept going through the rest of the Long Vacation was suspended. Episcopus was a mausoleum. There was no one about; even the lodge, after five o'clock, was unattended.

In fact, the problem solved itself because, after a chill and rather threatening morning, the rain-clouds drifted away and the afternoon was radiant and warm, with a promise of beauty and gentleness right up till the coming of the velvet summer night. Clearly the appropriate thing to do was to go for a walk in the country, and this suited me very well. I wanted to be alone with my memories for a while. Getting married, in however half-hearted a way, was so obviously a major step, a line of demarcation, that I felt the need to think back over the years that had gone before.

As usual when such moods took me, I headed for Wytham. My intention was to follow the river towpath as far as Godstow and then take the road to the left. Ten minutes' walk would take me to Wytham village, and from there I could climb up into the woods. I needed those woods, the whole rich leafy, whispering, earth-smelling, fox-and-badger-haunted two thousand acres of them. This was before the days when the University owned Wytham Woods and issued permits to worthy persons; you had to trespass to get into them; but Colonel Ffennel, the owner, was fairly easy-going about it and didn't employ fierce gun-toting custodians. I had trespassed there all my life, and never been made to suffer for it. Five o'clock found me entering the picture-book village with its jumble of thatched roofs and glowing walls in soft Oxford stone. As I crossed the little bridge over the Seacourt stream and passed between the first few houses, it seemed to me that I was entering a place that breathed perfect tranquillity. That impression, of course, was the signal for a major shake-up. It usually is. To believe that the next few hours will be totally peaceful is a very effective way of tempting Providence.

I needed something, I forget what, from the village shop, the one right opposite the pub. I went in, clanging the bell as I pushed open the door. It had the usual village-shop interior – dim light from small windows whose sills were cluttered with objects, a stone flag floor, a heaped counter, heaped shelves, cards of this and that hanging up, jars of boiled sweets ranged on the shelves, and, to one side of the counter, a slicer with a sharp wheel for cutting ham.

Behind the counter stood Vinnie. I thought she was a hallucination at first. The light inside the shop was so different from the bright sunshine outside it that I wondered if I was making some grotesque mistake. I blinked a few times. No, it was Vinnie. She was serving in the shop. The counter came up almost to her waist, but I could see she was wearing an orange skirt. Her top half, blouse or shirt or whatever she would have called it, was white – startling white, crisp, dramatic. On her ear-lobes she wore little shell-like clips, made of some substance that shone like pearl. The sunlight from the side window, falling on her brown hair, brought out auburn lights in it, which didn't precisely echo, but complemented, the orange of her skirt. I stopped dead, with the door swinging shut behind me.

When Vinnie saw it was I she gave her little secret smile and said, 'D'you come here often?' I couldn't tell whether she was joking.

'Once in a while,' I said. 'I'm on my way to have a walk in the woods. I just stopped off at the shop because I need some … I need some …' I couldn't for the life of me remember what I *did* need. 'It's a surprise, seeing you here. I'd no idea you –'

'My auntie owns this shop. I've just come over to tea. I'd be at work, only I'm having my holidays just now. She was just busy with some scones and I said I'd mind the shop. It's what I'm used to, you remember. Retailing.'

'Yes, I remember.' I remembered a lot about what she was used to. 'Well, it really is quite a surprise.'

'Vinnie, can you come in now, dear?' somebody, obviously the aunt, called from the room behind the shop. 'They've turned out all right, I think.' The voice was clear, like Vinnie's, and had a soft Oxfordshire accent.

'Yes, Auntie,' she called over her shoulder; then to me, in an undertone, 'I thought I'd go for a walk in the woods myself after tea. I do sometimes. I like it up there. D'you specially want to go alone?'

'No,' I said. 'Now I know you're here, I specially want to go with you.'

'Be in the car park behind the pub in half an hour,' she said so quietly that I almost didn't hear her. 'No, wait a minute. Buy something before you go. I shall have to say I was making a sale.'

'Buy what?'

'Anything. But *now*.'

I bought a pair of shoe-laces. As she took my money, and put the laces into my hand, her fingers touched mine. Suddenly I remembered how they had looked round that long, elegant shoe she was arranging in the window of the shop in Cornmarket Street. Was I awake? Or was all this going to turn into a lascivious dream that I was dreaming in my solitary bed?

I pushed out through the door, making the bell tinkle like an invitation to Fate, and, going across the road, waited for half an hour in the car park. I didn't dare go for a walk and come back at the appropriate time because I had no watch on me and was too afraid of not being there when she showed up. The half-hour was a crawling agony, but at least I managed to keep my mind a blank. I pushed away the thought that Vinnie was not a very suitable companion for a rural stroll taken on the eve of my wedding day. I pushed away the thought that she herself might have anything in mind beyond an innocent ramble in the woods. I pushed away every thought. My brain, as I stood there in the heavy August air, spun on and on like a tape-recorder full of silence. The comparison wouldn't have occurred to me at the time, because tape-recorders weren't invented, but that was the effect. Finally, after no more than about thirty-five minutes, she showed up. She had no raincoat or handbag. She was just as she had been behind the counter of the little shop.

'I like that skirt,' I said.

'Glad you do. I have this friend, Mavis, she works in a fashion shop. Gets me all sorts of things at discount. That's about the only good thing about working in retailing. Apart from that it's rotten hours and rotten pay.'

I didn't ask her why, in that case, she stuck with it. I knew why. What other kind of work was she in line for, with her Jericho background, given the social and educational opportunities in those days?

My mind, however, was not really on such matters. It would have been hard to say exactly what it *was* on. For the moment, I was content just to be walking along with this lissom, pretty, brown-haired girl. We went into the churchyard through the old wooden gates, round the side of the church, and over the low wall into the field. This, both of us knew as local kids, was the usual route for anyone who intended to trespass in Wytham Woods. We walked, mostly in silence, up the field with the wood on our right-hand side. Finally, just to make conversation, I said, 'Has your auntie always kept that shop?'

'Yes. I can just remember going to see her and my Uncle Frank when they kept it together. That was before he was killed. The war.'

'Oh. I'm sorry. Been a widow ever since, I suppose?'

'Yes. It's a good thing they had the shop, else she wouldn't have had anything to do. Wouldn't have been much fun, living on a widow's pension. Ten bob a week.'

'My God, no.'

'Mind you,' Vinnie said, 'I don't feel that sorry for her. The part of her life that was worth living must have been over by the time my uncle got killed. She must have been, oh,' Vinnie was calculating and estimating, 'she must have been thirty.'

The lush moist grass under our feet, the heavy green foliage of the woodland beside us, spoke of life, of an inexhaustible abundance and fertility. But Vinnie's fresh, clear voice sounded so certain as she condemned this thirty-year-old woman to the still-alive graveyard. Life was for the young. Just to be alive was not life.

'You think,' I said, really wanting to know, 'a woman's finished when she gets to thirty?'

'Are you joking? *Thirty*? With a roll of fat round her middle and crow's feet at the corners of her eyes? What man's going to look at her unless he's got to?'

'What d'you mean, got to?'

'Well – can't get anything else, I s'pose.'

We climbed a little further and reached the gate that opens into the wood, with a moss-grown ride beyond it. Vinnie climbed lightly up and sat on the top bar, looking at the view. I leaned against the gate and did the same. Her neat haunches were within a yard of my face, but for once it was the landscape that claimed my attention: the broad, sloping field in front, rising again to another fringe of trees; the wide valley of the Thames, with its shining ribbon of water and the low bluish line of the opposite hills, away to our left; the classic cluster of towers and spires, just visible on the edge of the picture, so to speak; and, nearer at hand, the Abbey, looking as usual like a perfect stage set for Twelfth Night. Gazing down on the building, graceful, stately and yet domestic, one could hardly believe that in the next few minutes characters in the clothes of Queen Elizabeth's last years wouldn't emerge on to those lawns and walk between those shrubs and flower-beds: Sir Toby Belch and Maria, hatching their madcap scheme, Sir Andrew Aguecheek ambling peacock-like on his long fleshless legs, Malvolio lurking like a fox. Which were more real, they or we? Vinnie and I, children of the twentieth century, had no more logical claim to exist in this setting than the colourful ghosts of 1600.

'Thirty,' Vinnie was saying. 'I might as well have made it twenty-five. It's hard after that age for a girl to get married. When men are just out for fun they'll take anything, but when they want marriage they go for the young ones. And God help any girl who hasn't got a man by the time she's twenty-five.'

'It's not very hard to get a man, surely,' I said. *For someone like you*, I meant.

'You know what I mean. Not just fun. A steady. Someone with a plain gold ring in one pocket and a mortgage on a house in the other. That's the kind my mum and dad keep on at me to get. *A nice steady fella*, they call it. They're afraid of having me under their feet with no home of my own to go to. Only the other night my dad said to me, "How old are you, Virginia?" "Twenty," I said. "Well," he says, "if you don't get off your bottom soon and get out and find a man, you'll be on the shelf, mark my words," he says.'

'I don't think he knows you very well,' I said guardedly.

'He doesn't know some things about me, but I wouldn't say he was mistaken, not really. He wants me to start going steady with a fella that wants to get married. He thinks there's nobody in my life, and as far as that goes he's right. I mean there's nobody like that. And he'd think anything else was a waste of time.'

I could feel the smooth grain of the weathered wood under my hand. Her skin would be smoother. She was so close to me.

'He thinks that, Vinnie, but you don't.'

'P'raps I don't, but he's right according to his ideas.'

'What does your mother think about it all?'

'Oh, she's more noticing than my dad. She knows I go out with men. She knows I like them. But I don't think she knows anything more. She thinks I'm just having fun.'

'Well, you are, aren't you?'

Vinnie gave a soft giggle. 'You know what I mean. She thinks I'm just going out dancing and the pictures and stuff.'

That giggle penetrated straight through to the centre of my sexual being. I knew, now, that I had been deliberately avoiding the issue. When I first invited Vinnie to come for a walk, I had avoided thinking about my motive. Vinnie fascinated me, it's natural to want to spend a little time with someone who fascinates you, why not take a stroll? – Pitiful, paltry stuff. I had simply not allowed myself to know what I was doing in case my conscience, nudging me with the reminder that I was a man who had arranged to be married the next day, should intervene and force me to leave Vinnie alone. I did not want to leave her alone. I wanted to give her a bold, thrusting, buccaneering fuck, with all the trimmings that suggested themselves. 'Let's go into the woods a little way,' I said. 'It's a pity to come this far and not see them.'

My voice must have sounded hot and feverish, but Vinnie showed no sign of taking alarm. Unconcernedly, she swung her legs over the gate – ah, the swirl of that orange skirt! – and I joined her.

'Straight up here?' I asked, indicating the broad path in front of us.

'No, this way.' She pointed to a narrow, winding path no wider than a mountain sheep-track. 'I'll show you a favourite place of mine.'

Better and better. I began to suffer the embarrassing symptoms of excitement, and, falling into single file behind Vinnie, frantically worked with my pocketed hands to manoeuvre everything into the available space. Then, at a trot, I followed her. Must keep up the semblance of normality until I got a chance to let fly.

We entered a clearer space where the trees thinned a little and the undergrowth was bracken rather than bramble, so that it was practicable to walk side by side. Vinnie must have wanted to talk, because as soon as I fell in beside her she started, reverting to the train of her thoughts.

'I s'pose if I was going out just to the pictures and dancing, that kind of thing, they wouldn't mind that because they say themselves you've got to have some fun while you're young. There's no fun after you get old, that's true enough. When I look at my mum and auntie and the other women I know of their age, I swear I wonder why they get out of bed and go on living day after day. Once you've lost your looks and you're stuck with a husband making a slave of you, and kids pulling you this way and that, wanting you to see to them every minute of the day, well!' She exhaled as if puffing out the whole hopeless subject on to the air. 'But if you don't get married it's even worse, I don't need our Dad to tell me that. A woman who isn't married hasn't got a place to call her own – she hasn't got *anything* to call her own. She's just an unwanted body cluttering the place up, under everybody's feet, everybody wishing she'd go away and be somewhere else where they don't have to look at her. No, thanks. I'm not going to end up like that. I'll marry some bloke all right. But at least I'll be doing it with my eyes open. All that stuff they give you about your wedding day being the happiest day of your life – they know what they can do with that. Stuff it where the monkey stuffed his nuts.'

I walked beside her, listening intently. So this was the gospel according to Vinnie. Well, I had to admit she was clear-sighted enough. Too clear-sighted for her own comfort; or for mine, come to that.

I said nothing to interrupt her and she went on, half to me and half to herself. 'They agree with having fun while you're young. The only thing is, what's fun? I know what they'd say – my mum and dad and my aunties and that. They'd say fun was O.K. as long as you didn't do anything bad. But what's bad? They don't know any more than I do. They've just got these old ideas handed down to them. What the people years ago thought was bad, that's bad – that's all they can see. But the people years ago didn't have any way of stopping getting pregnant. If you let a man get too near to you you had a baby. And that was a crime, wasn't it? It was the worst thing a girl could do, and they gave her hell for it. She'd ruined her life and they never gave her another chance. One fuck and you were on the scrap-heap. Easy to see why, isn't it? It got in the way of all the neat little family arrangements, about who was whose child when it came to inheriting property and that. Got the books in a mess, you might say. Can't have that. Of course it wasn't a crime for the bloke. Only for the girl. He was expected to be as sexy as hell, and if he couldn't put up with not having it he could go and buy it for half a crown and as likely as not pick up a dose of something and give it to his wife on their wedding night, when she'd been a good girl and waited her turn and never stepped out of line. Well, what I say is, sod that for a game of soldiers. It's just not called for any more. There's lots of ways of stopping a baby. Things for the chap to wear, things for the girl to wear. And if it all goes wrong, there's pills you can take. They bring on your period. I had to do it once. I didn't like taking them but it worked all right. Life's modern now, isn't it? I don't wear a crinoline. And I don't see why I shouldn't have a bit of real fun before it's too late. It'll be too late all too bloody soon. In no time at all I'll be a walking dead body like my mum and my auntie. I want a few memories when that time comes.'

She halted and looked at me. The sun had gone down into a warm haze now, and the wood seemed foetid, tropical, a fit arena for the savage copulation of feral animals. So what if it was my wedding-day tomorrow? I was like Vinnie in one thing at least: I wanted a few memories.

I took hold of her and laid my mouth across hers. 'Wait,' she said, drawing her head back. 'Not yet. I don't feel like it yet.'

'Soon?' I asked thickly.

'I don't know. I'll see.' As if to soften my disappointment, she added, 'Now I've started talking it all out I want to go on. Not many of the men I go out with want to hear me talk.'

I wasn't altogether sure that I wanted to hear her talk, for that matter, but I saw what she meant. I expect most of her men were the type who stumped around on their knuckles emitting deep grunts and shrill barks.

'I'm talking as if I sat down and thought it all out,' she said. 'But it wasn't really like that. It's not how I go on. There was – something that started me off. If it hadn't been for that, I might be going out dancing and going to the pictures and holding hands in the pictures like a nice girl, holding myself back ready to make somebody a virgin bride. But it didn't happen that way.'

We had walked on, and now reached a spot where exceptionally thick bushes grew between us and the open field. On our other side, ancient tree-trunks, perhaps once felled for timber but neglected so long ago that they were covered with moss and interlaced with brambles, formed a protective wall. Vinnie sank down on the soft carpet of dead leaves, and I sat beside her.

'There was this fella,' she began. How had I known that she would begin her recital with those exact words? 'I was fifteen. He lived in Wytham. I used to come over to see my auntie, just like now. His name was Mike. I used to see him all the time. He used to go out with this girl, Rita her name was. I was just a kid. I didn't know anything about anything. The first I knew that I got a thrill out of Mike was when it came to me that I hated Rita – really hated her guts. Then I asked myself one day, What's Rita ever done to me? And of course when I sat down and thought about it, I saw what it was. I wanted Mike. I wanted to be where Rita was.'

Her face was rapt and her eyes distant; she was caught in the toils of memory. 'I spent night and day thinking about it all, for weeks. If I saw

Mike and Rita together, I'd go home and lie on my bed and picture everything I thought they must be doing – I mean quite ordinary things like eating ice cream, and having a good laugh. Not the sex stuff. That came later. And when it came, it did come.'

'Go on,' I murmured.

'I used to hang about in the shop, always offering to help my auntie out behind the counter, in case Mike came in and I could serve him. He did come in sometimes, too. For cigarettes mostly. I'd give him the eye, as well as I knew how to do it then. Must have looked funny. Then one day I got up the courage to ask him if he'd like to come for a walk in the woods. And he laughed! He stood there in the shop and laughed at me! Christ, that hurt. I suppose he thought I was just a funny kid. Kid be damned. I was a woman already – I'd started having periods and all of that. I could have given him what he wanted. Only he didn't want it, I s'pose.'

'I'm sorry,' I said. 'That must have been painful.'

'Yes, it was bad. I did feel hurt. Then a week or two later I was in Wytham village one evening and I saw him with Rita. They were walking along past the pub towards the corner. I wondered if they were going to take the road towards town, but they went past the corner and kept on going, and I was curious and followed them. I didn't have to follow them for long. They were going to the cricket pavilion. Mike was the secretary or something. He had a key. I kept well out of sight and I watched him open the side door and they both looked round to make sure nobody was watching, at least they thought nobody was, and they went in. I didn't know what to do. It made me feel hot all over to think of the two of them in there. Of course I knew he might only be going in to do the accounts or something and she might be helping him, but somehow I didn't think that was what was going on. The way they looked round before they went in … They wouldn't have done that if they'd just been going in on cricket club business. I went back to my auntie's and tried to sit at the table reading a magazine, but it was no good, I couldn't think of anything but Mike and Rita in that pavilion just down the road, and after a bit I slipped out and went along to it. I went round the back. There was a window there but it had curtains and they were drawn. But the curtains must have shrunk or something. It took me a long time to work up the nerve because I thought I'd just about die if Mike found me spying on him, but in the end I went up to where there was this little gap, not an inch, where the curtains didn't quite meet, and I got my eye to it.' She paused and passed the tip of her tongue over her lips.

'Well? You're surely not going to stop there?'

Vinnie swallowed. 'He had her down on a heap of matting or something and they were fucking. He was really giving it to her. I was looking straight at her face and all of a sudden I saw the whole thing, what she must be feeling and what a thrill she was getting out of it. I stood there for a bit not able to move, just staring and staring, and then suddenly she gave a lurch or jolt or something, or perhaps it was both of them did, anyway she moved and the position of her face changed, it was looking a different way, and I was terribly frightened in case she'd seen me. She hadn't though. I turned and ran and didn't stop till I was back in my auntie's kitchen, pretending to read the same magazine in the same place at the table. If anybody had asked me I was going to say I'd never moved. But I was terribly disturbed. That one look at Rita's face had done it all. In a flash, you know what I mean? One minute I didn't really know anything about it all, and the next, I suddenly knew pretty nearly as much as I do now. I saw what it's *about*, I mean. I tell you I was nearly going out of my mind. There I was, sitting at my auntie's table, in that cottage down there, looking at that magazine, and I could feel I was all wet. There was so much of it I didn't know what was happening at first. I thought I must be starting a period or something, but it was just excitement. I can see it now. I can even remember what magazine I was looking at, or trying to. It was *Woman's Weekly* – full of knitting patterns and all that. Knitting patterns! And all I could think about was how wet I was down below, and how I wanted what Rita was getting. And I wanted it from Mike. I felt as if nobody else could satisfy me.'

It was none of my business, and in a way I rather dreaded what she might tell me, but I couldn't help asking, 'And did you ever have it with Mike?'

'No. I never managed it. I tried once or twice again, and he didn't laugh any more, but he just brushed me off. He wasn't interested. Once I got that message I gave up going to Wytham. The next winter I heard he'd left the district and I took to going again. I don't know whether Rita went with him, or what. I never saw her again either.'

'But you haven't forgotten them.'

'No, and I never will. They were my sex education. Sixty seconds at a chink in a curtain and I knew from then on that I wanted it. I wanted the *lot*, and as often as I could get it.'

'But only from Mike.'

'Oh, that was what I thought at first, but after a while I thought, Sod it. If you can't get the exact thing you want, go for something that'll take your mind off it and be better than nothing at least. That's how women think. I've heard of men getting all steamed up about one special girl and if they can't get her they just dream about her for the rest of their life and never go after anybody else. Women aren't like that. They go for what they want and if they can't get it they go for the next thing. So I went for the next thing.'

'Which was quantity.'

She nodded. 'I soon forgot Mike. I was too busy to think about him much, anyway. That's one good thing about being a girl. You don't have to waste any time. When you meet a new fella, you don't have to stop and think, I wonder, does he or doesn't he? the way men do with a girl they've just met. You know damn' well he'll want the whole menu if he gets half a chance. That's what men are like.'

'All of them?'

'Well, I never met one that wasn't. And I've met plenty.'

Yes, I thought, eyeing her slender form as she half sat, half lay among the soft dry leaves, eying her pale, alert little face, you've been a quick mover. If you were fifteen when this awakening happened and you're twenty now, there must be a lifetime's worth of rocketing sexuality packed into five short years. Memories! It's a card-index you'll need.

'Before the end of that summer,' Vinnie went on, glancing round at the snug enclosed space we were in, 'I'd found this place. It's always quiet here. Never seems to be disturbed. Colonel Ffennel has a gamekeeper and there are one or two other men working about the place, but I never knew one of them come near this bit of the woods. I always felt as safe here as if I was in a hotel room, and I've been in plenty of those.'

Illumination now broke in on me. She had come for a walk with me because she felt like confiding, felt like putting her view of life, and summing up her experience, in words for a change, finding herself for once in the company of someone who was not afraid of words. But, almost mechanically killing two birds with one stone, she had walked me up here to her chosen nook among the greenery, the place where she felt safe from being spied on. This was where, at fifteen, she had solaced herself for not being able to attract Mike (I wondered, briefly, about him) and where she had conducted the local studs who didn't happen to have the price of an hotel room in their pockets. This was the sacred grove of Vinnie, the Priestess of Fuck.

The realization ought to have fired my blood. The erection which had been an embarrassment to me a little earlier when all I was trying to do was to walk sedately along a pathway ought now to have sprung out into joyous freedom. But the human being is not a machine. Usually, one's body functions in response to purely mechanical stimuli. Usually, but not always. My veins seemed to cool; I actually felt my phallus shrink, dejectedly, to the size of a gherkin.

Why? Obviously, because of the crowd of anonymous ghosts that swam in the air between me and Vinnie's knickers. Some vestige of pride in me rebelled at being one of that work-gang. The latest, but obviously not the last, of the conscripts who had been marched up here to serve their turn and pass on. I would not, if only because I could not, make one in the shadowy procession that had filed through the archway of her thighs.

I sat back and leaned my shoulders against a tree-trunk. 'Yes,' I said casually, 'it was clever of you to find this place. And you never found anyone else here when you … wanted to use it?'

'Never.' She laughed quietly and said, 'My auntie used to tell people how fond I was of going for walks in the woods. "Vinnie loves country walks," she used to say to people. "Whenever she comes to see me she takes a walk in the woods. Very fond of nature she is." Well, I s'pose it *is* nature, isn't it? It's the way we're made.'

The moment had passed. Instead of throwing myself on her, I had chosen to make small talk, and with perfect composure she had responded in kind. Just as I had my pride, she had hers, and her pride would never have permitted her to, as she would have put it, 'start anything' unless I showed the initial eagerness. She knew that in the sexual market-place she was in the commanding position. *That's one good thing about being a girl. You don't have to waste any time. You know damn' well he'll want the whole menu.*

We talked for a little while more, I forget about what, and then Vinnie stood up and said, 'I have to look in at my auntie's again before I start off back to Jericho. There's something I have to take back to my mother. I forgot it. It's just on the table.'

'I'll walk with you, if I may,' I said. That 'if I may' sounded absurdly stilted. But it was the idiom that had become natural to me, and I couldn't shake it off now.

Silently, as we moved off, I said goodbye to Vinnie's boudoir among the woods. What tales it could tell! But no, I thought, it was only the same tale over and over. An endlessly repeated play with one heroine and an enormous supporting cast.

We moved down the path, through the gate, out into the field, and down through the churchyard in the village. Goodbye, Vinnie. Goodbye, my bachelor life that never happened. We walked round the side of the church with its green-mantled slumbering dead.

Outside the little thatched shop she halted. 'I have to go in and get this thing for my mum. It's a recipe. You can stay outside or come in and meet my auntie, if you like.'

'I'll come in and meet her. I've never met any of your family. I'm interested to see what she looks like.'

I never did see. Inside the cottage, on the neatly arranged kitchen table, was a pencilled note.

'Vinnie. – I am at Parish Council Meeting. I forgot to tell you. Please take recipe to your mother. See you soon. Auntie Dot XX.'

We were alone with the ticking of the clock. Outside, the evening was green and silent all round us. Inside, the cottage was shadowy and safe. Vinnie was looking at me, and her look said it all. I had missed one chance, life had brought me another only a quarter of an hour later, why miss that too?

'I like it at your aunt's house,' I said, taking hold of her round the waist.

'Yes, you like it better than the woods, don't you?'

'A lot better.'

I kissed her, but she broke free and said, 'Not down here.' The kitchen door opened on the foot of a wooden staircase. 'Upstairs, it's better.'

She scampered up the stairs ahead of me, and I followed with a pounding heart. The mere fact of feeling my feet treading up, up, up, from one polished stair to the next, knowing that the objective was a quiet, discreet room with Vinnie in it, flooded me with such a wave of excitement that I had to steady myself against the smooth plastered wall beside me. The staircase made a U-turn half-way up, and the momentary glimpse of Vinnie's delicious shape in profile as she whisked round it jolted me with such a shock of raw passion that I thought I should have fainted. When I got to the top landing I saw that there were two rooms up there. The door of one was closed, the other open. I went through the open one. She was already in there, peeling off her orange skirt. With a couple of brisk movements it came off, and she was on the bed, kneeling up, unbuttoning her upper half.

'Come on,' she said impatiently. 'You're wasting good time, standing there. These parish council meetings don't go on for ever.'

In a trance I began fumbling with my clothes. Zip fasteners for trousers had not come in at that epoch, it was all buttons, and my fingers felt thick and clumsy because I was so eager and yet so hypnotized. She reached forward with those long, delicate fingers and began deftly unfastening the buttons, one, two, three, four, while I stared down as if I were watching her shuffle a pack of cards and waiting to spot a particular one – that's how hard I was concentrating. As she opened my fly, my prick sprang out at her like an enraged jack-in-the-box. It had never been so swollen, so livid or so threatening. Since she was kneeling and I was standing, it was just about level with her face, and impulsively she bent forward slightly and took it in her mouth.

These days, I gather, this kind of thing is standard practice and to be found in all the instruction manuals. In those days it was fairly uncommon. I certainly wasn't expecting it, and the shock-wave, combined with the artful work she was putting in with her tongue, was too much for me so that I began to come immediately, running my fingers ecstatically through her soft brown hair as I shot jet after jet into her mouth. She drank it down like custard.

That, of course, took me off the boil and I finished my undressing at a more deliberate pace, while Vinnie, to fill in time, got off the bed, removed the neatly ironed bedspread and hung it carefully over the chair.

'That'll stop it getting creased,' she remarked. 'My auntie's very noticing. She'd soon tell if her spare bed'd been used. You have to think of everything in this game.'

I was quite willing to think of everything, so long as I got another shot at her, in the normal target area this time, before the aunt came back. It all depended on how soon my infantryman would feel able to stand to attention. In the next few minutes she gave him some help which had him out on the parade-ground as fit and eager as ever.

Now she was lying on her back on the bed, and the only things she was wearing were the little pearly shells on the lobes of her ears. As I slid into her she brought her knees up level with my armpits and crossed her ankles in the small of my back. I already knew that was just about her favourite position, and it must have been a good one for her because she went into a string of orgasms so close together that it made me think of a crazy alarm clock that couldn't help going off every few seconds. As I worked my ramrod in and out, now fast, now slow, now thrusting it in to the last available millimetre, now deliberately allowing it to stay in the shallows for a while, a part of my brain remained detached enough to form thoughts, and the thoughts it formed were all to the effect that Vinnie was really something special. I had had my first fuck with her, that Sunday afternoon in Episcopus, back when the world was new and every experience was a voyage of discovery, and at the time I had no standard of comparison. Now, although my sexual experience had only just attained a plural number, I could at least compare her with Heather.

The two were, of course, completely different in every way, and the difference was nowhere more marked than in the thrust of sexual action, where passion and appetite swept aside all evasions and the naked personality advanced to be recognized. Was it possible to make comparisons? Weren't people just people, with their own way of doing everything including this, and wasn't it nonsense to think in terms of good, better and best? No, no, I thought as Vinnie went into another savage orgasm, shuddering through the whole length of her supple body, it wasn't nonsense, she was better, better than Heather, better than any other woman in the world, better than all of them put together ....

After that she insisted on our both getting our clothes on. 'If my auntie comes back suddenly, we'll have more chance if we're dressed.'

'More chance of what?'

'Oh, some kind of getaway.'

'What kind?' It seemed pretty hopeless to me.

'Oh, never mind talking, get dressed. I hope she won't come in till we're ready for her, but if she does, well, it's better if we're dressed than if we're stark naked up here.'

I got dressed, all but my underpants, which I slipped into my pocket. Having her skirt and blouse on seemed to inspire Vinnie to fresh heights. She seemed determined to try it in every possible position, including a few I wouldn't have believed possible till she showed me. We used the bed, the chair, the floor, and if there had been parallel bars on the wall we would have used them too. I began to wonder if even my trusty henchman could take much more of this. Vinnie's cunt was as special as the rest of her. Where Heather's was big and generous and welcoming, Vinnie's was narrow and voracious. Not only was it as long and close-fitting as a glove-finger, it was also totally prehensile, varying the pressure of its silken clutch from second to second and from inch to inch of its unusual length. I had known already that Vinnie was in the habit of thinking with her cunt, but now I realized that she could also talk with it, and what she wordlessly told me went into the marrow of my bones and corpuscles of my blood and the cells of my flesh and drove me insane for ever.

We finished up with Vinnie on her knees and elbows on the bed and me standing with my feet solidly planted on the floor, holding her lightly by the hips and letting her have it like a crazed mammoth. I wondered whether I would ever come again – whether, indeed, I would live to see another day. One thing I knew for certain. The intricately lascivious pressures of her elongated passage had altered the shape of my cock, perhaps permanently. I had the impression that if I were to take it out now and look at it, I would find it as long and thin as a frozen grass-snake. Not that there was any question of taking it out. I could tell from Vinnie's gasping and the gathering pace of her wriggles that she was about to hit peak again, and this time she went into such a frantic convulsion that *whoosh*! I felt the electric surge shooting up uncontrollably from the twin power-house down below, and a few moments later it was over and I was watching my deflating member swinging to and fro like a cow's udder.

'Come on,' Vinnie said briskly, getting off the bed and taking up the bed-cover again. 'We must get out of here. There's no time to lose.'

'Come *on*?' I said feebly, sinking down on the chair. 'For God's sake. I'll have a heart attack or something.'

'Well, don't have it here. I have enough trouble keeping things from my family as it is.'

Groggily, I laced my shoes and stood up. The floor seemed to be shifting beneath me. 'What now? God, I could do with a drink. Tell you what, I'll go across to the pub and have –'

'No, you won't. That'd mean you going out through the front door and if my auntie's coming back she'll see you. No, you're going out through the back door and down the garden. Wait – I'll tell you if it's safe to come down.'

She whisked down the stairs. Why had she so much energy when I had so little? She had been coming non-stop, but all it seemed to have done was leave her fresh as a daisy. I stood waiting in the quiet little bedroom. It smelt faintly of lavender. Such an innocent place. But then Vinnie had probably been up to her tricks here before. So what? The sheets, the bed-springs, the polished wood, the lavender flowers were innocent even if Vinnie wasn't. Even if I wasn't.

'Come on,' she hissed up the staircase. 'Get down here.'

I got down. She had the door open into the back garden. 'Go down there and get over the wall. You'll be on the bank of the stream. Follow it down. It comes very near the road a bit further on. Get on to the road and wait for me. We'll go into Oxford together.'

I went down the garden. It had all the right things, like sweet peas and hollyhocks. Silver bells and cockle shells. Pretty maids all in a row, well, that was Vinnie. She was pretty enough and there were enough of her if she were laid end to end … what was I maundering about? I was drunk with exhaustion, with satiety. What had happened to me? Vinnie had happened to me.

I reached the bank of the smoothly flowing Seacourt Stream, epitome of the small pastoral rivers of Southern England. How gentle it was. I bent down, looking at the minnows darting among the gracefully undulating water-weed. The sun was just setting. Calm, calm all round me. I walked down to the point where the road came close, and waited on it for Vinnie. In a few minutes she came in sight.

'You're going to walk me home, aren't you?' she said.

'Well, I'll come with you, of course, but I'm not up to much walking. Let's go to the end of the Botley Road and take a bus to Carfax.'

'What, and then stand and wait for another bus to Jericho? Can't you walk at *all*?'

'Well, not far. Christ, you know how much energy I've been putting out. And I've got to be ready for tomorrow.'

'Why, what's happening tomorrow?'

'I'm getting …' I went into a fit of choking just in time. My mind seemed to have gone off duty. 'I'm getting very behind with my work and I need to go and look up some things in the British Museum. I have to make an early start in the morning.'

'To London, you mean?'

'Yes, to London.'

'I could do with a day in London. I'm not doing anything.'

'Well, have it some other time,' I said. 'I'll be in the British Museum Reading Room all day. It wouldn't be much fun –'

'Oh, I'll go round the shops. You'll have to come out for meals and stuff.'

'Look, Vinnie, do please come to London with me some day when I can be with you and we can have a really good time. I'd enjoy it so much. I don't get many days with you, don't waste one on tomorrow.' I was sweating now. At any moment, I thought, I shall give up and tell her that tomorrow is my wedding-day.

'Oh, all right. Well, you can walk me a bit of the way home. It's a nice evening. I don't want to be in buses all the time.'

In the end we settled that we would get off the bus at the Botley Road bridge (just a few yards from the Bargeman's Arms where they would be expecting me and where I longed to be, but still), and walk to Jericho along the river towpath and then to Walton Well Road.

'That'll give us a bit more of each other's company,' she said and gave me a smile as if she were feeling pleased with me. I ought to have felt flattered and elated; she had never looked at me like that before, nor said anything that came as close to a compliment. But my weariness, and the anxiety that was beginning to build up inside me, proved too dampening.

We duly stopped the bus and went along the towpath, upstream, with the allotments on the opposite bank and, from the unseen railway station, the hiss and clank of steam locomotives plainly audible in the still, heavy air. Then we crossed the little arched footbridge over the canal cut and found ourselves, still moving upstream, on the raised path with the Thames on one side and Fiddler's Island Stream on the other. That stream is narrow enough to jump over, and on the other side of it is a large area of reeds. I knew that area. As a child I had played there for hours, sometimes whole days, together. It was and is a miniature jungle. The soil is too marshy to support any plant heavier than a clump of reeds, but the reeds grow thickly and when trodden down they make a carpet on which a child can sit all day, being a Red Indian, a Robin Hood outlaw, a cop or a robber. Here and there is a patch of earth that seems naturally drier than the rest, where a full-grown person can stand or sit without sinking in. I knew those patches too. So did Vinnie. Every Oxford child knows them; at least, every Oxford child who lives nearby and whose circumstances are too humble to allow of recreation in grander and more expensive places.

As we slogged along the raised path, meeting only an occasional person walking along the river-bank, and with just two or three boatloads of people coming back from an evening's trip on the water, the light was draining from the sky and we entered the cooling oven of an August night. The air would not become chilly till almost morning, and at present it was close, hot, stifling. Vinnie fanned herself with her hand.

'Let's sit down a bit,' she said, and immediately jumped across the Fiddler's Island Stream and set off into the wide reed-bed. Some ducks, nesting in her path, quacked indignantly and moved a little way aside.

Another few moments and she was nesting too, flattening reeds to make a carpet. She had, I knew, unerringly chosen one of the spots where the water wouldn't seep through them. Not for a long time, anyway.

'Sit down a bit,' she repeated, looking up at me.

'I really can't stay long.'

'I didn't say anything about staying long.'

I joined her and immediately our mouths met in a long kiss. I couldn't have said which of us made the initial move. We just seemed to flow together. Well, why not? I thought. A few kisses to round off the evening. To round off this whole chapter of my life. I didn't suppose for a moment I'd ever kiss Vinnie again. There's a lot of things a kiss can say, and goodbye is one of them.

I was sitting, she was on her knees, which gave her more leverage, and without taking her mouth from mine she gently pushed until I went over on my back. Behind her head I could see the tall fringe of dark green reed-tips and the dirty white of the sky.

'Vinnie ....' I tried to say.

'You did well back there,' she said softly, and as she spoke she was burrowing away with that slender hand. I thought what she found there was bound to be as uninteresting as a bootlace, but to my astonishment, under her magical touch, it swung up like a compass needle finding north. And then, by God, she straddled me, there and then among the reeds, with the wild ducks nesting a few yards away and the sound of a train going by headed for Birmingham. As she worked away I stared up into her face, the pale, intelligent, predatory little face that so haunted my dreams. Its gaze was directed entirely inward. Completely possessed by the pleasure that flooded her being, she was oblivious of me as she was of the ducks and the train, now fading off to the north.

I thought that fuck in the reeds was going to last all night. I had nothing to shoot, and Vinnie was unable or unwilling to let go. As she remorselessly pumped at me, a swan flew heavily overhead, its bulky body seeming as big above us as a quadruped's, the air hissing through its strong feathers at almost the same rhythm as the jockeying of Vinnie's pelvis. And at that moment, though I'll never know where the ammunition came from, I began to come for what I was now positive would be the last time in my life. When, finally, she sank down and disengaged herself, I lay on my couch of reeds like a beached whale.

When I managed to climb to my feet, I walked Vinnie to the end of Canal Street. We didn't talk much, but when we parted she gave me a gentle kiss, as if she were still pleased with me.

Which was more than my parents were, when I finally shambled in at the Bargeman's. My father, who had expected a pleasant sociable evening on my last-ever night at home, had got tired of waiting and gone to bed. My mother had kept a meal warm in the oven, but she said she was afraid it was spoiled.

*

Lying there in what was now my marital bed, thinking back to what had happened with Vinnie, picturing it all and re-entering the whole detonating series of sensations. I felt the stirring of libido under the mat of exhaustion that still lay heavy on me. My penis sluggishly lifted its head as if to see what might be going on. Should I tackle Heather now? I knew, as certainly as anyone can know anything, that the only way forward was to make love to her, to bury the feeling of neglect that made her smart so much and implanted in her such disappointment and such fears for the future. I moved towards her, testing the situation. But she seemed to have fallen into an uneasy slumber. Better, I thought, to wait till tomorrow. On first waking, she was usually in receptive mood, and it would start our first complete day of matrimony with a positive experience. For me too: I had to wipe away the Vinnie-traces before I could start living with Heather, and after all that was what I must do now, nor was I unwilling to. I sank to sleep in a more or less composed frame of mind.

I think the first hours were deep and restful enough, but the floor of my sleep sloped upwards to the final shallows, and before waking I came through a zone of troubled, lecherous dreams, first about Vinnie and then, as if in some region of my mind I had symbolically won a victory over my darker appetites, about Heather. Knowing that I was going to make love to her when I woke fully, I dreamt or half-dreamt that I was already doing so, holding her unresisting form in my arms and driving away at her. But the skin of her cheek against mine felt grainy and lifeless, and as I came to consciousness I realized that it was her pillow I had hold of. I reached out. There was no Heather. It was daylight. She must have got up early and gone to another room. The space beside me was empty.

At this I became seriously alarmed. I waited for a while, but she obviously wasn't coming back, and during the wait I became more and more tense and gloomy. Nor did I see any reason, objectively, why I shouldn't be tense and gloomy. Here I lay, in the bed in which we were supposed to start our married life, and already two things had gone badly wrong. Last night I had gone dead asleep without making love to Heather or doing anything at all to make her feel like a girl on her wedding night. And this morning she had got out of bed and taken herself off somewhere, without waiting for me to wake up. It was all just about as bad as it could be, and what made it all the worse was that I couldn't explain. If I could have said, 'Heather darling, I feel genuine tenderness towards you and I really care about making our marriage work. I know I disappointed you yesterday, by being *distrait* and lack-lustre all day, by not having anything to say to you over dinner, and then going straight off to sleep when we hit the sack. But you see, it was all because of Vinnie. I had no energy because I'd shot it all into her the evening before. It was only the second time in my life that I'd got down to it with her and it'll be the last. I swear to God I never want to see her again. Enough is enough. From now on I belong to you.' How could I say all that? How could I say any of it?

I got up. It was a dull, sticky August morning: the light seemed yellow, as if there were a shell of stale butter across the sky. I thought I would like to be walking with Heather on a mountainside, or along an endless beach with great salty breakers rolling in. Instead, we were in North Parade. It was nine o'clock in the morning and the shops would be opening. Everything was prosaic, predictable, ordinary, and my marriage was on the rocks. It was like being shipwrecked on the Oxford Canal.

I went into the kitchen. Heather was sitting at the table, already fully dressed, drinking coffee. I sat down opposite her. She looked at me across the table without speaking.

'Heather ….' I began at last.

'There's some coffee in the pot,' she interrupted me. 'Not much, though. Better get on with it if you want a cup.'

'What I want,' I said, 'is you.'

She gave a glance round at the shabby little kitchen and said, 'Well, you've got me, haven't you?'

'No. I haven't got you and I don't deserve to have you, not yet. But I'm working on it.'

'Oh, *work*. You think work's the answer to everything.'

'I don't, I know there are lots of people who live very satisfactorily and very successfully without doing a stroke of work in their lives, but I'm not that type. I'm the kind of person who gets things by working for them or not at all. And the thing I want most is to be the kind of person you can love.'

'Have some coffee, for God's sake. It's too early in the morning for making speeches.'

I had just enough sense not to utter another word. I drank the coffee and then went and got washed and shaved and dressed. I took a little care over my appearance, picking out a clean shirt from the suitcase my clothes were stored in. We hadn't unpacked yet. The flat had only been ours since yesterday.

We ate boiled eggs and toast like an old married couple and then I asked, 'Now what?'

'I make a start on this place. The shelves need scrubbing out and lining with clean paper. All the holes and corners are dirty. I could tell they were from the way the agent rushed us through.'

'All right, so we tackle that.'

'No we. I. You'd be in the way.'

'No, I wouldn't, I'm very practical. I can look after a beer-cellar and knock the spigots in and keep the beer at the right temperature and everything.'

'Maybe, but this place isn't a beer cellar. I know what needs to be done and I can't keep stopping to issue instructions to you.'

'Oh, but Heather, surely I could –'

'Besides, there's your work.'

'Oh, never mind that. I can leave my work alone for a while.' I was going to add, 'This is our honeymoon, after all,' but stopped myself in time. Pretty funny kind of honeymoon, I thought, that starts off with a limp prick and a colossal guilt hangover. Better shut up about honeymoons.

Heather gathered up the breakfast dishes and took them over to the sink.

'I'll do those,' I said, pushing back my chair.

She turned to face me. 'Peter, will you please *go*. There must be some book or other you're in the middle of reading, go and read it.'

'I don't want to leave you alone when you're angry with me.'

'I'm not angry with you.'

'Well, in a negative state of mind, then.'

'Why? Are you afraid of what I might do? I don't see that you need worry about that. You've got me trapped securely enough in this rat-hole.'

'That's just it. I'm not afraid of what you might do, it's what you might *be*.'

'And what might I be?'

'Unhappy. Lonely. Disappointed with life.'

She turned on both taps. Water splashed into the sink. It seemed to be the only answer she was prepared to make.

'Heather.' I tried one more time. 'Listen to me, please, darling.'

'No, you listen to me. I've got to face three years in this hole, either this one or one just like it, skulking away from the light of day because you won't be able to tell them at College that you've gone and got married.'

'Well, that was the deal. If they know I'm married they'll give the Fellowship to someone else and then I'll never be an Oxford historian. I'll have to go and be a schoolmaster somewhere. You agreed to go along with it.'

'All right, I agreed, and your work's so bloody important to you that it comes before me and before anything else. So I'm stuck with it.'

'No, you're not. If that's really how you feel about it I'll write to Bax and tell him I've got married. He's away at the moment, they all are, but when he comes back and finds the letter he'll simply take my name out of the list of candidates for the Research Fellowship and cross it off. At the moment it's at the top. And you won't have to bother to scrub out those shelves. We shan't need this place. We'll be moving on.'

Why was I talking like this, sounding so bitter, so sullen and disappointed? I meant to be tender and understanding and healing. I meant to tell her that our relationship was all that mattered in my life and to hell with Episcopus, to hell with Oxford, to hell with being an historian. So why couldn't I? Because it would have stuck in my throat?

Standing there on the linoleum of the kitchen floor, I paused motionless, like Buridan's ass, between two equally powerful magnets. At that moment I saw with merciless clarity that my life, to be worth living, needed two things. On the one side, a meaningful relationship with a woman. Love, for short. On the other, meaningful work, and the only meaningful work I could imagine was trying to understand the past through the study of original sources. History, for short. And historical study, to me, meant working in Oxford.

It didn't seem to me that either of these objectives was, in itself, ridiculous or over-ambitious. Both were perfectly normal, the kind of ambitions most people had. Why did it seem, in my case, so impossibly difficult to fit those two halves together?

I think my face must have registered utter bewilderment, and I suppose I looked funny standing there like a waxwork, because to my surprise Heather burst out laughing.

'Go on out, Peter Leonard,' she said. 'Leave me to make something of this place and come back when you've done some work. And don't you dare go writing any silly letters to Bax.'

'I'll come back at lunch-time.'

'No, you won't. I'll have dust in my hair and I'll be sweaty and bad-tempered. Come back at pub opening time this evening and take me out for a drink.'

'You bet. And we'll go out to dinner afterwards.'

'No, we won't, we're not made of money. I'll cook something nice here. We might as well christen this place, have our first meal in it.'

Yes, I thought as I went down the narrow stairs, and after that we'll have our first fuck in it too, or my name's not Peter Leonard. I knew that would build a better bridge, and more quickly, than any amount of speechifying.

I cycled down to the Bodleian. It was true that I was in the middle of something.

All the same, interesting though this topic was, I couldn't feel much interest in it on that particular morning. I felt, instead, as if I were looking at it through a sheet of tinted glass that had been suddenly dropped down between me and it. Everything was there, and yet it seemed unreal. Finally, on making the discovery that I had been reading the same sentence over and over again for some minutes, I stacked up the books neatly, took them back to the Reserve counter, and went down the stairs and out.

The morning haze had burnt away now; the sun was strong and the shadows inky and hard-edged, as if an artist from a different school had been invited to take his turn at delineating the world. I knew there was only one part of Oxford where I wanted to be: the river-bank. And only one spot on the river-bank that I wanted. The Bargeman's Arms, Oseney Town. I cycled down there, knowing as I went that I would have some explaining to do. My father would be out at the Brewery, but my mother would be behind the bar, and I was supposed at this moment to be off in the blue with Heather, enjoying our glorious honeymoon.

The willows on the grassy verge of the water rustled their leaves at me in the small disturbance of air that I made by passing close to them. The rustling was a gentle, welcoming sound. It said, 'Come home, all is forgiven.' I didn't know whether to believe them.

The Bargeman's Arms slept in the sun. I leaned my bike against the wall. Two youths were in the back yard, playing Aunt Sally, that Oxfordshire version of skittles where you throw a wooden pin about the size of a rolling-pin and try to knock off a wooden ball about the size of a coconut. Behind the metal stalk that holds the coconut is an oblong of canvas stretched over a frame, and laced securely through holes all the way round. It has to be secure, because the pins come with considerable force, and their thudding is one of the Oxford summer sounds. I thought how often, at the beginning of a season, I had helped my father to lace up the canvas and throw the first few pins against it to test it. *Thud, thud*, they went. Here comes Peter Leonard declaring this season's Aunt Sally open. May God bless her and all who sail in her.

I went into the bar. The strong sunlight outside made the place seem very dark at first. But I could see that there was one customer sitting in a corner eating some of the 'Fresh Cut Sandwiches', reading the paper. He had a full pint of beer beside him and looked settled and contented. I could also see that my mother was behind the bar, but then I was expecting to.

'Peter!' she said in surprise. Her eyes opened very wide, and I could see for an instant how pretty she had been as a girl. Those big round eyes in that delicate-boned face.

'It's all right,' I said. 'You haven't seen a ghost.'

'But where's your – where's Heather?'

'In North Parade.'

'But I thought the two of you were off on a trip.'

'Look, Mum,' I said, 'can I come through into the kitchen?'

'Well, of course. Only I can't leave the bar for long.'

Work, work, always work. You lived by it, it put food in your belly and it ruled you.

'You can hear if anybody comes in,' I said. I led the way through into the kitchen and stood facing her. 'I shan't keep you long. Only some of what I want to say isn't for the customers, it's for you.'

'Go on then,' she said quietly.

'Number one,' I said, 'there's no wedding trip. When we went off on that train, we only went as far as Witney and then we got off and took another train back. It was just a manoeuvre. I didn't want to show up in front of Heather's family as the kind of failure who couldn't afford to take his wife away on a honeymoon, even a short one.'

I paused and my mother said, 'Well, we did wonder how you were going to afford it.'

'What we afforded was precisely one dinner. Chicken chasseur and white wine. Then home to bed in North Parade.'

'I'm sure it doesn't matter. It doesn't matter a bit as long as everything else is all right.'

'Everything else is just what I'm coming to. Number Two. Are you ready for Number Two, Mother?'

'Yes.'

'Heather's pregnant.'

She smiled calmly. 'How many months?'

'Why d'you ask? Is it important?'

'Well,' she said, 'it was the only thing I didn't know already, so naturally I was curious.'

I was silent while this sank in and then said, 'You knew she was pregnant? Did someone tell you?'

'No.'

'You just guessed?'

She shook her head. 'It wasn't a guess. I knew.'

'How?'

She gestured, pushing away the question. 'Oh, so many things, Peter. I can't stand here finding words for all of them. Let's just say, you're my son, and I know you well enough to know there's only one reason why you'd get married so suddenly, and before your career's settled and all that. And in the middle of the summer with all the College people away.'

'So it was the timing that made you realize we were rushing it.'

'Partly. Other things too. But I'm sorry, I have to get back to the bar. You've told me now.'

'Pretty unnecessarily, it seems.'

'I wouldn't say that. I'm glad you've talked to me. Of course it couldn't have been a secret much longer.' She was moving towards the bar entrance.

'Just a second, Mum. Just one more thing. Does Dad know?'

'I think he does.'

'You *think* so? Hasn't he said anything?'

She turned her gentle, all-knowing, all-fathoming eyes on me. 'Saying isn't everything, Peter. Finding words for things is very important for you in your world. But we ...' That leave-it-aside gesture again. 'Often when Jack's got a thought in his head, I know it's there and I know what it is. He doesn't have to talk it out. When I'm lying close to him in our bed, I can *feel* the thoughts in his head. They seem to go from his head into mine without any sound, without making that journey through the air. I feel them and he knows I feel them, and we don't need words. We're better without them.'

How wise she is, I thought.

We went back into the bar. The solitary customer was still reading the paper and eating his sandwiches. The level of his beer had gone down about two inches. He barely glanced up at me as we came back in. I went round to the other side of the counter like a customer.

'May I have a pint of your excellent bitter, please, Ma'am?' I asked.

My mother drew it and said, dead-pan, 'Any sandwiches?'

'If they're on the house.'

She would have to cut them herself, I thought suddenly. Brian and I used to do it once.

'It's against the rules of the house to give away free food,' she said primly. 'I'll make an exception as you're on your honeymoon. No charge for the sandwiches. But the beer you pay for. Your father's strict about that.'

The two youths who had been playing Aunt Sally now came in, followed by more customers in ones and twos. I sat down with my sandwiches and while I ate and drank I looked over now and again at my mother, quietly getting on with running the pub. I admired her so much. Everything she did was so instinctively perfect. She was pleasant to the customers without brassily intruding on their conversations or jollying them along. She knew where everything was and never forgot anything or made a mistake in the change. Her movements were quick and deft, and when she poured out a bottle of beer over her finger, as my father had painstakingly taught me to do, she did it perfectly. I thought of her life with my father: I thought of what his life would have been if he had not had her strength and support. He would have been finished, hopeless, out of it from the start, without the luck to marry Katie or some woman just like her, if there were any women just like her. And it wasn't just work and partnership and attending to detail; it was something that ran through the whole texture of their lives. My parents were poor. They were insignificant in the world's eyes. They ran a side-street pub. No one except their immediate neighbours had ever heard of them. No one except their sons would remember them when they were dead. But they were rich and successful because they had been given the greatest gift of all, and they had accepted that gift and shared it between the two of them, and the sharing had made it richer and stronger.

I stood up. I was going home. Not straight away, because I didn't want to tell Heather I had not, after all, spent the day working. She, presumably, would have spent the day turning our dreary flat into something like a home, and I saw no harm in at least letting her suppose that I, too, was doing what I was supposed to do.

And deep down, that would be true. I wasn't going to spend the day poring over a book, but I was going to spend it in preparing myself, as a human being, for those two objectives I wanted to follow. Heather and history! Domesticity and documentation! Conjugality and continuity! Both needs had their origin in the roots of my being, and it was these roots I proposed to refresh this afternoon.

I knew exactly what I would do. I would walk out of the open door of the Bargeman's on to the river towpath. I would go down past Oseney lock, over Folly Bridge, and all the way down, with Christ Church Meadow on my left hand and the University Boathouse on the other, to Iffley.

I trod steadily on, noticing everything, feasting on everything. When I drew level with the south-east corner of Christ Church Meadow I saw the dark streaks and tourbillions in the water marking the deep but quiet disturbance where the Cherwell pours itself into the Thames. The Cherwell is not a big river but it is strong and deep, with a lot of water and a big thrust. It changes the nature of the Thames in a few yards. After the Cherwell joins it, the Thames ceases to be a young country river and becomes large, authoritative, the Father Thames who presides over so much of English history. The river I had always seen from my bedroom window when I was growing up, though it was barely twenty minutes' walk from where I was now, was not the same river. That was still an *ingénue*. This was the river full of time and experience, suffering and knowledge, the river that flows past Sinodun and Reading Abbey and Westminster, and finally through the great marshes to the sea.

Thinking all this, I walked on. When I was about half-way from the Boathouse to Iffley, just at the most unfrequented point, I decided to have a swim. It was rather soon after lunch, but my lunch had only consisted of a couple of sandwiches and I wasn't afraid of cramp. The fields on the right-hand bank were still agricultural in those days, and there was a thick hedge running right up to the towpath. I took off my clothes in the shelter of the hedge. If it had occurred to me when I was back at the Bargeman's that I might go in the water, I could have dug out my old swimming trunks. But it didn't matter. I went in as naked as I had been with Heather that morning, just below Eynsham Bridge. God be with that time.

I'm not skilful enough to dive, but I lowered myself quickly into the water and struck out, feeling the lovely keen coldness on my limbs, my belly, my back, streaming round me, singing in my ears. My heart pranced for joy; I knew my scrotum was tightening like a fist. I rolled over and floated on my back, glancing down at my underside exhibiting itself to the sky like a seal's. The words formed in my head: Happiness is a navel full of Thames water. A boat with two girls in it passed quite near me. They glanced over at me and then one said something and they both giggled. I wondered if they had had a clear view of my erotic instrument. Well, whether or not, they weren't having it. It was not for them. It was Heather's.

I pulled myself out, bracing my knees against the yellow clay of the bank and taking a firm hold on great handfuls of the thick sweet grass. Then I walked quickly across to the hedge where I had left my clothes and stood there, naked and dripping, drying my body by brushing off the water with the palms of my hands. My knees were capped with clay; I wiped them clean with my wet hands.

In the close warmth of the August afternoon it felt good to be cool. I put on my clothes without waiting for my body to become completely dry. My flesh felt hard and firm, not relaxed and sweaty as an Oxford summer day generally makes one feel. The coolness of the river came with me like a blessing.

I went back to the towpath and stood for a moment looking at the river. Two swans, headed downstream, came in to settle on the water. Their strong wings shoved at the heavy air as they brought their big bodies down, feet running a few steps on the glassy surface of the water, taking care to bring their weight down without damage, like the pilots of flying-boats. Then, side by side, they moved on down the river, seeming to take no notice of one another but unshakably, indissolubly together, as married as Jack and Katie Leonard, as fixed in their relationship while life lasted and as content to be so.

Now I would walk to Iffley Church, and after spending a little time looking at that perfect example of a Norman doorway, taking it into my bloodstream like an injection of the Middle Ages, I would go down the Iffley Road and over to St Clements and across the Parks to North Parade. Heather would be there and I would take her my love. I would love and protect and serve her, and I would love and protect and serve the new young life she was carrying in her beautiful generous body. We would go down that stream together as proudly as the two swans.

I set off towards Iffley Lock. The river, at my side, was moving at the same pace as I was, but tirelessly, calmly, needing no rest. The water slid onward between its banks, as unhurried and purposeful as always, and the meadows beside it were as rich and green and fragrant as I remembered them from the time of my beginning. Only the fritillaries had gone.